Thessaloniki

The Savage Brood: Book Two

Emyll O'Bryan

Cover design by Emyll O'Bryan, featuring *View of Thessaloniki* from *L'Illustrazione Italiana*, 1876.

This book is a work of fiction. Names, characters, places and incidents either are a product of the author's imagination or are used fictitiously. Any resemblance to actual persons, living or dead, events, or locales is entirely coincidental.

This edition published by Jade Publishing Company, P.O. Box 240, Austin, AR 72007.

NOTICE: This work may contain descriptions of adult situations, including language, nudity, sex, and violence some readers may find objectionable. It is intended for mature audiences only, and reader discretion is advised.

ISBN:
978-1-944040-04-8

Acknowledgements

My goodness, what a long, strange trip this has been. I'd like to thank Phil for keeping me on track. I never would have kept going if you hadn't pushed me. It's all your fault! And Ann, as always. We are test tube twins in some weird genetic experiment, and we got separated. Only fifty more pages to go!

Again, I want to thank all of the researchers who have provided information for the era I use in this novel…and the entire Savage Brood series. Without your input, this book would not have been possible. I'd like to express special thanks to John Andela from Age of Sail (ageofsail.net). Dude, your site rocks! I told you I would give you an acknowledgement if you told me what a channel was, and it only took eight years for the book to be in print to finally give it to you. To everyone else who's written on the Regency era, the United Kingdom, the Mediterranean, archaeology, Greece, and on and on, thank you. I could not have known these things off the top of my head.

Last, but most certainly not least, thank you, reader, for taking another trip with me.

Emyll O'Bryan
May 5, 2016

This one is for all my friends and family. Your belief in me makes me more.

Chapter One

It would *not* suit. Psyche sat on the settee and shifted around, but the items under her gown were making her very uncomfortable. She reached up to the bottom of her bodice and adjusted it, attempting to keep it from rising to gape at the neckline. Her skin was tingling with perspiration, and it was difficult to breathe. All of that was compounded by her nervousness.

The pink- and white-striped muslin walking dress she wore was not meant to contain the package attached to her midsection, even with the bodice coming just beneath her breasts and the fullness of the skirt. It might have been a better fit if it weren't a prosthetic, but Psyche had no intention of finding out whether or not that was the case at any time in the immediate future. There would have to be several odd occurrences to take place in order for it to happen at all, and they were so unlikely it would border on miraculous.

"How much longer will I have to stay like this?" she hissed frustratedly to the person crouched on the floor behind the piece of furniture.

"He'll be coming any second! Just sit still and *quit* squirming!" hissed her sister from her hiding place.

"I can't breathe! This thing is too heavy!" griped Psyche.

"Now you know how I feel!" said her sister, Pandora, tartly. "At least *you* will be able to take it off soon!"

"I don't know why I ever let you talk me into this," groaned Psyche, shaking her head.

"*Shh!*" hissed Pandora. "I can hear him coming!"

Psyche attempted to compose her features into something less anxious as she, too, could hear the sound of approaching footsteps in the hall. She picked up the book that had been lying on the couch beside her and flipped to a likely point and pretended to read.

"He's never going to—" began Psyche under her breath.

"Shh!" hissed Pandora again.

Psyche rolled her eyes, but she continued to pretend reading. She didn't think Islington would be fooled for an instant, but her sister had insisted they pull the prank. Psyche decided it was so much the better if he wasn't fooled. She could not breathe, and she was ready to call the nonsense to a halt. The door opened, and Pandora's husband walked into the sitting room.

"Hallo, Pan, my poisoned hussy," Islington teased. He smiled warmly as he closed the door and came to sit beside Psyche on the settee. "Did Psyche leave already?"

"She wanted to go home and work on her translations a little more before going to the Stranraers'. She said she's to a particularly difficult part at the moment," said Psyche with a smile, setting her book aside.

Islington took both of her hands in his and slid closer to her on the settee with a teasing smile.

"Hmm. Mother is gone to visit Selena at Aberdare House, so that leaves the two of us to our own devices," said Islington suggestively with a grin. He slid even closer, and Psyche leaned back nervously.

Her brother-in-law of nine months' standing was handsome, with rich blue eyes and dark blond hair. He was looking particularly fine in a dark brown frock coat with black velvet cuffs and collar over a brocaded gold waistcoat worn with fawn-colored breeches and his riding boots, but he was married to her sister, who happened to be hiding behind the settee. She might be an innocent, but Psyche had no doubt regarding what he thought he and his wife should do to pass the time.

"What about the servants?" she asked faintly with a weak smile.

Islington chuckled and leaned closer. "We can go upstairs to our room. I'll even carry you," he said with a grin, and he pulled her closer and stood up with her in his arms.

"Oh, no!" gasped Psyche in alarm. "Put me down, please, before you drop me!"

Islington chortled. "Oh, m'dear, I can't believe you are still not over that." He kissed her forehead affectionately and gave her a squeeze. "Aside from that, you have not gotten so heavy that I am unable to carry you."

"What about your shoulder?" she asked quickly.

Islington gave her a half-smile. "I would say it is *obviously* not bothering me at the moment."

"How could you possibly think of something like *that* when I look like *this*?" wailed Psyche anxiously, quickly running out of ways to forestall things.

Islington laughed outright and shook his head. He bent his head toward hers to nuzzle her cheek. "Pandora, that is *not* what you were saying this morning."

"*Theo!*" gasped Pandora in shock, and she rose as quickly as she could from the floor behind the settee.

Psyche sighed with relief as her brother-in-law placed her feet onto the floor. His shoulders were shaking with silent laughter as he looked at his wife, who was still looking at him in round-eyed disbelief as she came around the couch to stand beside her sister, her hands resting on her hips. Islington turned to look at Psyche with a barely apologetic expression.

"You knew I wasn't Pandora," she said calmly.

"Of course," said Islington, giving her a huge grin.

He looked at the two sisters standing beside each other. For the moment, they did look alike. Both had the same golden blonde, spiraling-tendriled hair and almost feline, grass green eyes. They shared the same impish nose, sensual lips and determined chin. They had the same refined bone structure and soft beige skin. Psyche and Pandora were identical twins, and at present they both appeared to be *very* pregnant, but only Pandora really was. He had never had a problem distinguishing between the two of them, but this current difference in their conditions was the only thing that saved many people from confusion.

"How did you know she wasn't me?" asked Pandora disappointedly with a frown.

Islington tilted his head sideways as he looked at her incredulously. "You mean other than knowing my own wife?" he asked with an amused smile. "She was holding the book—which happened to be Pringle—in her right hand; you don't have a dress like that; and she looked much too guilty. You have never been able to fool me, Pan. You know that."

"But we look exactly alike," said Psyche dully, and at the moment she was wishing they didn't because she was feeling very hot and uncomfortable.

"True enough," agreed Islington mildly, "but I still know the difference. Call it a benefit of matrimony." He winked at Pandora.

"All right," said Psyche diffidently. She turned to look at her sister. "Can we take this off now, please? I honestly can't breathe."

"Very well," sighed Pandora. "Islington, turn around for a minute."

He smiled amusedly and did as he was told.

Psyche sighed with relief as she lifted her gown and chemise to let Pandora undo the ties that held on the blanket-wrapped melon attached to her abdomen. She felt much better once the weight and extra fabric were removed. Psyche was still unsure what it was that Pandora had hoped to accomplish with this charade, but it seemed her husband had managed to turn the tables on her. Psyche had to express a moment of admiration for Islington because so few people were able to catch Pandora in one of her pranks. Psyche knew from years of observation…and sometimes participation.

Pandora and her husband had been married at the end of the previous September (actually, at the end of the previous August if one wanted to consider their "elopement" to Scotland). She had gone from being Lady Pandora Savage, daughter of Alexander Savage, the Duke of Aberdare, to Pandora, Marchioness of Bardsey. Islington, her husband, had only started using his marquessate for address at the beginning of this year's Parliament session and Season, even though he had been the marquess for five years. Before that, he preferred to go by one of the lesser titles he possessed, Viscount Islington. Most everyone in Psyche's family (including his wife) still called him Islington, but the *ton* had readily and easily taken to calling him Lord

Bardsey. Psyche suspected the only reason he had started using it was that Pandora was due to deliver their first child around the middle of July, and Islington was anticipating the birth of a son, who would use the viscountcy for a courtesy title. They were blissfully happy together, and Psyche was relieved for her sister.

The twins had their debut the previous Season. Pandora had met her future husband almost immediately. Psyche had not found anyone who struck her in that fashion, and she was perfectly content to let it remain that way. Pandora had been lucky in finding a spouse who gave her the freedom to carry on her activities in chemistry, mathematics, engineering, and mechanics. He had even went so far as to allow her to oversee the implementation of a new plumbing and gas system in their houses similar to the one the two girls and their father had designed for the Aberdares. It would be completed by the middle of June, in plenty of time for the birth of their baby.

Psyche had no luck finding someone who she felt would be willing to let her continue with her work in antiquities and her quest to decipher Egyptian hieroglyphs and other ancient languages. Most men of the *ton* viewed a woman's study of such things as freakish, if they even considered a woman might have the intelligence for it at all. The men who didn't find it disagreeable were either already married or not interested in women. So Psyche was content to stay to home, where her interests remained unfettered and respected.

Psyche was still trying to convince her parents to let her go to Greece and Egypt, but she had quickly decided she was *not* getting married just to make it so. She had become all the more intent to go when she discovered her oldest brother, Myron, would be going by the end of the Season. He was not keen on taking her with him, but she was sure if he told her parents he would be her chaperone, they would allow it. She wasn't even sure *he* was against it. It more likely had to do with whom he would be traveling.

Myron shared Psyche's interests, and they both held them in common with their father. Her brother had studied at Oxford, but he readily admitted Psyche was the better scholar. They both made frequent visits to the British Museum, and he had pleased her to no end when he was able to obtain rubbings of the Rosetta stone for her. She was sure he told the staff he wanted them for himself, but Psyche didn't care how he had gotten them, only that he had. She had carefully created a second copy for him, but she had made much more progress. After he had broken his leg at the close of the previous Season in a riding accident while he was looking for Pandora on her way to Scotland, once it had healed, his interest in deciphering had waned. He was not spending as much time at home, and he often seemed to be preoccupied.

As far as Psyche knew, Myron still wanted to go to the Mediterranean and North Africa, but she wasn't sure that he would go there the same way he had originally intended. If those plans fell through, and it seemed as if they would, the only other way he would go was with their brother, Gregory. That also did not seem to be a possibility.

Pandora and Islington had gone the rather circuitous route to Bermuda by way of Edinburgh for their honeymoon. Psyche had been invited along, much to her joy. However, while they were in Hamilton, they had a bittersweet reunion with their next-eldest brother, Gregory, who happened to arrive there during their sojourn to have his Bermuda sloop, the *Julia* (named in honor of their mother), fitted with more cannon. He had determined that delivery of supplies and relaying dispatches across the Atlantic was not a sufficient contribution to the war effort for him. When the girls returned home, they had the distinctly unpleasant task of informing the duke and duchess. Gregory had only been home once, at Christmas. His family had tried to make him change his mind, but it was set.

Now that it appeared the conflict with Napoleon was coming to an end with the Bourbon monarchy restored in France, Britain would be able to focus more of her attention toward settling the disagreement with the United States. Psyche didn't hold out much hope that it would be over immediately, thereby preventing any harm from coming to Gregory and giving Myron an alternate passage to Greece and Egypt. Perhaps by next year, when Gregory was home, she would have had time to convince her parents that she should be allowed to go as well.

Psyche dropped her garments and adjusted them back into place. She looked at Pandora as she placed the blanket and melon onto the settee. The two of them truly had, for a time, looked identical again. Other than the enormous bulge at the front of her dress, Pandora looked much the same as she ever had. She hadn't encountered much in the way of morning sickness, and her appetite was as healthy as ever. The only odd craving she had encountered (and it had been *only* once) was for lampreys. Their physician, Dr. Hinton, had tried to place her onto a restricted diet and regimen, but Pandora would have none of it. Her husband was a trained physician as well, but Islington knew better than to issue her orders, especially when it came to food. The only complaints she had were a heartburn that would never quite go away once her girth began to enlarge and a constant ache in her lower back. Considering how large she was, the backache was no surprise.

"Oh, Psyche, you've got to feel this! Quickly!" said Pandora excitedly as she turned from her task, beckoning her sister with her hand.

"Can I turn around now?" asked Islington dryly.

"Yes, yes," said Pandora unconcernedly.

Pandora took both of Psyche's hands in hers and placed one to either side of her stomach. Psyche looked down at her twin's swollen belly intently, waiting for whatever it was that had Pandora in a dither. She didn't have long. She felt and saw as the baby moved with such force that it made her hands bounce outward. She looked up at her sister's rapturous face and giggled. When she looked back down, with her hands holding the folds of Pandora's gown smooth, Psyche watched in amazement as a ripple of activity made her sister's stomach change shape from a perfect roundness to an odd lumpiness. She looked up at Pandora speculatively.

"I think there's more than one in there," she chortled.

Pandora's eyes grew round in alarm. "No, there isn't. There's just one," she said firmly.

"How do you know?" asked Psyche with a grin. She looked over at Islington. "What do you think?"

Islington moved closer with a half-smile and put his own hands onto his wife's stomach. He didn't seem to be nearly so anxious about the prospect of Pandora carrying twins. He and Psyche both felt as Pandora's stomach rippled out of shape once again. He shook his head.

"I'm not sure," he said slowly, giving Pandora a wink.

"There's only one," she said hotly.

"See? Feel that," said Psyche, taking Pandora's hand and putting it onto one of the lumps. "That has to be a bum or a head." She moved her sister's other hand to another bulge. "That's also either a bottom or a top."

"Yes, one or the other of *each*," said Pandora obstinately.

"No," said Psyche patiently, giving a shake of her head. "Look where they are. There is no possible way those can belong to the same baby unless you are giving birth to Cerberus."

Islington rubbed a hand over his mouth to hide a smirk. He hadn't really considered it until then, but now his sister-in-law had mentioned it and demonstrated it, he was inclined to agree. He thought his wife was larger than expected. Carrying twins would explain it. He looked at Pandora. She saw his barely contained amusement, and she became all the more panicked.

"There's only one!" she huffed, pushing their hands away.

"Would you like to wager on that?" asked Psyche with a giggle.

"There's no need to wager because there's only one," said Pandora testily.

Psyche's shoulders shook with amusement. "Then there's no loss for you in placing a wager."

"Fine," said Pandora, relenting and giving her sister a determined smile. "What is your wager?"

"Do I really want to know about this?" asked Islington with a chuckle.

"Oh, it will be perfectly respectable," said Psyche. She grew thoughtful for a moment and tugged at her bottom lip as she tried to decide on the stakes.

"As long as it doesn't involve cravats," said Islington with a smirk. "I understand it was you who masterminded that ingenious scheme."

"Oh, pooh," said Psyche, waving her hand in the air dismissively. "It was harmless enough."

"Speak for yourself!" hooted Pandora.

At the beginning of the previous Season, Psyche and Pandora had placed a wager regarding who would be able to obtain the most cravats from gentlemen with a pair of earrings as the prize. Pandora had managed to get two, both from the same man, and he wound up becoming her husband. She had also managed to get one for Psyche from a different man, and he was now barely on civil terms with her twin. After some consideration, both sisters realized it had not been the wisest thing for them to gamble.

"I have it!" said Psyche victoriously. "If you have only one jack in a box, I'll sing *Those Endearing Young Charms* at Mamà and Papà's anniversary dinner."

"And what if there are two?" asked Islington with a raised eyebrow, folding his arms across his chest.

"Then Pandora will," said Psyche with a grin, folding her arms in front of her smugly.

"I think it would be less dangerous if you went after another piece of a man's articles," chuckled Islington. Pandora thumped him on the shoulder with her palm. "Ow!"

Pandora thought about the wager for a moment. Neither she nor her twin was more than passable at singing, and that particular song was devilishly difficult. She silently agreed with her husband's assessment it would be just as much torture for *her* as it would be for the *spectators*. Still, her parents' anniversary was about the same time she was supposed to give birth in July, and if she was still in her confinement or recovering, she wouldn't be able to leave the house, much less sing. Besides, she *knew* she was only having one baby. It seemed to be a safe enough bet.

"Very well, I accept," Pandora said with a grin. "You need to study those lyrics and let Dorian know you'll need accompaniment. You'll want to let Mamà know, too."

"I could say the same to you," said Psyche with a smirk, holding out her hand for a shake.

"I think I'll be ill that night," said Islington smartly. Pandora tried to hit him on the shoulder again, but he caught her hand with a grin and placed a kiss on her palm.

"Hmm, I think I'll have a word with Keung. You're becoming entirely too quick," said Pandora with a fond smile, tweaking the end of his nose.

The clock on the mantel struck the hour, and Psyche realized with some alarm that she was running late. She was due home to get ready for a ball at the Stranraers', and her maid, Chrissoula, was intending to put her hair into a style that would take some time to complete. She also had to be back early enough to see that their younger sister, Eurydice, was togged as well.

"I have to be getting home," she said reluctantly.

Pandora chuckled. "Yes, you've got to see that Eurydice puts away her violin. Papà and Mamà should really let her go to Vienna."

"Only if they let me go to Greece and Egypt first," said Psyche flatly.

"I don't see them letting either one of you go anywhere." Pandora shook her head. "I'm sorry to say that was my fault."

"Yes, Mamà and Papà have become a bit stricter about us leaving the house alone. The only reason they let me come see you without someone else is that I come in a carriage, and Jim is *not* going to let me run off." Psyche shrugged with a grin. "It's not so bad really. Things are fairly the same as ever. It could be much worse." She gave Pandora a hug and a kiss, and then she hugged Islington as well. "Are you two coming tonight?"

"Of course," said Pandora. "The Stranraers are friends. I don't mind attending functions given by friends."

"Pan, you've become a drudge," said Psyche with a giggle.

"And proud of it, too," said Pandora with a grin.

Psyche left the house after Waldon, the butler, retrieved her belongings. She went out to the coach waiting at the curb, where Jim, one of her family's coachmen and one of their few English servants, assisted her in. She leaned back against the cushions and chewed the side of her thumb contemplatively as she looked out the window when the carriage got under way. She loved spending time with her twin, and it made her sad when she had to go home. She visited three or four times a week, and they saw each other at social functions, but it was never enough. Psyche missed seeing Pandora every day.

Psyche was lonely without her sister. It was odd she should feel that way in some respects. They were from a large family. The duke and duchess were the parents of eleven children, and Pandora was the only one that no longer lived under their roof. Of the eleven, including the twins, five were girls, so it wasn't as if Psyche lacked for female companionship. Perhaps it was because she and Pandora had been inseparable before Pandora's marriage, even though they didn't really share the same interests.

They had shared the solarium at Wilderland, their family's estate in Wales, as their private domain. One side had been filled with Pandora's chemistry sets, experiments, and models, the other with Psyche's books, scrolls, and artifacts. All of Pandora's things had been packed up and moved to her new home Marshcliff, in Bardsey, and the solarium seemed empty and incomplete without them. Psyche's other sisters had no interest in filling the void. She had even asked her mother if she wanted to start using the solarium for her plants again, but the duchess was satisfied to have her rare specimens stay in the greenhouse where she knew they would remain perfectly safe.

Arachne, Psyche's older sister, had no interests that would require the room. She read literature and wrote, both of which she was able to do at the desk in her sitting room. She painted and sketched, which she was also able to do in her room or out of doors. She assisted the duke and duchess with tutoring their youngest brother, the eight-year-old Damon, who was deaf and wouldn't be able to go to Harrow, and she also helped with tutoring the next-youngest boys, the nearly eleven-year-old identical twins Cosmo and Christopher, but that also did not require the empty space of the solarium.

Eurydice, Psyche's eighteen-year-old, next-youngest sister, who had just come out that year, also didn't need the space. Her only interest was her violin, and she played it in her rooms incessantly. Her debut had provided a respite to her family. She played divinely…unless she thought she made a mistake, and then she would start the piece all over again or practice the few bars where she had erred several times until a family member felt the urge to go to her room and break her instrument. She didn't need more room.

Most of the pursuits of her youngest sister, the seventeen-year-old Persephone, didn't require her to be indoors at all. The only thing she did that required room indoors was having a table for playing cards. The rest of her interests were much better suited to outside, things like shooting, fencing, archery, racing, and sailing. She was a tomboy, and she was more often found in britches than a dress when they were at home in Wales, and since Gregory was away in America, he had charged Persephone with the care of his skiff on the lake.

Psyche had thought for a time about rearranging her own possessions in the solarium to make it seem not quite so empty, but it didn't feel right. She knew Pandora wouldn't be returning to reclaim its use, but Psyche would always consider the other side of the room to be Pandora's half. She had, however, started using it as a place to practice her *wǔshù* and *t'ai chi ch'uan*, but that was something else she used to do with her twin and no longer could.

Her brother, Dorian, the next-to-oldest of the Savage children, had married Islington's sister, Selena, in the same ceremony the previous September, but she also had no interest in using the space. She spent most of her time with the duchess doing needlework or knitting. The renovations were almost completed on the hunting lodge on the far edge of their estate, where Dorian and Selena would be taking up residence at the close of the Season regardless.

Psyche had asked Myron if he was interested in using the space for his own studies, thinking it would give them the perfect opportunity to collaborate on their deciphering, but he declined. Psyche wasn't sure what was happening with her brother. He had been away from home often once his leg healed. He didn't tell anyone what he was doing when he left, but he was a twenty-four-year-old man. Her parents' new rules on outings did not apply to him.

Psyche could only assume he was spending the time with his friend, Lord Barneville. Actually, he was Lord Sheerness now, and that would take some adjustment in Psyche's mind because she had taken to calling him *Barneville the Bastard*. As much as she loathed him, she couldn't bring herself to be so uncharitable, at least for a while, and give him a new sobriquet to go with the new title, considering the circumstances behind his acquiring it. She was compassionate enough to admit that, regardless of how beastly he often was to her, no one deserved to suffer the recent misfortunes he had.

Sebastian Nichols, the newly-titled Earl of Sheerness, was one of Myron's best friends. They had known each other since before Myron was at Oxford. Until about two weeks ago, he had been styled Baron de Barneville. The first stroke of bad luck for his family had happened at the beginning of December when his younger sister, Monique Yeardley, the Baroness Yeardley, had been killed in a riding accident, leaving behind a husband and three small children. She was only twenty-nine. Then, his youngest sister, Amalie, had become engaged to the Earl of Westerkirk by the close of last Season, but after her sister's death and the start of her mourning period, the earl had broken it off, deciding he didn't want to wait. The final tragedy had struck two weeks ago, when Barneville's father, the former Earl of Sheerness and a very close friend of Psyche's father, had died from a heart attack after a loss in the first running of the One Thousand Guineas at Newmarket. What made it all the more tragic was that he had been misinformed, and the filly had actually won. Psyche wasn't confident his death and the false information were actually related.

Psyche's parents had been friends with the deceased earl and the Countess of Sheerness for years, before their children had even been born. The countess was an émigré from France prior to the Revolution, until her marriage known as Josephine, comtesse de Fourmies, which was why all of her children had Gallic given names. She had taken the death of her oldest daughter and husband very hard. When Psyche had attended the earl's funeral with her family on the Isle of Sheppey at the chapel on the Nicholses' estate, Belle Glade, Lady Sheerness had not seemed the same woman. Psyche had always known her as energetic and humorous, with a quick wit and ready laugh. The countess had leaned on her oldest son's arm for support, her features pale beneath her black veil. Psyche could only imagine the heartbreak she felt.

The new earl had—outwardly, at least—appeared to be the same as ever. He had graciously accepted everyone's condolences, even Psyche's, and had attentively remained at his mother's side throughout the entire affair. Psyche knew from her friendship with Amalie that the Nicholses shared a close familial relationship, much like Psyche's own family, and Psyche knew Barneville had been close to his father. Regardless of how calm and composed he seemed, she knew he couldn't be finding his father and sister's deaths any easier to manage than the countess. Psyche knew that, despite their mutual dislike for one another, most people found him to be charming and conscientious, including her twin; it seemed unlikely he was as unaffected as he tried to pretend.

Psyche couldn't understand why he was always so hateful toward her. She would have thought they would get on well together, considering he shared her and Myron's interest in ancient Greece and Egypt. The only thing she could assume was that he thought her a simple female, who couldn't possibly know one Greek letter from another, never mind knowing Demotic from Hieratic. Psyche knew she had earned part of his dislike because she had corrected one of his translations and disagreed with his reasons for acquiring artifacts. He obstinately believed the corrections had been done by Myron rather than Psyche, despite her and Myron's assertions to the contrary. Barneville thought her disagreement regarding his acquisitions was irrelevant because she herself had never done any field work.

That Pandora had done something to him at a ball at the Sheernesses' last Season that had made him speechlessly angry while she was pretending to be Psyche had not improved matters any. Pandora did eventually tell Psyche what she had done while they were in Bermuda (where she had confessed to a multitude of other things as well), and Psyche couldn't really blame him for being furious. She did have to admit, however, that he had deserved it. Still, from that night on, he had been more determined than ever to argue with Psyche, and he incessantly took an opposing view from her own on everything, no matter how trivial it was or how obtuse it made him appear, simply because he refused to say or do *anything* that would agree with her.

Psyche knew Barneville was the reason Myron didn't want to let her go with him. If her brother went, he would go with Barneville. Myron knew his sister and his friend didn't get on with each other. He wanted to *enjoy* his trip; constantly being their mediator would make that impossible. Psyche was willing to be civil to Lord Barneville, if he would treat her with a modicum of the same, but she had to agree with her brother's assessment the earl would be unlikely to do so.

At the moment, however, the concern was null. Due to Barneville's recent calamities, Psyche doubted he would be going at any time in the near future. He was in mourning, and while it was not as strict for men as it was for women, she was sure his grief for the loss of his family members and concern for his mother would dissuade him from leaving for the Mediterranean for quite some time. When coupled with the necessity of taking up his father's seat in the House of Lords, Psyche knew it would be at least after the close of Parliament and sometime after that before he would have the freedom to go anywhere.

Psyche focused her gaze out the window and brought herself back from her wool gathering. They had just turned onto Bond Street and would soon be to the mews behind her family's home, Aberdare House, which was on Bruton Street off Berkeley Square. She looked at the watch on the chain around her neck. She would be home with just enough time to get ready to leave…no chance to catch her breath and relax. She didn't think she would even have time for a quick bath.

She wasn't looking forward to the ball that night. She liked the Stranraers, but it was another social function. She couldn't understand for the life of her why she had agreed to another Season. It probably had to do with her sister, Eurydice, needing a guiding hand, although her grace and Arachne were more than capable of attending to it. Still, Psyche had agreed to another Season to offer her sister and mother some relief from supervising Eurydice.

She had some consolation in that her calendar this Season was not as active as it had been the year before. Last year, she had gone somewhere almost every night because she had wanted to comply with her parents' wish that she should have a full Season. This year, they were content to let her go as she willed. That made Psyche happy because it gave her more time to work on her translations. It also saved her from being nice to people she didn't like. There were two or three social functions that had been cancelled because they would have been at the Sheernesses'. After the earl's death, they wouldn't be held.

Eurydice viewed the Season with as much disdain as her older sisters, possibly even more, but her grace had informed the girl she would have at least one, just as Arachne and the twins had. Persephone's turn would come the following year, and Psyche suspected there would be a minor battle, possibly with bladed weapons involved, to get the tomboy into a ball gown. At least Eurydice had no qualms about wearing dresses, and she was able to comport herself in a ladylike fashion.

Her only unusual pastime was her music, but it seemed to be the only topic of conversation that held her interest. So far, at the balls they had attended, her only comments had been on the capabilities of the musicians that had been hired. She had difficulty remembering the names of the guests and sometimes even the hosts. When she was presented at court, it had been all the duchess and her sisters could do to keep her from taking her violin with her. She had been certain the Prince Regent would want to hear her play. He was certainly enchanted by Eurydice's unique beauty, created by her flawless skin, auburn hair and amber-colored eyes, but her ability to play a violin was not something that would have intrigued him; Psyche was sure.

Psyche felt the carriage come to a stop and looked out the window to see they had arrived in the mews. Psyche felt the carriage shift slightly as Jim alighted to open the door for her. He helped her down and touched the brim of his hat politely. Psyche paused and looked up at him with a grin.

"Did you ever imagine you would be relegated to nursemaid?" she asked him cheekily.

Jim chuckled. "Cor, Lady Psyche, I wouldn't consider meself a nursemaid. Bodyguard would be more fittin'," he said with a smile. "A lady shouldn't 'ave to walk anyhow."

"Yes, but you also have to ride with me in Hyde Park every morning."

"That's not bad," said Jim. "It gives me a chance to exercise the horses that don't get out much, like Amati." (That was Eurydice's horse.) "Gives *me* a chance to exercise because I don't get out much, either," he chuckled.

Psyche patted him on the shoulder appreciatively and went to the gate that opened to the garden path to the back of the house. She walked past the gazebo and inhaled deeply the scent of her mother's roses. They were looking quite extravagant this year, and the inside of the house was drowning in their perfume from the open windows and the vases placed everywhere. Psyche greatly appreciated her mother's gardening ability, as well as that of their gardeners. Psyche lifted her watch to look at the time, and her eyes rounded in alarm as she quickened her step. She was running very late…again.

Chapter Two

The Earl of Sheerness was sitting at the table on the terrace, peacefully drinking his coffee and reading the paper, when his mother, the newly-widowed Countess of Sheerness, came through one of the sets of French doors at the back of the house to join him. A nearby footman quickly came to the table and poured a cup of coffee for her before retaking his attentive yet unobtrusive position. She waited a few minutes more, and another footman brought her a plate with toast, eggs, and sausage. Lord Sheerness continued to calmly read the paper, occasionally turning the page as he reached the end of an article, studiously attempting to ignore his mother's impatient glare.

Lord Sheerness knew what she wanted to discuss, and he was through talking about it. She had given him only three days respite after his father's death—just the amount of time it had taken to deposit his body in their family's mausoleum—before she started. Lord Sheerness didn't doubt his mother had loved his father and would probably continue to grieve for him for the rest of her life, but she also had a strong sense of duty. Her son shared her sentiments on most things, but the subject she wanted to continue debating was not among them. However, he soon finished with the paper and was left with little choice but to look up at her annoyed countenance.

"Was there something you wanted to discuss, *Maman*?"

"Sebastian, you know full well what I want to talk about," said Lady Sheerness perturbedly.

"No, *Maman,* I do not," he said dryly. "To know your mind would require an otherworldly skill I do not possess."

"Don't be impertinent with me, Sebastian. I am your mother, and you will *never* be so old that I won't hide you."

Lord Sheerness smiled at her amusedly, but he wouldn't be moved. "We're finished with that. I've already told you my mind. It's not going to change."

"It better," said his mother stonily. "What about your father's last wish?"

"He didn't give me a bound, *Maman,*" said Lord Sheerness firmly.

"Even if he didn't, you know what he intended, and do not try to pretend that you don't."

"I'm afraid it will not be something speedily or easily—nor should I say willingly—attended to, *Maman.*"

"Is that right?" said Lady Sheerness shortly. She took a sip from her coffee. "You should go to the Lundeys' tonight."

"*Maman,* I am in mourning," said Lord Sheerness exasperatedly. "Can you not wait a year?" He took a sip from his coffee. "Preferably longer," he muttered under his breath.

"No, I cannot, and you *will* not," said his mother determinedly. "You *will* go to the Lundeys' tonight." Her expression softened to one of mischief, and Sheerness was almost reminded of how she was before his father's death. "The Aberdares are going to be there. I think all their daughters who have come out are going to be there as well. They are all very exquisite, aren't they?"

"*Maman, mon dieu!*" groaned Sheerness. "Enough!" He rubbed a hand over his face and shook his head. "You may be my mother, but I'm a full-grown man, not some bantling in short pants! This isn't for you to decide."

Lady Sheerness wiped her mouth on her napkin and stood, tossing it on the table. Josephine could see discussing it with him further at that point would not yield any better result, but she didn't intend to let him sit and mope. It was true he was an adult, but she was still his mother. She still remembered how he was when he was a child, almost as if it were yesterday. That part of him was still in there somewhere, and she knew *it* very well. She went to stand by his chair and looked down at him with a pleading expression.

"Sebastian, *mon cher,* you are thirty-one years old, and now you are the Earl of Sheerness. You had *better* get yourself a wife…soon." She gave him a sympathetic squeeze to his shoulder before she went back inside.

"Thea, you need to hold still. I can't get this wound through your hair properly if you continue to squirm."

Psyche looked up at Chrissoula's reflection in the mirror. Psyche was fidgety because she was late, as usual. It didn't matter how early she rose from bed, she never seemed to have enough hours in the day to be on time…for anything. She was late for breakfast. She was late going to dinner. If she ate supper at home (or anywhere else, for that matter), she was late. She was late going to social functions, although that was becoming fashionable. Psyche would probably be late for her own wedding *and* her own funeral. The only time she could recall being early was when she was born twenty minutes before her twin. Pandora often mentioned how odd it was that Psyche never seemed to be on time for anything, and yet she was always up at the crack of dawn. Psyche had to admit it was peculiar. She didn't think she dawdled, but since she was always tardy, that apparently was the case.

"I'm sorry, Chrissoula," she said softly with an apologetic smile. "I'm just behind."

"Thea, you are always behind," said her maid tartly, but she softened it with a smile.

Psyche gave Chrissoula a half-smile and did her best to remain calm. She watched as her maid deftly threaded a strand of pearls through her hair, which had been braided and coiled into a loose knot on top of her head with a few tendrils left loose at her nape. Once the pearls were threaded, Chrissoula secured them in place with a golden comb studded with more of the jewels. Psyche's maid always did a wondrous job taming her hair, and tonight was no exception. The style went perfectly with the gown she had chosen.

The dress she wore was composed mostly of soft pink silk, but the short puffed sleeves were split, and a white silk under sleeve showed through. The bodice was covered in intricate embroidery of silver tinsel, and there were strips of matching embroidery at three levels along the skirt and at the bottom edge. It was comfortable and attractive, and the pink complimented Psyche's complexion and made the green of her eyes seem even brighter. She chose not to wear a necklace because she was wearing the pearls in her hair, but she wore small diamond studs in her ears with a single pearl hanging by a thin chain from each.

"Now, gloves, shawl, and slippers, and you'll be ready to go," said Chrissoula with a nod.

Psyche rose from her seat to put on her slippers. They were made of black kid, and Psyche liked the soft suppleness of the leather as she put them on her stockinged feet. Chrissoula held her gloves to put on, and Psyche appreciated her maid's assistance in sliding on the elbow-length satin. She was luckily not affected by the itchiness that wearing gloves prompted in her twin. Psyche could only assume it was caused by the bleaching or tanning process because Pandora didn't seem nearly so bothered when they were crocheted from undyed yarn. Chrissoula draped the embroidered burgundy cashmere shawl she had chosen around Psyche's shoulders, and Psyche was ready to leave.

"Thank you, Chrissoula. Magnificent work, as usual," she said with a pleased smile.

"Thea, it is easy to create a masterpiece when the original piece of stone comes already the right shape," said Chrissoula amusedly. "Do you need me to be up when you get home?"

"No, I think I'll be able to manage. If you can just do the usual things. Have you gotten another letter from your brother yet?"

Chrissoula nodded and smiled happily. "Yes, it came today."

"How are he and Ioanna?"

"They have a new little girl!"

"Congratulations!" said Psyche excitedly, clapping her hands. "What did they name her?"

"Yelena Christina Sofia Andreanopoulos."

"What a beautiful name," said Psyche happily. "How many is that now?"

"Five."

"My goodness!" said Psyche in amazement. "And still no boys?"

"Not yet. I suppose once they have one, they will stop."

"Well, let's hope that's soon," said Psyche with a chuckle.

"Oh, yes," agreed Chrissoula with a laugh of her own.

Psyche looked at the door expectantly after there was a brief knock, and Arachne came into the room.

"Mama sent me to retrieve you," she said with a grin.

"I was just coming," said Psyche hurriedly.

"Mm-hmm," said Arachne doubtfully, adjusting her wrap on her shoulders. "She said if you don't hurry, Eurydice is going back to her room and will start playing again, so please hurry."

Psyche laughed. "Good night, Chrissoula."

"Good night, Thea.*"*

Chrissoula knew better than to tell Psyche to have a wonderful time. She had listened to all of Psyche's grumbling and railing the previous Season. There was less so far this year, but it had barely begun. Chrissoula was going to her room in the servants' quarters to answer her brother's letter, and then she was going to, thankfully, retire early. She would have to be up early in the morning to attend to her mistress.

Psyche followed Arachne downstairs to see her parents and younger sister impatiently waiting for her at the bottom. Dorian and Myron, as well as Selena, had already left. As the number of members of their family participating in the Season grew, it became necessary for them to take two carriages, but her siblings had gone to avoid being too terribly late. Psyche and the rest of her family were just going to avoid being inexcusably so.

The function they were attending that night was a bit peculiar. It was a ball held at the home of the Earl of Lundey on South Audley, celebrating the engagement of his son, Viscount Drake, to a woman named Victoria Manson. That, in and of itself, was not what made it odd. The cause of the awkwardness was that Drake had been celebrating his engagement to Victoria's younger sister, Lilane, at about the same time the previous Season.

Lilane, also known as Lilly, was one of Arachne's best friends. Lilly had been invited to attend the anniversary dinner party for the Duke and Duchess of Aberdare the previous Season, but she had sent her regrets the morning of the day the function was to take place. No one in London had seen her since. Arachne had written her several letters, but Lilly never sent an answer back. Drake had similar results. About three months after she had seemingly disappeared off the face of the earth, the viscount received a letter from his fiancée informing him that she had eloped with her sister's fiancé, a soldier named Sean MacNeil, and gone with him to where he was stationed in India.

Arachne had been astounded when Drake informed her. She didn't believe it. She *knew* her friend had been truly in love with the viscount. She couldn't believe Lilly would have jilted him, let alone that she would elope with another man and go to India. But there was nothing she could do to disprove it, especially not after Drake showed her Lilly's letter. Arachne recognized her friend's handwriting. She had no choice but to silence her doubts about the matter.

The viscount had been upset over Lilly's defection. It could only be assumed Victoria had felt the same about her betrayal by MacNeil. The Savages were surprised when they learned the two jilted parties had become engaged to each other. Still, Drake was a grown man, and the Mansons, while not titled, were a respectable and wealthy family. Most people in society felt that one sister would be as good as the other when it came to marriage. The Savages, particularly the three older girls, who had all been friends with Lilly, felt Drake had repaid one betrayal with another.

As bizarre as the events surrounding the engagement had been, the Savages were even more surprised when they learned the Mordecais intended to have a ball to celebrate it, especially considering it had been almost a year to the day since the first one. But the Savages would never think of refusing to attend. The Earl and Countess of Lundey were longtime friends of the duke and duchess, and the older girls, while they may not have agreed with his choice of bride (especially Arachne), were friends with Drake and wanted to wish him the best of luck and happiness for his marriage.

Psyche intended to follow Pandora's suit (for the most part) on accepting social invitations. She would go to Almack's more than her twin (if only to keep Eurydice's attention on matters at hand), but most functions she would attend were only those held by family or friends. Now that she wouldn't have to worry about torment by Lord Barneville (*Lord Sheerness!*—she could not seem to remember that), she thought she might be able to tolerate going to more. Although it did take her away from her studies, she did like to dance, and after one Season, she had met almost everyone. Most of the *ton* she was able to tolerate, even if they were a bit shallow. The majority of them were harmless, and she was well able to avoid or fend for herself against the ones who weren't.

When Psyche and her family arrived, the first thing she did was look for her twin. It wasn't difficult to find her. She and her husband were dancing to a waltz. Despite her large belly, Pandora moved across the floor gracefully, and Psyche smiled affectionately as she watched them. Her sister looked lovely in a burgundy velvet gown trimmed in tiny seed pearls and lace, her hair piled on top of her head in a loose, curling bunch, tied around with a scarf. Psyche would have to ask how Pandora's maid, Maiyin, had done that because she really liked it. As her sister was otherwise engaged, Psyche decided she might as well go offer her congratulations to the guests of honor.

Psyche noted as she walked toward Drake and Victoria Manson that his face wasn't quite as happy as it had been the last time there was a ball for this purpose. As a matter of fact, she thought he seemed to be subdued, almost resigned. Psyche felt that he found the whole affair to be disagreeable, including his engagement. He would smile and nod, graciously accepting all the well wishes from his guests, but there was something about his eyes, the smile never quite reaching them, that made it obvious he would rather be anywhere else but there.

His prospective bride, however, seemed almost manic in her happiness. Victoria kept his arm in place around her waist and would not let him move from her side. Psyche didn't think Victoria was as pretty as Lilly, but she was not unattractive. She had the same blonde hair and blue eyes, but she was taller and thinner. She was also very pale, almost pasty, and her eyes were feverish in a way that made Psyche uneasy. She would laugh and giggle occasionally in what *might* pass for a simpering manner, but to Psyche's ears it sounded affected…and a little deranged. Victoria's expression changed to one of possessive suspicion as Psyche approached them, and Psyche had the impression the woman found her presence unwelcome.

"Lady Psyche, I'm so glad you were able to come," said Drake, placing an affectionate kiss on her hand.

"Lord Drake," said Psyche with a smile. "You know I couldn't possibly refuse to attend an affair celebrating such a happy occasion for you." She winked at him conspiratorially. "Aside from that, your parents *and* my parents would tar and feather me if I did."

Drake laughed with genuine amusement, and Psyche was cheered to see that it reached his eyes. She smiled amiably at his future wife and was taken aback to see a venomous hatred in Victoria's expression…directed at her. Psyche had never met Victoria before; the older girl spent the previous Season in Edinburgh, where she had met Sean. Psyche hoped she was mistaken in what she saw because it was definitely unwarranted. If she was capable of having that much proprietary hatred for anyone who dared to talk to her future husband, it did not bode well for their marriage.

"Did Lady Arachne come with you?" he asked mildly, still holding Psyche's hand in both of his.

"Yes, she did. I imagine it won't be long before she comes to offer her own congratulations. If not, I'm sure you'll be able to figure out where she's hiding." Psyche continued to look at Victoria, and she could swear the girl looked as if she could do murder.

"Oh! Where are my manners?" said Drake, shaking his head. "Lady Psyche Savage, may I introduce my fiancée, Miss Victoria Manson?"

Psyche grinned at him. "You certainly may." She held out her hand to Victoria with a calm smile. "How do you do?" Victoria did not accept her hand. "You're a very lucky girl," said Psyche amiably. Victoria didn't say a word, but she continued to look at Psyche resentfully. Psyche gave Drake a teasing smile. "I can think of several girls who were upset to learn he was no longer an available commodity."

"Who?" spat Victoria.

Psyche tilted her head sideways and looked at Victoria suspiciously. She could see Drake grow uncomfortable because of Victoria's behavior. There was something very odd about her. Psyche wasn't quite sure she could say it was insanity, but she had no doubt Victoria was off kilter. At that moment, it was impossible for Psyche to understand why Drake would want to marry her. If it was simply to avenge himself on Lilly, there had to be a less unpleasant way to go about it. She knew Drake well enough to know Victoria was going to make him miserable. Psyche shrugged her shoulders and gave Drake another teasing wink, trying to lighten the tone of the conversation.

"Why, every available young miss in London, of course," she said with a chuckle. Drake had the modesty to blush. Victoria was not appeased.

"Including you?" asked Victoria coldly.

Psyche's eyes rounded in surprise. "*Me?* Most certainly not. This man used to dip my hair in ink when I was a little girl." She shook her head. "I refuse to have anything to do with someone so unchivalrous."

Drake laughed again. "Yes, but I only did that because you and Lady Pandora would steal my clothes when your brothers and I went swimming in the lake. Then you would hide them from me. It would take *hours* to find them, and you would always put them in the most difficult places to reach."

Psyche giggled. "That was only *one* summer. Besides, it was all Pandora's doing. I'm too afraid of heights to climb trees and up cliffs. I would just wait at the bottom, in case she fell. I don't know why I thought I would have been able to catch her, but there I was nonetheless."

"Don't try to blame it all on me," said Pandora with a chuckle, coming behind her sister, her arm casually linked through Islington's. "I may have been the one to hide them, but you were the one who decided where to put them and that they should be taken in the first place." She shook her head. "You try to make it seem like I'm the only one of the two of us who can be shifty, but you are every bit as inventive as I am. It is simply that I will follow through on it."

"Perhaps that's because my twenty minutes of seniority gave me a bit more common sense," said Psyche with a grin.

Islington and Drake looked at the two sisters, their shoulders shaking with silent amusement. Drake laughed because he had known the two girls since they were seven years old. Islington laughed because he was married to one of them. Neither man believed one twin had more common sense than the other, and both were equally capable of causing mischief in her own special way.

The only person who wasn't amused by the whole exchange was Victoria. She looked at the two girls angrily, jealous of the long association they had with Drake. Her expression grew sullen as she turned to look at her fiancé. Psyche supposed Victoria was trying to be attractively pouty, but Psyche thought she looked whiny. It was not becoming. Yes, Psyche predicted much unhappiness for Drake in the near future. He would be much happier if he married Arachne; even when she was bossy or unsociable, Psyche's older sister was at least not possessive.

"Darling, could we dance the cotillion, please?" asked Victoria, and Psyche *did* think it sounded like a whine and not the least bit like a charming simper.

Drake looked down at his fiancée, and his relaxed expression faded. Psyche watched as a nerve began to tick in his jaw, and she knew he was a little irritated. "Yes, of course," he said flatly. He looked back at the two girls and Islington. "If you'll excuse me."

The three watched him stiffly escort his future bride onto the floor for the dance.

"I say, Psyche, but I think she's a worse actress than you are," said Pandora softly as she watched the two of them dance. "And she dances worse than Persephone."

"I have to agree…on both counts," said Psyche mildly, as she watched Victoria miss a step in the figure and nearly collide with another couple. That she hadn't stepped on Drake's toes yet was miraculous.

"I think you two are being uncharitable," said Islington. "I thought she was perfectly acceptable."

Psyche looked at her brother-in-law and arched her eyebrow. "Acceptable does not imply *likable.*" She calmly folded her arms in front of her. "If their marriage goes ahead, I foresee an eternity of misery for Drake, which is unfortunate because he deserves to be happy. They are *so* unsuited to each other."

"And how would you know?" asked Islington with a grin. "You don't even know her. That's very unfair. Maybe she has some hidden charm that appeals to him."

"I wouldn't consider being barmy a *hidden charm,*" said Psyche, shaking her head.

"She didn't seem that way to me," said Islington, wincing as he watched Victoria miss another step in the dance. He had to agree with his wife and Psyche that she was a *terrible* dancer.

"Perhaps if you had been looking at something other than her apple dumplin' shop, you might have seen she had crazed eyes," said Pandora, giving him a grin to show that her words did not stem from jealousy. Islington flushed in embarrassment. "It's all right, *àiren.* You're a man," she said with a chuckle, patting his arm soothingly. She inhaled with a slight grimace and put a hand to the side of her stomach. "I'd like to sit down for a bit."

"Are you all right?" asked Psyche worriedly.

Pandora waved a hand through the air dismissively. "Yes, I'm fine. It is just that standing still for a long time makes him cranky." She patted the side of her stomach as she looked down at it.

"I think you mean *them,*" said Psyche with a chuckle.

"*Him,*" said Pandora firmly, her lips setting into a line. She didn't even want to contemplate that it might be anything else. Her expression changed to one of amazement as she remembered something. "I almost forgot! You'll *never* guess who is here tonight."

"Well, if I'm not likely to guess, please, enlighten me," grinned Psyche.

"Go on—three guesses," coaxed Pandora.

"The Prince Regent?" asked Psyche indulgently with a smile, her forehead wrinkling thoughtfully. Pandora shook her head negatively. "Hmm, the Duke of York?"

"Not bloody likely," said Islington with a grin.

Psyche looked up at the ceiling intently as she thought. She looked back at her sister. "Lord Byron?" Pandora and Islington both shook their heads and laughed. "Well, then? Who is it?" asked Psyche leadingly.

"Lord Sheerness!" said Pandora excitedly.

Psyche's face paled. "But he's in mourning," she said dully. "His father's not even been in his grave more than two weeks!"

Pandora shrugged. "It does seem disrespectful for him to be out and about so soon, but it is not socially unacceptable. He *is* a man." She gave her sister a mischievous grin. "I just thought you might like to know."

"Thanks for the warning," said Psyche dimly.

She distractedly watched as her sister and brother-in-law went toward the supper room. Once they disappeared from sight in the throng of people, Psyche began to look everywhere for her nemesis. Wherever he was, she did not want to be. She grew panicked as she scanned the faces in the ball room, but she didn't see him anywhere. She wondered if he was in the supper room, but she was certainly not going there to find out.

She looked at her watch. It would be a while before her family decided to leave. They had only just arrived. She could just walk home, but her parents would be worried (not to mention angry) if she did. In addition to that, the part of Westminster where she and the Lundeys lived was safer than other parts of the city, and she was capable of defending herself, but she would rather not have to. She tapped her foot anxiously as she tried to decide what to do. In the end, she determined the best way to avoid the earl would be to go outside, into the garden, and hide until it was time for her family to leave.

Psyche nonchalantly walked around the dance floor toward the back of the room and the wall of French doors leading onto the terrace. They were open to allow air to circulate into the room, and it was easy enough for her to slip through one of them without attracting attention. She went to the balustrade, rubbing at her arms through her gloves. It was cool outside after the heat accumulated inside from the mass of bodies, and she wished she had her shawl.

She didn't know why she didn't want to see Lord Barneville (*Lord Sheerness!*). Well, actually, she did. She didn't want to see him because he was always hateful and tried to make her feel stupid no matter what she said or did. When he danced with her last Season, it was only because duty required it, and he would either ignore her or insult her the entire time. She had discovered that whenever she was at a function where the earl was present, she was unlikely to enjoy herself for long…as the evening's turnabout had shown. She hated that she had been reduced to hiding from him, but she would rather be bored to tears in the garden than bullied to tears inside.

Psyche had been shocked when Pandora told her what the man had done last year that made her sister knock the wind out of him while pretending to be Psyche. She couldn't be sure Pandora was being entirely honest, though, because it seemed unlikely he would have tried to kiss Psyche, which is what her twin said he had done. As Psyche thought about it, that would have needed to be the entire purpose behind what he did because if Pandora (or Psyche, for that matter) were a typical female, his winning the wager would have been inevitable. Psyche was sure Pandora had made up the stakes of the wager in an effort to make her twin think her feelings were "reciprocated." Psyche had no doubt on that, but they weren't the feelings her sister thought they were.

Psyche knew Pandora thought the feelings between her and Barneville were of the tender persuasion, but she couldn't be more wrong. Psyche couldn't fairly say she hated the man because even though he was hateful toward her, she knew from observing his interactions with other people that he could behave conscientiously and warmly as long as Psyche wasn't the object of his attention. He was also intelligent and honest (at least, she was relatively sure he was). Psyche couldn't hate someone with those qualities. It did not mean, however, that she couldn't *dislike* him intensely. She didn't doubt the feelings were returned in kind.

She looked into the sky at the half-moon above her. It was turned on its side like a bowl, clouds passing over it. It was a beautiful moon, colored a dark yellow, almost orange, shade. The stars would sometimes show, but the clouds and occasional stiff breeze indicated it was going to rain before long, most likely before dawn.

Psyche walked down the stairs into the garden to look at the beautiful Rococo fountain with its charging stallions, roaring lions and unclad nymphs. She was sure the sculptor had meant to depict some scene from ancient Greece or Rome, but he had used so much artistic license in its creation, what it was could be anyone's guess. It was a well-done piece, but Psyche knew from seeing them firsthand in the British Museum that it could not compare to the real sculptures from the Mediterranean.

Psyche didn't think she had ever been into the Lundeys' garden before, but the fountain was meant to be the focal point of its design. It was difficult to see the exact plan of the garden in the dark, but Psyche didn't think there were very many flowering plants. It didn't smell as if they had any roses. Most of it was box topiary and neatly-shaped privet hedge.

As she went onto the path beyond the fountain, the paving stone turned to gravel, and she could feel some of the sharp pieces poking her feet through her slippers. She walked along the path carefully, wincing occasionally at a particularly sharp jab to her sole, and she hoped she wasn't tearing her slippers; she liked her slippers, and she didn't want to go back to the house with them ragged.

Psyche stepped on what felt like a knife, and she raised her foot with a yelp of pain. She put out a hand to brace herself against the nearby tall hedge to examine the bottom of her foot and yelped again when she pierced her palm on a protruding privet thorn. She lost her balance as it seemed the garden started to attack her, and she pinwheeled through an opening in the hedge, landing soundly onto her backside on the stone pavers that floored a small courtyard.

"*Bloody hell!*" she gasped as she added bruising to her tailbone to all her other afflictions.

She continued to mutter colorful expletives as she tried to examine her injuries in the dark. She pulled the glove off the hand that had been poked by the thorn and put her palm to her mouth. It didn't feel like it was bleeding, but it stung terribly. She removed her other glove and raised the foot that had been poked by the rock. She inspected the bottom of her slipper with her hand. It felt like it was still in one piece, if a bit dimpled. She pulled off the shoe and gingerly massaged her heel. She would be limping, at least slightly, for a little while. She hoped it wouldn't be too obvious when she returned to the house. She could hide it well enough until she got home to ache in peace if necessary.

She put her slipper back on and grabbed her gloves. Her bottom was becoming numb from sitting on the cold stone, but she could still feel the ache in her tailbone. She carefully stood up and sucked in air through her teeth as straightening out her posture caused a stab of pain.

"Damn, damn, *damn!*" Psyche hissed, and she blinked back tears.

She stood still for a minute, and the throbbing began to subside, especially after she reached back to gently massage her buttocks and get the blood flowing again. Once she got the pain under control, she reached up to examine her hair. Chrissoula's work still seemed intact. Psyche looked down at her bodice, and she put her gloves in her mouth to reach up both hands and adjust it. She shook out the back of her skirt to clean off the dust and small rocks. At least it wasn't torn. She could only hope her tumble hadn't left the light pink silk too dirty. It wouldn't do for her to go back into the brighter light looking a mess, and Chrissoula would throw a fit if Psyche ruined the gown.

Once Psyche was satisfied she was still in one piece, she gave her surroundings more attention. She had landed facing the exit. The hedge was about eight feet tall, and the opening was about four feet wide. She turned around to look at the rest of the grotto, wondering if she might bide her time there, and she yelped in surprise when she realized she was not alone. Then she colored a bright red with embarrassment when it dawned on her that someone had witnessed her clumsy entrance. She was absolutely mortified when she discovered it wasn't just anyone.

"I must say, Lady Psyche, your command of the slang of several extinct and not-so-extinct languages is quite impressive."

The Earl of Sheerness sat on a stone bench facing the entrance not far from where Psyche stood; so close in fact, he could probably reach out and touch her. She was unable to see his expression in the darkness of the shadow cast by the hedge, but his tone had been a drawl of belittling amusement. She felt humiliated, and to know he had simply sat there without offering any help when he could have possibly saved her from at least falling onto the pavement distressed Psyche enough that she could feel her eyes start to sting with tears.

"Lord Barneville…I'm sorry…I mean, Lord Sheerness," Psyche said quietly. She wanted to be swallowed by the Earth. She didn't think she had ever been so embarrassed in her life. She nodded her head shortly. "I'm sorry," she mumbled again. "I'm leaving now. Good night."

She turned and limped toward the exit with as much dignity and grace as she could muster. She still wanted to find a place to hide, but now it was somewhere she could cry and lick her wounds in peace. She wondered if she could find her way to the mews and hide in her family's carriage. Jim wouldn't mind the company. She would just have to make sure she cried quietly. If the coachman found out, he would brain the earl.

Psyche gasped in surprise when Sheerness grabbed her arm and turned her around.

"You've hurt yourself. Come sit on the bench for a little while," he said benignly, giving her arm a gentle tug.

Psyche carefully freed herself from his grip. "No, thank you," she said dully and started to leave.

He took her arm again more firmly. "Quit being so pigheaded, and come sit down."

Psyche reluctantly did as he asked. She didn't want to stay, but she hurt too much to leave. She sat on one end of the bench, facing away from Sheerness. She blinked several times to clear the threatening tears from her eyes and folded her hands decorously in her lap. She would only stay as long as it took for her foot to feel better; then she was going. If the earl tried to stop her again, Jim wouldn't have to brain him because she would do it herself.

She could faintly hear a galop playing at the ball, and she wondered what time it was. She didn't know how much longer she would have to wait before her family left. She didn't want them to be ready to leave without her; if they couldn't find her, once they did, she would be in trouble. Her parents had become more interested in their daughters' whereabouts, but they didn't become overly concerned unless one of them didn't arrive at an expected time.

Psyche unfolded her hands and looked at her palm. It was still tender when she brushed her fingers over it, and one of her fingers felt stiff when she tried to bend it. She suspected part of the thorn had broken off and left behind a splinter. She would look at it when she got home and use the tweezers. She tested her heel, the one with which she had stepped on the rock. It was feeling somewhat better, and she was confident she would be able to leave the courtyard soon. She just knew she didn't want to remain near Sheerness any longer than necessary because sooner or later he would want to argue...it was inevitable. It was almost as if he couldn't stop himself.

They remained sitting in silence, Psyche doing her best to ignore him. She should have stayed in the house, but she had wanted to avoid him. Now, here she sat, less than two feet away from him. She did have to wonder what he was doing in the secluded courtyard, but she wasn't going to ask him. He would tell her it was none of her affair anyhow, and it really was.

She couldn't understand what he was doing at the ball in the first instance. It was almost two weeks since his father died. The etiquette of mourning for women was stricter than it was for men, but surely attending a social function, a ball no less, only a fortnight after your parent's death was not something even men were supposed to do. Then to have that coupled with his sister's death in

December…. Surely, mourning *two* family members required more than two weeks. If something like that happened to her family, Psyche couldn't imagine going to a ball after only two weeks, whether it was allowed or not.

Pandora hadn't mentioned whether Alex and Amalie were attending, but Psyche was sure that at least Amalie was not there. Psyche thought she might go by to visit her friend soon. The death of her father could not have been easy for Amalie, and she had already been through so much after the death of her sister and being jilted by Westerkirk. That was a shameful bit of business. Psyche never would have agreed to marry someone who only saw it as an arrangement, but her family's views weren't the same as those of the rest of society. Still, Amalie had to have felt insulted, and Psyche couldn't quite believe her friend would have agreed to marry him if she hadn't felt at least a small amount of affection for him. Psyche wasn't sure if her friend was up to company yet, but she thought she might go by sometime next week.

Sheerness continued to sit quietly and leave Psyche in peace. That made her happy. The tears she had felt were gone, and she was slowly beginning to regain her composure. She didn't think she would ever be able to look at him again without coloring in shame, but hopefully she wouldn't *have* to see him again. She would have to ensure that she didn't. The only way she wanted to see him again was if she got to go on his ship with her brother.

She had tried to get Myron to talk to the earl again about letting her go with them to Greece and Egypt, but her brother still didn't seem agreeable. Psyche had given her word that she would be on her best behavior, that she would be civil, but Myron didn't think the earl would agree because *he* couldn't be civil towards *her*. Myron knew how much she wanted to go, and he was slowly coming around to the idea. She wasn't sure he had talked to the earl about it. The soonest he would have been able to would have been that night. Aside from that, there was no guarantee Sheerness was still going. Considering he was able to attend social functions so soon seemed to indicate his leaving the country was not beyond possibility.

The earl was at least wearing mourning dress, if he wasn't doing anything else etiquette required. Everything he wore was black, except for his shirt, instead of wearing just a black band on his arm and hat. He was at least that respectful of his father's passing and not as uncouth as he first appeared.

Psych still couldn't believe her rotten luck at having him witness her ungainliness. She and Pandora were both accident prone, but she seemed to have a run of it that night. Then as she sat there, it dawned on her: it was Friday, and it was the thirteenth. She had never been one to consider superstitious nonsense as a reason for things, but it would explain it perfectly. If it was due to the date, then she needed to get away from Sheerness as quickly as possible before something more dire happened. Considering how bad she thought everything had been thus far, *more dire* would be horrific.

Psyche tested her foot and decided it was well enough for her to leave. She thought she could return to the ball. Her desire to cry had abated, and if Sheerness stayed in the garden, it would be safe enough for her to go back to the house. She did appreciate that he had remained quiet and had not tried to torment her; otherwise, she would have burst into tears already. She put her gloves back on and stood in preparation to go back to the ball.

"Leaving so soon?" drawled the earl. "You talked my ear off."

Psyche turned to look at him where he still sat on the bench.

"I sat for a while, and my foot is much better. You seem to be desirous of solitude, so I'll leave you to it," she said flatly.

She watched in astonishment as he stood up, giving her a formal bow. He took her hand and brushed her knuckles with his lips.

"Might I have this dance?" he asked politely.

Psyche could hear a waltz beginning to play. She was taken aback as she looked at him, surprised by the request. There was no need for him to request it, and that he would ask it of *her* startled her even more.

"Are you allowed to dance?" she asked softly, arching her eyebrow.

"I don't think so, but who will know?"

Psyche looked at him doubtfully for a moment. She should just turn and leave before things went from bad to worse. He seemed to be in a strange mood, but at least he was being civil. She hadn't been able to dance yet that night, and she did like the waltz.

"All right," she finally said hesitantly.

He took her in his arms and began to guide her around the small courtyard. It was almost too small for them to dance, and Psyche became dizzy as they continued to spin about. She needed something to focus her eyes on before she became queasy. She looked up at his face. As Psyche took more than a casual glance, she noticed something that had escaped her attention before.

"You've cut your hair!" she blurted in surprise.

The earl tilted his head and nodded with a slight smile. "Yes, I did."

All the previous Season, up to the last time she had seen him at his father's funeral, the earl had worn his hair longer than was normal, keeping it tied back in a queue. It was now cut short, and it had a wavy unruliness to it that keeping it brushed back and tied had hidden. She wondered if keeping it under control had been the reason he wore it that way, because unless he used pomade or something else, and lots of it, there was no way to keep it from looking unkempt. She couldn't decide which she preferred because he was equally handsome with either, but Psyche realized her preference was irrelevant.

It was true he was devilishly attractive. That he was mean and hateful toward Psyche didn't detract from it. For her to say he *wasn't* handsome would make her a liar of the worst sort, and she was no liar. His hair was a brown so dark it was almost black and wavy (now). He had beautiful eyes. On first glance, they appeared to be blue, but on closer inspection one realized they were a shade of green. That the outer edge of the iris was rimmed with a dark blue gave the initial impression the entire thing was that color. He had long, dark eyelashes that would make many women jealous. He had a low forehead and strong jaw with high cheekbones and a straight nose. His chin was firm with a slight dimple, and he had chiseled, sensual lips. He was tall and athletically built, and he was incessantly pursued by the marriageable women of the *ton*…and even some of the married ones.

"Why did you cut your hair?" asked Psyche curiously without thinking. She blushed. "I'm sorry. That's not my business."

Sheerness shrugged. "I just decided it was time."

Psyche nodded acceptingly. "How is your mother?"

"She's fine," he said calmly. He looked down at her with a raised eyebrow. "Could you, please, be quiet? I just want to dance," he said dryly.

Psyche colored hotly in embarrassment and looked away. He had yet again managed to make her feel foolish. He was right, of course. She needed to keep silent because if she tried to have a conversation with him, it would only end in an argument. It always did. Arguing with him always left her drained, and she really disliked feeling that way.

Sheerness looked down at her profile as they danced. He should have let her leave when she wanted to—both times, and he wasn't sure why he hadn't. He had gone to the courtyard to avoid her. When Bardsey and her sister had arrived and informed him Psyche would be attending, he decided coming to the ball was a mistake, and he couldn't believe he had let his mother convince him otherwise. He was not ready to be there or to see Psyche. Then Myron arrived and talked to him about their plans for Greece and Egypt and that Psyche was pleading with her brother to be allowed to go along. Sheerness had, of course, flatly refused. He had been tempted to leave the ball immediately, before Psyche arrived, but then he would have to listen to no end of harping from his mother if he didn't stay away from the house for a decent interval, and he didn't want to spend it at the club. Finding somewhere secluded to bide his time seemed the wisest choice.

He had been stunned by Psyche's entrance… amused as well. He might have tried to prevent her from falling onto the pavers if it all hadn't happened so quickly. Once he determined she wasn't seriously injured, he decided to keep silent, hoping she would leave without realizing he was there. He couldn't understand why she was there, alone in the dark. It almost seemed as if she, too, was looking for a place to hide, but that made no sense. She wasn't happy to see him there, and she was discomfited he had seen and heard her ungraceful activities. Even in the dimness of the moonlight, it was easy for him to see the way her face had colored.

She looked stunningly beautiful, as she always did. The scent of her perfume had changed, and he couldn't determine what it was. It suited her perfectly, and he found it intoxicating. Even though he hadn't wanted to see Psyche, now that he had, Sheerness wasn't ready to let her leave. He was consistently vexing to her, and he didn't know why he felt the need to be. It was only that someone who seemed so perfect could not possibly be. So far, he had been proven wrong.

The song ended, and they came to a stop. Psyche was dizzy and disoriented from all the spinning, and her stomach was feeling a bit unstable. That would eventually go away, now that she was no longer turning in circles.

Sheerness continued to hold her, and Psyche looked up at his face curiously. She was surprised when he pulled her closer.

"Lord Ba—Sheerness, please, let me go," she said somewhat nervously.

He smiled roguishly and pulled her closer still. "Make me," he taunted softly.

Psyche looked up at him uncertainly as he continued to look down at her with a sensual half-smile, as if he were expecting her to do something. She didn't know what it was he anticipated. His odd behavior since she had tumbled into the courtyard left her feeling perplexed, and she couldn't clearly determine what part in this bizarre interlude she was meant to play.

Then he kissed her. Psyche was at first too stunned to react. She felt something like an electrical charge at the contact of his lips against hers, and it made her jump slightly. The pressure of his mouth was gentle but insistent, and she let him continue partly out of shock and partly out of curiosity. Her hand that initially rested on his shoulder moved to the side of his neck, and the one that had been hanging relaxed at her side moved to his waist. She tentatively began to respond, her inexperience and amazement making her unsure.

She could feel him deepening the kiss, slowly teasing her lips apart with his tongue, and Psyche felt her knees go weak from the sensations his embrace produced. One of his hands rested at the small of her back, and she felt him move it to her side and splay it across her ribs just below her breast, his thumb pressed against the side of it. Then, just as suddenly as he had started the kiss, he ended it.

Psyche was addled. She couldn't believe he had kissed her. He was always so hateful, his kiss left her feeling nonplussed. What shocked her even more was that she had enjoyed it…immensely. It did make her realize Pandora had not been lying about the wager from the previous Season after all.

He looked down at her befuddled expression with amusement. He shouldn't have done that, but it was every bit as enjoyable as he had imagined it would be. She continued to look up at him dazedly, her forehead wrinkled with confusion. The kiss answered one question he had been pondering since the previous year.

"I knew that wasn't you," he said softly.

Her brow creased even further. "I beg your pardon?"

"Last year on the terrace, that was your twin, wasn't it?"

Psyche's cheeks colored with embarrassment, and she tried to move away from him. He continued to hold her against him and smiled victoriously. She struggled in his grasp, and her lips tightened into an angry line at his smugness. He had apparently been testing her, and she had failed. Psyche thought it was a bit unfair; if one were being given an examination, it was the decent thing if one were aware that was the case.

"Why would you think that?" asked Psyche as she continued to struggle.

"Because I'm still holding you," he said amusedly.

"I wasn't aware you expected me to cause you bodily harm, my lord. Do you like that sort of thing?"

He chuckled softly. "No, but I don't think you can."

"Please, let me go, Lord Barneville," she said coldly.

"Not until you admit it was your sister," he said calmly, tightening his hold even further.

"I'll do no such thing," said Psyche flatly. "I *can* make you let me go, but I am trying to be nice."

Sheerness laughed outright. "When have you ever?" he chortled.

"*Always!*" she spat. "If you weren't such an insufferable lout, you'd know that. Now, let me go," she ground out as she struggled against him.

Sheerness enjoyed the feel of her body moving against his, and he thought he might kiss her again. Her anger heightened the color on her cheeks and made her eyes sparkle. He would eventually let her go, but he was sure it had been her sister last year, whether Psyche wanted to admit it or not.

"Please, don't make me hurt you," she said softly.

"If you think you can, I dare you to go ahead and try," he taunted.

Psyche hated she would have to do it, but he really had left her with little choice. Even if it had been Pandora on the terrace, Psyche was no less capable of defending herself. She would try not to leave any marks and only do what was necessary to make him let her go. He was already mean and hateful, so making him angry wouldn't make it any worse. After a moment's thought on what she should do, Psyche gave him a tight smile of resignation and a nod.

She boxed his ear to stun him enough to loosen his hold on her. Once that was accomplished, she gave a slight push to his chest and hooked her foot behind one of his as he lost his balance, making him topple backward onto his backside on the pavement. Psyche calmly straightened out her dress as he looked up at her with an astonished expression.

"I'm sorry, my lord. I did ask nicely, and you dared me," she said softly, her expression regretful. "Just be grateful I didn't leave you incapacitated."

He stood and calmly adjusted his clothes after dusting off his hands. The earl looked at her with a tight expression, and his jaw clenched as he tried to regain his composure. He was furious, Psyche knew, and she was surprised he wasn't shouting. She did regret she had to do it, but the only thing injured was his pride.

"I see I was mistaken," he said flatly.

"I'm sorry," said Psyche again quietly, and she turned to leave the courtyard, as she had been trying to do for more than an hour.

Chapter Three

Psyche galloped across the turf at Hyde Park with a happy smile. Her white gelding, Achilles, was in top form, and the pace they maintained was the one he had chosen. He enjoyed their ride more when they had company, but Pandora had not been able to ride her horse, Bellerophon, at a fast pace for a few months. At the beginning of May, she had quit riding altogether until after she had her baby (or babies). That had been a difficult decision for her to make because she loved riding her horse, but it was for the best.

Neither Arachne nor Eurydice liked to ride as much. Persephone, although she loved to ride, did not like to be up quite as early as Psyche. Besides, she detested wearing a habit, which would be required if she went riding in the park. Psyche was lonely riding without any of her sisters, but she wouldn't dream of not having it. Her day did not feel right if she did not have a ride through the park just after dawn, before the rest of society came to clog it up and make it impossible to set her own pace. She occasionally saw her brother-in-law, Islington, riding in his phaeton in the early morning hours, but Pandora often kept him too occupied for it to be a regular occurrence.

She looked back over her shoulder and saw Jim trotting along at a sedate pace on Eurydice's bay gelding, Amati. The poor horse was probably enjoying the outing. Her sister rarely rode him, and Psyche wondered why Eurydice had even bothered to bring him to town. The animal would have been much happier at Wilderland where he could run freely in the fields instead of being cooped up in the stables. Psyche appreciated that Jim was there. He gave Psyche her privacy but kept himself within sight to make sure nothing happened. Psyche didn't know what instructions her parents had given the man, but he was so unobtrusive, Psyche sometimes forgot he was there.

Once she and Achilles passed back onto the regular riding path, she slowed him as they approached the Serpentine. She would let him graze for a little while as she watched the waterfowl. She wished she had remembered to bring some bread with her for the ducks. There was one drake, which she had taken to calling Waddlesworth, that would be upset she hadn't. She would have to bring something special for him tomorrow to atone for it.

Psyche reined Achilles to a stop and dismounted. She guided him over to a nearby tree and tied the reins to it firmly. Her horse was disturbingly gifted at untying knots. It would be complicated to untie, but she didn't want him to get loose and go grazing through Kensington Gardens, as he had done once or twice the previous Season. Jim wouldn't let him get that far, but the horse had to learn that he needed to stay where she put him.

She straightened out the skirt on her habit and strolled toward the edge of the lake. She was wearing a new habit made of a comfortable light brown velvet. She wasn't sure she liked it, though, because the skirt wasn't as full as that on her older ones; it made it difficult to ride astride, which is what she preferred. Still, it was pretty, and she liked the darker brown embroidery along the cuffs and the front edges of the open redingote. If she hadn't actually *liked* to ride her horse, then wearing it would have been fine.

She flopped down on the grass with her legs tucked underneath her. It wasn't long before Waddlesworth swam to the edge of the lake and climbed the bank. He quacked at her when he realized she wouldn't be feeding him. After giving her a disgusted hiss, he turned and went back to the water to begin diving for his breakfast. Psyche knew he would eventually return because he liked to be petted.

Psyche would see Amalie that afternoon. She didn't think it was too soon. It would be quite some time before Psyche's friend would be able to go out into society—none at all that Season. She was undoubtedly still upset about her father and sister, but Amalie probably disliked feeling so isolated. She had her brothers and her mother, but Psyche didn't want her to feel she had been forgotten by everyone. She had enough of that from Westerkirk after Monique's death. After the death of her father, the *ton* considered Amalie an untouchable. She was, after all, twenty-one years old and still unmarried. That made her on the shelf but not quite a hopeless spinster. Psyche found society's attitude completely asinine.

After Psyche went to see her friend and made a few other social calls, she intended to go shopping. She had a long list of things to buy: more paints and chalk for her studies (and more for Arachne for her birthday); another pair of riding gloves; birthday presents for Cosmo and Christopher, whose birthdays would be at the end of the month; a birthday present for her mother (and one for her parents' anniversary); and gifts for several other family members and friends. She wanted to buy a gift for Yelena, Chrissoula's new niece, but she would have to ask her maid when the baby was born. If Psyche still had the energy after that, she wanted to go to Beacham and Bagley and see if they had any new volumes. She already had lots, but it wasn't as if she didn't have the room for them in the solarium.

She might see if Pandora was interested in going shopping with her, but Psyche's twin was no longer able to spend large amounts of time on her feet.

Taking a carriage from store to store would be time-consuming, inconvenient, and a bit ridiculous. Still, it wouldn't hurt to ask.

That night, Psyche would go to Almack's. She was not fond of the assembly hall because it was always stuffy and crowded. They did not allow the waltz yet (which was her favorite dance). And she had to tolerate the most obnoxious people. That was the thing she disliked most. She had so far avoided attending, but she would go once a month. Aside from that, Pandora and Islington were going…and Eurydice. The duchess was staying home, but then she rarely, if ever, went to Almack's. Psyche didn't think her mother even went once last year, or any that Season yet. She used Wednesday for her whist night. Arachne had a cold, so Psyche would *have* to "chaperone" Eurydice.

Waddlesworth tried one more time for a treat. Psyche watched as the greenish-black duck came to the edge of the lake. He waddled to where she sat and looked at her speculatively with one eye, cocking his head sideways and giving a brief quack.

"No bread today, Waddlesworth," she said amusedly. He sidled a little closer and nipped at one of her bootlaces. Psyche chuckled. "That's not edible!" she chortled. He grabbed the edge of her skirt in his bill and shook it. "You silly duck," said Psyche affectionately. "I promise I will bring some crumbs tomorrow, but you *cannot* eat my clothes today. That's not polite."

Waddlesworth came closer, and Psyche reached out to pet him. He climbed into her lap and settled in comfortably, the fabric of her skirt forming a perfect nest. Psyche absentmindedly continued to pet him as she watched the other birds glide around on the surface of the lake.

Psyche lifted her watch on its chain. She still had a few minutes before she needed to leave and avoid the flibbertigibbets. She looked down at the duck in her lap; he had fallen asleep. She smiled and leaned back onto her palms on the ground. She lifted her face to the slowly rising sun and closed her eyes, enjoying the sounds of the morning.

The peace was soon disturbed by raised voices. Psyche turned to look over her shoulder and was surprised to see Sheerness involved in an argument with Jim, who was holding the reins of both Amati and Achilles. Psyche looked down at Waddlesworth, who continued to sleep in her lap. She gently lifted him in her arms and walked toward the altercation.

"What is going on?" she asked in shock.

Sheerness turned to look at her. He was in mourning dress, a riding crop in one hand, the reins of a beautiful, dappled gray mare in the other. His lips were compressed in an angry line, but his jaw went slack as he looked at her burden.

"You're holding a duck," he said dumbly.

"Yes, this is Waddlesworth," said Psyche absently. "Why are you accosting my coachman?"

"Your coachman?" asked Lord Sheerness, still eyeing the sleeping duck disbelievingly.

"Yes, Jim is my coachman." She turned to look at the tall, burly man with a grin. "He untied himself again, didn't he?"

"Cor, Lady Psyche. He beats all I've ever seen! I watched you tie that, an' it wasn't five minutes before 'e was loose."

"He may be a one-trick pony, but what a trick it is," she chortled. "He didn't get to the Gardens, did he?"

"No, mum. I caught 'im about the Keeper's Lodge when this gentleman accused me of 'orse thievery." He gave Sheerness an offended glare.

"Here, hold Waddlesworth," she said, giving the duck to a startled Lord Sheerness. "I need to have a chat with my horse."

Psyche went to Achilles' head and proceeded to scold him roundly. At one point, the gelding showed his teeth and shook his head, as if he were laughing, which made Psyche all the more vociferous. Once she said everything she thought the horse needed to hear, she turned her attention back to Sheerness, her eyebrow raised with amusement, her lips twitching with barely contained laughter.

The duck awoke when Psyche turned over his care to the earl. Sheerness, to his credit, attempted to maintain a firm grip, but Waddlesworth was not tame, and he was most displeased. The earl was in danger of losing a finger or an eye.

Psyche calmly retrieved the duck. He settled quickly, and she tucked him under her arm. She strolled back to the edge of the lake and shooed him on his way. She dusted off her hands and skirt and walked back to Sheerness and Jim. The coachman barely managed to control his mirth. The earl looked as if he had swallowed a bee.

"So, Lord Sheerness, I believe you owe Jim an apology," said Psyche expectantly.

"I beg your pardon?"

"You owe my coachman an apology," said Psyche slowly. "You have impugned his character," said Psyche with barely controlled amusement.

"No, I don't think so," said Sheerness coldly.

"In that case, I demand satisfaction. Jim is not your social equal, but I am, and if you will not apologize, I will have satisfaction for him."

"You cannot be serious," said Sheerness in disbelief.

"Oh, but I can be. However, I don't feel this requires a duel to the death or even first blood." Psyche's face wrinkled distastefully. "I think the countess has enough to mourn already."

Sheerness's eyebrow shot up in disbelief. "Then what do you propose?"

Psyche looked at the earl's mare. She was a lively Thoroughbred of about the same build as Achilles. Psyche looked at Jim.

"What do you think?" she asked him, looking at her watch. It would be close, but there was still time.

Jim rubbed his chin speculatively. "I don't know, mum. Achilles 'as already 'ad a fair run today. She looks to be a rum goer."

Psyche waved her hand in the air dismissively and looked back at the earl.

"Very well, this is what I propose: my horse against yours, from that walnut there—"she pointed to a nearby tree—"to the corner at Tyburn. If I win, you will offer your humblest apologies to my coachman. If you win, Jim's a big boy." She looked at Jim and gave him a wink. "Not a *word* to Mamà and Papà, right?"

"Not on your life!" agreed the Cockney.

"Well?" asked Psyche of the earl. "It's either this, or we choose seconds, and don't think I'm bamming you."

Sheerness tightened his jaw angrily. She was serious, even though her tone was bantering. He could only imagine Myron's reaction should he find out about the whole business. Sheerness could save himself the bother and simply apologize, but it was an honest mistake, and he didn't feel it warranted pardon. What was he to think when he saw a strange man leading away a horse that Sheerness knew was hers? He found everything since spotting the man too strange for description, but because it involved Psyche, he couldn't understand why it surprised him.

"Come on, Lord Sheerness," said Psyche impatiently, looking at her watch. "If you don't decide soon, we'll have an obstacle course. Racing or sabers? It's an easy enough choice to make."

"If you think that's so, then you really have no understanding of what honor means," said the earl coldly. "But then, you *are* a woman."

The lightness faded from Psyche's expression, and her anger showed in her tone. "One more insult, sir, and I'll *own* your horse before I'm satisfied."

Sheerness scoffed doubtfully. "Very well. I accept your terms."

Psyche grinned. "Bloody marvelous!" She turned to look at Jim. "You go ahead and cut across to the corner with Amati."

He handed Achilles' reins to Psyche and touched the brim of his hat before mounting and going across the park diagonally at a canter. He knew how fast Achilles could run.

Psyche rubbed Achilles' nose and whispered in his ear before patting his neck affectionately. She mounted and adjusted her skirts, but there was still a fair amount of brown- and white-striped stocking exposed above the top of her boot. She looked down at Sheerness with a raised eyebrow and gave him a jaunty grin.

The earl gave her a half-smile and shook his head, still not quite believing he had been reduced to participating in a horse race with a *woman* to avenge the honor of a *coachman*. He did not in any way consider this to be a legitimate matter of honor, but it would be entertaining. He mounted his mare, Troia, and he looked at Psyche with another resigned shake of his head. They lined up with the tree, and he glanced at her.

"This is so unnecessary," he said with some exasperation.

"Will you apologize to Jim?" asked Psyche mildly.

"No," said Sheerness with a stubborn grin.

"Then it is necessary," said Psyche. "I'll not have the reputation of such a decent man besmirched."

"As you like it," said Lord Sheerness, touching the brim of his hat.

"On my mark?"

"Why yours?"

"Why not?"

"I don't trust you."

"The feeling is mutual," retorted Psyche tartly.

"Then we are at an impasse."

"Do you have a handkerchief?"

"No."

"How can you, as a gentleman, not have a handkerchief?" muttered Psyche to herself. "What about your cravat?"

"I'll not give you another cravat."

Psyche groaned aggravatedly and shook her head. "Oh, for the…!"

Psyche took her foot out of the stirrup and unlaced her boot. Sheerness watched in disbelief as she removed it and took off her stocking. He was at just the right distance to see she had no hair on her leg, much to his astonishment and intrigue. She draped the silk over her shoulder and replaced her boot. Psyche looked up at him in irritation after she completed her task, disliking that she would lose one of her new stockings because of his orneriness, and saw his bemused expression. She did suppose it was out of the ordinary for a woman to remove her stockings in public, but Psyche didn't see that she had a choice.

"Now, I'll throw this in the air. When it touches the ground, we go. Agreed?"

"Agreed."

Psyche threw her stocking in the air, and both of them watched with anticipation as it fluttered down slowly.

"*Yala!*" cried Psyche as it touched the ground, and Achilles shot away energetically.

Psyche laughed as he sped along. Sheerness was gaining on her, but Psyche wasn't concerned yet. Achilles was a slow starter, and he had not reached his full stride. She leaned forward in her saddle and raised herself out of it, keeping the reins slack in her hands. Achilles always did much better without any guidance from her.

She glanced over and saw that Sheerness was almost abreast of her. His mare was moving quickly, but Psyche didn't think she would be able to get ahead. The earl grinned and urged his horse to go faster. Psyche returned his smile and leaned near Achilles' head to whisper in his ear.

"*Yala!*" Psyche cried, and she whooped as Achilles finally lengthened his stride.

They soon turned the northern rim of the circle, going toward the front of the park, and Jim was waiting at the corner. Achilles pulled another length ahead of the gray mare, and Psyche could tell the Thoroughbred's strength was waning. Her gelding had a few years' experience, and Psyche suspected he was worked more frequently, but she was not about to say the race was unfair; she just had the better horse. She grinned at Jim as she went past and began to slow Achilles. She patted him appreciatively on the neck. Unfortunately, he didn't have a sweet tooth like Pandora's horse, or she would have given him lots of sugar. She would just let him have extra grazing time when they went riding the following day.

She turned Achilles to be met by Sheerness's furious expression. Psyche wasn't surprised he was angry; she always seemed to make him that way without much effort. If he weren't mad, she would wonder if he was ill.

She hadn't seen him since the night in the courtyard, which was a bizarre episode by itself. If she hadn't known better, she would have thought he had an identical twin who had pulled a switch like she and Pandora sometimes did. He had been almost civil, and the kiss he had given her was pleasant in a way she found disconcerting. If it hadn't been for the privet thorn stuck in her palm, she might have believed she had hallucinated the entire thing and would have found that to be much less disturbing. She was relieved to find him behaving as obnoxiously as ever; it made her feel less confused.

"Well, Lord Sheerness, I believe you should apologize now," she said calmly as she came abreast of him.

"That wasn't a fair race," he said testily.

Psyche raised her chin and looked at him with moderate irritation.

"How can you say that? Just because my horse is better than yours doesn't make it unfair. You may weigh more than I do, but Achilles had already had a good run before this debacle. You saying it wasn't fair is like saying a gut shot is only a flesh wound."

"You cheated," he persisted.

"How *dare* you?" hissed Psyche angrily. "You accuse me of having no understanding of honor, and yet you have the audacity to say something like that? You pompous, obnoxious, despicable…*ooh!*" Psyche groaned and shook her head. "How could I have possibly cheated?"

"You were talking to your horse," said Sheerness churlishly. "You said something to make him run faster."

Psyche rolled her eyes. "That is not cheating. All I did was ask him if he was going to let himself be beaten by a girl." She scoffed derisively. "It appears he isn't the only one who can't stand losing to a female." She adjusted her gloves on her hands and glared at him. "I suggest you begin to behave like the man of honor you proclaim to be instead of an infantile, *whiny,* sore loser and go apologize to Jim. I beat you fair and square."

Psyche watched as he clenched his jaw and a nerve began to tick there. He was going to argue further, but he knew she was right. While the race may not have been a legitimate duel, for him to contest it further would be childish to the extreme and dishonorable. He should have just apologized once he had realized his mistake and been done with it, but he had been certain he was the better rider, even if he didn't have the better horse. He turned Troia and went back to Jim where he waited with Amati. Psyche watched as Sheerness removed his hat, and she was actually somewhat astonished that he was going to follow the terms to the letter.

"I would like to offer my humblest apologies for any offense you may have taken at my calling you a horse thief," he said mildly.

Jim waved his hand in the air dismissively and gave the earl a grin. "Cor, tweren't nothin', my lord. Besides, I *did* used to be one."

Sheerness turned to look at Psyche in shock, and his mouth began to work soundlessly in outrage. He turned and led his horse at a canter across the turf of the park. Psyche watched after him until he disappeared through the trees. Jim came beside her on Amati, watching the earl depart as well.

"Mum, I don't think 'e was very 'appy with you," said Jim, tilting his hat back to scratch his forehead thoughtfully.

"No, but then he never is, Jim," she said, giving him a cheeky grin. "Come on; let's get home before this place is so thick with people we can't move."

Jim gave her a smile of his own. "Too right."

Psyche arrived at the Nicholses' residence on Curzon Street later than she had intended. If she stayed only the customary fifteen minutes, she would still have time to do most of her shopping, but Psyche never stayed anywhere for just fifteen minutes. She had paid her other social visits, so that would not be a constraint on her time, but she really wanted to get her shopping done. She decided resignedly there would always be tomorrow.

Pandora had declined to go shopping with her. That had been one of Psyche's social calls, which was why she was so late going to see Amalie. Her twin was always in a flurry of activity (when she wasn't sitting with her feet propped up to reduce the swelling in her ankles). If she wasn't seeing to preparations for her lying in, she was overseeing plumbing and water supply renovations in the Marshalls' town house. The dowager marchioness was not convinced her daughter-in-law could do it without completely destroying the residence, but so far, she had been proven wrong. The system at Marshcliff was also being completed, and Pandora was constantly sending messages back and forth with the builder, Mr. Gribble, in Bardsey. As for her lying in, Pandora had the nursery in the town house redecorated and updated, as it had not been used since Selena was a baby and had become a storage room. It was now freshly painted and had new furnishings. All it lacked was a nanny.

Pandora wanted to hire Nanny Bixley away from her parents, but Dorian refused to let the woman go. The two siblings had begun something of a battle over the nanny. Pandora's younger brothers were old enough now that they didn't require a nanny any longer and would soon be old enough to have their own rooms and valets. Cosmo and Christopher would be going away to Harrow in less than two years. Damon was looked after by Arachne. Dorian and Selena weren't expecting a baby. Pandora didn't see why Dorian wasn't willing to let Bixley go. Their parents had no objection, with the understanding the nanny was only "on loan." Pandora was agreeable, but Dorian was not.

Pandora was now considering Kwan, one of the nursemaids. She was excellent with children and had been with the family for many years. She was Chinese, like Pandora's maid, Maiyin, and Maiyin's husband, Keung, who had gone with Pandora from the Aberdares' service when Pandora married Islington. That would give Kwan people she knew and liked. Now Dorian was also refusing to let Kwan go.

The duke and duchess wouldn't get in the middle. They were amenable to letting either Catherine Bixley or Hua Kwan work for Pandora and were also content to let them stay. Gregory, the usual mediator between siblings, was in America for the war, so Psyche was acting as go-between. The negotiations were not going well. It hadn't come to blows, and there hadn't been any gross insults tossed, but Psyche had to agree with her twin that Dorian was being intransigent and selfish. If Selena were expecting, Psyche might understand his reluctance to let one of them go. To her knowledge, her sister-in-law wasn't. Aside from that, they worked for Psyche's parents, not Dorian. If one of the siblings should have say over whether or not Pandora should be able to hire one of the nannies, temporarily or otherwise, it would be Myron, the future duke, who was unmarried and seemed content to stay that way.

Part of the reason Psyche had gone to see Pandora was to relay the latest round of reasons Dorian had for not letting her hire Bixley or Kwan. Dorian's reasons were becoming moderately ridiculous. He was beginning to realize that as well. On this visit, Psyche was able to tell Pandora that Dorian might be relenting on letting her take Kwan. That made Pandora happy. Islington was neutral on the entire thing. He refused to get between his wife and his best friend. Psyche would have preferred not to go between her siblings, but she had been left with little choice in the matter.

The two nannies, meanwhile, were flattered over all the flutter. They adored all the Savage children, and they were looking forward to assisting with the raising up of another generation, wherever that might be. It warmed their hearts to know the affection they felt was reciprocated. Psyche wished one or the other would express a preference and settle the matter. Dorian wouldn't make them stay if one or the other said she wanted to go. Psyche had no such luck, but she was hopeful it would soon be decided, if only so her twin would not be left looking for a nanny at the last minute.

When Psyche arrived to see Amalie, the footman escorted her to the terrace. He informed her that Amalie had gone to her room for a moment but would soon be returning. Psyche shrugged agreeably and went to sit on a bench near the stone balustrade. The weather was mild, and the mid-afternoon sun was pleasant. She much preferred being outside.

She had changed from her riding habit and put on a walking dress of white muslin in a fairly simple design. The only adornment it had was a row of several pin tucks along the hem. She wore a ruched, light blue cashmere coat with a ruffled edge that came to just above the hem of her dress and a narrow-brimmed, low-crowned bonnet of a matching color. The family's seamstress in Wales, Janet Davies, had recommended a poke bonnet to accompany the costume, but Psyche refused to wear a poke bonnet; she thought they were hideous. Her gloves were tan to match her walking boots. She didn't have a parasol because the weather was fair, and she didn't care if she tanned or not. The only other thing she carried was a light blue, drawstring bag.

Psyche only sat waiting for a few minutes when she began to grow suspicious she was not alone. She looked around herself on the terrace and wasn't able to see anyone, but she could hear breathing. She looked up at the windows on the back of the house and the two balconies there, but she didn't see anyone. Psyche didn't think she was hearing things. She looked behind herself into the garden, but she didn't see anyone there, either. That only left one place. She calmly moved her legs up onto the bench beside her and bent down to look underneath it. Her gaze was met by that of a startled young one.

"Hi," Psyche whispered with a smile.

"Hallo," the boy whispered back with a shy smile of his own.

Psyche thought he was six or seven years old. He had dark brown, wavy hair that flopped about in a familiar way and eyes of a deep, velvety brown that reminded Psyche of chocolate. He also had a slight dimple in his chin that Psyche recognized. The boy was curled up under the bench on his back, and Psyche couldn't believe she had not noticed him there when the footman led her onto the terrace. He appeared to be hiding, which was why Psyche had whispered when she saw him.

At the sound of approaching footsteps from inside the house, she quickly sat up and straightened out her skirts, providing the boy with even better cover. She didn't know why he was hiding, but she was always willing and able to aid and abet, as Pandora would readily testify. Psyche could tell from the heaviness of the steps that it wasn't Amalie. She calmly folded her hands in her lap and composed her features into the picture of innocence.

That was how Sheerness found her when he came onto the terrace. He was surprised to see her. He was in his shirt sleeves with a waistcoat; he was at home and saw no reason to wear a coat or a cravat. His anger with her over their *duel* still remained, and a nerve began to tick in his jaw as he saw her sitting there, looking for all the world as if she was exactly where she belonged. The fact that he found her to be looking particularly beautiful at the moment only made him all the more irritated.

"What are you doing here?" he asked coldly.

"Why, yes, Lord Sheerness, it *is* a lovely day," said Psyche tartly with a cheeky grin.

"Don't be impertinent," he snapped.

Psyche looked at him calmly. His behavior was becoming predictable (at least usually), and she was beginning to find it tiring. She was prepared for him to be home, and she was also prepared for his anger. She was enjoying a bit of revenge. All the previous Season, he had consistently made snide remarks, insulting her intelligence and several other aspects of her character. She was pleased to see that so far this Season she had the upper hand and was enjoying it immensely.

"I came to see your sister. I didn't want her to feel like everyone had forgotten about her," said Psyche evenly.

The earl's eyes widened, and his cheeks colored with embarrassment. Psyche managed to keep her features perfectly composed, but it was difficult. Inside, she was rolling on the ground, laughing with glee.

"Thank you. She'll appreciate your visit, I'm sure," Sheerness said dully. Psyche tilted her head sideways with a slight nod. He looked around himself, a slight frown furrowing his brow, and then he looked back at her questioningly. "I don't suppose you've seen my nephew, Philip, have you?"

"I don't think so. What does he look like?" asked Psyche calmly. She heard a nervous intake of breath at her feet and tried to keep her features blank.

"Oh, I don't know…dark hair and eyes. Stands about so tall—"he measured out a height about even with his waist. "We're playing hide and seek. I've found Josie and Jerome, but Philip has hidden himself well."

"Josie and Jerome?"

"My other nephew and my niece…Monique's children. They're twins, like Alex and Amalie."

"Ah," said Psyche with a slight smile and a nod. She found it surprising he would play children's games. She imagined he would have found that beneath him. "Hmm, I don't *think* I've seen him, but I'll let you know if I do."

Sheerness looked at her suspiciously, but she seemed sincere.

"If you'll excuse me, I need to look for my nephew. I'm sure Amalie will be down shortly," he said finally.

"Good luck, Lord Sheerness," said Psyche with a pleasant smile.

He gave her a slight nod and went down the stairs to search the garden. Psyche grinned amusedly as she watched him disappear. Their garden was infinitely suitable for hide and seek, with its mixture of trees, shrubbery, and flowerbeds. However, he was wasting his time, and she was glad she could contribute to that.

"Thank you," whispered the boy under the bench.

"Think nothing of it, Philip," she whispered back with a smile.

Psyche lifted her watch on its chain at her neck and looked at the time. She wouldn't be doing any shopping, but she should have plenty of time to visit and get home to dress for Almack's. She sighed patiently, wondering if she should have let Amalie know she intended to visit. It served her right she had taken for granted her friend would be idling her time waiting for someone to come visit her.

Psyche looked up in surprise when she heard small feet trundling toward the door. The boy and girl nearly tripped over each other in their haste to exit onto the terrace, and Psyche laughed silently. They were about nine years old, both having the same dark hair and eyes as their younger brother.

"Stop pushing!" said Josie.

"*You* stop pushing!" said Jerome.

"I'll tell Uncle Sebastian on you!" yelled Josie with a pout.

"I'll tell Mamère on *you!*" returned Jerome.

"Uncle Sebastian will send you to bed without *any* supper!"

"Mamère will *spank* you!"

Psyche began to giggle amusedly at their argument. When they noticed her sitting there, their eyes grew round in surprise.

"Who are you?" demanded Jerome suspiciously.

"Use your manners, Jerome!" hissed Josie loudly, elbowing her brother in the ribs. "How do you do? My name is Josephine Renée Yeardley," she said formally, reaching out her hand to Psyche.

Psyche took her hand and shook it politely. "I am Lady Psyche Savage, and it is a pleasure to make your acquaintance, Miss Yeardley."

"You're *very* pretty," said Josie, sitting beside Psyche on the bench and beginning to swing her legs back and forth as she looked at Psyche assessingly.

"Thank you," said Psyche with a smile. She leaned a little closer to whisper to the girl. "You might want to be careful swinging your legs like that. Philip is still hiding under there."

"Oh!" said Josie in surprise, her eyes going round. "Uncle Sebastian hasn't found him yet?"

"Not yet," said Psyche, shaking her head with a grin. Josie giggled.

Psyche turned to see Jerome approaching. She watched as he bowed formally, his face very serious.

"I am Jerome Yeardley, Lady Psyche," he said, taking her hand to place a kiss on her knuckles.

"Oh, my!" said Psyche, placing a hand to her chest and fluttering her eyelashes. "Such a handsome gentleman you are, Master Yeardley."

Jerome blushed, but he took a seat on the other side of her. "Why are you here?" he asked flatly.

"Jerome!" groaned Josie.

Psyche laughed. "I'm here to see your Aunt Amalie."

"Hmm, I don't think you'll get to see Aunt Am today," said Josie.

"Why is that?" asked Psyche curiously.

"She's gone to her room for a nap. I can go wake her!" said Josie brightly.

"No, that's not necessary," said Psyche quickly, as the girl looked as if she intended to fly away and do just that. "Hmm, I suppose I should be going then."

"Don't go yet," said Philip under the bench.

Josie and Jerome watched in amazement as Psyche easily bent backward to look under the bench, her feet still on the ground in front of her. She reminded them of an acrobat they had once seen at a carnival. Philip was awed as well.

"If your aunt is not available to see me, it would be rude of me to stay," Psyche told Philip calmly.

"What if you changed your mind and came to see *us*?" asked Jerome.

Psyche straightened back up to look at the boy. "I suppose I could," she said thoughtfully. "We *have* been introduced now."

"It's decided then," said Josie. "Lady Psyche, how kind of you it was to come call on us this afternoon," she said with a smile.

Psyche giggled and shook her head. She should really bring her younger brothers to see the three children. They would get along famously together.

"Can you do any more tricks?" asked Jerome excitedly.

"Tricks?" asked Psyche confusedly.

"Philip! You win!" Psyche heard Sheerness shout from the bottom of the stairs. That was shortly followed by victorious cackling beneath the bench. Sheerness arrived at the top of the stairs just in time to see Philip crawl out, giggling and hopping merrily. The earl looked at Psyche accusingly. "I thought you hadn't seen him."

Psyche looked at him innocently. "Your description was very vague, and I couldn't tell how tall he was all scrunched up under there." She watched his jaw tighten angrily.

"Lady Psyche was going to perform tricks," said Jerome excitedly, oblivious to the ire of his uncle.

"Tricks?" it was Lord Sheerness's turn to ask confusedly.

"She just bent over completely backwards on the bench without moving her feet from the ground," said Josie. "It was marvelous! Just like an acrobat!"

Psyche's confusion cleared. "Oh, you meant *that.*"

"I thought you came to see my sister," said Sheerness tightly.

"No, she came to see *us,*" said Philip, crawling familiarly into Psyche's lap. Psyche looked down at him in surprise, but gave him a grin, playfully tweaking the end of his nose.

"Aunt Am is asleep," said Jerome dismissively, "so Lady Psyche changed her mind and came to see us instead, and now she's going to perform tricks."

Sheerness looked at her with a raised eyebrow. "Indeed?"

Psyche looked at the expectant faces of the children. They could probably do with a bit of diversion; mourning could be very oppressive to children. She knew that from the deaths of two of her grandparents. Her Grandfather Sanders, her mother's father, had died when she was nine. Her *Babushka* Alexa, her father's mother, had died when she was fourteen. Her mother's mother and the duke's father had both died before she was born. It had not been easy for her or any of her siblings to understand the mourning requirements of society; then they were trying to come to terms with their grief at the same time. As children, they wanted to laugh and play, but they were afraid to do so without seeming disrespectful to the dead. It was the uncertainty that had made it so difficult and unfair.

She *was* inordinately flexible from the things Keung had taught her, as were most members of her family, and she was fairly agile (usually). She had never thought of the things she could do as being tricks, but she supposed most people would think of them that way because not everyone could do them. Still, they weren't very ladylike to perform in a dress.

"I'm not attired for it," she said, but her forehead wrinkled thoughtfully.

"Oh, *please*, Lady Psyche?" said Jerome appealingly.

"Yes, please, show us some more," said Josie excitedly.

Psyche started to chew on the side of her thumb in thought and quickly took it out of her mouth when she tasted the leather of her glove. Her face brightened as an idea came to her.

"Oh, very well," said Psyche with a grin.

"Huzzah!" shouted Philip, hopping out of her lap.

Psyche took off her bonnet then bent down and began to unlace her boots. Sheerness watched as she took them off and set them beside the bench, revealing white silk stockings. She looked up.

"The gentlemen in the audience will turn around, please. Oh, and you, too, Lord Sheerness."

The earl scowled but turned his back. Josie watched expectantly as Psyche removed her stockings and folded them neatly into her purse for safekeeping. Psyche then stood up and removed her coat and held it up to examine. She tied the arms around her waist and tucked the rest of the material in as necessary, forming a pair of loose-fitting pantaloons that came to just below her knee.

"I could really do with a pair of trousers or breeches, but I hadn't realized I would need them," said Psyche to Josie with a grin.

Then, almost as if through divine providence, a pair of chamois breeches came floating down to land at her feet. Psyche looked up at the sky in surprise, as did Josie. She looked up at the windows on the upper floors of the house, but she didn't see anyone standing at any of them to indicate where the garment had come from.

"Oh, my goodness, it's raining pants," said Psyche in pretended shock. Josie giggled.

"*What?*" said Sheerness in disbelief, beginning to turn around.

"No peeking!" said Psyche quickly, grabbing up the breeches to examine them. They looked as if they would fit. She quickly unfastened her coat and pulled on the breeches in its place. She lifted up the skirts of her dress and chemise and tied them around her waist, securing them in a bundle out of the way at the back. "There! You can turn around now," she said calmly.

The boys and their uncle turned around to look at her. All three faces bore expressions of surprise, but Sheerness was particularly stunned.

"That's indecent," he gasped. And then his forehead wrinkled confusedly. "Where did those britches come from?"

"I'm not sure, really," said Psyche honestly. She shrugged. "Still, they'll work much better than what I had planned." She clapped her hands. "Shall we start with something simple, then?" she asked the children. They nodded happily. "Oh! I need a stage," said Psyche with a flourish, standing on the bench. "Perfect!"

She bent down and touched her toes a few times to stretch the muscles in her legs and raised her hands above her head and bent side-to-side to stretch those in her upper body. She had done her exercises that morning, so she didn't need as much preparation as she might have otherwise.

Her audience watched as she lifted one of her feet behind her, and then, by using her hands and arching her back, she touched the sole of her foot to the crown of her head. The children clapped appreciatively. Sheerness folded his arms across his chest and yawned, clearly not impressed.

Psyche then bent forward and put her hands to either edge of the bench and slowly raised her legs into the air until she was completely upside down. She walked her hands down the sides of the bench until they were slightly closer to one end, and then she bent her legs over in the other direction, placed the soles of her feet onto the bench and came once again to a standing position. The reaction from her audience was about the same.

She stepped down from the bench. She looked from one end of the terrace to the other, estimating the distance. There would be enough. She walked from one end to the other, making sure there were no sharp objects that might get stuck in her palms or feet. She looked at the children.

"You might want to move to the side a step or two," she said with a smile, shooing them with her hands.

They expectantly did as she recommended and were rewarded with watching her perform flips and somersaults along the path she had chosen. Jerome whistled through his teeth, and all three clapped appreciatively. Sheerness was becoming grudgingly impressed.

For her finale, Psyche climbed onto the balustrade. She kept her eyes focused on the stone beneath her feet because if she looked to her right, the distance she was above the ground on that side would make her dizzy and faint. She couldn't tolerate heights of more than a few feet. Even the distance from the balustrade to the stone of the terrace made her nervous, but as long as she looked at what she was standing on, she would be fine. The children watched in amazement as she performed more somersaults, handsprings, and flips. Once she reached the stairs, they gasped when she performed a leap and gracefully landed on the stone at the opposite side and continued to tumble to the other end of the terrace.

Once she was done and back on the terrace, she curtsied and grinned. The children clapped and cheered happily and gathered around her with admiration. They were all chattering at once, and Psyche giggled at their enthusiasm as she tried to listen and reply to everything they were saying. Luckily she was familiar with deciphering the cacophony from dealing with her younger brothers, who also had a tendency to talk over one another. Psyche thought she would definitely bring her brothers to see the Yeardley children. Although, she was sure they would cause no end of mischief together.

She looked at Sheerness and saw his amazed expression. He hadn't wanted to be impressed, but she had accomplished it. For once he was looking at her with something other than disdain or disbelief. Yes, this Season was her turn to have the upper hand in their battle of wills, proving that his impression of her as a silly female was unbelievably misguided and unfair.

He was more astonished than his niece and nephews because he knew women of society weren't supposed to do things like that. He was also surprised by how quickly the children had taken to Psyche. This was the most animated he had seen them for quite some time. Their father, Baron Yeardley, had sent them to stay with their grandmother because he wasn't able to bear looking at them without thinking of Monique. Then Sheerness's father, their grandfather, had died, making them even more somber. Sheerness was cheered to see them laughing and behaving like children. While he was still displeased with Psyche regarding a few matters, he greatly appreciated what she had done.

"Lady Psyche, I would not have thought you agile enough to tumble like *that,*" he said with a smirk.

Psyche colored hotly with embarrassment at his reminder of her entrance into the courtyard. That was uncalled for. She didn't know why he always had to be so mean to her. It sometimes seemed as if he couldn't help himself. Psyche looked at her watch and was only moderately surprised she had stayed well past when she had intended to. She would be late again.

"Well, children, I'm afraid it is time for me to be on my way," said Psyche calmly, looking down at them with a smile.

"Must you?" asked Philip disappointedly. "I want you to stay and play hide and seek with us."

"Perhaps another time," said Psyche with a grin. "I think I should bring my brothers along then." She sighed. "Now, I need to change, so if you'll all turn for a moment, please."

The boys did as she asked, and Sheerness did so reluctantly. Psyche unfastened her dress and chemise then reached under to unfasten and remove the breeches. She folded them neatly and set them on the bench. The skirt of her gown was horribly wrinkled, but Chrissoula would be able to straighten it with an iron. Psyche retrieved her stockings from her bag and pulled them back on, and then she sat down to put on her walking boots.

"You can turn around now," she said as she finished lacing up her boots. She put her bonnet back on and stood up.

"Will you come again tomorrow?" asked Josie.

"Oh, I don't think I can," said Psyche. "How about Wednesday next?"

"Yes, please," said Jerome.

"I'll let Amalie know you came to call," said Sheerness politely.

"Thank you," said Psyche. She looked up at the back of the house. "Thank you for the pants," she called.

She waved her hand at the children and went through the French doors back into the house to go to the front door where Jim would be waiting with the carriage. After she had disappeared, Sheerness looked up at the back of the house to one of the balconies.

"Did you hear that, *Maman?*" he asked dryly.

The countess walked onto the balcony and looked down at him with an amused smile, her arms folded across her chest with satisfaction.

Chapter Four

Psyche arrived at Almack's with Eurydice and Myron. He would leave for Boodles before long and would return just as it was time to leave. The women were constantly fawning over him, trying to tempt him into a proposal of marriage, and he found the whole business tiring. Psyche couldn't blame him. She could never imagine doing some of the things women of the *ton* did to get a man to marry them.

She had learned last Season that marriage was the main purpose behind most of the social functions, but she found it distasteful. Marriage shouldn't be the sole reason for one's existence. It certainly wasn't for her...or for any of her family. Her twin had married a man who adored her to distraction, and Psyche knew Pandora felt the same about Islington. She and her sisters were lucky in that their parents supported their decisions on matters of matrimony. They had no need of money; their family was highly respected; and they were all more than capable of protecting themselves. The things that usually motivated a woman to marry didn't apply to them, and even if they had, Psyche knew her parents would still not arrange marriages for them. She wasn't sure if her parents would make them marry someone to avoid a scandal...maybe, but Psyche thought it highly unlikely.

Psyche had chosen to wear a gown of two layers, the top layer made of beautiful dark lavender silk embroidered with flowers in white thread trimmed with tiny seed pearls. The bottom edge of the short, puffed sleeves and this top layer, which ended at about her knees, were trimmed in delicate Irish lace. The bottom layer was made of a white silk. She had a shawl made of dark purple cashmere trimmed at either end with tassels, and she carried a feathered fan in a matching color. She wore her favorite black kid slippers, which had survived the walk through the Lundeys' garden without too much damage. Chrissoula had managed to recreate the style Maiyin had used for Pandora for the Lundeys', and Psyche thought it went well with the dress. She wore a delicately filigreed gold choker and matching bracelet that had been bequeathed to her by her grandmother, and the white satin gloves she wore came to just below her elbows. Psyche didn't think she was too vain when she felt she looked very pretty.

Eurydice was wearing a gown made of gold silk, embroidered with black on the bodice and at the bottom edge of the short sleeves and skirt. There was a sash of black velvet tied just below her breasts, and the cashmere shawl she wore was also black. The gold color suited her complexion well, and as she had already discovered, much to her dismay, the men of London found her to be transcendently beautiful. There hadn't been any who came to pay their respects, but Psyche was sure that was because her sister had threatened them with bodily harm if they did.

Eurydice had no intention of marrying unless she was allowed to go to Vienna first. Psyche suspected her parents would allow Eurydice to go after she had performed her duty and attended one London season. The duchess had a friend, Leilah Mahone, who resided there for most of the year, and she would be more than happy to chaperone Eurydice while she was in Vienna. Their parents wouldn't let Eurydice go unless that was arranged, but Psyche didn't see that it was going to be a problem.

When they arrived at the assembly hall, late again, thanks to Psyche, the rooms were already very crowded. Myron dutifully took each of his sisters onto the floor for a dance, and then he excused himself, saying he would return by one. Psyche grimaced because she was hoping they could leave earlier. Eurydice felt the same. Psyche disliked the rubbing elbows with *everyone* in society that attending Almack's entailed. Eurydice detested the whole Season. After their brother departed, the two girls sat at the edge of the floor, scanning the faces present for Pandora and Islington.

"The musicians are being particularly loose," said Eurydice absently, almost to herself.

Psyche looked at her with a grin. "I'm not able to tell myself, so I'll leave that to your judgment."

"Just listen to it!" said Eurydice exasperatedly. "It's supposed to be crisp and airy. The violinists are playing as if their bows are made of lead."

Psyche chuckled. "Forgive me, Dicy, but I cannot tell. I believe you, and I will say they should be ashamed of themselves for murdering the music, but my ear is not so attuned as yours."

Her sister shook her head disgustedly, and Psyche amusedly thought for a moment that Eurydice was going to cover her ears with her hands. Psyche honestly couldn't tell how badly they were playing, but because Eurydice was such an accomplished violinist herself, she *knew* when it didn't sound right. When it was wrong, the tone was almost painful to her.

Psyche continued to look for her twin. Pandora wouldn't be difficult to locate. She would be wearing something in a vibrant color, most likely emerald green or burgundy, and she was very large around the middle. Most other women wore the typical white or some equally pastel color that would make

Pandora all the more conspicuous. So far, Psyche had not seen her. Pandora could have changed her mind and decided not to attend, but Islington had to attend a certain number of social functions in order to make things run more smoothly for his causes in Parliament. This was one of those occasions, but Psyche was unable to find him either, and his height and appearance would make him difficult to miss as well.

Psyche was about to turn her gaze in the other direction when a face in the crowd caught her attention. Her jaw tightened grimly as she looked at the woman, and she hoped Pandora had decided not to attend after all. The woman stood at the center of a small crowd of other women and men, simpering and laughing. Psyche could only imagine whose character she was attempting to destroy; that seemed to be the only time when she was that animated. Psyche recognized the faces of several society gossip mongers: Lady Ramsey and her niece, Lucy Cranston; Sarah Mitchell-Langworthy and her husband, Sir William; Baroness Fribourg; and Lady Asterwick. Most of the gossips didn't perform their duty of spreading tales maliciously, but the woman who had caught Psyche's attention certainly did.

She used to be called Jessica Wainwright, but since her marriage, she had become Countess von Weilheim. At one point, about seven years previously, she had been betrothed to Pandora's husband when he truly had been just Viscount Islington. Jessica had wanted to marry him for his money, and when she found out he didn't have any (or so she thought), she had jilted him for a German count. She had remained on the continent since then, but this Season she had returned to London to introduce her husband.

Enough time had passed that she had been provisionally accepted back, but the Marquess of Bardsey was well-respected and well-liked from a well-established family. The countess trod a very fine line between acceptance and ostracism. She was very beautiful, with an ivory complexion, violet blue eyes, and black hair. She was usually able to comport herself with charm and politesse. Both were points in her favor when it came to society. Her husband, while foreign, was a nobleman and very wealthy. These, too, were to her benefit. She had still not, however, managed to be welcomed back by everyone, particularly by those who were associates and friends of the Bardseys and the Aberdares, and their number was large. The countess balanced on the edge, and one wrong thing would push her out of society for good. For Psyche, for her sister's sake, it couldn't happen soon enough.

One of the things the countess had done to regain her position was spread rumors…particularly about Pandora and her husband. Pandora and Islington were aware of it, and the things she was saying could only have come from one source: Ector Marsh, the Earl of Hendon. After his involvement in a criminal conspiracy the previous year that Psyche's twin and her husband had foiled, the earl had gone to the continent to stay with his sister, the Countess von Stockerau, in Austria. Although Austria and Germany were two entirely separate regions, it could only be assumed that émigrés from England would seek each other out. To everyone's knowledge, the earl remained on the continent with his sister, but the Weilheims had come to Great Britain, at least for the Season.

The one rumor the countess had spread that had not been generated by Hendon was that Pandora and Islington had eloped to Scotland before the official date of their marriage. That was true. When the two of them had gone to Edinburgh to stop Hendon, they had married in the Scottish fashion. However, they *did* have a ceremony performed in the parish church in Bardsey in Yorkshire, officiated by a member of the clergy. Since they had married each other legitimately, society found the tidbit of little interest other than for its romantic flair.

But there were other things the countess was insinuating, things like participation in murder, royal assassination, and a suicide at Holyrood. None of it had been substantiated, and no one involved would provide details, but the *ton* was speculating. Pandora and her husband didn't care what society thought, but Jessica's remarks continued to grow more spiteful as she attempted to maintain her tenuous position. For most, it was beginning to wear thin; society's tolerance of malice only went so far.

"Oh, no," said Eurydice, glancing in the same direction. "Isn't that the *volchica*?"

"*Da,*" said Psyche flatly.

Psyche saw Pandora and Islington then. Pandora saw her sisters at the same time, and she and Islington came toward them slowly along the edge of the floor as they stopped to speak with people. The two eventually reached them. Both appeared cheerful and relaxed, which made it obvious to Psyche that they didn't know the Countess von Weilheim was there. Psyche and Eurydice stood up to kiss both of them on the cheeks happily.

"Here, take a seat, Dodo. You look as if you're going to explode any day," said Eurydice, chuckling with amusement.

"Oh, yes, *please* to both," sighed Pandora with relief. She carefully eased herself into one of the uncomfortable chairs with help from Islington and started to wave her oriental fan in front of her face slowly.

"Pan, you should know right away that *she* is here," said Psyche quickly.

Pandora waved a hand through the air dismissively. "I don't care. I swear if I wasn't so ungainly at the moment, I would twist her knob off just so I wouldn't have to listen to her ridiculous prattle anymore."

"I could do it for you," said Psyche with a grin.

"No," said Islington flatly, "we'll have no knob twisting at Almack's." Psyche pouted teasingly. "I mean it. She is digging her own hole."

"Very well, I shan't," said Psyche resignedly, "but if she says one wrong thing within my hearing, I will not hesitate to correct her."

"Now, *that* you can do," said Islington with a grin, "and hopefully I will be close by to witness it."

The musicians began to play a rigadoon, and Psyche let Islington lead her onto the floor while Eurydice sat with Pandora. Psyche was glad her sister and brother-in-law had come, even if they would have to tolerate the countess.

Psyche chattered with Islington as they danced, and she was soon able to forget her concern because neither of the two seemed to be bothered by it. When the dance was done, they walked back to the edge of the floor to her sisters.

Psyche wasn't there for long when Sir James Klein came to claim her for the galop. She went with him for the dance and talked with him about various topics, including his work with the British Museum. He was helping to sort their collection of cuneiform tablets and transcribing the glyphs that were on the more fragile pieces before they disintegrated. Psyche was overjoyed when he said he would be happy to make her a copy of what he had so far. When the dance was done, he escorted her to the supper room for some lemonade, which led her close to the gaggle surrounding the Countess von Weilheim.

"Who would ever think to name their daughters so ridiculously?" the countess was twittering. "Honestly, there should be a law against things like that. If it's not biblical or native, it should be illegal. Some of them are impossible to pronounce. What's the one that come out this year?"

Someone supplied the answer to her question, but Psyche was too far out of earshot to hear. She couldn't be certain, but she was fairly sure Jessica was talking about her and her sisters. Psyche knew her parents had given them unusual names, but she wouldn't say they were difficult to pronounce and most definitely not ridiculous; anyone with a classical education had no trouble knowing how to pronounce them. Aside from that, she *liked* her name. She clenched her jaw and took a deep breath through her nose. It appeared the countess was now intent on blanketing her venom over the entire family. That would not suit. However, since Psyche couldn't be certain (but it really was not in doubt), she couldn't go back and call the woman on it.

She sat in the supper room with Sir James, enjoying lemonade and a piece of cake, continuing to talk with him about his work on the tablets. He readily admitted there had been no progress on deciphering the script, but once it was begun they would have a plentiful source for more. Psyche didn't find cuneiform nearly as fascinating as Egyptian hieroglyphs, but she was still interested. After they finished, Sir James escorted her back to her family. She skipped a step in surprise when she saw that Lord Sheerness had joined them, but she managed to continue talking with Sir James without seeming alarmed.

She hadn't expected to see Sheerness there, but then she hadn't expected to see him anymore for the rest of the Season after his father died. She still could not understand why he was already attending balls. This was the second function where she had seen him, although he had been hiding (she was fairly sure) in the garden at the previous one. Last Season she had seen him only once or twice a week, and now it was three times in one day. She wasn't sure she liked that. He stood talking with her sisters and Islington as she and Sir James approached.

"Thank you, Sir James, for everything," said Psyche with a smile as they reached her family.

"You are most welcome, Lady Psyche. If you'll come by the Museum around the first, I should have that ready for you."

"Marvelous," grinned Psyche. "If I'm able to learn anything, you'll be the first to know."

"Wonderful," said Sir James, giving her a kiss on her knuckles. He turned to look at Eurydice. "Would you care to dance the louvre, Lady Eurydice?"

"Of course, Sir James," said Eurydice with a polite smile, and she took his hand to let him lead her onto the floor.

Pandora turned to look at Psyche. "Have you seen Lord Georgie tonight?"

"No, I haven't," said Psyche blankly. Her forehead wrinkled. "Sir James didn't mention whether he had gone somewhere or if he was feeling unwell. It is unusual he wouldn't be here; they're like a matched set."

Pandora shrugged. "Oh, well, I'm sure he's somewhere. We just haven't seen him yet." She looked at Psyche curiously. "So what were you and Sir James discussing?"

"Nothing really," said Psyche dismissively.

She didn't want to talk about it in front of Sheerness because he always seemed to find her studies in antiquities more annoying than anything else about her. Pandora raised an eyebrow, and Psyche could see she wasn't going to let it go with that. She sighed resignedly, preparing for a row.

"He has simply promised to give me copies of all the transcriptions he has done so far on the cuneiform tablets at the Museum."

Pandora chuckled. "Don't you think you have enough already? You have a whole wall-full in the solarium at home."

"Those aren't all cuneiform," defended Psyche. "Some are hieroglyphic or other Egyptian languages and some are Greek or Latin...Hebrew...other languages," she trailed off.

"Still, you have a lot. What can you need with all of them?"

"Yes, Lady Psyche, what can you possibly need with all of them?" interjected Lord Sheerness flatly.

Psyche pursed her lips and ignored him. "Somewhere in all that mess is a clue to deciphering them. I'm very close; I can feel it, especially now I've got the rubbings of the Rosetta stone."

Pandora smiled at her sister's earnest tone. She didn't doubt for an instant that if Psyche said she was close, she meant it. Deciphering ancient languages for her was like solving a calculus or chemical formula for Pandora, and she could spend hours working on them without ever losing interest.

"I've already translated the Greek and the Demotic," continued Psyche, "but the hieroglyphs make no sense." She shrugged. "It's almost as if they couldn't make up their mind what language they were writing."

"Indeed?" retorted Sheerness darkly. "Perhaps it's an issue with the translator."

Psyche shook her head. "Oh, I don't think so, and perhaps I didn't phrase that the way I should have in order for *you* to understand it," she retorted in the same derogatory tone.

Sheerness folded his arms condescendingly. Pandora and Islington looked at each other with raised eyebrows. They knew how Psyche was about her translations. Surely by now, the earl knew, too. Pandora had been between them during an argument about the subject the previous Season, and—at least for her twin—it had nearly come to blows. Psyche was not prone to making statements regarding her theories unless she had tested them and found them sound. It was as if she were applying the scientific method to the subject of antiquities. That was why if she shared her thoughts on the matter, she was seldom wrong. If she was proved wrong, it was simply that the initial information she was working with had been inaccurate, not her capabilities. Psyche frowned at Lord Sheerness.

"What I meant to say is: in English, for example, we have the word boat to describe exactly that. It doesn't change. *Boat* means *boat*—not banana or horse. We also have twenty-six letters in our alphabet and ten digits to create an infinite number of words and numbers, but there is a structured formula to how they are made, and you don't change your mind about how it's written and switch from words to symbolic pictographs. Most any language has a set of characters used to represent what is written or spoken—Greek, Arabic, Cyrillic, Japanese, Chinese, Hebrew…any of them. Hieroglyphs are not like that, it seems. It almost appears as if some things are represented by one glyph, some by a set of glyphs representing letters or syllables to spell a word, and perhaps even some that are made up of *both*. That's why I said it almost seems as if they couldn't make up their mind. To the Egyptians, I'm sure it seemed entirely logical, but to me, so far, it makes not one iota of sense."

Psyche finished and looked at Sheerness calmly. She had never shared her thoughts on the matter with him because she didn't want to argue with him about it. She was on the right path, and she wasn't about to have his antipathy confuse her and make her begin to doubt it. His anger over her having papyri, clay tablets, and other samples of ancient languages had been enough for her to remain silent. She wouldn't have said anything at all if they had been alone.

Sheerness looked at her doubtfully. He had to wonder how much of what she said had been fed to her by Myron; his friend believed the same thing. He admitted her idea was a logical determination based on his own studies, but he wasn't about to believe Psyche had arrived at it by herself.

He suspected her rubbings of the Rosetta stone had been provided by Myron, much to his surprise. On her first mentioning it, the earl had to wonder if Myron had given them to her simply to humor her whimsy because Sheerness still couldn't believe she was as knowledgeable as she purported to be. He knew from the night in the garden that she was able to *swear* in several different languages, but that was often the easiest part of any language to learn. He was curious what items she had in her collection in the solarium. Myron said it was extensive, and it was *her* collection, not Myron's or the duke's.

"I think I'll have my hubby escort me to the supper room for tea or lemonade. I may not be dancing, but it is stuffy in here," said Pandora airily.

She knew an argument would soon escalate between the two, and she didn't want to see it again. Pandora believed the two liked each other, and a lot of their problems would be solved once Sheerness quit treating her twin like the town idiot. It had certainly cleared up a lot of the problems between her and her Theo.

Psyche watched as Islington helped her sister carefully rise from the uncushioned chair she had been sitting in for the better part of an hour. Pandora winced slightly as the movement caused a stitch in the small of her back and the bottom of her stomach. The weight lifted off of her backside made the blood rush back into it and caused an unpleasant tingling. The first of June, when she began her confinement, couldn't come soon enough for her.

"It's not any less crowded in there," Psyche warned with a grin. "I think the ladies provided too many vouchers this Season."

"I don't know that they supplied too many; it is just they will let *anyone* attend as a guest," said Islington dryly as he linked his wife's arm through his. He looked at Pandora with a slight frown of concern and thought they would leave earlier than they had planned. He gave Psyche a stern look as they prepared to leave. "Remember what I said about minding your manners."

Psyche giggled. "I will try," she avowed amusedly. She didn't feel threatened by her brother-in-law; she knew too many of his secrets.

She watched them weave their way to the supper room and sat on the chair her twin had vacated. Sheerness soon sat in the one beside it and looked at her curiously. He wondered what Bardsey had meant by his parting words to Psyche. She didn't seem concerned, in any event, but then she often behaved as if she had no manners…at least around him.

"I want to thank you for this afternoon," he said after a time.

Psyche looked at him with a preoccupied expression. Her attention was obviously focused elsewhere.

"For what?" she asked blankly.

"My niece and nephews are committing sacrilege and have begun to worship a goddess named Psyche," said Sheerness wryly with a half-smile.

Psyche had the modesty to blush. She was flattered by their admiration, but she was not sure it wasn't misplaced. A good time had been had by all, but she had never done it with the intention of gaining their adoration. She just thought they needed something to cheer them after all their recent misery, something that would let them escape from it for a time. That they held her in such high regard actually made her somewhat uncomfortable.

"I'm sorry," said Psyche quietly.

Sheerness shook his head dismissively. "Don't be. Everyone has been so worried about them. Philip hadn't spoken more than two words after Monique died; since this afternoon he hasn't *stopped* talking," he chuckled.

Psyche laughed as well. "Again, I'm sorry." She looked at him calmly. "You won't mind if I bring my younger brothers to meet them next Wednesday, will you? I should have thought to discuss it with you first."

"That will be fine. I'm sure they will like it. I told Amalie you came to visit her. She said she would make sure not to take a nap next Wednesday."

Psyche smiled absently and looked back across the room, her lips tightening grimly. The countess continued to hold court, but the number of people surrounding her had dwindled to only two or three. Psyche was trying to ignore the woman, following the suit of her twin and brother-in-law, but she couldn't stop herself from wondering and worrying over what horrible things the woman was saying.

"Are you ill, Lady Psyche?" asked Sheerness concernedly.

Psyche looked back at him in surprise. "No. Why?"

"You don't seem to be as contrary as usual."

Psyche raised an eyebrow. "I could say the same of you, my lord. I am surprised you had nothing more acerbic to say regarding my translations. Last Season, you would have been much harsher," she teased with a wry smirk.

Sheerness's relaxed expression tightened somewhat. "Yes, well, much has changed since then."

Psyche's eyes grew round in dismay. "Oh! I'm sorry…! I didn't mean to…," Psyche trailed off as her cheeks colored with embarrassment.

"I know. You never do," he said flatly.

Psyche colored even further and looked away from him. She could not believe she had been so thoughtless. Perhaps it was only that he seemed to be so much himself she had forgotten everything he had been through.

The louvre ended, and Psyche watched as Sir James led Eurydice to the supper room. The two of them walked past Countess von Weilheim, and her jaw began to wag as soon as they were barely out of earshot. Psyche's jaw tightened with frustration. Psyche thought she should leave. She would have no trouble convincing Eurydice to leave as well. Pandora and Islington would not stay much longer. Psyche just knew she couldn't continue to remain in the same room as Jessica without eventually causing her bodily harm, no matter what dire warnings Psyche had received from her brother-in-law.

But she couldn't leave until Myron returned from wherever he had gone. She looked at her watch, dismally noting it was only eleven. It would be two more hours yet to endure. She began to fidget, her foot tapping nervously on the floor, and she had to make herself stop. She couldn't decide if staying to watch more of the backbiting or if leaving and not knowing would be better. She was beginning to believe leaving would ultimately be more acceptable.

If she couldn't go home, maybe she could find somewhere else to wait for her brother's return out of the presence of the countess. She didn't like playing cards much, but she could go to the card room and watch. Eurydice had been introduced to enough people she could fend for herself alone in the dance room, and Pandora and Islington were still about somewhere; at least, Psyche was fairly sure they were. She didn't think they would leave without saying goodbye. She started to chew the side of her thumb, but she took it away when she tasted satin.

Pandora would know of some place to hide, and she would understand her twin's need of a place that was quiet where she could collect her thoughts. If Arachne were there, she would know of a place where one could go to be alone. Psyche recalled that her older sister had mentioned something of a storage room on the hall between the supper room and the powder room, but

Psyche couldn't remember where it was or how to get to it. It contained old furniture and things that had not been taken up to the attic or disposed of in some other way.

Sheerness watched her distracted behavior with curiosity. He didn't think she was purposely ignoring him. Her attention was focused elsewhere, for whatever reason. If he spoke to her, she conversed, but if left to her own thoughts too long, she became lost in them. Whatever they were, they didn't seem to set her mind at ease. He was confident they weren't about him, but he wasn't sure if that concerned him or not.

He was as surprised as she that they were behaving civilly. He had eventually accepted his defeat in the park that morning. As he thought about it, he had to admit the entire episode was—while bizarre—rather humorous, and it taught him a lesson. He realized that was her intention. Then, that afternoon when she entertained the children, she had earned his grudging respect. Their cheerfulness after her performance had made everyone optimistic they were going to come through the loss of their mother and grandfather soundly. That had been in question before. He didn't forget the original purpose of her visit. Amalie had been moved to tears when he told her.

Psyche sighed with relief when she saw Pandora and Islington coming toward them with Eurydice and Sir James. She was tempted to bound from her chair and meet them, but she was being too flighty as it was. She could wait until they arrived where she was sitting. Her anxiety was nonsensical, but she wouldn't be able to quell it until she had time alone. If she wasn't able to, she would break out in hives. Her twin got migraines; she got hives. Psyche couldn't decide which was worse. She stood up when they reached her.

"Pan, I am about to break out in hives. Tell me where I can hide because I can't go home until Myron comes back," she said calmly...in Russian.

Pandora and Eurydice looked at her in amazement. Her sisters knew she was speaking Russian because it wasn't a language other people commonly learned, while they had all learned it from their grandmother. Considering what she was saying, they could understand why she didn't want anyone else to understand it. Pandora could realize why her sister didn't want anyone to know she was about to break out in big, red splotches, but she wasn't sure what had prompted them. She looked at Sheerness suspiciously. She was feeling lubberly because of her belly, but a pressure grip didn't require grace.

"Why are you going to break out in hives?" asked Pandora with concern in the same language.

"Because I cannot get *that* woman out of my head."

"Don't worry about the *volchica*," said Eurydice with a grin. "I heard nearly everyone in the supper room talking about how full up they were of her."

Pandora chuckled. "She's right. Besides, if anyone should be concerned about it, it's me, and I couldn't care less."

"But she's not just talking about you and Islington anymore; I heard her talking about *all* of us. She said we have ridiculous names."

"So?" quizzed Pandora with a raised eyebrow.

Psyche groaned and shook her head. "Oh, I know, but I can't calm down in here. I just want to roast her over an open fire and be done with it. Having her become a social outcast isn't good enough. I've been sitting here imagining all the ways to make her die a slow, painful death."

"Psy, breathe in and out through your nose or something. Deep breaths from your diaphragm," said Eurydice helpfully. It didn't help.

"Why didn't you dance to take your mind off it? Lord Sheerness has been sitting right there the entire time," said Pandora practically.

"He didn't ask me to dance because he *can't* dance," said Psyche flatly.

Pandora frowned. "Psyche, that's not fair. I've danced with him, and I think he is an excellent dancer."

"*Nyet,* Pan. That's not what I meant. He can't dance because he's in *mourning.*"

"Oh, right," she said with a sheepish grin. "Well, you could have at least talked to him and not paid any attention to her."

"I tried, but I perpetually suffer from looby disease around him. I'd rather not talk than see how far I can shove my foot in my mouth. Aside from that, even when I don't, he makes me feel like I've done. It's best just not to talk."

Pandora and Eurydice chuckled. They found it amusing. There were very few things that would put Psyche into a dither. Having to lie was one. Trying to control her temper was another. Psyche did not often lose her temper; she would simply keep bottled inside the things that made her angry. If the source of annoyance disappeared, with some time to herself, the anger would go away. If the object of her wrath persisted, though, she was capable of being very *expressive* of her displeasure. When she wasn't allowed to express it, however, it resulted in hives.

"Can you, please, just tell me where I can find the room Arachne was talking about?" pleaded Psyche.

The three men stood talking with each other about goings on in Parliament (Sir James was a member of the House of Commons) as the girls spoke with each other in Russian. Islington was sure his wife would tell him the cause later, and he wasn't at all surprised to find them chattering as if they were from St. Petersburg. Sir James didn't speak or understand Russian, but listening to the three was making him think it was a beautiful language in its own right, and he might want to learn it himself. Sheerness was trying to divide his attention between both conversations because he *did* speak Russian, and while he realized the girls were using it for privacy, to hear them speaking with a native fluency was something he found astonishing. He was trying to keep his features unassuming, but he found their conversation much more intriguing than events in Parliament, and he wondered just how much Psyche was exaggerating about impending hives.

Pandora looked at her sister's panicked expression. She and Islington would be leaving soon but not soon enough to return Psyche to Aberdare House before she looked as if she'd been attacked by a swarm of bees. Aside from that, Eurydice couldn't stay by herself, and if they took her home as well, it would worry Myron when he returned and couldn't find them. Letting her have some time alone in the storage closet would remedy the situation.

"It's the second door on the left between the supper room and the powder room, just past the marble columns. What will you do if it's locked?"

"I have no earthly," said Psyche dully. She looked at her watch. "Myron will be back in about an hour and a half. If I can just have some solitude for a little while, I'll be all right."

"You would feel so much better if you wouldn't let things fester, Psy," said Pandora, her lips twitching amusedly.

"Maybe so, but I can't very well fly off the handle like you do."

"I do not!" said Pandora in an affronted tone.

"You do," said Eurydice sagely with a nod. "I think both of you could do with a bit of contemplation on things that are worthy of anger." She looked at the three nearby gentlemen. "In any event, now you know where you can hide, Psyche, we need to quit talking to each other in Russian before we seem ruder than we already do."

Pandora turned to slip her arm through Islington's and looked up at him with a smile. Islington looked down at her suspiciously from what he was saying to the other two men. She had a conspiratorial glint in her eyes. That made him nervous, but he didn't think she could get up to too much mischief in her present condition. Eurydice began to chat with Sir James about any manuscripts that might be available at the Museum on Renaissance music. Psyche prepared to excuse herself. Sheerness looked at her, and he felt a mischievous urge overcome him.

"Would you care to dance the quadrille, Lady Psyche?" he asked mildly as he heard the beginning strains.

"Wh-what?" stuttered Psyche disconcertedly.

"Oh, yes, let's do," said Pandora to Islington, tugging at his arm.

"Would you like to dance, Lady Eurydice?" asked Sir James kindly.

"Yes, of course, Sir James," said Eurydice agreeably with a smile. She liked Sir James. He was completely innocuous.

Sheerness raised a questioning eyebrow as he continued to look at Psyche.

"Are you supposed to?" asked Psyche weakly.

"I will if I want to," said Sheerness with a grin.

Psyche *really* wanted to go to the closet, but perhaps if she danced, it would assuage the necessity of hiding. If she could just take her mind off Countess von Weilheim, she would be fine.

"A-all right," said Psyche reluctantly, taking his arm to let him lead her onto the floor.

Her sisters and their partners had already taken their places at the bottom of one set. Psyche and Sheerness had to take their positions in another set, and to her dismay, she found herself standing beside Countess von Weilheim. She bit the inside of her lip to stifle a curse and began to follow Eurydice's suggestion of taking deep breaths through her nose. She would do her best to ignore the woman. She smiled politely at Sheerness across from her, and when the countess turned to look at her, Psyche managed an amiable smile. She was not surprised when the woman lifted her nose and rolled her eyes pretentiously then looked away to begin chatting with the woman on her other side, Baroness Fribourg, one of the society tabbies.

Psyche made a noble attempt at maintaining her composure. She followed the steps of the dance, but she couldn't ignore the chatter between the countess and baroness. They spoke in German and made no effort to keep their voices quiet, and it wasn't Baroness Fribourg so much as Jessica who prattled spitefully about Pandora, Islington, and anyone else that suited her. The countess thought she was being sly by speaking German, but Psyche doubted very seriously there was *any* language the countess could speak that Psyche couldn't speak better. Psyche smiled absently at Sheerness when he made eye contact, but her cheeks were becoming flushed with growing irritation at the woman beside her.

"How could she even show herself in public looking like that?" Jessica was saying spitefully. "It's unseemly. Surely she knows how scandalous it is, and that white swell is the size of a barge!" she cackled.

Psyche moved out of hearing for a step or two and was relieved at the brief respite, but she inevitably moved back into her position beside the woman.

"She has the manners of a slattern. You should have heard the things she said to me! *Outrageous*! She's no better than a common trollop."

Psyche could hold her tongue no longer. She looked at the woman coldly when she caught her eye.

"My sister has more dignity and grace in her little finger than you could ever hope to attain, and at least she isn't a jilt," stated Psyche chillingly in perfect German.

Jessica's eyes rounded in surprise. Baroness Fribourg tilted her head back to look around the countess to see who had spoken. Her lips pursed as she tried to contain her amusement. She had taken Countess von Weilheim under her wing when the young…lady arrived from the continent, feeling it was her duty for a fellow "countrywoman," but the baroness had wearied of her constant, vindictive railing about the Aberdares and Bardseys. Even as Baroness Fribourg loved a good tidbit of gossip, there was no truth in what the woman said, and she couldn't abide empty malice.

Sheerness looked at Psyche with concern. He had been listening to Countess von Weilheim prattle on venomously and suspected the person she was insulting was Psyche's twin. He also felt this was the *volchica* Psyche had wanted to avoid. He was disconcerted to realize his actions had brought her into close proximity. He was consoled that Psyche couldn't understand what the woman was saying (even if he could) and was dismayed when Psyche responded in German with as much ease as she had spoken to her sisters in Russian. He hoped for Psyche's sake that the countess would now be silent.

Jessica sneered at Psyche and moved away from her for the next steps of the dance. By the time they were beside each other again, the countess had begun to converse with the baroness in Italian, still spouting insults. It was a useless activity on her part; Psyche's family had several servants from that country, and the duchess had lived in Venice for many years; her grace's mother had *been* Italian. They even had a palazzo in Venice that Psyche's mother had inherited from Grandfather Sanders, which he had inherited from *his* Italian mother and had used during his time serving as an ambassador there.

Psyche watched in outrage as the woman had the effrontery to look directly at her and smile politely as she continued to rant.

"I have it on good authority that she used to give three-penny uprights on Drury," said Jessica, "and that she follows men through the streets in the hopes of sharing her favors."

Psyche clenched her hands at her sides to restrain herself from throttling the countess. She could hear the blood rushing in her ears as her anger threatened to overwhelm her. She waited until they were back beside each other, and she returned Jessica's smile with a vicious one of her own.

"Before you try to spread further scurrilous prattle to impugn the character of my sister, Miss Pickthank," said Psyche with a moderated tone in perfect Italian, "you should first consider that your source of information is nothing better than a hushing molly and a piddling shite sack."

Sheerness coughed and put a hand over his mouth to cover his amusement. Other dancers could hear the women talking in the foreign languages, but he suspected he was the only one, besides Baroness Fribourg, who could understand what they were saying. He looked at the baroness and saw she was finding the confrontation entertaining as well. He knew she would relish the opportunity to recount its details to the rest of society and would not hesitate to do so. Sheerness was chagrined he had played no small part in staging it, but he was finding Psyche's command of languages very impressive.

Countess von Weilheim looked at Psyche frustratedly, and it was obvious that she was angry. She had still not, however, become cognizant of the fact that Psyche's knowledge of languages was far superior. The countess had also not learned it would serve her better interests to remain silent on the subject within Psyche's hearing…whatever the language. When she came back to her position beside Psyche, she had switched to French, and Psyche was disappointed it wasn't something more complicated, like Polish or Croatian.

"I understand she played no small part in the death of a young nobleman last Season, and she went to Scotland to provide assistance to the *French*," spat Jessica. "She's a devious little shrew, and I, for one, wouldn't be surprised to learn she trapped Bardsey into marrying her."

Psyche smiled tightly and shook her head. "You're just jealous my sister got a well-hung Adonis who's nuts about her, and all you have is a piss-proud drip of a man who is probably a bad shag, most definitely reeks of rotten cabbage, and lets his eyes rove where putting his hands would get him shot!" she said hotly. "Now, shut your potato trap and give your tongue a holiday!"

The song ended. Psyche curtsied gracefully to Sheerness, and her anger at Countess von Weilheim prevented her from seeing the way his shoulders shook with silent laughter. The countess's decision to speak in French, however, had been a mistake because most people of the *ton*, if they were able to speak a foreign language, spoke that one. The music was quiet enough at the end of the tune that most everyone in the set heard Psyche's comments regarding the count and telling the countess to shut her mouth. While Sheerness attempted to give the illusion he was oblivious, most everyone else did not. Baroness Fribourg was twittering with hilarity, and the other couples were looking at Countess von Weilheim with satisfied smirks at her come-uppance.

Psyche began to turn red with mortification when she realized her words had been heard by several other people besides the intended recipient. When Jessica realized what had happened, she, too, colored with embarrassment and rage. She mindlessly flew at Psyche, her hands shaped into claws. Psyche's eyes widened for a moment in surprise, but she easily stepped aside and casually put out her foot, making the countess trip and fall ungracefully to the floor. The people nearby who either had not heard or understood what Psyche had said looked at the countess sprawled on the floor in shock, which grew even further as she began to throw a wild tantrum. No one (except Sheerness) realized Psyche had been the cause of her tumble.

Psyche put her hands to cheeks that had become hot with agitation. She looked down at Jessica's continued fit and knew the woman was done for socially. That kind of behavior was not tolerated by the *ton*. Psyche hoped no one in her family (or anyone else, for that matter) would have to be the victim of Countess von Weilheim's acid tongue ever again.

As many pairs of curious eyes as there were on Jessica's continued performance, there were a few looking at Psyche, too, especially those who knew what she had said. Psyche didn't think anyone knew she had been responsible for making Jessica fall, but the woman's intent to physically attack Psyche had been obvious. The room was full of a hissing noise as people began to whisper to each other. Whatever was not common knowledge up to that point would soon become so, thanks to Baroness Fribourg. Psyche wished the floor would open and swallow her.

She needed to go to the closet. Pandora and Eurydice were looking in her direction. Psyche gave her twin a helpless glance, and Pandora could fairly well determine what had happened. She blew Psyche a kiss and nodded understandingly. Psyche looked at Sheerness's dumbfounded expression. She gave him a tight smile and a nod and gracefully turned to leave the room, her back ramrod straight with discomfiture.

She ignored Jessica's continued screaming and crying and calmly wove her way through the people already in the room and others who were attempting to enter and see the spectacle. No one tried to stop her or noticed she was moving *away* from the commotion. Once she was into the hallway, it was easy for her to make her way to the closet. Everyone was trying to go to the dance room. She was able to slip in without attracting attention. Once the door was closed, she leaned her back against it and sighed gustily.

After a few minutes of just standing there with her eyes closed, attempting to calm herself, Psyche moved further into the room, waving her hands in front of her as she felt for objects in her way. She missed a low piece of furniture and yelped when she barked her shin. She put her hands lower and realized she had located some type of couch. It was a chaise, covered in brocaded fabric. She eased herself onto it and rubbed her leg where she had bumped it. That was going to leave a bruise.

She turned on the chaise and brought her knees up to her chest, putting her feet on the cushion and clasping her arms around her legs. She slowly began to rock back and forth and blinked several times to keep herself from crying. It didn't work, of course, and while she wasn't sobbing uncontrollably, she couldn't stop the tears from coming.

She shouldn't have done that. She should have held her tongue, and she shouldn't have tripped Jessica. Her part in the debacle was going to be the cause of as much tongue-wagging as Jessica's scandalous behavior. Baroness Fribourg had heard everything, and to Psyche's knowledge, she was incapable of discretion. Psyche didn't care what people said about *her*, but she could only speculate about what kind of difficulty it might cause for her family. And, while she had no concern for what people might say about her, she disliked attracting attention.

She removed her gloves and wiped her hands at her cheeks, sighing fitfully. How was she going to leave the assembly hall when there would be people staring at her? It would be unseemly to crawl out a window to escape. Psyche hoped that after some time to compose herself she would be more tolerant of whatever the results of the spectacle were.

Pandora and Eurydice would be informed what had happened by witnesses. Psyche would eventually talk to them and give them the *truth*. If not that night, she would tell them tomorrow. Pandora would hold her blameless in the matter, and she would understand that Psyche had felt she had no choice. Their parents would find out as well—it would be impossible for them not to. Psyche didn't think they would be angry. She had tried to be as discreet and dignified as she could under the circumstances, except for the things she had said to Jessica. Besides Baroness Fribourg, though, Psyche didn't think anyone else had understood what she was saying…other than the French. But that would be enough.

Psyche started in surprise when the door to the closet opened and closed quickly. She kept silent, hoping whoever it was would exit again. She might have thought someone had mistakenly opened and closed the door without coming in if it weren't for the soft breathing she could hear coming from the direction of the door. She also heard the unmistakable click as it was locked. Because her attention was elsewhere when the light from the hall entered, she didn't see who it was, and she wasn't sure from the breathing if it was a man or a woman. If it was Pandora, she would have already spoken, so Psyche could only assume it was someone else. The room was windowless and lampless and very dark; as long as she stayed quiet, the person wouldn't know she was there.

She carefully straightened her legs out in front of her and sank lower onto the couch, trying to do so without making the springs in the cushion squeak.

The person moved toward her in the darkness, and she tensed as he came nearer. She squeaked in surprise when the person found the chaise in much the same way she had, except he didn't just bump his shin; he completely tripped over it and grunted as he landed on it…directly on top of Psyche.

Psyche fought her panic and began to struggle under the weight on top of her, especially when she realized from the heaviness of the body and the texture and cut of the clothes that it was a man. Her arms were pinned to her chest between them, and she tried to work them loose. If she could get her arms free, she could push the person off…or whatever else might be required. She worked them free at about the same time the man raised himself up slightly.

"Lady Psyche?"

Psyche stilled in surprise and attempted to look at the face above hers in the darkness.

"Lord Sheerness?"

"Yes."

Her brow furrowed in confusion. "What are you doing in here?"

"I came to see if you were all right."

"How did you know where I was?"

There was a contemplative silence. "I speak Russian," he said quietly.

Psyche colored hotly with embarrassment when she realized he understood everything she had spoken about with her sisters. He shifted and took a little more of his weight off of her by settling between her thighs, but he seemed to be in no hurry to sit up and get off completely. She found his closeness disturbing in several ways, but she didn't want to call his attention to just how compromising his position was.

"What happened to Jessica?" she asked breathlessly.

"Her husband hauled her away…kicking and screaming the whole time that *you* had caused it all."

Psyche's agitation returned, and her chest began to heave emotionally.

"But I didn't…," she began, and her voice cracked. She blinked back anxious tears and bit her lip.

"No one believes her," soothed Sheerness, and he surprised Psyche when he gently brushed a hand against her cheek. "Baroness Fribourg has been happily telling everybody that the countess had been insulting you and yours, while you were the picture of gentility and grace. When the Countess von Weilheim couldn't rile you, she resorted to a physical attack."

"But that's not what happened either," said Psyche softly, and she was amazed the baroness was an ally in her defense.

"That's true. She did rile you, and you had every justification in saying everything you did to her. No one else understood what you were saying to contradict the baroness's account of things, and there were several witnesses to Countess von Weilheim's attempt to harm you."

"You understood what I said to her?" asked Psyche with dismay.

"Oh, yes," said Sheerness amusedly. "Let's see, you speak Russian, German, Italian, and French—all very fluently, I might add, but I do, too.

Don't worry, I'll not tell a *soul* what actually happened…not even that you tripped her."

Psyche squirmed in discomfiture, knowing he saw and heard *everything*. He already thought she was an ignoramus with the manners of a bitch booby. Her night's activities had done nothing but confirm it for him.

Sheerness enjoyed the feel of Psyche beneath him, and he was intrigued by the scent of her perfume. It was light and crisp but entirely feminine in a way he found intoxicating. He could tell the entire episode in the dance room had left her feeling humiliated. Her sisters and Lord Bardsey were preoccupied by the tumult that followed, so Sheerness decided to see to her since he knew where she had gone. He hadn't expected to trip over the couch and fall on top of her, but he found it to be a pleasing experience.

After several minutes of no further conversation, Psyche waited for him to get up. She wasn't physically uncomfortable, now that he wasn't squashing her; his weight rested between her thighs and on his forearms to either side of her. But his continued, intimate nearness made her nervous. She hadn't forgotten how pleasant their kiss was in the courtyard, and she unnervingly found herself wishing he would do it again. He had been infinitely more civil so far this Season, but her growing fascination for him couldn't be right. When he still showed no signs of moving, Psyche decided to ask.

"Lord Sheerness?"

"Yes?"

"Are you going to get off me?" she asked hesitantly.

"Not right now," he murmured after a moment of thought.

Psyche tensed in anticipation as his face drew closer to hers in the dark. His breath caressed her cheek, and then his lips brushed against hers gently. He placed teasing kisses against her lips until she started to respond, despite her misgiving, and then he covered her mouth with his hungrily. He coaxed her lips apart by softly nipping at the lower one with his teeth, and when he massaged his tongue against hers, Psyche instinctively returned the favor.

She slowly moved her hands from their place at her sides up his chest to run them through the silky tangle of his hair. Despite its wavy unruliness, she was fascinated to discover it was very soft and fine and that he didn't wear any oils or pomades. She moved one hand to the back of his neck, the other to the side of his head, where her palm rested on his cheek. She returned his kiss artlessly, and a soft moan escaped her as she felt herself becoming enthralled.

Sheerness skimmed his lips along her jaw down to her neck, and Psyche sighed as he nuzzled the point just below her ear. She arched her neck as his lips moved to its juncture with her shoulder, then lower still to brush across the tops of her breasts exposed by the bodice of her gown. When he brought his mouth back to hers, Psyche returned his kiss with a yearning that startled her.

She gasped against his lips as she felt him cup one of her breasts through the fabric of her gown, and when she arched against him excitedly as he began to circle the nipple with his thumb to make it pucker almost painfully, she was astonished as it made her aware of his arousal.

Sheerness moved his hand down her side in a caress and slowly began to raise the skirt of her gown. He groaned as Psyche shifted her hips against him to allow the fabric to be moved. He lifted her leg to place it around his waist, and he worked her stocking loose from its garter and pushed the silk down to expose the bare skin of her calf. He found it to be infinitely softer than the fabric as he smoothed his hand over it, working his way up from her ankle, to her thigh, along the edge of her bottom to finally rest at her hip. He moved his pelvis against hers suggestively, and Psyche moaned at the sensations it caused.

He moved the hand that rested at her hip up her stomach to her ribs beneath her gown and chemise, and when he reached the bottom edge of the bodice, he worked it higher with his fingers and freed her breast. Psyche moaned again at the feel of his warm palm against her bare nipple, and she shuddered and arched toward him when he drew the tip between his fingers as he kneaded her breast.

Psyche clutched her fingers in his hair convulsively when he moved his lips to her nipple, gently biting it with his teeth before taking it into his mouth and rubbing his tongue against the tip. She instinctively moved her hips against his as her breathing became ragged with her excitement. She felt as if she couldn't breathe, and her stomach quivered with anticipation.

Yet even as she was aching for him, Psyche knew they shouldn't do this. Innocent though she might be, she knew what the natural culmination would be. As much as she might want it, she would have to stop it…soon. Considering how much they professed to dislike each other, she was astonished it was happening at all. People who disliked each other didn't do things like this.

"Lord Sheerness?" she sighed.

"Hmm?" He had left her breast and was placing kisses along her ribs.

"Will you stop, please?"

His lips paused in their ministrations for a brief moment, and he moved his way back up her body to kiss her soundly, leaving her breathless and flustered.

"Hmm," he said thoughtfully. "Would you rather I did this?"

Psyche bit her lip to keep from crying out when he moved his hand to begin teasing her button, and her hands clutched at his shoulders spasmodically at the indescribable shockwaves it sent through her body.

"Wow!" she gasped, and she arched toward him mindlessly, thoughts of ending their lovemaking momentarily forgotten.

Sheerness laughed lowly at her reaction, and he trailed kisses up her throat to her lips. He was delighted as she responded passionately to his kiss. He knew, of course, what she had meant when she asked him to stop, but he wasn't quite ready to yet. When she cried out against his lips and began to shudder uncontrollably as she orgasmed, then he was ready to stop.

Psyche was dizzy from the sensations that washed over her. She had felt as if something had been building inside her, growing larger and larger until it had suddenly exploded. She was left awed and gasping as she floated back to reality. Psyche smoothed a gentle hand along Sheerness' jaw to his chin then up to his lips, which were parted in a slight smile. Psyche raised her head to kiss him warmly.

The earl slowly, reluctantly, began to put her clothes back into place. He pulled down the bodice of her gown after one more teasing bite to her nipple. He sat up on his knees and rested her foot on his shoulder, and he placed tiny kisses along her leg as he pulled the stocking back onto it and secured it beneath the garter just above her knee. He pulled her dress down to cover her after he put her leg back onto the couch, and then he pulled her to a sitting position, bringing her close against him in an embrace. He placed a tender kiss against her lips and smoothed his hands across her back to rest at the top of her buttocks.

Psyche looked at him in surprise when she felt he still had an erection. "But…you…," she trailed off.

He chuckled lowly and nuzzled her throat. "You can owe me next time."

"How do you know there will *be* a next time?" asked Psyche doubtfully.

He moved his hands lower to cup her bottom. "Well, if there isn't going to be, then I guess we can take care of it right now," he said silkily.

Psyche jumped in surprise when she heard someone try the knob on the door and found it locked. That was followed by a light rapping.

"*Psyche?*" she heard Pandora call softly through the door.

"Oh, my giddy aunt," Psyche gasped anxiously. "Just a second!" she called to the door.

She pulled away from Sheerness to feel around for her discarded gloves, fan, and drawstring bag. She quickly pulled on the gloves and stood up to make sure her clothes were actually where they were supposed to be. She started to go for the door when Sheerness reached for her in the dark and pulled her close to him to kiss her passionately. Psyche felt confused when he released her and shook her head to clear it. She went to the door and opened it.

The brightness of the light in the hall made her blink in momentary blindness after the darkness of the room, and she closed the door behind her quickly before her sister happened to see she had not been alone. Pandora looked at her curiously, her head tilted sideways.

"What were you doing in there?" she asked wonderingly.

"Looking for my gloves," said Psyche calmly. It wasn't a *complete* lie.

"Myron is here, and Eurydice is waiting for you at the cloak room," said Pandora as she linked her arm through her sister's. "Baroness Fribourg had a very fanciful tale to tell. You can come over after breakfast tomorrow and tell me what *really* happened," she said as they walked down the hall.

"I'm just glad I won't have to go back to the dance room. As a matter of fact, I don't think I ever want to come to Almack's again."

Pandora chuckled. "I think Countess von Weilheim by far got the worse end of this engagement, but I completely understand."

There were several people lining the hall as they walked toward the cloak room. Psyche grew uncomfortable as the people would stop whatever they were doing to look at her and smile as she walked past. She tightened her grip on Pandora's arm anxiously, and she began to wonder if going through a window would have been an unwise decision after all. Psyche's cheeks steadily turned pinker. She started to panic when the Countess de Lieven, one of the matrons of Almack's, stepped into the center of the hall, effectively blocking Psyche's escape. She could only imagine the woman intended to revoke her family's voucher to the assembly hall after Psyche's activities. She had only small relief in knowing that no one was aware of what she had been doing in the storage closet with Lord Sheerness.

"Countess de Lieven," said Psyche quietly when she reached her.

The beautiful Russian countess looked at Psyche with a raised eyebrow before smiling amusedly. She surprised Psyche when she embraced the younger woman and kissed both her cheeks. After the countess released her, she began to clap appreciatively.

"*Brava!*" called the countess.

Her applause was soon joined by that of the people nearby. Psyche's cheeks turned an even deeper shade of red, and Pandora watched with alarm. She was as astounded as her twin over the countess's reaction and the response it had prompted from everyone else, but she was waiting for Psyche to break out in hives any minute, and there was really no way to quickly—tactfully— extricate themselves.

Psyche put her hands to her cheeks, her eyes round with amazement. This was far worse than whispering and gossiping. Psyche was beginning to believe that would have been preferable. She looked around herself at all the beaming faces. Myron, Eurydice, and Islington were standing at the edge of the crowd looking at the spectacle in disbelief. Psyche was unsure what to do, but she finally decided she could only do as those in the theater would when cheered by the audience: she gave a deep, graceful curtsy and smiled pleasantly.

She linked her arm through Pandora's and calmly walked toward the rest of her family. Her willingness to be an object of public scrutiny only went so far, and her skin was becoming very itchy.

Chapter Five

As many invitations as she had been prone to receiving before, Psyche was inundated by them after the night at Almack's. She had no intention of accepting any of them. The entire episode was something she would just as soon forget. The only person she had done it for was her twin. Now that Pandora's good name remained untarnished (and made perhaps even slightly more pristine), Psyche just wanted to forget about it and wished society would do the same. That did not seem likely.

There were other things about that night she would be more than happy to forget, but they were permanently etched in her memory. A week later, she still had to fight a flush that rose in her cheeks when someone said the name *Sheerness*. For some peculiar reason, he was a frequent topic of discussion in the days that followed. For a man in mourning, supposedly conducting a subdued routine, everyone in her family had something to say that either involved him or a member of his family.

Her mother, the duchess, had gone to visit his mother, the countess. Dorian went riding with his brother, Alex. Psyche was going to visit his sister, Amalie, that afternoon, and her younger brothers were greatly looking forward to meeting his niece and nephews at that time. She couldn't understand why he had suddenly become so inescapable.

For a while she had considered begging off the visit, but she wouldn't because several people would be disappointed, and Sheerness would not be one of them. She was hopeful she wouldn't have to see *him*. If she did, then she would do her best to ignore the awkwardness she was sure would exist.

Myron had told her that he had mentioned her request to accompany them to Greece and Egypt. Psyche couldn't say she was surprised the earl had flatly said no. But perhaps things had changed since Myron had talked to him, so Psyche told her brother to ask again. It was Myron's turn to flatly refuse. He said he had asked, Sheerness had said no, and it was not up to him to make the man change his mind. Aside from that, he had other matters to occupy him. That led Psyche to believe that if Sheerness was going to reconsider, she would have to make him do it herself. She just had not figured out how yet.

She went for her usual ride in the park accompanied by Jim and took bread for Waddlesworth. He was most appreciative, as were his friends. He didn't want to let her leave, but he also didn't want to waddle too far from the lake, so she was able to escape with only a few nips to her bootlaces. She made sure she gave him plenty of crumbs that morning because she wouldn't be able to go riding the next, but it was for a worthy cause: the Derby.

All of her family would attend. There was no way her parents would stop Persephone, even if she had to sneak out by climbing down the ivy outside her bedroom window. Luckily for her, that would be unnecessary. Even Pandora planned to endure the two-hour carriage ride to go with Islington. There weren't many social events her family made it a point not to miss, but this was one of them. They had a temporary pavilion (which workmen had already gone to set up that day), and many of their friends joined them for the occasion.

Psyche was looking forward to attending, if only to see if she could maintain her winning streak. She had picked the winner for the last nine years. She never directly bet money on the races herself, but her father and brothers had, as had several of their friends. Her wagers usually involved something between her and her sisters. After she had won so many times, her sisters were reluctant to place a wager anymore. Psyche was curious to see if she could make it for ten successive years. She might even try to pick place and show. She didn't usually, but she had good luck with that, too.

After breakfast, she went to run a few errands and to visit Pandora. She also, reluctantly, went to visit Baroness Fribourg. After the baroness had put herself firmly on Psyche's side in her encounter with Countess von Weilheim, Psyche felt she owed it to the woman. It wasn't as unpleasant as Psyche had feared it would be. The baroness was disappointed to learn Psyche would not be going to Almack's that night, but she was somewhat mollified to learn Arachne and Eurydice would be. Psyche discovered to her surprise that Lord Georgie had become engaged to Lucy Cranston. That would explain why he had not been with Sir James at Almack's the previous Wednesday. She found the news just the least bit disturbing.

Psyche's younger brothers were almost uncontrollably exuberant when it came time to go to the Nicholses' home, Barneville Court, on Curzon Street. She supposed it was still considered the Sheerness residence, and it was owned by the current earl, now that his father was dead. She had to remind the boys that she expected them to be on their best behavior. They assured her they would be, and she believed them. Damon was nervous about meeting the children because of his disability, but Psyche soothed him by assuring him that the Yeardley children were very nice and were very much looking forward to meeting him. She also told him that she would make sure they were aware of how special he was. That prompted one of his cherubic smiles, and Psyche knew he would be fine.

When the footman answered the door, Psyche first informed him that they were there to see the Yeardleys. Then she told him that she was there to see Lady Amalie. She wanted to make sure the children were introduced first. He escorted them onto the terrace and said he would inform the children of their arrival.

Psyche could barely restrain her brothers. They were fascinated by the garden. They could see the small pond with goldfish and lily pads. There was a large weeping willow with a small bench hidden beneath its droopy boughs. Several fruit trees with perfect limbs for climbing were planted here and there, and large, bushy shrubs perfect for hiding abounded. It almost seemed untended, but Psyche was sure it wasn't. She applauded their gardening staff.

It wasn't long before she could hear several pairs of small feet barreling across the wooden floor inside the house toward the terrace. Once Josie, Jerome, and Philip made it through the door, they all went to Psyche and hugged her enthusiastically. She was overwhelmed. For them to show so much affection after one brief meeting was unexpected. After a brief hesitation, she smiled and returned their embrace. They soon released her, and all six children looked at each other shyly.

"Hallo," said Psyche with a chuckle. "Josie, Jerome, and Philip, this is Cosmo, Christopher, and Damon."

"Hallo. Hi," said everybody.

"Why are you moving your hands like that when you talk?" asked Philip curiously.

"Because I am talking with them," said Psyche with a smile, continuing to sign. "Damon cannot hear, so I use hand signs for him to understand what I'm saying. He can read lips, but we use sign, too."

"You mean he can't hear anything at all?" asked Josie, her eyes round in amazement.

"No, but don't let that fool you," said Psyche with a chuckle. "As long as you look at him when you're talking, he can understand what you're saying even if you don't sign."

"Wow!" said the three Yeardley children in wonder.

"I can talk a little, too," said Damon shyly.

"Yes, you can," said Psyche affectionately, tweaking the end of his nose. She looked back at the Yeardleys. "You just have to remember that if you have something you want Damon to *hear*, make sure he can see your mouth. Cosmo and Topher can sign, too, so if need be they can translate." Psyche smiled. "I really don't think that will be necessary."

Psyche looked on as the children became acquainted. It wasn't long before they ran down the stairs into the garden to play. Psyche chuckled as they went directly for the pool. Her brothers loved animals, on land or in the water. She wouldn't be surprised if they were wading around in it before they were through. After she watched them for a little while, she was surprised when the footman showed Sir James Klein onto the terrace.

"Sir James! What a pleasant surprise!"

He took her hand and kissed her knuckles. "Likewise," he said with a smile. "Are you here to see Lord Sheerness as well?" he asked curiously.

"No, actually. I brought my younger brothers to play with the Yeardleys and to see Lady Amalie myself. Are *you* here to see Lord Sheerness?"

"Yes. I've some maps he requested for his trip to Greece and Egypt."

"Oh, I see," said Psyche a bit breathlessly. She still hadn't been able to determine how to make him let her go with him and Myron. "Old maps?"

"Not so very…only fifty years or so."

"Oh," said Psyche dully. Her expression turned somewhat pensive. "Sir James, I heard Lord Georgie has become engaged to Lucy Cranston. Is that true?"

Sir James's face became pale at the mention of it, and Psyche didn't need him to confirm it.

"Yes, I'm afraid so," he said quietly.

"Does that mean that you two…? What I mean to say is…," Psyche trailed off at his startled stare.

"What *do* you mean to say?" he asked calmly.

Psyche looked at the garden to see the children playing happily, and then she looked at the back of the house to make sure no one was standing there to overhear what she was about to say. It could be very dangerous for both Sir James and Lord Georgie if the wrong person were listening.

"Does that mean you are no longer together?" she asked quietly. "I will *never* tell a soul!" she swore when she saw his alarmed expression. "I'm sure no one realizes!"

"You're mistaken," he said weakly.

Psyche took both of his hands in hers. "If I am, I truly, humbly beg your pardon. If I'm not, then I would like to say he's a fool for choosing that ninny over you." She shook her head. "You seemed so perfect for each other."

Sir James was silent for quite some time, and Psyche was afraid her intuition had been wrong. All of her sisters thought the same thing, and they would never tell anyone for anything. If she was wrong, she hoped she had not terribly offended Sir James; he was a wonderful man.

"He said he's only marrying her to carry on the family name by producing an heir," said Sir James quietly.

"That would explain why he didn't choose someone more comely and genteel, don't you think?" asked Psyche hopefully.

"I suppose," said Sir James morosely.

"But he didn't want to end it?"

"No." Sir James shook his head. "But I don't see how we can continue."

Psyche gave his hands a comforting squeeze. "Marrying just to produce an heir is a silly reason, but you know as well as I do that it happens all the time. Men have mistresses, even when they have a perfectly good wife at home."

"I know, but our situation is somewhat different."

"Somewhat, yes," agreed Psyche with a shrug, "but not all that different. Sometimes, you just can't marry the person you love, and that happens all the time, too. Granted, I do believe Lord Georgie should have chosen someone who is less of a gossip, but perhaps it could work to your advantage to have someone that aware of what tongues are wagging about."

"Perhaps," said Sir James contemplatively.

"Sir James, it's often difficult to find someone who loves you for who you are, not *what* you are or what you *have*. If you find something like that, regardless of how wrong others might think it is, you should try to hold on to it," said Psyche plaintively.

"You know, you're right," said Sir James happily after some thought.

"Of course I am," said Psyche softly with a fond smile.

Sir James impulsively kissed both her cheeks and handed her the rolled up maps he'd had under one of his arms.

"See Lord Sheerness gets those, will you? I'm off to see Georgie."

So saying, he turned to go back through the house just as Amalie was exiting. He tipped his hat to her as he strolled past.

"Hallo, Lady Amalie," he said cheerily.

She watched him go with amazement, and then she walked onto the terrace to see Psyche's amused grin.

"Did I just see you kissing him?" she asked in shock.

"Somewhat, but it's not anything to cause alarm. I just helped him solve a problem, and he wanted to show his appreciation."

"Indeed?" quizzed Amalie with a raised eyebrow. "What kind of problem?"

"I can't tell you; it's a secret. I'm sorry," said Psyche calmly.

"Hmm," said Amalie speculatively. "You haven't formed a *tendre* for each other, have you?"

Psyche laughed. "Sir James and I? Oh, no!" she chortled. "We are so unsuited for one another."

Amalie linked her arm through Psyche's and went to sit with her on the bench.

"Well, I am happy that you're *unsuited,* but you do share interests," said Amalie thoughtfully.

"Shared interests do not form the basis of everything, especially not a marriage or a *tendre*, as you put it. Let's just leave it at unsuited," said Psyche with a grin. Then her forehead wrinkled in puzzlement. "Why would that make you happy? Sir James is a wonderful man!"

Amalie blushed and shook her head. "I have not one thing unfavorable to say about Sir James. I don't know that I should tell you why it makes me happy, though."

"Since you're not pressing me to tell you my secrets, I'll not make you tell me yours," said Psyche with a smile. She waved a hand through the air dismissively. "In any event, let's move on to other things. How are you?"

Amalie's face grew thoughtful. "I still miss my father terribly," she said sadly, but she shrugged. "There is always something that will happen or that I will see that will make me think of him. I sometimes forget he is gone. I'm sure in time it will lessen, but it has been less than a month, and the newness of it has still not worn off."

"I'm so sorry you have to go through this. I can only imagine how you must feel," said Psyche sympathetically.

"I'm very happy you came to see me. Other than Papa's close friends, no one has come to call."

"Society is full of fair weather friends; I just wanted to be sure you knew that I am not among them."

Amalie smiled. "I never thought so for a moment."

The children continued to giggle and play in the garden, and Psyche and Amalie turned on the bench to watch them. Psyche wasn't sure what they were playing, though. It appeared to be a cross between tag and living statues. Whatever it was, they were enjoying it immensely.

"Thank you for bringing your brothers to play," said Amalie softly.

"You're quite welcome. They actually have very few friends their own age and no close cousins, so this is a special treat for them, too. They won't meet very many chums until they start school...at least Cosmo and Christopher will."

"That's right," said Amalie in realization. "Damon is deaf, isn't he?"

"Yes. He has no trouble reading lips, and he is able to speak well enough now that he can be understood, but it is too much to expect the instructor to constantly be facing the class. Mamà and Papà aren't keen on letting him go to one of the special schools for the deaf, and Damon really has no interest in going to one in any event." Psyche shrugged. "Arachne is doing a marvelous job teaching him, and I would challenge Harrow or anywhere else to do better."

Amalie grinned. "You're probably right."

"How is your mother? My mother came to call on her, but she didn't say much, other than that she had a pleasant visit."

Amalie tilted her head sideways thoughtfully for a moment. "My mother is a strong woman. She loved my father very much, and she will probably mourn him for the rest of her life, but she also believes the best way to remember someone is to live your own life, to cherish the things that are precious and not waste time worrying over the things that are petty, so when your own time comes, the last thing to go through your mind will not be regret."

"That's wonderful," said Psyche admirably.

"Yes," said Amalie thoughtfully. "I can tell when she's been crying; I think that's how she goes to sleep every night, but I've never *seen* her shed another tear since my father's funeral. It helps to keep me brave," said Amalie in a cracked voice. "I think that's why she doesn't let us see, for me and for the children, for Alex and Sebastian, too."

Psyche looked at Amalie pensively. "What about Baron Yeardley? How are things with him?"

Amalie wiped at her cheek and shook her head. "William was beside himself with grief when Monique died. Thank God the children have such a wonderful nanny because he completely ignored them, and they desperately needed someone to comfort them. She finally wrote a letter to *Maman* and

Papa to let them know what was happening. *Maman* said she thought William had gone a little mad. They went to retrieve the children from Lincolnshire in February after Nanny MacBean wrote to tell them things had not improved. We haven't heard anything from William since then, and he didn't even try to stop the children from going. I think, in the beginning, seeing the children reminded him too much of Monique, especially Josie. We've all written him several letters…even the children, but we haven't received an answer."

Psyche's forehead creased worriedly. "Shouldn't someone go see to him?"

"Alex went up just the week before Papa died. He said *Maman's* assessment William was *slightly* mad was mild. He said William looked as if he hadn't bathed or changed clothes for a very long time. Most of the staff had deserted him, and the manor was in ghastly condition. Alex said William didn't even recognize him, but the most worrisome thing of all was that he continued to speak to Monique as if she were still there."

"My goodness!" said Psyche with dismay, a hand going to her throat.

"Alex arranged to have a nurse come stay with William to make sure he's cared for, and Alex did what he could to keep the rest of the staff on hand and attending to their duties. He didn't want to go so far as to have William confined to an asylum, and we hope he will recover, but it will be quite some time, if ever, before the children will see him again."

"That's terrible!" gasped Psyche. "Oh, Amalie, I'm so sorry for everything your family has gone through. And those poor, wonderful children! It just breaks my heart!"

"Thank you, Psyche. I truly appreciate your concern. Did Sebastian tell you that up until you came to see them last week Philip had hardly spoken a word?"

"Yes, he did mention that," said Psyche, coloring slightly.

"I don't know what you did, but it has made all the difference in the three of them."

Psyche blushed even darker. "I only did a few flips and somersaults."

"They must have been *very* impressive," said Amalie and chuckled.

"I suppose," said Psyche with a shrug. "I just remember how upsetting it was for me when two of my grandparents died. I couldn't imagine what it would be like to lose my parents, either of them, especially at the children's age. I thought they could use something to distract them for a little while."

"*Maman* wanted you to know how much she appreciated it."

"Honestly, it was nothing," said Psyche with some exasperation, but she smiled to soften it.

"So modest," chortled Amalie. "I have it on good authority that you've become the darling Almack's by dressing down a vicious gossip."

"I can only assume your brother told you that, and I don't know how good an authority you can consider him," said Psyche flatly.

"Oh, I think he's a very reliable source of information. Did you or did you not socially deflate Countess von Weilheim?"

"I guess I did, but—" began Psyche.

"And did you or did you not exit the building to applause that was initiated by Countess de Lieven?"

"Yes, but—"

"There you have it," giggled Amalie. "Very reliable."

"Oh, pooh," dismissed Psyche. She pursed her lips with embarrassment as her cheeks colored hotly again. She folded her arms across her chest and looked at her friend thoughtfully. "Why is your brother going to social functions anyhow? He may be a man, but he's supposed to be in mourning."

"*Maman* made him," said Amalie simply.

"What?" asked Psyche in dumb amazement.

"Papa's dying request was my brother should marry and produce an heir. *Maman* took it to mean right away, but Sebastian didn't think so. *Maman* has won that argument, which is why he's going to balls so soon. It has been very difficult for him, but he says he *is* looking for a wife."

"Really," said Psyche dully.

She felt as if she had been doused with cold water. She was confused and dismayed to learn Sheerness had not re-entered society so soon by his own choice. Yet it made sense in some ways. Psyche just didn't know what her part was in all of it, and that was what troubled her. For him to go from being barely civil to seductive had been a disconcerting change, and she was beginning to realize her feelings of misgiving about his reversal of demeanor were not misplaced. She felt queasy, and her ears had started to ring.

"Well, he says he is. *Maman* and I have already decided who he should marry, but of course, the decision will have to be completely up to Sebastian."

"Of course," said Psyche absently.

"Aren't you curious who we've chosen?" asked Amalie excitedly.

"I'm sorry, but not really, no," said Psyche in the same flat voice.

"Oh, all right," said Amalie with some disappointment.

Psyche saw Amalie's crestfallen expression and decided to set aside her own concerns about the matter for the moment. "I'm sorry, I can see you really want to tell me, and perhaps you should, if only for me to send my sympathies to the poor girl," she said with a chuckle.

"Shame on you!" said Amalie with a chuckle of her own. "I don't know why the two of you can't get on with each other."

"Because he's an opinionated lout, that's why," said Psyche with a pout. "I've tried to be nice to him, but he's mean to me all the time, no matter what I do. I've decided a little *quid pro quo* is in order."

"What is that?" asked Amalie confusedly.

"I'm being mean right back," said Psyche with a grin.

"Oh, no!" said Amalie in dismay.

"Actually, I think it's working. He's much nicer. I think he likes it."

"Oh, I don't believe that," said Amalie, shaking her head.

Psyche was about to tell Amalie she had also threatened to shoot him at one point for insulting her driver, but the object of their discussion chose that moment to make an appearance. Sheerness walked through the doors to the terrace and looked around uncertainly. He was dressed more formally than the previous week, wearing a coat and cravat. At that moment, Psyche decided he looked much more handsome with shorter hair. He walked over to his sister and Psyche, and she had to control a quivery sensation in her stomach when he looked at her.

"Lady Psyche," he said mildly with a slight smile, kissing her knuckles.

"Lord Sheerness," she returned in the same impersonal tone.

"Have either of you seen Sir James? George informed me that he had arrived and was waiting for me on the terrace."

"Oh, he left," said Amalie casually, "after Psyche said something to him, and he kissed her."

"*What?*" Sheerness roared.

Psyche blushed profusely and wished her friend hadn't mentioned Sir James kissing her on the cheeks or that he had left after she told him something…especially not in the phrasing Amalie had used. It made the encounter sound risqué. Amalie had to fight back a giggle. She was gratified to see her brother was jealous, and she considered her work to be done. Her mother would be pleased as well.

"Oh! I believe I hear *Maman* calling me," said Amalie calmly. "If you'll excuse me." She stood up and turned to look at Psyche. "Do not leave without saying goodbye if I don't come back by the time you're ready to go."

"A-all right," said Psyche in surprise, still eyeing Sheerness's angry glare with some alarm.

After Amalie departed into the house, Sheerness towered over Psyche on the bench irefully.

"What were you doing kissing a man in *my* house?" he yelled.

Psyche set her jaw, her worry being replaced by irritation. She thought Sheerness would be angry she had chased away Sir James, not that the baronet had kissed her. In her opinion, Sheerness had no right to be angry. She rose from the bench to stand close to him and had to look up to stare him in the eye.

"There are a couple things that I am about to say to you, Sheerness, and you had better listen well," said Psyche in a quiet voice that resonated with cold fury. "First, you will lower your voice in front of the children. Your niece and nephews have been through enough and do not need to be upset further, and my brothers will—believe me—beat you to a bloody pulp if they feel you're not showing me the proper respect. Second, I will not have you use that tone with me about anything I may or may not have done because I am not yours to command around as you like, and *I* will—believe me—beat you to a bloody pulp myself if you do not desist. Have I said that loud enough for you?"

Sheerness looked down at her in shock. The anger seemed to radiate off of her like heat, despite the coldness of her tone, and he didn't doubt her sincerity. He looked away from her into the garden to see that all six children had stopped what they were doing to look at the pair of them on the terrace. Their reactions were exactly what she said they would be. His niece and nephews looked at him in round-eyed worry. Her brothers looked at him sternly, their hands clenched into fists at their sides. He wasn't sure how much damage the three of them could actually cause, but he could see they were willing to do as much as they could if necessary. He looked back to Psyche's furious expression.

"Of course," he said quietly.

"Now, Sir James had to leave on an urgent private matter which I offered a few ideas on resolving. He was very happy about what I suggested to him, so he kissed my *cheeks.* He left you *these.* " She shoved the rolled up maps into his chest, and Sheerness had to grab them before they fell to the ground. "I'm going to play with the children now, and you're welcome to join us if you like."
Sheerness looked at her in dumbstruck amazement.

Psyche turned and casually walked down the steps into the garden. She took a few deep breaths to regain control of her temper and gave the children a happy smile as she approached them. They had all calmed by the time she reached them, when they saw that she was fine, and gathered around her excitedly.

"Psyche, Josie, Jerome, and Philip want to see you juggle," said Cosmo. "They don't believe you can do it."

"Really?" said Psyche with a chuckle. "Well, let's just show them, shall we?" She removed her gloves and shoved them into her reticule. She tugged at her lower lip thoughtfully as she looked around the garden, trying to find some likely objects, and snapped her fingers when she saw the apple tree. "Why don't you all go get some of the apples for me?"

The children happily scampered off to do as she asked, and Psyche giggled as she watched them attack the tree. She could see tiny pairs of arms outstretched in the air as they jumped up to grab limbs and pick apples, and she could see the tree swaying.

"Not too many!" she called.

They soon returned with far too many apples and placed them into a pile at her feet. Psyche set down her reticule and removed her spencer and hat to place with it on the ground. The children sat on the grass nearby, and Psyche picked up a few of the apples in her hands. She began to juggle just the three, skillfully tossing them behind her back and over her shoulder. The children clapped gleefully and laughed. She stopped briefly and picked up two more. The Yeardleys watched in amazement as she juggled them in a high circle in the air, and then as she dropped one and began to juggle two in each hand before seamlessly switching back to all four with both. When Psyche was done, she bowed and grinned as the children applauded.

"That's wonderful!" sighed Josie admiringly. "She's like an entire circus!"

"Will you play hide and seek with us?" asked Philip hopefully.

"I will," said Psyche with a smile and a nod. "What are your rules?"

"No hiding in the house," said Jerome.

"No peeking when you're counting if you're the seeker, and you have to count to twenty," supplied Josie. "Oh, and you have to yell ready or not, or it doesn't count."

"No sharing hiding places," said Philip.

"Those all sound perfectly acceptable. Is there a limit on how long it takes to be found before someone is declared the winner?" asked Psyche as she was busily signing all the rules to Damon.

"Only until you get tired of looking," chortled Josie.

"Fair enough," chuckled Psyche. "Who wants to seek first, or do you want me to?"

"I will seek first, if that is agreeable with everyone," said Sheerness as he joined them.

Psyche turned to look at him in surprise. "I have no objection," she said calmly.

He had put his maps down somewhere and discarded his coat and cravat. Psyche suspected he had only put them on to see Sir James, and now the man was no longer there, Sheerness saw no reason to keep them. That was perfectly sensible; Psyche thought cravats were ridiculous anyhow. He seemed much calmer. Psyche was willing to tolerate him for the children, but she had long since grown weary of his domineering behavior.

Sheerness had felt more than a little silly after she chastised him, and he knew she was right to do it. She owed him no explanation, and yet she gave him one after she had set him straight on the matter at hand. He shouldn't have yelled at her, especially not in front of the children, and he truthfully wouldn't have been surprised if she had slapped him. As modulated as her tone had been, there was no doubt that she was livid.

She was not his in any shape or fashion, and the intense jealousy he had felt on discovering Psyche had been kissed by another man had startled him. He could perfectly understand why Sir James might appeal to her. They shared the same interests, and the man showed respect for her thoughts and opinions, which was something Sheerness couldn't claim. Sir James was also kind, attentive, and the perfect gentleman, while Sheerness, by his own admission, was typically a contumacious boor in his dealings with Psyche. That she didn't trust him and found him somewhat detestable was not a revelation, but he was wishing she felt otherwise. She didn't find him physically repugnant, but she was inexperienced. Her opinion could change.

Sheerness put his hands over his eyes and began to count without warning. The children all giggled and scampered off to find a hiding place. Psyche looked around in panic, trying to decide where she should go. Her brothers had been able to familiarize themselves with the garden, but Psyche had not. She leapt over a low row of chrysanthemums and moved toward a tall clump of hydrangeas near the wall surrounding the yard. She managed to squeeze herself behind them and crouched low with a sigh of relief.

"Ready or not!" shouted Sheerness.

Psyche listened intently for the sound of approaching footsteps. Her hiding place concealed her well, but it also prevented her from seeing anything. She heard a shriek and a trill of laughter as Josie was found. That was soon followed by giggles as either Cosmo or Christopher was discovered. Then came Jerome, and Psyche thought from the sound of it that he had been hiding up one of the trees. So far, it sounded as if Sheerness was looking on the opposite side of the yard. The other twin soon laughed as he, too, was found. That left only Philip, Damon, and Psyche. After several more minutes of silence, Psyche heard Philip's disappointed utterances, and she thought from the distant sound that he might have hidden on the terrace again. She soon heard Damon's distinctive giggle as he was found, but she wasn't able to determine where he had hidden himself. Psyche calmly propped her back against the wall behind the bushes and began to wait. She didn't think it would be long before he found her; her hiding place was not very imaginative.

She idly watched as a row of ants marched in a column along one of the branches near her face. With some concern, she looked at the ground around her and sighed with relief that she had not managed to hide herself on an anthill. That would have been typical. She was still listening for Sheerness, but it was quiet. She wondered if he might be waiting for her to grow impatient and reveal herself. If that were the case, he would have a long wait. She yawned and looked at the watch on her chain. She and her brothers still had quite some time before they would need to leave, but she also didn't want them to overstay their welcome. She continued to watch the ants, and her eyelids began to droop. She hadn't thought she would be all that difficult to find.

Psyche was almost on the point of dozing off when she finally heard footsteps on the other side of the bushes, but they went past where she was hiding toward the back of the yard. She could hear the children chattering and playing near the pool and the distant sounds of splashing water. They didn't seem to be impatient for Sheerness to find her for them to play again. Psyche stifled another yawn and fought to keep her eyes open. She was comfortable; the area beneath the branches was fairly open, and she finally curled her legs beneath herself, lounging back against the wall. Her dress was going to get dirty, but she was tired of squatting. She was so close to falling asleep, Psyche didn't hear Sheerness approach again, and she jumped in surprise when he suddenly appeared on his hands and knees beside her under the bushes.

"Boo," he said softly.

"You finally found me," she said with a giggle.

Sheerness sat beside her and propped his back against the wall as well. He turned his head to look at her with a grin.

"If I hadn't smelled your perfume, I would have given up."

"Drat! Foiled by cucumbers and green tea," chortled Psyche.

"Is *that* what it is?" asked Sheerness in surprise.

"Let's see, what did Maiyin say it was?" mused Psyche to herself. "Cucumber, green tea, and sunflower…mostly."

"Who's Maiyin?"

"Pandora's maid. She created a wonderful perfume for Pandora last year, and I begged and pleaded until Pandora had Maiyin make one for me. Now Eurydice wants some…and Arachne." Psyche chuckled. "I think Pandora is in danger of losing her maid to perfumery."

"Cucumbers and green tea?" asked Sheerness in disbelief. He never would have guessed.

"Yes…and sunflower."

He startled Psyche when he leaned toward her to nuzzle her throat. He gave it a brief lick before he trailed nibbling kisses along her neck up to her jaw, and then he covered her lips with his. Despite herself, Psyche responded eagerly, raising a hand to the side of his neck. He moved one of his hands to rest on her ribcage, just below her breast, and his lips soon moved back down her throat, up to her ear, then back to her mouth again in feverish exploration.

Sheerness pulled her onto his lap, and Psyche went willingly, wrapping her arms around his neck. His hunger fueled her own, and she moaned lowly when his hand at her ribs moved up to cover her breast and squeeze it gently. She could feel his arousal pressed against her thigh, and she shifted slightly against it. To her delight, he groaned and pulled her tighter to him.

Eventually, Sheerness tore his lips away from Psyche's and rested his forehead against hers. He was almost panting as he tried to regain control of himself, and he caressed Psyche's cheek gently, his eyes closed. He wanted her so bad he almost couldn't help himself, but this was neither the time nor the place for it, no matter how willing Psyche might seem to be. The storage closet at Almack's hadn't been appropriate, either, and he would have taken her then without hesitation if she hadn't stopped him.

"We cannot keep doing this," he said quietly after a time.

"No," agreed Psyche.

She softly traced her fingers along his jaw to his chin and down his throat to rest her palm against his chest, where she could feel his heart beating rapidly. He didn't stop because he *wanted* to, but the things that caused her apprehension did not affect him. He hadn't been wrong to think she would have let him continue. Every time he touched her, it became more difficult to resist, and she was surprisingly disappointed when he stopped. Keeping in mind their behavior toward each other the previous Season and his purpose behind returning to society so soon after the death of his father, Psyche couldn't be sure of his intentions, and it would be dangerous to her if she let herself become too entangled. Yet she couldn't seem to stop herself.

Sheerness eventually opened his eyes to look at her, and his expression was unreadable. He kissed her softly, briefly, and then he helped her get off his lap. He crawled out from under the hydrangeas, and then he reached down his hand to help Psyche stand up after she had done the same. He gave her hand a brief squeeze before he released it, and Psyche felt an unexpected lump form in her throat. She looked around the yard and noticed the children weren't there. She couldn't hear them either.

"Where are the children?" she asked with concern.

"I believe Nanny MacBean took them inside for lemonade and biscuits," said Sheerness calmly as they began to walk toward the steps to the terrace.

They were almost there when Psyche remembered she had left her things laying in the yard. She turned and went to retrieve them, and she noted the pile of apples was nowhere to be found. She sincerely hoped the children hadn't eaten them; they were very green. Sheerness stood waiting for her where she had left him, and they continued to walk together once she returned.

"I understand the maps Sir James brought are for your trip to Greece and Egypt with Myron," said Psyche casually.

"Yes, they are," he confirmed, but Psyche detected a cautious note in his reply.

"What are they? That is, if you don't mind my asking."

Sheerness shrugged negligibly. "They're just survey maps of different places showing possible locations for tombs or other sites of interest."

They began to walk up the stairs, and Psyche chewed on the side of her thumb thoughtfully as she tried to choose her next words.

"Myron said he had talked to you about the possibility of my coming along," she said in as offhanded a manner as she could muster.

Sheerness stopped and turned to look at her as they reached the top of the stairs. His expression was neutral, but Psyche could see his mind hadn't changed.

"Yes, he did, and I told him that it was an *im*possibility."

"Can you tell me why?" she asked calmly.

"For several reasons," said Sheerness flatly, and she watched as he clenched his jaw stubbornly. Psyche raised an inquisitive eyebrow. Sheerness sighed exasperatedly and shook his head. "The first is that we constantly argue with each other."

"But we are getting on much better this year. We've hardly bickered at all," said Psyche pleasantly.

It was the earl's turn to raise an eyebrow...incredulously. "Second, you don't know enough. All you have is whimsy and no scholarly interest."

Psyche scoffed unbecomingly, but she managed to keep her modulated tone. "That's a piss-poor excuse, and you know it. I can read and translate anything you can and probably more. I've read anything and everything I can get my hands on, and I never miss a lecture given by anyone if I can help it when I am in Town. And, since I am a female, Oxford and Cambridge are barred to me at the moment, so my *whimsy*—as you like to call it—*is* my scholarship." She folded her arms across her chest and grinned at him.

"Third, you are a woman, and as I have said before, you are unable to take care of yourself."

"Being a woman doesn't make me any less qualified for this trip than Myron. You should be perfectly aware by now that I can take care of myself."

Sheerness clenched his jaw on an angry retort. She was still calm and pleasant, but he had grown only more irritated because he knew she was not being conceited in anything she said. Those used to be his main reasons for not wanting her to go, but he now had one in particular that overrode the rest by a large margin. It had slowly started to grow the previous Season, and it had fallen on him full force this one, especially since his father had died.

"Anything else?" queried Psyche politely.

"You would be a lone female on a ship full of men for a voyage that would last several months."

Psyche laughed amusedly. "I honestly don't think you would hire a crew that depraved, and a tar is no worse than a landlubber when it comes to manners around women, no matter how long he's been at sea. And, as I said, I *can* take care of myself."

"Yes, but I'm thinking of one in particular," muttered Sheerness to himself.

"I beg your pardon?" asked Psyche confusedly.

"No, I'm sorry, but it's my ship, my trip, and the answer is no," he said finally.

"No to what?" quizzed Amalie brightly as she walked onto the terrace.

Psyche looked at her friend and smiled, glad to see she had returned.

"I was just trying to convince your brother that he should let me go with him and Myron to Greece and Egypt…whenever it is they are going, but he is being intransigent," said Psyche mildly.

"That would be a marvelous idea!" sighed Amalie. "You've always wanted to go, haven't you?"

"Now, don't you start," said Sheerness exasperatedly.

"Yes, I have," said Psyche, "but the only way my parents will let me go is if I have a chaperone, and since Myron is going, they are amenable, but Lord Sheerness said no."

Amalie turned to look at her brother. "Sebastian, you should let her go with you. She is so clever when it comes to things like that."

"No." He folded his arms across his chest and scowled at his sister.

"Such a face," teased Amalie with a grin, and she reached over to playfully chuck him under the chin. It only made his expression more dour. She looked at Psyche. "I looked in on the children at their tea party a moment ago. Nanny MacBean has them all well in hand, but Josie, Jerome, and Philip were put out to learn your brothers will be going to the Derby tomorrow."

"Oh, yes, the entire family is going, and bloodshed would ensue if anyone tried to stop them…especially Persephone," confirmed Psyche with a chuckle. "We all love to watch the horses run, and the boys like it because it is one of the few social functions they can attend with Mamà and Papà."

"Myron has invited Sebastian to attend," supplied Amalie.

Psyche looked at Sheerness in surprise, and he glared darkly at his sister. Amalie was the picture of innocence. Neither Myron nor the earl had mentioned it, although Psyche supposed it really was an irrelevant bit of information. Then a thought occurred to her.

"I have an idea," said Psyche, and she tried to maintain her calmness.

"Only one?" shot the earl sarcastically.

Amalie reached over and hit him in the arm. "Sebastian! Manners!"

Psyche had ignored him, as she had learned to do last Season. "Since it appears your objections for me going with you and Myron are being maintained solely on principle now, why don't we settle it with a wager?"

"I wouldn't say it was principle only," defended Sheerness.

"It must be," said Psyche practically. "You gave me your reasons, I proved you wrong, so the only thing left is you simply don't *want* me to go."

"No, I don't."

"But I would be on my best behavior," averred Psyche. "I would do my utmost to not be a burden and try to be the very model of decorum."

Sheerness laughed. "Oh, *that's* likely." Amalie hit him again and glared at him. The earl rubbed a hand over his chin and groaned aggravatedly. "Fine, let's hear it."

"If I pick the winning horse in the Derby tomorrow, you'll let me go with you and Myron."

"And if you don't?" asked Sheerness mildly.

"Then I'll cease to utter another word on it, and I'll even stand on the dock to wave you off on a pleasant journey with a smile on my face."

Sheerness looked askance at her. It was tempting. To have her leave off about it would be a relief, but to have her wave them off with a smile would be an utter treat. He also had to consider what would happen if she won. Could he tolerate being in close proximity to her for the number of months this journey was expected to last? They wouldn't be sharing a cabin, and not all of the time would be on board. Aside from that, Myron would mediate, even if reluctantly, between the two of them if necessary, and Sheerness would just have to keep any other urges he might have under control. What were the chances she could pick the winning horse? It would depend on the field; the fewer the horses running, the more likely her chances. In the end, he decided it just didn't seem likely she could do it, and it was worth the risk.

"All right," said Sheerness with a self-satisfied grin. "I accept your wager. If you pick the winning horse in the Derby tomorrow, I'll let you go with your brother and me to Greece and Egypt without another objection. If you don't, then I'll not hear another word from you about it, and you will stand on the dock to wave us off with a smile."

"Exactly," said Psyche, and she grinned as well. "Amalie is our witness, and you will shake on it," said Psyche, holding out her hand.

She wasn't about to have him try crawfishing out of it. She was so close to realizing her dream she could almost touch it, and she wasn't about to have him back out of it by saying the wager never happened. The only thing that remained would be for luck to stay on her side for the tenth straight year and allow her to pick the winning horse.

Sheerness calmly took her hand and shook it firmly. He was so looking forward to watching her wave goodbye from the dock.

Chapter Six

Despite everyone needing to be ready to leave the house early to reach Epsom, the family had a late start, as usual, thanks to Psyche. She honestly didn't know what had caused her to be tardy. She had risen before anyone else in the family. She had also not gone riding in the Park. She had eaten breakfast at the same time as everyone else, and she had not chosen a complicated outfit or hairstyle. It left her in complete puzzlement.

Even though they started late, the two coaches required to carry the family were able to make decent time, and they would be to Epsom well before the race. The duke and duchess rode with the three younger boys and Arachne in one carriage while Psyche, Eurydice, and Persephone rode with Myron, Dorian, and Selena in the other. This would be the first year they had gone without Gregory, and it was strange to them that he was absent. They were hoping if he couldn't make it for the Derby, maybe he would come home at some point before the end of the Season.

The two coaches carrying the family was followed by a third carrying a few of their servants and food and drink for the family and their friends to enjoy. Most of the celebrating (or commiserating, as the case might be) would be done at a ball hosted by the Earl of Stranraer later back in town. The Aberdares were one of the few families that had their own pavilion. Psyche's father would love a permanent stand, but the Downs, for the most part, was empty grassland. The Rubbing House sold refreshments, but most people attending brought their own anyhow. Psyche's family always did. Most attendees only had small tents at the sidelines, if that, but the Aberdares' pavilion, while temporary, had steps that led up to its roof for the family and their guests to have a better view of the running. Their pavilion was usually filled to capacity, even with just their closest friends and their families.

The duke had designed the pavilion. It was made of several pre-constructed wooden panels that fastened together, over which the canvas was placed around the bottom level for privacy and protection from the elements. Stairs led up to the plank roof, also covered with canvas to waterproof the bottom. The pavilion could quickly be set up and taken down by a crew of only four men. Only the steward's box and the prince's pavilion provided spectators with a better view, and entrance to either of those was exclusive. Access to the Aberdares' pavilion was by invitation only, too, but it didn't rely on one's popularity in society, only one's familiarity with the family.

Psyche had a seat beside one of the windows of the coach, which made her happy because she tended to get motion sickness if she couldn't see where she was going…at least on dry land. She had never been seasick a day in her life. She looked out at the sky and smiled approvingly at its cloudless perfection as they traveled further into the countryside. It was harder to pick a winner in the rain because even if a horse wasn't a mudder, although it improved his chances, he could still win. Aside from improving her odds of selecting the right horse, Psyche just much preferred watching the races in the sunshine.

Myron looked at Psyche's nervous excitement and thought she seemed more anticipatory than usual. It could only mean she had settled on something particularly tempting as the stakes of the wager she had placed with one or the other of her sisters. Although, Myron couldn't determine which of them would have been foolish enough to bet against her again. Persephone would surreptitiously give him her wager to place with the bookmakers, and he would just as secretively give her back her winnings later. She had only made the mistake of wagering with Psyche once; she discovered it was much more profitable to use her sister's choice and put her money on the book, as their father and brothers did. Myron wasn't sure what Psyche did to make her decision, but her accuracy was phenomenal.

"So, Psyche, what bauble or chore have you settled on this year?" he asked with a smile.

Psyche chuckled. "I've gone outside the family for higher stakes this year."

Myron's eyes widened in surprise. "Indeed? How much and with whom?"

Psyche laughed again. "Sham, you know I never gamble with my money, no matter how much of a sure thing it is."

"Too right," snorted Persephone, "which is why I never play cards with you anymore. You're much better at it than I, and I would be much poorer…if it weren't for the fact you won't bet more than a penny a round."

"Then I am saving you from going broke."

"Where's the fun in that?" said Persephone with a wink and a grin.

"Tell us what it is, then," said Dorian.

"I've made a wager with Lord Sheerness."

"What kind of wager?" asked Myron nervously. He was already thinking he knew, but he could be wrong.

"If I pick the winner, I get to go to Greece and Egypt with you."

"What?" asked Myron in disbelief.

"If I don't, then I'll wave you off with a smile," continued Psyche calmly.

"He agreed to that?" asked Eurydice in amazement.

"He agreed to it and shook on it in front of a witness," chortled Psyche.

"Hmm," said Myron suspiciously. "Did you happen to mention your luck at picking the winner?"

"Of course not," said Psyche flatly. "He never would have taken the bet if he had known."

"Don't you think that was a little unfair?" asked Selena.

"No more unfair than him not wanting to let me go in the first instance, despite the fact I probably know more than he does."

"But Psyche, why must you insist the man take you with him if he doesn't *like* you?" asked Myron. "How would you like it if you had to be around Countess von Weilheim for months on end without chance of escape?"

"I wouldn't," said Psyche dully, and she began to have misgivings about what she had done.

Until that moment, it hadn't occurred to her that she might be cheating. That was something she disliked and would never intentionally do. She also hadn't thought about how miserable tolerating her might make Sheerness. Last Season, she wouldn't have cared and would have gleefully done anything she could to cause it. Now, it gave her hesitation. Her feelings for him were murky. She couldn't say she any longer found him contemptible, but she also couldn't say she had taken a liking to him, either. She found him physically irresistible, but anything else she felt for him was in flux.

"I will tell him the bet is off," she said finally.

"You're still going to pick the winner, aren't you?" asked Persephone in alarm.

"I will still *try* to pick the winner," said Psyche wryly with a half-smile.

"She'll pick the winner," said Eurydice matter-of-factly with a smirk. "Nine years of experience cannot be wrong."

"Too right," chuckled Myron. He looked at Psyche's much more subdued expression. "You *are* doing the right thing, Psy," he said consolingly.

"I know," she said softly.

Psyche was sad because the wager would have been the surest way for her to go to Greece and Egypt. Now, it was unlikely. Without the wager to force Sheerness to do it, he wouldn't let her go. There would be other opportunities eventually, with her father or brothers, but Psyche didn't know when. She was giving up the chance of a lifetime because she was too honest to do something that *might* be considered cheating.

The family reached the race course after following a long line of other people arriving. There were several more behind them. Psyche linked her arm through Myron's after they stepped down from the coach. Persephone thought she was being sly when she came up on Myron's other side to give him her wager money. If Psyche had not been directly beside him, she wouldn't have noticed her sister giving him the folded up bank notes when she held his hand and quickly pecked him on the cheek before catching up with their parents. Myron looked at Psyche in pretended innocence.

"You didn't fool me, but I don't care, either," said Psyche with a chuckle.

"I suppose you want to get a program and see the horses," he said mildly.

"I do," said Psyche with a nod. "We could just go to the pavilion, but there will be several unhappy people if we do."

It was easy enough for them to acquire a program, and Psyche began to scan over it as they walked toward the paddock. There were several horses she marked off immediately. She ignored the odds because they were irrelevant to her. By the time they were to the saddling area, after stopping to speak with several people along the way, there were only four out of the fourteen horses running that Psyche wanted to see.

"Have you decided yet?" asked Myron.

"Almost. There are just not many running that I like this year."

"Hmm," said Myron with a smile. "Just as long as there is at least *one* you like better than the others."

Myron and Psyche were almost to the entrance to the paddock when they were met by Lord Sheerness.

"Oh, good, Barneville. I was hoping we'd run into you before the race. My dad's pavilion is hard to miss, but the crowd is becoming large."

"Lord Sheerness," said Psyche calmly.

"Lady Psyche."

"Lord Sheerness, I'd like to call off our wager, if you don't mind."

Sheerness looked at her with an arched eyebrow. That she would want to call off the wager was a surprise...and also just the least bit dubious. After the way she had been so determined to make it a legitimate, unbreakable agreement the day before, he wondered what had caused her sudden reversal of intent. It made him think she was beginning to have misgivings about what she would have to do if she lost. Perhaps she thought she would still be able to change his mind, but not if she lost the wager. He was sure she was going to lose. It was a large field this year, and she didn't like her odds. Sheerness was not inclined to let her out of it. Their bet would decide the issue once and for all, and Sheerness, for one, would dearly appreciate that.

"Why do you want to call it off?" he asked suspiciously.

"Because I want to," said Psyche calmly. She didn't want to tell him the reason because he would think she was cheating. He had thought she was doing so by talking to her horse in their own race; to find out about her ability to consistently pick the winner of the Derby would completely infuriate him, she was sure.

"No, I don't think so," said Sheerness firmly.

Psyche and Myron both looked at him in surprise. Psyche thought he would jump at the chance to escape. Myron also thought Sheerness would welcome the opportunity to still freely be able to tell Psyche that she couldn't go. Myron would be overjoyed for Psyche to go with them, if it weren't for his sister and friend constantly arguing with one another. They did seem to be more civil these days, but that wouldn't last for months in each other's close company.

"But, Lord Sheerness, I really—" began Psyche.

"No, the wager will stand. If you weren't prepared to honor it, you shouldn't have made it," said Sheerness coldly.

"Barneville, I think you should—" began Myron.

"No," cut in Sheerness angrily. "She made her bed; now she'll lie in it."

Psyche blinked. She didn't know why he was so determined to let the bet stand, but she wasn't going to question it. She had given him the opportunity to call it off, but she felt no guilt about going through with it now. She hoped she had made the bed comfortable enough for *him* because she had no intention of sleeping in it.

"Very well, if you insist," said Psyche evenly, and it was difficult for her not to grin victoriously.

Myron was shaking his head very firmly in the negative and mouthing the word *no,* but Sheerness ignored him.

"I *do* insist," said the earl tightly. "Just you remember the stakes."

Psyche did smile then. "Oh, I do, and so will *you*." She turned to look at Myron and winked at him. "I want to look at the horses before it's too late."

"You go on then," said Myron absently. "I want to talk to Barneville."

Psyche pecked him on the cheek. "I'll be back. Ta, Sham." She giggled as she walked away, opening her parasol to shield her eyes from the sun.

Myron watched her search for the horses she liked, talking to the trainers and the jockeys. If they were reluctant at first, she would flirt and cajole until they were eating out of the palm of her hand. One of these days, he would learn her secret. Myron shook his head and folded his arms in front of him as he turned to look at Sheerness. His expression was one of amused sympathy.

"You ought not to have done that," said Myron evenly.

"I'm sorry, but it's her own fault. This will settle it once and for all."

"Oh, it will that," agreed Myron with a chuckle.

"After today, she will leave me in peace on the matter."

Myron laughed outright with hilarity. "Oh, I don't think so."

Sheerness scowled. "She had better. We made a wager on it."

"She tried to give you an out, man, and you have absolutely *no* idea how hard it was for her to do that."

"What do you mean?"

"I would have warned you if I had known beforehand, but you're stuck now," chuckled Myron.

"*What* do you mean?" repeated Sheerness exasperatedly.

"Only that you better have a cabin on your ship prepared for her. She likes a very thick, fluffy mattress and lots of blankets because she gets cold easily."

"Why are you so sure she's going to win?" asked Sheerness perplexedly.

"Because she's won the last nine years consecutively." He clapped Sheerness on the shoulder. "She's been picking the winner of the Derby since she was nine years old, and only a fool would bet against her."

"*What?*" gasped Sheerness in shock.

"Just you wait and see what happens when she announces her pick at the pavilion."

Sheerness went pale as he realized his friend was speaking in all seriousness. He glanced over to where Psyche was looking at one of the horses, petting his nose and talking to him as if he could understand exactly what she was saying. She then said something to the jockey, and both of them laughed. The horse nuzzled her neck, and Psyche patted him on the shoulder. She shook hands with the jockey and the trainer, and then she began to make her way back to where her brother and the earl stood talking. Her lighthearted expression faded when she saw him angrily glaring at her.

When she saw his face, Psyche knew Myron had enlightened Sheerness about her talent. She didn't feel any responsibility now. He had insisted. Even if he didn't know the reason why she wanted to call it off, she had given *him* the chance to do so, something she was sure he would have done if provided with an honorable way to do it.

"She could still lose," said Sheerness weakly.

"Sure, she could, but my money's on her pick," chuckled Myron. He turned to look at Psyche as she reached him and linked her arm through his. "So, which have you decided on?"

"I think Blücher wants to win today," said Psyche with a smile.

"*Blücher?*" hooted Sheerness. His worry began to ease.

"Yes," said Psyche decidedly as the three of them began to walk to the pavilion. "He is feeling very frisky."

Myron and Sheerness laughed, but for different reasons. Her brother was sure she had made her decision on more than how the horse was *feeling*; even if she did have a gift for animals, she wasn't foolish enough to base her choice on that alone. Sheerness laughed because he thought she *was* making her pick solely on that, and he was confident she had only managed to pick the winner so many times because of sheer, dumb luck.

When the three of them reached the Aberdares' pavilion, Sheerness was astonished when everyone went silent as Psyche entered the tent, looking at her expectantly, and he grew nervous again. This was the first time he had ever been to the pavilion, although he had heard about it. Perhaps if he'd been there before, he wouldn't have been stupid enough to take Psyche's bet. She smiled amusedly as everyone looked at her, and for once she didn't mind being the center of attention.

"Blücher is looking particularly fine today," she called clearly.

"Are you sure? He's only got five-two odds," said Lord Stranraer disappointedly.

"I guess you'll just have to bet more money then," chortled Psyche.

All the men laughed and excused themselves to find the bookmakers. She would have liked to give them one with longer odds, but the bay colt was going to win. Myron left to place his wager (and Persephone's), and the women and children were left alone. Psyche turned to see Sheerness was still there.

"Are you not going to place a wager?" she asked mildly.

"I've already made my bet," he replied neutrally, folding his arms in front of him and rocking on his heels.

"I won't hold it against you if you want to use my favorite. Everyone else does," she grinned.

"Blücher isn't going to win," said Sheerness determinedly.

Psyche giggled. "At least, you hope he won't."

"Too right," agreed Sheerness, and he grinned.

Psyche tilted her head sideways as she looked at his relaxed behavior. She was wondering if his *doppelgänger* had taken his place again. It was either that or he was extremely confident she would lose. She hoped he was wrong about that. She had almost lost her chance, only to surprisingly get it back. She felt fairly sure her chosen horse was going to win, but she could be wrong. Even after Myron had told him about her record, he let the wager stand, and Psyche had to wonder if he did fully realize that he was going to lose.

"You could still change your mind," said Psyche softly.

"Why are you so determined to end it?" asked Sheerness with a grin.

"I don't want you to accuse me of cheating when you lose."

"*If* I lose, I will bear it gracefully," said Sheerness, and he chuckled.

"Mm-hmm," said Psyche doubtfully. She started to say something else when someone behind her covered her eyes. She smiled. "Hallo, Pan."

Pandora took her hands away and moved into Psyche's view. "How did you know it was me?" she asked disappointedly.

"Because your belly was poking me in the back," giggled Psyche. She put her hands on her twin's stomach and rubbed it affectionately. "How did they like the ride out?"

"*He* liked it just fine," said Pandora airily. She put a hand to her lower back and grimaced. "But *I* would like it better if he would quit kicking me in the kidney." Psyche and Pandora laughed, and then Pandora looked at the earl. "Hallo, Lord Sheerness. I didn't expect to see you here."

"Yes, well, circumstances made it somewhat necessary for me to come today," said Sheerness, his lips twitching amusedly at their banter. He had to wonder why Psyche talked as if there were more than one baby and her sister insisted there was *only* one.

Pandora raised an eyebrow enquiringly as she linked her arm through Psyche's. She couldn't imagine what would make it *necessary* for a man in mourning to attend any social function, much less a horse race. Then she remembered the part of the conversation she had heard between Sheerness and her twin when she snuck up behind her. She looked at Psyche reprovingly.

"Psy, you didn't sucker him into a bet, did you?" Pandora demanded.

Psyche colored, and Lord Sheerness laughed at her guilty expression.

"No! I have tried repeatedly to get him to call it off, but he won't, so who am *I* to make him change his mind?" said Psyche hotly.

Pandora turned to look at Sheerness with concern. "Lord Sheerness, you should know, Psyche has picked the winner the last nine years' running."

"I know," said Sheerness calmly.

"Then *why* won't you call it off?" asked Pandora in shock.

"Because dumb luck can only last so long."

"Is *that* what you think it is?" hooted Psyche in an insulted tone. "If luck was all I had to go on, I wouldn't have been able to keep it up as long as I have, and do you really think *men* would be willing to put money down on it?"

Sheerness looked her up and down appraisingly, finding her particularly fetching in a pink- and white-striped walking dress with a matching darker pink spencer and bonnet. All she would have to do was flutter her lashes to have any man blindly do what she wanted, and he was sure she knew it.

"Yes," said Sheerness with a grin.

"Whatever it is you think you're going to win from Psyche, I hope you don't want it too bad because this is not the day you'll be getting it," said Pandora amusedly. She had not missed his appreciative perusal of her sister, and she had no doubt what it meant.

It had only taken Pandora twice to learn she did *not* want to bet against her twin on a horse race…unless it was one of their own. She had to wonder what he would have gotten if he had won (and his glance for her sister made Pandora twitch with curiosity). She didn't have to think twice about what Psyche would get. She was happy her twin was finally going to get her trip.

"Lord Sheerness, you should have made her pick win, place, and show. Then you might have had better odds."

"She can't do that, then?"

"Well, she's only tried four times," said Pandora thoughtfully, and she rubbed a spot behind her ear.

"So, she's not infallible after all?" asked Sheerness amusedly with a chuckle.

"No, no, she won every time; it's only that she hasn't done it as many times as *just* picking the winner, so there would have been a greater chance that she could lose."

"Excuse me, but *she* is standing right here," said Psyche flatly. "And *she* would appreciate it if the two of you would quit talking about her as if *she* were the Oracle of Delphi."

Sheerness and Pandora laughed amusedly at Psyche's put-out expression. Pandora linked her other arm through the earl's, and she directed them toward the table with refreshments. She wasn't sure about them, but she was starving. Her hunger was due to her pregnancy, but it had been a lengthy ride from London. Psyche laughed as her sister began to pick at the food on the trays.

"What?" asked Pandora innocently when she noticed her twin's amused expression.

"Perhaps you should get a plate."

Psyche looked at Jens, one of the footmen attending the table and nodded to him to get one. She handed the plate to Pandora and chuckled as her sister began to pile little sandwiches and biscuits and cake onto it. Psyche looked back at Jens, who was trying with difficulty to keep his face expressionless. He wasn't much older than the twins, and he and his two sisters had been with the family since he was about twelve. Signe and Merete were upstairs maids, and the three of them shared a cottage on the grounds at Wilderland.

"How are Signe and Merete?" asked Psyche in Norwegian, his native language. "I haven't seen them in a while."

"They're very happy now since the plumbing work is done on our cottage," replied Jens with a grin.

"Good! What about the stove?"

"Wonderful! You'll have to come for *sort gryte* and *potetboller* after the Season."

"Ooh, you can count on it," said Psyche with a chuckle. She had learned never to refuse his sisters' cooking, and chicken stew with potato dumplings was one of her favorite dishes.

She turned to watch Pandora amble away, blissfully lost in her plate as she went toward the stairs, her sister and the earl completely forgotten as she devoured her food. Psyche laughed and turned back to Jens.

"I'll have a glass of champagne, *vær så god*," she told him as she picked a strawberry from a nearby bowl. She then turned to look at Sheerness, who was looking at her in disbelief. She raised an eyebrow enquiringly. "Would you like something to eat or drink before we go up?" she asked him, fluidly switching back to English and ignoring the way his jaw was slack. *"Takk,"* she said to Jens as he handed her the champagne, continuing to look at Sheerness with a questioning glance.

"Is that champagne?" asked Sheerness dully.

"Yes," replied Psyche as she swallowed another strawberry and took a sip of champagne.

"That will be fine."

Psyche looked at Jens, and he nodded and poured another glass to give to Sheerness.

"Here you go," said Jens in perfect English.

Sheerness was so startled he almost dropped the glass. He walked with Psyche toward the stairs to the roof. He looked at her speculatively.

"That was...Norwegian?" he asked curiously.

"Yes," said Psyche calmly as they started up the stairs.

"Russian, Italian, German, French, Norwegian—are there any others?"

Psyche shrugged noncommittally. "Several. Why?"

"Spanish?"

Psyche blinked in surprise, but she decided to indulge him. "Yes."

"Prove it."

"¿Por qué se importa a usted?"

"Just curious."

"I can't tell you *all* of them," sighed Psyche as they reached the roof.

"Latin? Hebrew?"

"Yes."

"Arabic?"

Psyche laughed. "Tajik and his family would be very ashamed if I couldn't speak it."

"Tajik?"

"Our stable master…from Syria."

"Hindi?"

"Of course, along with several other languages from India."

"Greek?"

Psyche laughed. "Yes. Chrissoula says I can speak better than she does."

"Chrissoula?"

"My maid from Thessaloniki," said Psyche flatly. She unfurled her parasol and nearly hit him in the face with it. "Lord Sheerness, you are trying my patience. I told you I cannot tell you all of them. What languages do *you* know?"

"All of the ones I just named, except for Norwegian. I also know Romanche, Basque, Jèrriais, Breton, and a few others, like Amharic, Sanskrit, Avestan, Pahlavi, Syriac, Chaldean, Persian, and Ethiopic."

"Do you know modern or classic Greek?"

"Classic."

"I know both, *and* all of the ones you just named because of my *whimsy*, as you put it. Any others?"

"That's it."

Psyche laughed again. "If you were hoping to one-up me on the number of languages you know, I'm afraid it was a waste of time." Her forehead wrinkled as she thought for a few minutes. "I also know Polish, Hungarian, Albanian, Turkish, Croatian, Dutch, Portuguese, Georgian, Irish, Scottish, Manx, Cornish, and Welsh, of course."

Sheerness paled in disbelief, but Psyche wasn't done.

"Then there is Mandarin, Japanese, Korean, and Sioux."

"Sioux?"

"Yes, one of our servants, Wenona, is from America." Psyche's eyes rounded as she remembered more. "Oh, and Swahili, Yoruba, Igbo, Hausa, Akan, and Fulani."

"You're having me on. You can't possibly know all those languages."

"Those are the ones I can *remember* at the moment. I can't say for certain I've named them all, and why *can't* I know them all?"

"Because you just *can't*," said Sheerness frustratedly.

"Lord Sheerness, I am not going to argue about it," said Psyche mildly with a half-smile, and she took a sip from her champagne and gave him a wink.

Sheerness watched in open-mouthed incredulity as she went to her twin to whisper something in her ear. Both of them laughed, and he had to wonder if it was about him. He didn't know why he should think it would be, but it bothered him that he could not provoke Psyche to argue with him. She was in a particularly pleasant mood, and that he could not change it upset him. He couldn't say he wanted to make her mad, but to have *some* influence on her, to affect her in some fashion, would have pleased him.

Psyche looked over Pandora's shoulder at Sheerness frowning as he stood near the railing where she had left him. It had been difficult not to yell at him, but she had decided it was a waste of her time. She believed it was something he enjoyed, which she found peculiar, but she wasn't willing to indulge it. Every time they argued left her feeling drained, and she wasn't going feel that way on such a glorious day. He would have to wait for another time.

The men began to return from placing their wagers. When Myron ascended the stairs, Psyche and Pandora were astonished to see he was accompanied by Georgiana Jeffries-Marsh, the Marchioness of Morecambe. They weren't aware she was even in town, but their surprise was based more on her being there unaccompanied by her husband, the Earl of Hendon.

She looked much healthier than she had the previous Season. She had gained weight, and although still willowy, she no longer looked starved. Her golden blonde hair shined with good health, as did her soft beige skin, and her amber-green eyes were no longer sunken and shadowed by dark circles. She looked much happier and calmer than the last time the twins had seen her.

Psyche and Pandora knew Georgiana's husband abused her. Other people knew, too, but most didn't think anything of it; she was Hendon's wife, after all, and it was his right to do so. Hendon had left for the continent at the close of last Season and left his wife behind. His absence didn't leave Georgiana brokenhearted, and she dreaded his return, as he would eventually. Unfortunately, there was nothing that could be done to keep her away from him, unless he never returned...or died. He had been gone for nearly a year, but it was expected that he *would* be back.

The one thing about Georgiana that was not common knowledge (and would be the death of her if her husband were to ever discover it) was that she was having an affair with Myron. Pandora and Islington knew, but no one else did. Pandora had not even told Psyche. Although she was sure her twin would keep silent, Pandora felt the fewer people who knew, the safer Georgiana and Myron would be. Hendon was a dangerous criminal, who would try to kill them both if he found out. Aside from that, Pandora and Islington kept hoping they would end it. The two did not seem so inclined.

Pandora had exchanged several letters with the marchioness over the past months, but in the last one she had received, Georgiana didn't say anything about coming to town. Myron had neglected to mention it, and if anyone had been aware she was coming, Myron was. Whether or not he would have told Pandora, even if he *did* know, was open to speculation. He knew what a dangerous game he was playing by falling in love with another man's wife, and Pandora understood he was doing what he could to protect both himself and Georgiana until he could find a way to free her from Hendon. When Georgiana saw the sisters, she shyly walked over to them with Myron.

"Look who was wandering aimlessly near the Rubbing House."

Pandora grinned hugely and gave Georgiana a quick hug. Psyche rubbed her shoulder and gave it a welcoming squeeze.

"Georgiana! How could you come to town and not tell us?" said Psyche with a pretended pout.

"I received a letter from Hendon only two weeks ago telling me he was *embarrassed* I was still in Northumberland and that I had better get to London for the Season. Naturally, I did as I was told," she said with a giggle. "I might have told you I was coming, but he had sent the letter at least a month before I received it. I set off as quickly as I could without time for messages."

"Did he mention when he would be back?" asked Pandora worriedly.

Georgiana's brightness faded a little at the question. "No, but I don't expect it will be long now."

"Oh, well, we shall enjoy ourselves silly 'til he does," said Psyche with a grin. "Where are you staying?"

"Our house in Soho," said Georgiana with a moue of distaste. "I would love to air out the place on Park Lane, but Hendon says he'll not tolerate being that near the *ton.*" She shrugged. "Any place will do as long as *he's* not there."

"How is Lorelei?" asked Pandora.

"Growing like a weed," giggled Georgiana. "Actually, more like a wild rose. She gets prettier every day. She didn't want me to come to town without her, but I convinced her she would be happier in the country with Cosgrove."

Lorelei was the marchioness's younger sister, who was nine. Their mother had died when both girls were young, and their father, the late Marquis of Morecambe, had died the same year Georgiana married Hendon, only a month after, in fact. Georgiana and Hendon had become Lorelei's guardians; the girls' grandmother, their only surviving relative, was too infirm to take the young girl. So far, Georgiana had managed to protect her sister from the earl, but it came at great cost to herself. The twins had never met Lorelei, but Georgiana mentioned her often. Psyche and Pandora hoped one day to introduce Lorelei to their younger brothers. It was their understanding she didn't have any friends…just her sister and her nanny, Cosgrove.

"Can you attend the ball at the Stranraers' later?" asked Pandora hopefully.

"I don't see why not," said Georgiana happily.

The horn sounded to indicate the race was about to start. The men had returned from placing their wagers, and everyone moved to the rail to view the race. The Savage girls all lined up near each other, and Psyche found herself between Persephone and Pandora. Islington stood behind his wife to protect her from any jostling against the rail once the race started. Psyche felt a casual hand at the small of her back and looked up in surprise to see Sheerness providing much the same service for her. Neither of the tall men would have trouble seeing the race over the heads of the women in front of them.

Psyche reached into her drawstring bag and retrieved a set of spectacles with lenses tinted a dark shade of blue. She was able to see much better once she didn't have to squint against the glare of the sun. She would have used her parasol, but then Lord Sheerness and several other people behind her wouldn't be able to see. Aside from that, the glasses also corrected her nearsightedness, which would make it easier for her to watch the race.

Persephone gripped the rail beside Psyche as the horses lined up. This was one of the rare occasions when the seventeen-year-old wore a dress. When she was at home, she was usually in breeches unless they were due to have company. When her debut came next year, it would be torture for Persephone.

"So, you think it's going to be Blücher, eh?" she asked Psyche with a grin.

"I'm betting on it," said Psyche with a grin of her own. She looked up at Sheerness, and he blinked in surprise at her glasses.

"*What* are you wearing?" he asked with curious amusement.

"Spectacles," said Psyche flatly. "What does it look like?"

She turned to look back at the field and picked out her horse. She went by the jockey's silks rather than the color of her animal; there were a lot of bays running this year, and one bay Thoroughbred looked about the same as the next. She put her hands on the rail in front of her and tensed in anticipation. The starting gun fired, and the net was dropped for the horses to be off.

Psyche's heart began to race excitedly as the animals sped across the turf. Blücher was off to a slow start, but there was still a lot of distance to cover. She leaned forward slightly as the horses headed into the first turn, and she felt Sheerness put his hands to either side of her waist to keep her from falling over. Blücher had moved to the middle of the pack and was steadily starting toward the front. There was a collective gasp of alarm from spectators when one of the horses near the front stumbled, and the jockey was thrown to the ground. He rose from the turf under his own power, barely avoiding being trampled by the other oncoming riders, and grabbed the reins of his mount to limp off the track.

"Who put that monkey on horseback without tying his legs?" shouted Persephone.

There were several people nearby who laughed at her comment, and Psyche grinned amusedly. She gripped the railing tighter and watched as Blücher moved into fourth position, but he was still several lengths behind the horse in the lead as they started into the back stretch. If he didn't pick up the pace, he was never going to catch up in time. Psyche hopped up and down excitedly and slapped her hand against the rail.

"Come on, Blücher!" she shouted. "Come on, you bloody nag! Run like you still have a pair!"

Psyche could feel the breath catching in her throat as the colt moved into second position. He still had a length to gain on the leader as they rounded the far turn, but Psyche was sure it would happen...it had to. Second place wasn't going to be good enough—for her or anyone else. Psyche grabbed Pandora and Persephone's hands, and the three of them began to bounce up and down excitedly as Blücher seemed to grow wings taking the last turn toward the home stretch. He soon came up neck-and-neck with the colt in the lead, and Psyche held her breath anxiously. If he could just stretch out a *little* farther.

Time seemed to drag as he nosed ahead, and then he moved forward by half his body length. Within yards of the finish line he clearly came out in front, and Psyche screamed ecstatically as he crossed the finish line the undisputed winner. She hugged Pandora happily, then Persephone, and everyone in the pavilion roared with excitement at their victory. She was so happy she was speechless, and she couldn't believe she could feel that much joy over a horse winning a race. She put a hand to her chest and felt tears sting her eyes, and then she forgot where she was and looked down.

It really wasn't *that* high, and there was railing, but she felt herself begin to weave dizzily, and she couldn't make herself look away. Her breath caught in her throat again, and her vision went hazy as she grew faint. Her knees became wobbly, and she was on the verge of collapsing when Lord Sheerness put his arm around her waist and grabbed one of her hands to hold her up. She looked up at him in surprise, and the surge of panic she had felt began to dissipate as her attention focused on his face rather than the ten-foot drop to the ground.

"Honestly, Lady Psyche, I would not have imagined you as the sort to go buffle-headed from excitement," he said dryly.

"But…," began Psyche weakly. She couldn't tell him she was afraid of heights. "Perhaps it was the champagne," she said dully.

Sheerness grinned amusedly. "Of course," he said obligingly, his lips twitching.

He *was* surprised to see her become faint, but perhaps she was overly wrought from winning their wager. He didn't believe it was caused by the champagne for a moment. She only had one glass, and it wasn't even empty. He was sure it would take more than that to make her tipsy, but he wasn't sure how much more. She had seemed perfectly fine until the horse won, so that was the only logical conclusion he could reach.

Sheerness wasn't happy he had lost their wager. He didn't want her to go with him, and now he couldn't tell her no. He never should have agreed to it, and he should have taken Psyche's offer to end it. He could have said no from the beginning, and she had given him two further chances that day, but still he had let it happen. He had been so sure she would lose, even after he discovered she had not for the last nine years. At least, that's what he tried to tell himself. The question he asked himself was: if he hadn't wanted her to go, why did he follow through on something that made it a certainty she would?

"Congratulations, Lady Psyche, on a decade of luck," he said mildly as he released her.

"Thank you, Lord Sheerness," said Psyche quietly.

She had won their wager, and now she would finally be going to Greece and Egypt, something that should have made her euphoric with happiness. Yet, for some reason, it felt like a hollow victory. It didn't make her as glad as it should have because she was forcing Lord Sheerness to take her with him. She would much rather he had *asked* her to go with him instead of inviting herself. Still, after all the time she had wanted to make the trip, she was not going to change her mind. She would make the best of it and take what she was given.

Chapter Seven

Psyche and her family made it back to town with plenty of time to prepare for the ball at the Stranraers'. Their house wasn't very far away, easily within walking distance just across Berkeley Square, and Psyche, Eurydice, and Arachne all decided to do just that. Dorian, Selena and Myron rode in the coach with the duke and duchess. Psyche didn't think it was worth the trouble to Jim or one of the other coachmen to take them that short distance, and their parents allowed it because the three sisters would be together. Luckily, it wasn't raining, and the temperature was tolerable.

Chrissoula helped Psyche select her dress for the evening, and Psyche wasn't sure she liked it. Her maid assured her that she looked wonderful, but Psyche felt more conspicuous than was her wont. She looked like Pandora—at least, when her twin wasn't pregnant—which was why Psyche knew she stood out more than usual. She didn't know what had prompted her to have Janet make the gown. She had probably been particularly lonesome for her twin the day she went to the shop; that was the only way Psyche could account for it.

The dress was mostly composed of deep reddish-purple velvet. The bodice was cut very low, and Psyche kept expecting her assets to pop out any minute. Her maid had to make alterations to a chemise to keep it from being exposed. Chrissoula laughed as Psyche pulled the top edge higher and shook her head as she readjusted the bottom to its proper location. Psyche was tempted to be old-fashioned and wear a fichu. The sleeves were long and split to show an undersleeve of thin white mull, and the edges of the splits were intricately embroidered and gathered with black and gold. There was an opening at the front of the skirt, trimmed in the same embroidery and exposing more of the white mull. The bottom edge of the bodice was trimmed with even more embroidery, almost like a sash. It *was* a beautiful gown, but Psyche wasn't sure it suited her. She had considered changing, but her maid refused to help her. Psyche would just have to be careful how she moved.

Chrissoula had braided the length of her hair and twisted it onto the top of her head, adorned by golden combs studded with amethysts. She had also selected Psyche's amethyst earrings and pendant on a simple gold chain for her jewelry. She had a white cashmere shawl trimmed with black and gold tassels and crocheted wrist-length gloves. As Psyche examined herself in the mirror, she did think she looked beautiful, but she didn't look like herself, and that made her self-conscious.

Chrissoula was overjoyed to learn Psyche would be going to Greece. She was going to write a letter to Nikos and Ioanna to let them know Psyche would be going to the country. Psyche tried to impress on her maid that she had no knowledge of whether or not she would go anywhere near Thessaloniki, but Chrissoula said she was still going to let her brother know. She also told Psyche that she should make a point of finding Nikos; he would be of great benefit in their enterprise to locate antiquities. Psyche didn't doubt that.

Psyche was retrieved from her room by Arachne, as was usually the case. She wasn't *always* far behind in being ready to go when she was collected by her sister, but Arachne or Eurydice came looking for her because they were tired of waiting. She grabbed her bag with her watch and a handkerchief and left her room with her sister. Eurydice was waiting at the bottom of the stairs, pacing back and forth to pass the time. Their parents, brothers, and sister-in-law had left thirty minutes before, so the redhead was becoming bored.

The three of them left the house and walked down Bruton Street to Berkeley Square. They were chatting happily with each other, Arachne and Eurydice asking Psyche questions about her impending trip. Psyche wasn't able to tell them much. She didn't know when she would be leaving or what her itinerary would be. She had no affirmation from Sheerness that he would stand by their agreement, but it would be dishonorable for him not to. She didn't know how big the ship was, or what it was called, or even where it was berthed. She assumed it was on the Thames, but it could just as easily be near the earl's home in Sheerness. She would have to get the particulars that night at the ball. By the time they reached the other side of the square, they had moved on to other subjects. Psyche didn't like seeming vague, but she couldn't tell them what she didn't know.

Despite their tardiness, there were still other guests arriving. Lady Stranraer was at the door to greet them, and she gave Psyche a particularly fond squeeze for her success at the Derby. Part of the earl's winnings had been his wife's. Blücher's win had given the countess a nice boost to her pin money. They gave their wraps to the nearby footman after the countess gave them their dance cards; then they went down the hall to the ball room.

Pandora and Islington saw them and went to speak with them. Islington signed his name to a dance on each of their cards, and Psyche saw that he had selected a quadrille. Before anyone else had a chance to put their name on for any of the others, Psyche went down the card and marked through a few to give herself the opportunity for adequate rest. She had learned her lesson last Season. She left all of the waltzes, though. Pandora's card had *most* of the dances marked through, and she would only dance the waltzes with her husband. They didn't care if it was rude to dance more than three dances with the same partner; she was pregnant, she loved her husband, and a pox on 'em if society disliked it. Aside from that, this would be Pandora's last social function until after she had her baby (or babies, as Psyche insisted), so she intended to enjoy herself. Since the ball was given by friends rather than the *ton*, it was unlikely anyone would care if she only wanted to dance with her husband.

Dorian signed his name on Psyche's card for an Allemande, and her father chose a Scotch reel. Lord Stranraer signed on for a rigadoon and told Psyche with a twinkle in his eye that she was not to leave before the Sir Roger de Coverly, the closing dance. Psyche grimaced, but she promised she would stay. She couldn't imagine why it would be important. Her card quickly filled, and she was glad she had thought to mark through some of the dances.

Myron walked over to her accompanied by Georgiana, and Psyche looked at the pair of them curiously. She hadn't thought anything of Myron escorting Georgiana to the pavilion at the Derby, but to see him with her at the ball as well was suspect. Psyche couldn't believe the marchioness would be involved with her brother, considering the foulness of Georgiana's husband, and Psyche also couldn't believe her brother would become enamored of a married woman, but stranger things had happened...like her own feelings for Sheerness. She would ask Pandora what she thought; she knew Georgiana better.

"Hallo, Sham, Georgiana," said Psyche with a smile. "I do believe the two of you are becoming a matched set like Lord Georgie and Sir James."

Georgiana colored at the comment, and Psyche saw in that reaction that she wouldn't need to ask Pandora. It would be for the best if she didn't mention it...to anyone. She would pretend she hadn't noticed. She hoped for her brother's sake that he knew what a dangerous game he was playing.

"Nonsense," said Myron with a casual grin. He didn't seem the least bit guilt-ridden, but Psyche wasn't fooled. "She happened to be on the other side of the room and walked with me to see you while I put my name on your card. It's not as if I've been following her around like a puppy dog on a lead."

Psyche chuckled. "Understood. Not bosom chums." She cleared her throat and held out her wrist. "So, dearest Sham, what dance shall we dance?"

He perused the front and back of her card to see what was still available, and he was not surprised to see it was already half full. He spotted a cotillion near the end of the evening and penciled in his name. Psyche looked at it, and then she grinned at her brother.

"Wise choice," she said mildly.

"Are you going to tell me how you decided Blücher was going to win?" he asked curiously.

Psyche wiggled her eyebrows devilishly at him. "Well, I could tell you, but then I'd have to kill you."

Myron laughed hilariously, and Georgiana chuckled. They were still laughing when Lord Sheerness approached them.

"Hallo, Barneville," said Myron as he wiped at the corner of his eye.

"Neath, Lady Morecambe," he said with a nod to Myron and kissing Georgiana's hand. He turned to Psyche. "Lady Psyche," he said evenly, taking her hand to kiss it.

"Lord Sheerness," she returned in the same impersonal tone. "I didn't expect to see you here."

Sheerness grinned. "Everyone says that these days. I'm beginning to feel like a pariah," he said dryly.

Psyche colored in embarrassment. "I'm sorry! I didn't mean to make it sound—"

"I know. You never do," he said flatly, cutting her off.

"Psyche was just deliberating whether or not to tell me how she picked her horse today," said Myron.

"I was *not* deliberating," said Psyche calmly. "There's nothing to tell."

Myron chuckled. "Now, you're bamming me."

"No, I'm not," defended Psyche hotly. "I don't."

"Then indulge my curiosity and tell me what you do. I'm sure Barneville would like to know how you managed it."

"I admit I'm intrigued. A system for picking the winner of the Derby for ten years is remarkable," said Sheerness speculatively.

"But it's not," said Psyche exasperatedly. "It's a simple matter of statistics. I look at what's running and what their bloodlines are. Then I look at the jockey and the trainer. Then I see the horse. Simple."

"Why did you decide on Blücher, though?"

"His sire was a previous winner with good lines, and his mother had good lines, but there were a few of those. Arnull was his jockey, and he's ridden winners before, and riding is in his blood, but there were other good jockeys. Not all the good ones were riding good horses, so that narrowed it down even further. Boyce was the trainer, also a proven producer of winners, but there were a few others. Not all the good trainers had good jockeys on good horses. I narrowed down my choices to four before I even saw the animals."

"But you still had four. How did you know it was that one?" asked Sheerness perplexedly.

"Because Blücher wanted to win today," said Psyche simply.

"Yes, you said that at the track, but how would you know?"

"Because he told me." Sheerness raised an eyebrow. "He seemed like he wanted to win more than the others. And, I liked his name." She grinned.

Myron laughed. It really *was* simple, but for it to work, one had to have a good memory, and not everyone did. He was amazed she was able to remember things related to horse racing in addition to everything else she had stored in her brain. He didn't see how there could possibly be enough room.

"Good evening, Lady Psyche," said Sir James as he approached their small group accompanied by Lord Georgie Beckinsale, the Earl of Plimpton.

"Sir James!" said Psyche happily, and she held out her hand for him to brush her knuckles. "I'm so happy to see you. And Lord Georgie!" she said as she held out her hand to him. "I understand you are to marry Lucy Cranston."

He gave her a lopsided grin. "Yes, I'm afraid this fine specimen is no longer going to be a commodity. You've missed your chance."

Lord Georgie was humorous and good-natured, but he could never be what might be thought of as a *fine* specimen. He was mildly heavyset and tall with frizzy, ginger-red hair and profusive freckles. He was also slightly pigeon-toed and had jug ears. But he was an excellent dance partner, always quick with a joke, and extremely loyal to his friends.

Psyche giggled. "Drat! Now I'll have to die a spinster," she teased.

"Perhaps we can share one last waltz together," sighed Lord Georgie in mock-consolation as he looked at her dance card. "Egads! Remind me never to pick the Derby winner," he chortled as he penciled in his name on a line. "I imagine your dogs will be tired by the end of the night."

Psyche waved a hand in the air dismissively. "That happens every time I go to a ball. I'll just give them a soak in the tub when I get home."

Sir James laughed and penciled in his name on a line for a waltz as well. Psyche scanned her card. There were only four dances left unclaimed, and three of them were the last three of the night—two waltzes, a volta, and the Sir Roger. Psyche was disappointed the waltzes remained unclaimed because, like her sisters, it was her favorite dance, and she was fond of the volta as well. She was surprised the two waltzes Lord Georgie and Sir James claimed had remained available. There were five, and up to that point, only Drake had selected one. She didn't think there were any other men to dance them with either, unless someone arrived late.

Sheerness watched her playful banter with the two men, and his jaw clenched in irritation. He felt that odd prick of jealousy again, and he tried to get it under control. She was polite to him, sometimes even affable when he wasn't mean to her, but she was never relaxed and flirtatious. He had no one to blame for it but himself. There was always a part of herself that she kept reserved from him, and it was because she didn't trust him.

"Might I see your card, Lady Psyche?" he asked mildly.

Psyche looked at Sheerness in surprise. He had danced with her at Almack's, but she still wasn't sure it was appropriate for him to be dancing while so newly in mourning. It was also disconcerting that he had yet to dance with anyone else. Knowing he only began attending social functions for the purpose of finding a wife to produce an heir, that his attention seemed to be solely focused on Psyche made her anxious. She didn't want to seem like she was shunning him; the entire situation couldn't be easy for him. The way his manner shifted from irascible to pleasant in a way that sometimes made him seem to be two different men had to be a mark of that in some way. She politely lifted her wrist for him to look at her card with a slight smile.

Sheerness examined her card, and he was surprised that nearly every dance was taken…other than the ones she had marked through. Psyche continued to chat with Myron, Georgiana, and the other two men as the earl looked, oblivious to what he was doing. He was pleased there were still a few left and lifted the pencil.

Myron watched Sheerness, and he controlled his features to keep Psyche unaware as Sheerness put his name on for the four remaining dances. Myron wasn't sure why his friend was doing it, but he didn't think he wanted to be nearby when his sister discovered it. If Psyche actually danced all of them (and Myron didn't think she would) it was going to cause plenty of gossip, even among friends. He didn't think Psyche would like that; she found (as did all the members of her family) being the center of attention undesirable. Pandora was fond of theatrics, but only in private, and she would never do anything to make herself a public spectacle if she could avoid it. Psyche preferred to remain even more unobtrusive. After the goings-on at Almack's last week, Psyche was too embarrassed to show herself there again at any time in the immediate future, even though Countess von Weilheim had been far more damaged by it. Myron didn't know what Barneville was playing at, but his expression was completely impassive when he looked at Myron after he was done.

The tune for the first dance began, and Psyche was collected by her partner for the minuet, the Marquess of Ewes, who looked very fine in his uniform. Psyche had no time to examine her dance card to see what Sheerness had chosen, but she would see to it later. She was curious but not concerned. She actually hoped he had chosen one of the waltzes. It would be a shame if she didn't get to dance them, even if her partner for one would be Sheerness.

Psyche was enjoying herself immensely. The number of people attending was less than at some balls she had attended, in part due to the smallness of the Stranraers' ball room and also because they had only invited friends. All of her partners were happy to dance with her, celebrating the victory she had given them at the Derby. The wine and champagne flowed, and the ball had an almost carnival atmosphere. She kept expecting Lord Stranraer to ask everyone to step onto the terrace for fireworks.

Lord Georgie came to take her onto the floor for her third waltz. He was bubbling with excitement, and Psyche smiled at him fondly.

"Lady Psyche, I wanted to offer you my thanks," said Lord Georgie with a squeeze to her hand.

"It's all in the name of public service," chuckled Psyche.

"Well, I do appreciate the nice sum I won today, but I didn't mean that," said Lord Georgie calmly.

Psyche's eyes widened. "Oh! Oh! That," said Psyche in comprehension. "You're quite welcome," she said softly.

"I don't know that I would have been able to bear losing Jamie," he said quietly. "Especially not since I have to…well, what I mean to say is…," he trailed off, his cheeks coloring.

Psyche smiled. "I completely understand." She looked at him seriously. "Do you think you'll be able to go through with it?"

"I *have* to," said Georgie stoically. "And I am not the first to do it."

"No, you're right there," agreed Psyche. "Sometimes doing one's duty can be unpleasant. Oh, well, let's not think about it now. I want to enjoy my last waltz with the dashing Lord Georgie." She grinned and gave him a wink.

Lord Georgie laughed and spun her around the floor. Once their dance ended, he escorted her to the room the Stranraers had laid out with refreshments for some champagne and biscuits. They went to the table where Eurydice was sitting with Sir James and joined them for conversation and a few glasses of champagne. It was then time for Psyche to dance the cotillion with Myron.

While they danced, she asked him when they could expect to go on their trip with Lord Sheerness. He was able to tell her that it would be at the close of the Season in August. Psyche was glad to hear that. It would give her time to make her own preparations for the trip. She knew she would need to make copies of some of her research notes and maps to take with her, and she would also need to have some appropriate clothing made. She didn't think what she had on hand would be suitable for the desert conditions of Egypt. Myron said they had still not decided what places they would visit. Psyche mentioned Thessaloniki, and Myron agreed it would be a good place to visit. The city itself might not have very many things to see, but the area around it certainly did. They would still have over two months to decide.

She didn't ask him about Georgiana. She wanted to, but it was probably not something he wanted to discuss. Now that she suspected it, his long absences from home and his preoccupation made so much more sense. Surely, he had to know it would have to end when the Earl of Hendon returned, if only to protect Georgiana. And what would happen should Hendon return without warning and find them together? Psyche could not escape the concern it would not end well.

Psyche tried to put the worry from her mind and resume enjoying the evening. Because of the excitement in the air and her knowledge that there was little she could do about Myron's private matters, she soon did. That was until she finally looked at her dance card and saw what Sheerness had done. She scanned the room for his face, but she didn't see him anywhere. Her forehead wrinkled with irritation. He was probably hiding because he knew she was going to kill him when she found out. She was *not* going to dance four dances with him...two, perhaps, but most definitely not four. What was he playing at? After looking for Sheerness for several more minutes, she decided she would have a word with him when he came to collect her for their first dance, one of the waltzes, which happened to be the next one on the card.

Before the music began, Lord Stranraer went to the head of the room, Lady Stranraer standing beside him and smiling excitedly. He tapped the side of a glass loudly to gain everyone's attention.

"My friends, let me first begin by thanking you all for joining us this fine evening," he said with a smile. Everyone applauded, and there were even a few shouts of *huzzah!* "We had a lovely day today at Epsom courtesy of the Aberdares, and if *you* didn't, it was your own dem fault!" There was lots of laughter at the comment. He looked to the countess, and she handed him a small box wrapped in paper and ribbons. "For *ten years* now, we've all been lucky enough to have no worries about whether or not we would take away more than we went with to the Derby, and it's due to only one darling girl."

Psyche began to color a deep shade of red when she realized Lord Stranraer was talking about her. Several of the people nearby looked at her and grinned, and Psyche grew even more uncomfortable. It was too late for her to flee the room, and she now understood why the earl had insisted she stay to the end of the night. She looked for the faces of members of her family, and when she saw her mother and father standing with Dorian and Selena, they all smiled encouragingly at her, and she realized they knew the earl had been planning to do this all along. Her skin was starting to itch, and she began to panic because she was about to break out in hives. She wished someone had warned her.

Psyche began to take deep breaths in through her nose and out through her mouth. There was really no need for her to become so overwrought. She was with friends. It wasn't as if they would expect her to sing or dance ballet. She could maintain her calm. At least, she kept trying to tell herself that.

"I can see she's becoming a bit flustered from all this attention, so we'll not make this too grand a production," continued Lord Stranraer. "Lady Psyche, if you would come here, please."

He waved his hand toward her, and Psyche smiled weakly as she walked toward the earl and countess with an outward calmness. Inside, she was a jumble of nerves as she became the sole focus of attention. Everyone stood aside and smiled to let her pass, almost creating an aisle. When she reached the Stranraers, they both hugged her, and the earl kissed her hand.

"Lady Psyche, it is my honor to present you with this token of appreciation from all the poor sots you have saved from the bum bailiff at Derby time for ten years by your astounding grace and generosity," said Lord Stranraer, holding out the gift box.

"Thank you, Lord Stranraer," said Psyche demurely.

Everyone began to applaud loudly, and she could hear whistles and shouts, even over the ringing in her ears. She held the box up in the air and smiled appreciatively, nodding her head shyly.

"Well, open it, gel!" said Lord Stranraer amusedly, giving her an encouraging nod.

Psyche untied the ribbon and removed the paper covering a large velvet jeweler's box. Her eyes widened in surprise when she opened it, and she put a hand to her throat as she felt herself becoming overwhelmed with emotion.

"Oh, my goodness!" she gasped. She could feel her eyes start to water, and she had to blink several times, waving a hand in front of her face.

It appeared to be a normal jeweler's box from the outside, but when she opened it, she saw that it held an Egyptian necklace, a real one. There was a central triangular medallion made of gold imprinted with the figure of some ancient king driving a chariot pulled by four horses, his bow drawn for the hunt. Suspended from the bottom of it were four teardrop-shaped pendants made of lapis lazuli. The chain was covered with beads of more lapis, agate, hematite, carnelian, and gold. Between the top of the medallion and the chain was a round, flat piece of amber about half the size of the triangle, edged in gold, and carved with a cartouche and other hieroglyphs. It was breathtaking.

"Oh!" she sighed, and she moved her hand to her lips and looked up at the guests with watery eyes. "You shouldn't have spent all your winnings on me," she said brokenly, giving them an overwhelmed smile. "Now look, you've gone and made me cry, and my eyes are going to get all puffy. Thank you all...so much."

Everyone laughed as it seemed she was thanking them for giving her puffy eyes and began to clap again. Psyche closed the lid on the box and smiled gratefully. She performed a graceful curtsy and began to make her way to her family, who had all by that time gathered together. Lord Sheerness was standing with them as well. When she reached them, her family all hugged her and Pandora provided her with a handkerchief, which Psyche gratefully accepted.

"You all knew, didn't you?" said Psyche reprovingly. "How could you not warn me?"

"It wouldn't have been a surprise if you knew," said the duke with a chuckle.

"I could have pretended," said Psyche hotly.

"No, you couldn't," chortled Pandora.

"I almost broke out in *hives*!" gasped Psyche. She looked at Myron and her father. "Did you have a hand in deciding what they gave me?"

"We gave them a little direction, but Stranraer chose it," said her father.

"Will you hold on to this for me?" she asked of her father, holding out the box to him. "I don't want to lose it."

"Of course," he said with a smile.

The music for the waltz soon began, and Lord Sheerness looked at her expectantly. Psyche sighed resignedly and let him take her into his arms for the dance. She really would have preferred to have some time to herself to collect her thoughts, but she could see he had no intention of letting her do so. She then remembered what she had discovered about her dance card. She was preparing to ask him about it when he spoke first.

"So what did they give you?" he asked curiously.

"A necklace," she said simply.

"You don't strike me as the sort to become that excited over a bauble," said Sheerness, his forehead wrinkling.

"It was very pretty," said Psyche unhelpfully.

"Still....,"

"It was a very old, *Egyptian* necklace," said Psyche flatly.

"Would it have killed you to tell me that from the beginning?" he asked tightly.

"No, I don't suppose it would have," said Psyche calmly. "But more often than not when I say the words *Egyptian* or *Greek* it seems to annoy you immensely."

"Am I really always so mean?" asked Sheerness quietly.

Psyche looked at him in surprise. It was a question she wouldn't have expected from him.

"Can you not tell when you are being mean and hateful, or is it simply you are always that way and do not notice?"

"I don't know," said Sheerness pensively.

"You have been doing much better this Season, but there are still times when you are simply impossible." Psyche looked at him seriously. "It makes it very difficult for me to like you."

"*Do* you like me?" he asked curiously.

"I don't know," it was Psyche's turn to say honestly, her eyes wide. "I don't *hate* you," she said almost to herself. Sheerness raised an eyebrow. "There are some things about you that are very admirable. Everyone else likes you."

Sheerness gave her a wry half-smile. "That's comforting."

"What did you expect me to say?" defended Psyche. "If you had asked me last year, I would have unequivocally told you I loathed the very sight of you."

"That's harsh," said Sheerness tightly.

"I said *last* year, and if you don't want an honest answer to a question, then don't ask *me, "* said Psyche sharply.

"Oh, I think you're very capable of being dishonest when it suits you," said Sheerness angrily.

"When have I ever lied to you?" asked Psyche exasperatedly. "Ask anyone who knows me, and they'll tell you I cannot lie because it is almost physically impossible."

"You have lied to me before," said Sheerness crossly.

"When?" shot Psyche aggravatedly.

"You lied about telling your sister what happened on the terrace."

"No, I didn't," said Psyche, shaking her head. "I did *not* tell her what happened." Of course, she didn't have to tell Pandora what had happened because she was there, but Psyche was being honest about not telling her. "She didn't find out about it from me. When else do you think I've lied?"

"When I asked if you had seen Philip?"

"I told you I didn't *think* I had seen him, and that was an honest answer. I didn't know who he was, and I couldn't tell how tall he was. He could have been an East End urchin who snuck into your garden for all I knew."

"Now you're being insipid. That was lying."

"No, it wasn't. Perhaps you should learn to phrase your questions properly," said Psyche airily.

"And what do you mean it's *physically impossible* for you to lie?"

"I shan't tell you," said Psyche flatly, looking away from him.

"Fine. I'll ask Neath," said Sheerness with an amused grin.

"You do that," said Psyche stiffly, looking away from him arrogantly. She didn't think Myron would tell him, but it was possible. Sheerness was his best friend. "I'm *not* going to dance four dances with you, by the way."

"Why not?"

"For reasons," said Psyche angrily. Sheerness chuckled at her perturbed pout. "One is that it's unseemly. People might think you have intentions."

Sheerness laughed outright. *"Intentions?"* he hooted.

"You know—or you should know—it's rude to dance that many times with the same partner."

"But I don't want to dance with anyone else," said Sheerness mildly. "What else?"

"You are in mourning. I don't think you should be dancing *at all."*

"I will dance if I want to, as I told you last week, and it's not as if I'm dancing the night away. Only four dances is not so very many."

"Yes, and I shall refer you back to point number one: they're all with *me."* Psyche pursed her lips primly. "That you're in mourning and dancing four dances with *me* will cause speculation I'd rather not be related to."

"You don't strike me as the sort to be bothered by gossip," said Sheerness softly, his head tilted sideways thoughtfully.

"Yes, you often say I don't strike you as the *sort,* which only demonstrates you know nothing about me," said Psyche coldly. "It's almost as if.... *Ooh,* never mind! I'll not dance four dances with you," said Psyche finally.

Psyche wasn't going to finish voicing the thought she had because she didn't like it. She was going to say it almost seemed as if he *wanted* people to gossip about them. That didn't sit well with her because she didn't know why he would want that. Amalie had said he was looking for a wife. Causing a scandal involving her would result in either irreparably destroying her reputation or force her into marrying him...maybe. She wasn't sure her parents would make her marry someone to avoid a scandal or not. She would rather not find out. Psyche and Sheerness were physically attracted to each other (it was becoming apparent), and they did share common interests, but she didn't think that was a suitable basis for a lifetime together, not when they couldn't agree with each other. She expected more.

If he wasn't trying to cause a scandal to force her to marry him, then it would mean he disliked her enough he meant to make her a social disgrace. She didn't care what society thought of her really, other than if she were an outcast she wouldn't be able to see her friends or show her face in London. That would mean no more shopping, no more Derby, and no more British Museum. That would not suit.

"Perhaps we might compromise, then," said Sheerness after a time.

Psyche looked at him doubtfully. *"You?* Compromise with *me?* I find that unlikely."

"I am not completely hidebound," he said through stiff lips, his jaw setting in a firm line.

"No, only with me," snapped Psyche.

"You really don't like me, do you?" he asked in a tone of amazement, as if it were a revelation.

"I told you I *don't know,"* sighed Psyche tiredly, and she raised her hand from his shoulder to rub it across her forehead. "What is your compromise?" Their bickering was, as usual, leaving her drained, and she decided the only way to end it was to hear him out.

"One more dance, but the time for the other dances you spend talking with me. Perhaps we could take a stroll on the terrace or something similar?"

"Lord Sheerness, we don't talk; we argue, " said Psyche drolly with a smirk, finding his idea ridiculous.

"Not always."

"No, for about *two minutes* at a stretch, we can actually be civil, but then you decide to be a gollumpus," said Psyche sarcastically.

"Lady Psyche, I don't know how you intend to spend your time on board my ship, but if you don't at least make an effort to control your wagging tongue, I'll keep you locked in the hold," he warned darkly.

"Myron wouldn't let you," said Psyche shortly, "and if you weren't so mean all the time, I wouldn't be either. I try to behave far more civilly than you do, and it's only when you've gone too far that I return the favor."

"I am *not* always mean," said Sheerness exasperatedly.

"You are to me. Sometimes I think you're mean to me just because it *is* me."

"Don't be silly."

"I am *not* silly. People who are silly are impractical, and I am nothing if not *practical.*"

Psyche was glad the waltz was almost finished. He was wearing her out with his incessant needling. He could say he wasn't always mean all he wanted, but the way she felt at the moment proved otherwise. The only time he wasn't mean was when he kissed her, and since she didn't know his motives for doing it, that could be construed as mean, too.

She wished she hadn't promised Lord Stranraer she would stay to the end of the night. One waltz with Sheerness was all it had taken to exhaust her. It was barely midnight, and yet she felt so tired it could be dawn already. Psyche was beginning to wonder how she ever thought she would be able to tolerate living on board a ship with him for several months. Perhaps being placed in the hold wouldn't be such a bad thing after all. It would keep her away from *him.* The only consolation she had was knowing that Myron would be there to act as her shield…hopefully. She knew he didn't want to, but he would also not let Sheerness constantly pester her either.

"When do I get to see your ship, by the way?" asked Psyche after a minute, but just then the dance ended.

Sheerness kissed her hand and gave her a teasing grin, and then he shook his head.

"If you want to see my ship before the day you board it for Greece, you'll have to agree to my bargain."

"*Ooh! You!*" gasped Psyche in outrage.

"It's not very fun, is it?" asked Sheerness coldly. "I would say knight takes rook."

"This is not a game," said Psyche tightly, "but I'll accept your bargain."

"Most excellent," said Sheerness with a grin. "I'll come find you when it's time for our next dance."

Psyche watched him saunter away after he escorted her to the edge of the floor to be claimed by her next partner. She went onto the floor with Lord Fielding for the galop, her mind distracted. Luckily, she was a good dancer and didn't need to concentrate on what she was doing. She was able to answer any questions Lord Fielding put forward, but her mind was not on the conversation she was having; it was on the one she just had.

He couldn't possibly think they were playing some kind of game. Psyche certainly didn't think they were. She wasn't doing anything to purposely provoke him or make him angry, even though she knew she had done things with that effect. If he was doing the things he was simply as some form of tit-for-tat, Psyche would find that highly childish, even more childish than she would expect from Sheerness. If that was the case, she wasn't going to give him the satisfaction. She refused to play with him. She didn't have the time or the energy.

Psyche was soon able to put him from her mind, especially after she went to the supper room and had a few more glasses of champagne. She had made up her mind how she was going to address his intransigence. She had won her berth on his ship. And she was not going to let him do anything that might cause public speculation about the two of them. At least, she was going to try not to let him. She was treading a very fine line by being the only one he danced with while he was in mourning, but perhaps if she limited it to only two dances per social function, she could divert any rumors.

She was actually able to regain some of her good spirits by the time Sheerness came looking for her for the volta. Instead of leading her onto the floor for the dance, however, he led her through the doors onto the terrace. For someone intent to have her talk to him, he was being quiet. He had not said a word since he came for her, but Psyche would wait for him to talk first. She didn't want to expedite the beginning of another argument.

He kept his arm linked through hers as he led her down the stairs into the garden. Psyche looked up at him curiously, but he kept his eyes straight ahead, his expression impassive. He didn't seem willing to talk, but Psyche was just as determined to remain silent. She was not playing his game, whatever it was.

The Stranraers' garden was lovely in the moonlight. It reminded her of the Lundeys'. There was lots of box and privet but not very many flowers. The difference between the two that Psyche greatly appreciated was that all the paths were paved rather than graveled. There was also no large fountain. The Stanraers had a pool surrounded by benches and low flowerbeds, but Sheerness didn't stop there. Psyche was still not going to talk unless he did first.

The Stranraers didn't have a secluded courtyard, but they did have tall hedges and more trees than the Lundeys, and after the two of them turned a corner in the path, they found a wooden bench swing suspended from the boughs of a large oak tree. Without a word, Sheerness steered them toward it and sat down with her. He balanced one of his arms across the back of the swing behind her and started it rocking back and forth with a slow push of his feet. Psyche sat demurely beside him, her hands clasped in her lap.

Psyche wasn't chilled, surprisingly. The long velvet sleeves of her gown kept her arms warm. Her shoulders and chest exposed by the low neckline of her gown might have been cold, if it weren't for Sheerness sitting close beside her, close enough that their thighs touched, in fact. She wasn't going to bring it to his attention, though. She suspected he wanted her to, and she wasn't going to give him the satisfaction of making her speak first. Psyche did realize by *not* playing his game, she was participating nonetheless.

Then he slowly leaned toward her and inhaled. Psyche could feel the warmth of his breath against her neck as he exhaled, but he wasn't close enough to touch her. She couldn't understand his fascination with smelling her. She liked the smell of her perfume, too, but she didn't walk around with her wrist to her nose. Maybe she needed to quit wearing it if this was going to be the typical reaction it caused in Sheerness. She looked at the things around her, the tree, the bushes, straight ahead, but she didn't look at Sheerness and didn't say anything either. She sat stilly and tried to pretend she didn't notice anything amiss. Had it been lighter, though, it would have been obvious from the flush on her cheeks that she *did* notice.

He soon moved the arm behind her lower until it rested on her shoulders, and he applied the slightest amount of pressure so that she moved closer to him and rested tighter against his side. Psyche bit her lower lip and gave him a sidelong glance beneath her lashes. She knew he was just trying to aggravate her, to make her lose her temper or react in some other way. She was determined not to admit defeat, but she could feel her skin beginning to tingle, and her breath caught in her throat with nervous excitement as she waited to see what he would try next.

What he did wasn't what she would have expected. He calmly reached over and began to tickle her ribs. Psyche squeaked in surprise, and then she began to squirm and giggle uncontrollably as he moved his other arm behind her to begin tickling the other side. She tried to get him to turn her loose, but she was laughing too hard, and she began to slide sideways on the bench from a sitting position to almost reclining in her attempt to get away as he continued his assault. She was laughing so much that her back was starting to hurt, and tears were streaming down her cheeks as much from the laughter as from the pain and the fact that she couldn't catch her breath. Sheerness finally stopped tickling her, and he leaned over her with a grin.

"Are you ready to talk, or do I have to tickle you some more?" he teased.

"N-no," gasped Psyche as she tried to catch her breath.

"No, you won't talk, or no, don't tickle you?" he chortled.

"Oh...I...ow," gasped Psyche as she finally took a full breath, and it caused a stitch in her back.

Sheerness laughed amusedly, and he rested his forearm against the arm of the swing above her head. He looked down at her and used his other hand to wipe the tears from her cheeks. He traced one of her eyebrows with his fingertip, down her cheek to her jaw and then to her chin up to her lips. Psyche watched as a fascinated, almost reverent expression enveloped his features as he explored the contours of her face with his fingertip. It was an odd experience for her, and even though she was there and could feel his touch, Psyche almost felt as if she were watching from a distance, as if she were seeing something that was meant to be a secret.

He lowered his head to kiss her gently, and Psyche felt a lump rise in her throat at the feelings of tenderness that washed over her for him. At that precise moment, in that exact instant, Psyche felt as if she could love him more than anything or anyone else she could ever imagine. And it scared her to death. Psyche managed to slide sideways off the swing from beneath him and quickly stood up to put as much distance between them as she could. She straightened out her dress as he sat up on the swing, his expression one of total surprise. Psyche put her hands to her flushed cheeks and shook her head.

"I can't play with you, Lord Sheerness," she said in an even tone that was almost devoid of feeling.

Sheerness gave her a perplexed smile. "What do you mean by that?"

"I cannot be your playmate, and I will not play these games you seem intent on playing," said Psyche firmly.

"What *games?*" he asked tightly, rising from the swing to come stand just inches away from her.

"First there's the fussing and the *insulting*, and then there's the kissing and the *touching*." Psyche shook her head. "I don't know what you're playing at, but you're not doing it with me."

Psyche started to turn and leave, but he grabbed her arm to stop her from going. She looked at him in surprise.

"Our time isn't up yet," he said flatly. "The volta may be over, but we still have the waltz and the Sir Roger. You made a deal with me, and you will honor it."

"No, I won't. Not this time. I told you I'm through playing a game for which only you seem to know the rules. And if that means I don't get to see your ship, even if it means I never get to see it, or Greece, or Egypt, then so be it," said Psyche simply, giving him a straightforward glance.

What she had felt when he kissed her had made her realize her self-preservation was far more important than seeing the world or anything else at the moment. It had worried her enough she had determined she should redouble her efforts to avoid him in the future or at least not be alone with him anymore. She could bear him being one way or the other (yes, even insulting), but the continual switching from hot to cold with his emotions was causing a mental strain for her she felt she could no longer take. She didn't know what to expect from him anymore, and the constant tenterhooks was beginning to make her physically ill.

"Why do you insist that I am playing a game? What about *you?*"

Psyche blinked. "First, you say I have lied to you, when I never have. Now, you accuse me of playing games. I've never been anything less than forthright with you. If you're implying I was playing games when I made my wager for the Derby or when I raced with you in the park last week, you are most assuredly mistaken. There has never been any doubt about my motives for anything I have ever done or said."

"And you think there is for mine?"

"Isn't there?" she asked sharply. Psyche shrugged. "In any event, I'm tired of arguing with you…at all," she sighed. She tried to pull away from his grip on her arm. "Just leave me in peace," she pleaded.

Sheerness pulled her toward him to kiss her hungrily. He put a hand at the back of her neck to keep her from pulling away, but Psyche didn't struggle. She let him kiss her, but it took all of her effort not to respond. When he realized Psyche wasn't going to kiss him back, Sheerness stopped and rested his forehead against hers, smoothing his hand against her cheek soothingly.

"Come with me…and Myron," he said softly. "He'll be coming to look at the ship next Saturday. Come with him."

Psyche looked into Sheerness's eyes so near her own mistrustfully. They were pleading and sincere, but Psyche felt he was being far too magnanimous for the emotion she saw there to be genuine. He let her go completely and clasped his hands behind his back. Then she watched as he clenched his jaw and looked at her stolidly. There was something about the action that made her feel as if she were being cruel to him, as if she had managed to wound him in a way that affected more than just his pride, and she felt her chest tighten with that same emotion she had felt when he kissed her.

"I'll try to be less…confusing," he said woodenly.

Psyche gave him an assessing glance. She didn't trust him for a minute. His face showed her nothing one way or the other, and there was only what she had felt when he released her. He had finally asked her to go with him to Greece and Egypt, which is what she had wanted. He wanted her to come see his ship, and she wouldn't have to dance with him or *talk* with him to get it. He also said he would try to be less confusing, for whatever that was worth, because his being civil was leaving her no less uncertain than any of his other moods. He seemed to be giving her exactly what she wanted, but there was a nagging feeling at the back of her mind that he had ulterior motives which suited only his own ends. Sooner or later, he would make her pay for it. She thought about it intently. He was completely suspect to her, but she knew he could be honorable when it suited him.

"All right," she said finally.

Chapter Eight

Psyche spent the days following the Derby starting her preparations for her trip. Her parents were somewhat leery that she should be traveling so far without them, but they gave their consent after she and Myron talked with them together. Psyche had no doubt this would be the outcome. They knew her brother wouldn't let her come to any harm, and they had known the Sheernesses for years. Myron had known the young earl since before Oxford. The duke and duchess realized the only way she would be safer was if they went too, and neither of them truly felt it would be necessary. They couldn't refuse to let Psyche go on the journey; the Aberdares knew it was something she had wanted for as long as they could remember. Aside from that, she had, at least, asked their permission, which was more than Pandora had done when she went to Edinburgh.

The first thing Psyche did was make a list of all the items she needed to take with her and everything she needed to do before she left. All of it spanned several pages, and she realized it was too much. So she rewrote it…several times, until she shortened it to one page of things to take and one page of things to do. Her handwriting had gotten small and cramped, but she did it.

Her sisters were all happy she would get to go. Persephone recommended she wear men's clothes as often as possible because it would be much more comfortable and practical. Pandora agreed. Psyche herself wasn't sure she *wanted* to go around in breeches, and she definitely had no intention of wearing a cravat. Persephone and Pandora suggested she try on a pair of britches to see how she liked them. She replied she had already tried them on before, which resulted in her having to tell them about her acrobatic performance for the Yeardley children. Her sisters both found that entertaining, especially Pandora, who was pleased things seemed to be progressing quite nicely between her twin and Sheerness, but she kept that thought to herself for future discussion with her husband.

In the end, Psyche decided she *would* take some pants with her, but she would take some practical dresses, too. She also came up with an idea for an article of clothing that was a combination of the two. She showed a sketch to the seamstress they sometimes used when they were in London, but she didn't think she was up to the task. Had Psyche been in Wales, she was sure Janet would have found no difficulty with the design, but she didn't want to make a special trip to Cardiff to have it done.

Chrissoula and Eurydice's maid, Agniezka, and Maiyin told Psyche she should leave the preparation of her wardrobe, including the creation of her split skirt, up to them. After only a brief amount of consideration and a small amount of urging from Pandora, Psyche gave her consent. All three were excellent at sewing and alterations, and Psyche was sure she would be well-pleased with what they made for her. Chrissoula assured Psyche it would all be prepared in plenty of time for her departure. When Psyche asked about fittings, her maid laughed and said she knew what Psyche's measurements were and everything would fit perfectly. Psyche questioned her on it, and Chrissoula finally admitted that after consulting with each other, she, Agniezka, and Maiyin decided what they would make for her should be a surprise.

Psyche almost changed her mind at that point, but she trusted Chrissoula and the other maids. Had Psyche known Pandora was involved in the planning of her wardrobe and that the three had enlisted the assistance of three or four others of the Savages' exotic female staff, she would have sought other seamstresses. However, she was oblivious to exactly how great a surprise her wardrobe was going to be.

After she started the preparations for her clothing, she looked into the other things she intended to take. That part of the list was surprisingly short. She was going to take two or three sketchbooks, and she was sure she could acquire more in Egypt or Greece if necessary. She would take her chalks and watercolors. She would take her notebooks on hieroglyphs, and she was going to make a copy of her rubbing of the Rosetta stone. She also had two maps she wanted to trace, but she didn't think they would be needed, especially not considering the bundle Sir James had provided to Sheerness.

But Psyche couldn't finalize what she planned to take with her until she saw what her accommodations would be. She didn't think for an instant that Sheerness intended to keep her in the hold…at least, not for the entire journey, but she knew from being aboard Gregory's ship many times that space was limited. She could only plan to take, at most, two trunks, and they would have to be capable of being stacked. She didn't know what kind of ship Sheerness had or much of anything about it. Myron was vague on the subject, and the earl wouldn't tell her anything…not that she had asked.

She saw Sheerness twice after the ball at the Stranraers'. The first was at his own house when she went to visit Amalie and the children on Tuesday with her younger brothers. Sheerness was polite but formal. He made no personal enquiries, and from his behavior, it could have been thought they were merely acquaintances. Amalie and the children noticed the change in his treatment of her, and it made them all uncertain what their own behavior should be…including Psyche. She tried to tell herself that he was doing exactly as she had asked, but after enduring an afternoon of it, she started to wonder if it really *was* what she wanted. It surprised her when it occurred to her that she *missed* the way he used to behave, and she hoped he would stay true to form and revert to his normal self in due course.

The second time she saw him was Friday morning while she was at the Park for her ride. She had already gone around the circle once, and she stopped at the Serpentine to feed Waddlewsorth and the other birds as she usually did after tying Achilles to a nearby tree. Sheerness arrived at the lake just as the birds formed a frenzy around her, competing for the crumbs. She wasn't aware when he arrived, and she was laughing and talking to the birds unconcernedly over their antics. When she turned to see him standing there, holding the reins of his horse, for a brief moment she saw a tenderly amused smile on his face caused by her activities. When Sheerness realized she saw him, his expression changed to that same rigid impassivity she had seen at his house.

He kept his distance from her and the ducks, particularly Waddlesworth, who seemed to remember the earl and eyed him with what might pass for disdain. Psyche had no trouble seeing the feeling was mutual. After making only a few brief remarks about the weather and the scenery, he bade her farewell, remounted, and rode away down the trail. Again, he was civil, but it made Psyche oddly wish for things to be back the way they were.

Saturday morning—this morning, she didn't see him. Psyche was tempted to believe he didn't go riding as early because he wanted to avoid seeing her again. It was childish, considering they would be making a trip out of the country together, but then she wondered if he thought it was just the civil thing to do, to not see someone more than once socially per day. Psyche thought that was even more ridiculous than purposely trying to avoid her, but she wasn't going to question him about it; it was none of her affair.

After she finished her ride and ate breakfast with her family, she found out from Myron exactly *when* they would be going to see the ship. She was pleased to discover it would be in the late afternoon. That would give her time to visit Pandora and run by the Museum to collect the transcriptions from Sir James. She wouldn't need them for her trip, but she did want to get them from him in a timely manner. She would go get them *before* she went to see Pandora. Then she could take her time visiting her sister.

When the post arrived, everyone was happy there was a letter from Gregory. He wrote as often as he could, but he was only able to manage one or two letters a month. He generally sent them on a ship departing from Bermuda, which was where he spent his brief terms of leave and put in for repairs to his ship. Any time he sent his family a letter, it was usually several pages, and he tried to keep them informed of everything that was happening in the war and his activities. He seemed optimistic (these days) that the conflict was soon to be at an end. He did not, however, think Great Britain would come out the better for it. Then again, he didn't think the United States would either.

Everyone passed around the pages to read them, and any plans for the day were postponed until they had all read and talked about what he had to say. This letter was particularly special and surprising. He had gotten married.

Gregory said his new wife was formerly Miss Annabelle Granger. Her father was Captain Harold Granger, who commanded a second-rate called HMS *Manticore*. She was born and raised in Bermuda, and her father was her only living relative, other than some distant cousins who lived in Nottinghamshire. Gregory hoped he would soon be able to bring her home to meet the family, and he was confident they would adore her as much as he did. He didn't tell them when the time for them to meet her would come, however.

Persephone was not pleased. Finding out her doting brother had married someone left her feeling entirely jealous. She didn't voice her thoughts on the matter, though, because she realized it was childish for her to feel that way, and everyone else was very excited about welcoming a new member of the family. He had never mentioned any plans to marry…ever. Persephone thought he would be like Myron: perfectly happy in his state of bachelorhood. She knew she would have to come to terms with it because she could tell from the tone of his letter that Annabelle made him very happy.

Psyche was as surprised by Gregory's marriage as everyone else, and she felt an intense curiosity about her new sister. The only part that was not surprising to her was that he had married the daughter of another seaman. As the younger son of nobility, Gregory was left pretty much to his own devices when it came to making his way in the world. He had inherited enough from their Grandfather Sanders and their Grandfather Savage that he would never have to work if he had no desire to do so, but, like everyone else in his family, idleness was not in him. He had always loved the water, and for him to follow a course that permitted him to be near it was natural. Even before the conflict with the United States, he was often gone from home on his ship. Psyche knew any woman able to bear his long absences would have to be of a special sort. For him to marry a woman born to that life was a practical choice, and that he loved Annabelle only made it so much the better.

She wondered what Annabelle looked like. Gregory offered no description other than to say she was pretty, charming, and practical. Psyche thought those were all features in her favor, but he offered no physical description and didn't provide them with a miniature or any other visual points of reference. He didn't say how old she was or what her coloring was, whether dark or pale. Psyche decided in the end that it didn't really matter. Gregory was happy with her, and that was all the recommendation that was needed.

Pandora would be as happy and amazed as everyone else to learn Gregory was married. It would be a new bit of information to share, and it would make for a great topic of debate and speculation between the twins. Psyche also looking forward to telling Pandora that Dorian had relented in the Battle of the Nannies. Hua Kwan would be changing employment from that of the Savages to the Marshalls, and Psyche suspected the cease fire had come not a moment too soon. Pandora looked as if she were about to explode any day.

The discussion among her family over Gregory's letter put Psyche a little behind on her schedule, but she fully intended to get everything accomplished that she had planned. She was making her best effort to be punctual or at least determine what it was that she did to cause herself to be late for everything and fix it. It wasn't oversleeping; not only did she suffer from insomnia, but she also rose very early. Sometimes, the only way she managed to fall asleep was with the use of a draught prepared for her by Keung. Regardless of when she finally went to sleep, she was up before the sun. She went for a daily ride in the park, provided the weather allowed, but she was back home no later than eight, even if she stopped to feed the birds. That gave her plenty of time to change and be down for breakfast, but she was usually late. From that point on for the rest of the day, she more often than not was running behind.

She went to the Museum first, and she spent time visiting with Sir James as he showed her some of the new acquisitions the Museum had made that had not yet been put on display. There were a few pieces of pottery and statuary from Mesopotamia which she found very impressive, but there was nothing new from Egypt. She thanked Sir James for providing her with the transcriptions from the tablets, and then she was on her way to see her sister. She was only an hour later going to see Pandora than she had intended.

The door was answered, as usual, by Waldon, the Marshalls' proper British butler. Since Pandora had come into the family, he was not quite so stiff, and he had a slight smile on his face when he saw that it was Psyche at the door.

"Lady Psyche, we've been expecting you," he said mildly, a veiled reproof for her tardiness. "If you'll come this way, I believe Lady Bardsey is waiting for you in the sitting room."

"Thank you, Waldon," said Psyche meekly, knowing a chastisement when she heard one.

She followed him the short distance down the hall to the family's private sitting room where she often met her sister. Once Waldon opened the door to let her enter, Psyche found her twin lounging on the settee, her stockinged feet propped up on one arm, her back relaxed against pillows at the other. She had her hands to either side of her stomach, and she had a frown on her face as she slowly released a deep breath. Pandora looked up when Psyche entered, only marginally concerned someone might come in and see her so casually seated.

"There you are," she said exasperatedly. "I was expecting you ages ago."

"Sorry. Sir James had new things to show me at the Museum," said Psyche, a frown furrowing her own brow. "Are you all right?"

Pandora waved a hand in the air. "Yes, I'm fine." She looked at the butler, who stood waiting at the door. "Can you bring us some tea, please, Waldon?"

"Of course, mum," he said with a slight bow and left the room, closing the door behind him.

Psyche went to one of the armchairs adjacent to the settee and sat down. Pandora continued to rub the sides of her stomach and breathe in and out slowly.

"You're not in labor, are you?" asked Psyche concernedly.

"No, not yet. Theo said these are *false* labor pains. Hunh," Pandora grunted. "He said I'll be able to tell the difference when I have a *real* one." She shrugged. "Like *he* would know."

Psyche chuckled. "Well, at least you can be comforted in knowing you now will have a nanny on hand when that happens."

Pandora looked up happily. "Did Dorian finally give in?" Psyche nodded. "Wonderful! I've been going mad waiting for him to leave off. He doesn't even *have* children. I don't know why he would need two nannies."

"He said to let you know Kwan is now at your disposal."

Pandora sighed in relief. "I must admit I was beginning to worry."

"I have some other wonderful news for you," said Psyche excitedly.

"You're getting married?" asked Pandora teasingly.

"Not ruddy likely," said Psyche shortly. "There's not a man in this town I can tolerate for more than five minutes at a stretch, much less a lifetime."

"Surely, there's at least one," said Pandora with a grin. "Handsome, intelligent, charming, excellent dancer—"

"Chuckle-headed lout," cut in Psyche. She was not going to let Pandora continue to sing the praises of Sheerness.

"He's not so bad as that," chided Pandora mildly. "He was *never* so detestable as that, and you two are getting on much better these days."

"I don't know if it's *better*," sighed Psyche. Pandora raised an eyebrow. "He's not insulting me anymore…at least, not this week. This week, he barely even goes far enough to say: 'how do you do?'"

"What?" asked Pandora in surprise.

"I told him I couldn't play with him anymore, and now he won't talk to me," said Psyche simply.

Pandora's jaw dropped, and then she began to laugh with great amusement. Psyche didn't find it funny. She didn't find any of Sheerness's treatment of her funny. Pandora wrapped her arms around her stomach as she tried to regain her composure, and Psyche looked at her with concern.

"Oh, Psy, I think you hurt his feelings," sighed Pandora. Her expression calmed, and she looked at her twin thoughtfully. "He's *kissed* you, hasn't he?" she asked knowingly. Psyche blushed mightily, and Pandora didn't need her confirmation. "And you *liked* it."

"That's beside the point," said Psyche flatly.

"No, it isn't. Psy, that *is* the point," said Pandora softly.

Psyche raised her hands in surrender. "Let's not talk about this, please. I have to see him this afternoon, and I don't want *you* putting ideas in my head."

Pandora laughed again, and Psyche looked at her pleadingly.

"Very well. We'll talk about it again, though, I'm sure," said Pandora knowingly. "What *is* your wonderful news, then?"

"Gregory got married," said Psyche happily.

"What?" asked Pandora in shock.

Psyche nodded. "In Bermuda. He married a girl named Annabelle Granger, a captain's daughter."

"Oh, my giddy aunt!" gasped Pandora. "I don't believe it!"

"We had a letter only this morning giving us the news. He doesn't know when he'll be bringing her home, but he said she's very lovely."

"Wow!" gasped Pandora. "I will be so glad when he comes home. Maybe this is a sign he'll be home for good before too long."

"It looks that way," agreed Psyche. "I don't think he would have gotten married if he thought he was going to be away from home much longer."

Waldon entered the room then to bring their tea. He placed the tray on the table in front of the settee and quietly left. Pandora struggled to sit up to begin pouring, but Psyche held up her hand to make her twin stay as she was.

"I'll get it," grinned Psyche as she began to make their tea. "You know I don't care if I have to pour my own. Do you want a biscuit?"

"Oh, yes, please. One of the orange snaps."

Psyche poured Pandora's tea and added a lump of sugar, and then she put a few thin brown wafers on the edge of the saucer and gave it to her sister.

"I thought you would like more than one," said Psyche with a grin. She looked around the room. "Where is everyone else today?" she asked curiously.

"Oh, Theo decided he wanted to go rowing with Dorian and a few of their mates this afternoon. *Mǔqin* has gone back to Bardsey."

"Already?" asked Psyche in surprise. "Is she coming back?"

"No, she isn't…at least, not this season. She's convinced the workmen are going to destroy her three-hundred-year-old home, so she wanted to be there to see it," chuckled Pandora. "She also wanted to be there to make sure everything was in order for the nursery."

"But the system was put in here without any problems; why would she think all will not go well in Yorkshire?" asked Psyche perplexedly.

Pandora waved a hand dismissively. "It is new for her. She's not used to running water and *plumbing*." Pandora grinned and winked. "But she's certainly starting to appreciate it."

"Don't we all?" agreed Psyche with a laugh, taking a sip from her tea. "I would dearly miss not having a hot bath whenever it suited me." She grimaced. "I think that will be the thing I'll dislike most while I am away from home."

"Do you think you're going to be happy being at sea for so long?"

"I hope so," said Psyche thoughtfully. She shrugged. "I think the end will be worth it."

"You'll have to write me as much as possible. I'm going to miss you while you're away," said Pandora sadly.

"I *will* be coming back," said Psyche with a chuckle.

"How long will you be gone?"

"I don't know. It depends on how well things go. It will take almost a month just to reach Greece, provided the winds are favorable and we don't stop anywhere else along the way."

"Won't you be home for Christmas?" asked Pandora in dismay.

Psyche shook her head unhappily. "No, I would expect not." She shrugged. "I'll ask Lord Sheerness when I see his ship this afternoon."

"Oh, I almost forgot. We're having a supper party tomorrow, and you are to come."

"I thought you were doing your lying in?"

"I am, somewhat, and I should be fine since I'm not leaving the house."

"What's the occasion?"

"No occasion. It's just supper," said Pandora mildly.

Psyche looked at her twin suspiciously. It was unusual for her to organize any type of social gathering, and to have one for no reason was highly suspect.

"Psy, it is just a very small gathering. Dorian and Selena will be coming, and so will Myron."

"All right. I'll come. I have no plans for tomorrow evening."

At that point, Psyche was surprised when Myron and Georgiana entered the room. They seemed just as surprised to see her there as she was to see them. Georgiana had a guilty expression, but Myron, as usual, did not. Psyche looked from the pair to Pandora, and her twin also looked as if nothing were amiss. It was then that Psyche realized Pandora was fully aware of the relationship between their brother and the marchioness. All three would provide her with some tale that seemed perfectly logical for Georgiana and Myron walking into the room at the same time, but it would *only* be a tale.

Then something occurred to Psyche that caused her no small amount of shock and alarm. The pair had entered without Waldon showing them in. That would mean it was likely they had been in the house. If that were the case, it also meant they had been having a tryst, and Pandora was helping them. Psyche had to wonder how long her twin had been aware of the relationship between Myron and Georgiana, and why Pandora had never told her about it.

"Hallo, Myron and Georgiana. Did you enjoy your ride in the park?" asked Pandora casually.

"Yes, we did," replied Myron just as casually. "I do much prefer the park when it's empty, but it's rather sparsely attended in the afternoon as well." He looked at Psyche after checking his watch. "Why don't we leave from here to go see Barneville?"

"That would be an excellent idea," said Psyche agreeably, and she let them believe she suspected nothing.

Myron brushed Georgiana's knuckles. "I'll see you here tomorrow evening?" he enquired.

"Of course, Lord Neath," said Georgiana softly.

"Shall we go, then?" he asked Psyche.

Psyche looked from her brother back to Pandora. She wanted to stay and visit longer, but after a brief glance at her own watch she realized it *was* time for them to be on their way. She set her cup and saucer on the table and rose from her chair to give Pandora a hug and a kiss.

"I'm sorry to drink and run, Pan," she said sadly. "I'll be here for supper tomorrow, and then I'll come visit on Monday."

"Perfect," said Pandora with a smile, squeezing her arm. "Georgiana will stay and keep me company for a while."

Psyche left the house with Myron, her arm linked through his. They went through the back of the house to the garden, past the beautiful gazebo made of stone and constructed to resemble a Greek temple. Psyche was proud to say she had helped design it. It had ornate Corinthian columns and was open on three sides. The back was solid stone with a fountain in the shape of a man's head in the middle of the wall, the water pouring out of his mouth into a semi-circular basin. The edge of the basin was wide enough to sit on, but one always risked getting wet from the splashing water. Pandora had gauzy sheets of beige muslin hung around the sides for further shading from the sun and to soften the starkness of the little raised shelter, at least until the wisteria and other vines that were newly planted around the sides could grow tall enough to perform the same task. It also provided some privacy to those inside the gazebo as long as the wind wasn't blowing too strongly. There was a double-ended, wide reclining couch with throw pillows inside for sitting and lounging, which only seemed to add to its appearance as some type of idyllic Mediterranean oasis. Psyche always loved sitting there when visiting with her sister.

Keung had been steadily working with the Marshalls' gardening staff to transform the garden into something less formal and rigid to compliment the unfussy air of the temple. There were new plantings of gardenia and hydrangea, and it was obvious where box and privet had been removed. It would probably be a year or two before the garden reached its full potential in appearance. When that happened, it would be pretty and relaxed, and a perfect place for children to play hide-and-seek.

Psyche and Myron walked through the gate in the back wall to the mews, where his curricle was waiting. He untied the reins after he helped Psyche into the high seat, and climbed up himself. Myron left the mews and turned left onto Park Street, heading for Oxford, and then he made a right onto that street. Psyche turned to look at him.

"Where is the ship?" asked Psyche curiously.

"It's at the Surrey where Gregory docks when he brings the *Julia* into town," said Myron calmly, turning to look at her.

"Then why are you going this way? It would be quicker if you took Westminster," said Psyche.

"Would you like to drive?" asked Myron with a chuckle, holding the reins in her direction.

"I'd love to," said Psyche with a cheeky grin, taking the reins from him.

After a brief look of surprise, Myron laughed and relaxed back against the seat. He sometimes forgot his sisters were very capable at whipping up a pair when the mood suited, and he was quite happy to let someone else be responsible for driving. He was tired after his afternoon's activities, and he wouldn't mind the opportunity for a brief nap.

Psyche turned the carriage right at the next intersection to head them toward Piccadilly and in the direction of Westminster Bridge. She was familiar with the way to the Surrey Commercial Docks in Rotherhithe and wouldn't need the exact location of the ship until they neared it. She was sure Myron had intended to take them down Oxford to Holborn and Cheapside to cross at London Bridge, but Psyche always thought it was quicker (and cheaper) to get into Southwark as quickly as possible, which meant Westminster Bridge.

Psyche was surprised Sheerness hadn't chosen a dock further east, like Woolwich, or even Sheerness itself. It would take him a day just to get the ship back to the Channel when he set sail from London. Gregory used Surrey because it was close to Westminster and was one of the safer ones to leave his ship moored at as opposed to directly on the river. That was probably the same reason Sheerness had chosen it. It would take at least two days to go to and from the ship if he had docked in Sheerness. She hadn't thought to ask what kind of ship he had, and Myron hadn't mentioned it. She didn't even know he *had* a ship last year.

She looked at Myron and was about to ask him how long Sheerness had owned the ship, but she saw he was sleeping, his chin propped onto his chest. She smiled affectionately and shook her head. They hadn't even reached the bridge yet. Perhaps it was just as well that she was driving, she thought amusedly. She would wake him up once they reached the dock if he didn't wake up on his own by then.

As Psyche drove through Whitehall, she let her mind wander to Myron and Georgiana. As hard as she tried not to, she found herself becoming filled with worry about the two of them and what was going to happen when Hendon returned from Austria. Georgiana had said at the Derby that she didn't know when that would be but suspected it wouldn't be long.

Surely, they didn't intend to continue the relationship once Hendon returned. That would be reckless. Psyche couldn't see how they would possibly be able to; she knew that even though Hendon obviously—oddly—didn't care for his wife, and more likely because of it, he didn't give her freedom to come and go at her leisure. He often made a point of attending social functions to which she had been invited and he expressly had not simply to make her miserable. He kept a constant accounting of his wife's whereabouts. If he hadn't left the country, the affair between Myron and Georgiana would never have had the opportunity to begin.

When the affair ended, Psyche knew Myron was going to be heartbroken. She *knew* he had to love Georgiana immensely to have embarked on an affair with a married woman. He was too honorable for it to be any other way. She believed Georgiana must feel the same in order to risk the wrath of a dangerous man like Hendon. It was very unfair they couldn't be together.

Then Psyche began to wonder if there was any way they *could* be together. Georgiana could not, or would not, divorce Hendon. It was next to impossible to get one but not out of the question. Psyche didn't believe Georgiana would let concerns about her reputation dissuade her, not if it meant the difference between being happy or being miserable. She didn't need to stay married to Hendon for financial reasons; she was probably wealthier than her husband. It couldn't be a matter of needing his protection; Georgiana needed someone to protect her from *him*. They had no children. Then Psyche remembered Lorelei.

Hendon was her guardian. Georgiana wouldn't leave Hendon without her sister, and that would happen if they divorced because *he* was the man.

There would have to be a way for both sisters to leave together. Psyche was practical enough to know that wasn't likely…at least, not unless something drastic happened. Nothing *legal* could be done. Of course, Psyche didn't let the legality of a solution deter her from considering it, but she did weigh it on just how *illegal* it was.

The quickest way would be for the earl to die. As much as everyone disliked it, Hendon was hale and hardy and unlikely to kick the bucket from natural causes. He was known to have participated in many duels, but he had come through all of them without even a scratch. Psyche could hope someone in Austria would put an end to him, but that, too, didn't seem likely. As much as she (and most everyone else) loathed him, she couldn't condone outright murder. Therefore, his becoming deceased was not the solution.

Having Georgiana and Lorelei "disappear" could be a possibility, but how to accomplish that was the problem. Psyche continued to think about it as she crossed Westminster Bridge into Lambeth. She watched the boats plying up and down the Thames, and a thoughtful frown came over her features. Then her face cleared as the solution came to her. She looked at Myron still sleeping beside her. It would mean talking to him about it. He would be reluctant to do so. It would also involve a sacrifice on her part, but it would be for a worthy cause. She would have to talk to Sheerness, too, but Psyche would wait until she discussed it with her brother before she came to a firm decision. Georgiana would also have to agree, but Psyche believed the marchioness would see the logic and simplicity of it. It would be the perfect solution.

As she neared Surrey Docks, Psyche pulled out her watch. They had made good time, but Myron had slept for an hour; it was time for him to wake up and direct her to the ship. She nudged him in the ribs, and he awoke with a start.

"There already?" he said with a sleepy smile and a stretch.

"You slept for an hour!" chortled Psyche. "Where do I go now?"

Myron looked around them to get his bearings. "Turn down the far side of the quay on East Country Dock."

Psyche did as instructed. The horses shied at the loud noise and busyness of the quay, and Psyche carefully steered them around crews loading and unloading cargo from the ships they passed. Psyche kept her eyes on where they were going, but she was able to see that most of the vessels they passed were small sloops and shallow water crafts. They were about halfway down the dock when Myron had her come to a stop.

Psyche looked at the ship. It had been freshly painted and gleamed with newness. The bottom of the hull had been painted white, the waterline edged in black. It had ornate carving at the stern and at the railing that had been gilded. The stern had a row of four large windows, and the side had three small round ones in an aftercabin. Psyche assumed there were three on the other side as well. The stern and the upper edge of the hull at the gunwale to the railing were painted a rich burgundy.

It was of a good size, bigger than Gregory's ship and not a sloop. Psyche wasn't sure what kind of ship it was. The bow was snubbed rather than prow-shaped. The figurehead was a woman with her arms outstretched in flowing robes, as if she were flying, and gilded like the rest of the carving. Psyche was looking forward to seeing belowdecks.

Even though it was a private craft, there was no less activity taking place around it on the dock and on the deck. The main difference, though, was that the workmen were loading on cured lumber…and not very large amounts of it. Psyche could hear the sounds of hammering and sawing. It became apparent that Sheerness had not been in possession of the ship for very long. She couldn't believe he would be making all of these modifications *now*, not if he had owned the ship for more than a short while.

Myron helped her down from the curricle, and Psyche looked up at the stern of the ship where the name had been carved and painted below the transom in black and gold that stood out clearly from the burgundy. Psyche's eyes grew round in alarm, and she turned to look at her brother. His lips were twitching amusedly at her reaction.

"You can't breathe a word, Sham," she moaned, shaking her head. Myron started laughing. "I *mean* it," she said warningly. She gave him a surprised look. "You knew, didn't you? And you didn't tell me!" Psyche punched him in the arm, and Myron grimaced despite his amusement, rubbing his shoulder gingerly. "How long have you known?"

"Since he bought it in November."

"Sham, don't tell him," pleaded Psyche, clasping her hands to her chest.

"Why not?" asked Myron impishly.

"I just don't want you to tell Sheerness he's named his ship one of my middle names. He'll want to rename it and repaint it."

"How do you know he didn't do it on purpose?" he teased.

"Sham, don't be a clunch. He doesn't *know* my full name," sighed Psyche exasperatedly. "Promise me you won't tell Sheerness."

"Tell me what?" asked the earl mildly at her side.

Psyche had been so anxious about getting Myron to be quiet that she didn't hear the earl join them. He was dressed as she often saw him at his house—no cravat, no coat.

"Nothing," said Psyche, coloring guiltily.

Sheerness raised a doubtful eyebrow and turned to look at Myron expectantly.

"Psyche doesn't like the red, Barneville," said Myron with a grin.

"Myron!" gasped Psyche in outrage.

"Indeed?" said Sheerness, giving her a scowl.

"No. She says it *and* the gold make it look like a floating brothel," said Myron with barely controlled laughter.

"Sham, you lout!" grated Psyche, and she smacked him on the back of his head.

"Ow!" he chortled with a pained grin.

She looked at the earl's disgusted expression and was secretly relieved to see him showing some other emotion for her besides indifference. She looked at him apologetically, her cheeks coloring over her brother's fun at her expense.

"I said no such thing," she averred solemnly, shaking her head.

"Hunh," said Sheerness noncommittally, clasping his hands behind him.

"Yes, you did," continued Myron. "You said all he'd need to do is add some brocade sails, and you'd feel like an abbess in her nunnery."

"You liar!" gasped Psyche. "I would *never!*"

"I'm sorry you find the colors not to your liking, Lady Psyche," said Sheerness coldly, obviously not believing her. "Would you rather it were painted something paler? *Pink* perhaps?" he asked snidely.

It was true Psyche often wore shades of pink and happened to be wearing a walking dress composed mostly of that color at the moment, but she only wore it so often because it suited her coloring and also helped her to be less conspicuous. She would never say it was her favorite color. Her favorite color was actually amethyst purple, but she didn't think he'd want to paint his ship that color either. In any event, she was insulted he believed Myron's taradiddle about a brothel. Apparently, Sheerness was often so dishonest himself he thought everyone else was as well…even her…especially her.

"No, actually, lemon yellow would be grand if you could arrange it," she said tartly, lifting her chin.

"I'm afraid not," said Sheerness flatly through stiff lips.

"Well, enough of this jaw-wagging," said Myron brightly, clapping Sheerness on the shoulder and linking his arm through Psyche's. "Let's see what you've done with your collier."

"This is a coal barge?" asked Psyche in amazement.

She never would have guessed its previous use. Now the shape was familiar. Psyche had seen them often enough in Swansea and Cardiff, but comparatively those were plain. She didn't know if Sheerness had been responsible for directing the modifications himself, but he had to have at least approved them. The ship was not made for speed, but it was perfect as a private vessel meant for exploration. The hull was round-bilged, almost flat-bottomed like a barge, which would make it suitable for shallow rivers and bays, and Psyche suspected it could be beached if necessary. Its rounded shape also made it more roomy belowdecks than might be expected, considering that its size would also make it easy to operate with a smaller crew. He had made an excellent choice, and Psyche was disappointed she would never get to sail anywhere in it, not if Myron, Georgiana, and Sheerness agreed with her plan.

The earl looked at her stormily in response to what he mistook for her dislike of his ship. He clenched his jaw and tightened his hands behind his back. There was no pleasing her! She thought she was perfect, that her ideas were *better*. What irritated him most was that she *was* perfect…apparently. As hard as he had tried, he had yet to find anything imperfect about her, inside or out. The only flaw he had found so far was that she was sometimes dishonest, and even then, her lying wasn't really lying, and still she was *good* at that, too.

She seemed to have no need for him at all, except for the use of his ship, and even that was apparently below her expectations.

"It is not a coal barge," he ground out. "It is a *bark.*"

"As you say," said Psyche diffidently.

She wasn't sure what she had done to earn his ire, but she was becoming more pleased by the minute that he was starting to behave true to form. She determined she was going to make sure it was permanent. She gave Myron's arm an excited squeeze as Sheerness stiffly turned his back to lead them up the gangway aboard the ship. He then turned to look at them again, and Psyche was relieved the gangway had been short but sturdy. It had been rather high above the water's surface.

"Welcome aboard the *Medea*," said Sheerness formally with a slight bow.

Psyche looked around herself pleasantly. Everything was so new and shiny. The deck gleamed, but that wouldn't last long once it actually went somewhere; the salt air would see to that. Most of the activity of the workmen seemed to be focused on the forecastle, and Psyche could feel the deck below her feet shake slightly as workers hammered on the berth deck beneath them. The waist deck was not very large because of the size of the forecastle and the aft deck, and it would be even smaller if Sheerness decided to carry any rowboats or launches. Psyche didn't see any, but she would be surprised if he didn't have one or two by the time he sailed.

"What a very pretty boat," said Psyche amiably.

Myron guffawed with hilarity.

"It's not a *boat;* it's a *ship,*" growled Sheerness.

"Boat, ship—same difference," said Psyche airily.

Psyche was well-aware it was a ship; she just knew her calling it a *boat* would annoy Sheerness. She and her sisters would have been hoisted into the rigging on Gregory's sloop long ago if they hadn't learned the difference. She was quite familiar with watercraft, and she was even capable of performing some of the tasks involved in the running of a ship. Others, especially those involving climbing into the rigging or suspension over the side were beyond her because of her fear of heights. Persephone had no such problem, and neither did the rest of Psyche's sisters. Gregory had never taken them on any of his longer voyages, but all five of them had been known to help crew on their family's trips across from Swansea to Lundy Island on more than one occasion. That was why Myron found her comment so funny.

Sheerness clenched his jaw before he said something unseemly. It appeared she didn't know everything after all, and he wasn't surprised ignorance of nautical terms was her one failure. He gestured with his hand to direct them up a short flight of stairs to the poop deck.

There was not much unusual to see, except for one thing that Psyche found fascinating. Instead of having an open grill to let in light and air to the deck below, there was a leaded glass skylight. It was very ornate with intricate sections and geometric patterns. The sill was made of wood and rose about six inches from the sole of the deck. The window itself was pyramidal in shape with four edges slanting inward to its peak. It was rectangular, and the longer sides were designed to be raised for air circulation in fair weather and lowered in foul. Psyche briefly looked down through the glass to the deck below and could see a beautiful wooden table and chairs. Her only concern was what would happen to the window should something fall on it.

"How beautiful," she sighed. She looked at Sheerness curiously. "Aren't you worried someone might fall through?"

Sheerness shook his head. "No. The glass is inlaid in wrought iron."

He closed one of the sides, and Psyche watched in amazement as he easily walked onto it. The framework didn't budge. Then, to Psyche's alarm, he grabbed her hand and pulled her onto it with him. She should have had every confidence she was perfectly safe, but she knew from her brief look through the skylight how high she was. If the glass or frame broke…. To Sheerness's surprise, Psyche clung to him anxiously and paled.

"Honestly, it's perfectly safe," he said mildly, and he bounced at his knees a few times to demonstrate it further.

"Mm-hmm," agreed Psyche weakly. She looked at Myron and held out her hand for him to help her down, which he promptly did.

Sheerness stepped down himself with a puzzled expression, and they strolled around the edge of the deck before taking another short set of steps back to the waist deck. He took them to a set of steps that led into the after cabins below the poop deck.

This part of the ship appeared to be finished. After taking just a few steps down a short hall, they entered the room Psyche had seen through the skylight. It was the officers' mess, if Sheerness intended to have officers. She suspected this was where she and Myron would dine, too. The table was big enough to seat eight, and the chairs were carved and cushioned. There was a beautiful, large buffet and hutch made of tiger maple and cherry against one wall that held china and glassware…probably the silverware as well. There were several doors leading off the room, and Psyche could see through the ones that were open that some of the rooms were for the officers, again, if Sheerness was going to have any. The skylight made the room very bright, which was difficult to accomplish belowdecks on a ship, and it made the room seem much larger.

"These cabins are for the surgeon, ship's master, and the first and second mates," explained Sheerness, pointing to some of the open doors.

"Oh, you've managed to find a surgeon, then?" asked Myron with surprise.

"No, not one I think will be adequate," said Sheerness bluntly. "I don't need someone capable of performing an amputation in two minutes or less, but one able to tend to most of the common ills would be nice."

"I might know of one for you. He's not a Navy surgeon, but he will be up to the task."

"Who?"

"Dr. Simon Felton. He's from up at Lickey End. I don't know how he is with cuts, and while I agree you won't need one, he could probably do an amputation if necessary, too. I can guarantee he's excellent at setting bones."

"That's right! He's the one who set your leg last year, isn't he?" asked Psyche as she recognized the name. "He was a nice man. I can't believe he traveled with you all the way back to London to make sure your leg stayed sound. Some of them are just happy to have your copper in their pockets."

"Hmm," said Sheerness contemplatively. "Do you think he can handle being at sea?"

"I don't see why not. I'll send him a letter of enquiry, maybe have him come up to meet with you before the end of the month?"

"Couldn't hurt," said Sheerness agreeably. "I just don't want to sail without one."

"When will we be leaving?" asked Psyche curiously.

"The first Saturday after Parliament dismisses, provided the weather is favorable," said Sheerness mildly.

"How long will we be gone?" asked Psyche, her brow furrowing thoughtfully as she performed some mental calculations.

"As long as it takes," said Sheerness flatly.

"For what?" asked Psyche blankly.

"To find what we need," said Sheerness impatiently.

"Oh," said Psyche dully. That probably meant she would *not* be home for Christmas. "And what is it that we are needing?"

"Whatever we can find that is useful," said Sheerness patiently, as if explaining to a child.

Psyche blinked. That didn't really narrow down the length of time they would be gone or exactly what it was he hoped to accomplish. The usefulness of something was subjective.... Cravats, for example. Men couldn't seem to live without them, while Psyche thought they were a waste of perfectly good linen. Did he want to find more examples of hieroglyphs? Did he want to find more statues? Jewelry? Mummies? Psyche personally hoped to find things that would help her to learn more about the people who created all these objects Sheerness seemed intent on collecting. To Psyche, simply collecting objects without taking their history, too, made them worthless. That was one of the things she and the earl had argued incessantly over the previous year. To her, finding just *one* item of historical significance would accomplish what she was sure the earl would think filling the hold to capacity would take.

"Can we see the rest of your ship?" she asked quietly, deciding it would be best for her to change the subject before an argument ensued. She wanted him to talk to her, but she didn't want bickering.

"Of course," said Sheerness, his forehead furrowed again in puzzlement. She didn't seem to be quite like herself, other than her dislike of his ship.

He led them through a door to the right of the buffet into a small room with three more doors opening off it. The room would have been very dark if not for the oil lamp fixture on one wall. The paneled walls were painted white, as they had been in the dining room, which helped to further dispel the gloom.

Sheerness opened the door of the room to the left, and they entered a long rectangular cabin...well, long comparatively speaking. The end of the room near the window was taken up by a bunk. It was larger than a usual ship bunk, almost the size of a regular bed, and the mattress was stuffed with feathers. The frame was raised, and the space underneath was full of drawers for belongings. There was also a small writing desk, but there was no other furniture. The rest of the room would be taken up by the occupant's trunk…or trunks. It was almost spacious without those, but even with them it wouldn't be cramped. There were two oil lamps attached to the walls, and the walls were, again, painted white.

"This will be Myron's cabin," said Sheerness. He looked at his friend. "If there's anything else you think you'd like to have, let me know."

"This will be fine, I'm sure," said Myron with a grin. "I don't expect to be spending much time in here."

Sheerness escorted them out and closed the door. He then opened the one to the portside of the ship. This cabin wasn't quite as long as Myron's, but it was no less roomy and actually seemed to be bigger. It contained the same furnishings and fixtures, but Psyche thought the bunk was slightly wider, the mattress just the least bit fluffier. There were also a few extra blankets folded at the end of the bunk, and there was a small rug on the floor.

"This will be your room, Lady Psyche," said Sheerness mildly. "Does it meet with your approval?"

Psyche was almost reluctant to ask because it *was* a very nice cabin, but she did have one request. If he refused, she would make do, but he had asked.

"Would it be possible to get a washstand and a decent-sized mirror?" she asked hesitantly.

"I believe that can be arranged," said Sheerness agreeably.

"Thank you," said Psyche with a relieved smile. It would be one less thing she would have to bring with her.

"Anything else? A chair? A settee? Pink brocade wallpaper?" he teased.

Psyche colored. "No, thank you," she said evenly. "So, what does your cabin look like?" she asked brightly, changing the subject.

Myron and Sheerness both chuckled at her embarrassment over having her vanity exposed. Sheerness took them to the final door in the alcove and opened it for them to enter ahead of him. Psyche was filled with envy.

The room was large enough to easily be as big as Psyche's, Myron's, the alcove, and part of the dining room combined. The walls were paneled in oak of a light stain, but it wasn't gloomy because of the bank of windows at the stern and the two round windows on the port and starboard sides. It had a small, copper-enclosed, raised fireplace in a small nook just to the left of the door with a comfortable-looking wingbacked chair placed near it. The floor was covered by rugs, a large one of Turkish design in particular that Psyche thought was exquisite. Given the size of the room, there were several brass oil lamps on the walls. He had a large desk on the same wall as the fireplace and a bookcase in the wall above it. There was a small, drawered commode on the starboard wall, centered beneath the windows, with decanters sitting on top of it. On the port wall, there was a chest of drawers of a similar size.

On the corners of the wall with the doorway, there were two built-in, floor-to-ceiling cabinets. One had a solid wood door, possibly a closet. The other, however, had a glass-fronted door and looked peculiar. Psyche curiously walked closer. She opened the door and looked inside from the top to the bottom, noting that it was lined with tin on all the interior surfaces except for the glass in the door. There were handles and a faucet, and Psyche's eyes rounded in surprise. She turned to look at Sheerness.

"You have a *shower-bath?*" she said in disbelief.

"Myron suggested it, and I have to agree it's an excellent addition," said Sheerness, giving Myron a grin. "It will be supplied with heated seawater, but it *will* be a hot bath...much better than a bucket on deck. We'll arrange something should you wish to use it, Lady Psyche."

"And what about the crew?" asked Psyche curiously.

"What about them?" asked Sheerness blankly.

"Will they be using it, too, or have you made one for them elsewhere?"

"No, and no," said Sheerness calmly. He clasped his hands behind him and rocked on his feet. "I don't expect they'll require a shower...or want one."

"Have you asked them?" she asked tartly.

"No, but they *are* sailors."

"And that makes them less desirous of being clean how?"

"They can use a bucket on deck, like most usually do."

"My arse on a bandbox!" said Psyche hotly. "If that's how you'll be expecting *them* to get clean, then *I* will do the same."

"Psyche," sighed Myron soothingly.

Psyche looked at him. "No," she said agitatedly, shaking her head. "Maybe there are some of them who don't feel the need for bathing, and that's their choice, but the ones who do should have no less acceptable facilities for doing so than I do." She looked at Sheerness, her chin lifted determinedly. "Surely you can find a place? Even on the deck would be better than not having one at all. I'd be willing to bet if you had one, it would be used...often enough to make it worth the effort and expense," she finished reasonably.

"I'll consider it," said Sheerness calmly.

"But—" began Psyche.

"I said I'll consider it," restated Sheerness finally.

Psyche nodded and decided to leave it be. It wasn't likely she would see the outcome of his *consideration* in any event, but she hoped he took her suggestion. Her family enjoyed bathing more than most people, but they weren't alone in that, not even among the lower classes. A bucket of cold water on the deck just was not acceptable. If he didn't give the crew a shower-bath...and if she did get to make the journey, she *would* follow through on her threat to bathe the same way they did.

Psyche finished her examination of the final piece of furniture in the room: his bed. The bunks for her and Myron were Spartan by comparison. She was sure their beds were more luxuriant than those of the rest of the crew, so the captain's bed would probably seem decadent. It was built in a fashion similar to a typical four-poster, but only in that it had four posts, one at each corner, reaching all the way—and fastened—to the ceiling. One long edge abutted the stern of the ship, centered on the windows. The two posts on that side were fairly plain. The short edges had high panels divided into three sections, with ornate carving in the outside center of each, framed by beaded edging.

The posts and top of the frame at the ceiling on the front-facing side of the bed were exquisitely carved in a pattern matching the side panels, with lots of tracery that made the carving almost seem like vines twining around the posts down to the floor. It looked Indian in origin, and Psyche didn't think it had started out as part of a bed. There were two short panels at the front of the bed to either end, slightly less in height than those on the short edges but similarly carved, which would prevent the sleeper from rolling out in rough weather. Psyche couldn't tell which end was the head or the foot because the pillows (and there were lots of them in different shapes and sizes) were lined up along the back edge beneath the windows.

Along the bottom beneath the mattress and support frame, there were drawers for storage. The wood of the bed was of two different types, one for the frame and another for the intricate carving on the front panel (which made Psyche suspect even more that it hadn't started out as part of a bed). Both were a shade or two darker than the walls, and Psyche thought it might be made of mahogany and teak. The bed was large for one found on a ship, even larger than her bed at home. It would easily be big enough for two people...maybe more. Psyche was tempted to climb onto it to find out if it was as comfortable as it looked, but that might be unseemly, even with Myron present.

Sheerness led them out of his room and gave them a brief tour of the rest of the ship. Psyche discovered the work in the forecastle was for creating bunks for the crew...at least, some of the crew. There would only be enough room for about half of them. To her surprise, she found they would have actual bunks with straw mattresses rather than hammocks. The bunks were set two high, with drawers for storage under the bottom one in each set for stowing possessions, which seemed to be a typical and practical feature Sheerness had used for all the beds on the ship. There was railing and webbing to keep them snug while they slept, even in a storm, and Psyche was happy to see he had taken the comfort of his crew into consideration. Now, if he would just find a way for them to take a decent, occasional bath, it would be excellent.

There were sleeping quarters at the stern end of the berth deck to accommodate more of the crew. At the bow were the quarters for the bosun, ship's carpenter, and gunner, as well as a large cabin with more bunks for the crew. Near this end of the ship was the large hearth that would be used to prepare the meals on the ship. It was of quite impressive size and design. Midships was the mess for the crew and the large hatch covered by a grill that would open into the hold. That was also where any livestock might be kept for feeding the sailors and the officers.

Psyche had thought the shape of the hull would make for plenty of room, and she was pleased to see she hadn't been wrong. Sheerness would have no trouble finding sailors ready to hire on, even if he didn't pay as much as others, simply because the quarters for the crew were so spacious and well-appointed. Even Gregory's crew conditions were not this grand, and her brother's were better than most. Once Sheerness finished giving them their tour and taken them back to the waist deck, Psyche turned to look at him.

"Where is your crew?" she asked curiously.

"I've not completed hiring them yet," said Sheerness calmly. "I've hired the officers—the ship's master and first and second mate, the bosun, the ship's carpenter—obviously, the gunner, and the cook. I am hoping I will have my surgeon—or physician—by the end of the month. Of the actual working men of the crew, I've only taken on about half. Why do you ask?"

"I was just wondering, that's all." It was the truth. "I think you have a very lovely ship, Lord Sheerness. Thank you for showing it to me."

Sheerness looked at her in surprise. She seemed sincere, but then she had been able to tell him things before that seemed completely honest which he discovered later were not, or at least, he *thought* were not. Still, his learning of her penchant for fibbing had been recent. Last year she had been consistently, bluntly, honest. She had also told him she was incapable of lying. He doubted that and suspected she was quite capable of being dishonest when the need arose. Myron had said she thought the ship was gaudy, but Psyche had heatedly denied it. This time, Sheerness decided to take her compliment on its appearance.

"You're most welcome, Lady Psyche," he finally replied evenly.

"We'll be seeing you at the Bardseys' tomorrow evening, yes?" asked Myron.

"I do intend to be there," said Sheerness noncommittally.

Psyche tried to control the panic that wanted to take hold, and she realized Pandora had tricked her into coming because Sheerness would be there. Psyche couldn't understand why her twin consistently tried to force the two of them together. That the earl seemed to be agreeable to it as well, even after Psyche had begged him to leave her alone, was bothersome. She reluctantly admitted that she would rather have him behaving in his usual argumentative manner than with his impersonal politeness of the past week or so, but she didn't trust him...not any further than she could throw him, which wasn't likely to be far. Psyche decided if there was going to be any distance kept between them, it would have to be up to her, so she would have to do her best to be polite, make sure they weren't left *alone* together, and keep him talking to her without arguing. It was going to be a difficult task, but she would only have to perform it until he left for Greece and Egypt...without her.

Chapter Nine

Psyche was, for some reason, looking forward to dinner at Pandora's with dread. It was an odd sensation for her to have for something that involved her twin, but it was probably because Pandora had manipulated her into going to another social function where Sheerness would be present. The entire thing was untenable, and Psyche decided if she were given the opportunity that evening to be alone with her sister, she was going to set her straight on exactly what her feelings were for Sheerness. Perhaps then Pandora would not be so keen on putting them together.

It was undeniable Psyche found him physically attractive, and these days every time she saw him caused a peculiar flutter to begin in her stomach. There was also, however, a warning bell that would begin clanging in her ears in counterpoint to the pleasant flutteries in her midsection that would make her feel something akin to the dizziness caused by her fear of heights. One or the other sensation had to cease. Until she was able to determine what would need to be done to affect that, Psyche decided the easiest way to not cause either was to avoid him as much as possible. That task was not so easy. Their families had close ties socially (Lady Sheerness was even Cosmo and Christopher's godmother), and his sister was her best friend…aside from her own sisters. She couldn't avoid him completely without avoiding Amalie and the Yeardley children, and Psyche wouldn't do that.

She had not had the chance yet to discuss her plan with Myron. She could have when they rode home from seeing the *Medea* the previous day, but she had wanted to think about it herself a little further and decide if it were the right thing to do. She wanted to find any suitable arguments to that effect for when she discussed it with her brother, Georgiana and Sheerness. Myron had been absent from the house that afternoon, and she had been getting dressed to go to dinner at Pandora's by the time he returned. Discussing it with the three of them at the dinner party wouldn't be appropriate. Aside from that, she wanted to talk to her brother alone before breathing a word of it to the other two.

Psyche had chosen a simple dress for dinner. Since Sheerness would be there, she didn't want to wear anything that he might find tempting. It was made of pale green mull with long, gathered sleeves, slightly puffed shoulders and ruffled at the cuffs. The bodice was covered in lace and went all the way to her neck with a ruffed collar. There was a subdued amount of embroidery at the edge of the skirt in a darker green, and a narrow satin ribbon of matching green bowed at the front where the bodice met the top edge of the skirt. It revealed as little as possible. Psyche thought it was perfect. Chrissoula wasted no time telling Psyche that it made her look like a drudge…a very pretty drudge. Psyche ignored her with an unconcerned smile. She would not let her maid cow her into wearing something more stimulating for Sheerness.

She walked down the stairs to meet Myron, and surprisingly, she was on time. Psyche wore a dark green velvet cloak because it started raining shortly before sunset, and it had yet to cease. With the rain came a chill breeze Psyche knew would blow straight through the thin material of her gown. Myron escorted her down the front steps to the waiting carriage, and Psyche hated that their driver, Ivan, was going to get wet. She was sure Pandora's stable master would have something available to warm him and dry him out when they got there. She hoped the rain would stop by the end of the evening so he wouldn't have to drive back home in it. Myron took the seat behind the driver and grinned at Psyche as he took off his beaver hat and shook the water off of it onto the floor of the coach.

"Lovely weather," he said dryly.

"It *is* England," said Psyche with a chuckle. "It will be much drier in Greece and Egypt."

"Not for long. In winter, they'll have plenty of this wet stuff, too."

"True." Psyche rubbed her arms to smooth away the chill that had managed to drift through her clothes to her skin. "Still, going to another country is such a wonderful thing."

"And you know that from personal experience?" teased Myron.

"Well, *you* would," shot Psyche with a grin of her own. "It must be grand to go somewhere else, where no one knows you."

"It can have its benefits," agreed Myron with a shrug.

"I suppose if one wanted to, one could go to another country and pretend to be someone *completely* different from who one really was."

Myron's eyebrow shot up. "I suppose," he said slowly.

"Well, I imagine an entire group of people could go somewhere else and pretend to be different from who they really were quite easily, provided they had the resources to do so and it was far enough away from where they left so no one would know their true identities. It would be a great way to escape from one's past…to start over."

Myron frowned. "Psyche, are you trying to tell me something? Have you done something you shouldn't?"

Psyche's eyes rounded. "Oh, no, Myron! I haven't done anything, I swear." Her face grew pensive. "I was just thinking maybe *you* have."

"And what does that mean?" he asked perplexedly.

"Myron, I *know* about you and Georgiana," said Psyche softly. "Don't try to tell me I'm imagining things, either."

Myron looked at her angrily. "You *are* imagining things," he said tightly.

"Myron, if you want to continue pretending there's nothing between the two of you, I understand that, but you know as well as I do that when Hendon returns it would be foolish to let it continue."

"There is *nothing* between Georgiana and I," he stated exasperatedly. "Why would you even think that?"

Psyche looked at him incredulously. For a moment, she almost thought she *had* been mistaken, but she could just *feel* she was not.

"I've seen the way the two of you behave toward each other when you're together in public. It's very subtle, so it would take someone who knows you as well as I do, as well as your family does, to see it. I know Pandora knows about it, too, and that she's been helping the two of you."

"Psyche, I say again, there is *nothing* there," said Myron plainly, his expression impassive.

"Well, in that case, what I'm about to say is going to be utterly ridiculous, but I'm going to say it anyhow," said Psyche firmly. "What if, when you went to Greece and Egypt with Sheerness, you took Georgiana and Lorelei instead of me and never come back?"

"What?" asked Myron in disbelief.

"I understand why Georgiana can't divorce Hendon. She would never leave her sister with a monster like him. It would be dangerous for you to continue what you're doing when he comes back from Austria, and you know as well as I do that even if you don't, he's going to keep on until he kills her. He is not so sickly that he will die and leave her in peace. The best way for the two of you to be together and keep Lorelei safe is to go somewhere far away and never come back…at least until Hendon is no longer a problem somehow."

"You're not serious," said Myron weakly.

"I am," said Psyche softly. "The means is already there in the *Medea*. You and she both have enough money you would never want for anything no matter where you were, and if no one knows who you are, then there is no one to condemn it. In less than two months you could be on your way to freedom and happiness…together."

"But you really want to go," said Myron carefully.

"Yes," said Psyche with a sigh, "I do, but Greece and Egypt will always be there. Sooner or later, I *will* go. Hendon will be coming back any time now; we all know that, and you *need* to get Georgiana and Lorelei away from him."

Myron reached across the carriage with a fond smile to take her hands in his and give them an affectionate squeeze.

"I'm very lucky to have such a clever sister," he said softly.

Psyche blushed at the compliment and sighed. "Yes, well, you still have to convince Sheerness to go along with it."

Myron shrugged. "That won't be a problem. He owes me a favor."

Psyche raised an eyebrow inquisitively. "Really? For what?"

Myron grinned impishly. "I'm not going to tell you."

"Hunh," said Psyche diffidently, and she relaxed back against the cushions with her arms folded in front of her thoughtfully.

It was only a few short minutes before they reached Bardsey House on Upper Grosvenor. The rain had still not lessened, and Psyche and Myron hurried for the stoop to knock on the door as soon as Ivan opened the door of the carriage. Waldon opened the door for them and took their things to hand to a footman standing nearby. He escorted them to the formal sitting room and opened the door.

Pandora and Islington were talking with Dorian and Selena, who were driven over by Jim. Psyche personally would have preferred the four of them had ridden together and saved at least one of their coachmen from a drowning in the downpour, but Dorian wanted to be early. Psyche had no idea *why* he wanted to be there before anyone else arrived, but it didn't matter, except for the rain. Besides, the ride over alone with Myron had given her a chance to talk with him about her plan.

Pandora was sitting on the settee, her feet propped up on a low stool. Psyche suspected that if they had no company, her twin would have reclined across the entire piece of furniture and propped her feet in her husband's lap. She looked miserable as her stomach grew even heavier. Her back constantly ached, and she was not sleeping as well as she used to. Psyche couldn't believe Pandora still insisted she was having only one baby. Psyche remembered how big their mother was when she gave birth to Cosmo and Christopher. Pandora actually looked bigger than that. Psyche chuckled at the sight she made.

"Are you going to need a litter to carry you to the dining room?" she asked amusedly.

Pandora looked at her tartly. "No, I have three burly men here to carry me," she said sarcastically.

"I don't think my back would survive," teased Dorian.

"Two, then. I won't have any trouble waddling down the hall to the dining room, though. Putting on the feedbag is worth any effort," she said amusedly.

"Where's everyone else, then?" asked Myron curiously. "I didn't think we were that early, especially not where Psyche's concerned."

"Sham, I was not late this time," said Psyche exasperatedly. "If you'll look at the clock, you will see it is only fifteen past."

"Is it really?" said Pandora in mock surprise. "How did you manage it?"

"I have no earthly, and you may want to mark the occasion somewhere because it's not likely to happen again," Psyche chortled.

"We're only waiting on Sheerness and Georgiana," said Pandora after a brief chuckle. "Theo, will you go check with Mrs. Hensley for me? I just don't think I can walk right now."

"Absolutely," he said agreeably, watching the pained expression that crossed her face as she shifted her position slightly. He left the room to go check with the cook.

Psyche went to sit beside her sister on the settee. "Pan, why are you even having this supper?" she asked with a concerned expression.

"Because today is Georgiana's birthday," said Pandora mildly, "and I thought we should help her celebrate it."

"Oh," said Psyche with surprise. "I didn't know, but I agree." She grinned for a moment, but then her eyes widened in alarm. "Why didn't you let me know? I haven't gotten her anything!"

"Yes, you have," said Myron with a grin. Pandora looked at him curiously.

The door was opened by Waldon for the arrival of Sheerness. He entered the room with his usual, graceful saunter and went to Pandora to kiss her hand.

"Good evening, Lady Bardsey. I apologize for my tardiness," he said with a slight smile.

Pandora gave him a pretended look of outrage. "Just don't let it happen again. It's never a good thing to come between a pregnant woman and her food," she said, her lips twitching.

He laughed with hilarity and bowed slightly. "I am truly chastened." He kissed Selena's hand. "Lady Glamorgan."

"Lord Sheerness," said Selena with a slight smile.

He then kissed Psyche's hand, and she looked at him neutrally. His face was no more expressive than hers, but she thought she detected a slight amusement at the corners of his eyes due to what she was wearing.

"Lady Psyche," he said evenly.

"Lord Sheerness," she replied in the same tone.

He surprised her when he sat down beside her on the settee. The piece of furniture wasn't very large, and she found that his thigh touched hers when he did so. She could have moved a little closer to Pandora to put more distance between them, but she couldn't do so without drawing attention to the matter. It didn't bother her overly much that they were touching…at least, as long as she didn't think about it. Psyche found it difficult not to.

Islington soon returned to give Pandora the status of supper from Mrs. Hensley. The cook thought it would be ready by eight. That would give Georgiana plenty of time to arrive. In the meantime, the five of them talked about idle things like the weather and rowing. For a brief time, the men started to talk about fly-fishing in Yorkshire, but Pandora quickly steered them away from the topic. Discussion of fishing of any type tended to make her lose her appetite, and she had not eaten fish (except for the lampreys she had craved earlier in her pregnancy) since the previous summer. By fifteen minutes until eight, however, the conversation began to dwindle, and the guests began to grow more introspect. When Waldon came to announce that supper was served precisely at eight, Georgiana had still not arrived.

Everyone except Sheerness knew the purpose of the party, and to find the guest of honor had not arrived was a matter of concern. It was even more worrisome for those who knew of the relationship between Georgiana and Myron. Pandora did her best to enliven everyone, but unease about the marchioness settled in and began to grow as the minutes passed. Pandora only waited until five after before she decided they would have to go into supper and hope Georgiana would arrive soon. She walked down the hall to the dining room with her arms linked through those of her husband and Myron, who would have gone in with Georgiana had she been there.

Sheerness had a thoughtful frown as he escorted Psyche to the dining room. He had begun to notice the lag in conversation and the preoccupation of the other guests, particularly of Psyche, who continued to exchange uncertain glances with her sister and Myron. He wasn't sure what the cause of the unease was, other than that Lady Morecambe had not arrived without a word of regret, but the three of them, and Lord Bardsey as well, seemed to find it extremely troubling. Their concern was beginning to settle onto him, Dorian and Selena, and the supper party was starting to feel less like a party and more like a funeral. Sheerness didn't like that.

The first thing Psyche did when she sat down to the table and removed her gloves to eat was begin to chew on the side of her thumb nervously. It was bad manners, but it was an unconscious habit she often didn't realize she was doing until something, or someone, brought it to her attention. Usually, she realized she was doing it, or starting to do it, when she had on gloves. If her hands were uncovered, there was nothing to make her notice. She had lost her appetite as her anxiety for Georgiana began to grow, and the cucumber soup that was placed in front of her smelled delicious but untempting.

Sheerness surprised her when he reached over and gently moved her hand away from her mouth. She looked at him, and he gave her a slight incline of his head toward her bowl. She smiled at him slightly and picked up her spoon, but she wasn't sure she could eat. It was then that she realized he was left-handed as he continued to hold her hand in his right one under the edge of the table as he picked up his own silverware and began to eat the soup. He gave her hand an encouraging squeeze, and Psyche finally lifted the spoon to her mouth. It was tasty soup, but now in addition to her worry over Georgiana, she had to contend with the fluttery feeling his holding her hand created.

Conversation was subdued, but it wasn't silent. There was no laughter though. Psyche was glad Pandora and Islington didn't have a clock in the room because everyone would have continually looked at it. The soup was taken away and the next course brought in. Psyche was pleased she had managed to eat most of her soup despite the topsy-turvy sensations in her stomach.

The next dish was braised ham with macaroni casserole and greens with mashed turnips. Psyche was able to do a fair amount of justice in disposing of the food on her plate, especially once Sheerness had to use both of his hands to eat his own food. Mrs. Hensley was an excellent cook (although Psyche thought their own, Mrs. O'Flaherty, was better), and Psyche couldn't help but tuck into the fare placed before her. Psyche needed to eat something because she had drank three glasses of wine with the first course, and the Moselle had started to go to her head. The wine with this course was a nice Welsh white that she suspected had come from the vineyard at Wilderland, and Psyche could feel her ears starting to ring.

At one point, Psyche realized she had not been talking to Sheerness or Myron, who was seated on her other side, and decided she should at least *try* to have a conversation.

"Lord Sheerness, I've asked Myron already, but I thought I would also ask you: do you have anywhere particular in mind that you plan to go in Greece?"

"I have a few thoughts but nowhere specific yet. Why? Do you?"

He was relieved to see her attention was focused on something other than Georgiana or her food, even if the topic she had chosen was not one he thought they would be able to discuss without arguing. He knew as well as she did that their goals for going to Greece were not the same.

"Well, I thought Thessaloniki would be a good place to start or at least go to at some point," said Psyche calmly. "Where have you been before?"

"I've not," said Sheerness casually as he finished a bite of his food.

"You've not what?" asked Psyche blankly, drinking more of her wine. It really was delicious.

"I've not been before."

Psyche looked at him dumbstruck. "You've never been to Greece before?" she gasped.

"No," he said flatly, drinking some of his own wine.

"But…you…oh, that's not fair," stammered Psyche, growing flustered.

"What's not fair?" he asked with a slight smile at her speechlessness.

Psyche was furious. All last Season and this, he had treated her as if she didn't know anything and that her opinion on antiquities didn't matter because *she* had never been to Greece or Egypt, when the entire time, *he* hadn't been either! It was unfair, and it made her angry he had made her feel the way he had and talked to her the way he had, belittled and bullied and bothered her in the superior way he had. It was mean, and she was so upset she was ready to punch him. She couldn't do that, and she also couldn't tell him exactly what she thought either…at least, not at the dinner table.

"Lord Sheerness," she said quietly, "you are a hypocritical prig." That fairly well summed up everything she was seething to tell him.

"I beg your pardon?" he asked in shock.

"Psyche," said Myron in quiet warning, as he had been listening to their conversation.

She turned to look at her brother. "Tell me I'm wrong," she said heatedly.

He simply lifted his glass to his lips and swallowed to hide his amusement. He knew this was going to happen eventually, and he had warned Barneville it was going to. Psyche detested injustice and thought everything should be *fair*. His friend had not been fair, and he should have told Psyche the truth a long time ago. Barneville had been unnecessarily mean to her on the subject of antiquities despite everything he had been told, and Myron had told him that he was playing with fire. Myron hoped he would be able to keep her temper in check, but if he couldn't, they were—at least—with family. He leaned past her to look at his friend with a slight smile.

"She does have a point," he said mildly, his lips twitching.

Psyche turned to look at Sheerness. "Hah!" she hooted.

She was preparing to say more when the door opened. Waldon moved, and Georgiana slowly walked into the room. She was very pale, and her eyes were unfocused. All the men stood as she came in, and she gave them a faint smile. Psyche looked at her with concern. She didn't seem to be herself, and Psyche thought her step was unsteady. Georgiana looked at Pandora and Islington.

"I'm terribly sorry to be late," she said quietly, and before anyone had a chance to prevent it, she collapsed to the floor in a faint.

"Oh, my giddy aunt!" squeaked Psyche in alarm.

There was a rush as everyone stood up from the table to go to her. Myron was the first to her side with Islington not far behind. He knelt down and put a hand to her neck to check for her pulse. On closer inspection, they were able to see that at least some of her paleness had been caused by the heavy coating of white powder she had used. One of her eyes was blackened, and there was a cut in her lower lip. It was also easy to see the unmistakable handprint bruising on her throat. It appeared Hendon had returned.

Once Pandora looked down at Georgiana over her husband's shoulder and saw her condition, she looked at Waldon, who was still standing at the door, his face impassive.

"Go and fetch Keung, please, Waldon. Quickly," she said urgently.

"Yes, mum," he said softly. He turned and went to do as she asked, leaving the door open.

"Son of a bitch! I'll kill him!" roared Myron furiously, standing up in preparation to leave.

"Don't you go anywhere!" said Psyche and Pandora together, and Psyche put her hand on his arm to restrain him.

Islington continued to gently probe Georgiana for other injuries, his forehead wrinkled with concern.

"Let's get her onto a couch," said Islington quietly as he lifted Georgiana's limp form from the floor and started down the hallway to the sitting room.

Everyone followed after him silently, and Psyche kept a firm grip on Myron's arm. Islington placed Georgiana on the settee and sat on the edge of it as he continued his examination. Pandora handed him a napkin she'd dampened with water in the dining room, and he took it from her and placed it on Georgiana's forehead. Psyche watched with relief as the moisture and coldness of the compress began to revive her somewhat. Islington turned to see Keung enter carrying a small wooden box and noticed everyone had followed him into the room.

"I'm sorry, but all of you except Pandora and Keung need to leave," he said gravely.

"I'm not going," said Myron flatly, his jaw set.

"Come on," said Psyche, and she pulled at his arm toward the door as everyone else turned to leave.

He wouldn't budge. Psyche was very concerned about Georgiana as well, but Islington and Keung needed to have some privacy with their patient. Myron set his jaw determinedly and gave Psyche a glare. She rolled her eyes and shook her head. Sighing resignedly, she shifted the grip she held on his wrist and applied pressure. Myron winced, and Psyche was able to make him leave the room. Just as they reached the door, she turned to look at Pandora.

"We'll be in the other sitting room," she said calmly, and she gave Myron's arm another tug to make him follow her as she closed the door.

Sheerness curiously watched the way Psyche held Myron's wrist. His friend was not willingly doing what she said, but there was something about the grip she had that seemed to leave him little choice. Whatever she was doing, it didn't appear to require much effort on her part. Once they were to the other room with the door closed, she let him go, and Myron rubbed his wrist gingerly with a sullen expression. She turned to look at Sheerness.

"Do *not* let him leave this room," she said flatly.

Psyche walked over to a nearby sideboard with several different bottles of alcohol placed on top of it. She retrieved a glass from the cabinet at the front and lifted one of the bottles from its place to fill the glass. She walked over to Myron and handed it to him.

"Sit down and drink that," she ordered. He looked as if he were about to refuse, but she raised a warning eyebrow and he did as he was told. She turned to look at her brother and sister-in-law and Sheerness, who had placed himself in front of the door. "Would any of you care for a drink?"

"I'll have a whisky," said Dorian from where he sat by his wife on the couch, rubbing her shoulder soothingly.

"Madeira, please," said Selena, and she was slightly pale at the night's turn of events. Psyche wondered if the girl could use something stronger.

Psyche looked at Sheerness. "And what about you?"

"Brandy."

Psyche nodded and went back to the sideboard. She poured the whisky and Madeira and took the drinks to Dorian and Selena. She went back to the sideboard to pour two glasses of brandy and took one of them to Sheerness. She then went to sit beside Myron on the settee with her own glass. She linked her arm through his and gave it a comforting squeeze before resting her head on the side of his shoulder. Myron leaned his head on top of hers, his expression morose. Once it appeared Myron wasn't going to attempt to leave, Sheerness took a seat in a wingchair beside the fireplace near the settee where his friend and Psyche were sitting.

The five of them sat in silence for what seemed like an eternity. They couldn't hear any sound from the rest of the house, although Psyche was sure the staff was clearing away what was left of their dinner. She hoped Mrs. Hensley wasn't too terribly put out over half of her hard work going to waste. It was doubtful any of them would be returning to their meal. Psyche *had* regained her appetite, but it was now completely gone.

She eventually linked her fingers with Myron's and gave his hand a squeeze. She could tell he was worried about Georgiana, and it was also obvious he was enraged over Hendon. But her brother was reasonable, and if given enough time, Psyche knew he would calm down and become more rational. She could already see that his concern for his lover was greater than what he felt for her husband at the moment. Psyche hoped it stayed that way.

It was a certainty Hendon was responsible for Georgiana's condition. No one else would ever think to be so cruel to such a wonderful person. They had all known the earl would be returning, but they had unfortunately assumed the time would be further away. Psyche was curious what Hendon had used as his excuse to abuse his wife this time. She could only hope he didn't know about Georgiana's affair with Myron. Psyche didn't see how he could know...unless he had been back in London far longer than just that day.

Psyche didn't think any of them would be able to see Georgiana once she regained consciousness, except Myron. Psyche didn't *want* to know what Hendon had done to her friend. The things she imagined made her queasy. She hoped Georgiana didn't tell Myron everything. He had only started to calm down; knowing the details would be likely to rile him again. That would not be the wisest thing.

Myron was usually very even-tempered, but he had come very close to calling Hendon out the previous year for involvement in the murder of one of his friends. The only thing that had prevented it was Hendon's leaving the country while Myron's leg was still healing. Pandora said she had never seen their brother so enraged as when he found out Hendon had killed the Marquess of Tarlborough. Psyche could only base her feelings on Pandora's description, but Psyche thought he was angrier this time, and she couldn't blame him.

She still thought Myron taking Georgiana and Lorelei out of the country was the best solution. Getting Lorelei from Northumberland would be the biggest difficulty, but she had the impression Nanny Cosgrove was loyal to Georgiana rather than Hendon. That would ensure the girl's safe passage to London, but now that Hendon was back, would Georgiana be able to send word to her servant without Hendon finding out? Psyche didn't know how closely he kept an eye on her. Did he think she was too cowed to do anything rebellious, or did he read her mail and have her followed everywhere she went without him? Psyche disliked it, but she suspected it was probably the second one.

She was surprised he hadn't had someone following Georgiana while he was out of the country, but Psyche was sure Georgiana would have been aware and taken precautions. That would explain why she met Myron at Pandora's; it would have been an unsuspicious way for them to be together, but Psyche had to express a slight irritation that her sister had helped them conduct their affair. Psyche eventually grew resigned to it, however; there were so many things that shouldn't have happened to make it possible that Psyche's singling out her twin's participation was useless. The best thing to do now would be deciding how to get Georgiana away from Hendon for her to go to Greece.

There was still Sheerness to convince. Myron said Sheerness wouldn't refuse, that he *owed* Myron for something, something Myron wouldn't clarify. It must be a very *big* debt for him to help Myron cuckold another man. Myron seemed confident it was, which made Psyche all the more curious about it.

Psyche looked up in surprise when Dorian and Selena rose from the couch.

"We're going home. Selena is tired," said Dorian. "You'll let me know how Lady Morecambe is doing?" he asked his brother and sister.

"Of course," said Psyche as she stood up to give them both a hug. She looked at Selena. She *did* seem tired, but it wasn't even eleven yet. "Are you feeling unwell?" she asked concernedly.

Selena smiled amusedly. "Not so very, but I'll be feeling much better in about five months."

Psyche's eyes widened in realization. "Really? That's wonderful," she said happily, giving Selena another hug. "We shall have to go shopping," she said with a grin.

Dorian looked down at Myron where he still sat on the settee. "Don't do anything you'll regret," he said quietly.

Psyche sat back down on the settee beside Myron after the two of them left. She had finished her brandy, and it had combined with the wine she had at their brief supper to leave her feeling very relaxed. She wouldn't go so far as to say she was drunk. She was just at the point where she wasn't feeling the anxiety about Myron and Georgiana. She was even able to look at Sheerness without the feeling of wanting to throttle him anymore. Maybe she *was* drunk.

He continued to sit in the chair by the fireplace, a reflective frown on his face. Psyche wondered if he had realized what was going on. He would have to be completely self-interested not to have. He was still not done with his brandy, and she watched as he continued to roll it back and forth in his hands meditatively, occasionally taking a small swallow from it almost unconsciously. She had to wonder what he thought about this whole affair.

Myron had finished his whisky, and Psyche thought about getting him more. She decided not to. She wanted to give him enough to help calm him, but if he drank too much, it would make him more likely to be uncontrollable. His features were almost blank as he sat beside her on the couch, and she could see he was thinking about things rather than letting his feelings overpower him. She wasn't sure if that made her feel relieved or not.

All three of them turned to look at the door in surprise when it opened. Islington stood there, and he silently motioned for Myron to come with him. Psyche didn't see any blood on his clothes, so that was a good sign…maybe. Both men left and closed the door. Psyche's forehead wrinkled thoughtfully after they were gone, and she began to chew on the side of her thumb. She jumped when there was a loud pop from the wood burning in the fireplace. She disliked the silence. The alcohol she had consumed had done much to soothe her nerves, but she was still not calm. She kept waiting to hear some form of outburst from the other room, but the house was as silent as a tomb. Other than the crackling of the fire and the ticking of the clock on the mantel, it was still.

She eventually stood up and began to pace, still chewing on the side of her thumb. She wished Islington would have at least said what Georgiana's condition was. His face had been impassive. Other than the bruising on her neck and face and her busted lip, Psyche hadn't seen anything obviously injurious, but the marchioness had been wearing a long-sleeved gown, much like her own, except for the ruff. It could cover a multitude of marks, and some things left no outward mark. The frown on her forehead deepened as she tried not to think about those things.

She had completed her circuit back to the fireplace when Sheerness surprised her by reaching out a hand to grab her arm and pull her onto his lap. She looked up at him with round, startled eyes and tried to get back to her feet. He set his glass on the nearby table and used his now free hand to hold her by the upper arm. She continued to wriggle in his grasp, and Sheerness tried very hard not to become excited by the sensations her movements created.

"Please, let me go," she said coldly.

"Be still," said Sheerness softly, and he wrapped one of his arms around her waist to pull her closer.

She didn't do as he asked, of course, and continued to struggle against him. Sheerness moved the hand he had been using to hold her upper arm to the side of her neck and kissed her in an attempt to make her quit moving. It worked, and she stilled in his arms with astonishment as he kissed her with a restrained gentleness. When Sheerness stopped, he surprised her even further when he used the hand at her neck to rest her head onto his shoulder. He sighed with relief when she stopped moving and stayed put. He wasn't sure he could have tolerated her squirming without reacting for much longer.

Psyche had a puzzled frown. When she started to put her thumb to her mouth to chew on it, Sheerness grabbed her hand and held it against his chest. She tried to look up at his face but couldn't see it from where her head rested on his shoulder, nestled beneath his cheek. She frowned even more. She didn't know why he was holding her on his lap. She could only assume her pacing had annoyed him in some way. Telling her to sit down would have been sufficient, and if someone were to walk in and see her sitting on his lap, it would cause an uproar. There had been enough of that already for one evening.

Psyche could feel her eyelids beginning to droop after a time, and she fought very hard to keep them open. She felt oddly relaxed and content where she was. It had to be a combination of the alcohol and the warmth of the fire nearby because it couldn't possibly be due to the closeness of Sheerness. Besides, she needed to be awake to move quickly if someone started to open the door. She couldn't be found on his lap. Sheerness wouldn't care; he seemed intent on causing a scandal involving the two of them. Just because this was her sister's home didn't mean it would not create a problem of some type for her. But Psyche couldn't seem to stay alert, and even as she fought to prevent it, she soon drifted off.

Sheerness could tell when she went to sleep. The constant movement and tenseness he associated with Psyche when she was awake was no longer there. He rubbed his cheek against the top of her head and gave her hand a gentle squeeze where it rested against his chest. Sheerness enjoyed the feel of her pressed against him without the suspicion he knew was there. He was surprised she had fallen asleep, considering how little trust she had for him.

He hadn't intended for Psyche to sleep; he only wanted to make her calm down before she made herself sick. The chewing on the side of her thumb was what she did when she was thinking intently about something; when it combined with the pacing, the things she was thinking about were only going to make her grow more worried. He only wanted to help her, and he supposed he had. She wasn't pacing; she wasn't chewing her thumb; and she wasn't worrying about things over which she had no control. As an added benefit for him, he got to hold her without the arguing or hesitancy she often exhibited.

Sheerness had suspected his friend was involved with a woman; he just hadn't known who. He really couldn't say he was surprised it was Lady Morecambe, but he certainly wished it wasn't. Neath was going to ask for her hand two seasons previously, but her father had arranged her marriage to the Earl of Hendon before he could. No one ever understood why the marquis had done it. The marriage hadn't been an advantageous one for the Morecambes either socially or financially…especially not socially. Everyone knew of the rumors involving the earl: raping, poisoning, other things. It was also known he had been in several duels (the number was officially given as fourteen), mostly incurred over his rumored activities. Most people in polite society did not welcome him; if it hadn't been for his wife, he would have been completely discarded by the *ton* long ago. Sheerness thought his friend should have chosen more wisely; even a *different* married woman would have been better.

He held Psyche for just a little while longer. He knew as well as she did they couldn't be found like this, but it felt wonderful. What would have made him happier would have been to have her sit in his lap willingly, to have her trust him enough to come to him for comfort when she was troubled. It was his own fault she didn't. He had made a terrible mistake in being so consistently abominable to her, and he wasn't sure there was any way to repair it.

Sheerness eventually lifted her in his arms and gently placed her onto the couch, resting her head on a small pillow propped against one arm. He placed a soft, lingering kiss on her forehead, and then he drained the rest of the brandy from his glass and refilled it. He sat back in his chair and watched her sleeping face thoughtfully as he finished the second glass. Even in sleep, her forehead had a slight furrow of concentration, as if her brain would not shut off.

He looked up at the door expectantly when he heard the knob turning. Myron walked in and looked at Psyche's dozing form with perplexity and concern. Sheerness put a finger to his lips and quietly rose to go with his friend out into the hall and pulled the door mostly closed behind them.

"Now what's wrong with Psyche?" asked Myron tiredly.

"Nothing's wrong with her; she's just sleeping," said Sheerness calmly.

"Psyche does not *just sleep*," said Myron doubtfully. "She has insomnia."

Sheerness's eyebrows shot up in surprise. "I never would have guessed. Honestly, there is *nothing* wrong with her." He folded his arms in front of him. "How is Lady Morecambe?" he asked concernedly.

Myron rubbed a hand over his face and sighed gustily. "She'll live. Dodo and Islington are seeing her home…at her insistence."

Sheerness frowned. "Back to Hendon?"

"Yes," said Myron flatly. "She said he would come looking for her if she didn't go home, and it would be worse." He gave a short bark of laughter. "Considering what he did to her, I don't know how it could be worse, unless he killed her." Sheerness raised an enquiring eyebrow. "I shouldn't say."

"Did she say *why* he did it? Such as finding out she'd been unfaithful?" Myron's eyebrows went up. "You figured that out, did you?"

"I suspected you had a lady somewhere, but I never thought it was her."

"Yes, well, anyhow, it's ended…at least, for now," said Myron shortly. "And Georgiana said he had done it with the simple excuse that he *missed* her," spat Myron.

"Oh?"

Myron shook his head regrettably. "I had thought to help Georgiana find a way to get away from him, but I don't think she can wait that long." He gave Sheerness a serious look. "I want you to be my second."

"Neath, don't tell me you're considering what I think you are. Hendon has never lost, and you can't fight a duel with a man over how he treats his wife when you're not related. Not even then, really."

"He raped and sodomized her and gave her two cracked ribs in the bargain! Do *not* tell me that I cannot demand satisfaction for that, and do *not* tell me that you wouldn't challenge the bastard if he did it to Amalie! Georgiana has no family, so who else is there? I'm well-aware he's never lost a duel. He's given enough gross insults to me and mine I won't even have to mention what he did to Georgiana. I'm not foolish enough to assume I will automatically come out the victor, and I don't want him to have an excuse to do her harm should I lose. I'm asking you to be my second because we've been friends for years, and I trust you more than anyone else besides my own family. I *will* find someone else if you refuse, but I know you'll do right by me."

Sheerness looked at his friend consideringly. He could see Myron's mind was set. He had gone from thinking to kill the man in cold blood to doing it honorably, but this was more dangerous. It didn't have to come to bloodshed, but Myron was not going to settle for anything less. In order for the duel to serve its purpose of freeing Georgiana from her husband, only Hendon's death would suit. Sheerness was reluctant to take on the task, but he couldn't desert his friend.

"Very well, if you can see no other way," said Sheerness finally.

Myron smiled gratefully and clapped him on the shoulder. "Thank you. Come by the house tomorrow morning, and I'll have my message for Hendon."

Sheerness nodded. "Does Georgiana know you're doing this?"

"No."

"What about your family?"

"No, and I don't want them to know either," said Myron firmly. "It will only worry them."

Psyche was sitting on the couch in the sitting room, her eyes glistening with tears. She had worn a blister onto the side of her thumb.

Chapter Ten

Psyche had dark circles under her eyes. She hadn't slept. The only sleep she had was the brief nap at Pandora's the previous evening. For most of the night, she had paced. For the other part of it, she had tossed and turned in her bed in an *attempt* to go to sleep. She should have taken some of the sleeping draught Keung had made for her, but she had run out. She would have him make more when she went to see Pandora later.

When the hour arrived for when she would have been waking had she rested, Psyche splashed cold water on her face from the basin and put on her riding habit. She had told Chrissoula she would dress herself; Psyche wanted *someone* to get a good rest. Her stomach was knotted and nauseous.

When Myron and Sheerness had returned to the sitting room, Psyche pretended to still be sleeping and did her best to act as if she had not overheard their conversation. For once, she was convincing. She could have railed at Myron then for what he intended to do, but she wanted to have time to think about it first…to find a way to talk him out of it…or have someone else convince him not to do it. She had spent most of the night thinking about the situation and had not been able to come up with a single solution. He may not have wanted his family to know or worry, but she did know, and she was worried, and she was going to tell Pandora. Perhaps both of them together would be able to talk him out of it, or at least make him tell their parents.

She walked down the back stairs and went to the stable after getting some stale bread from the kitchen for Waddlewsorth. Jim had Achilles and Amati saddled and waiting when she reached the mews. He looked at her concernedly when he saw her.

"Are you feeling well, Lady Psyche?"

"I didn't sleep much last night, that's all," she said calmly.

"You shoulda 'ad Mrs. O'Flaherty make you an 'ot posset," he said sagely. "That always fixes me right up."

"It was very late when I got home, Jim, and by the time I realized I wasn't able to sleep, it was far too late to be bothering Mrs. O'Flaherty." She gave him an appreciative smile for his thoughtfulness after he helped her into her saddle. "I'll live."

Jim smiled back and mounted Amati. They took their usual route to the park, and once they reached it, Psyche let Achilles set their pace. Her feelings of unease must have telegraphed to her horse because the gelding was skittish and unruly. Psyche wondered if she should have stayed home. Her ride in the park usually made her feel better, but this morning she couldn't move beyond her preoccupation with Myron and his intention to duel Hendon.

She went around the circle once and back to the Serpentine as usual, and once she arrived, she was almost surprised to find she was there. She tied Achilles to a tree, and he whinnied at her before dipping his head to begin grazing. She absently patted his shoulder before she removed her gloves and retrieved the bread from her saddlebag and walked to the edge of the lake to feed the birds. She felt distinctly out of touch with her surroundings, as if everything were unfocused and in a separate place from her.

The ducks circled around her as they usually did when she fed them, but today their antics couldn't rouse her from her anxiety. She finished giving them the crumbs and shook what was left out of the cloth. She stood dazedly at the shore, her mind so distant she didn't even hear as someone approached her.

"Good morning, Lady Psyche," said Sheerness calmly from behind her.

Psyche turned to look at him in surprise. "Oh, good morning, Lord Sheerness," she said dully.

The ducks started to disperse and go back to the lake as he came closer…except Waddleworth. He stood eyeing the earl suspiciously.

"Could you…?" he said gesturing at the drake with one hand.

Psyche frowned uncomprehendingly for a moment, as if it had taken her time to realize he was speaking, and then she nodded.

"Shoo, Waddlesworth," she said softly. The duck gave Sheerness one more disdainful look and a loud quack before he went back to the water.

When Sheerness came closer, he noticed her cheeks were flushed and the dark circles, and the way she seemed almost dazed, her eyes bright.

"Are you feeling well?" he asked concernedly.

"What? Oh, I'm fine," she said tonelessly. She began to weave on her feet and would have fallen to the ground in a faint if Sheerness hadn't reached out to catch her.

"Bloody hell!" muttered Sheerness, holding her to him to keep her from collapsing.

He looked around himself for somewhere to sit down with her, but there was no such thing. He picked her up and carried her further away from the mud near the shore, and then he set her down on the grass, balancing her back against his knee as he knelt beside her. He put his hand to her forehead, and his frown deepened when he felt that she had a high fever.

"Psyche?" he called uneasily.

She didn't seem to hear him. He gently patted her cheeks and called her name again, but she still didn't stir. He began to grow more anxious. At the sound of jingling harness and approaching feet, he looked up to see Jim heading toward them with a worried look.

"I didn't do it, I swear," said Sheerness flatly.

"No, I know that," said Jim distractedly, looking at Psyche worriedly. "She said she 'adn't slept well was all. I never would 'ave let her come ridin' if I'd known she was ill."

"Go get a carriage," said Sheerness as he continued to try rousing her. "I'll stay with her until you get back."

"I'm not supposed to leave her," said Jim nervously.

"She's burning up with a fever, and I can't get her to wake up. The Aberdares know me, and I give you my word I'll not let her come to any harm," said Sheerness patiently. "She can't ride a horse in this condition."

Jim looked at him uncertainly for a moment, and then he looked at Psyche, who still showed no signs of waking. He nodded his head finally and went to retrieve Achilles from where he surprisingly still remained tied to the tree where she had put him. Jim mounted Amati and looked down at Sheerness scrutinizingly before he urged the gelding to move on. Sheerness watched as the coachman guided the horses to a full gallop across the turf of the park and disappeared into the trees. He turned his attention back to Psyche.

He picked her up and carried her to a nearby tree, where he put her back down on the ground and propped her against the trunk. He walked to the edge of the lake and dipped his handkerchief into the water. It didn't look very clean, but the coolness might help to wake her, and he had no intention of letting her drink it.

He moved her again so that he sat against the tree and placed her halfway across his lap to balance her head in the crook of his arm. He smoothed the handkerchief against her forehead and across her cheeks, and he started to feel some relief as furrows began to form between her eyebrows. Her eyelids soon fluttered open, and she looked up at him with bright, feverish eyes.

"What?" she asked dazedly.

"Shh, don't move," said Sheerness softly as he continued to smooth the handkerchief over her face. "Jim's gone to get a carriage to take you home."

Psyche struggled to sit up but grew dizzy at the movement and reluctantly decided she would have to do as he asked. She looked up at him worriedly.

"What happened?"

"You fainted, and you have a fever. Do you have any pains? Nausea?"

Her forehead wrinkled. "I don't have any pains really, but I'm feeling a bit queasy. I thought that was because of something else, though."

Sheerness looked at her perplexedly. "Jim said you didn't sleep well."

"Actually, I didn't sleep at all last night, but that's not so very unusual," said Psyche dryly. She tried to sit up again, only to have the same result as before. She *was* feeling warm, and the skin on her face felt tight.

"Why didn't you sleep?"

Psyche looked up at him solemnly. "You can't let him go through with it."

"I beg your pardon?"

Psyche shook her head, and it made her feel as if the earth was moving without her.

"Don't play, Sheerness. You have to stop him. Take him, and Georgiana, and Lorelei away from here so Hendon can't get to them."

"What are you talking about?"

"*Don't* play with me!" said Psyche angrily, and the exertion made the blood rush in her ears. "Myron was going to talk to you about taking Georgiana and her sister instead of me when you left for Greece and Egypt in August, but don't wait. Take them all away on the *Medea* somewhere Hendon won't be able to find them as soon as you can. Then everyone will be safe and happy." She could feel herself growing faint again and tried to keep her eyes in focus. "He doesn't have to fight a duel with Hendon. There's another way."

"Why would you think Myron would go along with it? Or me?"

"Because it would be better for him to be alive and safe far away than near and dead." Psyche looked up at him and tried to keep her eyes focused on his face, but she could feel herself losing consciousness again as her fever began to climb higher. "Do you think you can stand to lose someone else?" she whispered as she drifted off again.

Sheerness looked down at her with astonishment. He tried to get her to wake again, but not even rubbing her face with the damp handkerchief would rouse her for the moment. At one point, he looked at his watch, noting it wouldn't be long before other people began to come to the park. He wondered if Jim would have thought to send someone for a doctor. That could be seen to once she was home. Getting her home and in bed was his main concern.

He didn't know what was wrong with her. If it weren't for the fever, he might have thought it was simple exhaustion or nervous prostration. Neither was usually accompanied by a high temperature. He was no physician, and he had no idea what would be causing it. There were so many things, many of which could kill her. He would rather not think about it. Thinking about that and the last thing she said terrified him. He knew she had meant Myron, but Psyche was the one he was holding unconscious in his arms.

He thought about her suggestion of taking her brother and Georgiana away on his ship. It wouldn't be ready to sail sooner than the beginning of August, and he knew without asking (even though he would anyhow) that his friend wouldn't wait that long for a solution to the problem. Even after sleeping on it for a night, Sheerness was sure Myron was determined to take some form of action…soon. The *Medea* was still being refitted and supplied. Sheerness didn't have a full crew yet, and the ship didn't even have her sails. He couldn't convince Myron to wait.

Sheerness could only assume Psyche had learned about the duel by overhearing their conversation in the hall. He thought she was still sleeping when he went back into the sitting room. She had been pretending. Myron hadn't suspected either. Sheerness would have to let his friend know when he saw him that morning. He didn't think Psyche would be in any condition to mention it herself. That would change once she was feeling better. Sheerness didn't know how Myron thought he could possibly keep his family from learning about it. Although he could understand his friend's reluctance to worry his family, it would be better if he told them.

After a few more minutes, Psyche began to come around again. She opened her eyes and looked at Sheerness, her face in a displeased frown as he continued to smooth the drying handkerchief across it. She lifted up a hand to his wrist to stop him, and he was surprised at how strong the grip seemed.

"Stop that, please," she said in a cracked voice. She grimaced as speaking caused her throat to hurt. "That thing smells like pond scum."

Her throat was so dry and sore it felt as if something were lodged there, and she coughed in an attempt to clear it. It only made her throat hurt worse. Her face felt dry and tight, and she felt as if she had a weight sitting on her chest. She had a headache, and if she moved too suddenly, everything started to go out of focus in a shimmer of dizziness. Added to all of that was a nausea that would come and go, and the smell of the handkerchief only made it worse.

"Do you have any water?" she whispered, trying to avoid putting a strain on her voice.

Sheerness looked down at her with relief. She seemed to be lucid and in no danger of fainting again, but it was obvious *something* was now causing her pain. He hoped he could keep her conscious if she kept talking.

"Only the Serpentine," he said with a teasing grin. Psyche made a moue of disgust and shook her head. He watched as the movement momentarily caused her eyes to go out of focus. "I have brandy," he supplied helpfully.

Psyche looked at him thoughtfully for a minute before finally nodding. Her throat was sore, but she was also very thirsty. She wasn't sure the alcohol would help, but she was *not* desperate enough to drink from the lake. He reached into the pocket of his coat to remove a small silver flask. After taking off the lid, he lifted her slightly and put it to her lips. She took a hefty swig and shuddered and grimaced after she swallowed it, but she was happy to find the brandy, at least temporarily, numbed the pain in her throat.

"How are you feeling now?" he asked amusedly.

"Terrible," croaked Psyche. "My throat hurts. My head hurts." She grimaced. "Actually, I don't think there's anything that doesn't hurt now."

"Jim should be here shortly with a carriage."

Psyche struggled to sit up again. "I don't need a carriage," she said waveringly before falling back again as the dizziness overtook her. She sighed frustratedly. "Very well, perhaps I do."

Sheerness chuckled, and she looked up at him with a sour expression, which made him laugh even more.

"I hope you catch it, too," she said tartly.

She was still thirsty, but she didn't think she should have more brandy; she was already dizzy enough. She had a cold, but she couldn't recall one ever setting on so suddenly with symptoms quite so harsh. She just hoped her parents didn't send for Dr. Hinton. He was more progressive than some of his colleagues, but he would want to bleed her, at least once, before moving on to something else. Maybe she could convince them to send for Keung.

Sheerness didn't try to rub her face with the handkerchief anymore, much to Psyche's relief, but he would brush a soothing hand across her forehead occasionally as he watched the front of the park for Jim arriving with the carriage. Although he was trying very hard not to show it, Psyche could see she had worried him, and she was making every effort to remain conscious. It wasn't easy.

"Are you going to stop him?" she asked Sheerness quietly, putting a hand to his chest.

He looked down at her thoughtfully and smoothed a hand down her cheek.

"I'll try. The *Medea* won't be ready to sail until August, and there's not anything I can do to change that." Psyche looked as if she was going to argue. "There's *not,*" he said firmly. "I will try to make him change his mind and follow your plan, but the decision is his."

"But...," she began, and Sheerness put a finger to her lips to silence her.

"Psyche, he's a grown man, and it is not up to me or you to make his choices for him," he said gently.

Psyche finally nodded resignedly and blinked her eyes to hold back the tears that stung them.

"Can you at least convince him to tell my family?"

Sheerness looked at her in surprise. "You mean to say you won't?"

"Only Pandora...at first. If she says not to, then I won't, but I'm sure she will say we should, and I already think we should, but Myron doesn't want to, so I will try not to, but they will eventually discover I'm hiding something, and I will *have* to tell them," rambled Psyche.

Sheerness looked at her confusedly as he tried to make sense of what she just said. "Are you becoming delirious?"

Psyche shook her head after some consideration. "I don't think so. I am thirsty and nauseous, and I fear I have been struck by an extraordinarily vicious cold and a fever from hell, but I don't think I'm delirious," she rambled again.

After some thought, Sheerness decided to give her the benefit of the doubt, but she seemed to be meandering more than usual. She was usually precise about what she said and definitely more logical. He opened his flask again and gave her more brandy. Against his better judgment, he let her have two large swallows. Her response to the taste didn't improve, and the fevered brightness of her eyes became heightened by the effects of the alcohol. She didn't seem to be inebriated, but she did begin to look dazed again.

At the sound of a quickly approaching carriage, he looked up to see with relief that Jim was arriving with one of the Aberdares' coaches. He thought something smaller would have been fine, but perhaps it was the quickest thing to arrange. The coachman pulled to a stop at the edge of the path near the lake and set the brake before hopping down to approach them. Psyche smiled weakly as he neared.

"Hallo, Jim," she said sheepishly.

"Cor, I'm sure glad to see you awake, mum," he said with relief. He looked at Sheerness. "I came as quick as I could, but I 'ad to wake somebody to 'elp do the 'itchin' an' get word to the 'ouse an' send for the doctor."

"Oh, not Dr. Hinton," moaned Psyche with a shake of her head. "He'll want to *bleed* me."

"Nah. I 'ad Tajik go to the Bardseys to fetch Keung for you," he said with a grin and a wink.

"Jim, you are a prince among men," sighed Psyche happily. "Now…if I can…just stand…up," she said, trying unsuccessfully to put action to words.

"Hold still," said Sheerness amusedly, and he braced his back against the tree to come to a standing position while holding her in his arms. "Jim, if you could tie Troia to the back, I'll see to getting Lady Psyche in the coach."

"Very good, my lord," said Jim agreeably. He was a bit more amenable to Lord Sheerness now that he saw the man could be trusted to keep his word, and he didn't think Psyche would be able to ride in the coach without someone to assist her in any event.

Sheerness carried Psyche to the coach while Jim went to untie his mare from the tree where he had left her. Psyche put her arms around his neck as he walked toward the coach, which proved to be helpful when he had to let go of her with the arm behind her back to open the door. He carefully placed her onto one of the well-cushioned seats, and she promptly began to slide sideways in an effort to lie down. Lying down seemed to alleviate the nausea.

Sheerness climbed in and closed the door behind him, and he sat on the seat beside her. After a minor amount of adjustment, he had her lying across his lap with her feet propped onto the seat, her head nestled into the crook of his arm again. Before long, they felt the coach shift on its springs as Jim climbed onto the driver's seat. There was a lurch as he started them in motion, and Psyche was relieved he wasn't driving quickly. She was afraid the jostling might make her sick.

Psyche was trying to remain conscious. Sheerness had a worried frown, and it wasn't all for the conversation they had about Myron. It was surprising to Psyche that he could be so concerned about her. He said he would try to be less confusing, and perhaps he wouldn't seem that way if she were feeling better, but at the moment, she was bumfuzzled. She impulsively reached up a hand to brush it across the furrows in his forehead.

"It's just a cold," she said gently.

Sheerness looked down at her in surprise. He wasn't aware his concern was so obvious. He hadn't meant it to be. She felt very warm pressed against him, and her eyes were glassy and slightly unfocused as she looked at him solemnly. He wanted to believe it was just a cold, but she had been steadily and quickly growing worse, much more rapidly than what would be expected for a cold. She simply couldn't know how unwell she was.

He bent down to kiss her, and Psyche responded without resistance. It seemed to her like the most natural thing that should happen at that moment.

She moved a hand to the side of his face, and her mind was detached enough because of her fever and the alcohol that she was able to forget everything else except how much she enjoyed being kissed by him. She noticed for the first time as she put her attention on nothing but Sheerness that his shaving lotion smelled of vetiver and a faint trace of lime. When he began to play his tongue against hers, Psyche found he tasted of brandy and chocolate. She had never realized that he smelled and tasted so divine.

He kissed her with tenderness and care, and Psyche could feel his restraint. She remembered the almost desperate way he had embraced her under the hydrangeas in his garden, and she suspected that was what he wanted to keep under control. Then she understood with astonishment what Pandora had meant when she said Psyche's enjoyment of his kissing her was the point. While she was sure he didn't find it to be a distasteful chore, Sheerness kissed her to please her, and Psyche had to wonder why. He had yet to disappoint her…except when he stopped to look down at her with amused exasperation.

"Psyche, just quit thinking and kiss me," he whispered appealingly, gently tapping a finger against her forehead before he resumed.

Psyche tried her best to accommodate him. She twined her arms around his neck and removed his hat to run her fingers through his hair. She really enjoyed the feel of his hair. Kissing Sheerness was a sensual experience, and Psyche found herself becoming lost in the smell, taste, and feel of him. She was dizzy again, and she wasn't sure it was due to her illness. He didn't try to take their embrace beyond kissing, and Psyche found herself wanting more.

Sheerness eventually ended the kiss, and this time Psyche was content to let him. She was very tired, and he would have found it insulting if she had fallen asleep while he was kissing her. She blinked slowly several times as she looked up at him, and she started to doze off just as the coach came to a stop. Sheerness gathered her up in his arms and stepped down when Jim opened the door. They were in the mews, and Jim opened the gate in the wall that would lead onto the path in the garden to take them to the back of the house.

Psyche looked at Jim's worried face and tried to manage a cheeky grin.

"I don't think I'll be going riding tomorrow, Jim," she said dryly.

"Just as long as you do the day after," said Jim lightly. "I'll go to seed if you don't."

Psyche smiled and rested her head on Sheerness's shoulder weakly as he carried her up the path. When he got to the terrace, he started to go through one of the sets of doors that would lead them through the ballroom. Psyche lifted her head and grabbed his collar to get his attention.

"Just go up the back stairs," she said softly. She lifted a wavering hand and pointed to another door further along the terrace.

He turned and went to it, and Psyche held on to his neck as he released her with the arm at her back to open the door. He closed it with his foot once they were through, and Sheerness went up the stairs. When they came to the landing, Sheerness looked down at her expectantly. He certainly had no notion of where her room or anyone else's was for that matter, and there were several to choose from. Psyche's forehead wrinkled for a moment as she thought about it. She was almost too tired to remember where her own room was.

"That way," she said, pointing to the left. "It will be the second door on the left after you cross the landing for the main stairs."

Sheerness wasn't surprised when he reached it to find the door was standing open. When he walked in, there were several people in the room. Pandora was there with Bardsey, as were the duke and duchess. He recognized the Chinaman, Keung, from the previous night, and there was a beautiful young woman with dark brown hair and light hazel eyes wearing an unusual dress that came to midway on her calf and was covered by an intricately embroidered vest. He wasn't sure, but he suspected that was Psyche's maid, Chrissoula.

As for the room itself, it wasn't what he expected. He thought it would be frilly and feminine. While he could tell it was the room of a woman, it wasn't cloying. He thought there would be lots of pink and white-painted wood; he was surprised to see burgundy, amethyst purple, and lavender, and the wood was all mahogany. There was a large writing desk with a hutch to one side littered with books and paper. The pigeonholes in the hutch were mostly filled with old scrolls, but some contained clay tablets. There was a low bench near the small fireplace, and there were two wingchairs placed in front of a set of windows with a small table centered between them. There was a dressing table and a low, wide clothes chest. The bed was an ornately carved half tester covered with amethyst purple velvet brocade hangings and bedspread. The room smelled faintly of her perfume, and Sheerness paused for a moment in the doorway. It was not what he had expected, but it suited her.

All the people stopped talking when he entered with Psyche and looked to the doorway expectantly. Sheerness thought it was amusing so many people would be there waiting for her and that they would all suddenly stop whatever it was they were doing when they realized Psyche was there. One would almost think he was entering with the queen. He calmly began to carry her to the bed, and the silence and stillness only lasted for a few seconds before everyone rushed toward him to look at her. He could tell from the way she clung tighter to his neck that she found it almost as overwhelming as he did.

Psyche managed to smile at them weakly as Sheerness carried her to the bed. She wasn't expecting so many people, although she was happy to see them. She had thought Chrissoula would be there to help her into bed, and then Keung would give her something to make her feel better. She should have realized it would be late enough for Pandora and Islington to be awake, and Psyche's twin would not let Keung go without her once Pandora found out Psyche was ill. Considering Pandora's due date was fast approaching, Islington would not be likely to let her leave the house without him, and he was a physician. When Jim sent someone to the house to let the family know she was ill, her mother and father would be the likely ones notified. Since the only thing Jim would have been able to tell them was that she was unconscious with a fever, they would have been desperately worried and would want to see her the minute she got home. And, of course, Chrissoula would have been waiting for Psyche to return from her ride to help her dress for breakfast. But she really didn't think they all needed to be there; it was just a *cold*, and all she wanted to do was curl up in bed under her blankets.

"Mamà and Papà, there is no need for you to look so worried. I have a cold," said Psyche affectionately…if hoarsely.

They were relieved to see her conscious and to hear her talking lucidly, but they wouldn't stop being concerned until Keung gave them his verdict.

Psyche was almost reluctant to have Sheerness put her on the bed, but he had to be tired from carrying her all the way from the mews to her bedroom. It had been a long way, and she thought it was quite impressive. She found herself ridiculously thinking she would feel fine if she could stay snuggled up to him for just a little while longer. Once he put her down, he would have to leave the room, and she found herself wishing he didn't have to go. She wondered if she was becoming delirious because she couldn't believe she would be quite so mawkish about the man otherwise. When he laid her onto the bed, as Psyche removed her right hand from the back of his neck, on the side that wasn't visible to her family, she softly moved it across his cheek in a caress.

"Thank you," she said quietly.

He looked at her in surprise for a moment then gave her a warm smile. "Not a problem," he said mildly as he straightened up.

"Thea, I will get you some room to breathe," said Chrissoula suddenly, clapping her hands together. She began to wave her arms at everyone. "Shoo!" she said.

"Oh, let Pandora stay," called Psyche in a cracked voice as loudly as she could manage, which was barely above a whisper.

Chrissoula nodded her approval. "Very well, Pseudo-Thea can stay, but the rest of you: shoo!"

Psyche found it quite comical to watch her maid herding everyone out of the room like a farm maid gathering up her chickens into the coop. The duke and duchess took the direction with equanimity; Psyche did not appear to be at death's door, and they were willing to leave her in Keung's capable hands. In a matter of seconds, there was only Pandora, Chrissoula and Keung left, and the door was closed. Psyche did feel as if she were able to breathe a little easier, although she still wished Sheerness could have stayed.

"Did he carry you all the way from the *mews*?" asked Pandora amusedly as she went to the other side of the bed to sit down on the edge.

Psyche turned to look at her sister thoughtfully as Chrissoula came to the side of the bed and started to unlace her boots.

"Yes, he did," said Psyche with a pleased smile. Then her face turned serious. "Oh, Pan, you are not going to believe what I have to tell you."

Chrissoula clucked her tongue. "That will wait until we have you in your shift under the covers," she said reprovingly. "And only then if Keung says you can."

Out in the hall, the other four people stood a bit uncertainly for a moment. Then Sheerness turned to look at Islington.

"Did she just call her *Thea?*" he asked disbelievingly. The duke and duchess and Islington all looked at him amusedly before nodding in confirmation. "No wonder she has such a big head," he muttered to himself.

The duke, who was standing closest to him, didn't miss what he said and laughed heartily. Sheerness colored in embarrassment when he realized Aberdare had heard him insulting his daughter, but he was relieved the duke didn't seem offended. Aberdare clapped him on the shoulder and looked at Islington with a wink.

"The two of you may as well join us for breakfast," he said mildly, leading them to the stairs with his arm linked through that of the duchess.

≪ ≫

"Pan, I don't think you should get close to me. If this is contagious, you don't want to catch it," said Psyche once Chrissoula finished sliding her shift over her head and helped her under the covers.

"Oh, pooh," said Pandora unconcernedly, waving her hand through the air. "It's not like I'll be kissing you," she said with a teasing smile.

Psyche's eyes grew round in alarm. "Oh, no," she moaned.

"What?" asked Pandora blankly.

"Oh, nothing," said Psyche quickly, and her cheeks flushed an even brighter shade of red that had nothing to do with her fever.

"Mm-hmm," said Pandora doubtfully, her eyebrow raised. "I foresee a very bad cold in someone else's immediate future," she said with a chuckle.

Psyche waved a dismissive hand through the air. "Never mind that. Pandora, I have something important to tell you," she said seriously.

Chrissoula clicked her tongue. "No, you'll let Keung look at you first."

"But—"

Chrissoula clicked her tongue again and shook her head. "No buts!"

Keung looked at her amusedly as he came to the edge of the bed. He began by feeling her neck before lifting each of her arms and feeling under each of them, and then he repeated the action at her stomach near her pelvis. He looked at her eyes, and then he had her open her mouth for him to look at her throat. He put an ear to her chest and listened to her breathe. It only took ten minutes to complete his examination.

"You did not sleep last night, did you?" he asked mildly.

"No. I've run out of my sleeping draught, or I would have taken it."

"Psy, why didn't you tell me you were out? I could have had Keung make you more," said Pandora in gentle reproach.

"I forgot the last time I was over—and last night. I was going to tell you when I came over today," said Psyche defensively.

Keung shook his head. "I will make you more, but this will be last time," he said firmly. "You need to learn to turn off brain when you turn off light," he said, poking her in the middle of her forehead. "Sleep time is *not* time for brain work. If your brain is not working, you have no insomnia. When you go to bed, think about something peaceful that not require lots of concentration, then you will go to sleep, *dŏng?*"

"I'll try," said Psyche resignedly. She had to admit she couldn't sleep last night because she couldn't stop thinking about Myron.

"Now, you have influenza…but not too bad yet," said Keung with a smile. "It would not be so bad already if you had slept last night."

He stood up from the bed and went to a large wooden box he had brought with him and placed on the table between the chairs by the window. He opened the lid and pulled out small shelves that contained several different jars. He pulled an empty bottle from the bottom of the box and proceeded to put several different ingredients from the other jars inside it. He put the stopper back in and gave it a shake to mix them all together. He set the concoction aside and pulled out another bottle to mix other herbs together. He then pulled out a pencil and wrote on the paper labels already attached to each bottle. He closed the lid on the box and carried the two bottles over to the bed and set them on the night table.

"One of those is for sleeping, and the directions are same as before," he said calmly. "The other is for influenza. You mix five drops in one cup of water. You take it every four hours until you are feeling better."

"*Xièxie*, Keung," said Psyche with a relieved smile.

"Right now, you need to sleep," said Keung.

"But—" began Psyche.

"You sleep *now!*" said Keung firmly. "You take influenza medicine, and you sleep."

He looked at Pandora, and she stood up reluctantly. She really wanted to know what was so important that Psyche needed to tell her, but it would have to wait for another time. Neither Keung nor Chrissoula was going to let her twin speak. Chrissoula was already getting a glass of water and mixing a dose of the medicine for Psyche to take.

"Get well, Psyche," said Pandora fondly.

"I hope so," said Psyche with a grin. "Tell Sheerness that I said to tell you about Myron…or else," she said, looking around Chrissoula at her sister as Pandora went to the door where Keung was waiting for her. She took the glass from her maid and began to drink the bittersweet concoction just as the door closed. She looked at Chrissoula dourly after she finished it. "What I had to tell her was a matter of life and death," she mumbled just before she dozed off.

"Humph," scoffed Chrissoula unconcernedly as she tucked the blankets in around Psyche. She went to the fire and put some of the embers into a warming pan to place at Psyche's feet.

≪ ≫

Sheerness left Aberdare House a few hours later with a grim expression. He carried a letter in the pocket of his riding coat that he was not looking forward to delivering. He had hoped to convince Myron not to go through with it, but he was dead set. An hour of arguing with him had not changed his mind and only seemed to make him more determined. His friend had decided Hendon's death would be the only acceptable resolution. Sheerness wished that were not the case.

It had taken another hour to convince him to tell his family. Myron had been upset to discover Psyche knew and that she was going to tell Pandora, but when Sheerness told him she said she wouldn't tell anyone else, Sheerness was surprised Myron believed her. Sheerness finally made Myron realize he needed to tell his family when he pointed out how devastated they would be to discover it after something went terribly wrong. Myron finally relented and promised to tell them after Sheerness left. Everyone was there, except for Gregory, so there would not likely be another time for it.

Sheerness looked at his watch as he walked down the path to the mews to get his horse. It was a little too early to go to Hendon. He had eaten breakfast with the Aberdares and their family. That had been a lively adventure, but Sheerness enjoyed it. They did not stand on ceremony simply because he was there, and he found himself participating in their debates and teasing as if he always had. For a time, he almost felt the way he had before his father died, before Monique died, and he regretted it when the meal was over because he then retired to the library with Myron to discuss his plans for dueling Hendon.

When he reached the gate to the mews, he paused for a moment before opening it to look at the back of the house. He picked out the set of windows he thought were Psyche's. The curtains were drawn. He was concerned when Keung stated she had influenza, but that began to ease when he saw no one in her family was particularly worried. They seemed to have every confidence she would make a full recovery in due time, and Sheerness wanted to believe that as well. He opened the gate and closed it behind him, finding Troia tied not too far away, munching on some hay that someone had provided her.

He would go by the *Medea* to see how work was progressing before he went to see Hendon. It was irrelevant now to find out if work could be completed sooner because Myron intended to have the duel, but Sheerness wasn't looking forward to giving Hendon the letter. Once it was done, there would be no going back. He wondered what time and place Hendon would choose, and he also wondered who the man would be able to have as his second. Sheerness didn't think Hendon would be able to immediately find someone to take on the dubious honor. He could think of a dozen men without much effort who would be just as likely to challenge the earl themselves. It was also unlikely that Hendon would decline the challenge.

Sheerness thought about stopping by Barneville Court before going to the ship, but he finally decided against it. His family would just be sitting down for their own breakfast, and he had been so well-fed by the Aberdares he wouldn't be able to join them. After a month, everyone seemed to have settled into a routine, and even if it wasn't the same as before—and was never likely to be—it appeared they would all survive.

When he arrived at the *Medea* and spoke with the carpenter, he was not surprised to find it was just as he suspected. Work was progressing, but there was no way for it to move quicker, especially not after he told the carpenter about the modification he wanted made in the crews' quarters in the berth deck. The carpenter, Mr. Laing, felt the change would be an unnecessary one, but the cost would not be coming out of his pocket. Laing assured Sheerness the ship would be ready to sail by August but definitely not before then.

After his discussion with Mr. Laing, Sheerness took his time traveling back to the other side of the Thames at London Bridge. He didn't grow impatient at the delays (unlike he usually did) as he went through Cheapside and Newgate to Holborn. This chore before he could return home was one he had accepted, but it was certainly not one he relished. Like Psyche, he didn't think it was necessary or that it would end well. He could not, however, see any way to prevent it. He guided his horse into Soho Square once he reached Oxford Street and reluctantly dismounted when he reached his destination.

The Hendon residence was neat and tidy, and looked much the same as every other terrace house on the square. There was nothing unique and nothing charming about it. It was a house. The curtains were all drawn, and Sheerness might have thought no one was stirring yet if he hadn't glanced at his watch to see it nearing one. Even the very late risers were up. He tied Troia to a nearby post, and after giving her a soothing pat to her shoulder, he went through the wrought-iron gate up the stairs to the door. He knocked twice and patiently waited for it to be answered. He could only hope there really was no one home and perhaps delay things a little longer. He could have no such luck. The door was opened by a stodgy housekeeper who peered down her nose at him, even from a height that was far shorter, as if his arrival were an inconvenience.

Sheerness presented her with his card. "I'm here to see Lord Hendon on a matter of business," he said calmly.

She looked from the card to him for a moment before she quietly gestured with her hand for him to enter.

"Wait here," she said stiffly, and she left him standing in the foyer while she disappeared further into the house.

Sheerness calmly removed his gloves and his hat while he stood waiting. The house was as silent as a tomb. He couldn't even hear the sounds of servants about their daily work. It was odd the house was so quiet. His house on Curzon Street certainly wasn't, even before his niece and nephews came to stay with him, and Aberdare House most definitely wasn't. He couldn't even hear the ticking of a clock. The silence made him feel uncomfortable. It wasn't natural for a house to be that quiet.

The housekeeper momentarily returned, but she didn't offer to take his things. That led Sheerness to believe either Hendon would not see him, or she did not expect he would be staying very long.

"If you'll come this way, Lord Sheerness," she said quietly, and she turned to lead him back in the direction she had gone before.

As Sheerness followed her, he noticed her shoes made no noise as she walked. He looked down at her feet in curiosity and was startled to see the soles of her shoes were covered in chamois to muffle the sound. His forehead wrinkled as he thought about it. That would explain why he didn't hear anyone walking around, not if *all* the servants were required to have their shoes made that way. The thing he found most bizarre, however, was that someone would have their servants do that. *Why?* He made no presumption of understanding the foibles of others, but this bordered on insane. She led him to a closed door, and her brief, quiet knock was answered by a muffled call from inside. She stood out of the way after she opened the door to let Sheerness enter before she closed it back on silent, well-oiled hinges as she left.

Sheerness saw the room he entered was an office of some type. There was a large ebonized desk with two stiff-backed chairs in front of it. One wall contained a floor-to-ceiling bookcase, but Sheerness could see the spines on most of the volumes had not even been cracked, and he was sure if they were pulled from the shelves, the pages would not even be slit on some of them. There was a large fireplace with an ornate black marble mantel and a large gilded mirror above it, and there was a sideboard along another wall that held decanters and glasses. There was a small settee with two matching chairs and a low table in front of the fireplace. All of the woodwork was dark, and the walls were covered in a dark red brocade paper. The room was lit by candelabras, and the dark green velvet drapes over the windows were closed. The appearance of the room only affirmed Sheerness's opinion that the house was a mausoleum. He did *not* like this house.

Hendon was seated behind the desk, and Sheerness was surprised to see that one of the chairs in front of it was occupied by Count von Weilheim. Sheerness could only speculate the reason behind the German keeping company with Hendon. He could only assume the foreigner simply didn't know any better. Of course, after his wife's unbecoming display at Almack's, his presentation to London society was less than stellar, and they had associated with each other on the continent. Being the exact bottom of the barrel himself, Hendon was not concerned about a little scandal.

Both men came to their feet when Sheerness entered. Weilheim looked at him pleasantly, and Sheerness was sure the man was associated with Hendon only because of happenstance. His wife was a vicious harpy, but Sheerness believed Weilheim just happened to be a misguided individual. Hendon looked at Sheerness suspiciously. The two earls did *not* socialize with each other. At one time, Hendon had been a member of Boodles, but his membership had been revoked by a majority consensus of all the other members because they had grown weary of his less-than-gentlemanly pursuits. Hendon had even, for a time, attended Oxford while Sheerness was there, but he had not stayed to the end and achieved a degree. Hendon came from behind the desk as Sheerness came near and casually leaned against the front of it.

"Sheerness," he said calmly. "Mrs. Brown said you came to see me on a matter of business?"

Sheerness shook hands with Weilheim and gave him a brief nod, and then he reached out a hand to Hendon out of politeness. Hendon did not take it, and Sheerness's jaw tightened in irritation.

"Yes, I've come to see you on behalf of Lord Neath," said Sheerness evenly.

"Lord Neath?" quizzed Hendon, his eyebrow rising in mild curiosity.

Sheerness reached into the inside pocket of his coat and removed the sealed letter from Myron. He held it out to Hendon. The earl looked for a moment as if he weren't going to take it, but he finally took it from Sheerness and went back behind the desk to sit down. He gestured at Sheerness to take the other chair in front of the desk as Weilheim reseated himself in his own. Sheerness declined to take the offer and calmly stood while Hendon retrieved a small knife from a drawer to open the letter. Sheerness didn't anticipate this transaction would take long.

Hendon's lips began to twitch with amusement as he read, and by the end of it, he was chuckling with malicious humor. He looked up at Sheerness after he finished and tossed the letter onto the top of his desk.

"Do you know what that says?" Hendon asked him.

"No, but I do know what it's regarding," said Sheerness mildly.

Hendon looked at Weilheim. "The pup has challenged me to a duel!" he chortled. "He says he cannot let my spreading of scandalous tripe about his sister, the Marchioness of Bardsey, go unanswered."

"Truly?" said Weilheim moderately.

"Oh, ho, but wait, there's more," chuckled Hendon. "He says it has come to his attention that *I* was in some way responsible for the death of the Marquess of Tarlborough last year, and he wants to see me punished."

"Really?" said Weilheim weakly.

"But *this* is the icing on the cake," said Hendon, still chuckling as he picked up the letter. "He says: *I simply cannot tolerate you breathing the same air as myself any longer.*"

Weilheim did manage a slight chuckle, but it was obvious he did not find dueling to be quite so amusing. Hendon threw the letter back onto the table and looked at Sheerness where he stood patiently waiting for Hendon's reply.

"You are to be his second?" asked Hendon, and he wiped a finger at the corner of his eye.

"I am," replied Sheerness evenly.

Hendon looked at Weilheim. "What say you? Would you care to be *my* second?"

"If you believe I am capable of such an honor, it would be my pleasure," said Weilheim agreeably.

Hendon nodded and pulled out a sheet of paper and a fountain pen to compose his reply to Myron. He scratched the end of the pen against his temple as he thought, and then he began to write, speaking aloud as he did so.

"Dear Lord Neath, As you seem to find my person so offensive, how could I do anything but accept your invitation? If it is agreeable to you, we shall meet at Hyde Park near The Ring with pistols at 5:30 in the morning a week from this Saturday. I trust you will have your affairs in order, as shall I. Count Heinrich von Weilheim will be my second, and you may direct any further enquiry to him." Hendon scratched his temple again as he thought of a suitable closure, and he chuckled and shook his head amusedly as he finished. *"With most sincerity, Hendon."*

He blotted the sheet before folding and sealing it. He came from around the desk and gave it to Sheerness, who calmly placed it into the pocket where Myron's letter to Hendon had been. He would go home for a little while before he took it to Myron.

≪ ≫

For the moment, the house was silent. Myron had gotten all of his family, with the exception of Psyche and the three younger boys, to join him in the drawing room. When he made his announcement, there was lots of shouting and argument. Of course, Pandora made sure to tell him that defense of her honor was not necessary and no longer his concern, but she knew her being maligned by Hendon was only an excuse anyhow. The true reason for his demand of satisfaction was Georgiana. She realized this had to be the thing Psyche was so desperate to tell her, and she had to wonder how her twin had managed to discover it before Myron told everyone else.

The duke had threatened to disown him if he insisted on going through with it, but Myron told his father he would have to do whatever he felt was necessary, but it would not alter his course. Everyone in the family considered dueling to be a distasteful way of settling a dispute and in no way a suitable method of avenging one's honor, but Myron knew there was no court that could touch Hendon for the crimes he had committed, and it wasn't *his* honor that demanded it. No one could make him change his mind.

Psyche had briefly awakened from her sleep when the shouting began, but her fever and the medicine Keung had given her prevented her from staying awake to worry over it, especially not after Chrissoula gave her more of the medicine. Psyche had expected there was nothing that could be done to make Myron change his mind, no matter how much she wished otherwise. She was sure Sheerness had done his best to convince her brother not to go through with it, but she realized, just as Sheerness had told her, that her brother was a grown man who would have to make his own decisions, even if they were the wrong ones. She was grateful, however, that Sheerness had at least been able to convince him to tell the rest of his family.

There was no way Hendon would not go through with it. Psyche had never spoken with the earl, but she knew enough from what Pandora had told her and what she had seen herself that the man was a monster and would have no compunction about dueling. There was nothing to be done from that point except pray for the best, whatever that would be worth. She hoped she was over the influenza before it happened; she wanted to spend more time with Myron…just in case.

≪ ≫

Sheerness arrived home to find his mother and sister in a panic. Alex had left for Lincolnshire shortly before noon after a letter arrived from the nurse he had hired to care for Yeardley. The children had been kept to the nursery from that point as they waited for Sheerness to return. The day was only half over, and he was exhausted. He would have to deliver Hendon's message to Myron, but he had wanted to spend some time alone and not think about anything, perhaps even take a nap. That was not to be.

Baron Yeardley had hung himself and truly left his children orphans. If there was to be one more thing that would happen that day, this would not have been the thing Sheerness would have chosen. In the terse letter the nurse had sent by messenger, she stated it had happened sometime between Saturday evening and Sunday morning. She had followed the family's request and kept all firearms away from the baron as well as all knives and other sharp objects. No one had really thought he was suicidal, and those steps had only been practical precaution. She had seen to it that he was in bed and sleeping before retiring to her own room. She had not noticed any behavior more unusual than was normal for him. She found him Sunday morning when she brought in his breakfast tray, hanging from the top rail of his tester bed. Because she was not a member of the family, she had requested someone come see to his funeral arrangements and final computing of her wages.

It had been almost four months since the children had seen their father, and they understood he was ill, but they had thought they would see him again at some point. As Sheerness was their only surviving male relative (besides Alex), he automatically became their guardian. Jerome was now the Baron Yeardley at barely nine years old. Sheerness didn't know how he was going to tell them that their father was gone, and he didn't know how they would be able to bear it when he did. He only knew he could *not* make them go to another funeral. Alex would attend to that and agreed with his sentiments.

After calming his mother and his sister and telling them he would attend to it, he calmly went to his study and closed the door. He sat at his desk for a while after he drank two glasses of brandy, his arms folded across his chest, his feet propped on the edge of the desk, and a despondent look on his face. He couldn't understand how so many things could go so horribly wrong in such a short time, and he didn't know how much more he could bear. He didn't want any of it, and he felt helpless because he wasn't able to stop it.

He finally rubbed a weary hand over his face and stood. First, he would see to the children; then he would go see Myron if there was any daylight left.

Chapter Eleven

Psyche was feeling much better. The fever had only lasted a day or two. It had taken her nearly a week to get beyond the coughing and runny nose, but she was feeling almost like her old self again. She was able to go riding in the park the following Monday, and she was even able to convince Myron to go with her. She had tried to keep herself sequestered from the rest of her family while she was ill because she didn't want them to catch it, but they had all, with the exception of her younger brothers, come to see her in her room several times while she recuperated.

She was glad Myron had told her family of what he intended to do, as glad as she could be for that type of news. He wouldn't change his mind, and it irritated him that everyone thought he should. It seemed to make him all the more determined to go through with it. She thought that logic was backwards, and she was sure he understood everyone wanted him to call it off only because they didn't want to see him come to any harm, but it was almost as if he felt he needed to prove he would pull through. She would never have thought Myron considered honor to be so fine a point.

Myron would not be straightforward enough to tell the family when and where the duel was to happen. He didn't want them to stop him, and they would try if they knew the specifics. Although she had no intention of going to the duel, Psyche firmly decided she would go stay with Pandora until it was over. Islington had agreed to be Myron's attending physician, and Psyche was not going to leave her sister all alone while they awaited the fate of their brother. Dr. Felton had arrived in town, and he found much to his surprise that he would be attending the duel as well since he was staying with the Aberdares as Myron's guest.

Psyche hadn't seen Sheerness since she had fallen ill. She did hear from Myron that he, too, had caught influenza, but she was distressed to learn his recovery was not quite so speedy as her own. It was traveling through the city at the moment, so no one was suspicious he might have caught it from her, but she felt guilty because she *knew* he had, had told him that she hoped he would. By the time she was well on Monday, he was still sick and in bed. She decided to take him what was left of the medicine Keung had made for her; there was still half a bottle. She couldn't give it to him directly, but she could go visit Amalie and have her give it to her brother. Maybe Psyche would take him some flowers, too.

Something else she learned from Myron that made her all the more determined to go visit Amalie was about the death of Baron Yeardley. Her heart broke for the children, and she wasn't sure what she could do for them. This time, no amount of acrobatics or juggling would be able to rouse them. Still, she wanted them to know she was thinking about them.

Psyche enjoyed her ride with Myron. She did not mention his duel with Hendon. She didn't want to argue, and she didn't want their time together dampened by the uncertainty thoughts of the duel would bring with them. Instead, she talked with him about the trip to Greece and Egypt. They discussed the plans as if he would come through his appointment successfully. Since both of them knew it would be unnecessary for him to flee the country with Georgiana with that outcome, and Psyche didn't want to think of any other, their conversation was based on Psyche going again, too.

While they were in the park, Psyche introduced Myron to Waddlesworth. He found the way the drake and his compatriots nearly overwhelmed his sister in their excitement and competition for the bread she brought amusing. He almost expected them to fly up and land on her shoulders or head at any time, but the only one that showed any interest in being handled was Waddlesworth. Myron almost believed the bird would follow her home if he had a stream to paddle along in behind her. But the duck showed no more interest in being held by Myron than he had for Sheerness. It was nothing personal.

Surprisingly, word of the duel had not become common knowledge among the *ton*. The Aberdares weren't talking about it; neither would Sheerness…not that he had been well enough to speak anyhow. Apparently, Hendon wasn't telling anyone either, and Psyche was surprised Weilheim had not told his wife and made it the talk of the town. Of course, all the parties involved didn't want it widely known because they didn't want the authorities to stop it.

The duke, however, *had* notified them, as far as he was aware of events, but there was little chance they would be able to stop it. No one would tell him where or when the duel was happening. Myron said he would let them know the night before, but not sooner because he would not let them interfere. Pandora would have told her father the details if Islington would have told her, but he had given his word to Myron that he would keep mum. He was the only one they might have been able to get the details from, and Pandora had unsuccessfully tried everything she could think of.

That afternoon after she had gone shopping for a new pair of riding gloves, Psyche went to see Pandora. Waldon informed her that her sister was in the garden, and Psyche gave him a cheeky grin and said she would find her own way. Waldon pursed his lips and bowed, thinking that one sister was no less impertinent than the other, but they did have a tendency to grow on one.

Psyche trotted down the stairs at the back of the house into the garden. The sun was shining, and the air was warm, and she was not surprised Pandora was outside. She didn't have as many rosebushes as their mother…yet, but there was one in particular that was covered in white blooms so fragrant there may as well have been no others. Psyche stopped once she reached it and bent her head to inhale, her eyes closed and a happy smile on her face. After standing that way for a few minutes, she straightened and continued on her way to the garden temple where she would find her sister.

Pandora was lying on her side on the couch taking a nap. She was in a somewhat odd position, a large cushion behind her back, another one under her stomach to support its weight. The couch, under normal circumstances, was wide enough for two people, and Psyche supposed that with her sister in her current condition, it was technically holding *three,* but it wasn't likely that a separate person would fit unless they were snuggled close together. Pandora had a warm, large cashmere blanket draped across her legs, and she appeared to be sleeping comfortably despite her unusual pose. Psyche sighed wistfully at her twin's ability to sleep under any circumstances; she could never recall a time when she was able to sleep so easily.

Pandora didn't stir as Psyche climbed the low steps to the gauzy-curtained platform. The sound of the water falling into the basin of the fountain at the back of the building, the scent of the roses, and the shade from the curtains created a very inviting place for a snooze, and the couch was very comfortable, Psyche knew. She carefully settled herself onto it beside her twin. There was just enough room at the edge for her to lie there facing her sister with her head resting on the pillow, her stomach touching Pandora's.

Psyche felt very peaceful. Perhaps it was because they were identical twins, but she always felt calmed and re-centered just being near Pandora. The fact that her sister was married and expecting a child didn't alter it. Even though they resembled each other on the outside, the two of them had always been two distinct people, but their differences seemed to be pieces that completed and complemented rather than caused discord. Psyche couldn't imagine how she would ever survive if she was never able to see her twin. Just a short time with Pandora helped her regain her normal, calm outlook no matter what she might have been feeling before. This time was no exception.

She continued to lie there near her sister for some time not moving, a contented smile on her face as she watched Pandora sleep. She actually started to doze off herself when she was startled to alertness by the most wondrous and peculiar sensation: Pandora's baby moved, and she felt it against her own stomach. Psyche knew the experience could in no way compare to what Pandora felt herself, but Psyche was almost overwhelmed with the joy created by knowing it was caused by a tiny person who would soon be in the world.

Pandora's eyes slowly opened, and she smiled sleepily as she looked at her sister. She saw Psyche's ecstatic countenance and looked at her curiously.

"Why are you so happy?" she asked softly.

"Because I love you, Pandora," said Psyche with a watery smile.

"I love you, too, Psyche," said Pandora, and she hugged her sister affectionately. After she released her, she gave Psyche an amused grin and a chuckle. "I don't suppose you love me enough to help me sit up, do you?"

Psyche chuckled and sat up herself, putting her feet on the floor. She grabbed Pandora's hands and leaned back toward the opposite end of the couch. It did take some effort, but she was finally able to help Pandora sit upright with her back resting against the cushioned, scrolled arm of the couch.

"Did Islington tell you when Myron will meet Hendon?" asked Psyche after Pandora was adjusted.

Her sister's expression grew sour. "No," she said flatly. "I threatened to make him sleep on the floor at the foot of the bed for a month, and he said he would just find a couch."

"Do you think Dorian knows?"

"Maybe, but I doubt he will say anything either. This whole business is just absolute rubbish to me, but you can't come between a man and his *honor,*" she said derisively. She shrugged. "I'm glad you're feeling much better. I don't think I could have tolerated another carriage ride to see you," she said with a teasing grin.

"I'm sure you're not as glad as I am, and I am also *very* happy you didn't catch it. I don't want you to be here alone when Islington goes with Myron." She gave Pandora a solemn look and held her hands. "I want to be here with you when it happens."

"Oh, Psyche, I'm sure Myron will be fine. He's an expert shot."

"How expert is he going to be when he turns and shoots on a signal with very little time to aim? And what about Hendon? Who knows how many duels he has fought, and not to anyone's knowledge has he ever even been hurt. You know the man is not going to delope, and he *will* aim to kill if he has the opportunity."

Pandora's optimistic expression faded somewhat. "I know, but I just have to believe Myron will be fine because I can't bear to think of the alternative."

"Neither can I," said Psyche gloomily. She looked at Pandora thoughtfully. "Why did Georgiana come to dinner Sunday in the condition she was? Didn't she realize Myron seeing her that way would set him off?"

"Yes, she knew," said Pandora evenly, and Psyche could see she was choosing her words. "Hendon made her come because he knew she was coming to *my* house. He doesn't know about the two of them, and we can be thankful for that. Hendon wanted *me* to see her that way, not Myron."

"Why would he do that?" gasped Psyche. "He didn't...he didn't rape her just for you to see her that way, did he?" Pandora looked away from her, and Psyche felt tears sting her eyes. "Why would he *do* that?" she repeated in a cracked whisper.

Pandora looked back at her sister with a grim expression. "Because he's a *lunatic!*" she bit out. "He wanted to remind me of Drury, to show me what he would have done to *me*. I wish Theo hadn't *saved* me from Hendon because the bastard would be dead by now and none of this would be happening!"

"Do you really think you could have killed him?" asked Psyche quietly.

"I don't know," said Pandora honestly with a shrug. "I certainly would have given him a drubbing that would have made him think twice about trying to do it again to someone else, even his wife. If I had felt I had no choice, I think I could have."

"Was he there when you took her home?"

"No, thank God. Theo was so angry he was ready to just break the man's neck and be done with it."

"It is terrible Hendon has been able to get away with the things he has done, but I don't think Myron should be the one to make him answer for them."

"I agree," said Pandora heartily, "but, please, let's not talk about it anymore. It will be what it will be, and we will just have to accept things as they come."

Psyche chuckled. "You've been around Maiyin and Keung too much. You're beginning to sound like a Buddhist monk. The next thing I know, you'll be wanting to shave your head and start wearing red and yellow robes."

Pandora chuckled, too. "I'm not quite so placid as that. Ask my husband." She looked at Psyche with a mischievous twinkle. "I understand Lord Sheerness has influenza."

Psyche colored but tried to remain as nonchalant as possible. "Yes, I understand it's going through the city right now."

"Mm-hmm," said Pandora with a raised eyebrow.

"I thought I might take him what is left of my medicine. Since it worked so well for me, I thought Sheerness might find it useful. He is Myron's second, after all, and it wouldn't do for him to be unable to get out of bed, especially since we don't know how much longer it will be before the duel. It surely cannot be too long now."

"Perhaps it would make Myron reschedule."

"I doubt it, and Sheerness really doesn't need to be ill right now."

"Oh?"

"You mean you haven't heard?" said Psyche in surprise.

"Heard what?" asked Pandora blankly.

"Baron Yeardley has died!"

"Oh, my giddy aunt!" gasped Pandora. "What happened?"

"Myron said he killed himself."

"No!" said Pandora with a horrified expression. "What about the children?"

Psyche shook her head uncertainly. "I suppose Sheerness is to be their guardian now. Going to see them and Amalie is my reason for visiting. Giving Sheerness the rest of my medicine was a side purpose, not the main one, but now is really not a convenient time for him to be ill...if there's ever a *convenient* time for anyone," she finished on a mumble.

"You wouldn't be feeling guilty, now, would you?" teased Pandora.

"No," said Psyche with amused exasperation. "But I thought taking him some flowers would be a nice gesture."

Pandora started to laugh with hilarity, and she put a hand to her side as it caused a stitch.

"You made him sick, admit it!" chortled Pandora.

"Ooh! All right! I admit it. It was my fault," groaned Psyche. "Does that make you happy?"

"Yes…deliriously," sighed Pandora, and she continued to rub her side in an effort to make the baby remove its foot from behind her ribs before it slipped off and kicked her in the diaphragm. "I think you should take him some of the white roses. Even with a stuffy nose, he'll be able to smell them."

"Roses? I was thinking of daisies or mums."

"Eww, no," said Pandora, wrinkling her nose distastefully. "Have Keung cut you some of the white roses."

"All right." Psyche leaned forward to hug her sister as she prepared to leave. "I think I'll come stay with you as soon as Myron lets us know. Can you tell Waldon to expect me in case I show up in the middle of the night? I could only imagine him turning me away in his nightcap," said Psyche with a chuckle.

Pandora grinned as she had an image as well. "Of course. I'll have a room made up for you, too," said Pandora as she slowly stood up from the couch to link her arm through Psyche's so they could go in search of Keung to retrieve her roses.

Psyche left for the Sheerness residence almost two hours later. It was still only mid-afternoon, and she would have plenty of time for a nice visit. She had the bottle of medicine in her reticule and a dozen of the white roses from Pandora's garden. She let Jim smell them before he helped her into the covered landau they were using, and he thought they smelled lovely as well.

Psyche wasn't sure if the children would be up to seeing visitors, but she was sure Amalie could use some company. She had no doubt Sheerness would be in bed and in no condition to see anyone. That suited her fine. She was feeling *very* confused about him at the moment; he had said he would try not to make her feel that way, and it had only steadily been growing worse. She was sure seeing him would not help matters any. Considering how other things in her life were at the moment, she didn't need confusion as well.

The door was answered by George, the footman, as usual. He was friendly, as always, but she could see the troubles of his employers worried him. She sympathized with his circumstances. This family had seen enough misery in the last six months to last a lifetime. George showed her down a hallway and opened the door to what she immediately realized was the family's private sitting room. She hadn't expected that, but apparently he had grown so accustomed to her visits and those of her younger brothers, he felt confident the Nicholses would not mind receiving her there.

That proved to be the case. Amalie was there with the children and Nanny MacBean (at least, Psyche felt fairly certain she was). Psyche might have thought the room was empty before George opened the door because the noise she associated with small children was absent. As George opened the door, Psyche saw Amalie seated in a chair by the fire reading a book of poetry. Nanny MacBean sat in a chair opposite, knitting something made of dark blue yarn. And all three children ranged about on the floor or the couch either drawing or reading as well. All of them looked up when the door opened, and there was only a momentary pause before Josie, Jerome, and Philip bounded from their places and charged toward her.

"Lady Psyche!" they cried excitedly, and she thought they were going to knock her over in their enthusiasm as they grabbed her about the waist and legs in a hug.

"Whist now, children!" said Nanny MacBean. "Mind how ye go!"

Philip turned to look at her over his shoulder as he continued to hold on to Psyche's legs happily. "But this is Lady Psyche!" he said incredulously, as if manners and calmness only applied to other visitors.

"E'en so, Master Philip. Tha's no way ta greet yer elders," said the nanny sternly. "An' there's other reasons it's nae fittin'."

The children looked at their nanny for a moment before they reluctantly released Psyche and stepped away from her with downcast expressions. Psyche felt sorry for them, and she was tempted to have them defy their keeper and hug them to her just to see them happy again. She walked the rest of the way into the room, and George, who had been patiently waiting behind her, closed the door. Nanny MacBean began to gather her things into a small wicker basket at Psyche's entrance, and Psyche hoped the woman did not intend to leave with the children. Psyche wouldn't let her.

Amalie smiled and put her book aside. She stood up and went to give her friend a warm hug.

"Psyche, it's so wonderful to see you," she said fondly but in a somewhat subdued tone. "I thought you had influenza," she said, and she held Psyche's empty hand and stood back from her to give her a disbelieving once-over.

"I did, but I'm better now...except for the occasional sniffle," said Psyche casually.

"And what marvelous roses!" sighed Amalie as she inhaled their perfume. "I could smell them as soon as the door opened."

"Yes, well, I understand I'm not the only one who has come down with influenza, and as Lord Sheerness took pity on me in my time of need, I thought it only fair I return the favor and bring him something he could smell, even...."

Her words died as she watched Amalie's face grow so pale it was almost white. Psyche's forehead wrinkled in puzzlement.

"Amalie? Whatever is wrong?" she asked, reaching out a hand to rub her friend's shoulder soothingly. "If he doesn't like roses, then you can have them, and I'll just bring him some ragweed," she said mildly. Amalie looked as if she were about to burst into tears. "Amalie? What is it?" she asked worriedly.

"Come along, children," said Nanny MacBean quickly, and she reached out an arm to escort them from the room.

Psyche looked from her friend to the nanny's activities with worried confusion.

"Oh, but....," began Psyche disappointedly, but the MacBean had already guided them out and closed the door.

Psyche looked back to Amalie nervously and took her by the hand to lead her over to the couch and sit down beside her. She placed the roses on the cushion and took both of her friend's hands in hers. She felt as if she were missing something, something that was a very important piece of all this.

"Amalie, please, tell me what's the matter," she said softly.

"Oh, Psyche, Sebastian is so very ill," choked Amalie.

"What?" gasped Psyche in shock. "I thought he had influenza."

Amalie nodded and attempted to calm herself, but she couldn't stop her tears. "He *does*. The doctor has been to see him every day since he's become ill, but he just keeps getting worse."

Psyche felt the blood rushing in her ears, and her hands went limp in the grasp that Amalie had on them.

"What are you saying?" she asked breathlessly.

"Oh, Psyche, I can't lose Sebastian, too!" choked Amalie, and she began to sob as she weakly leaned her head against Psyche's shoulder.

Psyche hugged Amalie almost reflexively as the thoughts spun around in her head. She rubbed Amalie's shoulder comfortingly and leaned her head against her friend's. Psyche's confusion and worry had not lessened.

"But he has influenza," she said softly, almost to herself. "How can he be so ill just from influenza?"

Amalie lifted her head from Psyche's shoulder in surprise.

"What do you mean: *just* from influenza?" asked Amalie, almost angrily.

"Well, I had it last week, and while I certainly *felt* like I wanted to die, I was never in any danger of actually doing so." Psyche looked in her reticule and pulled out her bottle of medicine. "As a matter of fact, I brought this for you to give your brother because I thought he might find it helpful, but if he doesn't have influenza, I'm not sure how effective it will be."

"He *does* have influenza!" said Amalie exasperatedly. "That's what I've been telling you! What is that?"

"It's the medicine I took while I was ill last week," said Psyche simply, and she was trying not to think about the fact that Sheerness could be dying.

"Are you sure *you* had influenza?" asked Amalie doubtfully, raising an eyebrow.

She didn't see how her friend could possibly be well already if she had influenza. People *died* from influenza; they didn't get well in a week. Her brother became ill on Wednesday, and he had only steadily gotten worse. But if Psyche had....

"Well, yes, I *did* have it." Psyche wasn't going to tell Amalie that if she was sure Sheerness had it, there could be no doubt Psyche had because he caught it from her. "I am absolutely certain I had it."

Amalie looked at the bottle in Psyche's hand. "And that's all you took?"

"This and the occasional horehound lozenge and a little eucalyptus oil for my nose."

"Come again?"

"Well, at one point my nose was so stuffy I had to do something to make it open up again."

"Eucalyptus oil?" asked Amalie blankly then shook her head dismissively. "Oh, never mind. Come with me," she said hurriedly, grabbing Psyche's wrist holding the bottle to pull her up from the couch.

"But…," began Psyche in a startled tone, and she reached down to grab the flowers as Amalie rushed her toward the door and into the hall.

Psyche let her friend lead her through the house with a puzzled frown, but she didn't begin to feel reluctant until they started up the stairs for the next floor. She grew suspicious about their final destination, and she wasn't sure what purpose it would serve to have her go as well. She could see Amalie did not intend to let her go until they got there, and while Psyche did not drag her feet, she did not move quickly either.

When they reached the top of the stairs, Amalie turned to go down the hall to the left. They were almost to the end of it when they stopped in front of a door on the right. There was light in the hall from a window at the end of it, but she could not see any from beneath the edge of the door. Amalie opened the door slightly and stuck her head into the room through the crack to look in for a brief moment before opening it further and pulling Psyche in after her.

The first thing Psyche noticed was the darkness. The room was barely lit by low-burning lamps on either side of the bed and a raging fire in the small fireplace. The second thing she noticed was the stifling heat. Psyche could scarcely breathe because it was so hot, and the small amount of fresh, cooler air that was created by opening the door was quickly consumed by the fire burning on the grate. Her sinuses started to seal shut from the heat in the room, and Psyche thought it was no wonder Sheerness was only getting worse.

The countess was sitting in a chair near the bed, and she stood to go over to her daughter and Psyche where they waited by the door. Psyche could barely see the earl lying in the bed, and she might not have realized it was the countess if she hadn't come closer. Lady Sheerness looked from Amalie to Psyche curiously when she reached them.

"Amalie, *chere,* why have you brought Lady Psyche in here?" she asked in quiet reproach.

"*Maman,* Lady Psyche had influenza," said Amalie in the same soft tone, but she still managed to sound very excited.

"Still, this is your brother's room, and he's very ill," said Lady Sheerness, and she spared a glance toward the bed where her son continued to sleep.

"No, *Maman,* you don't understand. Lady Psyche had influenza only *last week!*" said Amalie impatiently.

"*Shh!*" said the countess quickly, looking back at the bed with concern.

It was quiet in the room for only a moment before Psyche could hear Sheerness being overwhelmed by a racking cough. The countess looked at her daughter reprovingly, and Amalie's face went pale and anxious. Psyche's forehead wrinkled worriedly as she looked from the two women to the figure on the bed. The fit continued for several minutes until he finally became too weak to cough anymore, and Psyche could hear him gasping for air. Even with the room not being inordinately large, it was too dark for her to see him, and the dark velvet brocade curtains pulled to each of the corners of the large four-poster bed didn't help matters any. Psyche had had enough.

"Love a duck!" she muttered, shaking her head exasperatedly, and she made her way to the nearest window and pulled open the curtains to let in the sunlight. She ignored the astonished expressions on the faces of Amalie and Lady Sheerness.

"Oh, no, you mustn't!" said Amalie with alarm.

"Amalie, get her out of here!" cried Josephine in much the same tone.

Psyche continued to disregard their fear until she had opened every curtain in the room. It was certainly much brighter, and she was able to see the earl on the bed. When she looked at him in the light, her face paled, and a hand went to her throat in dismay. She almost didn't recognize him. She had thought at first that Amalie had only been exaggerating, but he *did* look like he was dying.

His skin was very pale, and he was drenched with sweat. There were white bandages on his arms, and from the places where the blood soaked through, Psyche knew they were there to cover the cuts the doctor had made for bloodletting. Sheerness had on no shirt, and his chest was red and blistered as if he had been burned by a flame or something caustic. His eyes were closed, and she could hear a soft, whistling noise every time he took a breath.

"Oh, my God!" gasped Psyche, and she felt tears sting her eyes as she looked at him. "What in the world have they done to you?"

"Quickly, Amalie, we must close the curtains!" said Lady Sheerness, and she went to the nearest set to put action to words.

"Leave them open!" shouted Psyche angrily.

"But the doctor said—" began Amalie.

"Your doctor is—at best—a draconic imbecile," cut in Psyche.

She went to the nearby writing desk and retrieved a pen and piece of paper. She quickly scribbled a brief message, blotted it, and folded it. She took it to Amalie.

"Take that to my driver, Jim, and tell him he needs to go to Bardsey House as quickly as possible. That is for Keung." Amalie looked at her in shocked awe. "Can you remember that?" Amalie nodded. "Then get moving!" said Psyche impatiently.

After a brief look from her mother, to her brother, then back to Psyche, Amalie quickly fled from the room. Psyche turned to look at Lady Sheerness, who glared at her angrily, but Psyche could also detect something that might have been relief just beneath it.

"Lady Sheerness, please, forgive me for taking over your house, but your son *is* going to die if this doesn't stop. I don't know who your doctor is, but the man's method belongs in the Dark Ages. All this bleeding, heat, and darkness nonsense. No wonder he's at death's door." She raised her hands from her sides and shook her head incredulously. "Didn't you wonder at all after a day or two that the man might be making things *worse*?" she asked sadly.

She moved closer to the bed and examined the items on the night table. She clicked her tongue as she looked. Laudanum. The makings for a mustard plaster, which explained why his chest looked so terrible. A pitcher of water and a small glass. At least those two items might be useful. She poured some water into the glass and retrieved the bottle she had placed back in her reticule and realized she was still holding the flowers. She didn't want to put them in the water pitcher. She turned to look at Lady Sheerness.

"Do you have a vase for these?" asked Psyche distractedly as she looked worriedly at the earl.

Lady Sheerness had calmed considerably, and she nodded numbly as she retrieved the flowers from Psyche.

"There's one downstairs," said Josephine quietly. "I'll just go get it." She looked at Psyche assessingly. "You will keep an eye on him."

"Absolutely," said Psyche soothingly.

She calmly watched the countess leave the room and went back to what she was doing. She added some of the medicine to the glass and set both it and the bottle on the table. She tossed the laudanum and mustard plaster into the nearby trash basket and retrieved her handkerchief from her reticule when she couldn't find another appropriate piece of cloth. She dampened it with some water from the pitcher. The room still felt unbearably hot, and she went to a nearby set of glass doors onto the balcony that had been hiding behind a set of curtains and opened them to let in the gentle afternoon breeze. *She* was able to breathe easier almost immediately, and she walked back to the bed. Sheerness hadn't moved.

Psyche climbed the step stool at the edge of the bed after she had moved it a little closer to his head, but she still had to lean forward quite a bit to reach him. She put the wet handkerchief on his forehead after she had patted the rest of his face with it. She couldn't believe his condition. She had seen him only last Monday, and he had been the picture of health. Psyche felt more than a little guilty for him being this way. He never would have gotten sick if it weren't for her, even if the doctor had made it worse. She removed the handkerchief from his brow and wiped his face with it again. She was hoping the coolness might wake him enough to give him the medicine, but it seemed the coughing fit had, for the moment, drained him.

Psyche soon grew tired of bending over and sat on the edge of the bed. It was much easier to reach his face, and she could reach the pitcher on the table by bending slightly. She wet the cloth again and smoothed it across his chest. It looked terrible, and she hoped it wouldn't take long for Jim to fetch Keung. She had briefly explained the situation in her message, and she knew he would bring everything necessary to get this sorted out…if it could be sorted out.

She wasn't concerned about seeing Sheerness without his shirt. Had the circumstances been different, she might have given him more than the clinical glance she did now. The red and blistered area covered most of what was exposed. She could only imagine how much it must have hurt, and it was all for nothing. It was an almost perfect square, starting a few inches below his collarbone to just beyond his sternum and crosswise from the edge of one nipple to the other. Even the light matting of hair that covered his chest had offered no protection from the caustic nature of the plaster. The paleness of his skin elsewhere made what Psyche could only think of as a wound look even more vicious.

Her head jerked up as he started to cough again, and it sounded almost as if he were drowning. As he continued to cough, she realized that was exactly what he was doing. He was lying almost flat on his back, and he wasn't strong enough to turn to his side or sit up. Without thinking, she hiked up her skirts and climbed further onto the bed and straddled him. She grabbed him under his arms and pulled backward to sit him upright. Once he was sitting, she moved off of him and kept him leaning forward, balanced against one of her arms, and began whacking him between the shoulderblades with the other.

She could hear a rattling sound in his chest as he continued to cough, and she watched as he expelled large quantities of phlegm. Psyche grimaced and controlled her queasiness as she continued to pound him on the back until the coughing abated. When he had finished, the rattling had lessened, and even though he was still having trouble breathing, Psyche thought it did sound a little better. Before she laid him back again, she arranged the pillows into a higher pile so he would be almost sitting. She grudgingly used her handkerchief to wipe up the phlegm before she straddled him again to gently lean him back.

Amalie came in just as Psyche had settled him onto the pillows, and the girl's face flushed a bright red in shock and embarrassment at catching Psyche in such a compromising position with her brother. When she had left the room, this was certainly not what she had expected to return to.

"What are you doing?" gasped Amalie.

Psyche calmly climbed off of Sheerness and used the step stool to get back on the floor. She disgustedly held the handkerchief with two fingers and tossed it into the trash basket before she turned to look at her friend as she dusted her hands together.

"I was helping him cough. I'll show you how before I leave because you'll need to do it a time or two yourself." She looked for another cloth to put on his forehead, but she didn't see anything. "Did you send Jim to Pandora's?"

"Yes, he's on his way there," said Amalie calmly. She looked at Psyche uncertainly. "Is Sebastian going to be all right?"

"I don't know," said Psyche honestly. "But I suggest you don't let that doctor anywhere near him again."

"*Maman* is dressing him down in the drawing room right this minute," said Amalie with a slight smile. She noticed Psyche looking around. "What are you looking for?"

"I need a flannel or something to put on his forehead."

"Oh, of course," said Amalie agreeably.

She went into a room through a doorway hidden in a panel in the wall and soon returned carrying a large pile of neatly folded cloths in various sizes. Psyche didn't think quite so many would be necessary. She took them from Amalie and placed them onto the night table. She wet one with water from the pitcher and reseated herself on the bed to smooth it across his face. Sheerness was still very pale, and the whistling noise as he breathed still remained. She really wanted him to wake up to give him some of the medicine, and the wet cloth wasn't doing any good.

She looked at the bandages on his arms distractedly as she adjusted the blankets further up on his chest, and she pondered what she might try to get him to wake up. He was very weak, but she would have thought he would wake up with the coolness and damp against the heat of his face. Then she actually counted the blood spots on the bandages. She turned to look at Amalie.

"How much blood did the doctor take in his lettings?" she asked stilly.

Amalie shrugged negligibly as she thought about it. "Oh, I don't know, really. I wasn't here every time, but he took at least a pint each of the three times I was here. Why?"

Psyche felt the breath catch in her throat, and she unfastened the bandage on the arm nearest to her to count the actual incisions. She filled with even more alarm when she saw they matched the number of blood spots, and two of them had become red with the beginnings of an infection. She crawled over him and did the same with the other arm, only to see much more of the same.

"Oh, my God," she whispered brokenly, and she put a hand over her mouth to choke back a sob as her eyes filled with tears.

She took a deep breath in an effort to calm herself, and she turned to look at Amalie. Lady Sheerness had returned to the room, carrying a beautiful crystal vase filled with the white roses. Josephine felt a surge of panic when she saw Psyche's stricken face, but she calmed somewhat when she saw her son was still breathing and Amalie didn't seem as upset. She also felt no small amount of concern as she took in the results of Psyche's activities while she had been absent from the room. She carried the vase to the table on the opposite side from that holding the pitcher and flannels and set it down carefully. She then looked at Psyche again.

"Dr. Phelps has been told his services will no longer be required," said Josephine evenly.

Psyche nodded because she didn't trust her voice to speak for the moment. She couldn't blame the countess or Amalie. They didn't know. Most of the things this Dr. Phelps (whoever he was) had done were considered perfectly acceptable methods of treatment…not to *her* family, but to most everyone else. Practices were changing, but technically, the man had done nothing wrong. She couldn't bear to tell them Dr. Phelps had nearly bled Sheerness to death. She didn't doubt if he had been bled one more time (which is probably what the doctor had been coming to do), he would have been dead by nightfall. As it was, Psyche wasn't sure even Keung could save him. She took another deep breath and looked at Amalie.

"Jim should be returning with Keung soon. He's a bit…unusual, so you may want to be downstairs when he arrives to make sure he is let in. You need to bring him to me the minute he gets here," she said as steadily as she could.

"A-all right," said Amalie uncertainly.

"I will go ahead and tell you that he is Chinese, and he is the kindest, wisest, most gentle man you are ever likely to meet." She looked at Sheerness again and sighed preparatorily to voice her next words. "And if there is anyone who can save your brother now, he is." She didn't want to believe things could be as bad as that, but it would be impractical to think otherwise.

Both Josephine and Amalie looked at her in dismay as she said it, and Amalie nodded her head soundlessly as she turned to leave the room. Psyche crawled back over Sheerness to re-dampen the cloth and wipe his face with it. She realized there was not much she could do at this point except be there, and she was trying not to cry. Unless he woke up, and she wasn't sure he would after losing so much blood, Psyche was desolate to think he might not ever do so. She couldn't believe how what she thought would be a brief sympathy call could go so horribly wrong, and how much of it was her fault.

"Please, give me something to do," pleaded Josephine in a whisper.

Psyche looked up at her in surprise. What *was* there to do? She chewed on the side of her thumb as she thought.

"I imagine Keung will want hot water while he is here."

"I will go to the kitchen to make sure that is ready," said Josephine with a decisive nod as she prepared to leave the room.

"Oh, Lady Sheerness?" called Psyche softly. "Can you tell me when the last time was that Lord Sheerness was awake?"

"Saturday," said Josephine sadly.

"He's not had anything to eat since then either?"

"No," answered the countess with a puzzled frown.

Her answer put another piece of the puzzle into place for Psyche and caused her another stab of panic and guilt.

"He's going to need something mild to eat at first. I found that chicken soup and—believe it or not—cabbage and potatoes with ham made me feel much better while I was ill last week."

"*D'accord.* I will see to that as well." Lady Sheerness started to leave the room, and she almost reached the door when she turned to look back at Psyche beside her son on the bed. "This Keung…he treated you last week?"

"Absolutely," said Psyche soothingly, and she gave the countess what she hoped was a comforting smile.

Josephine nodded and left the room. The countess began to feel hopeful, and now that she had a purpose, she began to feel not quite so helpless.

Psyche continued to rub the flannel across Sheerness' exposed skin. He didn't move except for his breathing, and the whistling had settled into a slow rhythm Psyche found in no way soothing. She hesitantly reached up a hand to smooth it across his hair to his cheek, covered by several days' growth of beard. She had to make this right.

"I am *so* sorry," she whispered.

Sheerness began to cough again, and Psyche was not surprised to hear the same gurgling rattle. She grabbed one of the cloths from the table and draped it across one of her shoulders. She straddled his lap and pulled him upright, but instead of moving, she rested his chin on her shoulder where she had placed the large flannel and pounded his back with the heel of her hand. She didn't want to see what came out, and this would be a better way to prevent it. When he finished, she gently eased him back onto the pillows.

The cough had sounded very productive, and she hoped she would be able to prevent him from developing pneumonia, which would happen if he didn't cough it up. She had helped Keung tend to enough of the families on their estate to know what she needed to do and what she needed to look for. Sometimes, if the family had waited too long to send for him, it was too late, but she was optimistic that for Sheerness there might yet be time.

She carefully removed the cloth from her shoulder and folded it over without looking at it. The last bit had sounded nasty, and she didn't want to know. She used the folded cloth to wipe his nose and mouth, and she sat there for a moment considering what she should do with it. She could care less whether she lost her handkerchief, but the flannels might be missed. She bent sideways slightly and dropped it onto the floor by the bed. She would ask Amalie or Lady Sheerness about a suitable place for it when they returned, but that would do for now.

She looked back at Sheerness after she straightened up and prepared to climb off of him. She leaned forward to retrieve the cloth to put back on his forehead, and she jumped in surprise when she saw that his eyes were open. After Lady Sheerness said he had not been conscious since Saturday, it was the last thing she expected. But his eyes were open, and he was looking at her. His gaze was glassy from fever, but he was looking at her as if he knew her, and she was hopeful.

"Hallo, Lord Sheerness," she said calmly with a pleasant smile.

"What are you doing here?" he asked weakly.

Psyche could see that he found the condition of his voice disconcerting. She could imagine hearing only a cracked whisper come out no matter how hard he tried to make it louder after being accustomed to a baritone—almost bass—would be disturbing. Psyche climbed off of him and straightened out her skirts before answering.

"I brought you some flowers," said Psyche casually, giving him a slight smile and nodding in the direction of the table on the other side of the bed as she put the cloth back onto his forehead. Then her eyes rounded as she remembered why she had hoped he would wake up. "Oh! I need to give you some medicine."

"Not laudanum," whispered Sheerness, and he weakly tried to lift a hand to stop her.

"Eww, no," said Psyche with a moue of disgust as she reached for the glass on the table.

She helped him raise his head and put the glass to his lips. She supposed one of the benefits of a stuffy nose was that he wouldn't be able to taste it, but as far as Keung's concoctions went, this one actually did not taste too bad. She personally had tasted much worse. After he drained the glass, she helped him settle back against the pillows again.

"Do you want some water?" she asked.

"Wasn't that?" he asked hoarsely, and he almost began to cough again but managed to keep it under control.

Psyche's lips twitched amusedly. "No, *that* was the medicine, and it should actually work."

Sheerness nodded and blinked his eyes tiredly. "All better?"

"You will be soon," said Psyche quietly, and she hoped she was right. She reached over to adjust the flannel on his forehead, and he grabbed her wrist to get her attention.

"No. You. All better?"

It was taking him a lot of effort to talk, but it seemed important to him to find out. His grasp was so weak, she could feel an emotional lump beginning to form in her throat. She could not bear to see him like this. It was so wrong.

"I am as fine as frog hair," said Psyche quietly with a soothing smile.

That seemed to set his mind at ease, and he smiled and nodded. He didn't let go of her wrist, but continued to hold her hand in his against his chest where it had come to lay when his strength gave out. Psyche let him keep it captive. She was becoming more positive with every passing minute he stayed awake that he would be able to recover. Only Keung would be able to say with more certainty. She shifted a little closer to him so she would be able to reach him with her left hand and began smoothing the cloth across his face again.

"What day is it?" he whispered.

"Monday...the thirteenth."

He frowned and shook his head and tried to sit up on his own without much success. Psyche put a hand to his shoulder, and gave the hand that held hers a gentle squeeze.

"Shh. You can't go anywhere in your condition, and I can't believe you actually want to try." She looked to the doorway for a moment to listen for anyone approaching; she didn't want Amalie and Josephine to hear. "In addition to catching *my* influenza, Dr. Phelps nearly bled you dry. Whatever it is will wait," she said firmly.

"Myron."

"Myron will have his duel with or without you," said Psyche evenly, and as she said it, she had come to accept there really was *nothing* anyone could do to stop him. "I know he entrusted you with being his second, but honor will do neither of you any good if you're dead." Psyche watched in disbelief when his jaw clenched...as if he were going to *argue* with her about it. "Dorian or Islington can take your place if need be, I'm sure. Besides, you would *die* before you made it to the door of your bedroom, and your mother and sister are beside themselves with worry just thinking of the possibility."

Further argument was halted when he began to cough again. Psyche quickly grabbed another cloth from the slowly dwindling stack on the table and repeated her previous actions. Once she had him settled back onto the pillows and had tossed the flannel to join the other on the floor, she rubbed a hand across her forehead to clear off a slight film of perspiration. He was heavy, and she thought it might take both his mother and sister to do it.

"Dizzy," he croaked.

"Too right," said Psyche with a wink and a humorous grin at his expense. He frowned, and Psyche smoothed an apologetic hand across his forehead. "I'm sorry, but you asked for that one," she said quietly. She shrugged and sighed thoughtfully. "It is probably from blood loss. If what Amalie says is right, you've lost at least six pints since Wednesday. You've had nothing to eat since Saturday, and I don't imagine what you had then was very nourishing. You're probably more ill from that than the influenza. Your doctor is an idiot, and I don't imagine he's had very much success in treating his patients who actually had something wrong with them."

"*Maman* and Amalie?"

Psyche's forehead wrinkled for a moment as she tried to decipher what he was asking, and then it cleared when she did.

"Oh! Amalie is waiting for Keung to arrive so she can bring him up to look you over. Your mother has gone to the kitchen to make sure there is hot water in case Keung needs it when he gets here and having some soup and cabbage made for you to eat when you're able." He grimaced at the thought of cabbage. "It's very good for you, and if I can eat it, so can you."

Psyche realized she was still sitting on him, and she reached for the cloth and prepared to move off of him and re-dampen it. Sheerness put his hands on top of her thighs just above her knees to stay her. Psyche looked down at him with a concerned frown. She patiently moved his hands without much effort and climbed back onto the bed and straightened out her skirts.

"Your mother and Amalie would be horrified to come in here and find me sitting there, and it would be my luck you would expire just as they came in the door," she said with an impassive expression. Sheerness smiled amusedly and actually began to chuckle silently. "You think I'm bamming you. Amalie's already come in to find me sitting there once, and I swear the look on her face would make you think I was some type of she-demon bent on doing you in."

Psyche ignored his silent laughter as she poured more water onto the flannel. She fully expected his amusement to cause another coughing fit at any time. She was glad he found it funny, but she did not find it so very. The next time one of his family members came in to see her straddled across his lap, she had better be hitting him on the back when they did because the position looked erotic otherwise, which she didn't realize until after Amalie's astonishment brought it to her attention. She poured more water into the glass, noting the pitcher was almost empty. When Amalie or Lady Sheerness came back, she would request to have it filled again. She set the cloth aside for the moment and lifted his head to put the glass to his lips.

"Here, drink some water," she said tartly.

He did without complaint, and he looked at her happily the entire time. She was tempted to just let his head drop back with a thump onto the pillows, but his humor was also a good sign. She set the glass back on the table to pick up the flannel again and began to pat it across his chest. He still had a fever, and she thought it might have dropped a degree or two since she had opened the balcony doors to let in the air, but it was far from normal. He didn't seem to be quite as sweat-soaked as when she first saw him, and she hoped the fresh air would help with his breathing. The whistling noise had almost stopped, and that would continue to improve as long as he continued to cough up what was in his lungs.

"Kiss me?" he asked softly.

Psyche paused in what she was doing to look at him with gentle exasperation.

"Didn't I just explain this?" she asked patiently.

"Not sitting on me," he said calmly, giving her a tempting smile.

Psyche looked at him consideringly. It wasn't as if she would catch the influenza, as she had given it to him. The expression on his face was almost boyish in its appeal, and she found it oddly endearing. Yet she knew if his mother or sister walked in to find her kissing him, she would not be able to explain it away as *helping* him. She didn't want to do anything that would cause him undue distress and make him take another turn for the worse, but she couldn't decide if kissing him or denying him would make him more excitable. She gave another hesitant glance to the door. It was closed, and she thought she would hear someone if they were to open it. She scooted a little closer to him and put a gentle hand on his cheek.

"You are so ill you cannot speak or sit up, and yet all you can think of is placing me into a compromising position," she said softly as she brought her face closer to his.

"Die happy," he said with a grin.

Psyche pursed her lips and shook her head with a groan. "You're impossible."

She dipped her head and placed her lips against his tentatively at first. The growth of beard was scratchy, but Psyche didn't mind it, and she smoothed her hand across the rough texture of his cheek as she deepened the kiss. She did like kissing him despite herself, and he obviously found it enjoyable, considering he wanted it even if it killed him. She felt his hand move to her waist, then up her side to just below her breast, and Psyche was disconcerted when she found herself becoming filled with longing. She ended the kiss and looked into his eyes with a bewildered expression, and she could see he was surprised she had stopped. She couldn't understand why he always had to cause her so much confusion, even when she was sure it wasn't intentional.

She looked away from him with a slight frown between her brows and straightened up to resume smoothing the flannel across his skin. She didn't want to have feelings for him, and she shouldn't have kissed him because it certainly didn't make her feel indifferent. She felt almost panicked by the emotions rushing through her, and she could feel her hands trembling slightly as she tried to control it. His hand had dropped back to her waist when she sat away from him, and he tugged at her skirt to get her attention.

"Not hurt," he said, giving her a soothing smile when he saw her worried frown.

"No," she agreed, giving him a noncommittal smile of her own. *He* might not have been, but she wasn't so sure about herself.

He began to cough again, and Psyche grabbed another flannel from the pile. She waited to see if he would be able to recover from it on his own, now that he had been able to clear out some of the congestion, but it didn't take her long to realize he couldn't. She climbed back onto his lap and helped him sit up. He clung to her weakly as he coughed, and Psyche blinked back her tears and closed her eyes as she pounded his back. The fit seemed to last much longer than the others, and by the time it ended and she had placed him back against the pillows, she was alarmed to see a slight bluish tinge to his skin and that he had lost consciousness.

A slight noise beside the bed and a touch to her shoulder made Psyche turn in surprise to see Keung standing on the step stool beside her. She started to cry with relief and hugged him as she moved to the side of the bed.

"Oh, thank God you're here," she sighed.

"Tell me," said Keung soothingly, patting her shoulder.

Psyche briefly looked to the foot of the bed at Amalie and Josephine standing there, their expressions no less alarmed than Psyche's as they looked at Sheerness on the bed. His skin had regained its previous paleness, and he was breathing, but he had not opened his eyes. She didn't want them to hear what she told Keung because it would only make them more worried so she took a deep breath and began to speak to him quietly in Mandarin, telling him everything she knew, what she had been doing (except for kissing him), and that she had given him one dose of the medicine. Keung kept his hands clasped behind his back and would nod occasionally with approval as she talked to him, his expression thoughtful. She felt much calmer after she was finished, and he waited until she was done before he asked her any questions to clarify a few things. Having him there made her feel like everything would be fine.

Keung retrieved the cloths she had discarded to the floor to look at their contents. He then balled them up and dropped them back to where they were, his expression impassive. Psyche moved out of the way, and he climbed onto the bed to examine Sheerness in much the same way he had done Psyche the previous Monday. Keung listened raptly to the sounds in his chest as he breathed, and he nodded once as he straightened back up. He looked at the burns left by the plaster on Sheerness's chest, and he clicked his tongue as he looked at the incisions in his arms. The last thing Keung did was put a hand to the earl's forehead to assess his temperature.

The countess and Amalie remained standing at the foot of the bed, holding each others' hands nervously as the small stranger silently conducted his examination. They weren't sure how capable he was, but Psyche seemed to trust him wholeheartedly, and they trusted *her* judgment.

Keung hopped down quietly from the bed and went to his wooden box. From the bottom, he pulled out a small, wide-mouthed jar; a round, lidded, wooden box; and two small, stoppered bottles and set them on the table. He then pulled out an empty bottle and mixed just two ingredients together in it before stoppering it. He signaled to Psyche to come closer and explained things to her quietly in Mandarin. Her face began to grow relieved while she listened, and she nodded in understanding as he talked. He closed the lid on his box when he was finished and left the items he had removed sitting on the table. Psyche bowed to him reverentially with a happy smile.

"*Xièxie, dà shī. Máfan nǐle,*" she said quietly.

"*Méi shénme,*" he replied fondly. He picked up his box in preparation to leave the room. "Now, I am going back to my garden," he said with a smile and walked out.

Amalie and Lady Sheerness watched him leave with some concern. Psyche's face was much calmer, and she sighed gustily as she looked at the earl before turning to face the two women.

"Why has he gone?" asked Amalie nervously.

"He has several flowerbeds to attend to before dark," said Psyche mildly.

"What about my son?" asked Josephine, her tone consternated.

"Keung thinks he will pull through, but it will be a day or two before you get a full night's sleep," said Psyche in an even tone. "Did you see what I was doing, pounding his back and sitting him up while he coughed?" she asked hopefully. She didn't have the strength to show them again right away.

"Ye-es," said Lady Sheerness slowly, and she almost mentioned she had found the entire thing improper.

Her son was on the verge of dying, and while Josephine didn't think someone of Psyche's stature could actually—under normal circumstances—cause him undue injury, Josephine thought beating him was no less barbaric than using a mustard plaster. And then there was the way the girl had been sitting on him.

"Until he's strong enough to either turn on his side or sit up on his own, you or someone else will need to do that," said Psyche calmly. "If you don't, he could drown or choke."

"Oh," said Josephine in surprise.

"Can you send for some hot water, please?" Psyche requested of the countess politely. "I want to wash his arms and his chest before I put on the salve. Oh, and the pitcher needs more water as well." She picked up the wide-mouthed jar and opened the lid to smell Keung's fantastic ointment. She had always thought it smelled wonderful, and its results were nothing short of miraculous. She wasn't surprised it was what he provided.

Psyche didn't leave Barneville Court on Curzon for her own home until it was well into the evening. She had explained to Amalie and Lady Sheerness the things Keung had left, which included some horehound lozenges, eucalyptus oil, ammonia salts to wake the earl for medicine or to eat (if necessary), and a tincture to help him regain his strength from the loss of blood...in addition to the ointment. Psyche made sure they understood everything Keung said needed to be done, and she had no doubt they would follow his orders without fail.

Lady Sheerness had insisted she stay for supper with them after arranging for Sheerness's valet, Clements, to tend to her son, and Psyche was pleased to no end the children were allowed to join them. Nanny MacBean kept a watchful eye over the three imps, but Psyche found the Scotswoman was not nearly as stern as she had first appeared, and the children adored their nanny.

Amalie invited Psyche to visit Sheerness one last time before she left for the night, and she was relieved to see an improvement already. The whistling as he breathed had stopped, and Clements had even managed to shave him. The infection in the cuts on his arms remained in check, and the redness had already started to fade on his chest. He was sleeping when she looked in, and he had started to regain some of his color. Psyche felt the last traces of her earlier worry fade as she watched the peaceful way he slept.

By the time Jim helped her into the landau, she was exhausted, and as he started the carriage on its way to her home, Psyche began to cry quietly to herself, and she couldn't for the life of her understand why.

Chapter Twelve

"Thea, why do you want to pack so much? You're only going for the night," said Chrissoula amusedly.

"I don't know," said Psyche distractedly.

Chrissoula shook her head and gently put her hands over Psyche's where they were folding a walking dress into her valise with fidgety concern. The girl was extremely anxious and not in any condition to make practical decisions.

"Let me get your bag ready," said Chrissoula with a cajoling smile. "Are you sure you don't want me to come with you?"

Psyche smiled and shook her head. "No, Chrissoula. I can manage for one night. Besides, I don't know what kind of sleeping arrangements they would have, even if it is Pandora's house, and you know how I thrash about."

Chrissoula chuckled. She did know, but most of the thrashing stopped once Psyche actually fell asleep. Chrissoula removed everything Psyche had placed in the valise. She re-packed a shift and dressing gown, a chemise, a walking dress, and a morning dress and pelisse. She retrieved stockings and a pair of slippers that would match either of the dresses and placed those items into the bag as well. She left out the riding habit because Psyche wouldn't be going riding. She went to the dressing table and placed a few of the items from there into the bag. She fastened the clasp and held it out.

"There, all finished," she said with a grin. The entire process had taken her five minutes. Psyche had been trying to pack the bag for the last hour.

"Are you sure you packed everything I'll need?" asked Psyche doubtfully.

"Psyche, you're only going for a night," repeated Chrissoula exasperatedly.

Psyche nodded her head meekly. Her maid only ever used her actual name when Psyche was being particularly trying. Chrissoula could understand why Psyche was anxious, but she was being exceedingly buffle-headed. Psyche began to chew on the side of her thumb nervously after she had taken the bag from her maid.

"I suppose I should be going now," said Psyche, not making any move toward the door.

"Yes, you don't want it to get too late, and Jim is waiting," said Chrissoula encouragingly. Psyche still made no move to leave. "Thea, everything will work out as it should...you'll see. Even if it doesn't happen the way you would like, everything happens as it does for a reason," said Chrissoula sagely.

Psyche hugged her maid and gave her a warm smile as she released her.

"I'll see you tomorrow," she said, and she finally turned toward the door and left the room.

Chrissoula watched the young girl leave, and her expression faded to one of sad resolution after the door closed. She went to the closet and replaced the items Psyche had taken out and left lying around the room in her indecision. Once those were put away, Chrissoula went to the small sitting room she used for tending to Psyche's clothes and other apparel. She lifted the lid on one small trunk and looked over the clothing in it with a critical eye before closing it back and pushing it under the small table where it was usually stored...empty, and then she retrieved the garment she had been sewing for Psyche to take with her to see Chrissoula's homeland. It was one of the last she was making, and it was almost done. Chrissoula hoped Psyche would be able to wear it and not the clothes in the trunk.

Psyche could feel her palms starting to sweat nervously as she went down the back stairs to go to the mews. Jim was there waiting with a carriage to take her to Pandora's for the night. She didn't imagine for an instant she would be able to sleep, but she had brought her sleeping draught.

Myron had told his family at supper that he was to meet Hendon tomorrow morning. He still wouldn't tell them where. It had been almost two weeks since Myron had announced his intentions, and Psyche had actually begun to hope he had called it to a halt. He hadn't, though. Even after that length of time, he was still no less determined that Hendon should die.

Psyche wondered how her brother was going to feel knowing he killed a man. Even if Hendon was a despicable monster, he was still (technically) a human being. Myron shared the same sensibilities as the rest of the family, and Psyche knew he wasn't going to kill another person without being changed by it in some way. She only hoped it was something he was able to live with.

She didn't want to think her brother was doing it because of jealousy. Hendon mistreated Georgiana terribly, and the woman needed to escape, but Psyche had given Myron another way to free her. No one needed to die. It almost seemed her brother had appointed himself jury and executioner for the man, and Psyche wasn't sure it was something that should be left to Myron; he was too involved in the crimes Hendon had committed.

Psyche finally made it to the mews, and Jim stood waiting by the landau. He smiled when he saw her, and he took her bag while he helped her into the carriage. He knew the reason behind her going to stay with her sister, and he also knew she wasn't feeling up to idle banter by the expression on her face. He placed the bag on the floor of the carriage at her feet and closed the door after she had herself seated. It was nearing midnight, and he was looking forward to getting back to the house to get some sleep. He would be driving Myron and his attendants to the duel in the morning, but he wouldn't let one of the other drivers take Psyche to Pandora's house; *he* was her driver.

When they arrived at the Marshall residence on Upper Grosvenor, he helped her out of the carriage and carried her bag to the door while they waited for it to be answered. It wasn't a long wait before Waldon opened it. For once, he didn't look at Psyche with prim disapproval. He took her bag from Jim without complaint and stood to the side for her to enter.

"Good evening, Lady Psyche," he said mildly after he closed the door. "I believe Mum and Sir are in the private sitting room. I'll take your bag to the room that has been prepared for you."

"Thank you, Waldon," said Psyche quietly.

He nodded and turned for the stairs. Psyche went down the hall to the sitting room. When she opened the door, she found Pandora lying on the couch with her feet propped in her husband's lap as he read a book held in one hand and rubbed his wife's feet with the other. They both looked up at her entrance, and Pandora gave her sister a commiserating smile.

"Hallo, Psy," said Pandora softly.

Psyche managed to smile for only a few seconds before she started to cry and went to fall on her knees beside the couch and wrap her arms around Pandora's neck as her shoulders shook with sobs. Pandora exchanged a helpless glance with Islington as she tried to calm her twin. She whispered soothing noises and rubbed Psyche's back, and Pandora began to cry as well. Islington tolerated it for five minutes before he decided enough was enough.

"Both of you, cease!" he said sternly. "The man's not even gone yet!"

Psyche and Pandora looked at him in surprise, and he watched as both of them hiccupped and bit their lower lip in such identical gestures that he blinked in momentary befuddlement.

"You are working yourselves into hysterics, and I'll not have it," he said in a more moderated tone. He set aside the book he was reading and pulled out his pocket watch. "If you could possibly wait another six or so hours, then you have my full blessing on any weeping and gnashing of teeth you feel necessary."

Psyche looked at him in disbelief for a moment, and then she smiled slightly. He was right, of course. And she felt guilty she had made Pandora cry, too. She pulled a handkerchief out of her reticule and wiped her cheeks with it before offering it to her sister. Pandora took it and wiped her own cheeks. She also blew her nose and began to offer it back to Psyche, who shook her head with a grimace. Pandora shrugged and put it onto the table behind her head. Psyche got into a more comfortable position on the floor beside the couch and rested her head onto it beside her sister's.

"Thank you," said Islington once he saw the waterworks had abated.

"You're welcome," said Psyche and Pandora together.

Pandora looked down at the top of her twin's head after a thought occurred to her. "I meant to ask you before all that: how is Lord Sheerness? Do you know? Keung said he looked awful."

Psyche raised her head to look at Pandora. "Myron said he's up and walking now, whatever that's worth. I can only assume he's recovered."

Pandora exchanged a glance with her husband, and he rolled his eyes before retrieving his book and burying his nose back into it.

"What? What was that look?" asked Psyche in bewilderment.

Pandora gave her husband's profile a teasing smile as he continued to pretend disinterest in their conversation.

"It's simply that you can *assume* he has recovered, but you have to keep in mind he is a man."

Islington scoffed and shook his head. Psyche looked from her sister to Islington then back to her sister again with uncertainty.

"You don't think he has?"

"I can't say one way or the other," said Pandora as she rubbed the spot behind her ear, "but Keung seemed to think it would take at least a week or two for him to be well enough to be out of bed."

Psyche's eyes rounded in alarm. "But it's only been Monday since I saw him! It's not even been five full days!" Pandora shrugged. Psyche smacked herself in the forehead frustratedly. "That blasted duel! The man's going to put himself into the grave just so he can help Myron—" She put a hand over her mouth to stop herself from finishing the sentence out loud.

Islington decided to voice his own opinion then. "He could be perfectly fine, you know," he said dryly from behind his book.

Pandora hooted and pushed her foot against his shoulder. "Yes, and pigs may sprout wings and fly!" she chortled. "Have you ever known Keung to be wrong?"

He turned to look at her calmly. "No."

Pandora saw her sister's worried gaze, and while it pleased her that Psyche had so much concern for Sheerness's well-being, Pandora didn't want her so distressed she was up pacing all night. Psyche had enough trouble sleeping.

"I'm sure he's not in any danger of dying," soothed Pandora. "He'd still be too weak to get out of the bed if that were the case."

"Yes, you're probably right," said Psyche distractedly, and she began to chew on the side of her thumb.

Pandora stifled a yawn with the back of her hand and struggled to sit up. Her husband finally had to help her by pulling on her hands. Pandora groaned and rubbed her back as she stood up.

"Just one more month," she sighed tiredly to herself.

Islington put down his book and stood as well. Psyche did the same, as it appeared the two of them were going to retire, and she had no idea where she would be sleeping.

"I've put you in Selena's old room," said Pandora over her shoulder as she linked her arm through her husband's while they walked down the hall. "It's just down from ours."

Psyche watched with concern as Pandora climbed the stairs when they reached them. It took her some effort to make the ascent, and it worried Psyche when she saw her twin was slightly out of breath when they made it to the top. Before she got pregnant, she would have been able to *run* up the stairs without any trouble. Psyche followed them down the hall to the right. When they came to the first door on the right Pandora stopped in front of it and opened it.

"Here it is," she said with a grin. "I made sure to have Sarah put extra blankets in the room for you, and they should have put in a warming pan as soon as you arrived."

Psyche smiled happily. "You know me so well," she chortled. She hugged and kissed her sister and brother-in-law affectionately. "Good night," she said as she walked into the room.

"Good night," they both said.

"Our door is the last one on the left," said Pandora just before her twin closed the door.

"All right," said Psyche as she closed it.

She leaned against the door with her back for a moment once she was alone. She put her thumb to her mouth and began to chew the side of it as she walked further into the room to look around. The lamps were turned low, and there was a cozy fire burning on the grate. The bed looked very comfortable, and her valise had been placed on an antique coffer at the foot of it. There was a dressing table and a chest of drawers, but Psyche did not particularly see the need to unpack her bag for only one night.

She opened her valise to retrieve her shift and dressing gown and set them on the coffer beside it. She removed the four pins holding up her hair and went to put them on the dressing table for in the morning. She pulled off her clothes and folded them into a neat pile, which she placed to the other side of her valise, and put on her shift and dressing gown. She retrieved her brush and ran it through her hair before taking it over to the dressing table as well. After she brushed her teeth at the wash stand, she pulled out the small bottle that held her sleeping draft. She usually took it with water, but she didn't see a glass and water pitcher, so she put the three drops onto her tongue, grimacing and shuddering at the taste.

Psyche went to the window to look at the street below. She wished her sister had put her into a room on the back side of the house, so she would be able to look out at the garden. There was no moon to see by, but the streetlights cast everything in a soft yellow, made hazy by the slight mist that had settled into the air. She looked up at the sky. It was cloudless, and there were stars, and she could imagine they would be brighter if the man-made light below were not competing with them. The weather would be clear in the morning and dawn would be bright. She imagined that under a full moon, her sister's garden temple was a beautiful site, but as there was no moon, it was just as well

Pandora had put her in this room. Still, it would have been nice to look at it in the morning after the sun rose.

Psyche shrugged to herself and turned toward the bed. She removed her dressing gown and draped it onto the coffer before pulling back the covers and climbing in. She pulled her hair up out of the way and curled onto her side. The sleeping draught had yet to start working, but it would eventually, and it couldn't happen soon enough to suit her. She didn't want to think anymore because the only things she thought about caused her to worry, and if she worried, she wouldn't sleep.

She now realized Myron had misled her. He said Sheerness was out of bed and walking, but it had taken Pandora's apparent experience with a similar situation with Islington to make Psyche see that being well and being out of bed did not necessarily mean the same thing. Surely he had to know Myron would understand if he couldn't be there because he was ill. And it wasn't as if Sheerness were the *only* one who would be able to perform the duties as his second. Dorian would do it. Islington would do it. If it came down to it, Viscount Drake would be willing to do it. Psyche couldn't believe Sheerness felt so *honor*-bound to discharge his role he would risk dying to do it.

Psyche agreed with Pandora that Keung had never been wrong when assessing an illness before, so she couldn't think this time was an exception. If Keung had said one or two weeks, he wasn't exaggerating. Psyche remembered the last time she had seen Sheerness. He had started to look better, but he had not made some miraculous recovery. How could he think he would be able to act as a second if he was unwell? It could just as easily be him firing the gun tomorrow as Myron. It wasn't likely her brother would be unable to perform his own part in the morning, but stranger things had happened. She simply couldn't understand why Sheerness felt it was so immensely important for him to be there. It went beyond stubbornness.

She stifled a yawn and flipped in the other direction. Seeing Pandora walk up the stairs had worried her. It would improve after she gave birth, but Psyche could see the pregnancy was beginning to hurt her. It went beyond the backache and heartburn that had plagued her from even very early. She was constantly tired, and it was easy for Psyche to believe she was on the verge of exhaustion. Psyche could also see Islington was a little concerned about his wife. He didn't let Pandora see it, but there had been times when Psyche had caught an expression on his face that bordered on fear.

Psyche rolled onto her back and looked up at the ceiling with a frustrated sigh. She needed to sleep. She *wanted* to sleep—she really did, but her brain wouldn't stop working. Added to it was sleeping in a bed that didn't have the same lumps and smell of her own. The sounds she was accustomed to were absent, like the ticking of the clock on the mantel or the reactionary pendulum Pandora had made for her as a gift for Christmas one year. It might have been easier for her to sleep if she had something there she was used to.

She turned onto her stomach and buried her face in the pillows. She couldn't stop thinking about the duel in the morning. Islington seemed to be confident everything would go well, but Psyche could not be so. Actually, he hadn't said he thought it would go well; he had simply told them to wait until it was over before they mourned. Psyche couldn't decide if that meant he thought it would go well or if he thought it wouldn't. Either way Islington felt, Psyche couldn't escape her own dread, and no matter how often she was told not to worry about it until it happened, an anxious knot had formed in the pit of her stomach that would not go away.

Thinking about the duel made her mind turn once again to Sheerness. She had cried most of the way home Monday night. She had only managed to stop just before they reached the mews, and luckily it had been dark enough Jim hadn't noticed. Either that or he had thought it best not to mention it. Psyche couldn't understand what had prompted her tears. She didn't want to believe she was developing feelings for him, and she wanted to excuse them away as being caused by guilt over making him ill. She *wanted* to, but she wasn't able to no matter how hard she tried. Somewhere between the end of last Season and the beginning of this one, he had changed…*something* had changed, and Psyche could not sort out her reaction to it. She felt utterly confused.

She could not honestly pretend she disliked him any longer. Her feelings for him had changed so much from being dislike that when she had thought he might die on Monday she had found herself more anguished than she would have believed possible. It frightened her to feel that way about him. Perhaps had last Season never happened, or if his manner toward her the previous Season had been different, she would not be quite so confounded. It was as if he had gone from trying to earn her everlasting hatred to winning her devotion, and she couldn't trust that his manner would not go back to the former. She didn't think she would be able to bear it.

And she couldn't forget what Amalie had said about his looking for a wife. Psyche was not aware of his name in connection with any women in the usual gossip, even if there were several who had tried to accomplish it, but she also knew discretion was a valuable skill; Myron and Georgiana had managed to conduct their affair without the slightest hint of scandal. If there were any rumors to be heard, Psyche knew (unfortunately) that they would involve her, especially this Season. She didn't want to believe it, but it almost seemed he had determined he was going to marry *her*. It would account for why his attitude toward her had changed, why it seemed as if he were *wooing* her.

That realization put the situation into an entirely different light. That he should marry and produce an heir had been his father's dying request. Psyche had seen enough recently to know he took duty and honor very seriously. He was going to be Myron's second tomorrow even if it killed him because he had given his word. Even why he would have selected her made sense, and she didn't have to be conceited to realize it. Even though people married all the time without a thing in common, it sometimes made things easier if they did. They shared an interest in antiquities and languages, so they would have something to talk about, even if it did sometimes devolve into an argument. She was from a highly respected and wealthy family, and although she had never asked her father, she was sure she would have a very tempting dowry, and she had a sizeable fortune of her own that would prevent the necessity of him giving her an allowance if he chose. Then there was his need to produce an heir. There could be no doubt the women in her family were healthy and *very* fertile.

Psyche was aghast to realize his attitude for her from the previous Season probably had *not* changed. She had simply become a means to an end. But he was intelligent enough to know he couldn't simply go from being hateful to proposing marriage and achieve the desired result. He knew she would flatly refuse, and he also knew her father wouldn't arrange the marriage without her consent…unless there was a scandal. Her words to him about playing a game at the Stranraers' ball had been more true than she realized at the time.

She was curious just how far he would go, to what lengths he would reach to lull her into believing him. She suspected the physical attraction was not part of his dishonesty; she had the impression he found it just as surprising as she did at times, but it was only of added benefit if he desired his intended bride. She had to ask herself whether he would try to use that to his advantage as well. She wasn't going to be fooled, now that she was wise to the point of his game, but she did have to wonder. He was in for a nasty shock when he discovered it wasn't going to work. Pandora had been right when she said Psyche was just as capable of deception, even if she couldn't lie to save her life.

With that decision reached, the sleeping draught began to take effect, and Psyche drifted off on her stomach with her face buried in the pillows.

Psyche woke up as she heard the sound of footsteps in the hall. She lifted her face out of the pillows and rolled onto her back to look around herself in a moment of confusion in her unfamiliar surroundings. Then she remembered where she was and why she was there. It was still moderately dark outside, but it was starting to lighten. She estimated the time was somewhere around five in the morning, not much before her usual time for rising. The footsteps she heard were Islington's, and he was going to join Myron.

Psyche quickly jumped out of bed and went to the window to peek around the curtains and look at the street below. One of her family's coaches was waiting in front of the gate, and she could see Jim standing patiently at the door, waiting to open it for Islington to step in, which happened not too long after Psyche reached the window. Islington was carrying a small black valise in his hands, and Psyche realized it was a medical kit. A hand went to her throat in panic, and she was tempted to run down to the coach and try one last time to convince her brother not to go through with it.

She could just make him out through one of the side windows of the coach. He didn't appear to be anxious, but his expression was serious and composed. She watched as he greeted Islington calmly as he settled onto the seat at the opposite window. The one thing she noticed that seemed peculiar was that Myron was dressed in black, except for his shirt, almost as if he were in mourning. Her brother never wore black.

A sense of dark premonition caused the blood to drain from her face and ring in her ears as she looked at him, and she tapped her fingers weakly against the glass of the window, willing him to look at her. Almost as if he knew she was there, he did look up. He gave her a soft smile and touched the brim of his hat just as the coach pulled away, and Psyche put her palm flat against the coolness of the glass as the vehicle disappeared from sight around the corner.

Psyche's chest began to heave as she gasped for air, and she sank weakly to her knees. She tried to control the hysteria threatening to overwhelm her, but she was on the verge of screaming. She didn't want to be alone. She managed to raise herself to her feet, and she went to the door of her room and into the hall. She stood for a moment trying to remember Pandora's directions, and then she went down the hall to the last door on the left. She raised her hand and started to knock, but she couldn't wait. She opened the door and went in.

Pandora was awake in the bed, her back propped against the pillows as she drank a cup of tea, her Collie, Bo, lying asleep at the foot of it. Maiyin was sitting in a chair by the fire, sewing with a placid expression. The scene was so calm and domestic, it did much to soothe Psyche. Pandora looked up from her cup of tea with surprise at Psyche's harried entrance, and she set the cup aside on its saucer on the bedside table before she silently held out her arms for Psyche to come join her on the bed. Her twin did not hesitate.

Psyche got under the covers and huddled close to Pandora. They wrapped their arms around each other, and Pandora laid her head against the top of Psyche's where it rested on her shoulder. Pandora seemed to be outwardly calm, but Psyche knew her twin had to find the situation as distressing as she did. Being there with her twin helped to alleviate some of Psyche's fear and to restore some of her composure, but she still felt nauseous with anxiety and couldn't understand how Pandora could tolerate eating or drinking anything at a time like this. Psyche didn't know Maiyin had needed to force her to do it.

Psyche watched through a space between the curtains as the sky outside continued to brighten. She wished Myron had told her family the details of when and where the duel would be. As Islington had just left, she could only assume it was to take place very soon. She didn't expect it would happen very far away, either. Putney Heath was very popular, as was Chelsea Common. Battersea Fields and Tothill Fields were also used on a regular basis, but as the location would have been chosen by Hendon, she could only speculate. She didn't know enough about his previous duels to guess where he might have selected; the only thing she knew was that he had never lost one.

Psyche turned in surprise when she was poked in the shoulder by a finger from behind. She looked up to see Maiyin holding a cut crystal glass out to her containing some brown liquid that looked suspiciously like whisky.

"You drink this," ordered Maiyin.

"What? But it's barely five in the morning!" gasped Psyche in a shock.

"You drink this," said Maiyin again, taking one of her hands to put the glass into it. "You too upset, it will cause hives. You too upset, you will upset Missy Pandora. Drink."

Psyche looked as if she were about to refuse again, and she looked at her sister to come to her aid.

"She has a point," said Pandora mildly with a soothing smile and a pat to her back. "Drink it as quickly as possible, and hold your breath."

Psyche looked from her sister to Maiyin and back to the glass. It was rather full. Maiyin and Pandora were right, though; the alcohol would help to settle her nerves…if anything could at this point. She lifted the glass to her lips and drank it as quickly as she could, following Pandora's advice. When she finished, she grimaced and shuddered and felt her eyes water as the alcohol burned a path all the way to her stomach, but its effects were almost immediate as she had nothing in her stomach to slow its process. She felt lightheaded, and even if she might have been anxious, the whisky cast everything in a warm, fuzzy haze that made her incapable of caring too strenuously.

As Pandora watched her sister's gaze go out of focus with the effects of the eight ounces of whisky she had just inhaled, she spared a glance to her maid, who quickly took the glass from Psyche's limp hand before she dropped it.

"How long do you think it will last?" asked Pandora concernedly.

Maiyin scoffed and shook her head. "Not long enough."

The coach full of men pulled through the Grosvenor Gate to Hyde Park and continued down the path toward the Ring, not far from the Keeper's Lodge. Inside the coach was silent, except for the occasional cough from Sheerness, and he retrieved a lozenge from his pocket to quiet it. He sat beside Myron with a wooden box in his lap containing the set of Mortimer dueling pistols his friend had chosen to use. At the opposite window on the same side, Dr. Felton sat calmly, if bemusedly, giving the man beside him an occasional glance of concern when he coughed, holding a small valise in his lap with hastily-acquired surgeon's tools. Islington sat on the opposite seat, holding his own bag of medical necessities, which he hoped he wouldn't have to open. The last man was Dorian. Although he had no role in his brother's appointment, there was no way he was going to let Myron proceed without him.

The air outside the carriage was covered in a hazy mist, and although the previous night had been fair and cloudless, the sky looked as if it were soon going to rain. The deep gray clouds moved swiftly, and there was an occasional, distant rumble of thunder signaling the approach of the impending storm. It was possible it would simply pass over on its way to elsewhere, but no one really expected that would be the case.

As Jim pulled the coach to a halt, no one was surprised to find Hendon had not yet arrived. A glance to his watch by Islington showed they were about five minutes early. Decency demanded Hendon should have been there at that time as well, but all of the men (except Felton) knew Hendon didn't bother with something like decency. Even still, it wasn't long before the men heard the rumbling of wheels as another vehicle approached from across the park. It was exactly 5:30 when Hendon's open landau came to a stop nearby.

Jim jumped down from the driver's seat to open the door for Myron and his associates to exit from the coach. They all stood waiting patiently as Hendon's driver opened the door for the earl, Count von Weilheim, Sir William Mitchell-Langworthy, and (to Sheerness's surprise) Dr. Phelps to step out. All of the men stood assessing each other silently for a time, but then as seconds, Sheerness and Weilheim walked toward each other across the space separating the two groups. The two men shook hands as they reached each other.

"Weilheim," said Sheerness evenly.

"Sheerness," returned the count calmly.

"So what say you? Ten yards?" asked Sheerness tersely, quickly getting to the matter at hand.

Weilheim looked at him bucolically. "Yes, I would say that should suffice," he agreed with a nod.

Sheerness looked around the space in front of them, trying to select an area to count out the distance that would not have the two men aiming toward the coaches or the bystanders. There was a space between some nearby trees he felt would be suitable.

"That place there?" he asked Weilheim, pointing to the place he had chosen.

"Yes."

The two spent some time quietly measuring the agreed-to distance as the rest of the men waited patiently. The two principals didn't even look at each other as they waited, and the only sounds in the clearing were the jingling of harnesses from the horses and the occasional rumble of thunder. The field was soon measured and marked, and Sheerness stood looking at Weilheim again.

"Shall they fire on a mark, or shall they take turns?" asked Sheerness when it appeared Weilheim wasn't going to say anything. One would almost think the man was clueless about procedure.

"I prefer they fire on a mark," said Weilheim. "There is less time for them to aim then, don't you agree?"

"Yes," said Sheerness, and he was glad Weilheim was being so agreeable.

He had discussed arrangements with Myron the previous day, and so far, Weilheim had found them all acceptable. He was hopeful the engagement wouldn't last too long. He was still not well, and the walking and pacing he had done measuring the field had tired him slightly. They then opened the boxes containing the pistols for each other to examine. Sheerness saw that Hendon had selected a pair of Dumonthier and Houdan. He lifted one to examine the barrel and mechanism and didn't see anything out of the ordinary. They looked as if they had never been used before, but Sheerness sincerely doubted that was the case. Once they had looked over the others' weapons they closed the boxes and walked back to their respective groups. Dorian took the box from Sheerness as he began to load the pistols. Sheerness looked up at Myron as he did.

"Ten yards, fire on mark," he said tersely as he loaded a ball into a barrel.

"Good," said Myron briefly, and he looked at the area the men had measured.

Had it been later, or if the sun were shining, it might have presented a problem, but the gloom of the early morning and impending storm made it an excellent location. The field was even, and there were no overhanging branches that might interfere. He had gone to the range at Knightsbridge to practice the previous day, and he was fairly comfortable with his aim. Dorian had gone with him, as Barneville was still not well enough to stand for the length of time it required. Myron was sure his friend would go home and back to bed as soon as they were finished this morning. Myron had spent the previous three mornings with his solicitor making arrangements he hoped would not be necessary, but he was not so foolish as to think his victory would be a certainty.

"You can still change your mind," said Dorian calmly, looking at his brother over the lid of the box.

"No, no, I can't," said Myron determinedly, shaking his head. "This has to be done."

Dorian nodded resignedly. He had already tried to make his older brother call it off, but he had realized it was useless. No argument he had been able to offer was enough to dissuade him. Dorian couldn't help feeling there was something more than just Pandora's honor or the death of his friend urging Myron to do this, but he could only believe what his brother told him.

If he had known where they would be going before this morning, he would have told their father in an effort to stop it, but Myron knew his younger brother well enough to know that would have been the case. The only thing he would tell Dorian beforehand was the date and time. The location was something Dorian only found out that morning when they were in the coach on their way to collect Sheerness and Islington. If Myron was determined enough to remain that secretive, even with his brother, there would be no stopping him. All Dorian could do was hope for the best, as everyone else did.

Sheerness loaded both pistols, but he hoped only one would be necessary. Actually, his greatest hope would have been that *neither* would be necessary, but like Dorian, he had quickly realized from his first argument with his friend on the matter that persuading him to find another way to settle things was useless. And he felt just a little guilty he had been lax in his duties as second because of his illness. There would have been little he could have done in the interim between when Myron had issued the challenge to Hendon and that morning because neither man had any intention of not going forward with it, but he still felt he hadn't been there as he should have. He hadn't even been able to go with Myron to practice the previous day. He just felt as if he had broken his word, and that troubled him.

Both parties soon had their pistols loaded, and they proceeded to the measured spot. It was at that point when Myron and Hendon actually faced each other and spoke.

"Have you gotten a bastard or two in your young life?" asked Hendon amusedly with a sneer.

Myron looked at him coldly. "Trust you to be so borné," he said evenly.

"No, no, it was just I'm thinking it's going to be a shame for all that beauty not to live on somehow after I've put a bullet through it," said Hendon with a chuckle. "Since you're not married, if you haven't sewn it on the wrong side of the blanket, then it's gone."

"I appreciate your concern for my progeny," said Myron flatly, "but it is unwelcome and unwanted." He curled his lip as he looked at Hendon. "And what about you? You *have* a wife and still don't have any. Makes one wonder if there might be something wrong with you, don't it?"

Hendon gave him a mocking sneer and turned his back to go to his place. Myron looked after him for a minute with a loathsome stare before he went to his own. Sheerness and Weilheim stood together at the mid-point for a moment.

"On three?" asked Weilheim.

"Absolutely," agreed Sheerness with a nod. "You may do the honors."

Weilheim nodded and turned to take Hendon his pistol. Sheerness took the box to Myron for him to retrieve his as well.

"You're to turn and fire when Weilheim says three," said Sheerness quietly. Myron nodded as he chose his pistol. Sheerness looked at him solemnly. "Good luck."

Myron grinned encouragingly at his friend's sober expression. "You'll join us for breakfast?"

Sheerness clapped him on the shoulder and moved to the edge of the clearing.

Myron and Hendon stood across the field at their marks, their backs turned to one another. Islington, Dr. Felton, and Dr. Phelps turned their backs to the field according to the rules. The other four men stood at the edge nearby, facing each other from opposite sides. Sheerness watched as Myron took a deep breath and loosened his shoulders as he prepared.

"All's ready?" called Hendon and Myron almost simultaneously.

"All's ready," agreed Sheerness and Weilheim.

"One! Two! Three!" called Weilheim.

≪ ≫

Psyche and Pandora jumped when they heard the gunshots and gripped each other tightly. It had come from Hyde Park, and they knew what it meant. It was possible there might be two other men meeting for a duel or the guns were being fired for some other reason, but neither sister was foolish enough to believe it. Pandora began to cry and shook her head. Psyche began to weep silently and hugged her twin and whispered soothingly. The alcohol was already wearing off after less than thirty minutes. By six, she was completely sober and her panic had returned.

"That bastard!" sobbed Pandora. "He did that on purpose!"

Psyche didn't want to believe Hendon had chosen Hyde Park, so near her sister's home the shots would be heard in the early morning stillness, just to torment Pandora, but there was no denying the coincidence. For the moment, Psyche was able to maintain her outward composure as she tried to comfort Pandora beside her. Pandora could little afford to become overwrought in her condition, and Psyche tried to quell her own anxiety in an effort to calm her sister. It was her turn to be the optimistic one.

"Shh, Pan," she said quietly, rubbing her sister's back consolingly. "There were two shots. That has to be a good sign."

≪ ≫

All the men rushed onto the field after the shots were fired to see to Myron and Hendon. Both had fallen to the ground with their injuries, and it was unlikely there would be a second volley. There would be other things to attend to shortly, but the main concern at the moment was tending to their wounds.

Myron's associates ignored the screams of Hendon as he writhed in pain on the opposite end of the field. They all felt the urge to put him out of his misery, but letting him suffer seemed a more fitting punishment. Myron had crumpled to the ground slowly, and he remained silent and unmoving as they approached him, their faces ashen with worry.

Islington and Felton knelt beside him and slowly turned him onto his back. They looked at each other gravely once they saw Myron's injury. Islington pulled open Myron's waistcoat and pulled his shirt from the waistband of his trousers as Felton opened his bag to remove a large wad of cotton wool and linen to place on the wound in his stomach just above his navel. The ball had not gone all the way through but had lodged against his spine, instantly paralyzing him from the waist down. There was a steady stream of blood trickling from the corner of his mouth from the damage caused by the ball tearing its way through the organs in his abdominal cavity. He was conscious, but his pupils had already begun to dilate. He was dying, and both men watched helplessly because there was nothing they could do to stop it.

"No mercy!" howled Hendon. "No mercy! Let the bastard *die!*" he screamed as he continued to roll on the ground in agony as Dr. Phelps attended to his leg.

Both Sheerness and Dorian began to rise from the ground with the determination they were going to finish Hendon off. Islington managed to restrain Dorian, even as he wanted to kill the man himself, but Sheerness had risen to his feet before Felton could stop him and was stalking across the field in a rage. Jim, who had rushed onto the field after calming the horses when the shots were fired, managed to grab Sheerness in a tight grip around his arms and pull him back toward Myron. Although Sheerness was tall and athletically built, Jim was much taller and built like an oak, and the earl's recent illness made him even less capable of getting loose from the driver.

Both Islington and Felton had ignored Hendon's howls for no mercy. There was nothing they could do for Myron in any event except keep him comfortable. When Myron started to choke on the blood that continued to bubble up, Sheerness knelt at his head and raised it into his lap once Jim released him. The choking eased, but his breath came out in a slow, gurgling rattle. His eyes were unfocused and glassy as he steadily moved closer to inevitable death. Myron grabbed Dorian's hand to get his attention and tried to speak. Dorian frowned concernedly and wrapped his brother's hand in both of his and leaned closer to Myron's mouth to hear the words.

"Solicitor," Myron whispered.

Dorian looked at him. "I'll take care of it," he promised.

Myron nodded. "Psyche…Pandora…not their fault," he got out before he started choking again. "Don't…let them…think so," he continued. "My own."

Dorian nodded and swallowed an emotional lump in his throat, unable to speak, and he was trying not to break down. He could feel Myron's grip on his hand growing weaker, and he couldn't believe his brother was dying. Myron then looked up at Sheerness.

"You…take your…trip," said Myron. Sheerness nodded, his face stricken. Myron reached up and pulled Sheerness closer to tell him something he didn't want the others to hear, but he could feel the last of his strength leaving and wasn't sure he would be able to. "You…and Psyche…." He started to cough again, and an even larger amount of blood started to come up as a clot worked its way loose. "Needs you," he sighed, and they all watched helplessly as Myron closed his eyes tiredly and breathed his last.

Islington numbly pulled out his watch and looked at the time. It was 6:38. Dorian rubbed a shaking hand over his face and took several deep breaths in and out through his nose in an effort to control his grief. It would have to wait. He still had to tell his family and take Myron home. Then, he would be able to express what he was feeling, after he had attended to his duty. Sheerness sat looking down at Myron in stunned disbelief. This man who had been his closest friend for almost ten years was gone. He felt as if he had lost another member of his family, and his chest constricted almost to the point he could no longer breathe.

Hendon continued to whine from across the field, but the four men didn't notice or care. The only sound they were worried about hearing from that direction was the earl trying to leave the field. They didn't want him to go anywhere until the authorities arrived to attend to the other matter that concerned them: charging him with murder. Hendon had turned early and aimed precisely. He had done what amounted to cold-bloodedly killing Myron, and they wanted to see him suffer for it.

All of them could hear the sound of horses approaching from the south as soldiers from the nearby barracks were dispatched to investigate the gunshots. They weren't rushing, and it was probably because the sergeant knew what the matter involved. There was little need for them to hurry along—the damage had already been done.

Myron's friends and family could see Hendon attempting to have the men with him help him into his carriage as he heard the soldiers approaching, but both Weilheim and Sir William refused to move. They stood to one side and looked at him disgustedly. Hendon had acted criminally and dishonorably, and they wanted nothing to do with him. The elderly Dr. Phelps was incapable of carrying the earl by himself, and the driver remained holding the horses steady. They felt fairly confident Hendon would stay to answer for what he had done.

"Help me, you old fool!" Hendon shouted at Dr. Phelps as he attempted to rise from the ground, but they (especially Sheerness) were sure the doctor had already dosed his patient with laudanum. In addition to the injury, he was under the effects of the opiate and incapable of going anywhere without assistance.

Myron's shot had come after Hendon's had already struck, but even as he sank to the ground, he was able to hit the earl. The ball went into his knee, shattering the kneecap and splintering the two bones at the joint. Dr. Phelps had tightened a ligature around his thigh above the wound to check the bleeding it caused and promptly dosed him with a large quantity of laudanum. It was an agonizing injury, but not nearly so agonizing as what was about to happen next. Myron's compatriots watched in horrified astonishment as Dr. Phelps proceeded to remove a field saw from the bag he carried with him. Before Hendon or anyone else could react, the surgeon amputated his leg.

Hendon's terrified screams as he watched his limb removed before his very eyes in a matter of seconds were enough to chill the blood of the men in the clearing, but none of them could honestly say they felt any sympathy. Myron's associates felt he deserved that and more. Hendon collapsed from the shock, and the air was suddenly silent except for the sound of the approaching horses. Dr. Phelps proceeded with his surgery and calmly and quickly tied off the veins and arteries in the stump that used to be Hendon's leg. He smeared a thick coating of some ointment onto the wound and covered it loosely with a piece of cloth...to cover the sight from view. He calmly picked up the part of the leg he had removed and took it to the landau to place on the floor. Watching that made Sheerness very glad Psyche had rescued him from the man.

By the time the soldiers arrived, Phelps had completed his surgery and repacked his instruments into his bag. Hendon remained unmoving and unconscious on the ground. Sheerness used his coat to cover Myron, and he helped Dorian gently lift him from the ground and carry him to the coach and lay him onto the seat. It took about an hour to explain everything to the sergeant, who had arrived with four other men.

Under ordinary circumstances, the parties involved in a duel, especially those of the stature of the ones present, would have been sent on their way with what amounted to a scolding for being naughty, but when the sergeant was made aware of events, he had the soldiers with him place Hendon in his coach...but only to carry him to jail to await answering for his crime before Parliament. When the sergeant examined Hendon's brace of pistols, he was even more determined to have him placed under arrest for murder when he saw the barrels were French rifled—the rifling stopped within an inch of the end of the barrel, when good form dictated there should have been none at all. It would have been quite easily missed during Sheerness's cursory examination before the duel, and both Islington and Felton agreed the location of Myron's injury would have still been fatal had Hendon not used a rifled pistol. At best, he wouldn't have been paralyzed, but his death would have been more painful.

Islington decided he would walk home. His house wasn't far away, and he felt he could use the time it would take him to compose his thoughts before he told his wife and her sister their brother was dead. Dorian assured Islington he would be able to tell the duke and duchess what had happened, and Dr. Felton would be going with him. He promised he would get word to them as quickly as possible when the funeral arrangements were made.

Sheerness asked Islington if he might accompany him to tell Psyche and Pandora. Given recent events in his own life, he thought he might be of some help. Islington agreed it would be a good idea. After the men said their goodbyes and the coach pulled away, Islington and Sheerness stood tiredly in the middle of the blood-soaked clearing before they silently began to make their way across the park to Upper Grosvenor. Neither man was quite sure he wanted to go to Hyde Park ever again.

Chapter Thirteen

Psyche and Pandora finally managed to get out of bed and dress themselves…but only after Maiyin made Psyche drink another glass of whisky. It calmed Psyche enough she was able to go to her room and put on her morning dress and pelisse, but her hands shook so much when she tried to put up her hair, she gave up and put it in a braid. By the time she returned to Pandora's room, Maiyin had arranged a tray with breakfast to be brought up for the two girls and dressed Pandora. She stood over them as they sat down to the small table that had been brought in and placed by the chairs near the window overlooking the garden until they picked up their utensils and began to eat.

After they ate their breakfast (a major portion of which was surreptitiously passed to Bo where he sat beside the table when Maiyin wasn't looking), Psyche began to pace, looking from the clock on the mantel to the window, her thumb constantly being worried by her teeth. Pandora might have paced as well, but she just didn't have the stamina anymore, so she sat fidgeting in her chair, her eyes on the clock. It had been over two hours since they had heard the gunshots, and still there was no word. They were hopeful it meant things had gone well. Psyche looked at her thumb at one point and realized she had worn another blister.

Both of them stopped what they were doing and looked at each other when they heard the sound of the front door opening echo through the silent house. Psyche helped Pandora rise from her seat, and they gripped each others' hands tightly as they went into the hall and hurried to the top of the stairs to look down at the entry hall below. What they saw filled them both with fear.

Islington had chosen to wear a pair of gray trousers with a darker gray waistcoat and black frock coat. When he turned from having Waldon assist him with removal of the coat, the front of his trousers were covered in blood. To the sisters' surprise, Sheerness was with him, and the condition of his clothes was no better. Although the black of his breeches and waistcoat disguised any blood that might be there, the white of his sleeves had been dyed red as well. Both men looked very tired and heavyhearted.

Psyche continued to hold Pandora's hand in a mutual, blood-draining grasp and put her other hand to her throat with dreadful anticipation. When the men looked up the stairs and saw the sisters standing there, and Psyche saw the sadly apologetic expressions on their faces, she knew without them telling her that her brother was dead.

"No!" she sobbed. "I saw him…this morning! He smiled…and I thought…I thought…oh, no!" Her shoulders began to shake as she cried, and she felt as if her knees were going to buckle from the grief.

Pandora, standing beside her, was no less distressed at the news. She stood for a moment with an almost thoughtful expression before a slight frown formed between her eyebrows, and she placed a hand to the side of her stomach. There was a sound of something liquid draining to the floor at her feet, and her expression changed to one of intense pain as she began to weave unsteadily. Psyche felt the tug at her hand as her twin started to faint, and she managed to grab her before she went tumbling down the stairs.

Both Islington and Sheerness had started up the stairs at Psyche's distressed outburst, and they began to move even more quickly when Psyche began to lose her balance as she tried to help Pandora. Islington reached the landing first and took his wife in his arms with a worried frown just as Psyche felt her balance tipping even further and her foot slipped in the wetness on the floor from Pandora's water breaking. Islington had his hands full with his wife, and Sheerness was still a few steps before the landing. Both men watched helplessly as she toppled backwards and hit the back of her head soundly against the blunt side of the wooden newel post with a sickening thud.

"*Bloody hell!*" roared Islington in disbelief and horror.

"*Merde alors!*" gasped Sheerness, and all the blood drained from his face as Psyche remained still, her eyes closed.

He knelt beside her as he reached the top stair and put a hand to her wrist. She wasn't dead, at least that much he could tell, but the sound as her head hit the post had been disturbing. There was no blood, but there didn't have to be any for a cracked skull. He brushed a hand against her cheek, and it was still wet with her tears.

"Well, is she still breathing?" asked Islington impatiently as he lifted Pandora in his arms.

"Yes," said Sheerness.

"Peachy," said Islington distractedly.

This was the scene Maiyin and Keung happened upon as they came in from the servants' quarters: both sisters unconscious, the two men covered in blood.

"Ayah!" gasped Maiyin in shock.

"Maiyin, come with me!" said Islington quickly when he saw her. "Sheerness, get Psyche into the first room on the right so Keung can take a look at her. Bloody hell!" muttered Islington again, shaking his head as he carried his wife down the hall to the bedroom. "These bloody accident-prone women!"

As tired and weak as he felt, Sheerness managed to lift Psyche from the edge of the landing and slowly carried her down the hall. Luckily, the door was open. He didn't think he would have the strength to hold her with one arm and open it. He almost felt like he needed someone to carry *him*. He took her to the bed and gently laid her down, and then he weakly collapsed onto the edge of it beside her as he began to cough. He had left his lozenges in his coat. The coughing had lessened, unless he did something to over-exert himself...like walk all the way from Hyde Park, race up a set of stairs, and carry something heavy...all without breakfast.

His head lifted as he heard the bustle of feet go past the doorway. That was Maiyin, on her way to help Islington with Pandora. He slowly raised himself up on one elbow and looked at Psyche, and he had to fight a wave of dizziness. She hadn't moved, and his concern about the damage she might have done to herself made him anxious in a way he had never quite experienced before. Her breathing still seemed to be fine, and her color was good, but he could only imagine what she might have done to her head.

He waited for Keung to arrive and take look at her, and he finally tried to sit up. He was able to put his feet on the floor and only had a minor amount of weaving. He was regaining some of his energy, but when it was time to go home (whenever that would be), he would arrange for a carriage. He glanced to the door and wondered where the Chinaman was. He had been standing beside Maiyin, and it shouldn't have taken him any longer to go to the top of the stairs than she had. Sheerness lifted Psyche's head from the pillow to feel the back of it, noticing there was already a sizeable lump forming.

Sheerness looked around the room distractedly. It was decorated and had furniture, but there were no personal belongings. He suspected Psyche didn't stay in this room often. There was a leather valise sitting on the coffer at the end of the bed; it had to be hers. When he saw the pitcher on the wash stand, he took a preparatory breath and stood up to go to it. After splashing some of the water in it onto his own face, he took the flannel hanging at the front of it and wet it with water and carried it to the bed. He sat back down beside Psyche and began to pat her face with it, but she wasn't waking up.

He heard feet again and looked up to see Keung entering the room, carrying his wooden box and a bowl with a cloth covering it. That would explain why he hadn't come up the stairs immediately; he had gone to retrieve the things he carried. Sheerness should have realized the man would need his box. Keung set the box and the bowl on the night table, and he turned to look at Sheerness expectantly before he lifted his hand and briefly made a gesture to indicate the earl needed to move.

"She hit her head," said Sheerness helpfully, getting out of the way.

"Hunh," said Keung curtly.

Sheerness watched as Keung bent over her and lifted her head to feel the back of it, his expression intent. He opened her eyelids to examine her pupils and lowered his head to listen to her breathing. He opened the lid of his box and pulled out a small bottle. He removed the stopper and lifted her head for her to inhale the contents. Her forehead wrinkled, and she shook her head as the smell of the ammonia salts brought her around. Her eyelids opened, and she looked up at Keung standing over her. Sheerness had never felt so relieved as when she wrinkled her nose and stuck out her tongue with distaste.

"Eww," she muttered.

"No time for sleep," said Keung tersely as he settled her head back onto the pillow and placed the bottle back into his box. "You are lucky you are so hard-headed. You will have a headache, but you will live."

Psyche struggled to sit up. "Pandora," she sighed worriedly, and her vision spun dizzily as she sat up, but she was determined to go to her twin. Keung poked her in the shoulder with a finger, and she fell back on the bed.

"Stay," he ordered. "Always hurry, always worry. No time for that either."

"But—" began Psyche.

Keung put up his hand in front of her face and held up his fingers.

"How many fingers?" he cut in.

"Three, but—" began Psyche again.

"*Nǐ yào báifàn gēn nèige?*" cut in Keung.

"*Bú yào, xièxie,*" replied Psyche, "but—"

"Hunh," said Keung, and he turned his back to pull the cloth off the bowl. It contained ice, and Keung wrapped some in the cloth and gave it to Psyche. "Put that on your head for thirty minutes," he ordered. He saw Psyche's worried expression, and his face softened slightly as he looked at her. "Your sister in good hands. Women have babies all the time. Thirty minutes, and then you can go see Missy Pandora, *dǒng?*" He turned to look at Sheerness reprovingly. "As for *you*. What are you doing here? You should be in *bed*."

"But—" it was Sheerness's turn to begin.

"Hunh," said Keung, and he began a quick examination as Sheerness sat on the edge of the bed in stunned disbelief. Keung reached into his box and removed a small bowl to mix several ingredients together before giving it to Sheerness. "Drink that," he ordered.

Sheerness looked at the liquid in the bowl. It didn't smell appetizing in the least, but Keung stood over him with a dour expression, and the earl quickly swallowed it. He shuddered and grimaced at the flavor, deciding it had to be the foulest concoction he had ever tasted. He gave the bowl back to Keung, and the older man gave a brief nod of satisfaction before he put it back into his box and closed the lid. He gave the two of them a disgusted look and shook his head before he left the room, muttering to himself in Mandarin about flowerbeds and shrubbery that would not plant themselves. Sheerness didn't understand him, but Psyche did, and her lips twitched amusedly.

The lightness of Psyche's mood lasted only a moment before everything came back to her, and she stood up and began to pace the room, holding the ice in the cloth to the back of her head. She looked at the watch on the chain around her neck, marking the time, and walked distractedly from one edge of the room to the other. She felt dizzy, but it began to pass, and although the back of her head hurt, she pushed it to the side as she waited impatiently for thirty minutes to be over.

Sheerness watched from his seat on the edge of the bed as she stalked about the room, and it reminded him of a wild animal penned in a cage. Her cheeks were wet as she cried silent tears, and he could see the waiting only made her grow more anxious. She wasn't chewing the side of her thumb, but he watched as she clenched and unclenched her hand at her side tensely. He began to cough then, and when he finally stopped, Psyche was no longer pacing and was looking at him with a concerned frown. Then he saw her shrug her shoulders with a resigned look and a shake of her head as she removed the ice.

"I can't wait," she said shortly, and she started to leave the room.

Sheerness managed to stand up and grab her around the waist from behind.

"Keung said thirty minutes," he said soothingly, and he lifted her hand that held the ice and put it back on her head.

She was still for a moment, and then she began to shake, and it was all Sheerness could do to keep her from collapsing to the floor. He managed to pull her toward the bed and sat on the edge of it with her sitting on his lap. She weakly buried her face in his shoulder as she sobbed, and Sheerness began to rock her and rub her back comfortingly. She wrapped her arms around his neck and curled into him, and Sheerness rested his cheek against the side of her head and closed his eyes as he tried to control his own grief.

The thirty minutes came and went as he continued to hold her, and the ice eventually melted away to nothing. Sheerness placed the cloth back into the bowl. Psyche continued to cry until she made herself weary, and Sheerness kept her held tightly against him as she eventually drifted off to an exhausted sleep. His legs had gone numb, but he didn't want to lay her down and risk waking her. The best thing for her right now would be sleep.

He looked around himself for a moment, and then he decided to move to the chair near the fireplace. He held Psyche against him as he stood from the bed, and he had to stand still for a moment as the blood rushed back into his legs because the tingling sensation threatened to make his knees buckle. He carried her over to the chair and sat down. It was more comfortable for him with the support of the chair behind his back, and it wasn't long before he drifted off to an exhausted sleep himself.

Psyche slowly opened her eyes, and it took a bit of a struggle to get them open because they were stuck together from all the crying she had done. The back of her head throbbed from the lump, and when she reached up a hand to touch it, she could feel it was the size of a small egg. Then she realized the cozy place she was sitting was Sheerness's lap. She could tell from the way he was breathing that he was sleeping. His cheek rested against the top of her head on his shoulder, and one of his arms rested across the top of her legs. She felt very comfortable.

Then she looked down at his arm on her lap and saw the blood. Myron's blood. She inhaled with a shudder and scrabbled off his lap. Sheerness woke up in surprise at her sudden movement, and he looked at Psyche in puzzlement at her horrified expression. Then her eyes widened when she remembered her sister. She looked to the window and saw with alarm she had slept all day. Even with the gloom of the clouds, she could see it was late afternoon.

"Pandora," she said softly, and she fled from the room and quickly down the hall before Sheerness could call her back.

Psyche didn't bother to knock (as she hadn't that morning). Pandora was lying on the bed, still looking very pregnant. Her eyes were closed when Psyche first opened the door, but they opened as Psyche moved toward the bed. Islington sat beside her on one side, Maiyin on the other. She had a wet cloth on her forehead, but her face was still beaded with sweat. She gave Psyche a soft smile as she carefully climbed onto the foot of the bed.

"All right?" asked Psyche softly.

"Not too bad," said Pandora with a lopsided smile.

"Did Sheerness leave?" asked Islington quietly as he moved the cloth across his wife's forehead.

"No," said Psyche, her brow furrowing, "at least, not unless it's been in the last three minutes or so."

"Is he still asleep?" asked Pandora, managing a teasing wink.

"No," said Psyche, and *she* managed a blush when her sister's comment made it obvious someone had seen her sleeping on his lap.

"How's your head?" asked Islington over his shoulder.

"I have a headache and a lump on the back of my noggin, but I'll live."

Pandora nodded, and Psyche watched as she quickly grabbed Islington's hand and squeezed it tightly, her forehead wrinkling with pain. She bit her lip and breathed in and out slowly through her nose as she tried to control the pain of the contraction. She soon relaxed, but Psyche could see the ordeal had drained her. Psyche's face paled anxiously when she realized Pandora had probably been suffering like that all day. She looked at the watch around her neck. It was nearing seven in the evening.

Neither Islington or Maiyin were cheerful. When Psyche looked at Maiyin, her face bore a worried, determined look. That was when Psyche realized Pandora was not as well as she pretended to be. Islington had not looked away from his wife, and his tone had been distracted and strained when he spoke. Psyche began to grow agitated, and she began to chew on her thumb as she looked at Pandora, who recognized her twin knew something was wrong.

Pandora continued to hold her husband's hand, and she turned to give Maiyin a silent look. While Psyche and Sheerness had been sleeping, the three of them had been discussing plans for what to do about Psyche. They knew she was already distraught about Myron; once she discovered Pandora was unwell, she would be on the verge of utter hysteria. Pandora had wanted to wait and see how Psyche managed before taking any action. When her sister began to chew on her thumb, Pandora knew it was only a matter of time before she came to a full realization. After Pandora's silent look, Maiyin nodded and rose from the bed. She retrieved a glass of whisky and brought it to Psyche.

"Drink that," ordered Maiyin.

Psyche shook her head stubbornly. "I don't want it," she said firmly, closing her mouth in a tight line.

"Missy Psyche, you drink it *now,*" ordered Maiyin.

"Drink it, please, Psy," said Pandora quietly, giving her sister an encouraging look.

Psyche reluctantly took the glass from Maiyin and drained it. The results were very similar to that morning, and Psyche felt a numbness envelop her as Maiyin took the glass and left the room to tend to the rest of the things she had discussed with Pandora and Islington. Psyche watched her leave, almost with disinterest, and then she turned to look at her twin to voice the idea that had come to her before they began their attempt to make her drunk.

"It's not time yet, is it?" she asked dully.

Pandora shared a look with Islington before her gaze turned back to Psyche. She was trying to keep her features impassive, but Pandora's acting skill failed for the moment. Psyche could see she was frightened.

"No, it's not time," confirmed Pandora softly.

Psyche put her hands to her head in disbelief and stood up to begin pacing the floor anxiously. The whisky had, at least, delayed her bursting into tears, but her brain began to whir at the implications of the premature labor. None of them instilled much hope. Pandora and Islington watched her pace for a few minutes, and Pandora began to have another contraction with a pain so intense her eyes began to water with tears.

"Psyche, you're not helping!" bit out Islington impatiently.

Pandora had squeezed his hand so tightly he felt the bones grinding together. Psyche's pacing only further distressed Pandora, and his wife could ill-afford it. She was grieving the loss of her brother, and she had gone into labor a month early. Islington understood Psyche was no less upset than Pandora, but her method of coping—the pacing incessantly—was in no way soothing to those who had to watch it. Pandora needed calmness. After the pain of the contraction had abated, he rose from the bed and got another glass of whisky for Psyche. He blocked her path and held it out to her. Maiyin was making arrangements to keep her occupied for a little while longer, but this was the quickest way to attend to it right now. She gave him an irritated glance.

"I don't want that," she said flatly.

Islington gave her an arctic glare. "You'll drink this and stop that infernal pacing, or you'll leave the room."

Psyche looked at him in astonishment. She couldn't believe he would actually follow through on it. But she realized her agitation and Pandora seeing it could not be beneficial. She finally nodded and took the glass from him to down the alcohol quickly. Her eyes teared up as she finished and meekly gave him back the glass. The alcohol stilled her mind enough that she was able to see he had changed his clothes. He was in mourning dress. Psyche put a hand to her forehead and rubbed it numbly as it brought something else to her.

"Sheerness needs another shirt," she said absently.

"Maiyin is seeing to that," he said softly, his expression assessing as he tried to determine how soon she would need more whisky. He didn't expect it would be long.

"And I need to send word to Mamà and Papà that I'm still here. I don't want to leave until...until...." Psyche couldn't finish the sentence.

Islington rubbed her shoulder soothingly. "I arranged that while you were sleeping."

Psyche nodded. "Thank you."

Islington set the glass back on the table by the whisky bottle and went to take his place beside his wife on the bed. He remembered someone had once told him only a fool was a physician to his own family, and this day was making him inclined to believe it. He had been helpless to prevent Myron's death that morning, but he was determined not to let anything happen to his wife. This was, after all, the reason he had gone to school in Edinburgh. He wasn't unbearably anxious yet, but not having Psyche pacing like a caged lion helped keep it at bay for a little while longer.

Psyche went to sit on the other side of the bed and took one of Pandora's hands in hers. Pandora gave her an assuring smile and gently gave her sister's hand a squeeze. Psyche could see on closer inspection the tired circles under her sister's eyes and the paleness of her skin. She tried to control her anxiety, and the two recent glasses of whisky helped. She realized as much as Islington and Pandora did that she would be pacing without the alcohol. As it was, one of her feet was tapping nervously on the floor. Psyche looked at the window as there was a loud clap of thunder and a flash of lightning. The storm that had been threatening all day appeared to have finally arrived. Psyche looked at her watch. It was 7:30.

Maiyin returned to the room shortly after that. She was carrying a copper kettle full of water and several pieces of linen draped over one of her shoulders. She placed the kettle near the embers in the fireplace to keep it hot and temporarily put the linen into a nearby chair. She then went busily around the room and turned up all the lamps. Once she had finished with her tasks, she looked at Islington and Pandora and gave them a nod.

Pandora gave Psyche's hand a brief squeeze to get her attention. "Why don't you go downstairs for something to eat?" she asked gently.

Psyche shook her head. "Oh, I can't eat anything."

"Psy, you need to eat something. You've not had anything since this morning, and you gave most of that to Bo."

"Hunh," said Maiyin when she heard.

"I don't want to leave you," said Psyche anxiously.

"I'll be fine," assured Pandora. "Go eat dinner in the sitting room with Lord Sheerness."

"No," said Psyche flatly.

Pandora began to have another contraction, and her grasp on Psyche's hand tightened to the point Psyche had to bite her own lip to keep from crying out at the pain. Once it passed, Pandora looked at her weakly.

"Psyche, please, go," she sighed. Psyche began to cry and shook her head. "Psy, I can't do this with you here," said Pandora, and her voice broke.

Psyche put a hand over her mouth to cover a sob and finally relented. She gave Pandora a tight hug and a kiss to her cheek, and then she stood up and left the room quickly. She closed the door behind her and stood in the hall for a few minutes crying silently. She finally wiped her hands across her cheeks and took a steadying breath before she straightened her back and walked down the hall to the stairs.

As she walked, she noticed the servants had drawn the drapes and turned up the lamps against the storm and nightfall. She slowly made her way down the hall to the private sitting room. Sheerness was already there when she opened the door, and he stood at her entrance. Maiyin had found him another shirt, much to Psyche's relief, and he stood there without his coat or a cravat, a glass of brandy in his hand. His expression was impassive as he looked at her. Psyche looked at him in puzzlement. She had to admit she was surprised he was still there. She thought surely he would have wanted to go home to his own family by now. He wordlessly went to the sideboard and poured another glass of brandy and took it to Psyche.

She looked at it blankly. "I don't want that," she said calmly.

Sheerness shrugged carelessly and put it in her hand.

"It's not a question of whether you *want* it; you're still going to drink it," he said firmly, giving her a determined look.

"But—" began Psyche argumentatively.

"You *need* to drink that," he cut in sharply, and Psyche almost thought he would try to force it down her throat if she didn't drink it on her own.

Psyche groaned and rolled her eyes then quickly swallowed the nearly full glass of brandy. Sheerness watched with some alarm. He hadn't intended for her to drink it all at once. She set the glass down and turned to look at him with a hiccup, her eyes watering.

"Satisfied?" she croaked with a scowl.

Psyche felt unsteady on her feet. She had never consumed so much distilled alcohol in such a short span of time, or so much in one day for that matter. Her stomach was empty, and the liquor was quickly working its way through her system. The glass of brandy added to the two recent glasses of whisky made her feel as if her bones had turned to jelly. Her head felt fuzzy and everything else was beginning to feel just wonderful.

Sheerness looked at her expression. He couldn't decide if she'd had enough or not. He didn't want her drunk, just tipsy enough to remain calm, as Pandora and Islington (through Maiyin) had asked him to do. She didn't even look fazed. There would be wine with their meal, but he didn't think wine would be enough, much to his astonishment. He thought a glass of brandy would have done the trick. He picked up the glass and took it to the sideboard to refill it and his own. He carried the glass back to her and held it out.

"Why don't you try sipping it this time?" he asked with an amused smile before taking a swallow from his own.

Psyche scoffed and proceeded to drink the entire glass again without stopping. She grimaced and shuddered with her eyes watering and held the glass back out to him.

"So help me, if one more person makes me drink another glassful of whisky or brandy or anything else more potent than Chateauneuf-du-Pape-Calcernier, I swear I will scream blue murder," she said in measured tones.

"Whisky?" he asked, his forehead wrinkling with concern.

"Yes," said Psyche airily, and she looked at her watch. "Maiyin and Islington both made me drink a glass of whisky each about forty-five minutes ago, and now you've just made me drink two glasses of brandy. I think it *all* tastes foul, but now I don't care."

Sheerness didn't detect any slurring to her speech, but her lackadaisical demeanor led him to realize, rather belatedly, that she had probably already been tipsy when she walked in and was now completely pissed. Her eyes were red and teary, but it was not all caused by crying, he now recognized. He rubbed a finger across the bridge of his nose with the empty glass in his hand to hide his amused smirk.

"You may drink whatever you'd like for the rest of the night," he said politely.

"I don't need *your* permission anyhow," she said tartly, and she flounced over to flop down on the couch.

Sheerness tried not to laugh as he went to set her empty glass on the sideboard, and then he went to take a seat in the chair by the fireplace while they waited for dinner. A servant had already been in to lay two places for them at the table. If Islington ate anything at all, he would have a tray in his room. Maiyin had been vague when she explained Pandora's condition, but she had said enough for Sheerness to know it would get worse before it got better.

After Psyche's horrified exit from the room, once he had regained the feeling in his legs from her sleeping in his lap for almost nine hours, Sheerness had risen from the chair with the intention of going home. He had felt much better physically after the sleep and the medicine Keung had given him (whatever it was and no matter how rank it tasted), and after Psyche had gone, he didn't think there was much point to his staying. When he looked down at his sleeves, he realized what had disturbed Psyche so much when she looked at him; even *he* found it troubling.

Maiyin had waylaid him in the doorway. She had given him one of Islington's shirts (which surprisingly fit almost like one of his own), and apprised him of the situation. Pandora was in labor early, and it was not progressing quickly or easily. Psyche wouldn't leave her sister, but as difficult as it was for her to make the decision, Pandora didn't want Psyche in the room. Pandora and Islington wanted Sheerness stay and keep her calm and keep her out of the bedroom until one of the two of them said she could come in.

Sheerness had almost refused. He didn't know what they thought he could do. Surely, they knew that even when he was perfectly healthy his chances of physically restraining her were unlikely if she were truly determined to get in the room (or to do anything else for that matter). That was when Maiyin suggested he might try getting her drunk. That wouldn't have been his first choice, but he had to agree it would probably keep her calm…at least until it wore off. He had finally agreed. Now he sat watching her pout on the couch, her arms folded across her chest angrily. But she wasn't pacing.

It wasn't long before a footman entered with a cart carrying their food. Psyche looked at it disinterestedly. She wasn't hungry…. She wasn't drunk either. She *was* tipsy, and it helped to keep her from pacing, but it didn't stop her from thinking about Myron or worrying about Pandora. It also didn't make her regain her appetite, but she would *try* to eat because Pandora had asked her to. Once the footman had their food served, Psyche stood up from the couch. Sheerness stood up as well after finishing his brandy and helped her into her seat at the table. The footman poured them each a glass of wine, and then he went to stand unobtrusively yet attentively nearby.

Psyche started with her salad. All of their food had been served at once, and it looked appetizing, but Psyche wasn't hungry. She unenthusiastically ate her salad and moved the plate aside once she'd finished. The footman came over to refill her glass and remove the plate. She started on her pea soup then, and it wasn't long before she finished that as well. Eating went quickly when she wasn't required to talk, and Sheerness was remaining quiet, much to her relief. There was no curtain covering the bay window overlooking the garden, and Psyche would look out periodically at the storm as it raged on, particularly when lightning or thunder brought it to her attention.

She looked at Sheerness at one point and found him watching her consideringly. She raised her eyebrow as she took a sip of wine from her glass, unaware it was the third one the footman had poured for her. Psyche wasn't happy he had made her drink two glasses of brandy. Well, he hadn't *made* her drink the second one, but as he seemed to be intent on making her drunk (as everyone else did), she thought she might as well get it over with. But she wasn't drunk, and it didn't seem she was going to be. She didn't feel as anxious, but she wasn't drunk. She ate a few bites of the main course, a succulent veal filet with roasted potatoes, creamed spinach and Brussels sprouts, but her interest in chewing waned, and she spent more time looking out the window and drinking her wine.

"You should eat," said Sheerness finally.

She turned from looking out the window at the garden, which was now completely dark between flashes of lightning, to give him an indifferent stare.

"I'm not hungry anymore," she said brusquely before taking a sip from her glass. All day, people had been telling her what to do, and she was tired of it.

"Psyche, you need to eat," said Sheerness a little more firmly.

"Don't tell me what I *need*," Psyche ground out. "I have had enough of being ordered about for one day. I am heartily *sick* of it." She signaled for the footman. "I am finished. You may clear away my plate, thank you," she said, giving the young man a polite smile.

"Leave it," ordered Sheerness when the footman began to do as she asked.

Psyche spared him a stubborn glare, and she threw down her napkin and stood up from the table, taking her wineglass with her. She went to sit on the couch and did her best to ignore him. She wondered how Pandora was. She also wondered how the rest of her family was after the news about Myron. They would be preparing him for his wake and his funeral. She closed her eyes and pressed a hand against them to keep away the tears. She had cried so much already. Then she heard a scream from upstairs. She dropped her glass, and it shattered on the floor as she stood up to head for the door.

"Pandora!"

Sheerness grabbed her around her waist and lower arms and pulled her away from the door. Psyche tried to twist out of his grasp, and he had to lean to the side quickly as she tried to hit him in the chin with the back of her head.

"Let me go!" she bit out as she continued to struggle, and he pulled her further away from the door.

"No, Psyche," said Sheerness quietly, and he tightened his grip as she continued to struggle.

"Let me go!" she repeated on a sob. "Don't make me hurt you," she ground out.

"No," said Sheerness in the same gentle tone, and he realized with astonishment she was in no way drunk. "You don't need to go up there."

"How would *you* know what I need?" sobbed Psyche, and she almost managed to twist free of him.

"Pandora doesn't want you there."

"I don't care," cried Psyche, and she tried to stomp on his foot.

Sheerness had learned to expect that and managed to move his foot and avoid it. Pandora screamed again, and Psyche was almost frenzied in her attempt to get away from him. He bent her forward at the waist and put his mouth near her ear and shushed her, trying to get her to calm down. Psyche continued to sob helplessly, but she was slowing her struggle because she knew he was right. Pandora *had* told her to leave, and as hard as it would be, she would do what her twin requested. Psyche could *not*, however, listen to Pandora scream, or it would drive her mad. She waited a few seconds until Sheerness eased his hold, letting him think she was becoming compliant, and then she pressed out sharply against his arms around her and got loose.

Psyche ran for the door and opened it before he was able to stop her, but instead of running down the hall for the stairs to the first floor, she turned in the opposite direction and headed for the door to the garden. Sheerness raced after her and caught up to her as she reached the bottom of the stairs outside. She was still crying, her hands over her ears, and he realized what she was doing. He had his arms around her waist again, and she was still trying to get away, but she wouldn't take her hands away from her ears.

It was still raining heavily, and there was still thunder and lightning. He couldn't let her stay outside. Both of them were already soaked to the skin. Sheerness tried to turn her toward the house and back up the stairs, but she wouldn't go and began to struggle more fiercely. She managed to get loose from him again and ran further into the garden. She seemed to be heading for somewhere with a purpose, and she was able to move quickly. The best he could manage was trying to keep up and making sure she didn't come to any harm. There was a bright flash of lightning, and he saw the garden temple. He slowed and tiredly climbed the steps and sighed with relief when he was once again out of the rain.

He found Psyche curled up in a ball on the bench, her hands still over her ears, crying quietly. The sound of the rain falling against the copper of the roof effectively drowned out any other sounds. Sheerness stood helplessly for a moment watching her cry, and then he went to sit beside her.

He took off his waistcoat and draped it over the end of the couch. There was a blanket lying over the arm, and Sheerness looked heavenward thankfully. The wind wasn't blowing much despite the ferocity of the storm, but the air was cool and both of them had on wet clothing. He took the blanket to put over them and lay down. He curled up close behind her with his front to her back, and then he put one arm around her waist and put his hand over hers covering one of her ears. She would shiver occasionally as she wept, and Sheerness thought he had never seen a more forlorn figure. She didn't pull away and snuggled closer under the blanket. He realized she did it unconsciously, simply because she was cold, and even though he was no less wet than she was, their bodies pressed together generated heat. He remembered Myron saying she got cold easily. She had to be freezing.

She continued to cry until she just couldn't cry anymore. The rain continued to fall and protected her from hearing her sister's screams. Psyche was hopeful Pandora would be fine, but her agonized cries didn't make it easy to believe. Pandora had said she couldn't do it with Psyche in the room, and Psyche realized her screams were probably the reason. Sending her downstairs had not been far enough away. Psyche only knew she would be able to bear losing Pandora even less bravely than the loss of Myron. She wouldn't be able to go on if she lost her twin.

Sheerness remained pressed closely behind her. Their clothes were still wet, but their body heat had warmed them until now Psyche's garments just felt clinging and uncomfortable. They would eventually dry, but she could feel the seam of the bodice cutting into her ribs to the point she thought she couldn't breathe. Her legs felt bound by the skirt, and despite her more important worries, the way her clothes felt began to prey on her mind.

Sheerness began to cough then, and he moved away from her and put a hand over his mouth. Psyche turned over to look at him worriedly. He was still sick, and getting soaked by the rain was not good. The fit lasted for several minutes, and once it ended, his eyes were closed tiredly as his breath returned. When he opened them, he saw Psyche's concerned expression. He brushed a hand across her cheek.

"I'm fine," he said quietly.

Psyche's expression didn't change; Pandora said she was fine, too.

"You're still not well," said Psyche evenly.

Sheerness shrugged. "Well enough."

Psyche's lips tightened at his stubbornness. "You should have stayed in bed."

"I couldn't do that," he said quietly, looking away from her reproving stare.

"Yes, *honor* demanded you risk putting yourself into your grave…just so you could help Myron into his," she said brokenly, finally voicing the thought she had been unable to finish last night.

Sheerness looked at her with a stricken expression, and she realized Myron's death had caused him just as much anguish as losing a member of his own family, possibly more because he had helped cause it. Psyche watched in astonishment as he started to tremble, his face crumpling emotionally, and he began to cry. Psyche looked at him uncertainly, and then she hugged him to her. He clung to her helplessly as he sobbed. She hadn't meant for this to happen. She hadn't *expected* this to happen. She rubbed his back consolingly and whispered soothing noises. To see this man she thought of as strong and the definition of male fortitude reduced to sobbing was heart wrenching. She started crying again herself because she couldn't bear to see him this way, and she didn't know what to do to make him cease. Eventually, he stopped, as if realizing how distressing she found it. He lifted his head from her shoulder.

"I'm sorry," he said huskily. Psyche couldn't decide if he was apologizing for crying or for Myron.

He looked lost and confused, and Psyche reached up to put a soothing hand against his cheek. She had asked him if he could stand to lose someone else, and she could see he was *not* bearing it well. He would have been all right, at least for a little while (until he was alone), if she hadn't said anything. Even though she didn't trust him, even as bereft as she was herself, she couldn't refuse him comfort. She was the only one who *could* comfort him because he wouldn't let anyone see him like this to know he needed it. That he had lost control of himself to let *her* see it had been a mistake; she could tell by the look on his face. Psyche found it mournful he thought it was necessary to keep emotions like grief and sadness hidden, when they were the two one was least capable of facing alone.

She smoothed her hand across his cheek, and then she leaned toward him and kissed him gently on the forehead. He jumped slightly at the contact, finding her sympathy and tenderness unexpected but infinitely moving. He put a gentle hand to the side of her neck and looked into her eyes. Her gaze was uncertain, and there was a slight frown of concern furrowed between her brows.

Sheerness brushed his lips against hers, and she responded hesitantly at first, only to begin kissing him back in earnest. He was warm and solid, and Psyche *really* wanted to kiss him. She moved closer to him and teased his bottom lip with her teeth, and her hand that had been at his cheek moved to the back of his head to twine in his hair. Sheerness was startled by her reaction, and he was subdued in his response as he fought the emotions it stirred inside him. As she continued to press against him, her tongue slipping past his lips to play against his, he groaned in surrender and began to kiss her back hungrily.

He moved a hand to her hip to press her against him as he trailed his lips to her neck. He moved the hand at her hip to cup her bottom, and Psyche sighed longingly just before his lips returned to hers for a kiss that left her weak with yearning. His embrace reminded her of the way he had been in the garden of his home, and just as then, she couldn't resist it. When he moved a hand to her breast, she leaned into his touch with a sigh of pleasure.

Psyche was frustrated by her clothes. They were wet and constricting, and she couldn't move freely enough to suit her. She wanted to feel his hands. She remembered the closet at Almack's, and she wanted to feel that again. But she couldn't because of her clothes. She worked her slippers off her feet and dropped them to the floor. She undid the fastenings for her pelisse, and with a little bit of a struggle with the binding material, she was able to work it off her arms and pushed it to the floor behind her. She started to feel better immediately, and she reached back to unfasten her gown.

Sheerness could tell she was removing her clothes, and he was willing to help. He reached down to grab the skirt of her dress and pulled it up. She moved away from him momentarily and sat up on her knees to remove it and put it on the floor with her pelisse. She quickly got back under the blanket and sighed with relief and yearning as Sheerness pulled her close and began to kiss her thoroughly. She had on only her chemise and stockings, but she felt warm pressed against him...until the cold, wet leather of his boots brushed against her legs. She tried to ignore it, but she couldn't, and she moved away from him again to pull them off. The leather was hard to remove, and it required her to stand up completely. By the time Psyche finished, she was cold, and she quickly climbed back under the blanket again.

Sheerness pulled her toward him and placed one of her legs over his thigh. Her breath caught in her throat excitedly as she felt his erection, and she trembled achingly. Psyche pulled his shirt loose from the waistband of his trousers and worked it over his head to toss it onto the pile of her own clothes on the floor. She sighed happily as her hands smoothed over the powerful expanse of his back, and she marveled at the combination of the silken texture of his skin over the hardness of the muscle beneath.

He loosened her garters and removed her stockings, and he could feel the chill bumps on her calf as he trailed his fingers along the soft skin. He was still fascinated by the absence of hair on her legs, and he knew one day he would have to ask where it went. He rolled her onto her back and settled between her thighs, and Psyche kept her leg wrapped around his hips and moved against him instinctively. He put a hand to the side of her face and tore his lips away from hers to look at her solemnly.

"I can't stop this time," he said softly.

Psyche looked up at him pensively. She knew if she told him to stop right then, even if he said he couldn't, he would. But this would be her only opportunity. This was wrong, but he felt wonderful close to her, and she felt gloriously alive and happy to be that way. Whatever else would happen, she couldn't let that end yet. She took his hand from the side of her face and moved it to her breast and held it there, and then she put her other hand to the back of his neck.

"I *need* this," she whispered, and she pulled his head toward hers to kiss him passionately.

Sheerness groaned low in his throat and closed his hand on her breast hungrily as he returned her ardent kiss. He swirled his thumb around her nipple through the fabric of her chemise until it hardened exquisitely, and Psyche moaned low in her throat and arched against him. He reached for the bottom edge of her chemise and broke their kiss only long enough to pull it over her head. Psyche gasped at the erotic sensations caused by the hair on his chest brushing against her bare nipples, and she cried out and clutched her fingers in his hair achingly when he stopped kissing her to take one into his mouth and rasp his tongue against its aroused hardness.

Their lovemaking was almost frantic in their need for each other. Psyche fumbled impatiently with the fastenings on the front of his breeches, wanting to feel all of him pressed naked against her. She finally worked them loose and pulled the material down as far as her hands would reach, and she smoothed her palms across the bare skin of his buttocks before she gently raked her nails across them. Sheerness gasped in surprise and thrust toward her. Psyche moaned excitably when his bare erection brushed against her button, and she put her leg around his waist and moved against him. Sheerness kissed her lustily before moving off of her to completely remove his pants, and Psyche's disappointment was appeased when he came back to her completely bare.

Psyche twined herself around him, and she sighed silkily with a soft smile just at the overwhelming sensational pleasure of being near him. She moved her hands down his chest to feel the light matting of hair that covered it, and she brushed her palms lightly over his nipples on her way to cling desperately to his back. He trailed kisses along her neck to her collarbone and took one of her breasts into his mouth and suckled it until she arched against him and cried out with a pleasure so intense it was almost painful.

"Sebastian!" she gasped breathlessly, and she twined her fingers in his hair to pull his mouth back to hers.

Sheerness was momentarily stunned when she said his name, and he felt his chest tighten emotionally. Psyche had never used his given name before, and he had never thought her saying it would provoke such an intense reaction. He moaned delightedly and returned her kiss as one of his hands moved down between them to gently begin teasing her button. Psyche moaned low in her throat and arched her hips toward his touch, and she moved her lips down his chin to begin placing kisses along his neck to his shoulder. Her lips moved back to his just as she climaxed, and she shuddered against him with a soft cry of ecstasy.

He placed gentle, teasing kisses all over her face, across her jawline and down her neck as he waited for her to catch her breath, and then he nuzzled his face in the valley between her breasts before raising it to look at her tenderly. She moved her hands to his face to trace his features with her fingertips, and she found his lips and chin to be particularly fascinating. She lifted her face to run her tongue over the dimple in his chin before she did the same to his lips, and he smiled slightly at her activities. Psyche felt it with her tongue and smiled happily to herself before placing her lips against his for a warm, lingering kiss as she played her fingers along his shoulder and down to his chest. She could still feel his arousal between them, and she moved against him with renewed interest.

Sheerness looked at her with a sharp intake of breath and knew she was ready. He played his fingers along the soft skin of her outer thigh to her calf and moved her leg to his waist. He positioned himself to enter her and gave her a gentle kiss before placing a soothing hand against her cheek. She bit her lower lip in anticipation, and he found it to be extremely erotic. He slowly eased himself into her, his eyes never leaving hers. Her eyes widened in shock, and he felt her tense as he went further, and he smoothed his hand reassuringly against her cheek as he steadily filled her completely.

Psyche had felt an intense burning, and for a moment she had almost panicked. As he stayed still inside her and looked at her in that tender, careful way, the pain began to subside, and she felt a lump forming in her throat and had to blink her eyes several times in awe of the tide of feelings she had for him. She put a hand over his on her cheek, and she put the other to the back of his head to pull his lips to hers for an ardent kiss.

He raised himself out of her and pushed into her again, his gaze intent as he watched her face for her response. There was still a hint of discomfort in the furrow between her brows, but as he gently repeated the action, the frown faded, and her expression of anticipation and pleasure returned. He gradually began to quicken his pace with each thrust, and he watched with satisfaction as her features became rapturous, and her hips rose to meet his with an instinctive need. Her breath came out in short panting gasps, and her hands fluttered over him in a steadily more disjointed fashion.

Psyche was almost overwhelmed by the sensations coursing through her as he continued to move inside her. She had never imagined she could become so lost in a tide of emotions, but as she looked up at his rapt expression, she could feel herself drowning in ecstasy. She felt the tightness in her stomach grow until it snapped, and she mindlessly cried out his name and arched toward him as she orgasmed. She clung to him weakly as he thrust in and out of her, and she felt herself continue to spasm with the power of her release. She put a wondering hand to his cheek at the look of utter bliss that came over his face as he reached his own climax, and she could feel him shuddering uncontrollably with the intensity of it. He bent his head to kiss her passionately, and Psyche returned it with a soft sigh at the back of her throat, her hand gently curling in the hair at the back of his head.

He turned over on his side and brought her with him so they lay facing each other, their limbs still wound together as they both tried to catch their breath. Sheerness adjusted the blanket over the both of them to protect them from the cold and pulled Psyche closer to him. She lay with her eyes closed, a softly contented smile playing about her lips. He leaned forward to place a tender kiss against the corner of her mouth, and then he rolled onto his back and cradled her into his side. Psyche laid her head on his chest and wrapped her arm around his waist as she snuggled closer to him. The sound of his heartbeat beneath her ear and the steady rise and fall of his chest as he breathed lulled her to sleep before she even realized she was tired. Sheerness adjusted the blanket again and kissed the top of her head before he tightened his arm around her and drifted off to a troubled sleep himself.

≪ ≫

Islington stood at the bedroom window looking out at the garden with a pensive expression, a troubled frown furrowing his forehead. The rain had calmed to a slight drizzle, and the flashes of lightning were becoming fewer and more distant, but the storm had left behind a light covering of fog. He adjusted the bundle he held with one arm cradled against his chest, and his lips tightened into a grim line.

"Theo, quit watching the storm, and bring me your son so he can eat," called Pandora softly from the bed.

"Coming, *àiren,*" he said absently.

His hand gripped the edge of the curtain for a few seconds more before he let it fall back into place and turned to face the room. He walked toward the bed with a soft smile as he looked down at the tiny newborn he held in his arms. He sat down on the edge of the bed and carefully held him out toward his mother. Pandora was propped against several pillows behind her back, and she soon had the baby settled in and suckling at her breast. She looked exhausted but blissfully happy, and Islington had never thought she looked more beautiful. He reached out with a finger to brush it against her cheek, and she looked up from her son with a fond smile.

"I think it's all right for Psyche to come in now," said Pandora softly, "but I expect I'll never hear the end of it when she does."

Islington looked up as Maiyin approached him, and he held out his arms to take his other son from her with a delighted smile. He looked back at his wife, and his pensive look returned for a moment before it was replaced with a grin.

"I think that will wait until morning. I'm sure she's sleeping by now, regardless of the racket you made, and you should get some sleep, too."

Pandora's expression was thoughtful. "I don't imagine Sheerness was able to keep her *that* distracted."

"You might be surprised," said Islington dryly. "And like I said, *you* need to sleep."

Pandora yawned fiercely at the mention of it. The baby at her breast finished eating, and she placed him to her shoulder to gently burp him. She *was* incredibly tired, but she was safe, and her babies were safe, and the ordeal was finally over. She wanted to see Psyche before she went to sleep, but Pandora suspected her husband was right that Psyche was already in bed. If

Sheerness got her drunk, as Maiyin told Pandora that she had suggested he do, it was almost a certainty. It was the only thing to account for why she had not already burst into the room.

"I suppose you're right that it can wait until morning," she said softly.

She took her son away from her shoulder to look down at him adoringly. She placed a gentle kiss to his forehead and held him out for Maiyin to place in the cradle not far away from the bed. Islington handed their other son to the maid to settle in as well, and he helped his wife adjust herself on the pillows so she could sleep. He gave her a gentle kiss on the lips and brushed a hand against her forehead.

"Have I told you how much I love you today, wife?" he asked her with a tender smile.

Pandora gave him a teasing grin as she started to drift off. "You're just deliriously happy I gave you *two* sons," she chortled, and she opened her eyes to look at him briefly and take his hand in hers. "I love you, too, husband," she sighed as she went to sleep.

Psyche woke up with her head pounding. Her forehead wrinkled with the pain, and she lifted a hand to rub across it achingly. Her mouth felt as if it were stuffed with cotton, and her stomach felt entirely disagreeable as she tried to rouse herself. She opened her eyes and blinked a few times to focus them around the fog at the edge of her vision. It was still dark, but the rain had stopped, and she could feel a draft across the end of her nose as she poked it above the edge of the blanket. She could hear a thumping in her ear, and it took her a moment to realize it was a heartbeat that was not her own. Then everything came back to her, and she rubbed a hand across her forehead again in disbelief.

She still lay next to Sheerness on the couch in the garden, her head resting on his chest. She felt warm against him under the blanket, but she raised herself up from her cozy place to look down at him. Her head spun at the movement, but her vision soon steadied. His eyes opened sleepily when he felt her moving, and he looked at her with a soft smile. He saw her disconcerted frown, and he reached up a hand to the side of her neck and guided her lips toward his for a gentle kiss.

"Did you sleep well?" he asked huskily.

Psyche's unease with the situation did not lessen at his warm greeting. She must have been far more tipsy than she realized. It would certainly account for the throbbing in her forehead.... The throbbing at the back of her head was from the lump. She remembered everything, but she couldn't say she regretted it...at least, not yet. He looked at her drowsily, but she could also detect a hint of self-satisfaction at the corners of his mouth as he smiled. She didn't think that could bode well for her, but she did have more pressing matters on her mind at the moment.

She started to move away from him to get dressed, but he pulled her mouth back to his for another heated kiss, and Psyche could feel herself becoming enthralled as his other hand trailed down her back to cup her bottom. He turned sideways with her and brought her leg up over his waist. His lips trailed down her neck to her breast, and Psyche clutched her hands in his hair achingly as she felt the heat coiling in her stomach.

When he brought his lips back to hers, she inhaled sharply with wanting of him, and her lips clung to his thirstily as he explored her mouth with his tongue. She moaned low in her throat as she felt him enter her, and she wound her arms around his head in weak abandon as he began to thrust into her deeply. His hand moved to cup her breast and knead it as he drew the nipple between his fingers. Psyche whimpered and began to tremble as she orgasmed with an intensity that frightened her. After only a few more thrusts, Sheerness joined her, and he rested his forehead against hers, his eyes closed, panting as he fought to regain his breath. He brushed his hand down her cheek soothingly and placed a tender kiss on her forehead.

"I love you," he whispered.

Psyche jumped as if scalded, and her eyes flew open in surprise.

"What?" she asked numbly.

"I want to marry you," he said quietly as he moved his hand down her arm in a caress to take her hand. He brought it to his lips and placed a kiss on her palm.

Psyche's face paled, and she scrabbled away from him off the couch. She felt much colder away from him and the blanket, and she looked for her clothes to put them on quickly. Blessedly, they were dry, if wrinkled. Sheerness sat up on the couch to look at her in puzzlement. This was not the reaction he had expected.

"Psyche? Did you hear me?" he asked confusedly.

She looked up at him from pulling on one of her stockings and garters. "I heard you," she said brusquely, and she pulled on her other stocking and garter and began to look for her slippers.

"Then what—?" he began, and Psyche held up her hand to stop him after she finished putting on her slippers.

"I don't believe you," she said simply with a sad look, and she fled from the temple to return to the house.

Chapter Fourteen

Psyche made her way across the garden easily as the sky began to lighten. She looked at her watch as she strolled quickly along the path; it was after five. That explained why she woke up. She went in the back door near the private sitting room and made her way to the stairs quietly in the dark. When she got to the first floor landing, she was startled to see Maiyin standing there, holding a small bundle of towels. The Mandarin woman looked tired but not bereaved in the light of the lamp she carried. Psyche grew hopeful.

"How is Pandora?" asked Psyche nervously.

"She is sleeping because she was very tired," said Maiyin softly, "as we all are." She looked Psyche up and down, and her nose wrinkled. "Where have you been? You smell like liquor. You need a *bath.*"

"Yes, please," sighed Psyche gratefully, "but what about the baby?"

"The *babies* are fine," said Maiyin with a soft smile as she watched the relief fill Psyche's features.

"Oh, thank God," sighed Psyche, closing her eyes and putting a hand to her chest.

"You go to your room and get undressed. I will get your bath started and show you where it is."

"*Máfan nǐle,* Maiyin," said Psyche with a smile.

"Hunh," said Maiyin with a shake of her head as she continued down the hall in the opposite direction from Pandora and Islington's room.

Psyche went to her room and closed the door behind her. She leaned against it with a tired sigh and closed her eyes for a moment. She was overjoyed Pandora was all right, and she felt guilty her twin could have slipped so easily from her mind last night. She was often accused of thinking and worrying too much. She had become completely oblivious when she was with Sheerness. She couldn't decide if that had been a good thing or not. It was true that for a time she had no worries while she was in his arms, but his words of only minutes ago had ended it. She had wondered how far he would go. Now she knew.

She eventually moved away from the door and went to her valise. She had packed her shift and dressing gown, and she removed the wrapper from the bag and placed it on the coffer. She also pulled out her walking dress and laid it on the bed to let the wrinkles air out of it while she bathed. She would have to wear the same chemise, stockings, and slippers, but she thought she would be able to tolerate it. After all, it wasn't her clothes that felt dirty.

She got undressed and put on her wrapper, and she began to pace the floor as she worried her thumb. She would go see Pandora after she had her bath, but she would ask Maiyin if that would be all right first. Now she knew Pandora was fine, Psyche realized she was probably very tired...justifiably. After she looked in on her sister and the babies, she would go home.

It was going to be peculiar now Myron was gone. She would never forget the last glimpse she had of him through the window of the coach. She should have run down the stairs and tried to stop him. She had *known* something was going to happen to him. She should have tried harder to make him call it off. She should have convinced him to sail away on another ship with Georgiana and Lorelei. They didn't have to wait for Sheerness. He could have booked passage on another ship, and they could have been on their way to freedom and safety in less time than he had waited to meet Hendon for the duel. He hadn't needed to die.

"Don't start that again," said Maiyin exasperatedly as she opened the door and caught Psyche in mid-pace. "Come have your bath, and then you can go see Missy Pandora. She has been asking for you."

Psyche gave Maiyin a bright smile she was sure was brittle around the edges and followed her down the hall.

Sheerness sat in stunned silence after Psyche left the garden temple. She had seemed almost horrified at his proposal, and he was at a loss to understand why. He had been beastly to her last year; at times his behavior this year had not been much better, but he had been trying to make amends for that. He thought she cared for him. Apparently, he was wrong.

He sighed tiredly with a shake of his head and put on his clothes. His boots were stiff from their drenching, and he didn't think Clements would be able to soften them. The sky was getting brighter, and he saw by a glance to his pocket watch it was a quarter until six. In less than an hour, his friend would have been dead twenty-four hours. He rubbed a hand over his face and stood up, only to sit back down again as he was overcome by a coughing fit. He would see if he could locate a servant stirring in the house to arrange for a carriage to take him home, and then he would take some medicine and crawl into bed for a few hours until he could find out what the arrangements would be for Myron's funeral.

He walked up the path to the back of the house and went in the same door Psyche had. He was surprised to find Islington standing in a nearby doorway waiting for him. He had his arms folded over his chest, a pipe held in one hand.

"Sheerness, would you care to come to my study for a moment?" he asked mildly, but his assessing glance suggested it really wasn't a request.

Sheerness nodded silently and walked toward him. Islington moved out of the way to let the earl enter his study, and he closed the door behind them. The marquess went to his desk and leaned against the edge of it and invited Sheerness to take a seat in one of the two chairs.

"Would you care for some coffee?" asked Islington casually.

"Oh, that would be grand," said Sheerness heartily as he took a seat. He hadn't thought about it, but a cup of coffee would be just the thing.

Islington went to a silver service on a nearby sideboard and poured a cup. He looked back over his shoulder.

"Do you take cream or sugar?"

"Cream, please," answered Sheerness politely.

He looked at Islington speculatively as the man brought him the cup. The marquess resumed his comfortable pose against the edge of the desk with his feet crossed at the ankles and drew on his pipe composingly for a moment.

"How is your wife?" asked Sheerness concernedly.

"She's fine. It was touch and go for a while, but she's stronger than she looks. All the Savage women are."

Sheerness took a sip from his coffee. "And the baby?"

Islington grinned proudly. "Ah, there, you see, was part of the problem. She had twins. Boys."

"Congratulations," said Sheerness with a smile.

"Thank you," said Islington, and he took another draw from his pipe. "I've arranged for a carriage to take you home, but I wanted a word with you first."

Sheerness nodded appreciatively and looked at him questioningly, and Islington's light expression grew serious.

"You know, when my wife and I asked that you help keep Psyche occupied, we didn't mean that in the *literal* sense," said Islington evenly.

Sheerness nearly choked on the coffee he was swallowing, and it resulted in a coughing fit that, for once, could not be blamed on his illness. He set the cup and saucer on the nearby table and looked at the marquess.

"I'm sorry?" wheezed Sheerness.

Islington grinned at him dangerously. "Don't try to dissemble with me, Sheerness. I saw you through the window. There may not have been a moon or stars, but the lightning was *very* bright at times. Once Pandora had the boys, I just happened to glance out at the garden."

"Very well, I was with her, and I'll not deny it," said Sheerness stoically.

Islington chuckled with a shake of his head, and he reached behind himself on the desk to bring a pistol into view and place it beside his hip on the edge of the desk top, the barrels pointed at Sheerness.

"Yes, I didn't figure you would, and I'd shoot you if you did," said Islington mildly. "You *will* do the honorable thing."

"I'll try," said Sheerness evenly, looking from the gun laying on the desk to the marquess, and he could see that although the man's manner and tone were light, he was deadly serious.

"You *will* do the honorable thing," repeated Islington.

"I've already *asked* her to marry me," said Sheerness defensively.

"And?" asked Islington leadingly.

"She refused," replied Sheerness flatly, slapping his hands against the arms of the chair in frustration.

Islington rubbed a hand over his mouth to hide a smirk, thinking this sounded very familiar.

"Do you love her?" he asked calmly.

"Of course I do," said Sheerness testily.

"Did you tell her?"

Sheerness looked at Islington exasperatedly, finding the man's questioning just the least bit tiring, even if he did have a gun.

"I told her that before I asked her to marry me."

Islington's eyebrow shot up in surprise. He took a thoughtful draw from his pipe.

"What did she say, exactly?"

"She said she didn't believe me," mumbled Sheerness dully.

Islington's eyebrow shot up even further. "Does she have any reason not to?" he asked calmly, and he thought about reaching for the gun again.

"No, damn it all, she doesn't!" said Sheerness angrily, but after a moment's thought, he shrugged. "At least, she shouldn't. I do," he said quietly.

Islington scratched the back of his head. The man did seem honest. He was sure Sheerness didn't force himself on Psyche. But if she had refused to marry him even after he said he loved her because she didn't believe him, then the earl must have done or said something at some point that led her to think it wasn't true. Islington wasn't sure he should mention it to Pandora (although she would find it highly entertaining), but she knew her twin better than anyone else. She might also know something else, something Psyche might have mentioned to her, that would shed some light on the matter.

"I'm going to offer you some advice," said Islington after a time, scratching the bridge of his nose with the stem of his pipe. "You had better find a way to make this right, and just asking her father to arrange it won't work. Believe me. I tried that route. If the Duke of Aberdare finds out what you've done, he'll be asking for his Manton back." Islington patted the gun on the desk. "You don't want *anyone* in that family angry with you—male *or* female."

He took a draw from his pipe and gave Sheerness a friendly grin. The earl seemed a nice enough fellow and would probably be a decent brother-in-law, but it sounded like he was going to have no less of a struggle wrangling Psyche than he had with Pandora. It was going to be very entertaining to watch, even if it wasn't going to be any fun for Sheerness.

"I'll keep that in mind," said Sheerness dully. He picked up his cup to finish his coffee. He was tempted to ask the marquess for something stronger.

≪ ≫

Psyche went down the hall to her sister's bedroom excitedly. She was just finished with her bath, and Maiyin had taken pity on her and brought her some breakfast and styled her hair while she ate it. The maid made sure, however, that Bo was not in the room. Her grief for Myron still remained like a heavy weight on her heart, but she had isolated it and pushed it aside for the time being, to be taken out and attended to later. Psyche had found the strength to do that once she knew Pandora and the babies were all right.

She practically skipped to the door of her sister's room. She didn't hear any noise on the other side of it, and after a brief scratching, she opened it and poked her head around it to look in. Pandora was awake on the bed, and she smiled widely at her sister when she saw her. She put a finger to her lips, and Psyche tiptoed toward the cradle near the bed. Her eyes teared up as she looked down at the two perfect creatures lying there. Their heads were covered by a thick mass of dark brown fuzz, their rosy, bow-shaped lips puckered around their thumbs. Psyche put a hand to her chest and sighed emotionally. They were absolutely beautiful.

She quietly moved around the cradle and climbed onto the bed beside her twin to give her a happy hug. Pandora still looked tired but not ill. She was slimmer…except for one thing: her breasts had practically tripled in size over night. Psyche was astounded.

"Oh, my God, Pan!" she whispered. "You've not got just dumplings anymore! You've got a whole bloody patisserie!"

"Yes, and they're throbbing right now because the babies are sleeping. I swear, I don't know what happened. I went to sleep—they were normal. I wake up—this!" she hissed disgustedly, motioning at her chest.

"Those are beautiful babies, Pan," sighed Psyche.

"Thank you. I think so, too," she said cheekily.

"Have you decided what to name them?"

"We thought at first we would be naming only *one*, so we were going to call him Alexander Lambert after Papà and Theo's father." She took a deep breath and sighed. "Now with two…and everything that's happened…we're still going to name one that, but we'll name the other Myron Sanders."

Psyche felt her eyes tearing up again, and she tried not to give in to it. Even though she knew Pandora was out of danger, her twin still did not need to be upset. She rubbed at her cheeks and hugged Pandora happily.

"I think that would be wonderful," she said quietly. "I was so scared for you last night. I couldn't imagine what I would have done if something had happened to you."

"Yes, Theo said I was making quite a racket," said Pandora with a lopsided grin, "but it helped."

"I had to go outside," said Psyche quietly. "I couldn't bear it," she whispered brokenly.

"Maiyin said she told Sheerness to get you drunk. Did he?" asked Pandora, giving her sister a speculative glance.

Psyche scoffed and shook her head. "You tried. He tried. Didn't work. Almost, but not quite. Tipsy was about the extent of it."

"I'm sorry, Psy," said Pandora quietly. "We told him to keep you busy and out of here whatever way he could think of. I wouldn't have been able to yell if you had been here because I wouldn't want to worry you. It would have taken a lot longer."

Psyche looked her. "You told him to keep me busy?" she asked dully.

"Yes. I knew you wouldn't go home until you knew I was all right, but I couldn't have you here." Her forehead wrinkled. "So, if he didn't get you drunk, how did he keep you out of here?"

"I stayed out because you asked me to, not because of anything *he* did," said Psyche, looking away from Pandora's curious gaze.

That was only a half-truth. She had decided she would stay out of the room because Pandora had asked her to, but if Sheerness hadn't *kept her busy*, she would have been in last night instead of this morning. When Pandora and Islington had asked him to keep her out by whatever means necessary, they certainly had not meant by the method he used. If Pandora found out, she wouldn't be upset, considering she would have little room to condemn her twin for doing something she had done herself and because she was determined to have Psyche and Sheerness together in some romantic fashion. Psyche didn't want Pandora to think something *romantic* had been involved. There wasn't.

"I find it hard to believe you would have stayed out only because I asked you to," said Pandora incredulously.

"When you started screaming I couldn't stay in the house and listen to it, or I would have come back, so I went out to the garden temple. I couldn't hear you out there. I suppose I was just tipsy enough I fell asleep." She gave her sister a lopsided smile. "I had a headache when I woke up this morning."

Pandora continued to look at her twin speculatively. Psyche wasn't lying, but that didn't mean she was telling everything, either. Usually, she did tell everything, regardless of the consequences, but as a method of self-preservation, she had learned to leave out parts of the truth or to phrase things in a way that would forestall the anxiety she got from lying…like when she had helped to cover Pandora's going to Edinburgh. Her family had asked after Pandora at breakfast, and rather than blurting out where Pandora had gone, Psyche had been able to word it in a way that tricked her conscience into believing it wasn't a lie, at least for a little while. Hives had eventually ensued, but by then Pandora had been well away. This time, Pandora was sure Psyche wasn't telling everything, but what she was leaving out made Pandora wonder.

"Well, I'd say you needed to get drunk. I would have, if I could," said Pandora feelingly. "I hope they hang that bastard, but it's not likely."

"What do you mean?" asked Psyche blankly.

Pandora put a gentle hand on Psyche's arm. "Theo told me what happened yesterday morning…at the duel."

"Oh," sighed Psyche breathlessly.

"Hendon turned, aimed, and fired early," said Pandora angrily. "Theo said it was over quickly…and that Myron didn't suffer, but it was no better than murder."

"Oh, no!" gasped Psyche, and she put a hand over her mouth to hold back a sob, her eyes shining with tears.

Pandora hugged her sister to her and rubbed her arm soothingly. "Hendon's paying for it, though," she said firmly. "Myron shot him in the leg before he…before…." She cleared her throat and shook her head. "Well, Dr. Phelps amputated his leg right there on the field, quicker than a diver after a purse on market day."

"Dr. Phelps?" asked Psyche, raising her head.

"Yes, why? You've heard of him?" asked Pandora in surprise.

"He's the doctor who nearly killed Sheerness, if there's not more than one of them about at the moment." She wiped a hand at her cheeks. "We could only be so lucky that he would finish Hendon."

"Hendon is at Newgate right now. I don't know what will happen to him, but losing a leg is a good start."

"Too right," said Psyche feelingly. She looked at her sister. "Have you heard anything from Mamá and Papá about…about the funeral?"

"No, we haven't," said Pandora sadly, "but I expect they'll want to take him home."

"Yes," agreed Psyche on a shuddering sigh. "He's really gone," she whispered brokenly, leaning her head against her sister's, and squeezing her eyes closed as scalding tears fell onto her cheeks.

The two of them cried together quietly for a little while, but the babies eventually woke and needed to be fed and changed. Pandora was relieved to feed them. While she was crying with her sister, her breasts had begun to leak, and when the babies started crying, it was as if someone turned on a faucet. Psyche happily lifted the babies from the cradle and took them to Pandora.

Once the babies were done eating, the sisters each burped one, and Psyche didn't even mind changing their diapers. Pandora was relieved to have her sister's help. Kwan would be arriving that day, and Maiyin and Islington had been helping, but the diaper changing was not a favorite chore for any of them. Psyche did have to try a couple times before she could determine exactly how the cloth was supposed to go back on, and she wasn't sure she had put it on in the same configuration, but it was close enough that it would serve its purpose.

The babies were identical, like their mother and aunt had been, and so far neither had developed any marks to distinguish them. Psyche's birthmark had not appeared until she was a few days old, but once it had, there had not been any confusion as to which was which, and definitely not any once the two girls developed their individual personalities. Until the same thing happened with Alex and Myron, Maiyin had painted one of Alex's toenails with red nail lacquer. Islington was willing to tolerate it until they were able to tell them apart in some other way. No one imagined that would be very long.

Islington came to the room not long after they had settled the babies back into the cradle. Well, Psyche had settled them in. Pandora was still too weak yet to move from the bed because of the blood loss and length of her labor. If their parents took Myron home to Wilderland to be buried, Pandora wouldn't be able to go. Her babies were too small to travel any great distance, and she wouldn't go anywhere without them.

If their family did take Myron to Wilderland, even if they didn't return to London after the funeral, Psyche had already determined *she* would be coming back to stay with Pandora. Psyche wasn't positive, but she was fairly certain Dorian and her father would return to the city because of Parliament. Arachne, Eurydice, and Persephone would stay home. The Season was over for them, and none of them particularly cared for the city anyhow. Pandora wanted Psyche to be godmother to her new nephews, and after the scare she had the previous night, she could not bear the thought of being away from any of them for very long yet. She would stay with them until the end of the Season, by which time Pandora and the babies would be healthy and strong enough for the journey home to Yorkshire. Then Psyche would return to Wilderland.

Islington lounged companionably on the bed with them for a while, listening to the cooing and gurgling from the cradle, until Psyche decided it was time to return to Aberdare House. Her whereabouts were probably the least of her parents' concerns at the moment, but she knew they were concerned nonetheless. Islington had sent them word Pandora had delivered and that she and the babies were doing well. Psyche was sure they were expecting her.

Islington arranged a carriage to take Psyche home, and when she reached it, she noticed a change in the decor. The mirrors had all been draped in black crepe. All of her mother's cut flowers had been taken out. The house was quiet. She didn't hear her little brothers playing. For once, Eurydice wasn't playing her violin. Tannaz had been standing at the door wearing a black armband. It was very somber, and Myron's death weighed heavily on her mind in the subdued atmosphere.

She made her way up the stairs to her bedroom. Chrissoula was waiting for her. Her maid was dressed as usual, but she, too, was wearing a black armband. When she looked up from sewing to see Psyche enter, Chrissoula put it aside and stood up to hold her arms out to Psyche. Psyche's face crumpled, and she dropped her valise by the door and went to her maid with a sob. Chrissoula shushed her and smoothed her hair until Psyche managed to once again quit crying. She had never imagined she would have so many tears.

Once Psyche calmed herself, Chrissoula went to her work room and brought out a small trunk. When she opened it, Psyche was disturbed to see it contained nothing but black clothing. Black dresses. Black hose. Black hats with black veils. Even the chemises were black. And it wasn't just any black. It was a dull, lifeless black. Mourning black. Psyche almost started crying again. She turned from looking at the contents to look at Chrissoula.

"I prayed you wouldn't have to see this," said Chrissoula quietly. "Someone so young and full of life as you doesn't deserve to have it hidden away under so much bleakness. I don't think your brother would have wanted this for you."

Psyche put a hand to her chest. "Oh, Chrissoula, don't make me cry again. I don't want to cry anymore," she whispered brokenly.

Her maid pulled out one of the dresses and shook it to straighten out the creases. "Mourning black is no color for the living," said Chrissoula as she looked at it critically, and then she looked at Psyche with a slight smile of dark humor, "but you'll live anyhow."

She turned Psyche around and began to unfasten the buttons on her walking dress, made of soft lavender silk with ruffles of cream Irish lace. She helped Psyche out of the dress and retrieved one of the chemises and a pair of the black stockings from the trunk. Psyche put on the clothes with a shuddering sigh. Chrissoula was right: in wearing it to remember the dead, it made the living feel that way, too. Some welcomed it. Psyche dreaded it. She had been too young to wear mourning for either Grandfather Sanders or *Babushka* Alexa, and when she began to wear it for Myron, she felt constricted in a way that withered her spirit.

Psyche felt guilty as she went down the hall to her parents' sitting room. She should *want* to wear black for Myron. He was her brother. Besides Pandora, he had been her closest confidant. She had loved him to distraction, and she would always miss him. She tried to tell herself they were just *clothes*, that they should have no affect one way or the other on her mood. But when she put them on, she felt fettered; Myron would never have wished that for her. Unfortunately, he was no longer there to prevent it. Psyche felt on the verge of tears again as she opened the door to the sitting room, and she tightly gripped the handkerchief she held in her hand.

Her mother and father sat talking quietly with each other as she entered. They, too, were dressed in black. Their faces were weary, and they looked older than Psyche had ever seen them. Myron was their firstborn. He had been heir. He was deeply loved and would be sorely missed. Their family was uncommon from many others in the fact that the duchess had given birth to eleven children, and all eleven had survived to be hardy and healthy. Neither of them had ever thought they would outlive one of their children, not even when Damon had scarlet fever or when Pandora had meningitis. That was something that happened to *other* families.

Psyche went to her mother and father and kissed both of them on the cheek. She wiped at her face angrily with the handkerchief as she tried to control her tears. She felt as if she had done enough crying for one day. She would do more tomorrow. Her parents told her they would be leaving for Wilderland for the funeral in the morning. Psyche requested she be allowed to return to London to be with Pandora once it was finished. Her parents agreed. They felt certain that being with her sister would be the best thing for her. Next to Persephone, Psyche had been closest to Myron out of his sisters. She looked exhausted and distressed, and they were concerned she might make herself sick in her grief. Pandora would help to lessen that.

After her visit with her parents, Psyche went down the hall to the front stairs and took a steadying breath as she descended them to go to the drawing room. She was going to see Myron. His family had placed him there before he would be taken home. Her palms felt sweaty, and she wiped a hand at her cheek as she walked toward the closed door. She wasn't sure she wanted to do this. She would rather remember him the way he was the last time she had seen him. It would be better, she thought, but she felt she *had* to go see him.

She walked into the drawing room and closed the door behind her. A long table had been brought in to set the coffin on. It was draped in black crepe, but Psyche suspected it was the table from the library. She walked slowly toward it, her breath catching in her throat, and she clenched and unclenched her hands anxiously as she neared it. When she peered into the coffin, a hand flew to her mouth to cover a sob, and the other went to the edge of the table as her knees felt as if they were buckling beneath her.

He looked like he was sleeping. He had been washed and dressed. Someone had chosen a royal blue velvet coat and a waistcoat of a lighter blue silk shot through with silver and gold. His hands were clasped across his chest, and he looked very peaceful…just sleeping. Psyche reached out a trembling hand to brush his cheek, and she snatched it back when she felt the icy coldness of it. He could have been made of stone.

"Oh, Sham," she sighed breathlessly as she shook her head, "you should not have gone."

She bit her lower lip and wiped at her face with her handkerchief, and then she bent down to softly kiss his cheek and rest her forehead against his for a few seconds. She took a deep breath and straightened up, closing her eyes as she tried to keep herself from bursting into sobs. She wrapped her arms around her waist and slowly left the room.

Psyche's family left for Wales early the following morning. The belongings of the duchess, the younger boys, Persephone, Eurydice, and Arachne had all been hastily packed and loaded. Chrissoula had seen to packing Psyche's things as well. All of her beautiful ball gowns and other things would be taken to Wilderland. Except for a few items Chrissoula had packed into a valise for the journey to Wales and back, the rest of her things (including her mourning dress in the small trunk) would be taken to Bardsey House.

A few of the servants were remaining behind to close up most of Aberdare House. Selena would be staying in Glamorgan with the rest of the family, so with only the duke and Dorian there, it wasn't necessary to have the entire house open. They wouldn't need to do any entertaining. Once the necessaries were attended to, the rest of the servants would return to Wilderland, and the duke and Dorian would hire temporary servants from the city until the close of the Season except for their valets, Tajik, and Jim. Tajik's son, Tewfik, had ridden to Wilderland on Saturday to let Madame Meunier, their housekeeper, know what had happened and have the house prepared for their arrival.

The train of coaches and carriages was long that followed the hearse. And for once, when they reached the toll gates, the gatekeepers simply opened them to let the family pass without collecting a toll. It was a long, slow journey behind the coach carrying her brother, and Psyche slept for most of the trip, her head resting on Persephone's shoulder. For once, Persephone didn't ride her horse, and she was wearing a black dress like her sisters. There wasn't much talking in the carriage. The sisters kept their thoughts to themselves.

The train of carriages was lengthened behind the ones carrying the Aberdares and their servants by a few more carrying close friends of the family who wanted to attend the funeral: the Lundeys, including Viscount Drake, the Stranraers, including their son Baron Lambeth, who happened to be in England for a short time from West Africa, and Sheerness and his brother Alex. There were more who had wanted to attend, but because of the remoteness of Wilderland and the distance involved, they had only been able to send their condolences. Those who were coming would be guests of the Aberdares for the short duration of their stays. It would be two or three days at most.

They didn't stop once they left London except to change horses. When the carriage did stop, Psyche would get out for a few minutes to stretch her legs and work the kinks out of her back and neck. They were making the journey even more quickly than they did at the beginning and end of the Season, but not as quickly as it could be done by post. Psyche had thought to bring a book to read, but her history books reminded her too much of Myron at the moment, and she couldn't tolerate the novels Arachne enjoyed. The journey made her weary, and the sadness and somberness of everyone else did nothing to ease it. Her only consolation was that she would be going home for a few days.

It was late afternoon on Wednesday when the coach drove through the gates marking the edge of Wilderland Park. Psyche looked out the window and dropped the pane to inhale with her eyes closed. Knowing she was home where she was safe and free helped to lighten her spirits. It would only be for a few days, but she was willing to return to London after that because she would be going to Pandora, the only other place where she felt the same peacefulness.

They drove on for some distance more before they reached the set of ornate wrought-iron gates that led them to the circular drive in front of the castle. When the coach came to a stop, one of their footmen, Niall, hurried down the stairs from the house to open the door and help the sisters down. Psyche looked up at the front of the house as she stood on the gravel, and then she walked up the steps to go inside.

Psyche didn't wait for anyone. Chrissoula would see to having her things taken to her room. The funeral would be in the morning. She wasn't going to eat dinner with everyone else. She would have a tray in her room. But she wasn't going to her room yet. She went up the grand staircase to the first floor and went down the hall to the left. After only a short distance, she came to another staircase that would lead her to the second floor and the wing where her room was located. When she came to the second floor landing, instead of turning left again to go down the hall to her room, she went a short distance to the right to yet another staircase. She climbed the wide spiraling stairs past the landings for the lower tower rooms until she reached the very top. She pushed open the thick oak door and looked at the solarium.

She closed the door quietly behind her and looked around herself. The sun was setting, and the high tower room's windows allowed it to shine in and cast a warm, golden glow on everything it touched. Psyche removed her bonnet and placed it on her work table, and then she rubbed a tired hand over her brow. She walked over to the window seat and climbed onto it, bringing her knees up to her chest and resting her cheek on them as she looked out the window. The sun that brightened the solarium made the surface of the lake twinkle occasionally across its blue-green color, and the emerald green of the oak forest began to darken in the fading light.

Psyche sat looking out with a blank expression. Inside, her head was a confused jumble of thoughts, but she could specifically determine what they were. She was glad to be home, but she wasn't. She wanted to go back to London, but she didn't. She missed Myron terribly, but she had been more worried when she thought she might lose Pandora. She wanted to mourn for her brother, and she did, but she couldn't tolerate wearing the black it required.

She felt as if she was betraying Myron because she couldn't mourn for him that way. She was devastated he was gone, and she felt guilty she did not do more to stop him, but she didn't need blackness to remind her of it. She would never forget it. He had only been gone five days, and she already felt suffocated by the somberness and gloom. She was sure she was wrong to feel that way, and it made her ashamed.

Psyche sat in the window seat until the sun disappeared behind the horizon and there was barely any light left in the solarium. She finally put her feet back to the floor and went to her table to retrieve her hat. She took one last look around the room and inhaled deeply, finding comfort in the familiar sights and smells. There was still a trace of the odors from the chemicals Pandora had used in her experiments, and it helped to soothe and still Psyche's troubled thoughts. She left the room and walked down the stairs to her bedroom.

Chrissoula had a tray waiting for her when she arrived, and she didn't scold Psyche for being gone so long. She could easily imagine what Psyche was going through, and she sympathized. Mourning was not meant for the young. She went to draw a bath for her charge while she ate, and after she bathed, Chrissoula helped her into bed and made sure the fire was well-supplied. After she turned off the lights and left the room to go to the servants' quarters, she sadly wondered how long it would be before she would hear Psyche laugh again.

Chapter Fifteen

Psyche had Chrissoula bring a tray for breakfast in her room. She wasn't hungry, but she ate because she knew she needed to. Her supper of the night before had only been half-eaten, and breakfast didn't fare much better. She hadn't slept well, which wasn't unusual, and she had spent most of the night pacing, until she finally relented and took some of the sleeping draught Keung had made for her. There were dark circles under her eyes, and her features were pale and drawn.

Dressing was a brief affair. The only benefit of wearing black was that there was little chance of mismatching items or agonizing over what to wear. Black was black, and Chrissoula hadn't packed enough for her to be worried about what *kind* of dress to wear either. Chrissoula styled her hair into a simple twist without any combs or ribbons. She wasn't allowed to wear jewelry, but Psyche did wear her watch on its chain around her neck. She didn't consider it jewelry. It was a necessity. A fact that was proven when she looked at the time and saw she was going to be late if she didn't hurry. It was amazing that wearing nothing but black and being in mourning had not altered that for her. After a brief kiss to Chrissoula's cheek, she hurried from her room to the stairs and proceeded at a quick trot.

Her family was meeting with their guests in the great hall, and then they and the servants who wished to attend (which would be all of them) would go to the chapel on the castle grounds. The new assistant curate from Glyncorrwg, Mr. Thomas, who performed Sunday services for the family when they weren't in London for the season, would be officiating. There was a mausoleum attached to the chapel where members of Psyche's family had been laid to rest for centuries. The last to be buried there was her *Babushka* Alexa. Myron would be next. The local stonemason had been contacted to chisel the marble facing stone that would cover his vault in the loculi wall. The duke, Dorian, and Psyche, and the friends who had come, would return to London tomorrow.

When Psyche reached the great hall, she wasn't surprised everyone else was already there. She had slowed her pace to a sedate walk just before she reached the door and took a deep breath before she entered. She had the black veil on her hat covering her face, so no one would see the flush to her cheeks from her race to the hall, and she tried to keep her breathing steady and calm.

She walked over to Persephone and took one of her hands comfortingly. Her youngest sister was not taking Myron's death well. The way Persephone behaved was how Psyche thought *she* should be behaving, but she couldn't. Persephone's cheeks were wet beneath her veil, and she held Psyche's hand so tightly she could feel the blood starting to drain from her fingers. Psyche wasn't sure she could cry anymore. She had cried so much Saturday, and after she went to see Myron in the drawing room on Sunday, she hadn't been able to cry again. She felt drained.

Psyche linked her arm through Persephone's and walked with her to the chapel when it was time for the service. The coffin was at the front near the pulpit, draped in black crepe on a stand covered in more of the same material. Several bouquets of lily-of-the-valley and gardenias had been placed beside it, and the smell of the gardenias was so strong it began to make Psyche's eyes water. When they neared the coffin, Persephone hugged it tightly, and Psyche had to guide her away forcefully. She was surprised when she had to blink her eyes a few times to clear the tears out of them. It was exacerbated by the gardenias (she tried to tell herself), but to see Persephone—frolicsome, devil-may-care Persephone—so anguished tore at her heart. She helped her sister to the pew and reached into her sleeve for the handkerchief she had placed there to wipe at her eyes.

Mr. Thomas gave a lovely service, and Psyche continued to wipe at her eyes periodically throughout. Persephone leaned her head on Psyche's shoulder, and Psyche wrapped her arm around her sister and rubbed her shoulder comfortingly. She exhaled on a shuddering sigh and rested her head against her sister's as Mr. Thomas finished. Then it was time for Myron to be placed in the mausoleum.

Dorian, Islington, Sheerness, Viscount Drake, Baron Lambeth, and Alex Nichols stepped forward and lifted the coffin among them. The family stood as they carried it past, and Psyche kept her arm around Persephone's shoulders as they walked behind their parents and sisters after it. The stonemason and his assistant stood waiting to replace the facing stone once the coffin had been placed into the vault in the loculi wall, and Psyche watched as her brother and the other pallbearers carefully lifted it into the black square that was five feet above the floor. Persephone started to move toward it, and Psyche held onto her and did what she could to soothe her.

Mr. Thomas said a few more words and a prayer, and as Psyche watched breathlessly, the stonemason and his assistant lifted the slab of marble into place and secured it. She began to feel dizzy and took several deep breaths to calm herself. She did *not* want to begin weeping again, and she didn't want to faint either. It would only be a few more minutes, and then it would be over. If she could just leave and not look at the inscription on the stone, then she would be fine, but she did look at it.

"*Myron Sanders Savage*
18 June 1814
Aged 24 years, 6 months, 28 days
Only sleeping."

Psyche felt a lump forming in her throat, and she swallowed several times to make it go away. She could feel the heat of tears welling in her eyes that had nothing to do with gardenias. She turned and began to walk away as quickly as she could. Chrissoula was there near the back of the mourners, and she reached out a comforting hand to Psyche's shoulder as she walked past. Psyche paused briefly to give her hand a squeeze, but she kept walking. She couldn't stay. She wanted to be alone. She *needed* to be alone.

She went down the path as quickly as she could without running and went through the gate to the circular drive. She crossed over the gravel onto the grass in the center and then back onto the track again to reach the steps to the front door. She was so intent on where her feet were going she nearly ran headlong into the side of the carriage parked there. It was small and unmarked, and she didn't recognize it. The driver was nowhere to be seen. It was no concern of hers. She skirted around it and went up the steps into the castle.

She hurried up the grand staircase and removed her hat as she reached the landing, not slowing her stride. She almost broke into a run once she reached the second floor, and she lifted the front of her skirt to keep from tripping over it as she began her ascent to the solarium. Once she made it into the room, she closed the door behind her and leaned against it, her chest heaving from the exertion and the effort it took to keep herself from sobbing. She wiped at her cheeks with the handkerchief she still held in her hand, and then she reached for the heavy object on a nearby shelf and opened the door to set it on the landing outside before closing the door again. She didn't want to be disturbed, but the door didn't have a lock. That object was the only way to accomplish it.

She rubbed at her arms from the slight chill in the air, and she went to the fireplace and soon had a roaring blaze lit. Then she began to pace. Without Pandora's tables and experiments and inventions there, Psyche had plenty of room to pace. She walked from the hearth to the window seat, alternating between rubbing her cheeks with her handkerchief and worrying her thumb with her teeth. As she began to calm, her pace began to slow, until finally she was able to curl up on the window seat and lean her back against the cushions there with a tired sigh.

She didn't know where the tears came from, and she didn't know how to make them stop. When she would think it was impossible she could have any left to cry, there were always more. It was exhausting. She felt so tired, it seemed as if she had been up for hours on end. It was only eleven in the morning.

It had begun to rain while she was pacing, a steady, misty rain that made everything gray. Psyche thought it was only fitting it should be so gloomy outside, considering they had put Myron to rest that morning. It would be most unfair if the sun were shining. At least it was easy for Psyche to understand why the solarium had a chill. When the sun was shining, especially in the summer, there was never any problem with the solarium remaining warm.

Her eyelids began to droop as she sat nestled among the cushions, looking out as the rain beat against the window. She could still see the lake, but the mist that accompanied the rain made the edges hazy. The forest and mountains beyond it were almost invisible. The wind would shift the fog occasionally, and a peak would appear, only to vanish again as if it were an illusion. She was almost to the point of dozing off when she heard a rapping at the door. The sound echoed off the empty spaces in the room and made her jump.

"Go away," she called tiredly, closing her eyes. She didn't want to see anyone. She thought she had made that clear.

After a few minutes of silence, when she thought whoever was there had realized his mistake and left, when she was beginning to think she might be able to take a much needed snooze, there was a rapping at the door once again.

"Go away!" she called, putting a cushion over her head tightly.

Whoever was there was either blind or foolish because he knocked again more loudly. Psyche heaved a frustrated sigh and uttered a curse before she groaned and got up from the window seat to go to the door. She pulled it open and was startled to see Sheerness standing there, holding the heavy steel helm she had placed on the floor in his arms.

"Oh!" she gasped in surprise.

"Did you know this was sitting out here?" he asked perplexedly.

"Of course I do!" said Psyche angrily. "I put it there."

Sheerness raised an eyebrow, unaware of her irritation. "Why?"

"Because I don't want to be disturbed," said Psyche coldly. He looked from the helm back to Psyche with a puzzled frown. Psyche groaned frustratedly. "That sitting outside the door means go away. If you open the door, you better have it on, because you are going to get something thrown at your *head*." She took the helm from him and set it on the shelf. "Go away," she said tiredly, holding on to the edge of the door and preparing to close it.

Sheerness ignored her and walked further into the room. Psyche looked after him peevishly and closed the door.

Sheerness went to the middle of the room and stood looking around himself at the much-touted solarium. It really was very impressive. It was large, easily a thirty-by-forty foot rectangle. Except for the wall with the door, there were tall windows all the way around. The wall with the door had a fireplace that was large enough even he could walk into it standing upright, and there was shelf upon shelf holding books, scrolls, and manuscripts. Because it was at the top of the tower, rather than a level ceiling, the area beneath the high-peaked roof was open, and skylights had been built into it with the supporting rafters exposed so that it almost looked like a giant ladder.

As he looked around the room, it seemed lopsided. One side was almost bare. The other side held a tall writing desk littered with scrolls, clay tablets and writing paraphernalia. There were three other sturdy, thick-legged worktables that held more clay tablets, statues, vases, and other antiquities from all over the world. Under one table, it looked as if she even had a mummy in its wooden sarcophagus. It was very cluttered, but the items were organized in their small space. He was puzzled why she had all of it on one side of the room, when it was obvious she would be much more capable of working if she spread the items out and had more tables.

He walked over to one table and looked at the items sitting there. They were all fascinating. He picked up a small, black jade Buddha trimmed in gold. The workmanship was exquisite, and he was sure the British Museum would be hard-pressed to find something of the same quality in their own collection. He carefully set it back down and moved on to something else, a statue of Kali standing atop Shiva's prone body in a similar size to that of the Buddha, made of what appeared to be solid gold. It, too, was in perfect condition. He was astounded. Myron had said her collection was extensive and impressive. He had not been exaggerating.

He turned to look at her. "Where did you get all this?"

"My father…and Myron." She shrugged. "Some of it I bought myself." She shook her head and rubbed a tired hand across her brow. "What are you doing here, and how did you find me?"

"Glamorgan told me how to find you."

He walked closer to her, and he could see the dark circles under her eyes and the tired frown etched between her eyebrows. He had thought he heard her pacing last night. His room was apparently directly under hers. He had caught occasional glimpses of her on the way from London, and she had seemed almost lost in the aimless way she had walked about outside the coach. Once they had arrived at Wilderland, while he had seen other members of her family at supper and breakfast, he hadn't seen Psyche again until that morning. She had seemed to be coping fairly well at the service until they placed Myron in the vault, and then he had seen her flee with what seemed like panic. This was the first time he had seen her up close since Sunday morning, and he was saddened by the dispirited look on her face.

"Hmm, I think I'll have a word with Brother Dorian about that," she muttered darkly. "What are you doing here?"

Sheerness sighed heavily and walked over to the fireplace and held his hands out toward it to warm the chill from his fingertips.

"Neath's solicitor arrived and was waiting for your father and Glamorgan when we returned from the service."

"Oh," said Psyche softly, and her eyes widened in surprise. That would have been the carriage she nearly collided with.

"He's here to attend to Neath's last will. The duke and your brother are preoccupied at the moment, so I offered to take care of this for them."

"Take care of what?" asked Psyche with a frown.

"Among the other things your brother left with Mr. Daughtry, he wrote several letters, to be delivered after his death." He reached into an inside pocket of his coat and pulled out a folded, sealed letter and held it out to her. "This is for you...from Neath."

Psyche's face paled, and a hand fluttered up to her throat. She hesitantly walked toward him and reached out a trembling hand to take the letter. She recognized Myron's familiar scrawl, and she released a shuddering sigh as she smoothed her other hand over its surface. She closed her burning eyes until she felt the urge to cry lessen. She looked back at Sheerness.

"Thank you. Is there anything else?" she asked calmly.

Sheerness frowned. "Aren't you going to read it?"

Psyche was trying not to tear it open and begin reading it immediately, but she didn't want to read it with him here. What it contained was private; she didn't want him to share in something that was meant to be between her and her brother. Yet she had to wonder if Myron had left one for Sheerness, too.

"I will...later," she said evenly. "If that's all, will you, please, leave now?"

Sheerness looked at her in disbelief for a moment, finding it odd she wouldn't read the letter as soon as he gave it to her. He finally shrugged and rubbed a hand over his face. He did have other things he wanted to discuss with her, and this seemed like it would be as good a time as any.

"Actually, I did want to talk to you," he said neutrally. Psyche raised an enquiring eyebrow. "I want you to marry me."

"Leave now," said Psyche shortly, moving to her desk to set the letter on top of it before going to the door to open it.

Sheerness walked to the door and closed it back. "I'm not leaving until you tell me why you won't marry me."

"Because I don't *want* to," said Psyche testily, and she tried to open the door again. Sheerness leaned against it with his hand.

"That's not good enough," he said tightly.

"It will have to be," she ground out impatiently as she tried to move his hand off the door and pulled on the handle.

"You owe me a better explanation than that," he said angrily, and he surprised her when he grabbed her by the wrists and raised them above her head, pinning her against the door by pressing his weight against her.

"Let go," she said coldly, twisting against him as she struggled to get free.

"No."

Psyche gave him a baleful glare. "I don't *want* to marry you," she repeated heatedly. "There's a *reason* I call you Barneville the Bastard! Why would you possibly think I would want to marry you?"

"Because I love you!" he ground out as he tried to get her to stop struggling.

Psyche scoffed and rolled her eyes. "Nice try, but I've already told you I *don't* believe you."

"You *should*," grated Sheerness. "If that's not good enough, think about the fact I've ruined you. We need to do the honorable thing."

"*Ruined* me? *Honorable* thing?" hissed Psyche between her teeth, and she tried to slide down the door in an effort to make him let her go.

"Bloody hell, would you quit moving?" he groaned aggravatedly.

He put a hand to the side of her head to hold it steady as he covered her lips with his. Psyche was so shocked she did quit struggling, and she moaned softly as he continued to explore her mouth with his tongue. His hand moved down her neck to begin massaging her breast, and Psyche gasped against his lips as she felt an aching begin in the pit of her stomach and her knees began to weaken. He released her hands, and one of her arms wound around his neck as the other hand went to wind tightly in the hair at the back of his head as she clung to him longingly. He traced his lips down her neck feverishly, and Psyche felt him raise her skirt to her thighs and bring one of her legs around his waist. She sighed pleasurably as he moved his pelvis against hers, and she surprised him when she lifted her other leg to wrap it around his waist as well.

Psyche could feel his arousal pressed against her, and she reached down between them to unfasten the buttons at the front of his pants. Sheerness groaned excitedly when she took him in her hand, and he kissed her hungrily as he felt her settle herself onto him. He pressed her more tightly against the door and cupped his hands under her bottom, and Psyche cried out against his lips as he thrust into her solidly and gyrated against her to make her tremble.

"Marry me," he whispered pleadingly against her ear, and he thrust into her again.

"No," she said on a gasp, shaking her head weakly.

Sheerness turned and carried her to the window seat. He sat down with her straddled across his lap, and when he dropped to the cushions, the force of it buried him deep within her. Psyche whimpered and clung to him helplessly with longing. He unfastened the buttons at the back of her bodice and pulled it and her chemise down to expose her breasts. He took one into his mouth and began to play at the nipple with his teeth and tongue, and Psyche clenched her hands in his hair to pull his mouth away and bring it back to hers, where she nipped at his lower lip so hard it nearly drew blood before she kissed him feverishly.

Psyche lifted herself up on her knees and began to raise and lower herself onto him with exquisite slowness, one hand braced at the back of his neck, the other resting against his chest. Sheerness moved his hands to her hips and attempted to make her move faster, but she was not to be deterred. He moaned low in his throat at the torture of it and nuzzled her breasts and neck hungrily. She steadily began to increase her pace, and Sheerness's grip tightened at her hips as he felt himself moving nearer to his release. He could feel Psyche's movements becoming more disjointed as she drew closer to her own orgasm, and he looked up at her to see her head tilted back slightly in abandon, her eyes closed, her lips parted in a soft smile of pleasure.

"I lo—" he began.

Psyche's head jerked forward, and her features became almost agonized as she put a hand over his mouth.

"Shh," she whispered, and she closed her eyes and rested her forehead against his as she continued to move against him.

Her breath came out in short, panting gasps as her actions became more frantic, and Sheerness could feel a slight film of perspiration on her forehead where it rested against his. She eventually moved her hand from his mouth to kiss him desperately, and then her head dropped to his shoulder as she cried out and began to quiver as she orgasmed. Sheerness kissed her passionately on the shoulder just where it met her neck as he, too, began to climax. They clung to each other weakly and shuddered together as the waves of euphoria washed over them.

Sheerness smoothed a hand across her back and placed a line of gentle kisses up her neck to just below her ear.

"I love you," he whispered.

Psyche lifted her head to look at him aggravatedly, her chest still heaving from their exertions. She moved a hand down his cheek in a soft caress before she forcefully shoved at his chest with both hands and climbed off of him to the floor and began straightening her clothes. She calmly fastened the buttons on her bodice and shook out the folds of her skirt before smoothing a hand over her hair. Sheerness sat propped on his elbows against the cushions where the force of her push had landed him, an astonished look on his face.

"I am *not* going to marry you," said Psyche finally before she walked to her desk to retrieve Myron's letter and left the room.

Psyche walked down the stairs of the tower to the second floor, muttering under her breath angrily much of the way. She was just as upset with herself as she was with Sheerness because she shouldn't have had sex with him again, and she knew it. On Saturday night and Sunday morning, she might have been able to excuse it away to too much alcohol and emotional distress. This time, there was no excuse other than she had wanted him. She had lusted after him like a Drury Lane Vestal, and she had left the solarium *still* wanting him. She couldn't blame him for that.

As for her anger with him, his insistence on wanting to marry her and his *per*sistence in saying he loved her infuriated Psyche to no end. She supposed he kept saying it because he thought it would make her believe he was sincere. She had no doubt about his sincerity when he said he wanted to marry her, but she didn't trust for a moment that he actually loved her. She had no doubt he wanted her, not any more than she could doubt her own desire for him, but that wasn't enough. She wasn't going to marry him just so he could satisfy some obligation he felt to duty or honor. She couldn't believe he honestly thought she would believe him when he said it.

But she did care about him. She couldn't say for certain she loved him; she was almost afraid to believe that and knew she would be settling herself in for much heartache if she did. She respected his intelligence. She felt sympathy for him and the troubles of his family. Despite her finding it inconvenient and troublesome, she had to admire his sense of honor. She recently had found him to be extremely gentle and sensitive. There was no doubt she found him physically attractive; that had always been there, even last Season when he had been so mean and hateful, but it had been much easier to resist then.

Then there were the things she found irksome. He was stubborn and bossy at times. In belittling her capabilities when his own were no better, he had shown himself to be hypocritical. Considering the almost complete reversal of his behavior between the previous Season and this one and what Amalie had told her, she couldn't trust him or anything he said regarding love and marriage. It would be wonderful if she could, but it would be foolish.

She eventually quit muttering and heaved a sigh as she turned down the hall to go to her room. She would be returning to London tomorrow. She would be in mourning, and unlike Sheerness, she wouldn't be attending any social functions or making calls. She would stay with her twin and enjoy her new nephews, and then when Parliament was out, she would return home to Wilderland. Psyche didn't think she would go back next year. Perhaps she could convince Pandora to stay in Yorkshire for the Season and go stay with her. Psyche was sure it wouldn't be that hard.

When Psyche walked into her room, Chrissoula was waiting for her, sitting comfortably in a chair near the fire, sewing, as usual. Psyche wasn't quite sure what her maid was making, but she loved the rich purplish-red shade of the velvet and the intricate bead and embroidery work. She could only assume it was something Chrissoula was making to send home to her family in Greece because it would be quite some time before Psyche was able to wear anything other than black.

"Where is your hat?" Chrissoula asked without preemption, looking her mistress over.

Psyche looked flushed, but not ill, and Chrissoula thought it was an improvement over the pale, drawn look that had been on her face at the funeral.

"I left it in the solarium," said Psyche meekly. Her constant misplacing of clothing and other items caused Chrissoula no end of vexation.

"Then you'll just have to make sure you go get it before we leave for London," said Chrissoula firmly. "Your father has said we will be riding with Pseudo-Thea's husband since you will be going to stay with her."

"All right," said Psyche agreeably.

"I have brought you some dinner. You had better eat it all, or so help me, I will sit on you until you do," said Chrissoula adamantly.

There was a tray on a table near the window, and Psyche went to it and sat down reluctantly. Chrissoula had done her best to tempt Psyche, and it worked. She lifted the lid covering a plate and looked at Chrissoula with a smile.

"*Eycharisto,*" said Psyche softly.

"Just eat all of it," said Chrissoula evenly, the corners of her mouth twitching with amusement and pleasure at the way Psyche's face brightened.

Psyche set Myron's letter beside her plate on the table and began to eat the gyro with tzatziki and spanikopita with great relish. She lifted the lid on another plate and saw it was a Greek salad with goat cheese and lots of olives and tomatoes. For dessert, she had baklava. Psyche knew Chrissoula had made it herself, and she would do her best not to disappoint her maid. When they were in London, Chrissoula didn't have as much opportunity to cook, but at Wilderland, she would often make dishes from her homeland. Psyche loved it more than anything, and she ate until her stomach was so full she thought she might burst.

"That was wonderful, Chrissoula," sighed Psyche, patting her stomach when she was through. "It was exactly what I needed. Thank you."

"Mm-hmm," said Chrissoula with an arched eyebrow in her usual brusque way, but Psyche could tell she was pleased she had made Psyche happy. "We'll have to see if your sister's cook will let me into her kitchen while we are there."

"I'm sure she will if Pan tells her to, and I don't think I'll have to twist *her* arm to do that," said Psyche with a smile. "You know we both love your food, and I know she's not had spanikopita since she left home."

"I'll take the tray back to the kitchen." Chrissoula looked Psyche over critically as she lifted the tray. The flush to her cheeks had faded, and the wan cast to her features had returned. "Perhaps you should take a nap. I don't think you slept well last night, did you?"

"No," sighed Psyche heavily, "I didn't. I'll try to do that after I read this," said Psyche, touching Myron's letter where it rested on the table.

"Hunh," said Chrissoula doubtfully as she looked at the letter, and she left the room and closed the door behind her.

Psyche watched her leave with a fond smile. For all Chrissoula's gruffness, she cared for Psyche deeply, just as Psyche did for her maid. Psyche was sometimes forgetful and had a tendency to lose clothing or get it dirty, which created extra work for Chrissoula, but she was very protective and wouldn't stand to let anyone else say a harsh word to Psyche.

Psyche smoothed a hand over the letter and lifted it from the table. She took a deep breath and closed her eyes preparatorily, and then she broke the wax seal and unfolded the pages.

"*Dearest Psyche, if you are reading this letter, it will mean things did not go well in my appointment with the Earl of Hendon. Please, do not blame yourself for that. I know you will try to, and I want you to stop it this instant. You did everything you could to make me change my mind. There is no reason for you to let it weigh on your conscience. I am a grown man, and my mistakes are my own.*

"*I am sorry for the pain I am sure you will feel at my loss. Do not let it consume you. Miss me—if you must—but do not let it become the only thing you have. If you must do something to remember me, live your own life! Be happy! Do not let your gentle, giving spirit be extinguished by grief. You know I would never wish that for you, and I will come back to haunt you if you do.*

"*Mr. Daughtry will have this in my will, but I wanted to tell you that I am leaving all my books, research, and artifacts to you. You were always so much better at it than I, and I wanted to make sure those things would go where they would do the most good. If I could have applied myself like you, the answers to the most puzzling questions in the universe would have been solved. Do not ever stop your search for answers.*

"*I realize my leaving will—yet again—prevent you from going to Greece and Egypt. I apologize for that more than anything. You must promise me you will go one day, somehow. You deserve to see the Parthenon and Delos and Giza and Thebes, and there is no one who would find them more moving. You see the people who built them, and you understand those things are more than the stone that made them. That is something special and important.*

"*Psyche, I have one thing to ask of you, and I know you will try your best to accomplish it, even as I know you will think it most unfair of me to request it. Please, look after Barneville. You are the only one who can. He has lost so much and must bear so much, I am afraid he will break from the weight of it. You have made a difference to him already, in so many ways, just by being who you are. I know he has been unfair to you, but it is not for the reasons you think. He is like you in so many ways that are good and worthy. Please, do not let him drown.*

"*I hope I made clear to you while I was alive that I loved you with all my heart. I always cherished the time we spent together. I will miss your smile and your laughter. Your intelligence, honesty, practicality, and generosity of spirit are without equal and something we mere mortals could only aspire to emulate. Your modesty and humility are genuine, and I was better for having you as a sister.*

"*I love you and goodbye, Sham.*"

The pages fluttered from her fingers to the table, and Psyche put her trembling hands to her wet cheeks. Her forehead wrinkled, and she bit her lower lip until it bled as she attempted to hold back a sob. Her shoulders began to shake, and then she began to rock back and forth as a sorrowful keening rose out of her from the depths of her soul. She was still weeping uncontrollably when Chrissoula returned, and her maid took her in her arms and rocked with her, smoothing a hand over her hair and holding her tight.

Psyche cried until she exhausted herself, and Chrissoula helped her to remove her dress and got her into bed. Sleep would be good for her, Chrissoula knew, and as terrible as it was to see her crying herself to weakness, she knew Psyche would be able to go to sleep without any problems this time. As Chrissoula was tucking her in, she noticed a mark on Psyche's shoulder when the strap to her chemise moved. In the dimness of the light near the bed, it looked like a nasty bruise.

"What have you done to bruise your shoulder?" asked Chrissoula curiously.

Psyche turned her head and craned her neck in an effort to see what Chrissoula was talking about. She smoothed her fingers over it with a frown of puzzlement which slowly began to clear when she realized where it came from. It didn't hurt, but it did look like a bruise. Psyche's frown returned as she tried to come up with an excuse to tell Chrissoula. Nothing was coming to mind, and she was beginning to panic.

"Oh, well," said Chrissoula dismissively after a moment when it seemed Psyche couldn't remember or was too tired to remember. "It's obviously not hurting. I'm sure you'd remember where it came from if it hurt." She gave Psyche a teasing smile. "It looks like a lovebite."

Psyche tried her best to maintain her innocent expression and nodded her head. She closed her eyes tiredly, and Chrissoula was pleased to see she was asleep within minutes. She didn't know how long it would last, but she knew that *any* sleep would be good. Psyche didn't sleep nearly as much as she should. Chrissoula looked at the clock on the mantle as she went to retake her seat by the fireplace and her sewing. It was almost two. If Psyche would sleep until dinnertime, it would be a good rest.

≪ ≫

Sheerness sighed with relief when the crying above his head stopped. Psyche must have finally read her letter from Neath. It had taken all his effort not to go to her. He wasn't positive which room was hers on the floor above, but he would have been able to find it just by listening. But he hadn't gone. He couldn't. She wouldn't have wanted him there.

Her refusal to marry him was puzzling. He didn't know what more he could do to make her change her mind. For some reason, she still didn't trust him, and she didn't love him. He had hoped she had come round, since she had willingly given herself to him, but clearly his feelings were not reciprocated. She didn't seem to dislike him anymore; it was obvious she found him physically acceptable, but there was still something about him that did not meet her expectations...not even for a marriage of convenience.

Bardsey had told him to make it right. Without the duke arranging a marriage, it would be unlikely, and Aberdare wouldn't without her consent. Psyche was adamant she wouldn't do it. Now that she was in mourning, it would be as long as a year before she could—or would—marry anyone. Perhaps it would give him more time to make her change her mind. Bardsey didn't say he would tell the duke, but he might if it seemed Sheerness wasn't following through fast enough. He just needed to discover what it was she found so repulsive about the idea and convince her she was wrong.

He found himself uselessly wishing the previous year had never happened, but he couldn't honestly believe his behavior would have been different. It had taken him awhile to realize how he felt about her, and he had thought he would have more time. There wasn't any. These days, there was never enough time.

He looked at his own letter from Neath on the table beside him. He was surprised when Mr. Daughtry had given it to him, and he was hesitant to open it. He was tempted to wait until he returned home. He didn't want to read it at Wilderland. He put his hand out to it and picked it up with a thoughtful expression. He turned it over and fingered the seal on the back. He started to break it, but then he changed his mind. He would be going home tomorrow, and he would read it there. That would be soon enough.

Chapter Sixteen

Psyche was up early (as usual) for the trip back to London. She kissed goodbye those of her family who would be staying behind, and she promised her mother she would write. She would go to Aberdare House for dinner with Dorian and her father every Wednesday. Psyche expected to see them more than that, but the duchess was firm Psyche would be there at least that often.

Psyche hadn't slept the length of time Chrissoula had hoped she would the previous afternoon. She had awakened by four, but her mien was much-improved. She still looked tired, but the sad, haunted cast to her eyes had lessened. Chrissoula had been satisfied and only grumbled slightly that she hadn't slept longer.

Psyche had gone to the mausoleum after her nap. She had walked down the wall of vaults, looking at the names and dates. Some of her ancestors had led adventurous lives, and she had recognized the names of the ones who were frequently mentioned, either in infamy or admiration. When she had reached Myron's vault, she had traced her fingers over the letters carved in the stone before brushing her hand across the surface with a soft smile. She had no doubt he was in heaven. When she left, she had felt more peaceful than she had in days, and she had not felt the urge to cry.

Supper that night was the only meal she ate with the rest of her family and their guests. Psyche was seated, through no machinations on her mother's part—she was sure—between Sheerness and his brother. All the conversation around the table was subdued, but she was able to speak to both of them politely and calmly.

She was surprised when Alex mentioned the Earl of Westerkirk had been to pay a call to Amalie. Psyche didn't want to place too much importance on it, but she wondered if perhaps the man had realized he had feelings for her friend after all. If that were the case, she also wondered whether or not Sheerness would let him renew his suit. If Amalie was still willing to have Westerkirk, it would be unfair of her brother to refuse. There wouldn't be anything Psyche would have to say on the matter. It would still be a week or two before she would be allowed to call on Amalie, but she hoped Amalie would come to see her at Pandora's. She would like to ask her friend what her feelings were on the matter.

Eurydice obliged everyone after supper by playing a piece on her violin. It was the first time she had played since Myron's death, and the work she chose was his favorite: the *Follia* by Corelli. Psyche thought she played beautifully, but Eurydice thought she was less than perfect. No one else thought there was anything wrong with it either. Eurydice was always her own worst critic.

That night, Psyche tried to go to sleep without her sleeping draught, but she soon discovered she wasn't going to sleep at all unless she took it. She paced for a little while, hoping it would tire her out, but it didn't. She reluctantly took some of the medicine and went to sleep. She wasn't sure what Keung put in it, but it worked. He had told her to turn her brain off or to think of something sleep-worthy, but she wasn't able to. There was still plenty left in the bottle, but he had said when it was gone, he wouldn't make her any more.

She went to the solarium to retrieve her bonnet that morning before she left, and while she was there, she chose a book to read on the way to London. It wasn't that she thought the conversation in the coach with Islington and Chrissoula would be boring, but it was going to be a long ride, and there would only be so much they could discuss before topics ran thin. She couldn't discuss her trip to Greece and Egypt because she wasn't going. There was no need to talk about things happening in the Season, because the Season was over for her (and Islington, theoretically). She and Islington didn't share the same interests. They would be able to find things to talk about, but none of them were prone to idle prattle. It would bore her to no end if all she could do was look out the window or sleep the entire way.

She was glad she brought the book. It actually provided them with something to talk about. It was Tacitus, and whenever he mentioned something related to medicine, she would ask Islington if he thought it would have worked. Most of the time, he would say no, absolutely not, but at times, he would actually think about it for a minute and say maybe. Psyche had already read the book several times before, but it was entertaining, and the history was not nearly so involved as reading *The Odyssey.*

It was late Saturday when they arrived at the house on Upper Grosvenor. Psyche was tired, but she wouldn't be able to go to sleep. She was never so lucky as to actually go to sleep when she was tired. She was going to try Keung's suggestion that she think of something that would put her to sleep. It had never worked before (and it certainly hadn't on Thursday night), but she would have to come up with something once her draught ran out. When Keung said he wouldn't make her any more, he meant it.

Pandora was asleep by the time they arrived, so Psyche would have to wait until morning to see her and the babies. Psyche was determined to go riding. She didn't care if she was in mourning or not. Achilles had been moved to a stall in the mews behind the Marshall residence, but Jim wouldn't be with her. That was going to feel odd. Psyche had grown accustomed to his presence. Although she would never think of doing anything half so foolish as Pandora and run off on her own, Psyche was going riding whether anyone was with her or not. It would be awhile before Pandora was able to go riding again, but Psyche knew her twin missed it. They would go together before the end of the season…she hoped.

The Marshall residence wasn't as big as Aberdare House, let alone Wilderland, and Chrissoula would be staying in the small room adjoined to Psyche's. Neither one of them minded, but it would be a bit of an adjustment. Psyche was pleased when they arrived to find someone had arranged to have a writing desk placed in Selena's room where she could do her work. Her things still remained to be unpacked, but she and Chrissoula could see to that tomorrow. It still didn't feel like her room—there was entirely too much pink, but she would only be staying until the end of the season in any event, and she was sure it would be fine for that length of time.

Chrissoula put a warming pan under the blankets as soon as they came into the room, and then she helped Psyche dress for bed. It didn't take long. She tried to convince Psyche to put her hair into a braid and save herself from having so many snarls in the morning, but Psyche, as usual, refused because it made her head uncomfortable. Chrissoula shrugged and went to bed.

Psyche curled up on the bed and hugged one of the pillows to her, trying to think of *something* that wouldn't make her think of *anything*. Unfortunately, *nothing* was coming to mind. After tossing and turning several times, she started to get out of bed and begin pacing, but she didn't want to wake Chrissoula. She sighed aggravatedly and hugged the pillow again. She tried counting, forwards and backwards. She tried making the different parts of her body relax individually. She tried thinking about times when she had been able to go to sleep without any problems. She was unable to recall any.

Until she thought about Sheerness. Psyche came to the realization, and it startled her. She was easily able to fall asleep when she was held by him. In the chair in the sitting room. In the coach (granted, she had influenza at the time). In the garden temple (she *might* have been intoxicated). She was astonished that even when she had been upset, he had somehow managed to calm her and make her *go to sleep!* It was bizarre beyond belief. She didn't trust him (she tried to tell herself), and yet she would go to sleep when she was near him, when she was unable to do so anywhere else.

The only question she had for herself was: how was she going to use that to help her go to sleep? It wasn't as if she could have him come hold her until she went to sleep every night. Well, he would, quite willingly, she was sure, and all she would have to do is marry him. As much as she would love to have a good night's sleep, she wasn't willing to have one on those terms. She would have to use the knowledge to come up with something else not quite so drastic.

It wasn't a question of whether she felt cozy and warm. She had, but she felt cozy and warm in her bed at the moment with the warming pan and the soft feather mattress. It wasn't even a matter of whether or not she felt safe. She had never had any reason to fear for her personal safety. Her family would never let her come to any harm, and she had never been away from her family. When she realized what it was, it shocked her more than discovering he could make her sleep. He made her feel peaceful. When she was with him, she was able to believe there was nothing that couldn't be resolved, that everything was as it should be. It was the same feeling she got when she was with Pandora.

It was impossible. But there it was. He aggravated her; at times he infuriated her. He provoked feelings in her that were unseemly, to put it mildly, and yet he was able to create a stillness in her. He hadn't always. It had started about the time they had danced together in the Lundeys' garden…about the time he had decided to start courting her. She didn't want to think about what it meant if he was able to make her feel that way because it worried her. It still didn't solve the problem of helping her go to sleep. In fact, it made it worse.

She finally put aside the complicated parts and tried to focus on how she could use it to go to sleep. She snuggled closer to the pillow and imagined Sheerness cozied up next to her. It wasn't the same thing, but she had an active imagination, and it wasn't long before she was able to lull herself to sleep.

Psyche woke up at her usual time the following morning, and she was relieved to find a riding habit in the small trunk of mourning clothes. After she inspected it, she realized it was one of her old ones Chrissoula had dyed black. That was so much the better. They were comfortable to ride in. When she went back to the stables, no one had alerted the stable workers to her penchant for rising early. Either that or they didn't expect she would be going riding so soon. It took some effort, but located her saddle and bridle and her horse, and she saddled and mounted Achilles herself.

It was different leaving from the King Street Mews to Hyde Park. It didn't take nearly as long. Psyche enjoyed that. It would give her more time to ride. It did feel odd not having Jim with her, and she found herself looking over her shoulder several times expecting to see him there. After she went around once, she rode to the Serpentine and dismounted. She tied Achilles extra tight before she went to the lake edge. Jim wouldn't be there to catch him if he got loose, and if she didn't find him quickly enough, there was no telling what mischief he might cause. He wasn't a bad horse; he just liked to eat…a lot. If what he was grazing wasn't something he felt was suitable, he would go looking elsewhere.

She wasn't standing at the edge of the lake very long before Waddlesworth arrived. He wasn't happy with her. She was gone for a week, and then when she returned, she had no bread. When he discovered that, he went back to the water and ignored her. Psyche would have to make sure she had arrangements made for the stable to have her horse ready every morning and to have a small amount of stale bread bundled into a cloth to take with her.

She stood watching the ducks and swans glide across the surface of the lake for a time, occasionally looking back over her shoulder to make sure Achilles was still tethered, but without bread to feed the birds, there was really no point in staying very long. It was obvious Waddlesworth was put out she had not come bearing gifts, and she was sorry she hadn't brought him any.

She eventually went to retrieve Achilles after looking at her watch; it wouldn't be long before other people started to come to the park. She didn't want to see anyone, and she didn't think it would be appropriate for anyone to see her. She went across the park to the Grosvenor Gate and went back to the mews behind her sister's house.

The stable was in an uproar. The first of the hands to wake up had discovered her horse was gone and thought Achilles had been stolen. When she came sedately trotting in, he and the stable master were displeased. Psyche apologized, her cheeks red, completely forgetting *she* was their superior. She did, however, take the effort to explain they should expect to have her horse saddled and ready for her by six every morning unless it was raining or unless she told them she wouldn't be riding the following day. If they took exception to it, they should address it to the marquess or marchioness.

When she arrived at the house through the garden, she was dismayed to find everyone there in turmoil at her absence as well. The only one who didn't seem overly concerned was Pandora. She suspected her sister had only gone riding, and she had tried to explain that to her husband and Chrissoula, but both of them thought she had been spirited away by bandits. Islington was even preparing to notify the authorities to begin a citywide search to find her. When Pandora and Psyche looked at each other after he said that, they both dissolved into a fit of giggles. Islington wasn't pleased.

"I fail to see the humor in this," he said darkly.

"Oh, Islington, really," chortled Pandora. "I tried to tell you, and you should know it would be highly unlikely marauding bandits could abscond with her. She *is* my sister."

Islington was not appeased. "She shouldn't be gallivanting around town on her own. She is in mourning."

Psyche and Pandora's humor died, and his sister-in-law looked at him with a stricken expression.

"I was not *gallivanting,*" she said evenly, "I was riding my horse, and I may be in mourning, but I am *not* dead. Myron would have understood that." She turned and left the room with her back stiff.

"Psyche, I didn't mean—" began Islington. "Bloody hell," he muttered when he heard her door close. He turned to look at his wife, and she was lying in the bed with her arms crossed in front of her, one eyebrow cocked up mockingly. "I didn't mean to make it sound like she was being disrespectful."

"Oh, really?" said Pandora dryly. "You do realize that's the first time she's laughed since our brother died?"

"I'm only concerned what other people might think," said Islington evenly.

Pandora hooted. "Since when have any of us cared what other people might think? There was no one there to see her. As early as she goes to the park it's unlikely there will *ever* be anyone there to see her...except you...or me...someone from our family."

"Lord Sheerness," said Islington flatly.

Pandora waved a hand through the air dismissively. "He has no room to say anything about what Psyche may or may not do while she's in mourning."

"Yet," muttered Islington.

Pandora gave him a speculative look. "Whatever do you mean?" Islington set his jaw, and she could tell he was hiding something. "*Àiren*, is there something you haven't told me?"

Islington scratched his temple with a fingertip before he looked at her. "Well, we *did* tell him to keep her occupied."

Pandora's eyes rounded in astonishment. "No, he didn't!" she gasped incredulously.

"Oh, yes, he did," affirmed Islington with a drawl.

"How do you know?" asked Pandora suspiciously. "It's unlikely he said: 'By the by, I've docked your sister-in-law. Care for a game of billiards?'"

Islington scratched the back of his head. "Well, I—somewhat—saw them."

Pandora gasped in surprise. "Oh, my giddy aunt." One of the babies began to cry in the nearby cradle, ready to be fed, and Pandora got up from the bed to pick him up. She put him to her breast and turned to look at her husband. "Do they *know* you saw them?"

"Sheerness does," he said evenly.

"And what, pray tell, does the man have to say for himself?"

"He said he loves her *and* that he asked her to marry him, but she refused."

"Did he tell *her* that he loved her? It does make a difference between him telling you and telling her. "

"He says he told her, and he also said she told him she didn't believe him."

Pandora clicked her tongue and shook her head. "If she doesn't believe him, it must be that she thinks he has some ulterior motive for saying either."

"Such as?"

Pandora shrugged. "I don't know. You asked me to marry you because you loved me, but you made it sound like a proposal of convenience. Maybe she thinks something similar, and you know as well as I do she would never agree to that."

"But he told her he loved her," said Islington perplexedly.

"Maybe she thinks he said it because he knows she would never agree to a marriage of convenience, and for some reason, she thinks that is all he's offering." Alex finished eating, and Pandora put him to her shoulder to begin burping him. "Considering how horrid he was to her last year, doubting his sincerity isn't all that difficult for her."

"Yes, but you believed me. I wasn't the most gentlemanly fellow."

"Oh, he was worse…way worse." Pandora shook her head. "He went out of his way to be mean to her last year. He made a point of dancing with Psyche just so he could argue with her, and not even Myron could make him leave off. Would *you* believe someone who said they loved you under those circumstances?"

"But that was last year. He hasn't been that way this Season."

"Obviously not, considering why we're having this conversation," said Pandora with a wink. "Still, proposals of love and sex and marriage are three entirely different things, and while one may willingly consent to one of the three, it doesn't mean the terms for the others are acceptable."

"But she doesn't have a choice now. She's compromised."

Pandora raised an eyebrow as she laid Alex in the cradle and picked up Myron to begin feeding him. "If you hadn't tricked me into marrying you and had continued making it sound like a business arrangement when you proposed, I never would have married you. I would have been your bit of fluff, but I wouldn't have married you. If you had said you loved me from the beginning and *never* asked me to marry you, I would have been perfectly happy.

"As for the third part of it, one doesn't have to be married or in love to have sex. Just ask the tarts on Drury," she said with a grin, "but I can tell you that Psyche would never have let him lay a hand on her if she didn't care for him...a lot." She sucked in air through her teeth and shook her head. "There has to be something about the proposal itself. There has to be some reason she thinks he wants to marry her besides love."

"So what are we going to do? If your father finds out what they've been up to, it will not end well."

"Hmm," said Pandora thoughtfully as she sat down on the edge of the bed and began to rock the cradle with her foot as she continued to feed Myron. "We have the love. We have the sex. I'm not about to tell my father what happened and *force* her to marry him." She tapped at her teeth with a fingernail and shrugged. "I'm not really sure my father would do that anyhow. He would probably shoot Sheerness, though. I suppose we need to find out what her reason is for doubting him, and let him know so he can fix it...if he can."

Psyche soon settled into a routine at the Marshall residence. She would ride in the morning and feed the birds. She would have breakfast with Pandora in her room while she fed the babies, and then she would go to her own room and work on her hieroglyphs. After she had dinner with Pandora, she would go back to her room and work on her translations again. By the end of the first week, Psyche was bored to tears.

The first Monday, she went with Pandora, Islington and Dorian to have the babies christened. Dorian was to be their godfather. Pandora wouldn't let Psyche wear black to her babies' christening. She found a morning dress from her closet made of a dark mauve. It was very pretty, and Psyche felt like she could breathe again. There weren't a lot of people in attendance. Their father was there, and friends of the family. The duchess and their siblings remained in Glamorgan. There hadn't been enough time for them to return to the city to attend.

The Sheernesses were there, all of them, and Psyche was happy to see the Yeardley children. She greeted the earl politely, but she didn't go out of her way to be friendly. She asked Amalie to bring the children to see her, with the earl's permission, of course. He said he had no objection, and Amalie said she would be sure to bring them by for a nice visit. The children were overjoyed. The countess watched the exchange between her son and Psyche curiously. There was something different there that she couldn't quite put her finger on. Once the christening was over, Psyche returned home and reluctantly donned her mourning clothes again.

On Wednesday evening, she went to have dinner with Dorian and her father at Aberdare House. It was a nice meal, which they took in the private sitting room. The dining room was dustclothed and closed because it was unnecessary to have it open with only the duke and Dorian in residence. Before Psyche left, she went upstairs to her bedroom and lay on her bed for a short while. It, too, was closed and dustclothed, but it felt nice to be in her familiar space again for a time.

As much as Psyche was reluctant to admit it, she missed the Season. She enjoyed working on her translations. She adored her new nephews and spending time with her twin, but she began to wish she could leave the house. Because of her mourning, she was unable to go shopping as she would like. Buying new items for her wardrobe wasn't necessary because she would be wearing black for quite some time to come. She wouldn't be going to Egypt and Greece, so there was no need for her to buy anything for that (although, she had purchased most of what she needed already, and now it was fairly useless). She wasn't supposed to make social calls just to visit, not that she had anyone in particular she would want to visit except Amalie. She got to ride in the park every morning, but she never saw anyone except Waddlesworth, and she was always alone. Pandora was still not well enough to go riding yet. Psyche hoped that would change soon. She hadn't even seen Sheerness on her morning rides, and although she wasn't sure she *wanted* to see him, she was willing to see almost anyone to break the monotony.

Islington tried to hide it, but Pandora managed to spirit the paper away when he wasn't looking. A notice was in regarding the duel and the results of it for Myron and Hendon. Justice had apparently been swift, if not fair. Hendon would survive having his leg amputated, but he would be doing his recuperation in prison. He was sentenced to six months for manslaughter, and he was also charged with a one-hundred-thousand pound fine. Neither sister had expected he would be convicted of murder or that he would hang, but they had certainly hoped something miraculous would occur.

When they asked Islington about the conviction, he said it was likely the fine would ruin Hendon financially. He had money, but that was an enormous sum to pay. Islington could only speculate exactly how much money Hendon had, but he would be surprised if Hendon didn't have to sell most of his property to meet the mark. His reputation was already black; a conviction for manslaughter only ensured he would never be accepted by anyone in polite society again, whether he was with his wife or not. Psyche and Pandora tried to console themselves with that, but being broke and ostracized didn't seem to be worthy enough punishment.

Islington was able to find out Georgiana had left for Northumberland only days after the duel. They were sure she was devastated by what had happened, and what had to make it worse was that she didn't know the duel was taking place until after Myron was dead. If it weren't for her father, Georgiana could have been their sister-in-law, and they were sure she was mourning for their brother like a wife for her husband. She probably wished no less than they did that Hendon would have hanged. She would, at least, have six month's peace to do her grieving.

Psyche was pleased when Amalie brought the Yeardley children by to see her the following Monday. She was at a point in her translations where she was frustrated enough that some time away from it would be more helpful than continuing work. She almost skipped down the stairs to the sitting room, which looked out of place in the black dress she wore. When the children saw her, they didn't hesitate to run to her and wrap her in hugs. It never ceased to amaze her and bring a smile to her face.

"Hallo, you three devilkins," she teased. "Have you been practicing your juggling?"

"I have," said Philip, jumping up and down enthusiastically and raising his hand.

Psyche looked over their heads at Amalie. "The weather is nice enough; would you like to go out to the garden?"

"Lovely," said Amalie with a grin.

"All right, then," said Psyche. "Let's go see how well you are coming along with your juggling, Master Philip." She herded the children out of the sitting room and turned them down the hall to the back door. Once they reached the terrace, she had them stop. "Now, the rules are: you can play anywhere you'd like except the flowerbeds. Keung has just planted them, and he would be unhappy if he had to do it over again so soon."

The children hooted excitedly and ran into the garden to explore. Psyche and Amalie watched after them for a time, and then Psyche linked her arm through her friend's and started down the path to the temple.

"How are you?" asked Psyche gently.

Amalie waved a hand through the air. "I am doing better. But how are you? I am so sorry about your brother."

"I am better here, with Pandora. I have my moments, though. I miss him terribly. There are so many things I do that I shared with him, and now he's gone." Psyche scratched her forehead thoughtfully and looked sideways at her friend. "I suppose I feel a bit *lost* at times."

"I understand," said Amalie softly, patting Psyche's arm.

"And," sighed Psyche, "you're probably going to think I am most disrespectful when I say this, but I cannot tolerate being *in mourning.*" Amalie looked at her in surprise. Psyche shook her head. "I loved my brother, and I miss my brother, and I always will. It is the wearing *black* and being *secluded.* I don't need these things to *remind* me of what I've lost." Psyche blinked her eyes and swallowed. "I *know* what I lost," she said softly.

"Oh, thank God," sighed Amalie, squeezing Psyche's arm.

Psyche looked at her. "What?"

"I thought I was the only one," said Amalie quietly, and she blushed. "*Maman* will probably wear mourning for Papa for the rest of her life. I feel as if it is draining the very life out of me. Sebastian and Alex don't have it quite so hard. They at least get to wear a white *shirt*, and they're allowed to be seen in public. If it weren't for the children, I would go mad, I swear I would, and I felt almost delirious whenever you came to call."

"We'll keep this our little secret," said Psyche with warm smile. "But I understand I'm not the only one who has come to call on you lately." Amalie gave her a blank look. "At Wilderland, Alex happened to mention Lord Westerkirk came to see you."

Amalie blushed and nodded. "He did."

"Well? I see the color in your cheeks, and you cannot tell me he came to simply offer his condolences."

"No, that's true. He has apparently realized he can have no one else for a wife but me."

"Oh, my," sighed Psyche.

"He said he would wait for me as long as it took," said Amalie with a happy smile.

"Oh, wonderful," said Psyche, raising a hand to her throat. Her expression grew pensive. "And what about Sheerness? Is he going to let Westerkirk renew his suit?"

Amalie's features clouded. "He's not dead set against it, but he's not quite so happy about the matter."

"But Westerkirk loves you, doesn't he? I mean, what other reason could he have for saying something like that?"

"Yes, he has said that he does," agreed Amalie.

"Hmm," said Psyche thoughtfully. "He will come around. If he hasn't outright refused, then there's still hope. If not, there's always Gretna Green."

"Oh, pooh," said Amalie with a chuckle. They neared the white rose bush, and they stopped to smell the flowers. "These are so lovely," sighed Amalie.

"Yes, they are," agreed Psyche.

"Sebastian won't throw out the ones you brought for him. They're all wilted and dead in the vase, and he won't get rid of them because, he says, they still smell." Amalie shrugged. "I expect we'll have to send in the maid at some point while he's away. By the time he comes back, they will be long gone, and he'll have naught to say about it then."

"Away?"

"Well, yes, on his ship," said Amalie.

"He's still going?" asked Psyche dully.

"It would appear so."

"Oh," said Psyche softly.

She didn't know why it should surprise her that he would still intend to take his trip. It wasn't as if he weren't allowed to go. It was his ship, and

Myron would have only been a passenger. *She* would have only been a passenger. It wasn't as if he had lost another member of his family. She just thought it had affected him more than that. She was *sure* it had affected him more than that.

Amalie turned from the flowers to look at her solemnly. "I wanted to thank you for what you did."

"What did I do?" asked Psyche blankly.

"That day…if you hadn't come. You saved his life."

Psyche waved a dismissive hand in the air. "It wasn't so bad as all that."

"Always so modest," said Amalie teasingly. "It *was* as bad as all that. That day you came, we were expecting him to breathe his last." Psyche started to demur again, and Amalie took both her hands. "You've done so much for our family. You've made all the difference in the world to the children. They realize it's all right to be alive and be children *and* still miss their loved ones. You've kept *me* out of the dumps. *Maman* positively adores you. To her, you can do no wrong." Psyche blushed and looked away as she felt tears coming to her eyes. "And you *did* save Sebastian. No one knows that better than he."

"Now, look, you've gone and made me cry," choked Psyche with a watery smile.

Amalie hugged her tightly and rubbed her back soothingly. If her brother didn't marry this girl, she would never forgive him.

Friday morning, Pandora was finally able to ride with Psyche. Psyche was amazed when Pandora willingly rode aside. She also didn't try to race across the park, much to Bellerophon's disappointment.

"Trust me, when you have a baby, you'll be more than willing to ride aside and slowly, too," said Pandora, adjusting herself gingerly. "I feel much better than I did, but *lud.*"

Psyche was happy to ride with her sister at any speed. Pandora recognized Waddlesworth when they went to the lake, and she wasn't surprised the duck had taken to her sister. Psyche seemed to have an affinity for animals. The only ones Pandora had ever been able to exercise any control over were horses. Even Bo listened to Psyche better. Pandora was lucky if she could get him to stay off the bed. Her twin could make him sit, stay, roll over, play dead, and a multitude of other tricks. If Pandora ever tried to make him do any of them, his tongue would loll out of his mouth, he would blink his eyes lazily, and he would not do what she asked.

Pandora watched as the ducks horded around Psyche as she fed them. She fully expected them to trip Psyche and walk all over her. They would each other but not Psyche. When all the bread was gone, Waddlesworth remained behind to be picked up and petted. He was a very pretty duck with iridescent feathers of green and black, almost like the shell on a scarab beetle. She didn't see another one like him on the lake, and she couldn't recall ever seeing one that looked like him anywhere else before. He could be a hybrid, but he didn't have the speckling which sometimes resulted from that.

They took their time riding back to the house, and Pandora was grateful she didn't have very far to ride. She looked in on Jezebel, Islington's mare, while they were at the stable. The Thoroughbred was due to foal any day. The stable master, Mr. French, said she had been restless for the past few days and suspected it would be very soon. Pandora asked him to let her know as soon as it happened.

The twins walked toward the house arm-in-arm. Somehow, Sheerness became a topic of discussion.

"It's odd we didn't see him in the park this morning. He usually rides early, too, doesn't he?" asked Pandora casually.

"Oh, I don't think it's *odd*," said Psyche in the same casual tone. "I haven't seen him riding since we got back from Wilderland, and I haven't seen him at all since the christening."

"I wonder what he's doing these days."

Psyche looked at her sister suspiciously. "You're showing a lot of interest in the man." Pandora continued to look at her innocently, and Psyche shrugged noncommittally. "I suppose he's seeing to preparations for his trip."

"He's still going then?" asked Pandora in surprise.

"According to Amalie, he is."

"Hmm," said Pandora thoughtfully.

"What?"

"Oh, I'm just thinking it's unfortunate that now you won't be able to go," said Pandora evenly.

Psyche shrugged again. "I'll get there one day." She sighed. "Even if Myron were still alive, I might not have been able to go this time anyhow."

"But you won the wager!" said Pandora in disbelief.

"I had convinced Myron he should take Georgiana and Lorelei instead of me to get them somewhere safe...before Hendon...," she trailed off.

"You *know* everything he did?" gasped Pandora.

"I heard Myron and Sheerness talking in the hall. They thought I was asleep. Myron wouldn't wait, and Sheerness said there was no possible way the *Medea* would be ready to sail before August." She shrugged. "If Myron would have waited, then it would have been Georgiana and Lorelei instead of me. If he had won the duel, then I would have still been able to go. Now, even though Sheerness is still going, I can't go alone, and I *am* in mourning."

Pandora hugged her waist. "We'll get you there somehow."

"Yes, well, they *will* always be there."

Psyche had breakfast in Pandora's room while she fed the babies. At nearly three weeks, they slept most of the time...when they weren't eating, but they were starting to develop personalities. Alex was more fussy than Myron. Even when Myron was awake and hungry, he would wait his turn to be fed, and then he would eat with gusto. If one of the two was crying, it was usually Alex. Neither had yet to develop a birthmark, so Alex's toenail remained painted red.

After breakfast, Psyche went to her room to work on her translations, or at least, trying to decipher them. At one point, she opened the drawer on her desk to locate another nib for her fountain pen and found the jeweler's box the Earl of Stranraer had given her. She pulled it out and opened it and thoughtfully ran her fingers over the necklace. She lifted it out of the box and held it up to examine closer. There were scratches on the back of the giant amber. She frowned and stood up from her desk and went to the window for more light.

She held the necklace up to the window, and the sun shone through the stone. She didn't see the scratches from the front, but when she turned it to examine the back, she gasped in surprise. From that direction, the marks on the front and back combined into a peculiar configuration. She lowered the necklace and looked around herself. She found a small table nearby and dragged it closer to the window after she removed the objects from the top of it, and then she went back to the desk for a pencil and a piece of paper. She held the necklace back up to the light and began to sketch what she saw.

She worked painstakingly for several minutes, trying to capture every detail as correctly as possible. She could feel her upper lip begin to bead with sweat as the heat of the sun became absorbed by the black of her dress, and she impatiently wiped at it with her sleeve. She was almost finished when she heard the door open behind her.

"It *is* very pretty, but don't you want to have dinner? You know Mrs. Hensley graciously relinquished possession of her kitchen to Chrissoula, and your maid will kill us both if the meal is ruined because we're late," said Pandora humorously.

"Give me just one more minute," said Psyche intently as she drew.

"Hurry up. I've been positively drooling all day just thinking about hummus and flatbread."

Psyche added the last detail and grinned victoriously. She took the necklace back to the desk and placed it into its box in the drawer, and then she retrieved her drawing. She took it to her sister and held it out with a grin. Pandora looked at it, and her forehead wrinkled.

"Psy, that looks like…," began Pandora. She looked back at her sister in disbelief. "That was on the back of your necklace?"

"Yes," giggled Psyche.

"But where is it?"

"I have no earthly. I need to talk to Lord Stranraer about the necklace, but I can't go calling."

"What about Papà?" asked Pandora practically.

"Pan, you're a genius," said Psyche, giving her sister a kiss on the cheek.

"No, what I am is starving," chortled Pandora. "Put that down, and come on. We're having dinner in the sitting room, and Kwan has already taken the babies down."

The two of them walked down the stairs arm-in-arm to the private sitting room. Psyche had discovered since coming to stay with Pandora and Islington that they rarely used their dining room. They hadn't eaten there even once since Psyche had been there. She supposed it was fairly pointless to use the large room unless they were entertaining. It was only the two of them. The dowager marchioness was in Yorkshire, and it would be quite some time before the boys would be old enough to eat a meal at the table. At dinnertime, it was usually just Psyche and Pandora because Islington was at Whitehall. The two of them had been eating their dinner in Pandora's bedroom, but this would be a nice change.

When they reached the sitting room, the food was already on the table, and Chrissoula was there to oversee their sitting down to the meal and to briefly sigh over the babies. Pandora and Psyche asked her to sit down and eat with them, but Chrissoula declined because she needed to clean Mrs. Hensley's kitchen. Both girls watched her go disappointedly, but they soon forgot as they began to eat *spanikopita*, hummus with flatbread, and *souvlakia* with *tzatziki*. Both of them ate until they couldn't find another morsel, all the while talking about Psyche's discovery.

After the meal, Pandora went to the couch to feed the babies. Psyche held Myron while Pandora fed Alex, and she cooed and talked to him adoringly until she was able to coax a smile from him. His eyes had started to change color, and they were going to be the same pure blue as Islington's. He grabbed her nose at one point, and Psyche giggled as he tweaked it then patted it almost apologetically.

Once Pandora was through feeding Alex, Psyche exchanged one baby for the other. Alex wasn't as calm as Myron. Even as confused as others might be when telling the sisters apart, Alex knew Psyche was *not* his mother. But he was full and content after she burped him, so he wasn't crying. He did frown at her at one point, and Psyche chuckled when she thought he looked exactly like his father.

Once Myron had been fed and burped and both had been changed, the sisters sat holding the babies, playing with them. It was becoming apparent the lacquer on Alex's toenail wasn't going to be needed much longer. When they were awake, there was no problem distinguishing them now. Pandora and Psyche had just laid them into the cradle for a nap when Waldon came into the room. Pandora looked up at him expectantly.

"Yes, Waldon?"

"Mr. French wished me to inform you Jezebel is foaling, mum," he said mildly. There was a slight twitching at the corners of his mouth when he saw her excitement.

"Wonderful," sighed Pandora happily. She turned to look at Psyche. "Can you stay with the babies? They should sleep, and I'll not be gone long, I expect. I don't want to miss this."

"Of course, I can," said Psyche with a grin. "You go see whether or not you're going to win your wager. I'll sit and sigh over these gorgeous babies."

"Excellent," said Pandora rubbing her hands together. "If they start to get fussy, you can send for Kwan."

Psyche watched her sister leave and relaxed onto the couch with an amused smile. She didn't know how long it would take, but both babies had been fed and changed, and now they were sleeping. Her sister was very lucky to have babies such as these. Even when Alex was fussy, he didn't wail incessantly. They were actually both happy and easy to care for. Psyche sat for a time listening to them breathe as they slept. It was a peaceful, soothing sound that started to lull her to sleep when combined with her full stomach from dinner.

She finally shook her head and stood up to walk around the room. There were two new paintings on the wall to either side of the fireplace. One was a portrait of Pandora and Islington, the other of Dorian and Selena. Pandora had been very pregnant when it was painted, but the artist had painted it in such a way that it wasn't at all obvious. They were both excellent works, and Psyche moved closer to one of them to look for the name of the artist. She hadn't been there while he was doing the work, so she had never met him. Once she found the name, her eyebrow rose when she realized it was not painted by a *him.*

One of the babies started to fuss, and Psyche turned to go to the cradle. She was surprised to see it was Myron. She tried rocking the cradle to see if that would calm him, but he continued to fuss. Psyche picked him up because she didn't want him to wake Alex. She put him to her shoulder and rested her cheek against the soft down on his head and shushed him, and he soon settled and went back to sleep. When she placed him back in the cradle, he woke up and started to fuss again. She picked him back up and repeated the process, but she didn't put him down right away. Instead, she walked around the room.

She walked over to the window and looked out at the garden for any sign of her sister. She couldn't see into the stables because of the high stone wall. She hoped everything was going well for the mare. Pandora had grown very fond of Jezebel, and Bellerophon was the sire. She and Islington had a wager placed on what color the foal would be. Both parents were black, but Jezebel had white markings. Pandora was betting the foal was solid black. Psyche wasn't sure herself, but she was willing to agree with her twin.

Psyche heard the door open, and she turned just as Waldon moved out of the way to let Sheerness enter the room. She was surprised to see him, until he moved out of the way and let his niece and nephews come rushing in behind him. They started to race toward her for a hug before Psyche put a finger to her lips and rubbed Myron's back. It was comical to see them stop mid-rush to begin tiptoeing toward her to hug her around the waist. Psyche grinned.

"Two visits in one week, my goodness!" she said softly. "I can't play yet, but I'm sure Waldon will show you to the garden," she said amusedly, looking over their heads at the butler where he still stood by the door. He nodded agreeably. Psyche bent down and kissed each of them on the forehead before they quietly followed him out of the room. "Stay out of the flowerbeds!" she whispered loudly after them.

She adjusted the baby at her shoulder and looked out the window to see the children race into the garden. She was sure they wouldn't get into too much mischief. She turned to face Sheerness after she watched them for a few minutes as they skipped up and down the paths giggling.

"Hallo, Lord Sheerness," she said quietly. "Is Parliament out for the day, then?"

"Yes, they dismissed at noon. It's rather hot today, and the smell from the Thames was unbearable," said Sheerness evenly.

"Oh!" said Psyche in surprise, wondering why she hadn't seen Islington. "Islington is probably at the stables then, since Aysgarth is coming," she said almost to herself as the realization dawned on her. Sheerness raised an eyebrow. "His favorite mare is foaling," explained Psyche, "and they've already decided to name it Aysgarth Falls."

Psyche walked to the cradle and tried to lay Myron back down again. He was still going to have none of it. She picked him back up and soothed him.

"Oh, sweetie, you need to sleep in your cradle," said Psyche gently. "Your mama will have my hide if I spoil you. Alex is supposed to be the fussy one."

Sheerness watched Psyche with the baby, and his chest tightened. She was good with children. Her younger brothers were willing to have fisticuffs with him for yelling at her. His niece and nephews worshipped her. And seeing Psyche with her nephew made him long to give her several babies of her own. She turned to see him looking at her with a peculiar, almost covetous, expression, and she raised an inquisitive eyebrow.

"What?" she asked dryly.

"Have you—?" he began uncomfortably, and Psyche watched in amazement as his cheeks colored in what she could only think of as a blush. "What I mean to say is, are you...?" Psyche's lips began to twitch amusedly. "Have you gotten your flowers?"

Psyche looked at him blankly, and her forehead wrinkled with a puzzled frown. "What flowers?"

She watched as his cheeks began to turn even redder, and he nodded his head toward the baby, and then he held his hands in front of him in a way that made her realize what he meant. She chuckled and shook her head in amusement at his discomfiture. She never would have thought he would find the topic so uncomfortable.

"Oh, you mean my *courses*?" she asked mildly.

"Yes," he said weakly.

"I am not pregnant," she said evenly.

"Are you sure?" he asked, looking at her assessingly.

"Absolutely," she said flatly.

She clenched her jaw to hold back a further retort about yet again dashing his plans of getting her to marry him because she was trying to do as her brother had asked. She would try to be nice to him, but she was *not* going to marry him. She could see from his disappointed expression that her answer wasn't what he had hoped for. He nodded and clasped his hands behind his back.

"Amalie tells me Lord Westerkirk has asked for her hand again," she said casually, attempting to change the course of the conversation.

"Yes," Sheerness said noncommittally, and she watched his jaw tighten.

"Are you going to let him?" she asked evenly.

"I'm not sure. I think she needs someone less wishy-washy. I was thinking of arranging a marriage between Amalie and Sir James."

"Sir James Klein?" asked Psyche in surprise.

"Yes. He's not grandly titled, but he is from a good family and well-to-do. It would be a good match."

"Oh, you can't let Amalie marry Sir James," said Psyche, shaking her head dismissively. "I doubt very seriously that he's even expressed an interest."

"Why can I not let her marry Sir James, and why are you so certain he wouldn't be interested?"

"Because they're unsuited."

"They don't need to be well-suited for an arranged marriage," said Sheerness flatly.

"You should let her marry Westerkirk. At least he loves her."

Sheerness snorted. "Love is, apparently, not everything."

"Amalie deserves something better."

Sheerness raised an eyebrow. Psyche and Sir James were friends, and he knew she respected him. He had to wonder why she was so adamant Amalie shouldn't marry the man. It was true Sir James had not mentioned an interest in marrying his sister, and his only objection to her marrying Westerkirk was that the man had already jilted her once. He didn't want to see Amalie hurt again. Then he began to grow suspicious Psyche might have hopes of marrying the baronet herself. They *were* well-suited, and Amalie had said Sir James had kissed Psyche. Perhaps *he* was the reason she didn't want to marry Sheerness.

"I thought you liked Sir James," he asked neutrally, gauging her reaction.

"I happen to know Sir James is in love with someone else."

Sheerness looked at her with a scowl. "And who might that be?"

"Oh, I'll not tell you that," she said calmly.

"You, perhaps?" he asked coldly, feeling a jealousy he had never thought possible.

Psyche laughed. "Oh, no," she chortled. "Sir James doesn't love me."

She seemed to be sincere, but he had been fooled before. "Perhaps you would like to marry him yourself?"

"No," said Psyche airily, "I don't want to marry anyone."

"I've noticed that," he muttered.

"Pardon?" she asked with a puzzled frown.

She walked to the table and picked up the bell sitting there to ring it. She was going to send for Kwan so she could go out to the garden with Josie, Jerome, and Philip. Conversation with Sheerness was fast devolving, and she thought the distraction of the children would be beneficial. Myron started in her arms when she rang the bell so close to him, and she rubbed his back soothingly to calm him. Luckily, Alex still slept on in the cradle.

"Why shouldn't Amalie marry Sir James?" asked Sheerness evenly.

"Even if Sir James *has* asked for her hand, which I seriously doubt, she doesn't love him, and he doesn't love her. It would be an arranged marriage solely for the purpose of producing heirs, not based on any form of mutual attraction or respect. Just because of some sense of duty. That's wrong. Westerkirk has, on the other hand, stated he loves her, and she loves him. The man is no less respectable than Sir James in all ways. Even if they never have *one* child, *they* will still be happy. I can't believe you'd be willing to make your sister miserable just because you think Westerkirk is *wishy-washy.*"

Waldon opened the door to look at her enquiringly. "You rang, Lady Psyche?"

"Yes, Waldon. Could you, please, fetch Kwan?" she asked mildly.

"Certainly, Lady Psyche," he said with a slight bow before he closed the door.

Sheerness looked at her gravely after the door closed. "I don't want her to marry Westerkirk precisely because I *don't* want her to be unhappy."

"You do realize she's old enough to marry him even without your consent? And she may be in mourning, but who will know if she goes to Scotland?" Sheerness's jaw dropped in surprise. "She hasn't mentioned it, but she *is* determined to marry him," she said evenly.

"I suppose if he's still interested after I return, I'll give it my approval," he said neutrally.

Psyche smiled. "I'm sure Amalie will appreciate that," she said softly.

Kwan entered the room then and took Myron from her. Psyche reluctantly let him go after placing a kiss on the side of his head. Sheerness offered his arm, and she took it to walk with him out to the garden. Pandora and Islington entered the garden not too long after that to proudly announce Jezebel had produced a beautiful, solid black colt.

Chapter Seventeen

The duke didn't feel Psyche's sense of urgency on speaking to Lord Stranraer. She explained why she wanted to know, but while it was interesting, he didn't think it was extremely important. Myron would have, she was sure. Unfortunately, Psyche was at her father's pleasure for getting the information. She only hoped he would get it before the end of the Season. She didn't want to wait another year to find out.

It took Aberdare nearly two weeks, almost the end of July, before he talked to the earl about it. It proved to be fruitless in any event. The only thing Stranraer could say was that it was old and Egyptian. He had no knowledge of where it had originated in Egypt. He didn't know if it came from a royal tomb or that of some high official. He didn't know if it came from Upper Egypt or Lower Egypt. He knew nothing about the necklace that was useful.

Lord Stranraer's attitude was something Psyche found extremely frustrating about most others who dealt with antiquities. Was it real? What was it made of? What was it worth? Was it pretty, unique, or epic in size? Psyche was more interested in knowing who made it. Why did they make it? Did it serve a purpose in their daily life or their interest in another one? For her, knowing the context of something was far more important than the object itself because knowing that made it all the more valuable. Most people didn't care.

Once she got the useless information from Stranraer, Psyche made a second, larger copy of the drawing. She kept hoping Sir James would come by, but he didn't. She wrote him a letter asking him. Some people might have felt it forward of her, but Sir James would not. She briefly mentioned what she had found and asked him to come see her at Pandora's at his earliest convenience. It happened that his earliest convenience wasn't until the first of August.

Psyche was taking a walk in the garden when he arrived. She almost skipped up the path when she saw him on the terrace. She was so relieved.

"Sir James, I'm glad you came," she said happily.

"Forgive me for taking so long," said Sir James after kissing her hand. "I was sorry to hear about your brother. That was a nasty bit of business."

"Thank you," said Psyche softly.

"Now, you mentioned you'd found something on your necklace?"

"Oh, yes," said Psyche excitedly. "If you'll just wait here a moment, I shall run and get it."

"Of course," said Sir James agreeably.

Psyche ran through the house and raced up the stairs to her room. She retrieved the necklace in its box and the larger of her drawings and went back to the terrace. It was slightly cloudy outside, but she felt there was probably enough light. If not, she did have the drawing. She opened the box and pulled out the necklace to hand it to Sir James.

"Oh, this is a lovely piece," he said admiringly. "It's definitely pre-Roman, possibly late Middle Kingdom."

"That's more than Stranraer was able to confirm for me," said Psyche.

"Yes, well, I don't think he was buying it with the expectation it would be necessary information," said Sir James mildly, looking up from it to her with a smile. "You can see from this here—" he said, pointing to the crown on the head of the king driving the chariot—"that it was made after the uniting of Upper and Lower Egypt, but that still gives you a very wide time period."

"Yes," said Psyche, "I was afraid of that. What I really wanted you to see is on the back of the amber. You'll need to hold it up to the light, and if it doesn't work, I've made a drawing of it."

Sir James lifted the necklace toward the cloudy sky. He squinted his eyes, but he couldn't quite see, other than the scratches on the back of it. He thought at first they might have been imperfections created at some point during its very long life, but after examining them closer, he realized they were deliberate.

"It doesn't look like any form of writing, if I've got to make a guess," said Sir James as he continued to study the marks. He finally shrugged and handed the necklace back to her. "I'm afraid it's not something I recognize."

"I thought it might be too overcast out here for you to see, so I have this," said Psyche, unrolling her drawing and giving it to him.

"Oh, my," blurted Sir James in surprise.

"Absolutely," said Psyche with a grin.

"But what's on the back looks nothing like this," said Sir James as he looked from the sketch to the necklace.

"It does when the light shines through it," said Psyche calmly. "And it doesn't show through from the front. Whoever made that was a master craftsman and very clever. It would be unlikely someone would want to look at the necklace from the back, unless they knew something was there to look at. Hidden in plain sight," said Psyche with a grin.

"I'm not sure where this is. We do need to keep in mind that if this is the Nile as it was then, it has shifted its course somewhat since this was made."

"I know," said Psyche disappointedly. "That was why I was hoping Lord Stranraer might have been able to tell me where it came from, to possibly narrow down where I needed to look." She shrugged. "Even that might not have helped if it was buried or whatever a great distance away."

"If I might keep this—"he shook the drawing—"I can look at the Museum at the old maps...compare it to what we have and see if anything lines up."

"Would you?" asked Psyche hopefully.

"Of course," said Sir James with a smile. "You have piqued my curiosity."

Psyche bounced excitedly on her feet and impulsively kissed his cheek. "Oh, thank you, Sir James, and you may certainly have it."

"You're most welcome," said Sir James with a grin. "As a matter of fact, if you'll walk me to the door, I'll go get started on that right away."

"Sir James, you are simply wonderful," sighed Psyche happily.

They turned to go back into the house, and Psyche was startled to see Lord Sheerness standing in the doorway. He was positively livid. His jaw was set, and there was a set of lines etched deeply between his brows. Psyche looked at him in puzzlement, not quite understanding his rage.

"Hallo, Lord Sheerness, marvelous to see you," said Sir James jovially.

"Sir James," Sheerness bit out. "Lady Psyche, if I might have a word," he said stilly.

"Certainly, if you'll just give me a moment to show Sir James to the door," said Psyche agreeably, her forehead still wrinkled in confusion.

Sheerness moved silently from the doorway to allow them to pass, and Psyche looked up at him curiously as she walked past. Psyche bade Sir James farewell and calmly made her way back to the terrace.

"Now, Lord Sheerness, you wanted to see me?" she asked politely.

"Actually, I came to see Bardsey, but as I was on my way to his study, what should I do but look out the door to see you *kissing* Sir James again," he said tightly. He *was* managing not to yell.

Psyche blinked. "Well, yes, he made me very happy."

"Indeed," said Sheerness coldly. "And when's the happy occasion?"

"Pardon?" asked Psyche blankly.

"The wedding? When is the *wedding*?" he ground out.

"There isn't going to *be* any wedding," said Psyche exasperatedly. "Sir James is going to research something for me at the Museum. I *told* you, I'm not marrying Sir James."

"For a man you've no intention of marrying, you certainly have a penchant for kissing him," said Sheerness angrily.

Psyche raised an eyebrow and lifted her chin. "I've *kissed* you more, and I have no intention of marrying you either," she said flatly. She shook her head tiredly. "Go see Islington, Lord Sheerness. You've had your *word.*"

She turned and went back in the house, muttering under her breath as she went up the stairs to her room. She had no time for his anger, and he had no excuse for it. It wasn't as if she had to answer to him for anything, and she had done nothing wrong. When she walked into her room, Chrissoula was sitting in the chair by the fireplace. She looked up at Psyche's peeved entrance.

"Why are you muttering, Thea?" asked Chrissoula curiously.

"Ooh, Lord Sheerness," said Psyche disgustedly.

"What has he done now?" asked Chrissoula, trying to control the twitching in her lips to hide her amusement.

"He thinks I'm marrying Sir James, and he was angry because he saw me kiss the man on the cheek."

"Angry or jealous?" asked Chrissoula lightly.

Psyche tilted her head sideways. "I suppose he was jealous," she said thoughtfully. She scratched her forehead. "I guess he thinks because *he* wants to marry me that he has some type of proprietary control over me."

"Sheerness wants to marry you?" blurted Chrissoula in surprise. She would never have believed it. He had made Psyche miserable the previous Season. This one had not been so bad, but Chrissoula thought it was due to the earl not being in society to cause it. That certainly explained at least one thing.

"Yes, he wants to marry me just so he can produce an heir and honor his father's dying request." Psyche groaned aggravatedly.

"Are you sure about that?"

"Yes. No. I don't know," said Psyche, shaking her head. "But I'm *not* marrying him, and I've told him that. He has no right to be jealous."

She went to her desk and put the necklace back in the drawer, and then she pulled out another piece of paper to make another, larger drawing. Chrissoula watched her continue to mutter occasionally with an amused smile. She thought she would send a letter to Nikos.

Sheerness entered Islington's study still frowning. He hadn't liked Psyche's answer, and he was frustrated she had still not changed her mind. It was obvious she still had no intention of marrying him...ever, and he was at a loss to decide how to change it. He hoped his time away from the country would give him time to decide what to do, and maybe it would even give Psyche a chance to realize she missed him.

Islington looked up from the paper to see Sheerness's dour expression as he entered the room. It was a familiar look. Not on Lord Sheerness. Pandora used to make *him* look that way...often.

"Afternoon, Sheerness," he said mildly, setting aside the paper and leaning back in his chair to prop his feet on the edge of the desk. "Take a seat."

Sheerness slumped down in one of the chairs at the front of the desk, and his expression hadn't changed.

"I can see by your face that things aren't going well, but I thought I would ask anyhow," said Islington mildly.

"She's impossible," groaned Sheerness. "The devil take her!"

Islington's lips twitched amusedly, and he picked up his nearby glass of whisky to take a sip to hide it.

"Have you actually asked her why she thinks you're being insincere?" asked Islington.

"Yes. No. I asked her why she didn't want to marry me, and all she said was that she didn't want to." Some of the anger left his features. "I think she wants to marry Sir James."

"Sir James Klein?" asked Islington in surprise.

"Yes. I saw her kissing him on the terrace before I came in here."

Islington's eyebrow shot up. His wife had informed him about Sir James's proclivities, and he was sure Sheerness was completely off the mark. He was sure Psyche was aware as well. Aside from that, Islington knew she liked Sir James, but the baronet didn't strike him as the type of man who would be attractive to Psyche.

"Kissing him how?" asked Islington curiously.

"She very happily kissed him on the cheek and told him how *wonderful* he was," he said sarcastically. He saw Islington take another sip from his whisky. "Can I have one of those?"

Islington nodded and rose to pour Sheerness a drink. He took it to him then leaned against the front of his desk with a thoughtful expression.

"She doesn't want to marry Sir James," said Islington finally, "and I'm sure if all she did was kiss him on the cheek, she has no other interest in him either."

"How can you be so sure?" asked Sheerness darkly.

"Because Psyche is quite a bit like her twin in some ways."

"If you know her so well, what the bloody hell does she want from me?"

Islington shrugged. "I couldn't tell you." He gave Sheerness a speculative glance. "She thinks you want to marry her for something besides love." Sheerness started to speak, and Islington held up a hand. "Perhaps you should ask her why she thinks *that* instead of asking her why she doesn't want to."

"Isn't it the same thing?" asked Sheerness perplexedly.

"Not to Psyche. You have to understand that she has a very hard—if not impossible—time telling a lie, so she's learned to skirt around it altogether. If you want a direct answer, ask her a direct question. If you ask her something that could have multiple answers, she will take the honest one that saves her and still won't tell you what you want to know. You asked her why she won't marry you; she said she didn't want to. Perfectly honest."

"She's lied to me before," said Sheerness, setting his jaw.

Islington chuckled. "Oh, I doubt that. She might not have told you the whole truth, but she didn't lie. The other side of it is that if you don't want the truth, don't ask her because she won't lie to make you feel better. Trust me."

Sheerness remembered the ball at the Stranraers'. She had been brutally honest, and she had told him the same thing Islington just did. He still had to wonder why she couldn't lie and what happened if she did. She said it was physically impossible. He had asked Myron, but his friend had only laughed and said Psyche would break his legs if he told Sheerness.

"I'm going to be leaving for Greece in two weeks," he said thoughtfully. "I doubt very seriously I will be able to change her mind before then."

"No, I don't think you will either," said Islington mildly. "Did you yell at her when you saw her kissing Sir James?"

"I didn't *yell*, but I suppose I did—somewhat—accuse her of being *light.*"

Islington grimaced and sucked in air through his teeth. "That was very bad. You'll be lucky if you'll even get her to speak to you in two weeks."

"I suspected as much," said Sheerness dryly.

"I'll tell you one more thing that might help when you're dealing with Psyche, and this is something that applies to every woman in that family. If there's ever a question of whether something is honorable or right, even if it's dangerous or impossible, don't ask yourself what a *woman* would do under the circumstances because *she* won't."

Sheerness raised an eyebrow and took a swallow from his glass. Islington had given him quite a bit of advice, but Sheerness wasn't sure how much of it would be useful. It would have to wait until he returned to England.

≪ ≫

The Season was over, and Psyche and Chrissoula had packed her things for going home. Pandora and Islington were packed as well, but they would stay a few days more in town while Islington attended to some personal business. Psyche was going to miss her twin, but now she felt she would be able to tolerate being home. Her father and Dorian would be coming to collect her tomorrow, and they would all travel to Wilderland together.

Sir James hadn't been able to find much of help at the Museum in the two weeks he had the drawing, but he would continue to look and let Psyche know if he found anything. She would spend her time at home poring through her books as well. She didn't know when she would be able to use the information, should she find any, but she would at least have it.

Amalie brought the children to see her one last time that afternoon, and Psyche was sad she wouldn't see them for a while. She gave them a standing invitation to visit Wilderland whenever they liked, and the children brightened at the thought of it. Psyche didn't know if they could come, as Sheppey was nearly from one side of the country to the other away from Glyncorrwg, but they would be welcome. She would, of course, write as often as possible.

Amalie said Sheerness had spoken to her and Westerkirk regarding their marrying, and the earl stood by his assertion that he would wait for her however long it took. Sheerness told them if Westerkirk hadn't jilted his sister again by the time he returned from the Mediterranean, he would give it his blessing. Amalie was overjoyed, and she told Psyche it was, again, all thanks to her.

Psyche had supper with Islington and Pandora in the private sitting room. She thought she might at some point go to Yorkshire to see her sister. She had grown attached to her new nephews, and they would be walking, and possibly even talking, by the time she saw them again if she didn't go to Bardsey at least once before next year. Pandora and Islington said she should come any time, and it wouldn't even be necessary for her to let them know.

One thing that troubled Psyche was that Waddlesworth had been missing from the park when she went riding that morning. It wouldn't have bothered her so much, but she hadn't seen him the two previous mornings either. It wasn't unusual for him to be gone for a day, but three days in a row was disconcerting. He wasn't an old duck, so she didn't think he had died from age, and he was protected as long as he was in the park. She hoped he hadn't gone somewhere he wasn't safe and gotten shot. She was disappointed she wouldn't be able to see him one last time. She wouldn't be riding in the morning because Achilles needed to be fresh for the trip home, so this morning had been her last opportunity to bid her farewell.

Psyche's mind had briefly turned to Sheerness and that he would be leaving for Greece and Egypt tomorrow. She was disappointed she wouldn't be going, and she tried to console herself with knowing she would go one day. She wouldn't be seeing Sheerness again for some time. It gave her an odd twinge, and she realized she was going to miss him…a lot. He made her angry, and his incessant pestering to marry him aggravated her to no end, but she was going to miss him nonetheless.

Psyche didn't get much work done on her deciphering. She tried to dismiss the tense feeling in the pit of her stomach to excitement about going home, but she didn't feel excited. She felt anxious. It wasn't anxiety over Pandora. She was fine; the babies were fine; and Psyche had every confidence they were out of danger. She wasn't anxious about going home. She wasn't anxious about her necklace. She was making progress, if slowly, with it.

Then she realized it was Sheerness. She hadn't seen him since the day on the terrace. She tried to tell herself she didn't care, that she was and would be perfectly happy if she never saw him again. But when she had ruled out all the other possibilities, it was the only thing that remained. She hated that the last words she had with him had been unkind, and she felt ashamed she hadn't been living up to Myron's request. By the time she realized what was making her anxious, it was night and too late for her to change it.

After supper, she and Pandora stayed in the sitting room talking after Islington went to his study to do some paperwork before going to bed. Pandora noticed Psyche's withdrawn demeanor and looked at her with concern.

"Are you feeling well?" Pandora finally asked.

Psyche blinked. "I feel fine," she said. "Do I look ill?"

"No. You just seem a bit down in the dumps."

"I'm fine; just a little sad to be going home, I guess," said Psyche absently.

"I know what you need," said Pandora with a smile, rising from the couch to go to the sideboard. She poured some wine into a glass and took it to Psyche. "Try this."

Psyche took the glass and looked at it suspiciously. "It's not whisky or brandy, is it?"

"No, it's a spiced wine Keung made," said Pandora with a grin.

"Ooh, outstanding," said Psyche excitedly. She took a sip. It was sweet but tasted delicious. "This is fantastic. I may need another glass."

Pandora chuckled, and she watched as her twin drained the glass and held it out to her to refill.

"Are you sure? This has quite a kick. It might sneak up on you."

"Yes, please," said Psyche with a grin.

Pandora poured her another glass and gave it to her. She watched as Psyche quickly drained it again. She chuckled and brought the bottle from the sideboard to Psyche, setting it on the table in front of her.

"Here, you may as well finish it. I'll let Keung know you liked it."

"Yes," agreed Psyche heartily as she poured what was left in the bottle into her glass. "I want some of this at Wilderland. Do you know how he made it?"

"I think it's plum wine and a few things," said Pandora vaguely.

"This is great! I could drink this all the time," said Psyche as she swallowed what was left in the glass.

Pandora sat beside her on the couch. "I really don't think you'd want to do that," she said in a mildly amused tone.

"Oh, yes, I would," said Psyche with a yawn. "It tastes like plums and cherries and something I can't quite put my finger on." Psyche yawned again, and her eyelids began to droop. "Goodness, I am sleepy!" she said with surprise.

Pandora's face became serious as she watched her twin begin to lose consciousness.

"I hope you have a good trip," said Pandora gently.

"Thank you," mumbled Psyche, and her chin dropped to her chest as she passed out completely.

Pandora looked at the clock on the mantel, and then she went to the door and looked out. She signaled to Maiyin and Chrissoula, and they hurried quietly into the sitting room. Pandora went behind the couch and pulled the trunk she had hidden there to the front, closer to where Psyche was sitting. She opened the lid, and there was a pillow and a few blankets in the bottom. Pandora unfolded one of the blankets for a cushion and put the others on the couch and replaced the pillow.

Maiyin looked at the empty bottle on the table. "She drank *all* of it?" she asked in surprise.

"Wasn't she supposed to?" asked Pandora with a worried frown.

"No, Keung say to *not* let her drink all of it."

"Oh, no!" cried Pandora. "It's not going to kill her, is it?"

Maiyin thought about it for a minute. "No, but she's going to sleep for a *very* long time."

"How long?" asked Pandora with some trepidation.

"Two days," said Maiyin negligibly.

"*Two* days?" gasped Pandora.

Maiyin shrugged. "So much the better. Less likely he will turn around and come back."

"Yes, but *two* days!" said Pandora concernedly.

"She needs the sleep," said Chrissoula dryly.

Pandora looked at her sister sleeping peacefully. Chrissoula had a point, and so did Maiyin. It was just the thought her twin would be sleeping in a box for two days, and when she woke up, she would have no idea where she was. For a moment, she had second thoughts, but it was for Psyche's own good.

"All right," sighed Pandora, "let's get her in the trunk."

Chrissoula and Maiyin each grabbed a leg, and Pandora grabbed her under the arms. Pandora gave a nod, and they all lifted her at the same time. She was heavier than she looked.

"You've been giving her too much *souvlaki*," grunted Pandora to Chrissoula as they carefully settled Psyche into the trunk.

"No," panted Chrissoula, holding a hand to a stitch in her side once Psyche was in. "It's from Mrs. Hensley feeding her too much macaroni and cheese."

"We're going to need help getting her to the wagon," said Pandora. "That trunk is way too heavy for us to manage." She looked at Maiyin. "Go back to the mews and have Jim pull around to the front. Tell him to come in the front door when he gets there but don't ring or knock."

Maiyin hurried out, and Pandora and Chrissoula finished settling Psyche into the trunk. Pandora made sure the ventilation holes she had made weren't covered, and then she bent down to kiss Psyche's cheek and smooth the hair off her forehead.

"You are going to be angry with me, I'm sure, but I know you're going to enjoy this." She looked at Chrissoula. "Is her trunk ready?"

"Jim should already have it on the wagon. I put in the things you wanted her to have, and her clothes, and the things from Maiyin and Keung. It wasn't easy to get it out of the house without her noticing. I waited until you were eating supper."

"I'm sure we've forgotten something."

"Nothing else would fit in that trunk," said Chrissoula, shaking her head.

"You put my letter on top?"

Chrissoula smacked her forehead. "I'll be right back with it."

Chrissoula left the room, and Pandora scratched her forehead as she looked at the clock on the mantel. It was nearing one. Jim wouldn't drive very quickly with the cargo he was about to carry. The ship wouldn't sail before dawn, and it was less likely the sailor on watch would ask questions if he were tired, but Pandora was nervous about how closely they would be shaving it. It wouldn't do any good if the ship sailed without her. It was going to be *very* close.

Pandora turned toward the door and sighed with relief when Maiyin entered with Jim. After one last look at Psyche, Pandora closed the lid. She thought they would have to wait for Chrissoula to help carry it to the wagon. Jim astounded her when he lifted it from the floor by himself with seemingly little effort. Pandora went to the door first and looked toward Islington's study before she turned and waved for them to come out. Chrissoula came down the stairs with Pandora's letter just as they were going past, and the four of them went out the front door and down the steps to the wagon.

Jim carefully eased the trunk onto the bed to join the other one of the same size already waiting there. Pandora quickly climbed up to lift the lid on the other trunk and placed her letter on top of the items there after giving it a kiss.

Chrissoula was right: there was no possible way to fit anything else into it, but it didn't look like Psyche was going to *need* anything else. Jim helped Pandora down after she closed the lid.

"Do you know how to find the ship?" she asked him nervously.

"Of course, I do, Lady Pandora. I even went to it a time or two in the dark so I'd be able to find my way," he said with an assuring smile.

"Thank you, Jim," said Pandora, giving him a hug. "You should get going before it sails without her."

Jim climbed onto the driver's seat and urged the horses to move on. Pandora stood with Maiyin and Chrissoula for a moment until the wagon disappeared from view.

"She's going to be livid," said Chrissoula conversationally.

"She'll survive," said Pandora with a sigh. "This was the easiest way for both of us to do what Myron wanted us to do."

"I don't think this is exactly what he had in mind," said Chrissoula dryly. "This is good for her, though."

"Thank you for telling me what he told her," said Pandora softly.

"I only told you the parts I thought you needed to know. She doesn't need to be in mourning," said Chrissoula sadly. She sighed and nodded with a smile. "This may not be what your brother intended, but it somehow seems right."

"What are you three doing standing out in the street at nearly two in the morning?" asked Islington from the stoop.

Pandora squeaked in surprise and turned to look at him. She walked up the steps and took one of his hands to wrap it around her waist and pecked him on the cheek.

"We thought we heard something and came to see what it was," she said calmly.

Islington looked down at her innocent expression and kissed her on the lips. "Mm-hmm, a likely story," he said mildly.

"Very well. I've just drugged Psyche and sent her to be stowed away on a ship bound for the Mediterranean," said Pandora calmly.

Islington threw his head back and laughed with hilarity. "That's even less likely," chortled Islington.

"Of course it is," said Pandora agreeably.

≪ ≫

Jim took his time traveling to the dock. It was a faster trip at night than during the day, but he didn't go quickly because the wagon was not well-sprung, and Psyche wasn't riding on a seat. The trip during the day took about an hour because of the other traffic and pedestrians. By the time he made it to the dock, it was four in the morning. The sun would be up in an hour. Pandora was right about how close it would be. He pulled the wagon to the gangway and stepped down, mentally rehearsing what Pandora said he should say. It wasn't that complicated.

"Who goes?" called a voice from the head of the planking.

"I'm delivering some personal belongings of the earl," said Jim easily.

"Which earl?" challenged the sailor.

"Lord Sheerness, o' course," said Jim dryly.

"Bit late…or a bit early, ain't it?" asked the sailor suspiciously.

"Look, I don't make no question of 'ow the earl comes an' goes. 'E says take this to the ship, I takes it to the ship."

"Good enough, then," said the sailor.

"'E said these are to go in one of the guest cabins, and I'll need 'elp getting them aboard, if you please."

"Hunh," grunted the sailor.

He whistled loudly and another sailor joined him. They walked down the gangway to the wagon. The first sailor looked up at Jim.

"You're not going to fit belowdecks," he said plainly. "You help us get them to the main deck, and we'll take them below."

"All right," said Jim uncomfortably.

He lifted the trunk holding Psyche and carried it on. The two sailors grabbed the other trunk and followed behind. Jim set the trunk on the deck and stood aside for the two men to go past him. They carried the trunk belowdecks and soon returned to take the one holding Psyche to the same place.

"That's very fragile," said Jim hurriedly as they lifted it.

"We have it," said one of the sailors with a grin. "You can go now."

Jim nodded and watched them carry it below. They did seem to be taking care with it. He turned and left the ship to go back to the wagon and return to Aberdare House. He would be tired tomorrow, but he had the distinct impression he wouldn't need to worry about driving far. By the time the duke discovered what had happened, the ship would be well on its way to the mouth of the Thames. He gave the ship one last look and picked up the reins.

"Safe journey, Lady Psyche," he said softly.

≪ ≫

Bandy and Watkins carried the second trunk to the guest cabin on the right. Neither one would be occupied, but the door on that one happened to be open. They quickly determined the second one was the heavier of the two, and after some adjustment, they had it braced against the wall with the first, lighter, trunk sitting on top.

"Tie 'em down, would you, Watkins?" asked Bandy. He looked at the watch he carried for his shift. "It won't be long before the rest of the crew and his lordship arrives."

"Sure thing," said Watkins agreeably.

Chapter Eighteen

Sheerness stepped down from the hackney and looked up at his ship. She was ready to sail and gleamed with a brightness that made him proud. Sailors were moving around on deck making things ready to get under way. He would check with the first mate to find out how many had arrived. There was still a little time, and as long as they arrived before the anchor was raised, Sheerness didn't mind. He slung his sack over his shoulder and walked up the gangway.

Some of the sailors nodded to him respectfully as he went past on his way to the aftdeck. He went to his cabin and dropped the sack onto his bed. He would unpack later. He wanted to speak with the first mate and make a quick inspection before sailing. On his way through the alcove to the officers' mess, he glanced to the closed doors of the two empty cabins. He didn't like that they wouldn't be used; space on a ship was at a premium, and the cabins were large. His mother and sister couldn't go because of the children...not that either showed any interest in the Mediterranean anyhow. What bothered him more than their not being used, however, was the reason *why* they wouldn't be used.

It was just after seven when they unfurled the sails and lifted anchor. The crew was present and accounted for, and the weather was perfect for sailing. The sun was shining, and a stiff breeze was blowing. If the weather held, they could be to the Channel by nightfall. The ship wasn't going to be fast, but at least that was possible.

≪ ≫

Pandora sat calmly eating breakfast with Islington in their bedroom when there was a knock at the door. She continued to eat the piece of bacon she had in her hand, and Maiyin went to get the door and found Waldon there.

"His grace and Viscount Glamorgan have come to collect Lady Psyche," he said calmly.

Maiyin turned to look at Pandora with a raised eyebrow. The younger woman carefully wiped her mouth with her napkin and rose from the table. She looked down at her husband.

"You might want to come hear this," she said with a slight smile.

Islington looked up at his wife as he was taking a sip of coffee. His forehead wrinkled curiously, and he rose as well. They had been expecting her family to come for Psyche. It was odd Pandora's twin had not joined them for breakfast as she usually did, but he thought it was because she had taken breakfast in bed. That would have been a nice treat for her last day in the city. Pandora linked her arm through his, and they walked down the stairs to the sitting room where the duke and Dorian were waiting.

"Hallo, Papà," said Pandora calmly.

"Dodo, where's Psyche?" asked the duke. "We need to get going."

Pandora clasped her hands in front of her. "I'm sorry; she's not coming."

"What do you mean she's not coming? Has she decided to stay on with you and Islington?" he asked confusedly.

"No. She's not coming because she isn't here," said Pandora calmly.

"What do you mean she's *not here?*" asked Aberdare stilly.

Pandora looked at the clock on the mantel. It was after eight. Pandora felt fairly sure the *Medea* was somewhere on the Thames and well beyond reach.

"Through no intention of her own, she's on her way out of the country," said Pandora evenly.

"*What?*" roared Aberdare.

"Bloody hell, you weren't having me on," said Islington breathlessly.

Pandora looked at her husband. "No," she said softly. She looked back at her father. "I've stowed her away on a ship bound for Greece and Egypt."

"What do you mean *you* stowed her away?" he asked darkly.

"Psyche would never have gone, but she needed to go, Papà. Myron wanted her to go, and he asked me to help her. She would have waited for years if necessary before she went, but I thought *this* was the time. She was so unhappy. The only way to describe it would be to say she was *languishing*, and she would have stayed here, still doing it, if I hadn't knocked her out, put her in a trunk, and sent her to sea on the *Medea.*"

"Oh, Dodo, tell me this is a flim-flam," said her father softly.

"No, it isn't," she said plainly. "She wanted to take this trip. It was all she thought about before Sham died. She'll be safe. I'm certain Lord Sheerness will protect her. She *needed* to go," finished Pandora.

Aberdare looked at his daughter as a wide range of emotions battled inside him. He was furious with Pandora for taking it upon herself to shanghai her sister. He knew as well as Pandora did it was too late to get her back; it would be useless to go after the ship. His concern for Psyche was overwhelming. At least when Pandora had gone to Scotland, it was all her own doing. Psyche wouldn't know she was going until it was too late to come back.

But he wanted Psyche to be happy; he had noticed, like Pandora, that Psyche had settled into a melancholy existence. She never laughed, and she rarely smiled after Myron died. No one knew Psyche better than her twin, and Pandora seemed to think this was what was needed to bring her out of it.

Then there was the fact Myron had wanted her to go. Aberdare could only assume it was something he had told them in their letters. His grace could not, in good conscience, go against his son's last wishes. He knew Sheerness, and he believed, also like Pandora, that the earl would not let Psyche come to any harm. Going to Greece and Egypt had always been the only thing Psyche ever wanted. He didn't think she would have gone, though, after Myron died, not for a very long time…if ever.

Aberdare rubbed a hand over his face. "What am I supposed to tell your mother?" he asked resignedly. "She'll worry herself to death."

"No, she won't," said Pandora gently. "As long as she knows Psyche is safe and happy, Mamà will be fine. Psyche *will* be safe and happy. I know."

Aberdare looked askance at his daughter. She seemed so certain, and there was no question about her bond with her twin. Pandora was also a lot wiser than her years would give her credit for. His anxiety began to lessen, and he realized there was little that could be done about it now in any event.

"Very well," he said with a slight smile.

"We can send her letters. At least to Nikos Andreanopoulos in Thessaloniki, and I am sure she'll write to us, even if she never gets ours. She promised she would."

"Chrissoula's brother?" asked Aberdare in surprise.

"How can you be sure she'll write if she didn't even know she was going?" asked Dorian.

"She said she would write when she thought she was going before Sham died, and if she has anything she can do about it, she is *not* going to let Sheerness take her to Greece without taking her to Thessaloniki and Nikos. I gave her plenty of paper and pens. I didn't just stow her away with nothing. She already had everything she needed for the trip, but she didn't think she would be using it anymore after Myron died. It was a simple matter of setting it aside without her knowing and seeing it was put aboard with her. Other than her not knowing she would be going after all, she is as well-prepared as she would be otherwise."

"How long have you been planning this?" asked Islington wonderingly.

"Since the beginning of July, after I found out Lord Sheerness still intended to go," said Pandora calmly.

"You brazen hussy," said Islington with an amused smile.

"And don't you forget it," said Pandora with a grin.

≪ ≫

The *Medea* was making excellent time, and by dark they were nearing Calais. Sheerness went below to have supper in the officers' mess, and then he went to his cabin for the night after taking a tour of the main deck. He unpacked the bag he had brought with him, and then he sat at his desk doing paperwork, making notes in the log and checking his maps for their course. He eventually looked at his pocket watch and realized with some surprise it was after midnight. He rubbed a tired hand over his face before he put away what he was working on and stood up. He got undressed and stood looking out one of the windows at the Channel for a time before he went to bed, but he couldn't fall asleep.

He looked through the doorway of his cabin to the closed door of the cabin that would have been Psyche's. He was going to miss her. Even though she persisted in refusing to marry him, for reasons that confounded him, he was going to miss her a lot. The only consolation he had was that perhaps she would miss him, too. Perhaps when he returned to England, she would finally say she would marry him. At the moment, it was almost as if she was haunting him, and he hoped that would lessen. He would never get anything done. He had only begun to think about her incessantly when he was alone. He could smell her perfume, and he decided the best way to not think about her would be to spend as little time alone as possible.

It was going to be odd not having Myron there. He had grown accustomed and actually begun to look forward to having Psyche there, but he had never imagined he would make the journey without Myron. He almost *didn't* go without Myron. If his friend hadn't told him to take his trip, almost with his dying breath, he wouldn't have. Sheerness wasn't sure he *ever* would have gone if Myron hadn't told him to…not without Myron.

Sheerness still hadn't read Myron's letter. He had picked it up several times and looked at it. He had almost broken the seal on it once or twice, but he couldn't bring himself to read it. Once he read it, he would fully have to accept that Myron was gone. Sheerness wasn't ready to do that yet. Perhaps once he was in the Mediterranean, maybe even on a hilltop somewhere in Greece, he would finally break the seal and read his friend's last words for him. That somehow seemed appropriate.

He still wasn't sure where he would go and what he would do once he got there. He had something of a purpose in mind, but he had never been. Myron was supposed to help him with that, among other things. He had been to both countries before and had known of several good areas to explore. Psyche seemed to think Thessaloniki would be good. He never had the chance to ask her why she thought that. Sheerness sighed and rolled over on his side and put a pillow over his head. He would think about it after he had some sleep.

By the time Sheerness ate breakfast and went abovedecks the following morning, the *Medea* was nearing Cherbourg. They had, thus far, had excellent luck with the wind and currents. His crew proved capable, and he was pleased with the job his first mate, Mr. Higginbotham, had done with selecting them.

He spent most of the day talking to his crew. They all seemed to be friendly, decent men. Some were formerly in the Navy, but most were merchant seamen. None had ever crewed for a private vessel, let alone a research expedition. He had Mr. Higginbotham impress upon them that this was not going to be a treasure hunt. They would be paid their wages, but there would be no stake in anything Sheerness might discover. It was all intended for research and eventually—hopefully—the British Museum.

The crew didn't mind. The *Medea* was well-appointed, and Sheerness was compensating them at a more than reasonable rate. He also gave them better food than they were accustomed to; he wasn't going to eat better than his crew, and he was *not* going to eat hard tack. He had plotted their course to enable them to make stops in the larger ports along the way to resupply as necessary.

As Sheerness went below for the second night, they were nearing the tip of Brittany. They would round it at some point during the night and be into the Bay of Biscay by morning. The weather had remained fair and almost cloudless all day, but it would be foolish to think it was going to remain that way. Sheerness had sailed enough to know that was never the case, especially not once one entered the Atlantic.

Sheerness's expectation they would be into the Bay of Biscay by morning proved correct, as did his belief the weather wouldn't hold. When he came topside, the sky was steel gray, and they were going to face a large storm very soon. The wind had picked up considerably, which enabled them to make better time, but the water became rougher as the storm approached.

Sheerness thought for a while to head inland, where the storm might be less intense, but they were too far out to make land before the storm struck. The best thing was to stay their course and ride it out. They were about to find out how well the ship had been refitted. Sheerness had every confidence it would be fine. The *Medea* was about fifteen years old, but she had been refurbished almost to the point of being entirely new.

The storm struck just at sunset, and it was every bit as vicious as Sheerness had expected. The wind roared around the ship and tossed it, and it required a man to yell himself hoarse to be heard above it. The crew that worked to keep everything secured and maintain the ship on its course had tied off to keep themselves from being swept overboard as the waves washed over the deck. Sheerness remained topside, holding the *Medea* to her course the best he could.

Psyche woke up with a crick in her neck. She was disoriented, and she couldn't recall ever waking up that way unless she was ill. She was stiff and achy and hoped she wasn't coming down with something. She put a hand to her forehead and rubbed it. She felt like the bed was moving, and there was a loud roaring in her ears. She hoped she didn't have influenza again, but at least Keung would be nearby to make more medicine.

Her forehead didn't feel hot, but she felt unfocused and confused. She tried to sit up and bumped her head on something. Her eyes flew open, and she couldn't see anything. She tried to fight her rising panic and began to feel around herself. Something was not right at all.

She was curled up and tried to straighten her legs. There wasn't room to do so. She had a pillow under her head, and she was covered by a blanket. She had on a dress rather than a sleeping shift. She put her hands out in the pitch blackness as far as she could to the sides and above her, and she tapped her knuckles against it, recognizing the sound of wood. She was in some kind of box. She raised her hands above her and moved them to the corners and down to feel the edges of the lid. She was in a trunk.

Psyche's forehead wrinkled as she tried to remember how she got there. She couldn't. She tried to recall the last thing she *did* remember. That was dinner with Islington and Pandora. She put her thumb to her mouth and chewed on it worriedly, trying to remember anything else, but everything beyond that was a complete haze.

She still felt as if she were rocking, and there were a few times when she could feel herself going sideways as her knees pressed into the side of the trunk. The roaring noise in her ears had not lessened, and it was, in fact, so loud she could scarcely hear herself think. There were occasional, booming thunderclaps that would rattle her teeth, and all the while she was trapped in the dark. Her panic didn't slacken and only became worse when she suspected she was on a boat or a ship of some type and that it was being tossed about in a bad storm.

Psyche pushed her hands against the lid of the trunk, but it wouldn't move. She pushed even harder, but it remained firm. She pulled the blanket from over her to free her legs and tried to push at the lid with both her hands and feet. She strained and pushed until she was gasping from the exertion, and still it wouldn't budge. Her panic escalated to outright hysteria. She began to loudly pound on the sides of the trunk.

"Help me!" she yelled. "Let me out!"

She pounded as hard as she could and kicked and yelled. Other than the storm, she couldn't hear anything. She realized with terror that no one could hear her. Dark imaginings began to fill her head, things like the ship sinking and her being left in the trunk to sink to the bottom of the ocean and drown without anyone realizing she was there. Her chest began to tighten until she couldn't breathe, and she became frenzied in her efforts to free herself.

She continued to scream and yell, tears streaming down her cheeks. She turned over onto her knees and tried to raise the lid of the trunk using her back to no avail. She could only imagine there was something sitting on top of it. She turned onto her back again and tried kicking out the end. The trunk was too small for her to put any power behind it and apparently very well made.

"Please! Somebody! Please, let me out!" she sobbed.

She could feel the trunk had a lining of some sort, and she began to tear at it with her nails, hoping that if she could remove it, the sides would be made of slats that would weaken without the lining and enable her to break through. She could feel her nails breaking and shredding until her fingertips were throbbing. The lining held tight in most places, and it was made of solid wood beneath. All her efforts proved useless.

She put her hands to the side behind her head, and she felt three, one-inch, round holes. She turned over and put her eye to one of them to look out at her surroundings. She could see only darkness until there was a flash of lightning. All she could see then was a white wall about three feet away from the hole. She turned in the other direction and felt more holes. She put her eye to one and waited for another flash of lightning. There was a doorway. The door was open, swinging on its hinges in time with the rocking of the ship. Beyond it was another door that was closed. She had only minute consolation that she was not in the hold or the bilge, and the appearance of it seemed to confirm she was indeed on a ship. How she had come to be there and why were a mystery.

Psyche was tiring. She continued to beat her aching hands against the side of the trunk, but there wasn't much force behind it. She had yelled and screamed so much her voice was growing hoarse. She could barely manage more than a whisper. She continued to cry helplessly, and all she had left to do was pray the ship didn't sink before someone found her or that whoever had taken her would let her out soon.

The storm was still raging when Sheerness went below. He sent for Higginbotham to relieve him. He didn't like leaving, but he was exhausted, wet, and frozen to the bone from the rain that drenched him even through his slicker. If he didn't rest, he would do more harm than good. He would have a few hours sleep and dry out; then he would relieve Higginbotham.

He went through the door of the officers' mess to the alcove and secured it. He began removing his clothes as soon as he closed the door. He couldn't light a fire because of the pitching and yawing of the ship, but he could crawl into bed under a thick pile of blankets, which he did tiredly.

He was on the point of dozing off when the sound of wood banging against wood jarred him. The wind howling didn't bother him. The thunder also didn't bother him. The occasional soft thud as something shifted didn't even bother him. They were all expected noises, and there was nothing to be done for them. The sound of the door banging on its hinges, however, was something that would keep him awake and was easy enough to fix.

Sheerness sighed tiredly and got up. The door to his cabin was no longer there. As there were no guests in the other cabins, he had seen no point in having two doors to his room. A flash of lightning showed him that it was the door to the cabin on the left. He grabbed the handle on the door and was about to close it when another flash of lightning illuminated the interior of the room. He saw the two trunks stacked and tightly secured against the wall, and he frowned in confusion. He didn't recognize them, and he had no idea how they got there. He shrugged and started to close the door tightly. He would worry about it after he had some sleep...and after the storm was over.

"Please, help me."

Sheerness almost had the door closed when he heard the disembodied female voice. He opened the door and looked around. Other than the two trunks, nothing was out of place, and there was certainly no one—least of all a woman—in the room. He shook his head, deciding he was so tired his mind was playing tricks. He had his hand on the knob when it came again.

"Someone let me out."

He could barely hear it above the wind. It sounded so defeated and forlorn. If he didn't know better, he might have thought it was a ghost. He tilted his head sideways and looked at the trunks. He went to his cabin and returned with a lamp. He lit the one on the wall just above the top trunk and looked at them. Judging by the craftsmanship and materials, they were expensive. It was unlikely they belonged to any of the crew, with the exception of Dr. Felton. Sheerness thought they were too costly even for the good doctor.

It was while he was standing close to them that Sheerness could hear a soft thumping noise. He put his ear to the top trunk, but it wasn't there. He got down on his hands and knees beside the bottom trunk. His forehead wrinkled concernedly. There was someone in there, and judging by the voice he had heard, it was a woman. He went back to his room to pull on some pants and returned to the cabin to undo the trunks. Once he had the rope untied, he lifted the top trunk out of the way and moved the bottom one far enough away from the wall to lift the lid. When he did, his face paled in alarm.

Psyche lay curled up in the bottom with both her hands bleeding. The lining inside the trunk had been shredded, and there were smears of blood that made it obvious she had been trying to claw her way out. When her hands had given out, she had begun to pound with her knee, and it was scraped and bleeding. Her eyes were closed, and her hands were held closely against her chest. She was so out of her mind, she didn't even realize the lid was open. She continued to pound her knee against the side.

"Please, let me out," she pleaded quietly, and a pained expression came over Sheerness's face when she did it because he could see she was putting every effort she had into yelling at the top of her lungs, and it came out as no louder than if she had simply spoken in a normal voice.

"*Mon dieu,*" he whispered brokenly.

He bent down and gently lifted her out of the trunk to carry her to the bunk. He lit the lamp on the wall there and sat beside her on the edge of the mattress. She was still insensible, and he reached out a hand to brush it against her cheek. Her eyes flew open at the contact, and she reacted with a quickness and violence that astounded him.

She used one hand to push his away from her face, and then she raised the other to hit the heel directly upward against his chin with a force that snapped his teeth together and made him fall to the floor, his vision momentarily blurred. She scampered to the corner of the bunk farthest away from him and curled up with her arms around her knees protectively, her face pale with hysteria, and he could see she was delirious with exhaustion and mental distress. She might even have gone a little mad because it didn't seem she recognized him at all.

He gingerly rubbed his chin and slowly stood up from the floor, his feet unsteady as much from the storm as from the force of the blow she had given him. She started at the movement, and he thought she might attack him. This was something beyond him, and after he gave her one last look to determine whether or not she was going to move, he left the room and made sure to lock the door behind him.

Sheerness went back to his cabin and pulled on a shirt, and then he went to the officers' mess and the door of Dr. Felton's cabin. He knocked on it loudly to be heard above the storm, and it was momentarily answered by Felton, looking at him blearily after being awakened from a sound sleep.

"I'm sorry to disturb you, but there's something that needs your immediate attention. If you could come with me, please," said Sheerness urgently.

The doctor frowned for a moment as he tried to collect his thoughts, but he nodded and followed Sheerness. Once they were through the door to the alcove, Sheerness closed and locked it behind them. He paused with his hand on the door to Psyche's cabin and looked at Felton with a serious expression.

"You cannot breathe a word of this to any of the crew until I decide what to do about it. Do you understand?"

Felton's frown deepened even further, but he nodded. Sheerness unlocked the door and directed Felton to enter the cabin. The doctor took one look at the girl curled up in the corner, and his eyes rounded in shock. He looked at Sheerness as the earl shut and locked the door behind them.

"Oh, my God, that's…," he trailed off breathlessly.

"Yes," said Sheerness gravely.

"What on Earth's happened to her?"

"I found her shut in a trunk." He pointed to the open one on the floor. "That one. It was underneath the other one. She couldn't get out. I can only assume she's been in there since we left London. I don't know how she got there." He shook his head. "We'll worry about that later. Right now, you need to tend to her."

"Of course," said Felton quickly.

Felton started to approach the bed, and Psyche looked at him warily. She was still not herself. Sheerness hoped the madness was only temporary. He had heard tales of the lunatics in Bedlam. He had seen his brother-in-law and knew what happened to him. He couldn't bear the thought of her being this way. Felton raised a calming hand as he came nearer.

"Hallo, Lady Psyche. Do you remember me? It's Dr. Felton," he said soothingly. She stayed curled up in the corner, looking at him as if she might attack him any minute. "I understand you've had a nasty time of it," continued Felton. "Do you mind if I take a look?"

He was standing at the edge of the bed when she sprang at him, and Sheerness watched in astonishment as she easily knocked Felton down and tried to run for the door. Her knee was badly hurt, and she fell after only a step.

Sheerness knelt beside her and grabbed her wrists to keep her from striking out, which it was obvious she would have done from the way she struggled to get free and glared at him wildly. Felton calmly stood and looked at her.

"Slap her," he said quickly.

"What?" asked Sheerness in disbelief.

"That's what I would have done had she let me get close enough. She's in shock. Slap her," said Felton firmly.

Sheerness looked from the doctor to Psyche uncertainly. She was clearly out of her mind. She didn't recognize either of them. They couldn't tend to her injuries if she wouldn't let them get close to her. Sheerness held his breath and slapped her across her left cheek. He didn't hit her as hard as he could have, but the blow stunned her. Her eyes widened, and then he saw awareness slowly return. Her forehead wrinkled in confusion as she looked at him.

"What? I—" she stammered disconcertedly, and then she looked at her hands where Sheerness still held them by the wrists and saw her fingers. She remembered what had happened. "Oh, my God," she gasped brokenly, and her eyes filled with tears.

Sheerness pulled her close and held her, and she wrapped her arms around his neck tightly and buried her face in his shoulder. He picked her up and carried her to the bunk, but she didn't want to let go of him. He gave Felton a helpless glance, and the doctor nodded.

Felton came closer and examined her hands where she had her arms around the earl's neck, his expression critical as he looked at them. She had mangled them badly, but they would heal. The biggest problem would be infection. He left the cabin and momentarily returned carrying a basin and pitcher of water and his bag. Sheerness sat down with her on the edge of the bed.

"Felton needs to look at your hands," he said quietly, rubbing her back.

Psyche took her arms from around his neck after a minute and turned in his lap to hold them out toward the doctor. She kept her head resting on Sheerness's shoulder, her forehead nestled against his jaw. He felt her wince as Felton began to clean her hands with some water in the basin, and he smoothed a hand over her back while the doctor tended to them. Once he had put on some salve to help them heal, Felton started to put away his things.

"Wait," said Sheerness. "There's one more."

He lifted the skirt of her dress to show Felton her knee. The silk of her stocking had been shredded, and the area over her kneecap was raw and bloody. It was already starting to bruise, and a purplish-blue tinge to her skin covered her entire knee and well above and below it. Felton removed her slipper and stocking and cleaned it as gently as he could, and then he wrapped it with a bandage. He looked up at her face, and after a moment's thought, he pulled a bottle and small spoon from his bag. He poured some of the liquid into the spoon and held it out to Psyche.

"I want you to take this. It will help you sleep," said Felton gently.

Psyche looked at it for a moment, and then she reluctantly sat up to open her mouth. She grimaced at its bitter taste. She knew it was laudanum, but she throbbed and ached so much, she had to agree it would probably do her some good. Sheerness felt her grow even limper in his arms as it began to take effect, and he gently eased her onto the bunk. He laid her head onto the pillows, and she looked at him sleepily, her forehead wrinkled with a frown. He covered her with a blanket from the foot of the bed, and then he stood up to leave. Psyche reached out a hand toward him.

"Don't go," she whispered.

Sheerness looked to Felton then back to her. "I'll be back," he said gently.

He walked out with the doctor, carrying the lamp from his room and closed the door behind them to talk without Psyche overhearing. The storm had slackened considerably, but it was still raining. The rocking of the ship had become almost a gentle roll, and there was only an occasional rumble of thunder. Felton looked at him gravely as they stood in the alcove.

"She will be all right, physically at least, I think. The trauma of being locked in a trunk for three days, however, is not something she will easily overcome." Felton scratched his forehead thoughtfully as he looked at Sheerness. "You've no idea how she came to be locked in that trunk?"

"Absolutely none. Before Neath died, she was coming on this voyage, but afterwards, she could no longer go."

"Hmm, do you think she might have done this herself?"

Sheerness looked at Felton in disbelief. "I find it unlikely someone as intelligent as she is would intentionally have herself trapped in a trunk. You saw her hands and her knee. If she had known where she was, she wouldn't have been that frantic to get out."

"You're probably right," said Felton thoughtfully. "She should stay in bed for at least a day with that knee. She didn't damage the kneecap, I don't think, but she's probably bruised the bone. Were we on land, I would tell her not to walk any great distances or go riding for at least a week or two, but I don't see that as being a problem on a ship," said Felton with a slight smile.

"She paces."

"Hmm, well, she'll not be doing that for a week then," said Felton dryly. "This is completely improper. She has no chaperone or guardian." He looked at Sheerness calmly. "I don't expect you'll turn around and take her home."

"No, that's not possible," said Sheerness evenly. "As for her having a chaperone or guardian, she'll be under my protection, and that is as close to propriety as we will come. Her brother was my closest friend, and my family and hers have known each other for years...since I was wee. The crew is a decent one, but I'll try to keep her out of sight. I've planned to stop in Vigo to resupply. It's a big port, and it shouldn't be difficult to find a ship sailing to England. I'll send a letter to her family to let them know where she is."

"Why don't you send *her* back?"

"Then she'll no longer be under my protection. I will not let that happen."

"I understand," said Felton, yawning tiredly. "I'll return to my cabin now. Come get me if you need me. If she's still awake when you go back in, try to give her some water. Three days without any is not good for her."

"Thank you, doctor, and good night," said Sheerness quietly, giving him a clap to the shoulder.

Sheerness watched him go and latched the door. He went to his own cabin and retrieved a water pitcher and glass and took them back to Psyche's cabin. He caught her attempting to unbutton her dress. It was just not possible because of her fingers. He was amazed she was still awake. He thought the laudanum would have put her completely out. If she kept trying to use her fingers, she was going to rub all the ointment off of them, and that wasn't good. Her thumbs were the only digits that hadn't been damaged.

"You should be sleeping," he said quietly as he closed and locked the door.

"Can't breathe," mumbled Psyche hoarsely.

Sheerness set the pitcher and glass on the desk and walked over to the bed. "Turn around."

Psyche looked at him distrustfully for a minute, but then she turned to let him unfasten the back of her dress. Even with the laudanum, she couldn't sleep with so many clothes, and her hair would have to come down, too. Quite a bit of it had already come down anyhow, and she could only imagine how frightful she looked. She was actually afraid to go to sleep, and she wasn't sure she could even if she were more comfortable. She was afraid she might wake up and find herself locked in a box again. Sheerness helped her slide her dress off her shoulders and gently eased the sleeves over her hands.

"Can you stand up?"

Psyche nodded uncertainly and carefully moved her legs over the side of the bunk. She winced and sucked in air through her teeth as she bent her knee, and she put all of her weight on her right foot. She wove unsteadily as she stood, but she only had to remain upright long enough for the dress to fall to the floor. While she was standing, Sheerness quickly pulled the blankets back so she could get under them, and she sat back down as she began to feel dizzy from the laudanum. Sheerness removed her other slipper and stocking and helped her put her legs onto the bunk and under the blankets.

Psyche lifted her hands to her hair to remove the pins, and while she was able to locate them, she couldn't tighten her fingers onto them enough to pull them out. Sheerness leaned over her and took them out, and then he ran his fingers through her hair to unwind it and work out some of the tangles. She could do with a brush, but he wasn't about to tell her that. He fluffed the pillows for her, and she lay back against them.

He adjusted the blankets over her, and then he went to pour her a glass of water. Felton had said she needed to drink some if she was awake, and it didn't seem like she intended to go to sleep. For a moment when he took it to her, she seemed as if she weren't going to take it. She held it between her palms, and he wasn't surprised when she quickly drained the entire glass.

"More?"

Psyche nodded, and he refilled the glass. He brought it back to her and sat beside her on the edge of the bed. She continued to look at him with a frown etched between her brows, and he could tell she was thinking about something very intently. She had to be exhausted and was dosed with laudanum, and still she wouldn't stop thinking. Sheerness didn't know how she managed it.

"I'm on your ship?" she asked him quietly.

"Yes," said Sheerness with a nod. "Do you know how you got here?"

The furrows deepened as she tried to recall the time between supper and when she woke up in the trunk. She couldn't remember. She shook her head.

"You didn't...," she began, and he could see she found it distressing.

"Oh, no," said Sheerness soothingly. "I could never."

Psyche nodded. She didn't think he would have, but she had to hear him say it. She looked at the trunks against the far wall of the cabin. The one she had been in still sat with the lid open. From the outside, in the light, she recognized them as being her own...the ones she had intended to take aboard this very ship. As she looked at them, she realized one must have been on top of the other, and she saw the piece of rope lying nearby. Why two trunks? The wrinkles in her forehead would not go away as she thought.

"How long has it been?" she asked Sheerness softly as she continued to look at the trunks.

"This is our third night out from London. We sailed Saturday morning, the thirteenth, as planned." He reached out a gentle hand to smooth it across her forehead soothingly. "You should go to sleep," he said softly.

"Can't," said Psyche, and she raised her thumb to her mouth to begin chewing on the side of it.

Sheerness pulled it away from her mouth. "Then we have a problem because I'm not sleeping until you do, and I *really* need to sleep," he said dryly with a slight smile.

Psyche knew he was right, and she felt guilty she was keeping him awake. It had to be very late. The laudanum had eased the pain in her hands and knee, but she was afraid to sleep. Knowing she was there with Sheerness, someone she recognized, even if she didn't completely trust him, helped lessen her fear somewhat, but she had to have gone from Pandora's house to the *Medea*, and she trusted her sister implicitly. It was foolish, but she was afraid if she went to sleep, she would wake up locked in another trunk or somewhere else she didn't know. A tear escaped from the corner of her eye as she felt a knot of panic forming in her stomach.

"Oh, don't cry," he said soothingly, reaching out a hand to wipe the tear off her cheek. "You're safe now. I won't let anything happen to you." He lay down beside her and pulled her close protectively. "I'll stay right here."

Psyche sighed tiredly and relaxed against him, resting her head onto his chest. He smoothed a comforting hand over her back and kissed the top of her head. The sound of his heartbeat in her ear and his arms wrapped tenderly around her began to do what the laudanum could not, and she finally let her eyes close and drifted off to sleep. When Sheerness heard the steadiness of her breathing, he sighed with relief and finally went to sleep himself. There would be time enough tomorrow to determine how she had come to be there.

Chapter Nineteen

Sheerness opened his eyes with a start, for a moment unsure of where he was. As he felt the body pressed close to his, it all came back to him. Psyche continued to sleep, her head resting on his chest. The sun was shining brightly through the window, and he wondered what time it was. Well beyond the time he should have been up, he was sure. He looked at Psyche's head where it lay on his chest, and the sun glinted off something not far away from it. It was the watch she carried on the chain around her neck. He carefully picked it up to look at the time. He let it drop back and softly hit his head against the pillow a few times before he closed his eyes and rubbed a hand over his face.

He carefully eased himself off the bunk without waking Psyche. It wasn't easy with the railing, her injuries, and her head on his chest, but he did manage it. Once he was standing, he adjusted the blankets over her and bent down to kiss her cheek. He needed to meet with his officers, and then he would bring her some food. She had to be starving. He'd only missed breakfast, and he was famished. She was sleeping peacefully, and it could only be good for her.

He left the room and closed the door behind him. He made sure it was securely latched but not locked. He didn't think it would come open, and he didn't want Psyche to wake up, decide to leave her room, and find it locked. She would only find it upsetting. He went to his cabin and hurriedly put on some socks and his boots, and then he tucked in his shirt and put on a waistcoat. He looked in the mirror and combed his fingers through his hair, decided it was hopeless, and left the room.

He wasn't surprised there was no one in the officers' mess. It was well past nine, and everyone was tending to their duties. He first met with Higginbotham and the bosun, Stockbridge, to find out how the *Medea* fared from the storm. He was pleased she had weathered it well, and none of the crew had been injured. He then asked them, Felton, and the rest of the officers to join them in the mess for a meeting.

Most of the officers were aware Psyche was to have traveled with them, but they had also been informed she would no longer be coming. Sheerness explained briefly that circumstances had changed. He didn't elaborate on how she came aboard the ship, only that she was. They all knew why she was not to have been with them, and Sheerness made sure they understood she was under his protection. He was unsurprised none of them voiced any complaints. They were all intelligent enough to know having a woman aboard would only pose a problem if it were the wrong *kind* of woman. She definitely wasn't.

He asked the second mate, Broughton, and the ship's master, Blossom, to meet with the rest of the crew as time and duties allowed to make them aware a woman was aboard and to be on their best behavior. Sheerness didn't expect it to be a problem. Once he had that out of the way, he asked Mr. Higginbotham to find the sailors who were on duty the night before they sailed and bring them to him. Before long, Bandy and Watkins stood looking at him nervously.

He tried to put them at ease. They had no part in what happened. They gave him a description of the man who brought the trunks, and Sheerness recognized Jim, Psyche's coachman. It was easy enough for them to believe the trunks belonged to the earl, and he understood why they put the heavier one on the bottom and lashed them to the wall. The only puzzlement was *why* Jim had put her in a trunk and on the ship. Sheerness was beginning to realize part of what happened to Psyche was the result of sheer dumb luck. He thanked the two men for their information and sent them on their way.

After he had tended to all the necessary business and been given a status on their location and conditions, he went to see the cook, appropriately named Mr. Meals, and had him quickly put together a tray of food and a pot of tea. Meals offered to have one of the sailors carry it, but the earl said he would take care of it himself. He didn't want anyone to see Psyche yet—especially not in her chemise in bed—except him.

It wasn't easy to keep the tray balanced with the gentle rolling of the deck, especially when he climbed the stairs, but Sheerness made it to the waist deck and down the stairs to the after cabins without spilling anything. He went to the door of Psyche's cabin and put his ear to it to listen for any signs of movement. He didn't hear anything, and he carefully opened the door and walked in.

Psyche still slept, and she hadn't moved from where he had left her two hours previously. He set the tray on the desk, and as he did it, he thought he should get a bedside table of some sort. He also needed to get her washstand and mirror she had requested. He sat beside her on the bed and gently ran a finger down her cheek. Her eyes flew open, and she inhaled with a start.

"Hallo, sleepyhead," said Sheerness softly.

Psyche looked around herself in confusion, a little disoriented. She went to move a hand to her forehead and winced as her body felt like one massive ache, particularly her hands and one of her knees. She did recognize Sheerness, but it took her a moment to remember where she was and what had happened.

"Ow," she moaned, gingerly putting a hand over her eyes.

"All right?" asked Sheerness concernedly.

"I'm fairly sure I'll live," mumbled Psyche.

"Do you want me to get Felton?"

"No, I'll be fine," said Psyche quietly, her eyes still closed.

Her voice was still hoarse, and her fingers over her eyes looked terrible. He wasn't so confident Felton didn't need to come take another look at her.

"Are you sure?" he asked her gently.

She removed her hand and looked at him. The sun from the window was shining in her eyes, and she quickly determined if she was going to spend any amount of time in this room, she would have to move the pillows to the other end if she was going to sleep this late again. He was looking at her worriedly, and she did her best to give him an assuring smile.

"I'll be fine," she repeated quietly.

"Are you hungry?"

She thought about it for a moment. "I could eat," she said agreeably. She wasn't really hungry, but she was sure she should be.

Sheerness helped her sit up after raising the pillows against the wall, and then he retrieved the tray from the desk and carefully balanced it on the bed.

"I can't eat all that," said Psyche, shaking her head.

"It's not all for you," said Sheerness with a grin. "I haven't eaten since last night, and it's nearly dinnertime."

"Oh," said Psyche dimly. She lifted her watch to look at the time. He was right. It was almost noon.

The cook had provided them with bread and cheese and lamb stew. While she had no trouble with the bread and cheese, the earthenware bowl of stew was hot, and when she tried to hold it in her hand, the heat of it made her fingertips begin to throb. She tried balancing it against her stomach, using only her thumb at the edge, but that proved uncomfortable as well. She grabbed one of the pillows and laid it across her stomach to set the bowl on, and that was better. When Sheerness poured her a cup of tea, she even managed to keep that nestled onto the pillow so she wouldn't have to hold it the entire time.

As they ate, Psyche would occasionally glance over to the trunks. She was still puzzled at their number. She had been in one, so what was in the other? Was it empty? They were definitely her trunks, but she thought they had been sent to Wilderland. She hadn't seen a need to keep them in London after Myron died. She supposed during the hurried confusion of the family's abrupt return to Glamorgan, they could have been sent with her things to Pandora's. But it was odd someone had abducted her and carted her off in a pair of trunks that belonged to her. That could be coincidental, but stowing her onto the ship of someone she knew, heading somewhere she wanted to go, could not be.

Sheerness saw her looking at the trunks. He knew she had to be puzzling over how she had come to be there as much as he was. He would discuss it with her, but he wanted her to eat first. She was going to heal, but an empty stomach would not help matters any. Once she finished her stew, he left her with her tea and put the tray back on the desk. He sat beside her on the bunk and looked at her calmly.

"Have you remembered anything more about how you got here?"

Psyche's forehead wrinkled as she tried to see if anything else had returned to her. "I remember having dinner with Islington and Pandora on Friday night." She shrugged. "The next thing I remember is waking up in the trunk."

"I talked to the sailors on watch Friday night and Saturday morning." He paused for a moment as he tried to choose his next words. "I think, from the description they gave me of the man who brought the trunks, it was Jim."

Psyche's eyes rounded in surprise. "Jim? My *driver*, Jim?"

"Yes."

"Oh, surely not!" said Psyche, shaking her head. "Why would he do something like that?"

"I don't think he intended for you to be trapped," said Sheerness quietly. "At least, I don't *want* to think he intended to, but he is a criminal."

"No, he isn't," said Psyche flatly.

Sheerness raised a dubious eyebrow. "He said himself that he was a horse thief."

Psyche rolled her eyes exasperatedly and shook her head. "He *was* a horse thief…when he was about twelve years old, and he was never what you could call a *criminal*. His parents died of cholera when he and his sister, Mary, who happens to work in our kitchen, were both very young. They had no family, and they were living on the streets. They were *starving*. He fell in with a crew that worked near Lincoln's Inn. Luckily, Mary was still too young—only five, or she could have wound up a prostitute. As it was, she became a diver in Covent Garden. Jim tried to steal my father's horse, and my father took pity on him and gave him an *honest* job. Mary as well once she was old enough. If it was Jim, he had no intention at all of me being harmed."

Sheerness looked at her in dumbfounded silence. She knew the man better than he did, obviously. He also knew from what he had seen that she had the Cockney's complete loyalty. Considering what she had just told him, it was easy to understand why. He scratched his chin thoughtfully as he looked at her.

"The sailors who were on watch put the trunk you were in on the bottom because it was the heavier of the two. It's standard practice to put heavier on the bottom and lash things down if they're not going to be used often. It keeps them from getting tossed around if there's a storm. If Jim were familiar with ships, he would have thought to tell them not to stack them, or to put the heavier one on top."

Psyche gave him a sardonic grin. "Lovely. It just takes being accident prone to a whole other level."

She lifted her mangled hands and looked at them. Her thumbs were fine, but the rest of her fingers were horrible. She hadn't managed to completely rip out all the nails, just three of them. Of the other five, two were almost pulled out, and the remaining three were broken down to the quick. The ends of her fingers were bruised and swollen, and unsightly was a polite way to describe them. They also throbbed in time with her heartbeat. She looked as if she had been interrogated during the Inquisition. She looked back at Sheerness.

"Is there anything in the other trunk?"

Sheerness's forehead wrinkled. "I haven't looked. Does it matter?"

"Well, they *are* my trunks," said Psyche dryly.

"What?"

"They're the trunks I bought to pack my things in for the journey that I assume I am now taking."

"Yes, whether you were intending to or not, you're going to Greece and Egypt." He gave her a wry smile. "Are you sure they're yours?"

Psyche nodded. "Oh, yes, I bought them at Beacham and Bagley."

Sheerness frowned and got up from the bed. It was beyond coincidence she would have been put aboard with an extra trunk, let alone on his ship, if someone did it with criminal intent, especially not if they were *her* trunks. He closed the lid on the trunk she had been in because he couldn't bear to look at the blood smeared on the inside of it any longer, and then he opened the lid on the other one. It was carefully packed completely to the top, and he couldn't understand how the one she had been in could have possibly been heavier. It was true most of what he saw was clothing, but it was completely full. He turned to look at her, and her gaze was as dumbfounded as his own. He looked back down at the contents and saw the letter sitting there, centered perfectly in all of it, with her name on. He picked it up and brought it to her on the bed.

Psyche frowned as she took it from him. "This is Pandora's handwriting." She broke the seal and unfolded the letter. It was definitely from her twin.

"*Dearest Psyche, By now you are aware you are on your way to Greece and Egypt. I hope you have a good time, and don't forget you promised to write me as often as you can.*

"*Forgive me for drugging you and stowing you away, but I knew you would never go on your own—not now...not with Sheerness. Don't blame anyone else. It was all my idea. Myron asked me to make sure you went, and I could think of a no more perfect time or way than now...with Sheerness. You kept saying you would get there one day, but you have wanted to go for so long. I could not let you wait any longer.*

"*I will be sure to tell Mama and Papa where you have gone. I will also make sure they know it was not your fault. They will understand. We all want you to be happy, Psyche, and I know this will make you so very.*

"*I tried to pack everything you might need. I am sure I have forgotten something...probably many things. I am sorry if I did. Please, please, don't be angry with me for doing this. I love you, Pandora.*"

Psyche folded the letter and placed her hand on top of it where she set it on the pillow. She took a deep breath and closed her eyes. It was all a terrible accident. No one could have imagined things would unfold the way they had—not Pandora, not Jim, and certainly not Psyche. It was almost comedic the way something that had been planned with the best of intentions had gone so horribly wrong. She couldn't be angry, and there was no one to blame.

"Are you all right?" asked Sheerness concernedly as she continued to sit with her eyes closed.

She finally opened them and looked at him. "I will be," she said quietly.

"Am I understanding correctly when I think your sister did this?"

"No. No one did. Pandora drugged me and put me in the trunk, probably with Chrissoula's and most likely with Maiyin's help. Jim took me to the ship, and he probably carried me aboard. The sailors stacked the trunks and tied them down. None of them did any of it with the intention of hurting me. It was all just a misunderstanding."

"A *misunderstanding?*" said Sheerness in disbelief. "Look at your hands!" He pulled the blankets off of her and exposed her bandaged leg. "Look at your knee! You were *out of your mind* last night when I found you, completely unhinged, and you call it a *misunderstanding?*"

"Yes," said Psyche simply.

"Well, maybe you can't be angry with her, but I can," he said darkly.

"Then you'll have to be angry with Myron, too, because he told her to do it," said Psyche exasperatedly.

"What?" He looked as if someone had just knocked the wind out of him.

"In his letter to her, I suppose, Myron told her to see that I went."

"I don't think drugging you and locking you in a trunk was what your brother had in mind," said Sheerness stiffly.

Psyche shrugged. "Maybe not, but Pan knew I wouldn't go now, not without Myron...not with you. She thought there was no time like the present, and if I didn't go now...with you, I never would."

Sheerness looked at her. He couldn't understand how she could so calmly accept what had happened to her and call it a *misunderstanding*. Seeing her last night had frightened him far more than he would have believed possible. He could not accept it had been caused by a series of unfortunate events with the same placidity she seemed to have. He wasn't sure he ever would. He stood up from the bed and looked at her impassively.

"I cannot be so forgiving," he said in measured tones. "I have things I need to do. Is there anything you need?"

Psyche looked at him assessingly for a moment. He was furious, and she couldn't decide if it was all for Pandora. He would eventually have to come to terms with it, whether he wanted to or not. She could *not* be angry with Pandora, and he had no right to be.

"Now you mention it, I could use a...um...chamber pot, if you have such somewhere or something," Psyche stammered. "I don't see one anywhere in here, and...."

"How is your knee?" he asked her shortly.

"It hurts, but it will be fine. Why?" she asked in confusion.

"There is a water closet in my cabin," said Sheerness evenly.

"There is?" she asked blankly. "I don't remember seeing one. I remember the shower-bath."

"The other corner."

"Oh!" said Psyche, her eyes rounding in surprise. "I thought that was a regular closet."

"No."

"It is just around the corner," said Psyche reasonably. "I don't see any reason why I *can't* go that far." She started to swing her legs over the side of the bunk, and her knee felt as if someone hit it with a sledgehammer. *"Bloody hell!"* she gasped.

"Here, I'll carry you," sighed Sheerness, and he went to pick her up.

Psyche held up a hand. "No, no, I'll manage," she said evenly. "You go tend to your *things."* She put a hand on the railing and stood up. As long as she didn't put any weight on it, she would be fine.

"Do you intend to hop there?" asked Sheerness sarcastically.

"That's exactly what I intend to do," said Psyche through stiff lips. Her knee hurt.

"On a moving ship?" Sheerness shook his head and picked her up. "Always so pig-headed," he muttered.

"And you're not?" said Psyche tartly as he carried her out of her cabin and into his to the corner with the water closet.

He carefully put her down and opened the door. Psyche looked at it. It was simple but adequate. She recognized the design and suspected it was another one of Myron's suggestions. He hadn't come up with it; Psyche and Pandora had with their father, but the plan for it could only have been given to Sheerness by her brother. It was small, and when the door was closed it would be dark. Sheerness looked at her expectantly.

"Can I have a light, please?" she asked quietly.

Sheerness' expression softened as he saw the way her face paled at the thought of going into some place small and dark. He found a candle and lit it for her. She gratefully took it from him and hobbled in and closed the door. Sheerness walked over to his desk while she tended to things and looked at the papers sitting there. He would need to update the log, and he would also need to make a list of things he needed to get while in Vigo to make Psyche's accommodations more comfortable. He looked up when she opened the door.

"Better?" he asked her with a slight smile.

"Oh, yes, much. Thank you," sighed Psyche. "I need some crutches."

"Why?" asked Sheerness as he picked her up to carry her back to her cabin.

"Because you can't carry me around everywhere, and I'm *not* going to stay in bed or my cabin all the time."

"How do you expect to manage a pair of crutches with your hands the way they are?" he asked as he laid her back on her bunk.

"My thumbs aren't hurt," said Psyche stubbornly.

"Humph," said Sheerness. "Felton said you need to stay off it at least for a day, and then no walking long distances or riding for at least a week."

"I'm on a ship," said Psyche dryly. "Where am I going to walk? I doubt very seriously Jim managed to sneak Achilles into your hold, and even if he did, where would I ride him?"

"I'll see what I can arrange," said Sheerness mildly.

"Thank you."

"Is there anything else? Are you sure you don't want me to send Felton to look at you?"

"No, I'm fine," said Psyche calmly.

Sheerness nodded briefly and left the room, closing the door behind him. Psyche sat in bed for a time, looking around herself at the room, out the window, at the ceiling. It lasted for about thirty minutes before she became indescribably bored. Her eyes lit on the trunk Pandora had packed with her belongings. She was curious what her sister might have thought she would need. She would have no shortage of clothing. Looking at them from the bed, she didn't see anything black. She had to wonder about her wardrobe because Chrissoula, Maiyin, and Agniezka had made it without her ever seeing it.

Psyche looked from the trunk to the door then back again. Sheerness was tending to *things*. It would be awhile before he returned. She hoped her sister had packed a brush. Psyche needed one…immediately. It wasn't such a long distance from the bed to the trunk, much closer than Sheerness's cabin. It couldn't be more than eight feet. She carefully moved her legs over the side of the bed and stood. As long as she didn't put weight on her left leg, it didn't hurt too much, but when she bent it to make it easier to hop to the trunk, she sucked in air through her teeth and bit the inside of her cheek at the pain. She looked at the chair by the desk. It was even closer. She hopped over to it and pulled it out with the back toward her. She moved it toward the trunk and hopped after it, keeping her hands on the back. It proved to be very helpful, and once she had it close to the trunk, she was able to sit down on it.

Psyche bent over and began to pull out the clothing to look at it. Her eyes began to round in alarm. There was not what could be called a dress anywhere to be found. There were ganseys and her split skirts, breeches and linen shirts. She found waistcoats and a slicker, as well as what looked like a man's top coat. Thankfully, there were no cravats. There were a few outfits that looked like the traditional Greek costumes Chrissoula wore, only much more ornate, but there were definitely no *normal* dresses. She found two saris, two galabias and an abaya. And then she found the *tsifteteli* costume.

"Oh, Pan, what have you given me?" she moaned.

The rest of the clothing was no better. She found chemises, but they were shorter than normal. She found a few dressing gowns, and she put one on over her chemise. She found some sleeping shifts, but they were not what she normally wore and could only be considered provocative. She found slippers, fans, gloves, a reticule and a drawstring bag, a sensible pair of walking boots, *men's* riding boots, sandals, and stockings and garters. There was a small wooden box with very little jewelry, but it did contain her several pairs of glasses, and there was also a small box that contained combs and pins for her hair, her hairbrush, and a comb. She had nothing to wear. A trunk full of clothing, and she had absolutely nothing to wear.

There were other things in the trunk besides clothes. She found her notebooks, and Pandora had also packed her drawings from the back of her necklace and the necklace itself. Psyche sighed with relief that her sister had at least not sent her completely unprepared. She thought, however, that she could have made do with less of the exotic clothing and more of her books. Perhaps then *this* trunk would have weighed more than the one she was in. She found a thick stack of paper, and a narrow wooden box with fountain pens, pencils, nibs, ink, and sealing wax. Her sister had also packed several watercolor tablets, her paints and brushes, and her chalks. She was beginning to feel somewhat better. It wasn't everything she would have wanted to take with her, but it was far better than she could have expected.

She found two other small wooden boxes, and she was still amazed this trunk had weighed less. One of the boxes contained her perfume, lotion, soap, and shampoo, and she dabbed a little of the perfume behind her ears. It had her depilatory, which she looked heavenward with thanks for. It had a toothbrush and tooth powder, and there was a set of tweezers, a pair of scissors, nail files, and nail lacquer. She was relieved her sister had remembered to include her feminine supplies. It wouldn't be too long before she needed them. There was also a large stoppered bottle with a thick, milky liquid inside. Psyche had no idea what it was, but Pandora had, rather practically, attached a label. *Soapwort. For washing clothes or other things.* Psyche remembered Pandora's adventurous soapwort experiments from the solarium. It *was* very handy, and she could imagine she would have to wash her own clothes for much of the trip if anyone would.

The last box was smaller and was worn at the edges and scratched. It was obviously not one her sister had bought specifically for Psyche. She opened it and found several small, stoppered bottles tied in place in the velvet-lined lid, labeled in Chinese, containing various liquids and herbs. The labels described what each bottle contained, their purpose, and how to prepare them. In the bottom, she found her bottle of sleeping draught, a bottle of laudanum, bandages, cotton wool, scissors, tweezers, a sewing kit, and a decent-sized, wide-mouthed jar.

"Oh, yes," sighed Psyche, lifting out the jar.

She was preparing to open it when she spotted the note on the small piece of paper folded on its side against the edge of the box. She put the jar back and lifted out the note and opened it.

"This box was a life saver many times between London and Edinburgh. Keung has refilled it with the things he thought would prove useful for you between London and wherever your travels may take you. I hope it serves you well. Love, Pan."

"Ahh," said Psyche softly, "the infamous Medicine Kit."

At the very bottom of the trunk, she found three letters, one from each of the maids. She opened and read them, and she would occasionally find herself chuckling amusedly at their comments, especially Chrissoula's, which she saved until last. By the time she came to the last of it, however, she had to blink back tears that stung her eyes as she read.

"Thea, there should be no more mourning for you. We honor best the ones we lose by living. No more black. Laugh and be happy. Chrissoula."

Psyche looked at the things piled around her. The sun was setting, and she wondered at the time. She lifted her watch on its chain; it was after five. She couldn't believe she had spent so much time going through the trunk.

She sat for a moment contemplatively, trying to decide how she was going to put it all away. She didn't intend to put it back in the trunk. She had it all out; she might as well put it where it belonged. Her knee had grown stiff and pained from sitting in the chair, but she might as well get started. She carefully stood and stacked things onto the seat a little at a time. She started with the things that belonged on the desk. That proved to be the heaviest chore, but it was also the shortest distance.

Once she had her paper, pens, art supplies, and notebooks arranged to her satisfaction, she put her garments onto the seat and put them away in the drawers under her bunk. There were six of them, and they were roomy; she was able to put away all her clothing and accessories without having to cram them. There was one drawer she purposely left empty on the top row at the end near the pillows.

She hobbled back to the trunk and picked up the boxes containing her glasses and jewelry and carried them back to the bed. She put them in the drawer and went back to the trunk for the box with her toiletry items and took it to the bunk. She was almost back to the bed with the medicine kit when there was a knock at the door. She looked from the trunk, to the bed, and back to the door. Her dressing gown was tied, and she was as presentable as she would ever be until she could use her brush.

"Who is it?" she called.

"Sheerness."

She really hadn't expected it would be anyone else. "Come in," she said mildly and continued on her way with the chair to the bunk.

"What are you doing up?" Sheerness asked in disbelief when he saw her.

"Putting away my things," said Psyche matter-of-factly.

She started to open the drawer to put in the medicine kit, but she changed her mind and set it on the bunk. She wanted to use some of Keung's ointment. She looked back to the trunk to make sure she had everything, and then she turned the chair to go back and close the lid. Sheerness moved in front of her.

"Sit down."

"If you'll close the lid on the trunk for me."

He pointed at the bunk. "Sit."

Psyche raised an eyebrow, but she went to the bunk. "I'm not a dog, you do realize?"

Sheerness looked at her darkly and closed the lid on the trunk. He moved it closer to the wall and turned it sideways to go on the other side of the desk. Psyche's room was becoming dark, which she hadn't noticed while she was working. She was relieved as Sheerness filled the lamp on the far wall with oil from a small cask he had brought with him, and then he came to the one by the bed to refill it as well. He left and returned momentarily with a rush to light both of them, and the room brightened considerably.

While he was tending to that, Psyche lifted the lid on her medicine kit and removed the jar of ointment and some bandaging. She opened her dressing gown and unfastened the bandage Felton had put on the night before. It stuck to her knee, and she gently pulled it off as tears stung her eyes.

"Now what are you doing?" asked Sheerness exasperatedly as he returned from putting the rush into the fire in his cabin.

"I'm putting another bandage on my knee, and then I'm going to put ointment on my fingers. Is that all right with you?" she asked tartly.

His lips tightened into a grim line. He saw the open wooden box on her bunk. "Where did you get that?"

"It was in my trunk," said Psyche absently as she carefully tried to put some of the ointment on her knee.

It stung, and she bit her bottom lip as she applied it. It would start to feel better soon. While she had nothing against Felton's handiwork, Keung's ointment was nothing short of miraculous. Once Psyche had it on the skinned part of her knee, she worked some of it into the surrounding bruising, and then she temporarily replaced the lid. She selected the largest square bandage she could find from those provided and put it over her knee, and then she wound some of the long narrow strip around it, cut it, and tied it securely into place. She heaved a deep sigh of relief once she was done. Her leg had started to tremor, and her hands were shaking from the pain, but it was over now.

She reopened the jar and put some of the ointment onto her fingers and worked it into the bruising on the palms of her hands. She didn't want it to rub off, but she didn't want to put bandages on her hands. She leaned over the side of the bunk and opened the drawer where she had put her gloves and retrieved a pair of short silk ones. She carefully eased them onto her hands and put the lid back on the jar. She looked through the bottles in the top of the box and untied one of them.

"Can you get me some water, please?" she asked Sheerness calmly, looking up at him.

He stood looking at her in bewilderment. Her leg had caused her a tremendous amount of pain, but she had methodically finished dressing it and her hands anyhow. Her eyes were sparkling with tears, but she acted as if nothing was wrong. Sheerness didn't know how she could be so calm.

"Do you want me to get it myself?" she asked him quietly.

Sheerness poured a glass of water from the pitcher on her desk and brought it to the bunk. She took it from him and added five drops from the bottle. She swirled it around to mix it together, and then she swallowed all of it without stopping. She made a moue of disgust and shuddered at the taste of it, but that, too, would help her feel better with less undesirable effects than laudanum.

"What was that?" he asked her as she tied the bottle back into the lid.

"For pain," said Psyche dimly. She closed the lid on the box, and she carefully leaned over the side of the bed and put the box into the drawer with the rest of her kits. She looked at Sheerness with a placid expression. "Did you want to see me for something?"

"Other than to see how you are and ask if you are hungry?" He looked at his watch. It was after nine. "I could have helped with that," he said evenly.

"With which? The unpacking or the bandaging?" she asked with a raised eyebrow.

"Both."

Psyche gave him a wan smile. "I mean no offense, but I didn't need you to help me."

Sheerness clenched his jaw on a retort and nodded his head briefly. He pulled the chair from the desk toward the edge of the bunk, turned it backward and sat across it, resting his elbows on the back.

"Felton said for you not to be out of bed for at least a day," he reproved.

"Would *you* have stayed in bed?" she asked him flatly. Sheerness pursed his lips. "I didn't think so."

"Are you hungry?" he asked, deciding to change the subject.

"I am rather, actually, but a trip to the water closet would be grand," said Psyche pleasantly.

"Of course," said Sheerness calmly.

He picked her up, and when she was nearer, Sheerness could smell her perfume. He had to fight the desire to lean closer to her neck and nuzzle it. She had one of her arms around his neck, the other one balanced against his chest, and her neck was *so* close. She was completely oblivious to the way he tightened his grip, her eyes on the way in front of them. Luckily, the distance wasn't far. Sheerness wasn't sure how much longer he could have resisted. He carefully set her on her feet and opened the door, and then he went to retrieve the lamp from his desk for her.

"Thank you," she said politely and went in and closed the door.

Sheerness exhaled gustily and rubbed a hand over his face. He walked to the other side of the cabin and poured himself a brandy, which he downed quickly. He stood looking out the window as he attempted to control the urges he felt. His reason for not wanting her to come on the trip reared its head more than figuratively. He would have to do his best to ignore it, especially right now. By the time Psyche opened the door, he had regained his self-control, and he managed to maintain it while he picked her up and carried her to her cabin by holding his breath until he had her placed back on her bunk.

"I'll go get you something to eat," he said neutrally once she was settled in under the blankets.

Psyche was puzzled as she watched him leave. She supposed he was distant because he was upset with her for being up and not letting him help. She hadn't meant to offend him when she said she hadn't needed his help. She had even told him so. She didn't know why he would expect *her* to stay in bed when he wouldn't. That wouldn't be fair.

Sheerness returned carrying a tray much like the one he had brought in for dinner, and it held much the same thing. There was more bread and cheese and lamb stew, but there was also a pitcher of dark brown beer, a bottle of Bordeaux, and apple pandowdy with clotted cream for dessert. Although it had been hot, and her appetite had not been particularly sharp at dinner, the lamb stew had been tasty, and she wasn't going to mind having it again.

Instead of retaking his seat in the chair, Sheerness sat on the edge of the bed. He balanced the tray on one of her thighs and one of his to make a table. The wine had already been uncorked, and he poured her a glass. Psyche gazed disappointedly to the beer.

"What?" he asked her mildly as he poured some of it into a tankard.

"I would like some beer, please," she said quietly.

Sheerness shrugged and put the tankard in front of her and took the wineglass. "We'll share...if you can keep up," he said with a slight smile.

Psyche raised an eyebrow and calmly began to eat. Her fingers felt much better with the ointment and the gloves. She was able to break off a piece of bread to dip into her stew with only a minor amount of discomfort. Of course, the gloves were becoming dirty, but it wasn't as if she would need white silk gloves in Greece or Egypt. She finished the last of the beer in the tankard and held it out to Sheerness. She looked at the wineglass and saw it was still almost half full. Sheerness looked at the tankard in surprise, and Psyche gave him a grin and shook the cup.

"I guess I'm thirsty," she said pertly.

Sheerness gave her an amused smile and shook his head, but he refilled the tankard. She was at least eating, and eating and drinking (anything) could only be good for her. Three days in a trunk without could have killed her. He still couldn't understand why she didn't blame her sister for what happened. She had to know she could have died. It completely baffled him, but he was happy she seemed to be recovering well.

"So where are we, exactly?" she asked him calmly.

"We're nearing Vigo."

"Spain?" asked Psyche with some surprise. Sheerness nodded. "The *Medea* goes faster than I thought she would." Sheerness gave her an insulted look. "It's only that she's bluff-bowed and round-bilged. Something narrower through the beam and more hard-chined would go faster...theoretically...like a sloop," she finished lamely as he looked at her with his eyebrows raised in disbelief.

"Hunh," said Sheerness noncommittally.

She had just demonstrated to him that she had far more knowledge than the average person—especially a female—about the construction of a sailing vessel. Someone who would know the difference between a *ship* and a *boat*. It was beyond him why she would have said what she did when he had given her and Myron a tour.

"So where are we going?" she asked him brightly. "I know we're going to Greece and Egypt, but where, exactly?"

"I haven't decided yet," said Sheerness flatly.

"Um, don't you think that might be important?" she asked haltingly.

"We're still at least a week or more away from the Aegean," said Sheerness dismissively. "Do you have somewhere in mind?"

"I'd like to see the Parthenon because Myron said I should, but if we're going to find anything—what was it you called it—*useful*, then I think we should go to Thessaloniki."

"Why there?" asked Sheerness curiously.

"Because I know someone there who can help us," said Psyche calmly. "He's somewhat in antiquities."

"Somewhat?"

"Well, not really, he's actually more of a smuggler...somewhat," said Psyche lamely.

"*What?*" asked Sheerness in disbelief.

"He's not really a *smuggler* smuggler. Oh, I can't explain it, but I know he can help us."

"Who is he?" asked Sheerness stiffly. A *smuggler?*

"His name is Nikos Andreanopoulos. He's Chrissoula's brother."

"Hunh," said Sheerness noncommittally.

"He really is perfectly respectable," said Psyche quickly. She could see Sheerness didn't think they should go to Thessaloniki.

"Mm-hmm," said Sheerness doubtfully. "Anywhere else?"

"Not in Greece, no. I have somewhere I want to go in Egypt, but I'm not sure where it is, really."

"I see," said Sheerness.

"Well, of course, there's Alexandria and Giza and Luxor, but I don't think this is any of those places."

"How can you know there's somewhere you want to go, and yet you don't know where it is?" asked Sheerness as he switched the empty tankard and wineglass and refilled them.

"Because I have a map," said Psyche calmly.

"If you have a map, how can you not know where it is?" asked Sheerness confusedly.

"Ooh," said Psyche frustratedly. "Look there on the desk and bring me the jeweler's box and the piece of paper underneath it."

She held on to the edges of the tray while Sheerness stood up and went to the desk. He brought the things back and sat down to rebalance the tray on his thigh. Psyche took them and opened the box. She pulled out the necklace and held it up for him to take.

"Your Derby necklace?" he asked as he looked at it. It was a very lovely piece.

"Yes. I found a map on the back of it," said Psyche excitedly.

Sheerness turned it over, but he didn't see any map. There were a few imperfections on the back of the large amber medallion, but not anything that remotely resembled a map...at least, not that he could see.

"I don't see a map," he said dismissively.

"I don't know if it will work, but hold it up to the lamp so the light shines through."

Sheerness looked at her doubtfully, but he obligingly did as she asked.

"I don't see a map," he repeated.

"Look at the amber with the back *toward* you," said Psyche impatiently.

"I still don't see anything," said Sheerness in an exasperated tone.

"Oh, well, I guess it only works in sunlight," sighed Psyche. "No matter. I've drawn it."

Sheerness retook his seat, and she handed him the drawing. It was definitely a map, but he couldn't believe it was on the back of her necklace.

"That was on the back of your necklace?" he asked doubtfully.

"It *is*," said Psyche defensively. "Sir James looked through the maps at the Museum, but he wasn't able to find anything…at least, not in the two weeks he had it before…," she trailed off and shrugged. "Anyhow, he was trying to compare it to what was there, and it didn't match. All of my maps are at Wilderland in the solarium, so I wasn't able to look at them for myself. So, you see, I have somewhere I want to go, but I don't know where it is."

"Hmm," said Sheerness indulgently.

He wasn't so sure that she wasn't imagining things. The map was very detailed, though. He absently looked at his watch. It was nearing midnight. He took the tray to the dumbwaiter in the officers' mess to lower it to the berth deck. He would make a few notations in the log, and then he wanted to go to bed. They would anchor at Vigo sometime during the night, and he planned to go ashore in the morning.

When he returned to her room, he put her necklace and drawing back on the desk, and then he took her to the water closet again. He refilled the pitcher from the water barrel in the mess and brought it back to pour some into the glass for her to take more of her pain medicine. Once she was settled in, he started to turn off the lamps. He was reaching for the one near the bed when Psyche stopped him.

"Leave that one on, please," she said quickly.

Sheerness looked down at her and nodded. "Good night."

"Good night," she said quietly.

Sheerness left her room and closed the door behind him. He went to his cabin and made a few entries in the log, and then he wrote a few letters. Once he was done, he went topside to check with Broughton on their status before he went to bed. It was after 1:30, and he was looking forward to lying down. He could see the light of the lamp in Psyche's room coming from the crack under her door as he went past. He almost stopped to see if she was asleep but thought better of it and went on to his room. It had been over an hour since he had left; he was sure she had to be sleeping already. He got undressed and lay down with a tired sigh. Within minutes, he was sound asleep.

Sheerness jolted awake in surprise, almost as if something had shook him. He looked around his cabin in confusion, but he didn't see anything out of place. He could tell from the motion of the ship they had dropped anchor, but he didn't think that was what woke him. Someone might have knocked at his door, but when he didn't hear it repeated, he decided that wasn't it either.

When he didn't notice anything unusual, he dropped his head back onto the pillows and started to drift off again.

As his eyelids almost drooped closed, he noticed there was no longer light coming from under the door to Psyche's cabin. He frowned slightly and sat up. He rubbed a hand over his face and stood up to put on his pants. He walked to her door and put his ear to it, listening intently for any sounds. Then he could hear it, a soft, gasping whimper. He opened the door to find Psyche wide awake, curled up in a ball in the corner of her bed, looking around her at the darkness with utter panic.

"Psyche?" he said concernedly.

"I *couldn't* sleep," she said brokenly, "and then the light went out."

Sheerness went to the bunk and pulled her close to him soothingly. She was quivering with fear, and she clung to him anxiously as he smoothed a hand over her hair. He lay down with her on the bunk spoon fashion and covered them with the blankets, putting one arm under her head beneath the pillows and wrapping the other around her waist.

"Why am I afraid of the dark? It's silly to be afraid of the dark," she said quietly, almost to herself.

"Shh," said Sheerness soothingly, giving her a gentle kiss on her neck.

"I misunderstood, that's all. I simply overreacted," she continued to mutter, but he could feel her relaxing in his arms.

"Go to sleep, *chere,* " said Sheerness with a yawn, and he tightened his arm around her waist.

He placed a line of soft kisses from her shoulder up her neck and happily nuzzled the spot just below her ear where the scent of her perfume was strongest. He smoothed his hand across her stomach to her ribs and rested his head onto the pillow behind hers. He could tell from her breathing and the supple way she pressed against him that Psyche had gone to sleep. Sheerness smiled peacefully and went to sleep as well. He would be perfectly content to do this every night if necessary.

Chapter Twenty

Psyche rolled onto her back and stretched languidly with a happy smile. She hadn't felt this well-rested in a long time. She could tell before she opened her eyes that the sun shining into her cabin would be bright, but she was so relieved she had slept long enough for it to be shining at all that she didn't care. Her hands and knee ached, but she felt absolutely wonderful anyhow.

She carefully squinted open her eyes to look around her cabin, and she wasn't surprised Sheerness was no longer there. She really hadn't expected him to be. She hadn't even expected him to come to her cabin the night before, and she didn't know why he had. She had thought she was being quiet. She had tried very hard to be. She had thought about taking some of her sleeping draught, but not only had she been unable to sleep, she had been afraid to sleep. She hoped that would go away, and she had no problem doing so when Sheerness held her, but she couldn't have him do that all the time, as enjoyable as it was.

She would have to do away with her utterly ridiculous fear of the dark. Being afraid to fall asleep was more understandable than being afraid of the dark, and even that was not an acceptable phobia to Psyche. She had no need to fear falling asleep. If she was going to have a fear from all of this, perhaps it would be more logical to be afraid to take food or drink from someone else…anyone else. But phobias were never logical…they wouldn't be called phobias otherwise. She didn't expect they would immediately go away, and she wasn't even certain they were actual phobias, but she would have to move beyond them somehow because the list of things she was afraid of was becoming far too long. If she were able to dispose of these two irrational fears, then perhaps she would see what could be done with her fear of heights.

Psyche sat up and looked at her watch. She almost giggled when she saw it was nearly ten. As it was, she grinned widely. She looked at her hands in the gloves. They didn't hurt as bad as they had the day before. Her knee felt somewhat better, as long as she didn't bend it quickly or sharply. She reached over the side of the bunk and retrieved her medicine kit. She would have to send Pandora a letter to thank her for thinking of sending it along. It had proven very useful, and Psyche had only been aware she had it for a day.

She carefully eased the gloves off and sighed with relief that they hadn't stuck. She reached over the side of the bunk to get another pair of the useless silk gloves. She would also have to mention to Pandora in her letter that while the medicine kit was extremely useful, the gloves had been a waste of space in the trunk. Handkerchiefs. Handkerchiefs would have been helpful.

When she had the gloves removed, she gave her fingers a critical examination. Her palms were still tender, but the bruising had already started to fade to an odd yellowish-green. The ends of her fingers were still purplish-blue, and she had no idea how long it would take for her nails to grow back. The two that had not been completely removed would fall off when new ones began to grow. She could bend all her fingers without them throbbing, and she could even touch the tips of them without too much discomfort.

She unfastened the bandage over her knee. It looked slightly less bruised, but the area over her kneecap was as raw as the day before. She might leave the bandage off for a while after she put on the ointment to see if that would help it heal a little faster. If she ever got dressed, and Psyche certainly hoped she might accomplish that at some point that day, then she would put the bandage back on to keep the ointment from getting rubbed onto her clothes.

Her clothes. What was she going to do about her clothes? She had no intention of putting the black dress back on. She would keep the black chemise because she actually liked it, but she would wear what was in her trunk before she put on the dress. She was hesitant to wear the clothes because they were unusual; it was going to make her attract attention. Psyche did not like to attract attention.

Psyche was putting on the new gloves after reapplying the ointment when there was a knock on the door. She eased on her dressing gown and tied it before answering. It was Sheerness, of course. He came in carrying a tray of food, but there was only enough for Psyche. He didn't intend to stay, obviously. She was disappointed, but he did have other things to do. She couldn't expect him to spend all of his time with her.

After he had the tray settled onto her lap, Sheerness went out of the room again but shortly returned carrying a set of crutches. Psyche felt like Christmas had come early. Her hands and knee were feeling better, and now she had a way to move around the ship. All she had to do was brush her hair and put on some clothes, and she would be set.

"The crew has been told you are here, and they've also been told they are to behave themselves."

"Thank you, but I don't think it was necessary," said Psyche as she ate a piece of bacon. "Thank you for the crutches."

"It *was* necessary, and Mr. Laing, the ship's carpenter, is to thank for the crutches." He reached for a piece of bacon, and she slapped his hand. "Ow."

"*My* bacon," she said sharply, but she gave him a slight smile as she continued to eat. "You'll have to be quicker than that."

"I'll keep that in mind," he said amusedly. "So, you have food; you have crutches. Is there anything else you need before I go ashore?"

"Ashore?"

"Yes, we've moored in Vigo to resupply," said Sheerness matter-of-factly.

"Oh," said Psyche dully as she finished a bite of pancake.

"What?"

"If I had known, I would have written some letters to send home."

"Can you write with your hands like that?"

"If I can eat with them, I can write with them," said Psyche practically.

Sheerness rubbed a hand over his chin. "Give me the rest of your bacon, and I'll wait to leave until you've written them," he said with a grin.

Psyche looked at her bacon, and then she looked at Sheerness. She *really* liked bacon. Apparently, he did as well. She would, however, like to send letters home more. She held up the plate with an unhappy expression.

"You're an extortionist," she muttered.

Sheerness laughed and took the plate. "I don't have to be fast; I just have to be smart."

"Humph," said Psyche petulantly.

"I'll leave you to your letters," said Sheerness as he left the cabin, waving a piece of bacon in the air.

Psyche looked after him for a few minutes, but then she moved the tray to the end of the bunk out of her way. She grabbed the crutches, which he had conveniently left within reach, and went to the desk. Mr. Laing had done an excellent job, and they were very comfortable and easy to use. Perhaps she would try to locate him at some point that day and thank him.

Psyche first wrote a letter to Pandora. She didn't mention the circumstances for finding her way aboard the *Medea*. She didn't mention why she had already found the medicine kit useful. It would only upset Pandora to discover what had happened, and it wasn't her fault. Psyche told her sister where they were and to kiss Alex and Myron for her.

The next letter was to her parents. She apologized for not being home and sent her love to the rest of the family. She asked them not to be angry with Pandora for helping her leave. She didn't know how much of the truth Pandora had told them, but Psyche had wanted to go. Now that she was on her way, she couldn't imagine still being at home.

Once she had those two, most important ones, she next wrote letters to Amalie, Sir James, the Yeardley children, and Chrissoula. By the time she was to the last one, for Sir James, her fingers were aching. She thought about switching hands, but Pandora was more ambidextrous, and Psyche's writing with her left hand was barely legible. She was just sealing and addressing it when there was a knock on the door, and Sheerness came back. She blotted the address and added it to the stack.

"Are you finished yet?" he asked mildly.

"Only just," said Psyche. She turned in the chair to give him the thick pile of letters.

"Lud, woman!" he said in surprise. "Are you writing everyone in the country?"

"I intend to get my bacon's worth," she said pertly.

He looked at the name on the top letter, and his jaw tightened. Sheerness lifted the letter and held it up.

"He doesn't know I've gone, and I didn't want him to become concerned. He is such a worrier," said Psyche calmly.

"Hunh," he said noncommittally. He flipped through the rest, but that was the only one he took particular exception to…other than the one to her twin.

"That's very rude," said Psyche shortly as she watched him.

"This will not be going on a mail packet," he said stiffly.

"And that means you can be intrusive?"

"I *do* have to pay for it."

Psyche stood up and hobbled on her crutches to the bed. She opened the drawer where she had placed the box containing her spectacles and jewelry. She looked through what was in it and pulled out a platinum and marcasite locket on a chain and straightened to hold it out to him.

"Take it. I may not have any money, but that will more than cover the cost of mailing my letters," she said evenly. "And in the future, if you're going to look through my mail, the least you could do is not do it in front of me."

Sheerness took the necklace from her and bowed slightly at the waist, his jaw set angrily. Psyche watched him leave, closing the door tightly behind him. She sat on the edge of the bunk and listened as his footsteps first went to his cabin, then a few minutes later go to the door to the officers' mess.

Psyche hopped on her crutches to the window and looked out. She couldn't see the city. She could see islands in the distance and lots of beautiful blue water. She could see other vessels entering and leaving the port, but she couldn't see the city. She sat on the trunk looking out the window for a little while, trying to calm the irritation she felt for Sheerness. She'd had a wonderful night's sleep. The weather was beautiful. She had written letters home. As angry as she was at his outright prying, there were too many other things to be happy for.

Psyche eventually stood up and went to the door. She needed to go to the water closet, and then she would see about getting dressed. When she got to Sheerness's cabin, it was well-lit from the sun shining in through all the windows. His bed was neatly made, and everything was tidy and put away. It looked almost as it did the day he had given her and Myron their tour, except there were now volumes in the bookcase above his desk.

Psyche looked at the water closet nervously. She had no lamp or candle to use, and even if Sheerness had left one lit, she wouldn't have been able to carry it because of her crutches. Since Sheerness wasn't there, she *could* leave the door open, but it would be her luck someone else would come in, or someone would decide it was time to wash the windows. To be safe, she needed to close the door. She went to it and opened it. After standing and looking for five minutes, she still hadn't managed to bring herself to go inside.

In the end, she compromised. She went in and closed the door, but she left it open a crack, far enough she had a little light but not far enough someone might see her. She was able to tolerate it, but she was relieved when she was done, and it wasn't only because her bladder was empty.

She hopped to her room and selected her clothes. She looked through the items she had been given and finally chose one of the split skirts and a gansey. The shorter chemise proved to work well with the split skirt; it didn't bunch up as a regular one might have. Before she dressed, Psyche used the black dress and some water from the pitcher to wash herself. She would love a bath, but her knee wasn't well enough to stand in and operate the shower.

Getting her stocking and garter on over the bandage was problematic, but she didn't want to wear shoes without stockings, and she intended to put on shoes. She felt much better once she had washed and had on clean clothes. She couldn't see how she looked, and considering what she was wearing, she wasn't sure she wanted to. She only hoped it was decent. After she ran a hand over her outfit, she suspected it might cover *more* than a normal gown would.

Once she was dressed, she did what she could with her hair. Putting it up was too difficult wearing the gloves, so she made do with putting it into a braid. She wondered if Sheerness had a mirror in his cabin. Psyche was fairly sure she had done a decent job, but a mirror to make certain would be nice.

She went back to Sheerness's cabin and looked around. Psyche didn't see a mirror, but he had to have one somewhere, if only to shave. The top on his desk was closed, and she didn't want to open it because she didn't want to go through his things. She went to the chest of drawers near the water closet. The top looked peculiar, and when she pushed up on the edge with her thumb, she discovered it lifted. She hesitated before she raised it. She found his mirror and luckily nothing else. Unlike him, she did have some scruples.

Psyche had a few stray locks, but it was passable. It was not bad enough to warrant redoing it. She closed the mirror and went to look at the books on the shelves over his desk. It wasn't prying; they were in plain sight, and they weren't private. Psyche looked at the spines with interest. There were quite a few she had and had read many times. He had a few volumes by Pliny the Younger she didn't have. She started to take one down when she heard a loud commotion somewhere on the ship.

Psyche frowned and left the cabin. She opened the door to the officers' mess and looked in. It wasn't coming from there, but it sounded very close in Sheerness's cabin. It had to be coming from the berth deck. She hesitated to leave the after cabins, but she was terribly curious. She closed the door and went across the officers' mess to the door to the alcove at the bottom of the stairs. She made her way up to the waist deck and looked around.

No one was there. They were docked, but to have *no one* on deck was odd. At least one of the officers had to be aboard, and it was likely he was on the berth deck because of whatever was causing the problem.

Psyche looked down the stairs and listened. There was yelling and shouting with occasional clattering of pots and pans and thumping as pieces of furniture were knocked over. She thought it might be a fight amongst some of the crew, but then she heard the quacking of a duck. Once Psyche heard that, she only considered for a moment before she went down the stairs.

The berth deck was complete chaos. It was bright enough amidships from the entry for the hold, and there were lamps around the edges to brighten it even further. Men were standing on the benches as much to see what was happening as to get away from it. In the midst of it all was a burly sailor with a wooden leg running after something small.

As soon as the sailors close to the stairs saw Psyche, they moved aside, especially when they could tell she intended to get past one way or another. As she got nearer to the crux of the activity, she could see the grate covering the hold was open. About the time she got to the front and was able to see everything clearly, the sailor captured his quarry. The rest of the crew present yelled and applauded loudly. Psyche's face went pale with alarm when he turned in her direction and she could see what he was holding.

"It'll be th' cookin' pot for ye, ye wee beastie!" he said victoriously.

"*Unhand that duck!*" roared Psyche.

The effect of her voice was instantaneous. There was a collective gasp of surprise from the crew for a woman yelling loudly enough to be heard above the din, and then all was silent. The sailor holding the bird was so surprised he nearly dropped it, and his grip loosened enough the duck was able to turn and firmly grab him by the nose.

"Ow!" he yelled. "Get 'im off me! Th' little shite is possessed!" he cried as he tried to make the duck turn loose.

Psyche hobbled forward to come to the man's aid. The rest of the men were dumbfounded. When Psyche reached him, she kept her crutches balanced under her arms as best she could and reached over to disengage the duck.

"Now, Waddlesworth," chided Psyche gently once she had him in her arms, "that's no way to behave."

To everyone's amazement, the animal that had heretofore seemed to be some form of hellspawn calmly settled in her arms and began to preen. The sailor she had rescued reached up to gingerly touch his nose. He was relieved it was still in one piece, if a bit battered and bloody, but one more scar wasn't going to make much difference. He started to take Waddlesworth back from Psyche, and the duck turned to nip at his fingers with a loud quack.

"If ye'll 'old on til 'im, I'll go get me 'atchet," said the sailor.

"Oh, you're not cooking this duck," said Psyche flatly. "As a matter of fact, I'd like to know how he came into your possession in the first instance."

"'E was in a crate delivered til th' ship before we sailed from London wi' several others tha' were a lot less trouble."

"Hmm," said Psyche thoughtfully.

She could only assume Waddlesworth had strayed from Hyde Park and gone somewhere ducks were collected for human consumption, possibly even a farm. She didn't think this man was responsible, but Psyche wasn't going to let Waddlesworth be eaten.

"I'm sorry, what is your name?" she asked him calmly.

"Meals, mum," he said quietly.

"Mr. Meals, I will take this duck off your hands," she said with a smile. "He's old enough any meat will be tough, and there won't be a lot at that."

Meals looked from her to the duck, which sat calmly in her arms, eyeing him suspiciously. It was obvious they were familiar to each other, and he was curious how that was. It could have been her pet for all the tameness it showed. At that point, Higginbotham decided it was time to enter the conversation.

"My lady, I'm the first mate, Mr. Higginbotham. Might I suggest you let Meals tend to his business and cook the bird? It's obviously wild and could only create more havoc otherwise."

Psyche turned to look at him. "A pleasure to meet you, Mr. Higginbotham, but I can't allow Mr. Meals to cook this bird. I know he's wild, but I give you my word he'll no longer be a bother."

Higginbotham scratched his forehead uncertainly. "I don't know, Lady Psyche. I don't think the captain's going to like having an intransigent bird loose on his ship."

"Leave that to me," said Psyche determinedly. She shrugged. "I will *not* let anyone harm one feather on this duck. Judging by the rumpus just now, I doubt he would let you. See how calm he is for me? I'll keep him in my cabin, and that will keep him from under foot." Higginbotham was still dubious. "If I can get him to my cabin without carrying him, he will stay. Deal?"

"Fair enough. If you can get him to your room without further trouble, he'll stay. If not, once he's caught again, he goes in the pot."

"Thank you," said Psyche gratefully with a smile.

She gently set the duck at her feet. Everyone moved back nervously when he was loose again, but the drake stood calmly where she had placed him, eyeing the men. Psyche adjusted her crutches and looked at the cook.

"Mr. Meals, before I go, I'd like to offer my compliments on your cooking. Your lamb stew is most excellent."

"Thank you, mum," said Meals, his cheeks coloring.

"Now, there's a tray in my room. I would have brought it down myself, but it's a bit impossible with the crutches. If you could have someone retrieve it and bring me some dinner, I would be grateful."

"In a trice, mum," said Meals.

Psyche looked down at her feet. "Come along, Waddlesworth, and don't dawdle," she said firmly, and she turned to go back to the stairs.

The duck did recognize her, obviously, and he knew wherever she went would be safe, so when she started to leave, he waddled behind her docilely. The men cleared a wide path for the two of them, and although Waddlesworth did glare at them threateningly, he continued on behind Psyche as if he were on a leash. Once Psyche reached the top of the stairs, Waddlesworth flew up behind her and followed the short distance across the deck to the after cabins.

When Psyche got to her cabin, she closed the door behind the duck. She didn't know how well he had been fed in the hold. He didn't appear to be malnourished. All she had for him that he *might* eat was some leftover pancakes, and she wasn't too sure he would like it. She went to the tray and looked at what was there. She had some scrambled eggs left, but she couldn't feed that to Waddlesworth. That would be somewhat like cannibalism. She set one of her crutches aside and picked up the plate of pancakes. She took it over to one of the trunks and set it down, and then she picked up Waddlesworth and showed it to him. She was only marginally surprised that he did eat it.

Waddlesworth had just finished his food when there was a knock on the door. The duck quacked and flapped his wings nervously, but he didn't move from the top of the trunk. Psyche picked up the plate and put it back on the tray, and then she went to the door. To her surprise, Higginbotham was carrying a tray with her dinner.

"Mr. Higginbotham, you didn't need to bring that up for me," she said as she moved out of the way.

"Yes, I did," said Higginbotham evenly. He took the tray over and set it on her desk. He rubbed his hands together and gave Waddlesworth a dubious glance. "The rest of the men didn't want to go near the duck."

Psyche chuckled. "I'm sorry about that, truly. He will not cause them any further mischief, I promise."

"If I may, could I ask how you seem to be so familiar with a *duck?*"

"He is normally a denizen of Hyde Park, and I fed him on the Serpentine nearly every morning this past Season. I can only assume he decided to find lodgings elsewhere and was crated."

Higginbotham tilted his head and looked at the duck. Waddlesworth eyed him no less curiously.

"He is a peculiar thing," said Higginbotham thoughtfully.

"I agree," said Psyche. "I never saw another like him in the Park." She shrugged and looked at the first mate with a grin. "I guess that's why he took to me; we're both odd ducks."

Higginbotham smiled and picked up her breakfast tray. "I'll leave you to your dinner, my lady. I don't imagine the captain'll be back before nightfall. If you need anything, just let me know."

"Thank you, Mr. Higginbotham," said Psyche with a smile.

"Oh, call me Bothi," he said with a chuckle. "I realize my name's a mouthful."

"All right...Bothi," said Psyche pleasantly, nodding her head.

Psyche watched him leave and closed the door. He was a nice man. She judged him to be somewhere in his forties, perhaps, but years of working at sea had weathered the skin on his face to make him appear older. He was about her height and stocky, with dark brown hair that was becoming peppered with gray at the temples and brown eyes. His face, by its construction, was very stern, but his smile softened his countenance dramatically. Psyche could see he wasn't tolerant of nonsense, but he was also fair.

She was grateful he had let her keep Waddlesworth. He could have just as easily let Meals cook him. Even though her rank gave her certain privileges, aboard the ship, next to Sheerness, Higginbotham's word was law, whether he was a peer or not. It was his responsibility to keep the *Medea* disciplined and untroubled. Waddlesworth's behavior had been far from either. She could only imagine Sheerness's reaction when he discovered the duck aboard ship.

Psyche looked at her crutches for a moment and leaned them against the wall. She tried putting her weight onto both feet. Standing still, there was only a slight throbbing in her knee. When she tried to put all her weight to that side, however, it threatened to give way. It would be awhile before she could manage without the crutches. She would need to try using it occasionally, even if it hurt, if only to prevent it from becoming stiffer and weaker.

She took up the crutches again and went to Sheerness's cabin to use the water closet. Then she went to retrieve the book she had wanted earlier. She didn't think Sheerness would mind her borrowing it. She would just have to be careful with it. She took it to her cabin and found Waddlesworth still sitting on the trunk where she had left him.

She then went to the one she had been in. She started to lift the lid, almost changed her mind, but opened it anyhow. The blood had faded to a dark brown, and the lining hung in tatters. She ignored it and pulled out the pillow and closed the lid. She took the pillow to Waddlesworth and laid it on the trunk for him. She patted it and fluffed it until she had it shaped somewhat like a nest. The drake looked from her back to the pillow for a moment before he walked to it and settled himself in comfortably. Before long, he was asleep.

Psyche went to her desk and sat down to eat her meal. She was having cabbage and potatoes with ham, a nice brown bread, which she set aside a bit of for Waddlesworth, and a baked apple. Meals had also given her a large tankard of beer. Psyche began reading while she ate, and once she had finished with her food, she moved Waddlesworth sleeping on his pillow to the top of the other trunk and situated herself on the trunk by the window to continue reading.

She spent the rest of the day enjoying her borrowed book, stopping occasionally to put notes in a notebook or use the water closet. Waddlesworth woke from his nap, and she gave him the bread left over from her dinner. He would be happier with grain or something similar, but the bread would have to do until she could make arrangements for something else. She would also have to find a way for the duck to do his business. He couldn't do it in her room. She raised herself and looked out the window. The shroud for the mizzenmast came down not far from her window, and it presented the perfect place. She picked up Waddlesworth and took him to the window and looked down at him.

"Now, I'm trusting you'll come back when you're through, but this is where you need to go when you need to go," said Psyche calmly, smoothing a hand over his back affectionately.

She lifted him to the window and set him out on the channel. He fluttered his wings slightly and glided down to the water. She was afraid she might have set him free and that he wouldn't return, but him being free was better than being cooked. Psyche watched as he submerged himself, only to return momentarily with a fish. She laughed to see him so happy, and she knew this had to be the first time he had been in the water since he had been captured.

Psyche sat watching Waddlesworth for a while, but he didn't stray too far. She hoped he would return, but she couldn't deny him his freedom. So far, he seemed to be content paddling and fishing and had no intention of leaving. She picked up her book to read again, occasionally looking out the window to make sure the duck still remained close by. Eventually, the sun began to dip lower, and Psyche would have to find Higginbotham or someone else to fill the lamps in her cabin. She marked her page with a small piece of paper and set the book on her desk. She was about to grab her crutches when she heard the flap of wings outside the window. When she looked out, Waddleworth sat on the channel looking up at her expectantly. She happily reached out to pick him up and brought him through the window to place on the trunk with his pillow.

"Good boy," said Psyche as she smoothed a hand over his damp back.

She reached up to close the window, and then she grabbed her crutches. She was almost to the door when there was a knock. Psyche thought that was fortuitous and went to answer it. She was startled to see not Higginbotham but Sheerness standing there.

"Oh," she said breathlessly.

"You look surprised to see me," he said with a sardonic grin.

"Well, yes, I am. I was expecting Bothi," said Psyche calmly.

"Who?" asked Sheerness confusedly.

"Mr. Higginbotham."

"You call him *Bothi*?" said Sheerness in disbelief as he leaned a shoulder against the door frame with his arms folded across his chest.

"He did ask me to," said Psyche matter-of-factly.

Then Sheerness noticed her clothes. "*What* are you wearing?"

"Clothes," said Psyche flatly.

Sheerness looked at the intricately knitted, tight-fitting sweater made from a blend of dark mauve and lavender yarn. It resembled the ones worn by sailors, but only in how it was made, not in the color. The way it hugged her breasts made the breath catch in his throat. When he first saw her, he thought she was wearing a skirt, but it was trousers made of thin, flowing cotton in a shade matching the dark mauve of her sweater. The bottoms of the legs were wide and embroidered along the edges, which is why he thought it was a skirt, but at her waist and over her bottom, they fit closely like a regular pair of trousers. She had on women's shoes, but they were low-heeled, lace-up ankle boots and looked like something a kitchen girl might wear. Paired with the silk gloves and braided hair, it all looked very strange and a little provocative.

"Has my crew seen you dressed like this?"

"Yes, they have…at least the ones not with you," said Psyche neutrally.

"You cannot wear that," said Sheerness flatly, shaking his head.

"Why not?" asked Psyche perplexedly. "I am dressed more modestly in this than I would be in a silk ball gown."

"Yes, but a silk ball gown is made for a woman to wear. I don't know what this is, but it is definitely *not,*" said Sheerness, and he lifted his hands and made gestures in the air that made it obvious what he meant.

"Oh, pooh," said Psyche dismissively. She turned on her crutches and went to sit on the bunk. She looked at him once she was seated. "I regret to inform you there is nothing in my wardrobe that is better. I would say this is the least *not* of what I have. I do have actual women's clothes…somewhat, but I suspect you wouldn't want your crew to see me in those either."

"Then you can put back on the black dress, and I will get you something else in Vigo," said Sheerness flatly.

"No, I'm afraid not," said Psyche firmly. "I'm going to wear what I have, and I am *not* putting back on the mourning dress."

"Yes, you are," said Sheerness tightly.

"No, I am not," said Psyche in measured tones. It was sitting on the foot of her bunk from when she had washed earlier, and she picked it up and went to the window. She opened it and tossed the dress out, watching as it fluttered down to the water's surface before sinking below it. "*Not* wearing it."

Sheerness looked at her in amazement and nodded his head determinedly. "Then you'll stay in here until I can find you something else to wear."

"No, I won't, and no, *you* won't. I have clothes. I don't *need* something else. The only one bothered by it is you. No one else even noticed what I was wearing. Higginbotham didn't mind. The rest of your crew didn't mind."

"Perhaps that is only what you think."

Psyche shrugged. "I am *not* going to wear anything you buy me, so you may as well save your money, and if you try to keep me in my cabin, I'll bust your nose!" said Psyche hotly.

It was at that point Waddlesworth made his presence known. He stood on the trunk and flapped his wings, hissing at Sheerness. Sheerness looked at the bird in surprise. He shook his head and took a deep breath, his jaw clenching.

"What is *that* doing here?" he said stilly, pointing at Waddlesworth and giving her a dangerous look.

"I saved him from Meals…well, I saved Meals from Waddlesworth, too, since Waddlesworth had *him* by the nose," finished Psyche lamely.

"*What?*" roared Sheerness.

"Well, he was going to cook him! He was only defending himself," said Psyche exasperatedly.

"Oh, he's got to go," said Sheerness firmly.

"No," said Psyche flatly, shaking her head. "He was calm as could be until you came in here yelling like a field marshal."

"He's a menace, and I want him off my ship," said Sheerness angrily, raising his chin.

"Please, don't make me get rid of him," implored Psyche.

"As captain, I order you to get rid of that bird," said Sheerness coldly.

Psyche looked at him in stunned disbelief. She couldn't refuse. It could cause problems with the crew if she did. Even if she was a passenger, if there were some type of disagreement between Sheerness and the crew (although she didn't think there would be), her disobeying could lead them to do the same. Insubordination was not something that could be allowed on a ship...from anyone. She had to comply with the captain's orders.

She bit the inside of her lip and nodded defeatedly, and then she went to the trunk to pick up Waddlesworth, who calmly let her do so. She went to the window and opened it and placed him onto the channel. He looked at her curiously and didn't move. After a few seconds, Psyche closed the window. She took a deep breath and turned back to face Sheerness.

"Get out," she said quietly.

"I've come to see you about something," said Sheerness, acting as if the last fifteen minutes had not happened and insensible to how upset she was.

"I don't care; I said get out," said Psyche stilly.

"I've brought you something," said Sheerness genially, giving her a smile.

"I don't want anything from you. Not now...not ever," said Psyche tonelessly. "Please, go away."

Sheerness narrowed his eyes and tightened his jaw. He bowed stiffly at the waist and left the cabin, closing the door behind him. Psyche slowly went to the bunk and sat down, and then she began to cry quietly. She put her hands to her cheeks and rocked back and forth, shaking her head. She couldn't understand why he had to be so mean. Waddlesworth was like a dear friend to her. As she had told Higginbotham, his oddity suited her own, and she found comfort in that. With him, it was simple: food and occasional petting was all he wanted. There were no hidden motives, no other expectations. He was also special to Psyche because spending time with him at the park had been one of the last things she'd done with Myron before he died.

When someone knocked at the door a few minutes later, she jumped in surprise and looked at it, but she ignored the summons. After they tried a second time, and Psyche still didn't answer, whoever it was went away. She could only assume it was Sheerness returning to rail at her for some other infraction he felt she'd committed. She thought about locking the door, but she didn't feel like moving. Aside from that, if Sheerness wanted in, breaking the door would be just as easy, and then she would be without a door.

She looked around herself and noticed it was almost dark. It was nearing the point she couldn't make out shapes across the room. Still crying, she reached into the drawer under her bunk for her medicine kit, and then she went to get a glass of water from the pitcher on her desk. She put in some of her pain medicine and a double dose of her sleeping draught and quickly drank it. Then she went back to the bunk and curled up in a ball in the corner. She might be afraid to sleep, but now she wouldn't have a choice. If she was sleeping, she wouldn't have to worry about the dark. And if she wasn't worried about it being dark, Sheerness would have no reason to come into her cabin.

≪ ≫

Supper was a quiet affair. Sheerness was in a foul mood, and the rest of the men sitting around the table knew why. Neither the door to the officers' mess or Psyche's cabin was closed when they argued, and all of the officers had been there. The men were of the opinion Sheerness had been unfair to Psyche, but they wouldn't think of telling him that. When Sheerness sent Higginbotham to refill the lamps in her cabin, she hadn't answered the door. When he sent Felton to invite her to supper, she again had not answered. When Sheerness himself took a tray to her cabin, there was still no answer. He frustratedly decided she could pout all she wanted. He was not going to cater to her.

After supper, Sheerness took a round of the main deck before retiring. The sky was cloudless and the weather was fair. Sailing in the morning wouldn't be a problem. His step hesitated as he went past Psyche's door. There was no light coming from underneath it. He put his ear to it, but he didn't hear anything. He frowned and went on to his cabin, closing the windows and lowering the shutters at the stern and lighting a fire on the grate.

He sat at his desk doing paperwork, but he had it taken care of quickly. At one point, he looked up at his bookcase and noticed a book was missing. He realized Psyche must have borrowed it at some point during the day. He wasn't concerned about it. He finally put away the things on his desk and closed the top, and then he went to the sideboard and poured himself a brandy. He got undressed for bed and stood looking out the starboard window as he drank.

He looked back over his shoulder at the door to Psyche's cabin. The frown that had settled in when he noticed there was no light on had never gone away. Considering how frightened she had been of the dark, it wasn't something he thought she would have gotten over so quickly. He finished his brandy and set the glass down, and then he went to put his pants back on with a tired sigh. He grabbed the lamp off his desk and went to her door. He listened intently, but he still didn't hear a sound. There was none of the terrified whimpering of the night before. He didn't even hear snoring, not that he expected he would.

Sheerness tried the handle, and it opened quietly. He put his head around the door and looked in, but he didn't see anything out of place. His book was sitting on her desk, just as he expected. He looked at the part of the bunk he could see. She didn't seem to be in it. The small wooden box with medicines was sitting near the foot, but it didn't look like she was there. He opened the door further and went in, closing it behind him.

That's when he saw her, curled up in a ball in the corner, her arms around her legs, her cheek resting on top of her knees. She was completely dressed, even her shoes. She was sleeping...rather heavily. He looked from her to the box and realized she must have taken something to make her sleep. Considering her fear of the dark, she must have done it not long after he left. That would explain why she hadn't responded to any of the knocks to her door. She had been crying, and she hadn't been pouting at all.

He walked over to the bunk and looked at the box. He had no idea what the bottles contained or which one she might have taken. It was all labeled in Chinese. He saw the folded up piece of paper in the box, and after a brief glance to her, he took it out and read it. He put it back in the box where he found it and closed the lid, and then he opened the drawer where she kept it and put it away. He set the lamp on the desk, and then he gently eased her out of the corner and laid her down on the bed, carefully straightening out her left knee. He removed her shoes and pulled the blankets over her. She made no sign she even noticed.

He went back to the desk and looked at the things there. He found the letters from Pandora and the three maids folded neatly in a rear corner. Sheerness looked back over his shoulder to Psyche. He started to leave them, knowing he was prying, but he picked them up anyhow.

He couldn't read the one from Maiyin because it was in Chinese. He read the one from Agniezka in Russian, but all it contained were suggestions on what garments to wear with which and how she should style her hair. When he opened the one from Chrissoula, it was almost unintelligible because it was in modern Greek, but he could read it well enough. The tone of it was not what he would expect from a maid to her mistress but more like that of a friend or even a sister, and while it offered clothing suggestions, it also contained advice of a more personal nature. And then he read the letter from her sister.

Once he did it, he knew he shouldn't have. If Psyche were to discover he had, she would be terribly hurt. But it was as if he had been unable to help himself. There were things about her that he didn't understand, and he had hoped reading the letters would help. It hadn't, and now he felt guilty without being any further enlightened. The only thing they had shown was that she was well-loved, and he hadn't needed to read the letters to know that. He folded them and put them back where he found them.

Sheerness went to the edge of the bunk and looked down at her sleeping face. She had found one more way to make him irrelevant. She had no need of him, and it seemed there was nothing he could do that met her expectations. His love was not good enough. Nothing he had or did was good enough. She would rather take drugs than let him hold her. Her brother had said she needed him...*with his dying breath!* So far, he had found nothing to demonstrate she did. At times, he felt as if she used him until she was able to find something better, and in the end, there was always something—or someone—better.

But he wasn't willing to give in yet. He wanted to believe she could come to care for him. Sheerness couldn't believe Neath had used his last breath to tell him something that wasn't true. Before he knew she was on the ship, he thought their being separated for a time might make her realize she cared for him. He still thought that, but it wouldn't be easy to accomplish on the ship. Perhaps if he made himself as inaccessible as possible, she would realize he wasn't there for her convenience and that she needed him for more.

He bent down and kissed her softly on the lips before brushing a finger down her cheek in a caress. He straightened up and sighed resignedly.

"One day, you *are* going to need me," he whispered.

Chapter Twenty One

The following morning, the ship sailed with the tide. Once they were under way, Sheerness went for breakfast with Felton, Higginbotham, and Blossom, and then he went to his cabin to shower and shave. Once he was done, he made a few quick notes in his log and looked at his charts. He started on his way topside and paused at Psyche's door for a moment to listen for any sounds. There weren't any. He shrugged indifferently and continued on his way. It was barely nine. He would give her another hour, and then he would send someone with a tray. It wouldn't be him.

Psyche was up at dawn. She never slept beyond that usually. Since she had gone to bed before ten, it was not surprising. She also took it as a sign she was getting over the effects of being locked in a trunk for three days. She felt somewhat groggy from doubling the dose of her sleeping draught, but it had done the trick. She had gone to sleep quickly, and she couldn't recall having a single dream. She woke to find she was still in the same place she had gone to sleep, and she hoped her fear of going to sleep would soon be remedied. Her insomnia, however, wasn't something she felt would be as easily fixed, and neither would her fear of the dark or her fear of heights.

When she woke up, she was disturbed to find someone had come in to put her under the blankets and take off her shoes. She could only assume it was Sheerness. She didn't like that he had been able to come in while she was asleep and move her without her waking up. If *he* could, that meant someone else could, too.

She used some of the water from the pitcher to wash her face and brush her teeth. Since she didn't have a washstand, she spit out the window. Luckily, it was early enough no one saw her doing it. When she opened the window, she was sad to see Waddlesworth was no longer sitting in the shrouds. He was also not floating on the water nearby. He was gone, and she was heartbroken to see it. She unplaited her hair, brushed it, and rebraided it, and then she did the best she could to straighten out the wrinkles in her pants.

Her knee was stiff when she first woke up, but it began to feel somewhat better after she was awake for a little while. Once she finished with her hair and clothes, she pulled off her gloves and removed the bandage on her knee to reapply the ointment. The bruising was starting to fade and her kneecap was starting to scab over. When she stood up without her crutches, the twinge in her knee had lessened, and when she tested putting her weight onto it, she was able to bear it much longer. She could bend it and lift it without as much pain as before, and she might be ready to begin using only one crutch. She wasn't ready to walk on it without support yet but would be very soon.

Her fingers were looking better. She used her clippers to trim the nails that were only broken to a less jagged shape and did what she could to make the others less unsightly. The bruising on her palms had faded even further, and they no longer felt tender when she pressed them together. The bruising on her fingertips was changing from purplish-blue to a dark green. They looked very odd. Her nailbeds where the nails had been removed were starting to toughen, and although her hands looked terrible, after she had massaged some of the ointment into her fingertips, she didn't put the gloves back on.

Once she was done with her toilette, she went to sit at her desk and do some work in her notebooks. Without any of her scrolls or tablets and books, there wasn't much to do, but she could look through what she had and see if anything came to her. She poured herself a glass of water and continued to read quietly.

She heard Sheerness when he woke up. Well, she heard him use the water closet because it adjoined the wall to her cabin. It was actually well-muffled, but she could hear the flush. She also heard when he went past her door to go topside. After waiting a few minutes, she got up and went to the water closet herself. He would be gone for a while, which suited her perfectly. When she got back to her cabin, she retrieved her nearly empty pitcher and went to the mess to refill it from the water barrel. It was much easier using one crutch.

She sat back down at her desk and picked up the book she had borrowed. She could hear the ship coming to life and knew they would soon set sail. She heard and felt when they raised anchor, and it wasn't long after that when she felt a slight lurch as the sails caught the wind. She went to the window and looked out. As they turned about, she could see the city. She watched the passing landscape at the window for a while, but she eventually picked up her book and began to read again.

After a time, she heard several men's voices coming from the officers' mess; they were having breakfast. Her stomach rumbled unhappily, but she wasn't going to eat with Sheerness. She didn't want to see him unless it was absolutely necessary. Someone would be along to bring her food at some point. Until then, she would make do with the water in her pitcher.

She heard Sheerness go by her door to his cabin. After a few minutes, she heard the sound of running water and knew it was the shower-bath. She was envious. She longed to have a shower. Her hair was in desperate need of a wash, but her knee wasn't up to it yet. Perhaps tomorrow, but hopefully not longer than that. She felt grimy. The water eventually turned off, and she tried to concentrate on reading her book…well, *his* book.

About an hour later, she heard him leaving his cabin again. She heard when he paused outside her door, and Psyche tensed preparatorily as she waited for him to knock. She breathed a sigh of relief when he didn't and continued on. She *really* didn't want to see him, and she was seriously considering the next time they stopped that she might ask to go home…on a different ship. The only things that made her hesitate was knowing several people had gone through a lot of effort to get her on this ship, and Myron had wanted her to go. She couldn't let their work go to waste, and she had to do it for her brother.

With the decision reached she *couldn't* go home, after the previous evening, the only way she could bear it was if she avoided Sheerness. He hadn't needed to *order* her to get rid of Waddlesworth. He had no reason to take such umbrage at her clothing. The outfit was comfortable, and she was starting not to care that it looked unusual. He was the only one who minded.

Eventually, she would have to find a way to talk to him without arguing. Once they reached Greece, they would have to cooperate. She had no intention of staying on the ship all the time, and she had to find a way to convince him to go to Thessaloniki. If she could coexist with him until then, once she reached Chrissoula's family, he could leave her stranded for all she cared. Even if she had never met them, she knew them well enough from Chrissoula that she believed they would take care of her and see she found a way home. She couldn't believe the same thing about Sheerness.

Psyche tried to put it out of her mind and concentrate on her book, but after she read the same passage three times without absorbing any of it, she set it aside. She tried to read one of her notebooks, and that proved unproductive. She finally turned her chair to prop her left foot onto the nearby trunk and began to thoughtfully chew on the side of her thumb, but that was useless, too.

She turned her head slowly at a soft knock on the door, and she thought about not answering, but even if it was Sheerness, he would have food. She could tolerate him long enough for that. She stood up and went to open the door, and she was startled when she had to look down to see who it was.

"Oh," she said softly in surprise.

Standing there holding a tray of food was a young boy. He was blond and freckled with inquisitive brown eyes. He was about eight or nine, and Psyche couldn't imagine what he was doing on a ship at such a young age. She quickly moved out of his way to let him enter because the tray was heavy for him.

"Just set it on the trunk by the window," she said hurriedly.

He did so, and then he turned to look at her curiously, tilting his head.

"Did the man find you, ma'am?" he asked quietly.

Psyche's forehead wrinkled. "What man?" she asked blankly.

"The one that came looking for you," said the boy.

"Do you mean the captain?" she asked perplexedly.

"No, ma'am, the viscount," he said, and his forehead began to wrinkle in confusion as well. "I didn't want to tell him where you had gone, but he seemed like he knew you, and he said it was important."

Psyche sat down in her chair to be closer to his height, and she gave him a soft smile. He seemed to think he knew her from somewhere else.

"When did he come looking for me?" she asked.

"About this time last year," said the boy as he thought about it.

"What is your name?"

"Freddie, ma'am, Freddie Bunney." His face wrinkled disappointedly. "Don't you remember me?"

"I think you have me confused with someone else," said Psyche gently.

"No, I don't," he said definitely, shaking his head. "You had a big black horse, and you were—"he paused to look behind him at the open door to see if anyone was listening—"you were dressed like a man," he whispered conspiratorially.

Psyche's forehead wrinkled thoughtfully, and then her face paled as she realized who he was.

"Freddie? Frederick Leftwich Bunney?" she asked in astonishment.

He grinned cheekily. "See! You do remember me!"

Psyche smiled and shook her head. "Oh, no, Freddie, I've never met you."

"Then how do you know me name?" he asked confusedly.

"Because my *sister* has met you," said Psyche with a grin, "and she told me all about you and how much help you were." She shrugged and pointed at her face. "She looks exactly like me."

"Ohh," said Freddie slowly with comprehension.

"But what are you doing so far from Thorpe Satchville? Where are your parents?" asked Psyche as she grabbed a piece of bacon from the tray.

The brightness in his face dimmed. "They died from influenza this past January," he said softly.

Psyche's throat constricted, and she found it hard to swallow her food.

"Oh, Freddie, I'm so sorry," she said consolingly. "But why are you on the *Medea*? Haven't you any family?"

"Me Uncle Bothi's the first mate. He's not married anymore, so when he signed on, he got me hired as a cabin boy to keep an eye on me."

"How are you liking it?" asked Psyche curiously. She still thought he was too young, but many sailors had started their careers this way.

Freddie shrugged. "It's not too bad. I help Mr. Meals mostly. The rest of the time I watch me uncle."

Psyche smiled. "Well, I'm sure if sailing is what you want to learn, he is the man to teach you."

Freddie grinned. "Yes, ma'am."

"I'll let you get back to your work. If you come back in an hour, I should be done by then. All right?"

"Yes, ma'am," said Freddie agreeably.

"And we don't need to stand on using *ma'am*. If there's not anyone about, you can call me Psyche."

Freddie nodded and skipped from the room, closing the door behind him. Psyche looked after him and smiled, and then she began to eat her food. She was famished. The only problem with getting up so early was that her food was brought far too late. She would write a letter to Pandora once she ate and let her sister know whom she had found. She would also write a letter to Damon. His birthday was tomorrow, and even though he would be very late getting it, she wanted to let him know she had not forgotten.

≪ ≫

From near the helm, Sheerness watched Freddie skip across the deck to the stairs and go to the deck below. He could tell from the boy's exuberance that Psyche had worked her magic on yet another child. It boggled him how she managed it. All she had to do was say hallo or smile, and they were like putty in her hands. And it all seemed unintentional. Even adults liked her. He had yet to meet *anyone* who didn't. Psyche seemed completely oblivious to it.

Mr. Stockbridge came across the deck from the forecastle and took the stairs to the poop deck. He had a puzzled frown and was scratching his chin as he came to stand by Sheerness.

"What is it, Stockbridge?" asked Sheerness concernedly.

"Sir, you might want to come see this," said Stockbridge slowly.

Sheerness left overseeing the helm to Broughton and followed Stockbridge to the bow of the ship. He looked out at the sails and rigging, but he didn't notice anything out of the ordinary. He looked at Stockbridge.

"Look down, sir, at the figurehead."

The figurehead for the *Medea* was large because of the bluntness of the bow, and the carving had several nooks and bends to accommodate rigging for the foresails and windows to the forecastle. Sheerness frowned and leaned over the front to look at the carving. The curiosity in the frown changed to disbelief and irritation when he saw what Stockbridge found so astonishing.

Waddlesworth hadn't gone away; he had only found new quarters. He decided a spot on the figurehead's shoulder, which was bowl-shaped from the figure's billowing hair and outstretched arms, would be perfect. He had found leaves, straw, and other items to cushion his new roost, and it looked as if he had always been there. He had his head under his wing to protect himself from the wind the figure didn't block. He looked perfectly at home, and of the many places on the ship the duck could have selected, this one did not affect the operation of the ship or interfere with the crew's ability to work. Sheerness looked from the bird to the bosun, and then back to the bird again.

"What should we do with it, sir?" asked Stockbridge, and while the bosun was doing his level best to keep his features composed into perfect seriousness, the corners of his mouth were twitching with amusement.

Sheerness leaned forward to grab the duck with the intention of wringing his neck and being done with it, but as soon as the earl touched him, Waddlesworth's head snaked out from under his wing, and he bit down on Sheerness's forefinger with enough force it was bleeding by the time he turned it loose. Waddlesworth looked up at him angrily and hissed before putting his head back under his wing.

"Bloody hell!" yelped Sheerness, and he shook his finger and put it in his mouth.

Stockbridge stood beside him with his lips pursed to keep himself from grinning, and his shoulders shook as he tried not to laugh. Sheerness saw the bosun's amusement, and his lips tightened into an angry line.

"*Go get her,*" Sheerness bit out slowly.

≪　≫

Psyche had just finished her breakfast and was drinking her tea and starting her letter to Pandora when there was a knock at her door. She looked over her shoulder with a frown, but she grabbed her crutch and went to answer it. It was a member of the crew she'd never met before, but at least it wasn't Sheerness.

He looked to be in his thirties, slightly taller than Psyche, but not as tall as Sheerness. He had dark brown hair and gray eyes with a muscular build. He was actually very attractive, and she was sure from his charming smile that she was not the first female to think so.

"Excuse me, my lady, I'm Mr. Stockbridge, the bosun."

"Pleasure to meet you," said Psyche, holding out her hand to shake his. "What can I do for you, Mr. Stockbridge?"

"Begging your pardon, mum, but the captain's asked me to come get you," he said impassively.

Psyche frowned. "Certainly. If you'll just give me a moment to put on my shoes," she said agreeably.

Once Psyche had on her shoes, she followed Stockbridge out of her cabin topside. Instead of directing her to the poopdeck, however, he led her to the foredeck. Psyche's forehead was wrinkled with confusion as they went to the bow, where she could see Sheerness standing with an angry expression, examining his left index finger critically. When he heard them approaching, he clasped his hands behind his back and scowled at her. Psyche looked at him bewilderedly, unsure what she could have done to make him so angry again.

"You asked to see me, captain?" she said evenly.

"I want you to look at the figurehead," said Sheerness coldly, jerking his head in the direction of the bow.

Psyche's confusion didn't lessen, and her frown only deepened at his request. She was high above the moving water. She wasn't sure she could do it. She slowly moved closer to the rail and held onto it tightly as she leaned over slightly to look down. Even as she went dizzy, she gasped in surprise and quickly looked away. She looked at Sheerness and raised an eyebrow.

"Yes?" she said dryly.

"Get that *thing* off of there. Right now," he said in measured tones.

"No," said Psyche airily. "He's not hurting anyone or anything."

"Get that malevolent shite off the bow of my ship!" said Sheerness tightly.

"I'll not do it unless you let me take him back to my cabin and keep him there," said Psyche evenly, her jaw set.

"Woman, do as I say, or I'll keelhaul you for insubordination!" he shouted.

Psyche lifted her chin stubbornly and narrowed her eyes at him. "Do it. The water's warm enough, I'm sure, and I can hold my breath for a *very* long time. You'll *still* be left with a duck on your figurehead."

Sheerness raised his hand in the air, and for a moment Psyche thought he was going to strike her. She had only seen him that angry once before…last year. She tilted her chin higher and continued to look at him determinedly. Sheerness finally balled his hand into a fist and dropped it to his side.

"Fine," he bit out, and he tightened his jaw angrily and stalked past her to go back to the helm.

Psyche let out her breath with a whoosh and put a hand to her stomach nervously. She leaned back over the bow to look down and just as quickly straightened back up again. She couldn't get him that way. She couldn't reach, and it also made her dizzy. Stockbridge looked at her impassively.

"Can you come with me and see if anyone's in the forecastle? I want to use one of the windows."

Stockbridge nodded and went with her down the steps to one of the doors into the forecastle. He pounded on it loudly before he opened it.

"Woman on deck!" he shouted.

Psyche didn't think it was necessary to announce her. Simply looking to make sure everyone was decent would have been enough. She walked past him into the forecastle and went to the windows at the bow. There were a few men, but most were either working or on the berth deck. The ones who were there were all dressed, and it didn't appear they had needed to become so before she entered. She smiled nervously at them as she passed and went to the window that would open over the right shoulder of the figurehead.

She opened the window and looked out, deciding this would work. There was a bench placed directly beneath it, and she carefully stood on it. The window was smaller than the one in her cabin, but Psyche managed to squeeze through it. It was lower to the water, and the shape of the figurehead prevented her from seeing how high she was. She looked at Waddlesworth, who had turned to look when the window opened. She carefully reached for him and brought him in without any difficulty. She stepped down from the bench and lowered the window and grabbed her crutch from where she had propped it against the wall. She turned to look at Stockbridge.

"Thank you, Mr. Stockbridge, for your help," she said pleasantly.

"Anytime, mum," said Stockbridge with a grin.

"I'm sorry to have disturbed you, gentlemen," she said to the members of the crew in the forecastle, and she calmly left and closed the door.

Psyche went across the waist deck to the after cabins, Waddlesworth placidly tucked under her arm. She didn't look up at the helm because she was sure Sheerness was still furious. Once she was back to her cabin, she set Waddlesworth on his pillow on the trunk and pet his back affectionately.

"You are becoming a troublemaker, young man," she said with a grin.

She had gone to the water closet and was on her way back to her cabin when Freddie arrived to take her breakfast tray. He looked in the room uncertainly when he saw Waddlesworth on the trunk. The drake was looking at the boy but didn't seem to be concerned.

"He won't hurt you, Freddie," assured Psyche.

"He was awful mean to Mr. Meals," said Freddie doubtfully.

"That's because Mr. Meals was going to cook him," said Psyche with a grin. "It was nothing personal against Meals." She retrieved the leftover bread from her breakfast tray and broke off a piece to give to Waddlesworth, who happily took it from her. Psyche broke off another piece and held it out to Freddie. "Here, you try."

"Oh, no!" said Freddie, his eyes rounding fearfully and shaking his head.

"He won't hurt you," cajoled Psyche. "The secret to getting on with Waddlesworth, like with any other animal, is understanding what he wants. My sister and brother-in-law—the viscount—said you have a way with horses, so I think you know what I mean. Animals are far simpler to figure than people. With Waddlesworth it's *very* simple. He likes to eat, and he likes to be petted," said Psyche with a chuckle as she gave Waddlesworth another piece of bread. She tried to give Freddie another piece. "You try. The worst that will happen is he won't take it from you, and I've *never* known him to turn down food."

Freddie took the piece of bread and hesitantly held it out to Waddlesworth. The duck looked from Freddie to the piece of bread before he reached out and took it from Freddie's fingers without even a nip. Freddie giggled with giddy relief to see his digits remained intact. Psyche gave him another piece, and Freddie gave it to Waddlesworth. Freddie soon grew confident enough he reached out to smooth a hand down the duck's back, and Waddlesworth didn't even blink.

Freddie stayed until the bread was gone, and then he took Psyche's tray to the dumbwaiter in the officers' mess and went to the berth deck to retrieve it. Before he left, he told her he would bring her dinner around two. Psyche thought that would be fine and got back to writing her letters. She had only finished the letter to Pandora and was starting the one for Damon when there was yet another knock on her door. Psyche heaved a frustrated sigh and got up to answer it. She was faced by another crew member she hadn't met before.

He was an older man with gray hair and twinkling blue eyes behind a set of spectacles. He was somewhere in his fifties, about her height, and sturdy. He was carrying a wooden box full of tools and wore a leather apron over his white homespun shirt.

"Begging your ladyship's pardon, but I'm Mr. Laing, the ship's carpenter," he said pleasantly.

"Nice to meet you," said Psyche calmly, holding out her hand. "What can I do for you, Mr. Laing?"

"The captain's asked me to make a few modifications to your cabin."

Psyche frowned. "What kind of modifications?" she asked concernedly.

"He acquired a few fixtures in Vigo yesterday that he thought would make you more comfortable," said Laing with a pleasant smile.

"A-all right," said Psyche hesitantly. She looked from the carpenter to Waddlesworth. "Is it going to be noisy?"

"Could be a mite noisy," said Laing, looking to the duck as well.

"Then I'll just go across the hall to the other cabin while you work and take the duck with me. I don't think he will bother you, but the noise might bother him," she said with a smile.

"I'm afraid that's where I have the things stored that I'll be moving in here," said Laing apologetically.

"Hmm," said Psyche thoughtfully, scratching her forehead. "Well, then, I guess I'll sit in the captain's cabin. Is it going to take long?"

"Shouldn't be more than an hour or two, I think," said Laing with an assuring smile.

"Fair enough," said Psyche, looking at her watch.

That was about the time Freddie would bring her dinner. She went to her desk for her book, and then she went to the trunk to pick up Waddlesworth on his pillow. She stopped in front of Laing before she went out the door.

"I wanted to thank you for my crutches, Mr. Laing. They've been very helpful," she said with a gracious smile.

"Your quite welcome, ladyship," he said with a smile of his own.

"Did you do all the work on the cabins?" she asked curiously.

He nodded. "Most of it, yes. Some was to the captain's specifications, but I directed the workers."

"I love the drawers under the bunks. That's very practical."

"That was something the captain suggested, as well as the bunks for the crew. Not very common."

"No, it isn't," agreed Psyche evenly. "My brother has a sloop, but the crew all have hammocks. What about the captain's bed? It's very unusual."

Laing scratched the back of his head thoughtfully. "That was an interesting thing to put together. He brought me all the pieces, told me what he wanted it look like when it was done, and left it to me to figure out how to do it."

"Well, I think it's very beautiful," said Psyche with a smile, "and big."

Laing chuckled. "It is that."

"Well, I'll leave you to your work, Mr. Laing," said Psyche pleasantly.

"Thank you, ladyship," he said with a smile.

Psyche went to Sheerness's cabin and looked around uncertainly. The top was closed on his desk. She was not going to sit on his bed; although, she was tempted to, just to see how comfortable it was. Everything was just as neat and tidy as she had seen it before. If she didn't know better, she would find it easy to believe he was never in there. She almost wanted to move something out of place to see if he would notice and what kind of reaction it would cause. She decided not to. He was already displeased; she didn't want to make it worse.

She took Waddlesworth on his pillow and settled into the chair near the fireplace with him on her lap. There were still a few embers burning, but it was warm enough from the sun coming through the windows Psyche didn't think she needed to add more wood. She opened her book to read. Waddlesworth started nervously when Laing began his work, with loud hammering and sawing, but Psyche was able to calm him after smoothing her hand over his back a few times. She leaned her head against the wing of the chair to muffle some of the noise and continued to read.

She was curious what *modifications* Sheerness thought her cabin needed. There wasn't room to add much else, not with the two trunks unstacked. It was a roomy cabin, though…not as big as *his* cabin, but it wasn't cramped. She liked having the trunk by the window because it reminded her of the window seat in the solarium. It wasn't as comfortable as that, but having the window to look out occasionally to rest her eyes from reading was nice. It also made it easier to put Waddlesworth into the shrouds and retrieve him.

She tried to concentrate on her book, but she soon ran into the same problem she had earlier. Psyche leaned around the wing of the chair and tried to see into her cabin and what Laing was doing, but the angle was wrong. She started to straighten back out and caught the scent of Sheerness's shaving lotion on the wing of the chair. She moved her nose to the back, but it wasn't quite as strong there, and she tried to imagine why. Then it came to her. With the way the chair was situated toward the fire, he sat in it at an angle, probably with one leg or both over the opposite arm. She put her nose back to the wing and inhaled. It did smell wonderful. Psyche went back to her book, and she found it somewhat easier to follow what she was reading.

Laing soon had the work done in her room, and she nervously went in to take a look. He had attached a full-length mirror to the wall opposite the bed that had a small chest at the base which could be used for sitting and storing her shoes. Beside it was a washstand. He had stacked both trunks behind the door and lashed them into place out of her way. Under the window was a small coffer with a cushion, the perfect height for sitting and looking out. Beside it near the washstand was a small table where she could put her water pitcher and the tray for her food to keep them from cluttering her desk. It made her cabin more crowded but also more comfortable, and she was pleased with all of it.

"Thank you, Mr. Laing. Excellent work, as usual," she said with a smile.

"You're welcome, ladyship," he said with a pleased smile of his own as he picked up his things and left.

Psyche put Waddlesworth on his cushion on the chest at the bottom of the mirror. He wasn't going to be bothered by having his reflection looking back at him. Psyche sat down at her desk and resumed writing her letter to Damon, and this time she was able to finish it without interruption. She had folded, sealed, and addressed it when there was another knock on her door. It was Freddie, bringing her dinner. He was amazed at the change in her room between this and the last time he had seen it. He wasn't able to stay and feed Waddlesworth because he had to help Meals start work on supper.

Psyche occupied herself for the rest of the afternoon making another larger copy of the map on her necklace. She still had no clues to where it was or what it would lead to. She didn't really care. The thrilling part was finding the map, and even if all it led to was an uninhabited oasis in the middle of the desert without one thing of value, it would be worth it to her to find it. Without maps to compare it to, though, she was unlikely to even know where to begin searching. Sheerness had maps, but that would mean asking him to let her use them, and she wasn't at all confident he would let her.

Shortly before sunset, Freddie returned to take away her dinner tray and refill her lamps. Since they were fairly high, Psyche did it because he would need to stand on a chair. She let him pet Waddlesworth while she took care of it, and Freddie considered it a fair trade. The only problem she had when it was time to light them, however, was that she had no way to do it. It was all well and good to have full lamps, but they were useless if they weren't lit.

She opened the door to her cabin and looked out. The lamps in the alcove weren't lit. She went to the door of the officers' mess and looked in. They weren't lit yet, and when she looked in the other direction, the lights in Sheerness's cabin weren't lit either. When she went to look, there were still a few embers on the grate. She found a small container of rushlights and lit one from the embers after blowing on them a little to get them hot enough. She took it to her cabin and lit the lamp close to the door. She didn't turn it up high to conserve the fuel. She blew out the rush and put it where she could find it later because she would use it to light the one near the bunk. She didn't want to light that one yet because she would need it when she went to bed.

She finally got around to looking at herself in the mirror. She still didn't understand what Sheerness found so troubling about her clothes. It was more form-fitting in the space between her breasts and her hips, but it wasn't immodest, certainly not any more immodest than some of the dresses society considered fashionable, like the one she had worn to the Stranraers' ball. It was made of a good color for her and extremely comfortable. Although her split skirts weren't trousers or breeches, she found them liberating and was surprised more women didn't wear them. She could easily understand why Pandora and Persephone preferred them, and they would be perfect for riding.

She was adjusting a few strands of hair back into her braid when there was a knock on the door. She was amazed at the number of "callers" she had received today. This was her third day (somewhat) of being aboard, and she had seen more people today than on the other two…if she didn't consider her adventures on the berth deck the previous afternoon, and she didn't.

When Psyche answered the door, she was unsurprised it wasn't Sheerness. To see him would have startled her more. She knew he held her responsible for Waddlesworth taking up residence on the figurehead. She supposed she was, since she hadn't let Meals cook him. But Sheerness was angry with her before that, and she was trying to determine the exact point when it started.

Almost since she had woke up on his ship. It was even before then, and it was a combination—more likely an agglomeration—of many things.

She didn't want to marry him, and she didn't believe he loved her. That was probably the one thing that made everything else she did wrong all the more irksome.

She wouldn't let him wait on her, help her, or do anything for her. That wasn't anything personal; Psyche preferred to do things for herself, and it wasn't as if she refused to let him do anything. She had sense enough to know when she needed help; she just didn't need it as often as he liked (apparently).

She couldn't be angry with Pandora for putting her in the trunk. No one understood better than Psyche what a traumatic experience it was, but she really did bring it on herself.

She had justifiably taken exception to his going through her mail, and he seemed irritated she had asked him not to. She would never think of looking through his mail—or anything else—without his permission. Giving him her necklace irritated him more than her taking him to task for looking through them, but she didn't want him to have an excuse to keep doing it.

He didn't like her clothes, and while she had expected to have more actual dresses, her wardrobe was fairly well what it would have been had she overseen it herself and taken this trip the way she had originally intended: with Myron and *walking* up the gangway. While her clothes were unusual, they weren't indecent, and it was senseless for him to think it necessary to buy her more.

And then there was Waddlesworth. She didn't know what about the duck riled him so, but she supposed they *had* gotten off to a bad start. It could be remedied, but Sheerness didn't find it worth the effort.

It was apparent she could do nothing right in his opinion, and it was something he had demonstrated last year, which was why it was all too easy for her to believe he was being insincere when he said he loved her. She couldn't believe he would be so judgmental of everything she did if he loved her.

Dr. Felton was there to invite her to dine with the officers and the captain, at Sheerness's request. Psyche would have wondered why Sheerness didn't come himself, but that would have been silly. She let the doctor examine her hands, and he was pleased they were improving. She let him escort her to the table, and he set her crutch out of the way once she was seated.

She found herself sitting beside Sheerness, who sat at the head of the table, and she was across from Higginbotham. Felton sat on the other side of her, and she was introduced to Mr. Blossom. Mr. Broughton was overseeing the helm, so she had yet to meet him. Stockbridge and Laing ate with the rest of the crew on the berth deck, along with the gunner, Rolleston. Psyche wasn't sure how the meal would go. She would have no problem being polite to Sheerness, but she wasn't sure how well *he* would behave.

It actually went well. Sheerness ignored her, but with the other three men to talk to, there was no shortage of chatter. She did thank him for the new furnishings in her room, but after his terse reply, she didn't make any further effort to speak to him. She enjoyed talking with the other men about different things: places they had been, family, things they had seen. Sheerness's reserve did make the other men uncomfortable, but they were charmed to have a woman's company, and Psyche was a good conversationalist.

When supper was over, Psyche stood and thanked the men for their discourse. She went to her cabin and shut the door, and then she retrieved the bread she had secreted away for Waddlesworth out of the pocket in her pants. After he finished eating, she opened the window and let him out. She was glad he hadn't made a mess in her room. That would be one more thing to make Sheerness mad.

She made sure the window wasn't going to close, and then she looked through her drawers for a shift and a dressing gown and put them on. She needed to go to the water closet, but she wasn't sure if Sheerness had gone to his room yet. She hadn't heard him go by, but she had been preoccupied. She opened the door and carefully looked out. The door to the mess was closed, and when she looked in the direction of Sheerness's cabin, it didn't look like any lights were on. She went back to her cabin and lit the rush and hurried to the water closet. The light wouldn't stay burning long, and she wanted to be back in her cabin before Sheerness came in. He seemed to be in an unpleasant mood after the events of that morning and intent on trying to pretend she wasn't there. That was probably for the best.

She had to admit, however, that his actions were confusing. He had sent Laing to add the new furnishings. She assumed that had been what he wanted to talk to her about the night before, and it surprised her that he had them put in despite how furious he was. He had invited her to join him and the officers for supper, even if it was through Felton, even though he ignored her and didn't seem happy she was there.

Psyche finished in the water closet and opened the door, carefully holding the light with two fingers as it began to burn even lower. She was so intent on keeping the light burning without adding more injury to her fingers she didn't see Sheerness until she almost ran into him. That surprised her so much the rush burned her fingers, and it dropped to the floor and guttered out as she put her throbbing index finger in her mouth with a squeak. She gave Sheerness an accusatory look, which he could see from the light of the fire he had kindled.

"You should make more noise or something," said Psyche testily.

"Would you like me to walk 'round with bells on my boots?" he asked sardonically.

"Hunh," said Psyche. She tried to go past him to return to her cabin, but he stood in her way. "Will you move, please?"

Sheerness looked at her in the firelight. Her dressing gown was open, and it was hard to remember he was supposed to ignore her. The wrapper was made of thin white silk with ruffles and lace at the ends of the sleeves and around the edges. It looked like a typical dressing gown...mostly.

Her shift, however, did not look ordinary. It was made of burgundy silk as thin as her wrapper. The length of it came to about mid-thigh, like a chemise, with a ruffled edge at the bottom. The neck had more frills and came down in a point that ended midway between her breasts. There was a set of strings a little higher up, just below her collarbone, which were fastened to keep it from sliding off her shoulders. The ends of the sleeves were exposed under the ruffling of her wrapper. Sheerness was finding it hard to breathe. He would go back to being inaccessible, but right now, he couldn't for the life of him remember why he should.

He moved closer to her and put his arm around her waist under her dressing gown. He pulled her nearer and smoothed a hand across her back. He put his other hand to the side of her neck and bent his head to kiss her, softly at first, but he began to deepen it as he felt her yield against him pliably and return it, one of her hands moving to curl softly in his hair. Sheerness moved the hand at her neck down the exposed skin of her chest, between her breasts, and across her stomach to her back, and then he moved both of his hands to cup her bottom and press her hips against him.

Psyche moaned softly, and there was a muffled clatter as her crutch fell to the carpet when she raised her other hand to the side of his face. She hadn't expected him to kiss her, but she was willing to let him. There was a quivery tension starting in her stomach, and she wanted him so much her knees felt weak. His lips left her mouth to move along her jaw to her neck, and her fingers tightened in his hair as he nipped at her earlobe. Psyche didn't know why she was so willing and ached so much when he was always so mean.

When she understood what it was that she felt, the nature of the fluttering in her stomach changed to one of utter panic. She could feel the skin on her face starting to tingle as the blood drained out of it, and she felt like she couldn't breathe for entirely different reasons. Psyche loved him. She didn't want to, and knowing she did despite her wishes to the contrary frightened her. She couldn't be here with him right now.

Sheerness had unfastened the strings at the neck of her shift, and Psyche felt his hand go to her breast and squeeze it softly. Oh, she wanted him, and now she knew she loved him, but she couldn't do this...not right now. He brought his lips back to hers and kissed her hungrily, and it took all of her effort to break the kiss and turn her face away from his.

"I can't do this," she whispered sadly.

Sheerness moved his hands to her shoulders and placed a gentle kiss at her temple. "Of course, you can," he whispered longingly. "Don't take whatever it is you take to go to sleep, and stay here with me."

Psyche turned her head to look at him, and he saw her troubled expression. She reached up a hand to caress his cheek and brush her thumb over his chin before she put a tender kiss at the corner of his mouth. She moved her hand to the side of his neck and shook her head apologetically before she stepped back from him.

"I can't," she said again, and she bent down to retrieve her crutch and walked to her cabin.

When she had the door closed behind her, she leaned against it with her back and took a shaky breath, a hand going to the tight ball that had formed in the pit of her stomach. She kept her eyes closed and bit her lower lip to keep herself from crying.

When she felt she had more control of herself, she went to the window and brought Waddlesworth back inside and placed him on his cushion. Then she brushed her teeth and unbraided and brushed her hair. She retrieved the medicine kit from the drawer under her bunk. Psyche removed the bandage from her knee and put on more ointment but not another bandage. It was well enough now exposure to air would be better.

After she put more ointment on her fingers and put the jar away, she got a glass of water for her sleeping draught. She almost didn't take it, but that would be foolish. Tonight of all nights, she wouldn't sleep if she didn't take it, and the things she would think about to keep her awake were things she didn't *want* to think about yet. Tomorrow would be soon enough. She was going to try turning off the lamp before she went to sleep because she *had* to move past her fear of the dark.

She lit the lamp by the bed using a small piece of paper, and then she turned off the one by the mirror. She retied the strings on her shift and added an extra blanket to her bunk, and then she tried to go to sleep. Luckily, because of the draught, it didn't take long, and just as she felt on the verge of being unable to stay awake any longer, she turned off the lamp. Knowing the light was gone did cause anxiety, but the draught would work. It always did.

Sheerness lay in bed, watching the light under Psyche's door. He saw when it went off, and he frowned with dissatisfaction. He was tempted to go see if she was actually asleep, but he took her actions to mean it would be unwelcome. Something was worrying her. She had wanted him, and he could have convinced her to stay, but she wouldn't have been happy.

It was almost as if something had frightened her, and Sheerness couldn't think of anything it might have been. He hadn't been harsh, and he hadn't tried to force himself on her, but it almost seemed as if *he* had been the cause of it in some way. And yet the way she had caressed his cheek and kissed him before she left had made him feel as if she was unhappy to leave him. Her mind was always working; he couldn't even be certain what was troubling her had anything to do with what they were doing. She wouldn't tell him, either.

He had overheard her talking with Freddie about animals and how much easier they were to figure than people. He hadn't meant to eavesdrop, but he had heard it nonetheless. She had a point. He could understand nothing about *her*. He didn't know what she wanted, and it was driving him insane trying to discover it. He was beginning to believe it was something he couldn't give her.

Sheerness rolled over to face the wall and put a pillow over his head. He would have to do his best to follow through on his plan to be inaccessible. Perhaps it would work, but if it didn't, it would at least keep him far enough away from her that he wouldn't be overwhelmed by the urge kiss her.

Chapter Twenty Two

Psyche settled into a routine on the ship over the following days, and she found plenty to keep herself occupied. When she wasn't doing something in her cabin, she had found a comfortable place to read on the deck sitting in one of the tarped launches, which kept her out of the way of the crew and gave her a good view of the ocean. The small boat would rock slightly as the ship traveled, and she felt almost as if she were in a large hammock. She wore a pair of her tinted spectacles to keep the glare of the sun from bothering her eyes, and the weather remained sunny and warm. She much preferred reading in the boat than she did in her cabin. It gave her fresh air and also let her become more familiar with the men of the small crew.

Freddie would bring her breakfast and dinner to her cabin, and at night she had supper with Sheerness and the rest of the officers. She finally met Mr. Broughton, and she liked him as much as the rest. They were all friendly and honest, and Psyche always looked forward to having conversations with them. All of them had been sailing for years, and they had been to places Psyche found fascinating, including Greece and Egypt.

She was able to take her shower the following day with Freddie standing watch at the door to the officers' mess. The salt water stung Psyche's knee and hands at first, but she was so happy to be clean she didn't care. The pressure of the water was kept at a decent rate by the use of a foot pedal, which was why she had been unable to use it until her knee felt better, and the water was wonderfully hot. She would have been satisfied with the water coming out at barely a trickle and colder just so she didn't feel scummy anymore.

Sheerness came belowdecks while she was showering, and Freddie made him wait. Sheerness wasn't happy he was barred from his own cabin, by a child no less, but it wasn't as if he could go in while Psyche was showering, no matter how tempting it might be. When he was finally allowed in, he almost had to turn around and leave again. His cabin smelled of her soap, which smelled the same as her perfume. She had already gone to her cabin and closed the door, and he had to fight the urge to hunt her down and ravish her. He opened all the windows in his cabin, and he didn't stay very long. By the evening, the smell had lessened, but there was still a faint trace of it that lingered in the air, and he did not sleep well that night.

By Saturday, Psyche's hands were well enough she could submerge them in soapy water to wash her clothing. She had thought about hanging them outside her window in the shrouds, but there were certain items she would just as soon not let the crew see fluttering in the breeze. She had Freddie find her some rope, and Psyche put up a makeshift line in her cabin. Once they were dry, she took the rope down and stored it in the coffer. She would need it again. There was a clothes iron on board, and she carefully ironed the things that needed it before folding and putting them away. She had watched Chrissoula and the other maids do it often enough she was familiar with it, and with only a few burns to her already mangled fingers, she did it herself.

Also by Saturday, she was able to walk without her crutch. She limped somewhat, but she could move around without support. The bruising had faded to a pale yellowish green, and the area it covered had shrank. The skinned area over her kneecap was also growing smaller, and as the edges began to heal, she tried not to scratch it.

As they neared the Strait of Gibraltar, their speed slowed somewhat. While the weather was temperate, the wind had died down, and even under full sail, their progress was less. On Saturday night, they encountered a fog bank that made it even more difficult to travel quickly, but they were into the strait by the following morning. Her heart beat excitedly when she borrowed Higginbotham's spyglass to look to either side of the ship at the cliffs and mountains. Once they were through the strait, they were in the Mediterranean and that much closer to Greece and Egypt.

There was always at least one crew member in the crosstrees for the mainsail keeping watch for other ships. England was finally at peace with France after the Bourbons entered Paris in April, but there were pirates from the coast of North Africa. Once they got further into the Mediterranean, the likelihood of trouble would lessen, but the area around the strait was teeming with them. They wouldn't care the *Medea* carried nothing of value; taking the people prisoner and holding them for ransom to the British government would be a worthy enough prize. There were also Americans, and the conflict with the United States was not over.

They had already been hailed a few times by other ships, but they had all, fortunately, been friendly. One had even been a British first rate, and Sheerness met with the captain to discuss the conditions in the Mediterranean. After that meeting, he felt more confident, but he still had a lookout at all times. If anyone did try to board them, he wanted to be prepared and hopefully avoid having his ship commandeered.

By the time Psyche went to bed on Sunday night, their progress through the Alboran Sea, which was technically the Mediterranean, was slow. They had yet to reach a dead calm, but the sails were finding it difficult to catch even a small amount of breeze. She took her sleeping draught after brushing her teeth and hair and bringing Waddlesworth in from the shrouds, and then, just as she was unable to stay awake any longer, she turned off the lamp by her bed. She was no longer afraid to sleep, but her insomnia wasn't going away...especially not these nights. Her fear of the dark had lessened, but she still had to have a light when she went in the water closet, and leaving on the lamp by her bed had become a habit.

About an hour later, under Waddlesworth's suspicious glare, Sheerness silently came in to make sure she was tucked in and sleeping peacefully and to kiss her good night. He had started on Friday night, and it gave him peace of mind to see she was all right, even though it was drug-induced. The first night he came in, Waddlesworth hissed at him, but Sheerness was prepared and offered the duck a piece of bread after hearing Psyche's conversation with Freddie. The duck still didn't like him, but he was satisfied to let Sheerness come in for his brief visits provided the earl remembered to bring him a gift.

Sheerness brought a lamp with him the first time, and he retrieved the medicine kit to determine which bottle she was using. That was fairly easy to guess; it was one in the bottom rather than the lid, and its contents were decreasing. He lifted the other bottle in the bottom and realized it was laudanum when he opened it and smelled. He was relieved it appeared, as yet, untouched. He wasn't sure what Keung had put in the sleeping draught, but Sheerness was confident it was nothing nearly as harmful as opium.

After Thursday night when she left his cabin, Sheerness had noticed she was putting almost as much effort into avoiding him as he was into avoiding her. He would watch from the helm as she laughed and joked with the rest of the crew when she was topside, but she never came to the poop deck when he was there. The only time they were in close proximity to each other was at supper when she sat beside him at the table. She was polite, and she would speak to him, but she kept herself distant. It puzzled Sheerness. He had thought his being inaccessible would make her *want* to spend time with him, but it seemed to have the opposite effect. Coming into her cabin to make sure she was sleeping at least allayed his worries she might be unwell.

When Psyche woke up on Monday morning, she could feel the ship moving faster, but something wasn't right. She brushed her teeth and dressed after going to the water closet with a slight frown between her brows. Freddie brought her breakfast, and after she gave Waddlesworth his bread and put him into the shrouds, she sat at the window to watch him for a time as she ate, still frowning. She wasn't sure what was wrong, but it would come to her, probably when she quit thinking about it so much.

Psyche had still not come to comfortably accept she was in love with Sheerness. When she woke on Friday, it was the first thought that came to her, and it was no less unsettling then than it had been on Thursday night. She didn't know how it could have happened. She had tried so hard not to, but it was impossible to deny. If she were honest with herself, she would have to admit it had happened quite some time ago. What she was going to do about it was what troubled her. It wasn't as if she could take it back; it was much too late for that. She had come to think of it as an addiction, and if she could avoid him, maybe she could keep it from becoming worse…maybe even *wean* herself off of it. She was sure it was hopeless, but it was all she could think to do.

So far, it wasn't working. Every night she went to bed, he was what she thought of, and it was the same every morning. She couldn't get away from him on the ship, and she hadn't mentioned Thessaloniki again. He continued to avoid her as well. At supper, he was polite and spoke to her, but he didn't go out of his way to make anything more than shallow conversation. It reminded her of the week in London between the Stranraers' ball and her tour of the *Medea*. She didn't like it any more now than she did then, but it was probably for the best.

Her only problem was that she didn't know *why* he was doing it. Before, he had done it to make her feel *less confused*. It hadn't helped then, and it wasn't helping now. She hadn't done anything more to make him angry, other than not staying with him on Thursday night. Waddlesworth had been the model of good behavior. Her wardrobe hadn't become any more offensive. She didn't see him often enough to have said anything to irritate him, and considering how meaningless the discourse was when they did speak, it was unlikely that was the cause.

But she couldn't have it both ways. She couldn't keep her distance *and* not have him ignore her. If she was going to make that stop, then she would have to spend more time in his company and take whatever came with it. She wasn't prepared to do that yet. She would have to eventually because she had to get to Thessaloniki, and it was his ship. She didn't want to use him, and that is what it would be. When she stopped avoiding him, it would be because she wanted to…not because she had to.

Once Psyche realized what was troubling her about how fast they were going, she looked out the window with moderate concern to confirm it. Freddie hadn't mentioned anything was out of the ordinary, but it was very odd. Sheerness would be overseeing the helm. That would mean talking to him, but she was too curious; just talking to him about this seemed harmless enough.

She looked in the mirror at herself. She was wearing another of her split skirts and a matching gansey. The sweater was made of shades of darker and lighter green yarn that brought out the color in her eyes, and the trousers were in a matching color of olive green. Even though her fingers were well enough, she still kept her hair in a braid rather than putting it up, simply because it was easier. She looked as presentable as ever, and by this point, the crew had become accustomed to not seeing her in a dress. She wasn't sure about Sheerness, but he had made no further comment about it.

Once she retrieved Waddlesworth out of the shrouds and closed the window, she left her cabin and went topside. When she reached the waistdeck, she put on her tinted spectacles to shield her eyes from the sun and looked toward the bow of the ship. The temperature was balmy without being unbearably hot, something aided by the spray that would come up from the bow. The day was remarkably clear, and she could see some land mass in the distance, a large one. The sails were full and taut under the power of a good wind. Wherever they were going, it wouldn't be long before they got there.

It was nearing eleven as she glanced at her watch, and she turned to look through the railing to the poop deck. Sheerness was, as she suspected, standing near the helm. Psyche sighed resignedly and made her way up the stairs toward him. When he saw her approaching, he looked surprised. Psyche went to stand beside him and turned to look toward the bow, her hands clasped casually behind her back. Sheerness looked at her with a curious expression.

"Is there a problem?" he finally asked her mildly when it didn't seem she was going to say anything.

"You do realize east is that way?" she asked, pointing toward the left.

Sheerness feigned surprise. "Is it really? And all this time, I thought it was whatever direction the bow was pointing."

Psyche looked at him and lowered her spectacles on her nose to gaze at him directly and folded her arms across her chest. It was obvious from his waggish reply he was perfectly aware of where they were going and whatever it may be was south rather than east. Her concern evaporated, and Psyche decided to use this opportunity to find out if he was ignoring her because he was angry or for some other reason. He was in a pleasant mood, and she couldn't see any harm. She attempted to maintain her grave expression because she wanted to see what response her next question would provoke.

"Are we lost? Maybe you should stop and ask for directions," she said solemnly.

Sheerness threw his head back and laughed uproariously. Of all the things he thought she would approach him to speak about, this was not among them. She seemed sincere in her concern, which is why he found it so amusing. After he calmed somewhat, he looked at her and wiped a tear from the corner of his eye. She was looking at him with a teasing, wry smile, and he realized she hadn't been serious after all.

"Oh," he groaned with a sigh, "that was funny."

"Honestly, though, where are we going?" asked Psyche mildly.

"Melilla," replied Sheerness matter-of-factly.

"Melilla? As in, it's-actually-in-Morocco-but-it's-part-of-Spain Melilla?" she said with surprise.

"That would be the one," said Sheerness with a grin.

"Why?"

"Because I hoped we would be to Cartagena by now to resupply, but it's still too far away. The wind was favorable, so I decided to go to Melilla." He looked at her with a half-smile. "Do you not *want* to go to Melilla?"

Psyche shrugged indifferently and grinned. "I have no preference. I understand it has some very nice Moorish and Spanish colonial architecture, but I prefer something older. I just happened to notice we weren't heading toward Greece anymore, so I thought I would find out where we *are* heading."

"Well, now you know," said Sheerness with a wink.

"So I do," said Psyche, pushing her spectacles back up her nose. "Ta."

She turned and went back to her cabin. That had been painless enough. The only thing she hadn't thought to ask him was whether or not they would stay overnight. In the end, it didn't really matter. Now she needed to make sure all her letters were written since they would be stopping, and she wasn't sure when that would happen again. It seemed, however, Sheerness tried to stop every five days or so. Still, considering how amazed he was at the number of letters she sent from Vigo, it wouldn't do to let the amount grow too high. She still had credit left from the necklace she had given him, and she had more jewelry and nowhere to wear it if not.

She had two letters for Pandora. There was the one for Damon. She quickly wrote letters to her parents, Amalie, the Yeardleys, and Chrissoula. She wrote a letter to Selena and Dorian. Her sister-in-law still had a month or two before she was due, but Psyche wanted her to know she was thinking about her. Lastly, she wrote a letter to Georgiana. She had no notion of whether or not the marchioness would get it, but considering her husband was still in prison, there shouldn't be anyone to stop her from getting it. Psyche wanted Georgiana to know she had not been forgotten.

Psyche looked out the window when she was finished. They had entered the port and were close to mooring. It was a beautiful city, with high, crenellated walls and orange tile roofs, built on a rocky escarpment that jutted into the sea. The towering walls made it very imposing. She could see why Spain felt after the *Reconquista* that it would be wise to take it from the Moors. Better to use it to defend themselves than to try to attack it.

Psyche heard many feet moving around topside as the crew furled the sails and prepared to tie off, and as she continued to gaze out the window, the ship gently glided into its slip. There was a slight bump as it stopped, and she heard voices shouting in Spanish as the crew on shore called to that on the ship. She gathered her letters and left her cabin with the intention of finding Sheerness topside, but he was already coming below when she entered the officers' mess.

"Could you possibly mail these, please?" she asked, holding out the letters toward him.

"More letters?" he blurted. "You just mailed some five days ago."

"Yes, but I promised I would write as often as I could," said Psyche evenly.

Sheerness took them from her. "All right," he said agreeably. "Would you like to go ashore?"

"Thank you, and no, thank you," said Psyche with a slight smile. "Will we be staying overnight?"

"No, actually, we'll only be staying long enough to resupply and sail with the tide, if possible."

Psyche tilted her head sideways. "I may take a walk on the beach, but I don't feel an urge to see the city."

"Fair enough," said Sheerness with a shrug. "Just make sure you take someone with you...someone bigger than Freddie," he said with a grin.

"All right," chortled Psyche, and she went back to her cabin.

Sheerness looked down at the thick pile of letters in his hand. It was bigger than the first one. He almost started to look through them, but he tightened his hold and went to his cabin to get his coat. They were all going to England, and that was all he needed to know.

After dinner, Psyche went for a walk on the beach with Freddie and Stockbridge. They didn't go far, in part because Psyche's knee was not up to it and also because it wouldn't be long before they sailed. The sand was a glaring white, which made it easy to find seashells and other things washed up on the shore. Psyche had brought a net bag to put things in as they found them, and by the time they returned to the ship, it was full.

Psyche was surprised to learn Freddie didn't know how to swim. It was disconcerting he was on a ship and didn't know how. He wasn't afraid of the water, which was good, but his swimming was something that needed to be remedied as quickly as possible. She and Stockbridge tried to explain the basics as they walked, but he really needed to go in the water and learn. Had there been more time, she would have started while they were on the beach, but there wasn't, and she didn't have on the right clothes in any event.

Not long after they returned to the ship, it was under way. Sheerness was standing on the deck, and his jaw tightened when the three of them walked up the gangway, laughing and chattering with each other. He didn't like that she had taken Stockbridge. He was younger and handsome…with an easy charm. Sheerness didn't notice any flirting or familiarity between the two of them, but they got on well with each other. Sheerness was jealous, jealous she was comfortable with the bosun and that Stockbridge had been able to spend time with her while Sheerness could not.

The drop in latitude and brief stop proved helpful. The wind picked up, and the *Medea* was able to make good time once again in the direction of her intended destination. They continued to skirt along the coast of Africa, near enough Psyche could occasionally see it in the distance when she was topside. They would see other ships from time to time but none that hailed them.

Things on the ship remained in much the same pattern they had settled into since leaving Vigo. Psyche and Sheerness continued to avoid each other, except for his nocturnal visits to kiss her good night. Waddlesworth had grown so accustomed to them he didn't even glare anymore. Psyche still wasn't ready to spend more time with Sheerness, but she always looked forward to supper.

Psyche worked on teaching Freddie how to swim, but there wasn't much she could do by just *telling* him. They really needed an opportunity for him to try it. Four days later presented that. She just had to convince Sheerness to stop. There was an island looming in front of them, and the shallow water would be perfect. It wasn't out of their way, since they would be sailing directly past it, and Psyche was confident they were making decent time and could afford to stop for a while.

After she took her second volume of Pliny the Younger back to her cabin, she went topside and climbed the stairs to the poop deck. Sheerness was at the helm, Higginbotham standing beside him. That was perfect. Sheerness looked at her as she approached him, and he was curious, since it happened so rarely. He hadn't long to wait.

"What is that?" she asked as she pointed to the steadily-approaching island.

"That's probably Pantelleria. Why?" he asked suspiciously.

"Can we stop for one or two hours, please?"

"Why?" he asked with a frown.

Psyche glanced over at Higginbotham and gave him a smile. "Because Freddie needs to learn how to swim, and he can't do it while the ship is moving or if we're docked in a port."

"Freddie doesn't know how to swim?" asked Sheerness with surprise.

"No. I've been teaching him, but I can only do so much *without* water."

Sheerness looked at Higginbotham. It was unusual, but not unheard of, for a sailor to not know how to swim, and Freddie was only a boy. Still, Sheerness was concerned someone on his crew could not. He hadn't even thought to ask Higginbotham if his nephew could swim before taking Freddie on as a cabin boy; he had assumed he could. The waters around Pantelleria were warm and shallow. The crew had been sailing for two weeks with only brief stops to resupply. They were making *excellent* time; Sheerness anticipated they would be to Athens in less than a week. A slight detour wouldn't hurt, and he agreed with Psyche that Freddie needed to learn.

"I suppose we can do one or two hours," said Sheerness agreeably. He looked Psyche up and down. "What are you going to wear? You can't wear that. Did your sister pack a bathing costume, by chance?"

Psyche shrugged. "No, she wouldn't think I'd need one, but I'll find something," she said diffidently as she went back to her cabin.

Sheerness watched her leave and frowned. He wasn't sure he liked the sound of that. There would have to be some rules put in place. He could only imagine what she had in mind, and he was sure it was something the crew shouldn't see. It was probably something *he* shouldn't see either. He couldn't understand why her sister wouldn't think to give her something for swimming, but given everything else he had seen, he somehow found it unsurprising.

They approached the island and skimmed along its northern shore. He had the crew haul in the sails and drop the anchors when they began to turn further south. It was a shallow cove a distance away from any settlements, one edge of it demarcated by a rock formation that looked like an elephant dipping its trunk into the water. As they had been nearing the island and looking for a suitable location, Sheerness had Stockbridge and Blossom inform the crew what they were doing and what Sheerness expected. Once the sails were furled and the anchors set, Sheerness went below and knocked on Psyche's door. She answered with a pleasant expression, still wearing the same clothes.

"We are stopped," said Sheerness evenly. "The crew has been told to stay to the starboard side of the ship. You are to keep to portside. I don't think I need to mention they're not likely to wear anything should they swim, but I thought I would anyhow."

Psyche raised an eyebrow and quirked her lips. "Usually—at home—I don't either, but Freddie might find that a bit...unnerving."

Sheerness's jaw went slack, and he almost changed his mind about the entire thing. "So, what *are* you going to wear?"

"I was thinking my black chemise. It's short enough and light enough I can swim without being weighed down by it, and it won't be sheer once it's wet."

"A *chemise?* " said Sheerness breathlessly. It was worse than he thought. "Don't you have anything better?"

"Well, yes, I do, but it's far less modest," she said with a grin.

Sheerness blinked disconcertedly. Now he was definitely thinking they should sail on. He also found the way she seemed to be intentionally teasing him somewhat *unnerving* himself. He knew how he wanted to react to it, but he also knew that he shouldn't.

"Why don't you let me teach him?" he asked as calmly as he could.

"Because I've already been teaching him, and he trusts me," said Psyche blithely as she walked to her window and opened it.

She lifted Waddlesworth from his pillow to put him onto the channel, and he promptly flew down to begin fishing. She looked down at the water. It was very clear and blue, and it looked absolutely perfect. It was quite a distance from her window, but she wasn't concerned about falling into the water as long as the ship wasn't moving. She turned to look at Sheerness.

"Can I get a ladder rigged from the shrouds here?" she asked curiously.

"Why?"

"I was just thinking I could go into and out of the water from here rather than the deck. Would that be more *modest* for you?"

"Yes, actually, it would," said Sheerness dryly.

If she did that, then the only crew member who might see her would be the one in the crosstrees, and he shouldn't be looking at the water that close to the ship anyhow. And, of course, there would be himself.

"I'll take care of that for you," he said evenly.

After Sheerness left, Psyche went to his cabin for two towels. Then she went to her cabin and got her black chemise. As she looked at it, she realized the bottom edge wouldn't stay in place in the water. She had some breeches, but that would be too much cloth to suit her. She was completely serious when she told Sheerness she didn't wear anything when she went swimming at home, and that was the way she was most comfortable. She held up the chemise and looked at it thoughtfully. It was too short to tie between her legs, and it might constrict her movements. Then she had the solution.

Psyche opened the drawer with her kits for the one with the medicines. She got the sewing kit and the scissors. She put the chemise against the front of her and marked a spot up from the bottom edge. Then she laid it out flat on the bunk and cut both the back and front up to that point. She turned it inside out, threaded her needle, and began to sew. It wouldn't be pretty because she was doing it quickly, and she couldn't sew well, but it would suit. She retrieved a pair of garters and removed a belt from one of her dressing gowns.

She heard movement outside her window while she was sewing, and one of the crew tied a Jacob's ladder to the deadeyes. It was a good thing she hadn't begun changing clothes yet. He wasn't looking in her window, but there wasn't anything for him to see at the moment.

Once he was gone, she changed her clothes for the chemise. It wasn't easy to slide over her hips, and she began to grow concerned it might not go at all when she shimmied a little and it finally moved. She looped the belt from the front to the back then to the front again at her waist and tied it, and then she fastened the garters at the bottom of the legs. Then she went to look in the mirror. To say it looked bizarre was an understatement, but it would keep her from exposing herself...mostly. It was better than nothing, and it was better than no modifications at all. Freddie wouldn't be bothered by it; he was still at the age when girls were thought of as a nuisance.

When there was a knock at her door, she put on the beltless dressing gown and went to answer it. It was Freddie.

"Are you ready?" she asked him with an encouraging smile as she opened the door further to let him in.

"I think so," he said nervously.

"It will be fun!" said Psyche with a grin. "We'll teach you to float and tread today. If you can do that, the rest is a snap." Psyche put the towels on the table, and then she looked at Freddie. "You'll want to take off your shoes, socks, shirt and waistcoat." She took off her robe and began to climb out the window. "Ordinarily, I recommend not wearing anything, but perhaps it would be better if you were used to the weight of clothing at first."

Once Psyche was standing in the shrouds, she held onto the ropes as she looked down. It was awfully high up, but her fear was lessened because she knew it wouldn't hurt if she fell, and she could swim if she did. Heights above dry land or while the boat was moving were a completely different prospect, and this was about as high as she liked to be even above still water.

She let go of the ropes and held her arms out from her sides, and then she leapt into the air to perform a perfect somersault before putting her hands above her head as she dove into the water with barely a splash. She kicked to the surface and turned to look back at the ship. Freddie was standing on the platform with an awed expression.

"Wow," he gasped.

Psyche chuckled as she frog-kicked closer. "I recommend you use the ladder for now," she said with a grin.

Psyche waited near the bottom as he hurriedly climbed down, and then she began to teach him to swim. Freddie was a quick study, and it didn't take long to teach him how to float on his back and tread water. That salt water added buoyancy over fresh water helped, and Psyche tried to explain that to him so if he should ever happen to swim in a lake or river, it wouldn't take him by surprise. She also had him try holding his breath under water, so he wouldn't panic should it happen he went below the surface unintentionally. Once he had confidence with those, she taught him a few different basic strokes. By the end of an hour, he was climbing the ladder and jumping from the channel without fear, and Psyche was confident he would be able to fend for himself should he fall overboard. She felt better now.

Psyche dove down to the bottom a few times, which was less than thirty feet below. On the last one, she spotted something silver hidden among the seaweed and rocks, and she grabbed it and took it to the surface. She paddled over to the ladder and climbed up to sit beside Freddie, who was taking a rest. Once she was seated, she opened her hand. Her eyes rounded in surprise, and she gave a startled gasp.

"Wow," said Freddie.

It was a coin, an old one. One side had Athena, the other Pegasus. The edges were worn, and most of the writing was gone, but there was enough left for Psyche to see it was Greek. From the design, she thought it might be a stater, but she was in no way a numismatist. She held it out to Freddie.

"Here you go," she said with a grin.

"Really?" said Freddie in wonder.

"Consider it a medal for champion swimming," said Psyche with a chuckle. "Just don't try to spend it. That coin is over two thousand years old and worth far more than a shilling."

"But you found it," said Freddie uncertainly.

Psyche shrugged and bumped her shoulder against his. "I'll see if I can find any more, but that one is yours regardless."

"Thank you," said Freddie appreciatively.

Psyche stood up and prepared to dive off the platform. "Don't worry if I'm gone for a while. I'll be back."

Psyche dove in and swam on the surface until she was above the place where she found the coin. She turned to face the ship and waved to Freddie with a smile before she went under and headed for the bottom. It was easy enough for her to find the place where she had spotted the coin. It stood out because one of the rocks had been a different color and shape than those around it, white and square standing out against the rough, black basalt of the rest. She lifted the rock and moved it out of the way, and she was so surprised she almost forgot she was underwater and inhaled. She looked around the rest of the area for anything else unusual, but there was nothing. She began to gather her trove with the intention of taking it all to the surface. It would be heavy, but that was the nice thing about being under water: even rocks weighed less.

Sheerness went across the deck to the portside of the ship and climbed down the shrouds for the mizzenmast to the channel outside Psyche's window. Freddie was there looking at something in his hand, but Psyche was nowhere to be seen. Freddie turned to look at him as he climbed down, wearing a pair of black trews. Sheerness bent down to look into the window of the cabin, but Psyche wasn't there. Freddie didn't seem to be concerned.

"Have you learned to swim, Mr. Bunney?" asked Sheerness with a grin as he sat down beside him.

"Yes, sir," chortled Freddie. "Lady Psyche's crackin' good at it."

Sheerness looked at what Freddie was holding. "What's that there?"

"Lady Psyche found it for me. She said it was me medal for champion swimming," Freddie said with a grin.

Sheerness looked over the water's surface and beneath it just below the platform, but he still didn't see her. Waddlesworth was paddling about not far from the ship, but no Psyche.

"Where is she, by the by?" he asked mildly.

"She went to look for more coins," said Freddie casually as he looked at his coin. "Over that way," said Freddie, pointing about fifty feet from the ship.

Sheerness frowned. He had been sitting with Freddie for almost two minutes. "How long ago did she go looking?"

Freddie shrugged. "She went under a minute or two before you got here, I suppose. She said not to worry if she's gone for a while."

Sheerness *was* worried. She had been under water for at least three minutes, perhaps even as long as four or five. He didn't know how she could possibly hold her breath that long. He was about to dive in and look for her when he happened to look below his feet into the water.

"Bloody hell!" he said in astonishment.

Psyche came calmly swimming to the surface, leaving her find where she had carried it. She would need some rope, and some help, to get it to the surface and aboard the ship. It was heavier than she thought it would be.

"Hallo, Sheerness," she said slowly with a grin, not showing the least sign of distress as she began to tread water near the bottom of the ladder.

"Did you find more coins?" asked Freddie excitedly.

"Oh, I found more than that," Psyche purred. "Can you get the rope out of the coffer in my cabin, please?" Freddie got up excitedly to do as she asked.

"What have you been up to?" asked Sheerness suspiciously.

Psyche put some water in her mouth and squirted it out, giving him a playful grin. "You'll see." She gave him a speculative look as a thought occurred to her. "Is it time to leave?"

"Not yet," said Sheerness as he continued to look down at her curiously from the platform. "How long were you under there, exactly?"

"I don't know, exactly," said Psyche dryly, and she looked past him to see Freddie returning with the rope. "Toss it down to me, will you?"

"Can I come?" asked Freddie hopefully.

"No, I think it's best if you stay near the surface," said Psyche. "You can see it once it's aboard." Freddie tossed her the rope, and Psyche looked at Sheerness. "Don't go anywhere; this thing weighs a ton."

Psyche gathered the rope and gracefully dove under the water. Sheerness watched as she went to the bottom and swam a little further from the ship to tie the rope to something. Before long, she lifted whatever it was and walked with it across the seabed toward the ship. From how easily she managed to stay anchored to the bottom, she hadn't been exaggerating when she said the *thing* was heavy. He didn't believe it weighed a ton but definitely more than a few pounds. The water was clear enough he could see her occasionally lift her face toward the surface, trying to get as close as she could to the ship. Once she was near enough, she set the object down, held onto the rope, and brought the end of it with her to the surface. Sheerness tried to see what it was. From this distance, it appeared to be a big white box...with something in it.

Psyche climbed the ladder, and Sheerness tried to ignore how she was dressed but it was impossible. The black linen of the chemise (he *thought* it was the chemise) might not have been transparent, but the fabric clung to her like a second skin. He stood up on the channel and reached down to help her as she neared the top of the ladder. She had a belt tied around her waist to keep the extra fabric from floating, and she had tied garters at the bottoms of the legs to keep them from doing the same. His mouth went dry as he looked at her, and he was glad he had restricted the crew to the other side of the ship.

"I *think* the rope is strong enough," she said calmly, oblivious to his reaction. She offered the rope to Sheerness. "Are you going to help?"

Sheerness wrapped the rope around his hands and began to pull. He felt his breathing return somewhat to normal as he focused his attention on her find rather than her. Even with the water adding buoyancy, the object *was* heavy, but he thought he could manage on his own. As it came nearer to the surface, he became excited and began to pull on the rope even quicker. Once the object rose above the surface, however, its very weight forced him to slow down.

"Do you need me to help?" asked Psyche concernedly.

"No, I have it," said Sheerness calmly as he continued to pull.

Once he had it raised above the edge of the channel, Psyche helped guide it through the shrouds onto the platform. She carefully tipped it sideways to drain some of the water out, and then she began to remove items. The first thing to come out was the lid. It was broken in two, but other than the break that separated the halves, it was in excellent condition. She tipped it over again to remove even more of the water and pulled out a beautiful black-figured kyathos that remarkably remained in one piece. There was a bronze phiale that had greened over its time in the water but had only moderate corrosion. She pulled out several pieces of broken pottery that all appeared to belong to the same object, but Psyche wasn't quite sure what it was yet. It was covered with more black figures and also had writing. Then she removed a dozen or so coins made of gold, silver, and bronze.

"What have you found?" said Sheerness slowly in admiration.

Psyche looked at him and grinned. "I found a puzzle. What is an Etruscan cinerary urn with Greek coins and objects doing in the water off the coast of an Italian island?" She chuckled. "It boggles the mind."

Psyche climbed through the window to her cabin and carefully brought the objects inside. She placed the kyathos, phiale, and pottery shards on a blanket on her bunk until she could decide the best way to protect them from damage. She put the coins on a piece of paper on her desk, and then she carefully eased the base of the alabaster urn through the window and set it on the floor with the two halves of the lid. She wanted to let it all dry for a time before examining it, and she also wanted to go back where she found them and take a closer look.

She didn't think the cove had previously been above water, and she hadn't noticed any remains of a shipwreck. She could only assume the urn had been intentionally deposited where she'd found it, but whether the dumping had been contemporary to the items or whether they had been stolen and dropped there at a later time by thieves wasn't something she could determine. That she had found such disparate things together in one place could be explained by the second scenario, but she wanted to examine her trove before deciding.

She climbed back out the window onto the platform. "Do I have time to swim a little more?" she asked Sheerness calmly.

He squinted and looked at the sun. "One more hour…unless you find something else," he said with a grin.

Chapter Twenty Three

They docked in Valletta in Malta around six the next morning. Sheerness thought they would arrive earlier, but their stop in Pantelleria delayed them. He wasn't bothered. He had intended to moor and resupply in Malta, thinking they would arrive sometime during the night. That they were there by morning was sufficient. Their brief stop had been for a worthy cause, and Psyche's trove had made it even more worthwhile.

Psyche didn't find anything else when she went back to where she had found the urn and other items, and that had disappointed her. She was hoping she could find some clues to how and why it was put there, but there was nothing. She would have to use what she had found to determine that, and she didn't think it would be enough. She would know better once she had more time to look at everything.

Psyche was awake as they approached the city, and she sighed with wonder as she looked out her window. It was beautiful. She could see domes intermingled with spires, and as the sun began to touch the buildings made of varying shades of white and cream it looked almost celestial. There were soft, grayish-white clouds billowing in the pure blue sky above it, and it seemed to rise out of the deep azure of the water surrounding it like a jewel. If she was given the opportunity, Psyche would like to see this city.

Psyche heard Sheerness when he left his cabin. He still didn't realize she was always awake well before him. The only time she slept for any great length was when he was with her, and that hadn't been for almost two weeks. Her supply of sleeping draught was dwindling, and she had no notion of what she would do when it was gone. Her fear of going to sleep had ended, but her insomnia remained, and the only cure she had found for that was Sheerness. Her fear of the dark had gone as well, and she was very pleased.

After she heard Sheerness go topside, Psyche went to his cabin to use the water closet, and then she went to sit at her desk and write letters. She wanted to look at the coins she had found, but that could wait. She wanted her letters ready before Sheerness went ashore. It wouldn't be that difficult to find a ship sailing to England from Malta; Valletta was controlled by the British.

Then a thought occurred to Psyche. If Valletta was in British hands, perhaps she could find a British bank, one that would let her withdraw funds. She had no need for money at the moment, but what if there was a time that she did? It would be handy when Sheerness mailed her letters. Then she wouldn't have to give away her jewelry, even if she didn't wear it. If she did find a bank, would they believe she was who she said she was and let her draft money? She didn't need an inordinate amount. Of all the things it would have been useful for Pandora to give her (besides handkerchiefs), money ranked fairly high on the list, and Psyche couldn't believe her twin had forgotten to give her any.

Psyche sat at her desk chewing on the side of her thumb for a moment in thought. She couldn't believe Pandora *had*. Psyche was beginning to believe she had overlooked it among her things. She went to her bunk and opened the drawer containing her kits. She looked through the medicine kit, but there was nothing there. She looked through the one with her toiletries, and again found nothing overlooked. She went through every box, and didn't find any, not even in the box with her jewelry and spectacles. There *wasn't* any money. The only thing not thoroughly examined was the trunk she had been in.

Psyche looked at the trunks stacked atop one another by the door. She hadn't looked in them since she got the pillow for Waddlesworth. She chewed on the side of her thumb nervously for a few minutes as she gazed at them, and then she went to untie them decisively. Mr. Laing had stacked them again with the one she had been in on the bottom. Her forehead wrinkled, and she thought it was odd the carpenter would have put them that way after the crewmen had done so. They had both weighed the same when she bought them. If they still weighed the same when empty, what order they were stacked was unimportant. It was true the trunk that had held her belongings had been further from the corner by the door, so Laing could have simply stacked them closest to furthest.

Psyche lifted the top one and moved it out of the way and set the rope on top of it. She moved the bottom one out slightly from the wall, and after taking a preparatory breath, she opened it. The blankets were still in it, and she pulled them out and folded them and put them on top of the other trunk one at a time. Once she had the last blanket out, her eyes rounded in surprise. She supposed, given the circumstances of her sojourn in the trunk, it might have been easy and excusable for her to miss it, but she didn't know how she could have.

Inthe bottom of the trunk at the end where her pillow had been was yet another wooden box. The short ends were flush with the front and back of the trunk. It was about three inches tall and six inches wide with a hinged lid. It had two latches on the front and two brass handles near the ends on the top. Psyche bent down to lift it, and she found it was too heavy to raise with one hand. She grabbed the handles and pulled up on them, and she quickly discovered why the trunk that held only her had weighed more than the trunk with her belongings. It felt as if it were made of lead.

Psyche carried the box to her desk and carefully set it down with the latches facing her. She flipped them up and opened the lid, and she gasped in astonishment. It held a small mint, and she was flabbergasted. Stacked in neat rows across the bottom almost from edge to edge were guineas and shillings, and at the very end was a stack of bank notes pressed out neatly and wrapped, flush with the top of the coins. There was a note on a slip of paper sitting on top of all of it, but Psyche put aside for the moment as she figured how much money she was looking at. Once she was done counting, Psyche felt clammy. It was five hundred pounds in coins and notes. What could her sister possibly think she would need with that much money? She picked up the note.

"Psyche, This is your allowance for the rest of the year. Wellington was done with them, so I thought you could use them. I expect to have lots of lovely souvenirs when you get back. Love, Pan."

Psyche looked from the note back to the box. There was no way she would need all that money, no matter how many souvenirs she wanted to buy. It wouldn't be a good idea for anyone to know she had it. She didn't worry about the crew or Sheerness, but having that much gold and silver lying around made her break into a cold sweat.

She opened the drawer where she had the rest of the boxes and placed the one with the money at the back of it. Then she put back the rest of the boxes in front of it. Luckily, the drawer was strong, or she might have been concerned it would break. As it was, the drawer almost didn't want to slide back in. Should she have the opportunity to go ashore, she would get some of the money to take with her, but she would leave the guineas for as long as possible. The only consolation she had from having found the box was that she would at least no longer need to find a bank.

She restacked the trunks and lashed them, keeping out the blankets. Sheerness had provided her with plenty, but one never knew when another might be helpful. They needed a cleaning though. She added them to her laundry, and she would do the wash either later that day or tomorrow. She had no shortage of clothing, even if she didn't get to it, but her ganseys and split skirts were the most modest things she had. If they weren't clean, she would have to wear breeches or dresses that were either too fine to wear on a ship or too revealing to suit Sheerness.

Psyche went back to her desk to finish writing her letters after finding her allowance. She had just sealed and addressed the last one when there was a knock on her door. She went to answer it after putting the letter on the thick pile to let Freddie come in with her breakfast. She looked at her watch and was surprised it was 9:30.

"Goodness! I didn't realize it was already so late," she said in alarm. "Has the captain already gone ashore?"

"No, ma'am. He's in the mess having breakfast," said Freddie with a grin when he saw her panic.

Psyche reached onto the tray to give Waddlesworth his bread then grabbed the letters. She went to the mess and found Sheerness alone, standing over a chart on the table, his plate and other dishes moved to one side. He looked up expectantly when she came in and put down the gauge he was holding.

"Let me guess: you have more letters?" he said with a half-smile.

"Of course," said Psyche evenly, holding them out.

He took them from her and weighed them in his hand. The pile was not as thick as the last one, but there were still several.

"What could have possibly happened in the last five days, or even the fortnight since we left London, that requires so many letters?"

Psyche shrugged. "All sorts of things. We went to Melilla. I saw the coast of Africa. We stopped on Pantelleria. I taught Freddie to swim. I found the urn. We're in Valletta. We're almost to Greece," said Psyche practically, listing them on her fingers. "That's just the last five days."

"And you have to tell everybody?"

"I don't tell *everybody,*" she said defensively. "I tell certain people about different things, and some things I don't mention at all. And I don't just talk about things I'm doing. Sometimes people like to know you've been thinking about them and what's happening to *them.*" Sheerness raised an eyebrow. "Selena's due to have her baby soon, and I never did get to go shopping with her. The last packet had a letter to my brother Damon, who turned nine last Friday. This one has a letter to Eurydice, who will be nineteen on the fifth. I don't expect she'll get it by then, but at least she'll know I remembered. I always have plenty to talk about with Pandora, my parents, and Chrissoula."

Sheerness looked at her doubtfully and turned the stack sideways in his hand to count them. He was *not* going to look at who they were going to. The only one he could see was to his niece and nephews. He started to ask but thought better of it. Sheerness hadn't written to them, or anyone else in his family, since he left.

"I'll take care of it," he finally said quietly, picking up his cup of coffee and setting the letters to the edge of the table.

"Thank you," said Psyche relievedly. For a moment, she thought he was going to say no. "Are we staying overnight?"

"No, just long enough to resupply. Why?"

"I thought I might like to look around."

"For what?"

"Does that matter?" asked Psyche dryly. "I've been on this ship for two weeks, and I've gotten to walk on a beach and go swimming. I would like to see the market, perhaps buy some souvenirs."

"Souvenirs?" quipped Sheerness with an amused grin.

"For my family and whatnot. None of my sisters—except Pandora—have ever left Britain, and neither have my younger brothers." Psyche frowned. "Do I have to justify everything I do to you? Do I *always* need to have a reason for doing something? Don't *you* ever do anything just because?"

"*Just because?*"

"Yes," said Psyche simply. "You buy something for someone, or give something to someone, or write a letter, or anything else you do for someone else or yourself. You don't do it because you have to or need to, or because you expect something or because it's expected of you. You do it *just because*."

"Hunh," said Sheerness noncommittally. He set down his coffee and picked up the gauge again with an impassive expression. "We'll sail with the evening tide, and I don't want you going alone," he said without looking at her.

"All right," said Psyche calmly, her expression disappointed. She had thought *he* would take her.

She went back to her cabin to eat her breakfast. Once she had eaten, she began to examine the things she had found on Pantelleria. The kyathos was in almost perfect condition. There were only one or two small chips missing from the base, and the glaze had only a minor amount of crazing. When she examined the design on the outside of it, she found in one small part of it a brief inscription: *Phito made me.* She pulled out one of her notebooks to jot down what she had found.

Then she moved on to the phiale. It would take more work. It needed to be cleaned, but she didn't want to do something that might make it disintegrate even further. It was easy for her to see the chasing and etching on the surface, but she wasn't able to find anything that might tell her where it came from or who made it. Then she looked at the shards. She could only assume she had found all the pieces, and it was certainly too late to go back and look for more. She couldn't glue them back together, but she tried fitting them together, like a puzzle, particularly the pieces that had writing so she could begin translating it.

Psyche continued to work, her mind focused on the things she held in her hands. A knock on her door startled her, and she nearly dropped the shard she was holding. She got up to answer the door, and she was surprised to see Freddie standing there with her dinner tray. Her eyes rounded in dismay, and she looked at her watch. It was one in the afternoon.

"Oh, darn," said Psyche anxiously. She moved out of the way for Freddie to take the tray to the table, and she sat down to begin eating quickly. She looked at Freddie as he started to leave the cabin. "Do you know when we'll be sailing?"

"Not for a few hours I expect. The tide's just ebbed."

Psyche sighed with relief, but she began to eat even faster. She should have left hours ago. Now she wasn't sure she would have time to do anything. She had no notion of where the market or anything else was. She wouldn't have time to do anything except buy presents. Once she was done eating, she retrieved the one reticule Pandora had given her, and then she went to the drawer with her boxes and took out a few pound notes and shillings. She didn't anticipate she would need all of it, but she would keep what was left over in the bag for next time. The less she even had to look in the box, the safer she felt.

Then she looked at herself in the mirror. She was wearing another of her split skirts, made of burgundy linen, and a gansey made of soft mohair yarn in deep rose. The collar came high on her neck and turned down. This was her favorite so far; it was very soft and snuggly. Her hair was still in a braid. Her attire was going to prompt scandalized stares, but she had little choice in what she could wear. She *could* put on one of her outfits like Chrissoula's, which was at least a skirt, but she didn't have the time it would take to change. She still had to find someone to go with her. She took a pair of her spectacles to shield her eyes from the sun, since she didn't have a parasol or hat, and grabbed her reticule.

Psyche left her cabin and went topside to begin her search. She found Mr. Broughton on the poop deck, but he wasn't able to go and recommended she ask Stockbridge. Psyche thought it was an excellent idea. She went down to the berth deck and found him sitting at a table whittling a piece of wood.

"That's very good work," said Psyche with a grin as she looked at it. He wasn't finished, but once he was done it would be a mermaid, fish from the waist down, but completely naked woman elsewhere.

Stockbridge blushed and put it in his pocket. "What can I do for you, Lady Psyche?" he asked pleasantly.

"I'd like to go shopping. The captain said we sail with the evening tide and I cannot go alone. Would you be my escort?"

"Of course," he said with a grin and stood to go with her.

"Thank you," said Psyche gratefully as she walked with him. "I don't suppose you've been here before?" she asked hopefully.

He chuckled amusedly. "Many times. I was in the Navy before this."

"Ahh," said Psyche with a smile. "That explains a lot." Stockbridge quirked an eyebrow as they approached the gangway. "The discipline. You're more *orderly* than I would expect someone from a merchant background to be."

Stockbridge chuckled. "I've been trying to do away with that. It's one of the reasons I left the Navy. Now I can come and go as I please." He frowned as he looked at one of the ships moored not far from the *Medea* and paused for a moment. "Hmm."

Psyche looked at him curiously. "What is it?"

He pointed in the direction of the ship. "That is a corvette, and if I'm not mistaken, the one docked right past it is a frigate."

"French?" quipped Psyche in surprise, her eyebrows raised.

"Definitely French."

"I thought Valletta was British. What are French battleships doing here?"

Stockbridge shrugged. "Couldn't say. The captain we talked to near the Strait said there were several around, but Sheerness thought they'd be closer to Spain and France." He gave her a grin. "I don't think they're here to bombard the harbor, though. We *are* at peace with them…for now." He clapped his hands together. "So, do you intend to buy a lot?"

"I don't know. I want to buy presents, and I *really* need handkerchiefs, but I don't have anything specific in mind."

Stockbridge looked at his watch. "We have a few hours before we sail, but I think we should plan to carry everything with us rather than have it delivered." He turned to look back at the crew working on deck. "Oi! You! Bandy and Watkins." Both men put down the ropes they were gathering and approached Stockbridge. "We're going shopping," he said with a grin.

Both men looked at him with raised eyebrows, but they shrugged their shoulders and followed the bosun and Psyche. He was the boss.

One of the nice things about Valletta was its size. It was small, and walking from one place to another was not difficult. Stockbridge took Psyche to an area with several storefronts, and she bought several dozen handkerchiefs. She had a tendency to lose them, and it would be best to have lots. She also found better bath linens. The towels and flannels Sheerness used were sufficient, but she preferred something thicker and fluffier.

Her collection of packages grew as she went from store to store, and she realized she hadn't been shopping since Myron died. Bandy and Watkins were weighed down by items, but none of them were heavy. The storekeepers didn't quibble about taking her notes, and they gave her British coins in change. After she found what she could in the stores, Stockbridge recommended a tour through one of the open air markets near the cocathedral. Psyche thought it would be excellent; it was closer to the dock.

When Psyche walked into the plaza, she put on her glasses to shield her eyes from the late afternoon sun. She wandered among the stalls curiously. Most were selling produce and spices, but she occasionally found others with clothing and jewelry, sometimes housewares. To her surprise, she found strawberries at one vendor, and she bought several baskets. She would keep one for herself, but Mr. Meals and the rest of the crew might enjoy them, too. They were expensive and perishable, and they wouldn't be among the items Sheerness would choose to resupply the ship.

She ambled slowly through the stalls and turned down a side aisle only to come within a stone's throw of three French sailors. They were leaning against the side of a nearby building watching the activities in the market with bored expressions. Psyche wasn't familiar with French naval attire and was unable to determine their rank, but they saw her at almost the same moment. Her appearance piqued their interest in a way that didn't bode well. She had seen other French sailors in the shopping district, but they had been there to shop like anyone else, and while everyone had looked at her curiously, none of them had done more than stare. She wasn't so sure about these three. She turned to say something to Stockbridge, and she was alarmed that he wasn't there.

Psyche casually turned and began to retrace her steps. She remembered hearing the sound of a cart passing behind her at one point before she turned from the main row of stalls. She could only assume it had passed between her and the men, and they had become separated. It should be a simple matter of going back the way she came and looking for them…she hoped. She kept her step even and nonchalant, occasionally stopping to look at something in a stall to surreptitiously glance back in the direction she had seen the Frenchmen. They were following her and steadily moving closer. She was almost back to the main aisle when they finally got within arm's reach of her.

"*Excusez moi, mademoiselle,*" said the one that appeared to be of higher rank than the other two as he stood beside her where she had stopped to look at some oranges.

"*Oui?*" she said politely, her features placid.

"My friends and I could not help but wonder what such a beautiful and *charming* young woman as yourself was doing walking all alone," he said suggestively, slowly letting his eyes travel up her body and pausing hungrily at her breasts before moving to her face.

"I'm not alone," said Psyche calmly. "I'm waiting for the three men I was walking with to meet me."

He leered at her. "What a coincidence. There are three of *us* to walk with you." He reached out a hand to run a finger down her cheek, and Psyche jerked her head back.

"*Monsieur,* please, do not touch me," said Psyche coldly.

"*Pardonnez moi,*" he said slowly with a sly smile, and he reached out again. This time, however, his fingers went lower and brushed across the front of her sweater and the tip of her breast.

Psyche took a step back from him. "*Monsieur,* if you put your hand on me again, I'll break your arm," she said calmly.

All three laughed amusedly, confident she had no intention or probability of carrying it out. They also didn't believe she was waiting for any other men except them. To be dressed as she was and unescorted could only mean she was looking for company, especially since she was French in a British port.

Psyche smelled alcohol on the one who couldn't keep his hands to himself, and she could only assume the other two had been drinking as well. Since she didn't know them, she couldn't know whether or not they were actually drunk. Their sobriety, however, did not excuse ill behavior…not to her.

"But, *mademoiselle,* something so soft and perfect begs to be…fondled," he said seductively.

Before she could move, he firmly grabbed her left breast with his right hand. Psyche reacted instinctively. She gripped his wrist with her left hand and turned to extend his arm outward and behind him. She casually leaned on it with her right elbow just above the joint and pulled backward on his wrist to break his arm in several places. Then she used her foot to knock his feet from under him, and he crumpled to the ground, holding his arm and screaming in pain. She calmly stood looking at the other two Frenchmen.

"Do either of you have an urge to touch *soft* things?" she asked stilly. The men looked at her in wide-eyed shock and dumbly shook their heads.

Psyche vaguely heard the sound of several pairs of hurriedly approaching feet behind her. Stockbridge, Bandy, and Watkins had spotted her just as the French sailor reached out to touch her. Since her back was to them, Stockbridge could only assume what the man had done, but all three were astonished by the way she reacted. It had been quick and fluid, and seemingly almost effortless. All three looked down at the sailor where he continued to groan on the pavement, holding his right arm protectively to his chest. It had been soundly broken.

"Bloody hell, woman, what did you do?" said Stockbridge breathlessly, his expression one of disbelief, admiration, *and* dismay.

Psyche still eyed the other two sailors suspiciously. "He touched me," she said evenly.

Stockbridge looked at the crowd of onlookers beginning to grow, and there was a buzz in the air as word began to spread. This was not good. She had just assaulted a French naval officer, and while she had just cause *and* Valletta was controlled by the British, there was no way of knowing what kind of repercussions it might have. Luckily, the harbor wasn't far away, and the tide was coming in.

"We need to get back to the ship. Now," he said urgently, protectively putting his arm around her waist and taking her by the arm to make her turn the other way.

Psyche gave the sailors a disdainful glare before she turned to let Stockbridge hurriedly, yet as casually as possible, escort her back to the port. It wasn't far, and she almost had to run to keep up with his long stride as they went down the stairs to the quay on the Grand Harbor and boarded the *Medea*. Stockbridge kept his eyes on the two French ships as they crossed the gangway, and he did not take them off. It would be awhile before the sailors were back to their ship, but he couldn't say what would happen once they were.

Sheerness was standing on the deck when they arrived, and his already tight-lipped disapproval when he saw Psyche with Stockbridge grew worse when he saw how the bosun held her close with an arm over her shoulders.

"Get to your cabin," said Stockbridge firmly to Psyche once they were safely on the deck and he released her.

Psyche nodded dumbly, still confused by what was happening, and she turned to look at Bandy and Watkins. She took one of the baskets of strawberries from Bandy and the armfuls of packages from Watkins.

"If you can take the rest of those to Mr. Meals, with my compliments, please," she said with a slight smile.

"Yes, mum," said Bandy quietly, still awed by what he saw in the market.

Psyche went to the open door to the aft deck and went to her cabin as Stockbridge, his face grim and his eyes still on the battleships, went up to the poop deck where Sheerness was standing. Waddlesworth was waiting in the shrouds to be brought in once Psyche had her packages on the bed and the strawberries set on the table, and it was at the point when she was leaned out the window to retrieve him that she heard the roar.

"She did what?"

Psyche looked up at the ceiling, a frown on her face. She was still confused about exactly what it was she had done that was so terrible...other than breaking the sailor's arm. She would have done the same thing even if he had been as British as the Prime Minister. A few minutes later, she heard heated arguing in the officers' mess, and it was apparent Sheerness and Stockbridge had taken their conversation there.

"You were supposed to be watching her!" shouted Sheerness.

"We got separated!" countered Stockbridge. He said something else too quietly for Psyche to hear through her door and that of the officers' mess.

"You would have loved that, wouldn't you?" growled Sheerness.

She listened as they continued to argue, and it seemed Sheerness intended to blame Stockbridge for what had happened. She wasn't going to stand for that. The bosun had nothing to do with it.

"Love a duck," groaned Psyche tiredly with a shake of her head.

She went into the mess to see them standing toe to toe, and she thought they were about to start brawling. She whistled to get their attention, and both of them jumped in surprise, the sound echoing loudly in the room.

"Go back to your cabin," ordered Sheerness.

"I am *not* going to let you hold Stockbridge responsible. He wasn't there."

"He *should* have been," Sheerness said tightly, eyeing the bosun angrily.

"We were only separated a few minutes, and even that wasn't his fault. I wasn't paying attention to where I was going. It was already over by the time he got there. He did absolutely *nothing* wrong. There is no one to blame for this but me...if you're not going to blame the sailor."

Sheerness scowled at her. "You broke the arm of a *lieutenant* in the French navy, who is here as part of a *peaceful* envoy to begin trade negotiations...at the behest of the Bourbon monarchy."

"He touched me after I had told him not to," said Psyche simply.

"Did you *have* to break his arm?"

"He touched my face, and I told him not to. He touched my shirt, and I told him if he touched me again, I'd break his arm. He *wouldn't* listen!"

"In case you've forgotten, we've only just stopped being at *war* with these people. The *Medea* doesn't have the cannon or the ammunition to take on the French navy because a junior officer wouldn't *listen!*"

"He *grabbed* my *tit!*" she bit out. "He's lucky I didn't castrate him!"

Stockbridge wiped a hand over his mouth to hide a smirk. After what he had seen her do, he didn't doubt she could have. Given what the man had done, she would have had every right. Sheerness sighed tiredly and shook his head, raising his hands from his sides. He turned to look at the bosun.

"Send me Rolleston and Blossom, and have Higginbotham get us under way as soon as we're sure everyone's aboard. It would be best if we put as much horizon between us and this place as we can...and quickly."

"Yes, sir," said Stockbridge agreeably, leaving the room for topside.

Sheerness turned to look at Psyche. She was still standing in the doorway to their cabins with a perturbed expression, her arms folded across her chest. He walked toward her and gently brushed his hand down her cheek to her neck.

"Are you all right?" he asked her quietly.

"I'm fine," she said softly. "I was only defending myself."

He kissed her softly on the lips and pulled her to him in a comforting hug, resting his cheek on top of her head. "Yes, but you do it so well," he sighed, and Psyche could hear a slight amusement in his tone.

Psyche put her arms around his waist and kept her head resting against his chest, listening to his heartbeat beneath her ear. "I don't think the French navy is going to bother us," she said thoughtfully after a time.

"Why would you think that?" he asked curiously.

"Well, imagine if you were him. Would *you* want to tell your commanding officer you got your arm broken by a *girl* because you tried to assault her?" she asked practically.

Sheerness chuckled softly and smoothed his hands over her back. It felt wonderful to hold her. She was soft and snuggly, and she tasted of strawberries. He was glad she had been able to defend herself and that nothing worse had happened. He should have gone with her. Then perhaps none of this would have happened. He sighed and lifted his head to let her go. Blossom and Rolleston would be coming any time. He gave her another brief kiss before he stepped back from her.

"I'll have to remember in the future that if you tell me you'll break my arm, you mean it," he chortled, tweaking the end of her nose.

"Just don't put your hands where they're not wanted, and you'll never have to worry about it," countered Psyche with a wry grin.

Meals provided a delicious supper. There was roasted pork, asparagus, macaroni casserole, and Brussels sprouts, followed by strawberries with whipped cream and sponge cake for dessert. It was divine, and Psyche almost felt like she was at home, except her family wasn't there. She ate until she couldn't take another bite, and she felt wonderfully relaxed.

Sheerness was more talkative than he had been. He still didn't direct much conversation toward Psyche, but he told them what he had discovered about the two French ships while he was ashore. Of course that topic led to conversation about the French navy in general, and the war, and Psyche let her thoughts stray to Gregory in America. Her parents had written him a letter telling him about Myron and requesting he come home, at least for a little while. They had still not heard anything when Psyche left. She had to push the thoughts from her mind because it made her worry, and she didn't want to.

After dinner Psyche went to her room and dressed for bed. She was feeling very at ease, and she thought about not taking her sleeping draught. The bottle was less than half full. If she took a full dose every night, it wouldn't last the entire trip. After contemplating for several minutes, she put the bottle away. She would *try* to go to sleep without it. If she couldn't go to sleep after a while, then she would take it. She brought in Waddlesworth and shut the window, and then she went to bed and turned off the light.

She tried going to sleep using the method that had worked well for her while she was staying with Pandora—thinking about Sheerness—and tonight it actually worked. Tonight, it didn't cause the panic it had over the previous days, and in less than thirty minutes of lying down, she was sound asleep.

≪ ≫

Sheerness noticed after taking his nightly walk around the deck that the light in Psyche's cabin was already off when he went past. He frowned because she usually still had it lit when he came below. He went to his cabin to take care of the log and other things before he got ready for bed, and then he would go check on her as he usually did.

He sat at his desk once he was done with the log writing letters home to his family. Finding out Psyche had been sending letters to them when he had not made Sheerness feel guilty. He didn't think he was a great composer of letters, which was why he never sent them very often, but he was concerned when he thought his family might be worried about him, and he did miss them. He had no notion whether Psyche even mentioned him when she wrote.

He took a piece of hard tack from a sack he kept in the drawer of his desk for Waddlesworth. Just because he wasn't going to feed it to the crew or himself didn't mean there was none to be found, but it was only for use in an emergency. So far, there hadn't been one. The duck seemed to like it well enough, perhaps even better than bread.

He got undressed except for his pants, and went to the door of Psyche's cabin. He listened for a moment before he opened it and went in. Waddlesworth looked up at him expectantly as he entered, and Sheerness handed him the piece of hard tack and smoothed a hand down his back. The drake tolerated it and began to nibble at his cracker.

Sheerness tilted his head sideways thoughtfully as he looked at Psyche. He'd never seen her sleeping like that before. She had her head resting on one pillow as she lay curled on her side, another pillow hugged to her with her cheek resting on one corner of it. She looked comfortable, and her sleep was as sound as usual. Ordinarily when he came in to kiss her, she was lying flat on her back. It was curious, but it wasn't as if he could ask her what was different about how she went to sleep that night compared to any other night.

He brushed the hair away from her face and kissed her softly at the corner of her mouth, and he saw in astonishment when he raised his head that she was smiling in her sleep. Then he knew. She hadn't taken her sleeping draught. She had gone to sleep on her own, and that meant she was probably not sleeping as heavily and might wake up. Her reaction to finding him there would not be good. He looked at her one last time, the soft smile still there, and he quietly left the room and closed the door behind him.

Sheerness was awakened by a knocking on the door to the mess. He put his pants on and went to answer it, rubbing a tired hand over his face. When he opened the door, Broughton was standing there with a lantern.

"Sorry to wake you, sir," he said quietly.

"What is it, Broughton?"

"There's a storm coming, sir."

Sheerness frowned. The sky had been cloudless when he went below.

"What time is it?"

"Just after four, sir."

"How bad is it looking?"

"You might want to come see for yourself," said Broughton grimly.

That wasn't a good. Broughton wasn't prone to nervousness over a little wind and rain. To see him concerned meant it was looking…unpleasant.

"Let me get dressed, and I'll be up," said Sheerness, clapping the second mate on his shoulder assuringly.

"Yes, sir," said Broughton, leaving for topside.

Sheerness dressed quickly and grabbed his slicker before leaving. He looked at the door to Psyche's cabin, wondering if he should wake her and tell her about the storm. There hadn't been any rain, much less a storm, since the one in the Bay of Biscay. He didn't know how she would react. He would wait and see how bad it was before he woke her. He would need to though; she wouldn't sleep through it, especially since she hadn't taken her draught.

When Sheerness reached the deck, he looked up at the sky. As he watched, the stars began to disappear behind a solid black mass, as if someone were pulling a piece of cloth over them. The nearly full moon was nowhere to be seen. When he looked toward the horizon, he could see distant lightning barely illuminating the billowing clouds that produced it, and the ship was heading directly toward it. This looked as if it were going to be worse than the last one, and that one had been bad enough. With that one, it had been traveling across their path, instead of straight for them, and they had been able to keep just to the edge of it for the most part as they continued south. They would have to go through this one, and there would be no getting around it.

"What's our heading?" he asked Higginbotham when he reached the helm.

"Due east."

The sea was still calm, but it wouldn't be long until the waves began to swell. Sheerness needed to warn Psyche.

"I'll be right back," he said quietly. "Make sure everything's battened down and get to half-sail. We want to delay this as long as possible."

"Yes, sir," agreed Higginbotham heartily.

Sheerness went below to Psyche's door. He opened it and went in after a brief hesitation. She still lay in the same position, and she still looked so peaceful he was reluctant to wake her, but he had to. He sat on the edge of the bunk, and after he brushed the hair back from her ear, he leaned toward it.

"Psyche."

Her eyelids fluttered open, and she turned to look at him in surprise.

"What is it?" she asked confusedly with a frown.

Sheerness smoothed a hand over her forehead. "A storm is coming."

"How bad?" she asked nervously.

"It looks to be extremely bad," said Sheerness evenly, and he continued to smooth a soothing hand across her hair. "It won't be long before we reach it, and I wouldn't be able to tell you once we do. I didn't want you to wake up and not know what was happening."

"Thank you," she said softly, her expression worried.

Sheerness lowered his head to kiss her and rested his forehead against hers.

"It will be fine," he assured her as he sat up. "The *Medea* is a good ship, and we've a fine crew. Just stay below until it's over."

Psyche nodded, and she raised her hand to his cheek and kissed him. "Be careful," she said quietly.

Sheerness smiled soothingly and stood to leave the cabin. Psyche watched him go with a troubled frown and began to chew the side of her thumb. A storm didn't worry her. Even after waking up locked in a trunk during the middle of one, a storm didn't frighten her. What had scared her was being locked in the trunk with no way to get out and that she wouldn't be able to swim to the surface if the ship sank. She had no such worry this time. What concerned her was that Sheerness would be out in it. He would tie off, but ropes could break, and men were swept overboard all the time.

Psyche got up and went to the water closet, and then she lit a rushlight from the dying embers of the fire in his cabin to light the lamp by her bed. She dressed quickly, putting on a pair of linsey trousers, a shirt, and a waistcoat because she hadn't done her laundry. She didn't put on her shoes. She wasn't planning to leave her cabin, but she didn't want to be in her shift should she need to. By the time she was finished, the rocking of the ship had increased, and it had begun.

Psyche looked over the things in her cabin and tried to secure everything loose. She took the things from the tabletop, except for the water pitcher, and put them on her desk and closed the top. She put the pitcher in the drawer; if the water sloshed out of it, she didn't want it to get the things on her desk wet. The only other unsecured thing in the room was Waddlesworth, and he continued to sleep on his pillow without a care.

Psyche paced nervously as the storm began to build. There wasn't much room to do it in her cabin, so she opened her door and wedged it to keep it from swinging with the motion of the ship and added the distance of the alcove, but it soon became too rough to pace. She went to her bunk and curled up in a ball in the corner, chewing on the side of her thumb. She kept her eyes on the window, watching as the lightning flashed, sometimes so intensely it would be as bright as noon outside for as long as fifteen seconds at a time. Then the thunder would boom and roll so loudly Psyche had to cover her ears. Through it all, there was a constant roaring and howling as the wind buffeted the ship.

When the sky outside began to lighten, Psyche looked at her watch. It was after 6:30. The sun was usually brighter by then, but Psyche could barely tell it was daylight. She went to the coffer and looked out. The sky was a mixture of black and dark gray, and the billowy clouds moved slowly. She looked in all directions she could in the sky, and the edge of the storm was nowhere in sight. This would not be over quickly.

Psyche looked at the ceiling. Sheerness was outside in that. The crew was outside in that. At one time the ship pitched far enough to portside Psyche could have touched the surface of the water with her hand if she opened the window. Once the ship righted itself, she went back to her bunk. She could occasionally hear shouts from the deck as orders were issued or conditions were checked, but the voices were always unintelligible. She hoped all the men were safe, but her particular concern was for Sheerness. Then when she looked out her window again, she saw Freddie hanging from the shroud near its edge, his arms wrapped around the deadeyes as his legs dangled above the water.

"Oh, my giddy aunt!"

Psyche leapt to the window and opened it. She leaned out as far as she could to try to reach him, but she couldn't quite stretch far enough. She was drenched within seconds, and the rain pounded against her in heavy, stinging sheets. Freddie was holding on as hard as he could, but the wind was pushing on him unmercifully. He wasn't tied off, which meant Psyche was likely the only one who knew he was there.

"Hold on, Freddie!"

"I'm trying!" he cried, and he had a terrified expression as he looked at the roiling water below him.

Psyche tried to reach further out the window. She could almost touch him when the ship lurched to portside. She had to brace a hand against the window frame to keep herself from falling completely out into the water. As it was, she was hanging out the window far enough her head was submerged for quite some time before the ship righted itself again. When it did, Freddie was still holding on, but he was coughing and sputtering from the water he'd inhaled, and he was losing his grip. Psyche watched in horror as he slipped and fell.

"Freddie!"

Psyche looked down to see him bob away from the ship. Without a lifeline, there was no way he would survive unless someone went in after him. No one could survive it. She needed to go topside. The rope she had in the coffer wasn't long enough or strong enough, and she didn't want to go in after him without letting someone see she was going.

She hurriedly took off her waistcoat and watch and raced through the after cabins to the storage room beside the stairs. She found a coil of rope she thought would be sufficient, and then she opened the door to the deck. It wasn't easy. The wind was pushing on it hard enough it took all her strength to get it open, and once she did, it was ripped from her hands and slammed against the wall of the after cabins with a loud boom.

She stayed under the shelter of the overhanging poop deck and made her way to the portside of the ship. She tied the rope around her waist, and then she went to the rail to tie it off. She leaned over the side to look for Freddie, and she could see him still bobbing, miraculously managing to keep his head above water. But he was floating further away, up the side of a giant swell, and if Psyche didn't get to him before he reached the top, when he went to the other side of it, he would be lost forever. Psyche's heart thudded against her ribs when she realized what she would have to do.

She was making her way to the mainmast when Stockbridge spotted her. He ran to her and grabbed her arm. Psyche turned to look at him in surprise and struggled to get loose. Freddie didn't have very long.

"You should be below!" he shouted above the wind and rain.

Psyche pointed to the portside of the ship where she could see Freddie steadily making his ascent on the giant wave.

"Freddie's overboard!" she yelled back and finally managed to get free.

She hurriedly scampered up the shrouds of the mainmast, occasionally looking back over her shoulder to keep her sights on Freddie, but she didn't dare look down at the deck. When she stood on the crosstrees, she was at the same height as Freddie, and he was less than twenty feet away. All she had to do was leap toward him. The ship begin to yaw again to portside as they started over another swell. As it reached its farthest point, moving her even closer, and just began to go the other way again, Psyche sailed through the air, diving toward Freddie. She landed in the wave just above him, and as he continued to rise, she grabbed him.

He was shivering and exhausted, and on the verge of drowning, but he was still alive and mostly conscious. He wasn't strong enough to hold on by himself for long, and she needed her hands free.

"Freddie, we need to go under water for a few seconds. I need to wrap this rope around both of us, and it's the easiest way to do it."

"All right," said Freddie, his lower jaw shaking.

"Big breath," said Psyche encouragingly.

She took him under the water and began to twist on her side like a fish caught on a hook and wrapped the rope several times around her and him. When they came back up, they were on the other side of the swell. The ship had disappeared from sight. Freddie was bound tightly to her by the rope, and with her hands finally free, Psyche began to pull on it, coiling it in her hands to keep it firmly around them.

Eventually, she felt the line go taut and began to pull them back in the direction of the ship. She could feel the rope biting into her waist, and her palms were stinging where it would occasionally slip in her hands. She pulled and coiled almost mindlessly, her shoulders beginning to burn from the strain. She soon came to realize they were going under water again. They were at the same height as the ship on the other side, and with the line tight, unless the ship rose again, they had to go through. Freddie had his arms wrapped weakly around her neck, and he was on the verge of collapse.

"Freddie, you'll need to hold your breath again. We've got to go under water to get to the ship. Can you do that for me?" she panted.

"I'll try, ma'am," he said weakly.

Psyche gave him a reassuring smile. "We'll be back on the deck in a jiffy."

As soon as he took a big breath, she began to pull on the rope again, and they went into the swell. She was tiring herself, but she had desperation coursing through her veins. She could feel the water pushing on them, trying to hold them back, but she continued to pull hand over hand, coiling the rope around her forearm. They finally broke the surface again, and Psyche and Freddie gasped for air. She almost cried with relief when she saw the ship, and she could see men pulling on the rope to get them onto the deck.

Then the ship pitched away from them, and the force of it jerked Psyche and Freddie out of the water and slammed them into the hull. Psyche was stunned as the side of her head banged against the wood, and the rope burned her palms as her grip went slack. They began to sink under the water, and it revived her enough that she kicked toward the surface and tightened her hold on the rope again. She didn't have the strength to pull anymore.

Psyche felt them being lifted out of the water, and she wrapped her arms around Freddie as they were drawn up the side of the ship. Several pairs of hands reached out to pull them over the rail, and Psyche was shaking with cold and exhaustion. Without the water to help her support his weight, she started to sway from Freddie's feet not touching the deck, and he was dead weight from having finally lost consciousness.

Stockbridge and Higginbotham were there with Bandy and Watkins, and they quickly uncoiled the rope. Higginbotham lifted Freddie in his arms, and Stockbridge helped Psyche across the deck to the after cabins. Felton was there waiting for them. He had Higginbotham take Freddie to his cabin and put him to bed under some blankets. The doctor looked at Psyche's hands and shook his head reprovingly. There were raw, bleeding lines across her palms, particularly on the webbing between thumb and index finger. There was a cut on her scalp from hitting the side of the ship, and he gave her a cloth to put on it to stop the bleeding. The skin around her waist and across her back was raw from the rope chafing against it, but that was something she would worry about later. Higginbotham came out of his cabin and looked at Psyche.

"Is he awake?" she asked the first mate concernedly.

"No, but I think he'll be fine," said Higginbotham quietly. "What happened?"

Psyche shrugged uncertainly. "I don't know, really. I was in my cabin, and when I looked out my window he was hanging from the shrouds. I tried to reach him from the window, but he slipped and fell. I got some rope, tied off, and went in after him," said Psyche simply.

"In all my years at sea, and I've been doing this since I was Freddie's age, I've never seen anything like what you did," said Higginbotham quietly.

"Me either," agreed Stockbridge with amazement.

"I just did what I thought needed to be done," said Psyche, and she clenched her jaw to keep her teeth from chattering.

≪ ≫

To the men watching on the deck, her actions were astounding. When she jumped from the crosstrees, to them, it looked as if she had grown wings and taken flight. The way she looked as she went through the air, her arms outspread and hair unbound, reminded many of them of the ship's figurehead.

Sheerness had seen her pointing while she talked to Stockbridge, but he couldn't see what she was pointing at or hear what she was saying. It had been several hours since he had seen her. As he watched her climb the mainmast, he was afraid she might have lost her mind again. When he watched her leap into the sea, he was sure of it until he followed her arc through the air and saw Freddie. He was lashed to the helm, or he would have gone in after her. When they disappeared beneath the surface, the blood drained from his face, and it felt as if his heart had stopped beating. He didn't see her lifeline, and he thought she was gone forever. But then he saw Stockbridge and Higginbotham rush to the side of the ship and begin hauling on a rope tied very securely to the rail. He didn't start to breathe again until she reappeared.

It was impossible to hold the ship steady, and his stomach churned when they slammed into the hull. He watched the men pull them over the side, Freddie unconscious, Psyche staggering and blood streaming from her head. His only consolation was that she at least managed to make it to the aft deck mostly under her own power. He wanted to go to her, but he couldn't leave the helm until the storm was over. He didn't know how much longer that would be. It had been raging for hours. He couldn't see the edge of it, and it was only growing worse.

Before long, Stockbridge came out of the after cabins, tied off, and made his way to the poop deck.

"They'll be fine," yelled the bosun, looking ahead of them at the churning sea. "Freddie's resting in Higginbotham's cabin. Lady Psyche has gone to hers. She got her hands tore up pretty bad from the line, and she has a cut on her head."

"Is that all?" asked Sheerness, taking his eyes off their course long enough to give Stockbridge an assessing glance.

"She was cold, wet, and exhausted," replied the bosun exasperatedly. "I didn't *see* anything else, and she didn't *mention* anything else. Felton's main concern is with Freddie, and so is hers," shouted Stockbridge in a way that suggested perhaps Sheerness's should be, too.

"What happened?"

"She saw Freddie hanging from the side of the ship from her window, and when he fell she went to get him. We won't know why Freddie was there until he wakes up."

The storm didn't break until noon. By the time it was over, three more men had been swept from the deck. Luckily, they had all been tied off, and other than a thorough soaking that went unnoticed in the downpour, they were all safe. The ship itself, however, did not escape unscathed. The foremast broke from the wind, and when it did, it damaged the rigging, the railing, and the forecastle. Despite battening the hatches and sustaining no hull damage, the ship had taken on a lot of water. She had a slight list to starboard. To make it worse, the steam-powered bilge pump was damaged. There was a manual pump, but it was going to take several hours—the rest of that day and most of the next—working through the night, to pump it out. No one knew how to fix the steam pump. Myron would have, had he been aboard, but he wasn't.

Once Sheerness received an assessment, he put the crew to work on repairs. His biggest concerns were pumping out the water and repairing the mast…in that order. Laing explained he was a carpenter, not an engineer, so he would be unable to do anything with the steam pump. Now, if the manual one were to break, he would be able to repair that one. He had the supplies to fix the mast, but it would take until the following day to complete. Sheerness looked at the pump himself, but he was no more knowledgeable than Laing.

As tired as he was, Sheerness remained topside working with the crew, taking only a brief time to eat. Higginbotham came up from the aft deck after tending to Freddie and getting a much needed rest after being awake all night. Freddie was still sleeping, but he as yet didn't appear feverish or anything worse than exhausted. Once Psyche went to her cabin, she had not come out. Sheerness had Meals take her a tray, and the cook was able to say she was well, but he was sure he woke her.

It was after dark by the time Sheerness could go below. He had eaten with Laing, Stockbridge to discuss progress and plans for repairs.

Psyche did come out of her cabin to eat supper with Higginbotham, Broughton, and Felton. She had changed clothes and braided her hair, and she felt much better after a long nap. She was dismayed to learn the condition of the ship. It was easy to notice the list, but she hadn't been on deck to see the rest of the damage. She had bandages on her hands, and ointment on the cut on her head. Once she had taken off her wet clothes and had a nap, the skin around her waist felt better, but in the mirror, she could see red lines from the rope. Putting ointment on had helped…as long as she didn't touch them.

After supper, she went to bed, but she didn't take her sleeping draught. Unlike the night before, though, she could not go to sleep. Thoughts of Sheerness worried her. She hadn't seen him since that morning. She knew from talking with Higginbotham and Broughton that he was all right, but she would like to see him and judge for herself.

She lay on her side in her bunk, hugging her pillow, looking out the window at the wispy clouds floating in front of the stars. She wasn't sleepy at all. The sleep she had earlier was contributing to her insomnia, in addition to her worry about Sheerness.

She heard him when he came from the officers' mess, and she sat up in her bunk in surprise when he opened the door to her cabin. She could see by the moon that he was exhausted. He came to the side of her bunk without a word and pulled her toward him to kiss her thoroughly. Psyche was so happy to see him, tired but safe, and she held onto him tightly. She smoothed her fingers down his cheek tenderly as kissed him. Sheerness ended the kiss and rested his forehead against hers, smoothing a hand down her arm.

"I want to hold you tonight," he whispered.

"Yes," said Psyche softly without hesitation, smoothing her fingers across his cheeks to his hair. She couldn't think of anything she wanted more.

She helped him remove his coat, and he draped it over her desk chair. She watched impatiently as he removed the rest of his clothing, neatly laying each piece over the back of the chair. He sat on the edge of the bunk to remove his boots and socks, and the breath caught in her throat when he stood up to take off his trousers. He was bathed in the moonlight, and Psyche thought she had never seen anything more perfect. She had made love to him, but she had never *looked* at him completely naked. Had the ancient Greeks carved a statue of him, there would have been no need for artistic license; they could never have done him justice.

Sheerness came to the bunk and got under the blankets. He lay on his side and pulled Psyche close to him, wrapping his arms around her waist. She put a soothing hand to his cheek and rubbed her nose affectionately against his before giving him a soft kiss on the lips. Sheerness tightened his arms around her waist hungrily, and Psyche breathed in sharply through her nose and winced as it put pressure on the rope burns. He lifted his head to look at her concernedly, but she wouldn't say anything.

He smoothed a hand over her side, but he couldn't feel anything through her shift. He moved his hand lower and slid it under the fabric back to the skin at her waist. Then he could feel them, a wide line of welts at her side and across her back. He was gentle, but Psyche still found it uncomfortable.

"I'm fine," she finally said quietly.

"You have to quit scaring me," he said brokenly. "You do things...and I can't...I'm not...," he said emotionally, unable to voice his fears.

Psyche brushed a soothing hand over his hair and kissed him gently on the forehead before bringing his head to rest comfortingly against her breasts, wrapping her arms around him and smoothing her hand over his back. She blinked her eyes to keep from crying as she felt him shudder and cling to her desperately. She kissed the top of his head.

"I'm here. I'm fine," she soothed. "I'm not going anywhere."

She hadn't realized she had scared him. She had only done what she thought was necessary. During the entire storm, she hadn't been worried for herself, not even when she had gone into the water to save Freddie. She hadn't wanted *him* to drown. She had tied off and was an excellent swimmer, but Freddie wasn't. Once he was safe, her worry had returned to Sheerness and the rest of the crew, especially Sheerness. She hadn't thought about how it must have looked. All she could imagine was how she would have felt had he been the one in the water and she had been the one watching helplessly from the deck. She hugged him tightly and rested her cheek against the top of his head.

"Promise me you won't do that again," he said quietly after a time.

"I can't promise that," she said sadly. "I hope I'll never have to do it again, and I promise I'll *try* not to do it again, but I couldn't let him drown...not any more than I could let you, not if I could stop it."

He didn't move, and Psyche could tell from his stillness that he was troubled, but it would be a lie to unreservedly promise she would never try to save someone. It would go against everything that made her who she was. She couldn't make a promise like that, not even to him. He would never make a promise like that either. She smoothed a hand over his hair and across his shoulder, and then she adjusted the blankets over them.

"Go to sleep now," she said gently.

She began to run a calming hand through his hair, and he carefully tightened his arms around her waist. He was completely sapped of energy, and even as troubled as he was, he couldn't stay awake. It felt wonderful to be there with her, to listen to her heart beating slowly and strongly beneath his ear, to feel her breasts rise and fall with every breath she took. She was alive and safe, and for now, that was enough.

Psyche felt Sheerness settle onto her more heavily as he went to sleep. She continued to stroke his hair, loving the feel of it as it feathered over her fingers. Her countenance was pensive as she lay there, but she was not long for sleep herself. At some point during the storm, she had turned a corner. She still didn't want to marry him, but she couldn't bear the thought of not being near him. She was probably going to be hurt, but she couldn't resist it anymore. It was like an addiction, and she was starting to feel like she couldn't live without him.

Chapter Twenty Four

Psyche opened her eyes shortly after dawn, but she wasn't ready to wake up yet. Sheerness was still with her, still sleeping the way he had been the night before when she had finally drifted off. She relished the moment. She felt cozy and languid, and she blinked her eyes drowsily as she tried to go back to sleep. Although it was the time she usually woke, Psyche still had at least another hour before it was the time when he did, and she didn't want to move and wake him. She didn't want to go anywhere; all she wanted to do was lie there and let him stay pressed warmly against her because she didn't know when it would happen again.

She wasn't going back to sleep. She'd had a long nap the day before and a good night's sleep. Her body had had enough. She contented herself with being where she was. Psyche watched the sky become brighter through the window. Unlike the day before, the weather was going to be marvelous. The sky that she could see didn't have a cloud in it, and as it grew lighter, it settled into a warm, medium blue. The crew would be happy to see it.

Psyche looked down as Sheerness began to stir. He wasn't quite awake yet, but it wouldn't be long. He snuggled his head against her breasts and smoothed his hand up her side to rest on her rib cage just below the right one. She could feel the warmth of his cheek pressed against her chest exposed by her shift, and it caused a peculiar tickling sensation when his eyes finally opened and his eyelashes brushed against her skin. He lifted his head to look at her sleepily and was surprised to find her awake and looking back at him.

"You're awake," he said softly.

Psyche quirked her lips at him amusedly. "You noticed that, did you?" she asked dryly, reaching up a hand to gently comb through his hair.

Sheerness adjusted his position and lifted himself to lie on his side, propping his head on his hand very close to hers on the pillow. He leaned forward and kissed her softly, smoothing a hand down her chest to rest it on her stomach. Psyche wondered if he could feel the quivering that had started there as he continued to kiss her slowly. She was disappointed when he ended the kiss with a teasing nibble to her bottom lip, and she opened her eyes to look at him reflectively as he lifted his head.

"Did you sleep at all?" he asked, moving his fingers over the silk of her shift where it covered her abdomen.

"I did," said Psyche breathlessly.

"How are you feeling?"

"I'm fine," she sighed. She was actually beginning to feel wonderful as his fingers continued to rove. "Did you get enough sleep?"

"I think so," said Sheerness calmly as he watched his fingers play over the emerald green silk of her shift, oblivious to Psyche's reaction. "What are you planning to do today?"

"The first thing I want to do is look in on Freddie," Psyche managed to get out in a semi-normal tone. His fingers had moved higher, and he was trying to smooth the silk, fitting it to the form beneath it and seeming to have forgotten *she* was the form. "I need to wash clothes, and I think I'll take a shower."

"Hmm, I'm afraid you won't be taking a shower today…maybe not even do laundry either," he said absently, a slight frown of concentration on his brow as he attempted to make the silk go flat against the underside of her breast.

"Why not?" she sighed.

"Because the bilge pump is broken," he said simply as he continued his attempt to make the silk hug her breast.

Psyche was trying not to squirm, and her forehead wrinkled at his words. "What does one have to do with the other?"

"The boiler for the pump provides the hot water for the shower. Now it's broken, and no one knows how to fix it," he said calmly, and his lips formed into a pleased smile as he finally got the silk to smooth over the gentle curve of her breast. He ruffled his fingers over the silk to wrinkle it again and start over.

"Steam?" she said in surprise.

"Exactly."

Psyche watched his face as he continued to play with the silk of her shift, knowing she was there but forgetting she was beneath it. He had a boyish expression as he touched and smoothed, shaping it to her ribs and steadily working his way back up to her breast. She was past being mildly excited and was finding it hard to breathe.

"Why would you have a piece of equipment on your ship that no one knows how to repair?" she asked confusedly.

His hand paused momentarily. "Because your brother was supposed to be here," he said quietly.

"Oh," she sighed as his hand covered her breast. "I could…I could take a look at it," she tried to say casually.

Sheerness looked at her face then in surprise. Her cheeks had a heated flush, and he slowly realized what he had been doing. His hand was, in fact, still holding her breast, and he could feel the way the nipple was hardened pebble-like against his palm. His own cheeks colored with embarrassment, and he moved his hand back down to her ribs. He had not spent the night holding her with the intention of making love. He didn't have time right now.

"Why would you want to look at it?" he asked perplexedly.

"I don't know," said Psyche with a shrug. "I might be able to fix it."

Sheerness's eyebrow shot up. "You?"

"Engineering and mechanics *is* Pandora's area of expertise, but I did share the solarium with her. She had me help her with quite a few of her projects. If you got the plans from Myron, he probably got them from her." Sheerness continued to look at her doubtfully. "It wouldn't hurt for me to *look* at it."

Sheerness looked down at her watch. He had to get up. The ship still had a list, and it wasn't moving very quickly. The crew was capable of working without his supervision, but he wanted to find out their progress. Psyche continued to look at him with a put-out expression. He wasn't sure how much of it was caused by his incredulity and how much by his obviously (though unintentionally) exciting her and not following through on it.

"All right, you can look at the pump." Her face brightened, but he gave her a serious look. "*Most* of it is in the hold at the stern."

"That's what lamps are for," she said calmly.

Sheerness leaned toward her to kiss her properly and soundly, and Psyche sighed at the back of her throat, one hand moving to twine in the hair at the back of his head, the other going to his bare hip. He surprised her when he suddenly broke the kiss and rose from the bunk, leaving her looking after him dazedly. She rolled onto her side and watched him dress, sighing wistfully. He draped his slicker over his arm once he was dressed and came back to the bunk to kiss her on the cheek.

"I'll see you later," he said calmly, his lips twitching amusedly, and he tweaked the end of her nose before he left the room.

After he left, Psyche put a pillow over her face and groaned. He did that on purpose. He hadn't intentionally teased her in the beginning, but when he left, he knew she wanted more and had left her without it. That wasn't very nice. She pulled the pillow down and looked at the ceiling with a thoughtful frown. He didn't realize he shouldn't start playing a game like that with her.

After Psyche dressed, she went to Higginbotham's cabin to see Freddie. She was concerned when he wasn't there, but he came down the stairs from the deck, looking as chipper as ever. She was dismayed to learn he was trying to bring her breakfast the previous day. It would have only been bread and cheese, which he had put into the dumbwaiter with a pot of tea, but he had to go across the waist deck to retrieve it. He was almost to the door to the aft deck when a wave washed over the ship and swept him overboard. It made her feel guilty to think he could have died because he didn't want her to be hungry.

This morning he got her breakfast from the dumbwaiter without incident and carried it to her room. They sat and talked as he fed Waddlesworth, and he said she had bowled over the crew, between breaking a man's arm and rescuing *him* from the drink. That made her self-conscious. She didn't want them to be awestruck, and she couldn't understand why they were.

After Freddie left, she finished her breakfast and put Waddlesworth into the shrouds. She straightened her room and gathered her things to wash. There was a lot. She strung up her line, and then she went to the berth deck about the things she needed. If the water she used to wash her clothes was from the boiler, she might not get it...unless Meals boiled it on the stove.

She was a little flustered when Meals already had water ready, and then he wouldn't let her carry it. Sheerness stood on the poop deck watching in disbelief as she was followed by a string of sailors carrying her things. Once Psyche was to her cabin and the sailors left, she closed the door and rested her back against it with a sigh. She hoped that would not continue for long.

Psyche spent the rest of the morning and part of the afternoon washing clothes and the blankets from the trunk. She had just finished when Freddie brought her dinner. There was little room to move with everything hanging from the line to dry, and Psyche had the window and door open to let a breeze blow through to speed up the process. Psyche had just sat down to eat, and Freddie had not been gone more than five minutes, when the sailors returned to empty and take away the buckets and pails. This could not go on.

When she finished her dinner, she went to the deck to see how repairs were going. She had heard the sounds of work all morning. Laing was overseeing the raising of the new portion of the foremast while other men worked on replacing the part of the foredeck that was shattered when it fell. There was a piece of rope strung along the railing temporarily where that had been broken until it could also be repaired. The deck still canted slightly to starboard.

She decided to go look at the pump and see what could be done with it. She looked up at the poop deck and saw Sheerness there with Higginbotham and Stockbridge. Psyche calmly made her way up to join them. The first mate and bosun both greeted her warmly. Sheerness looked past her when she reached them, and Psyche looked behind herself as well in puzzlement.

"What?"

"I was looking for your entourage," he said with a grin.

Psyche blushed uncomfortably and pursed her lips on a retort. She didn't find it funny at all.

"I'm going to look at the pump," she said evenly.

"I'll come with you," said Sheerness mildly. He was curious to find out exactly what she thought she could do.

"If you'd like," said Psyche airily. She was still perturbed by what he had done that morning, but she wasn't looking forward to going into the hold.

Psyche walked with Sheerness down the stairs to the berth deck. The hold grating was open when she went down to get her things for laundry, a hose feeding out of it to one of the windows for the manual bilge pump. With only one pump, Psyche had no trouble understanding why the *Medea* was still listing. Even with two masts in good working order, it wouldn't be wise to have all the sails unfurled until the ship was back on an even keel.

Sheerness grabbed a lantern and directed her toward a set of stairs into the hold near the stern. She hadn't noticed them when he had given her a tour. Something that was different, however, was that he had put in a shower for the crew, just as nice as the one in his own quarters. It looked as if it had been used, too.

When they stood in the hold, Psyche heard livestock: chickens, sheep, pigs. She looked toward midship and saw them milling around. She frowned, but they sounded happy, and she couldn't have scrambled eggs or lamb stew without them. It was fairly bright in that direction, and crewmen were working the manual pump beneath the main hatch to the hold, the pipe feeding into the bilge through a small hatch.

Sheerness turned toward the stern and held up the lantern. The hold was larger than Psyche thought it would be, almost cavernous, and it reminded her of what the *Medea* used to be. There were hooks nearby with lanterns, and Sheerness used a piece of straw to light them from the lamp he carried.

Psyche looked at the boiler with a frown. She did recognize it. It was almost like the ones they used for hot water at home. It was coal-heated rather than gas, so it was raised slightly higher to allow for the firebox. There were coal bins to either side of it to keep the ship in balance. The tender could easily reach into them with the nearby shovel to reload the box as needed.

Three lines went out from the tank to supply hot water to the crew's shower, the one in Sheerness's cabin, and another that went toward the bow for Meals to wash dishes and for cooking. Having pre-salted water was probably handy, depending on the purpose. There was another line for the cold water to be heated.

The pump came forward from the boiler, with copper lines to supply the steam that operated the pistons and made the suction to draw out the water. A pipe went down into the bilge, and another came out from the pump and fed to the side of the ship to drain the water outside. It looked rather simple…in a somewhat complicated way.

"The boiler's not lit," she said simply.

Sheerness laughed. "That's not the problem."

"Then what is? What was it doing? Was it leaking?"

She walked closer to the boiler. It wasn't very well secured. The pitching of the ship yesterday probably came close to tipping it over. If it had tipped over, it would have turned over the firebox as well. The water in the tank might have extinguished it, but if not, a list to starboard would have been the least of his worries. She thumped the side of the tank and could hear it was full.

"This needs to be fastened more securely," she said evenly, and she put her hands on her hips and turned to look at him. "Well, what was it doing?"

"The boiler itself didn't have a problem, as far as I was able to tell. It wasn't leaking water or steam. The pump simply had no suction."

"Did it have pressure?"

"I believe so," said Sheerness with a frown.

"Were the pistons moving?" she asked slowly.

"Yes, I think so. It's designed to operate as needed rather than all the time. There is a float in the bilge. When the water reaches a certain height, the float trips a lever, which turns on the pump. Once the water goes back down, the float sinks, and the pump turns off. Considering how much water is in there, it's well above the height when the lever should have tripped."

"Has anyone made sure the float wasn't damaged...or the lever?"

"I don't think that's the problem," said Sheerness dismissively.

"You *believe* the pump had pressure. You *think* the pistons were moving. Yet, you seem *sure* there's nothing wrong with the float or the lever," said Psyche dryly, folding her arms across her chest.

"It would mean swimming through the bilge," said Sheerness darkly.

"You don't have a hatch here to access it?" asked Psyche in surprise.

"The fewer places there are to get into the bilge, the fewer there are for water to come out if it," he said evenly.

Psyche shrugged. "Fair enough," she said agreeably, "but then you have moments like this when it would save you from swimming through God-knows-what to make repairs." She grinned cheekily, and Sheerness scowled at her. Psyche cleared her throat.

"First then, we should light the boiler to make sure it *did* have pressure and that the pistons were working." She scratched her forehead. "If there wasn't a problem with the boiler, you should have at least left it burning to supply hot water for showers and whatnot. There's a valve here—"she pointed to a valve with a tube leading to the outside—"to relieve the pressure if it gets too high. It's going to take until nightfall for the water to get hot enough to produce the steam needed to operate the pump. It would have made this go much quicker if it hadn't been put out." She clapped her hands. "So, three things: secure the tank better before we have another storm and it tips over and catches your ship on fire; relight the boiler; and put in an access hatch near the pump."

"I'm not putting in a hatch," said Sheerness flatly.

"So, you intend to swim through the bilge?" she asked plainly with a raised eyebrow. "I'm not." Sheerness compressed his lips into a tight line. Psyche started on her way to the stairs to the berth deck. "Have someone come get me when the pressure gets up to fifty, or nightfall, whichever comes first. Ta."

Sheerness watched her leave with a sour expression. She did seem to know what she was talking about, which irritated him. And she was right: there *should* be an access hatch near the pump, and he couldn't remember why he didn't have one. He sighed resignedly and went to the stairs as well. He hoped Laing had the crew far enough along on repairs topside to come do the work in the hold. The carpenter might not know anything about repairing the boiler or the pump, but he knew how to brace the tank...*and* how to make a hatch.

≪ ≫

Psyche spent the rest of the afternoon on her laundry and writing letters. She wanted to get back to deciphering the shards, but she didn't want to keep her cabin looking like a laundry room. After she finished ironing and put away her things, she sat on her bunk and painted her toenails. It was a guilty pleasure she didn't indulge very often, but since Pandora had supplied the lacquer and she had the time….

The crews operating the manual pump drained enough water that the ship no longer listed, but Psyche learned from Freddie when he came to retrieve the iron that the bilge was far from empty. She had to suppress a chuckle when she learned Sheerness had Laing go down to the hold to build a hatch, but she *did* grin widely. The foremast was repaired, and once the list was corrected, the *Medea* was again under full sail…and it had only taken until nightfall.

Psyche had brought in Waddlesworth for the night when there was a knock at her door. She opened it to find Sheerness there with a mild expression.

"You said whichever comes first," he said with a half-smile.

"So I did," said Psyche agreeably. She closed the door on her cabin and followed him to the deck. "What is the pressure at?"

"About forty-five."

"Hmm," said Psyche thoughtfully as they went down the stairs.

The lamps were lit along the walls, and most of the crew was eating their supper. Psyche and Sheerness went down the stairs to the hold, and she tried to ignore the way her stomach rumbled. Meals had made his lamb stew again. Psyche went to the boiler and pump to look at the gauges. One of the crew was seated on a chair nearby, eating his supper. He started to get up, but Sheerness raised a hand to let him stay as he was.

Psyche opened the valve at the top of the boiler and quickly closed it as she satisfactorily heard the soft hiss from the other side of the hull as it released steam. She looked at the gauge. It had the right amount of pressure, but the pistons weren't moving. She looked at Sheerness.

"How deep is the water supposed to get before the lever trips?"

"A foot."

Psyche raised an eyebrow. That was fairly shallow. "How deep is the water right now?"

"Almost four feet."

"Is there a manual lever to turn on the pump?"

"I don't know."

Psyche bent down to take a look. She frowned as she searched, and then she glanced up at Sheerness.

"I need some water, please," she said as she unfastened a wing nut.

He pulled open the newly-built access hatch and grinned at her wryly. "How much do you need?"

"Not more than a pint, I should think."

Sheerness went to the berth deck and came back momentarily with a bucket attached to a rope. He dipped it into the hatch and took it to her. The bucket was unwieldy (a tankard would have been better), but she managed to pour it into the small reservoir removing the cover had revealed. Once it was full, she pulled a nearby lever, and the pistons began to pump. She heard a sputtering, airy sound, but it was soon replaced by a gurgling, which silenced as the air worked out of the system. She put her hand on the pipe that drained outside, and she could feel it vibrating as the water was pushed through it out of the bilge. She grinned and grabbed Sheerness's hand to put on the pipe.

"Bloody marvelous!" he chortled.

"Well, we know the pump works, and it will be safe to leave it running this way for quite some time since there is *a lot* of water to clear out, but eventually we'll have to look at the float in the bilge," said Psyche provisionally.

Sheerness waved a hand through the air dismissively. "We'll worry about that tomorrow. Are you hungry?" he asked with a grin.

"Absolutely famished," groaned Psyche. He linked his arm through hers as they started up the stairs. "What is the float made of, do you know?"

"A sheep's bladder," said Sheerness calmly as they started to walk across the berth deck to go topside.

Psyche started to ask another question when there was an eruption of applause and whistling from the crew. Psyche blushed in embarrassment and buried her face in Sheerness's shoulder. She didn't enjoy the attention. She was glad they were happy, but she didn't need applause. She eventually raised her head and smiled uncomfortably, and then she curtsied slightly and pulled on Sheerness's arm to continue across the mess to go topside.

"Do you know if your bilge has rats?" she was finally able to ask.

Sheerness looked at her in puzzlement. "You just received a standing ovation from nearly the entire crew," he said in amazement.

"Yes, I saw that," she said brusquely.

He frowned. "That doesn't make you happy?"

"I'm happy they're happy, but I don't need applause. I did what needed to be done. I don't think it warrants a cheer from the audience."

Sheerness continued to look at her in astonishment. "But you're always doing things to be the center of attention."

"Not by choice."

"But—"

"I don't *like* attracting attention. Why do you think I wear pink and white all the time?" she asked rhetorically. "Because all the other women do. I don't do things for recognition or admiration or notoriety. *Semper est quidquid.*"

Sheerness raised an eyebrow. "Your family's motto?"

"Exactly," said Psyche flatly.

"You do realize that could be interpreted several different ways to suit the purposes of whoever happens to be using it at the time?"

Psyche chuckled as they went down the stairs to the aft deck. "Judging some of the things some of my ancestors did, I would have to say: too right."

Sheerness grinned. "So the Savages haven't always been fine, upstanding citizens?"

"Where do you think we got our name?" chortled Psyche. "Besides, I do have somewhat ulterior motives in fixing the pump."

"Really?"

"I want to take a shower," she said pertly. Sheerness laughed.

The other men were almost done eating by the time Psyche and Sheerness sat down, but they stayed to talk while the two of them ate. Psyche was relieved conversation had not changed after her recent activities. She would just as soon have everyone forget about it. She didn't want deferential treatment, and she didn't want any of the men to feel as if they could no longer share a joke or a story or talk to her at all.

After she finished supper, Psyche went to take her shower. The water was hot, and she felt much better. She washed as quickly as she could because Sheerness was waiting to go into his cabin. He had stayed in the officers' mess talking with the other men after she left, and he also had a tendency to take a walk around the deck, but she didn't want to make him wait long. Psyche had to fight a yawn as she brushed her teeth, and she was ready for sleep. She got into bed and turned on her side facing the wall, hugging one of her pillows.

Psyche had been lying on her bunk for a while and was on the verge of dozing off when she heard her door open. She started to turn over but decided to stay just where she was. She wasn't going to give him the satisfaction of knowing she was awake. Psyche was sure he wanted to hold her again, and she was happy to let him, but she was plotting revenge for his teasing. By the time she was through, he would *never* do it again.

Sheerness could smell Psyche's perfume as soon as he opened the door. He closed his eyes and clenched his jaw as it assailed him, and he took a deep breath and shook his head as he went to his cabin to open all the windows. Her light was still on as he went past her cabin, but he had work to do. He had a hard time concentrating on his log entries and paperwork, and he was only halfway through before he was frowning impatiently.

By the time he was finished, her light was off, and he wasn't sure how long it had been that way. His cabin was still permeated by the scent of her, and he knew he wouldn't be able to sleep. Before, she had taken her shower earlier, and he was able to clear the cabin enough that he was able to go sleep. Not tonight. He owed her for that morning, and judging by how unhappy she was, he was fairly sure she wouldn't refuse to let him make amends.

He left the windows in his cabin open, and then he got undressed and had a glass of brandy. He got a piece of hard tack for Waddlesworth and went to her cabin. He listened for any sounds, but as usual, there weren't any. She didn't move as he went in, and Sheerness was disappointed that she was already asleep. He was tempted to wake her, but it was hard for her to fall asleep, and considering she had been awake before him that morning, she probably had a hard time staying that way as well. He couldn't bring himself to do it.

He gave Waddlesworth the piece of hard tack, and then he went to the bunk and climbed under the blankets. She stirred and slightly lifted her head from the pillow, but he shushed her and ran a soothing hand down her arm. He carefully worked one arm under her head beneath the pillow and put the other around her waist and settled in behind her on his side. He nuzzled her neck before placing a gentle kiss below her ear.

Then he sucked in air through his teeth and let it out in a strangled gasp as Psyche shifted in her sleep and nestled her bottom closer against him. The feel of the silk of her shift as her actions rubbed him against the cleft in her bottom was exquisite. He had been hard almost from the moment he entered his cabin, and now he was throbbing. He started to move away, but it rubbed his erection against the silk in a way that was excruciating. He was caught in a tender trap. He tightened his arm around her waist to keep her from moving and began to take slow, calming breaths in through his nose and out through his mouth. Thoughts of sleep disappeared. Trying to sleep in his cabin would not have been worse than this. At least there he could have found some relief.

With her back turned to him, Sheerness couldn't see the way Psyche smiled drowsily. It had seemed like such a natural ploy to try. She hadn't realized how fantastically it would work. She wouldn't be able to use it again without him becoming suspicious, but she would find other ways to torment him. By the time she was through, he would be *begging.*

The following day on the ship, things were much the same as they had ever been. Psyche picked back up her volume of Pliny the Younger and spent much of the morning on deck reading in the launch. She had been awake before Sheerness, but she pretended to still be asleep. She heard him sigh tiredly, and he ran a hand down her hip to her thigh before he placed a kiss at the corner of her mouth and got up. She didn't roll over until she heard him go topside. She noticed when she went on deck herself after having breakfast that he was decidedly grumpy, and she had to try not to laugh or grin.

She went down to check on the clearing of the bilge, and they would be able to look at the float that afternoon. To her amazement, when she shined a light into the bilge and put her head in, she didn't see any eyes shining back at her. It appeared there were no rats. Either they were in another part of the ship, or the ship had simply not been in service long enough to acquire them. Psyche was happy.

For the afternoon until the bilge was low enough, after dinner, she worked on putting together the shards. It was a vase of some type, narrow and elongated, with handles to either side of the neck. Something useful she found was that it had been made by the same artisan, Phito, as the kyathos. It was neither an amphora nor a krater. What Psyche really needed was glue. Laing had some, but it wasn't a kind Psyche thought would be suitable for piecing together a two-thousand-year-old vase. She might be able to get some when they stopped to resupply, but she didn't know where that would be.

Around five, she went to the hold with Sheerness to look in the bilge. She could see the pipe that fed in to drain the water, and not far from it was a small metal bar. The water was still too deep to see the float. She followed the bar where it fed up to the pump, and she found the lever. She pulled up on the bar where it came through the planking and found the lever was very sensitive; the slightest bit of rise on the bar would trip it and turn on the pump. That made it possible to rule out a problem with the lever. The problem had to be with the float. Psyche looked into the bilge unenthusiastically. It was dark and dank, and it smelled like stagnant water.

"We could wait a little longer," said Sheerness neutrally.

"No," sighed Psyche resignedly as she began to pull off her boots and stockings. "The sooner this is fixed, the better."

"What's wrong with your toes?" asked Sheerness in surprise.

"What?" asked Psyche alarmedly, and she began to look at them carefully.

"Your toenails are red!"

Psyche sighed and rolled her eyes. "It's lacquer. There is absolutely nothing wrong with my toes."

She dropped into the bilge, and she was glad her breeches were unbuttoned at the knees and pulled up higher on her thighs. The water was just above her knees. The bottom was slippery, and she moved carefully to avoid falling.

"Hand down the lantern," she said as she looked up at the hatch, where Sheerness sat looking down at her, his legs hanging through the opening. He held it for her, and she grabbed it. She carefully moved out of the way and looked up at Sheerness. "You want to be careful when you drop; it's—" The moment Sheerness's feet touched, they slipped from under him, and he landed on his backside up to his neck in bilge water. "Slick."

"Thanks for the warning," he said darkly as he attempted to stand without much success.

Psyche balanced her feet to either side of the keel and reached out a hand to help him up, trying not to laugh.

"I was going to say I have dibs on the shower, but I think you'll need it more," she grunted as she helped him to his feet.

"How kind of you," he said sarcastically.

"I think so," she said blithely.

Once he was upright, she turned the lamp in the direction of the pipes. The light helped her see where she was going and to see the pipe and bar above the water level, but it didn't provide much assistance for seeing below the water.

"Does the suction pipe have a bend?" she asked before she moved too far.

"Yes."

"How long?"

"Three, maybe four, feet."

The suction pipe came down in line with the keel, and she moved to the side. She didn't want to hit her toes on the end of it. It wouldn't hurt much if there was a screen to keep debris from clogging the pipe, but if it was bare metal, she didn't want to cut her toes. She had enough injuries already.

"Stay to the side, then," she called over her shoulder as she went toward the bar.

She slid her hand down the metal beneath the water's surface and could feel where the float had been attached. It was no longer there. She shined the light over the water, wondering if it had simply come loose, but she didn't see it anywhere. Then she heard another splash behind her as Sheerness fell again. Psyche closed her eyes, shook her head, and slowly turned to look at him.

"Pah!" he said disgustedly.

He had gotten some of the water in his mouth. He started to reach up to wipe it off when he realized both his hands were covered in it, too. Psyche walked toward him and switched the lamp to her other hand. She pulled her shirt loose from her waistband and bent forward to dry his mouth and face with it. He had a scowl caused as much from his predicament as the fact that Psyche was, for the most part, dry. Psyche coughed to cover a laugh and held out her hand to help him back up.

"Did you trip over the suction pipe?" she finally asked.

"No, the bottom had something particularly slippery on it right there," he said testily, pointing to a spot not far away.

Psyche walked over to it and carefully began to feel with her toes. There was something oozy and squishy like fungus, and she realized what it was.

"You found the float," said Psyche dryly.

"Humph," said Sheerness, clearly unimpressed.

"We'll need to replace it. Do you have a sheep's bladder lying about?"

Sheerness snorted. "I doubt it. Meals throws things like that overboard, which I greatly appreciate."

Psyche chewed on the side of her thumb thoughtfully, and then her face brightened. "What about a condom?"

Sheerness's expression lightened, and he gave her a suggestive half-smile. "I don't think this is the place for it, *chere.*"

Psyche pursed her lips. "Hunh. I was thinking we could inflate the condom with *air* and use it as a float."

"I'm not aware that we have any," said Sheerness dryly.

"A ship full of sailors, and there aren't any?" Sheerness scowled and raised an eyebrow. Psyche finally shrugged. "It probably wouldn't last very long, either. The bladder failed because it started to decompose in the water. If we had some gutta percha, that would be excellent."

"Gutta who?"

"It's the latex from a tree my mother has in her greenhouse. Pandora has found all sorts of use for it. India rubber would work, too, but it can sometimes be heavy," she mused, and she started to tug at her bottom lip before going back to chewing on her thumb. "Hmm…a sealed bottle? No. Glass would be too heavy. A pan? No. It needs to be closed. Oil? Wood?"

Sheerness watched as she continued to mutter to herself. He imagined if the hull weren't so slick she would be pacing.

"Aha! I've got it! Cork. Have you got any?" she asked calmly.

"How much cork?"

"Oh, a piece eight inches across in diameter and three inches thick."

Sheerness scoffed. "Is *that* all?"

"Does that mean you have it or not?" asked Psyche blankly.

"Yes, it just so happens I *do* have it," he said dryly.

He carefully made his way back to the hatch. He lifted his hands above his head and raised himself part of the way through it to speak to the sailor tending the boiler, and then he carefully lowered himself back down. Psyche lifted an eyebrow questioningly as Sheerness walked toward her.

"He's gone to get it. I am assuming you need it with a hole in the middle for the bar?"

"That would be helpful."

They had to wait a short while before the sailor returned with the cork. Sheerness went to the hatch to get it and carried it to Psyche. The hole in the center was just small enough to fit, and there was a threaded bolt at the bottom of the bar that would keep it from sliding off should the water level go below the bottom. The fitting that had been used to attach the bladder would keep it from rising and maintain it at the proper height.

Once she had the cork attached, it worked perfectly. She would have to let Pandora know; although, Psyche still wasn't sure her twin had designed the pump. It had a few design flaws Psyche didn't think her twin would willingly lay claim to. They made their way back to the hatch, and Psyche handed the lamp up to the sailor, Bolen. Sheerness cupped his hands and gave Psyche a boost up to the opening. Bolen helped her into the hold, and Sheerness climbed out by himself. After she put on her stockings and boots, Psyche went to the manual lever and turned it back to the off position. The pump didn't shut off, and when she looked at the lever tripped by the bar, it was in the on position.

"Well, your pump is repaired. What's my pay as the ship's engineer?" she asked with a straight face.

Sheerness raised an eyebrow. "You're not serious, are you?" he asked hesitantly.

Psyche grinned. "No, not really."

Sheerness shook his head as his lips quirked in a slight smile. "Come on. There's something you should be able to see by now on the deck," he said indulgently, linking his arm through hers.

Psyche looked up at him curiously, and then she looked at her watch. It was close to seven in the evening, and as they went up to the deck, the sun was well on its way to setting. She looked to the north, and she could see land. She looked to the south, and she could see even more land. Almost directly ahead of them was an island. She looked at Sheerness.

"Where are we?" she asked with a frown.

Sheerness grinned. "That to the north is Peloponnesus. That to the south is Crete, and the larger of the islands there—"he said as he pointed ahead of them—"is Kithira."

Psyche's eyes widened in astonishment. "Greece?" she squeaked. Sheerness nodded. "Whoopee!" she hooted excitedly, and she amazed Sheerness and the crew standing on deck who saw it when she performed a somersault in the air and landed on her feet with a giggle.

Chapter Twenty Five

Psyche was impatient to go ashore. They docked in Piraeus shortly after nightfall the next day. From the moment Sheerness had pointed out they were (technically) in Greece, she had barely been able to sit still. She was so excited it would be pointless to try to sleep on her own, and she had taken some of her sleeping draught. Sheerness *might* have been able to help her go to sleep, but she hadn't wanted to risk it. He was there when she woke up, but she had, as she had taken to doing, pretended to be asleep until he left.

That wasn't easy. She wanted to look out the window at Greece surrounding her, but she was still working on her retaliation. She wanted him to be near her and still not have her…at least for a little while, which meant she would have to actually be asleep or continue pretending a few days more. She wouldn't let it continue much beyond that because it was just as tormenting to her. She had other reasons for making him wait, but she thought Monday would be long enough. She was starting to *crave* him…just like a drug.

As soon as he left, after placing a kiss on the side of her neck, Psyche got up to sit on the coffer. She could look out her window and *see* Greece, and it was almost too fantastic for her to believe. She hurriedly got dressed and braided her hair, and as soon as Freddie brought her breakfast, she ate and went to the main deck. She took her book with her, but it was useless to attempt concentrating on it; she spent all her time looking at the scenery. Whenever a new island would come into view, she would ask whoever happened to be nearby if he knew what it was. It was usually Stockbridge, and it soon got to the point that he would come to the side of the launch and tell her before she asked, an amused smile on his face. Her giddy excitement kept the crew entertained for much of the day, and her good spirits were contagious.

The only one it didn't seem to affect, however, was Sheerness. As the day wore on, he became increasingly more surly. He was jealous…again. His duties kept him from being the one to provide her information, and he was jealous it was Stockbridge yet again who filled the role he felt should be his. Sheerness was jealous of the easy camaraderie they shared, and even though the relationship between him and Psyche had become less strained, he still felt reservation and knew she still didn't quite trust him and didn't love him. He was afraid of what other activities the bosun might take on.

Sheerness had never seen anything to indicate they were more than friends. He hadn't seen her touch Stockbridge, not even to take his arm for a turn around the deck, much less hug or kiss him as she had Sir James, and yet watching them made him feel inferior, as if she still didn't consider him *worthy*.

To add insult to injury, he was feeling a little sexually frustrated. He enjoyed holding her at night, but he wanted far more. He somewhat understood why she had taken her sleeping draught; he didn't think she had done it to purposely thwart any plans of seduction he might have had, but it had proven effective. He would have found a way to help her go to sleep, and it would have made him feel better, too.

Psyche reluctantly went belowdecks when the sun set. She wanted to stay looking at the sea and the land, but it soon became too dark to see anything except the moon and stars. The sunset was beautiful, and Psyche was looking forward to seeing many more. Even the sunsets over the lakes at home couldn't compare to the one she saw that night. The hues were warm and vibrant, so rich she felt as if she could reach out her hand and touch them.

She managed to eat at dinner and supper, but she was a jumble of nerves and hadn't really tasted what she'd eaten. To her, it was only food, but she would never let Meals know that. They moored in Piraeus sometime during supper, and Psyche was hard-pressed not to jump up from the table and go topside once the anchors dropped. She forced herself to slow down while she ate instead of bolting her food, and she managed to eat all of it *and* participate in the conversation at the table.

Once Psyche finished supper, she went to her cabin and sat at her window after she was dressed for bed. There wasn't much she could see in the dark, and Piraeus, while a large port, was not heavily used. There were one or two other ships and several small fishing skiffs and ketches, but there weren't any others. She sat for a time in the dark, waiting to feel tired but never did, so she reluctantly took some of her sleeping draught. It was steadily dwindling, and she wouldn't be able to get more.

She lay down and was adjusting her pillows and blankets when Sheerness came in…without knocking. Psyche propped her head on her hand and looked at him. He had seen her moving, so it was pointless to pretend she was asleep.

"You do realize a closed door is a sign you need to announce your entrance to a room in some fashion rather than just walking in?" she said dryly.

"You're usually asleep when I come in, so I don't want to knock and wake you. Do you *mind* me coming in?" he asked uncertainly. Sheerness hadn't thought she might not want him there.

"No, not really," said Psyche with a half-smile.

"Do you mind me *staying*?" he clarified.

"No, I've grown accustomed to it," said Psyche mildly.

"If it's only that you've become accustomed to it, then perhaps I shouldn't stay," he said stiffly.

"I'm sorry. I didn't mean it to sound like that," said Psyche quickly.

"Yes, I know. You never do," said Sheerness flatly.

Psyche sighed and moved over. He was standing there naked and perfect in the moonlight, and she *did* want him to stay. How could she *not* want him to? When she told him she had grown accustomed, she had meant it would seem odd for him not to be there. Even if she didn't know when he came in, it would be strange to wake up without him. She *liked* being held by him.

He came to the bunk and climbed beneath the blankets. He pulled her close, and Psyche turned on her side and rested her head on his chest. She was starting to feel drowsy, and she snuggled close to him, smoothing a hand over his chest. She found the covering of hair fascinating, and she ran her hand over it absently as she started to drift off. Now he was there, she didn't want to go to sleep, but it was inevitable.

"What are we going to see first tomorrow?" she asked with a yawn.

"I have business tomorrow," said Sheerness mildly. He enjoyed the feel of her hand moving over his chest, and he was glad she was awake.

Psyche frowned. "What kind of business?" she asked, and she looked in fascination as her fingers followed the ridge down the center of his stomach where the hair all but disappeared, only to begin again at his navel.

"I've got to arrange for permission to take things out of the country, should we find anything suitable," he sighed. Her hand had traveled below his navel, and she was very close to touching things even lower.

Her hand stopped at his words, and Psyche lifted her head from his chest to look at him with a puzzled expression. Raising her head made her dizzy, and she was having a hard time keeping her eyes open.

"With whom? Permission from Athens will amount to nothing, not even for taking things from Athens," she said slowly, and her expression changed to one of distracted curiosity as she started to trace her fingers over the hair on his chest again, fascinated by the texture of it and the way it disguised the hardness of the muscle beneath it. "Permission from the beylerbey *might* be sufficient, but even he is in Ioannina. What you really need is a firman from the sultan, and that would mean going to Constantinople."

Sheerness reached up to move the hair from her face. She had a dreamy, unfocused expression, and he realized she had taken her sleeping draught. She was fighting to stay awake, but she was drifting off. He sighed disappointedly and pulled her head toward his for at least a kiss before she went to sleep. She was warm and relaxed, and she kissed him back with a redolent sensuality that excited him. Her breasts were pressed against his chest, and he moaned low in his throat as her fingertips trailed down across one of his nipples to his side and came to rest at his hip.

Psyche left his lips to begin placing slow kisses down his chin to his throat as everything started to take on a dreamlike quality. She knew in a distant way that this was completely ruining her plans of making Sheerness wait, but in her hazy, disjointed state, she was unable to recall *why* she had wanted to. There was something vague at the edge of her mind that had she been more alert would have clanged like a warning bell. At the moment, it was no more than an occasional tinkle, like a chime, and it was very easy to ignore.

She explored the column of his neck with her lips and tongue, down to the shallow hollow at the base of it and across his collarbone to his chest. Sheerness's arm beneath her tightened at her waist as his hand moved down to cup her bottom through the silk of her shift, and his other hand went to the back of her head to clutch weakly in her hair as she continued her exploration.

Sheerness knew he should stop her. He could tell she was halfway asleep, but even as he knew this was not going to end well, he couldn't let it end. He ached for her almost to the point of desperation, and he found her currently uninhibited state too intoxicating to interrupt. He was willing to suffer the consequences, and he was fairly sure he *would* suffer.

Psyche explored his chest with her mouth, and he inhaled sharply through his teeth as she teased one of his nipples. She draped her leg over his and slowly worked her way lower, touching the places with her teeth and tongue that she had already felt with her hand. Sheerness worked her shift up over her bottom, and she sighed with delight as she felt his fingers splay against the bare skin and begin to knead its soft roundness. She was so tired she could barely move, but she didn't want to stop. There was still so much to discover.

She moved her mouth back to his, and Psyche was not surprised when he kissed her back hungrily. She knew what he wanted, and she wanted to give it to him, regardless of the reasons she shouldn't, but she wasn't sure she could stay awake. She had already been fighting it for quite a while, but whatever herbs Keung had put in the draught were powerful, and she *was* going to sleep…probably very soon. She moaned softly as she felt his hand move to the ties at the front of her shift to loosen them and slip inside to begin massaging one of her breasts, and she tried to fight her losing battle for just a little longer.

She lifted her hand from his hip with the intention of moving it back up his chest, but her hand brushed across the hair that started below his navel, and her curiosity led her in a different direction…lower. She had only ever touched his member once, very briefly, but her mind had been intent on other things then. She could tell when she neared it, when she realized his erection was lifting up the blankets almost like a tent pole, and she found that to be just the least bit impressive. She was intrigued by how the hair grew up to the very base of it, and even a little up the circumference. It was extraordinary, and if she hadn't been so lethargic, she might have lifted the blanket to look at it with her eyes rather than her hand.

She slowly moved her fingers over its surface before carefully wrapping her hand around it, and Sheerness's reaction was instantaneous. It was as if he experienced a paroxysm of pleasure at her caress, and Psyche was fascinated. He inhaled sharply and groaned as he nipped at her lower lip. His grip on her bottom and breast tightened, and Psyche felt his hips arch involuntarily toward her touch. His erection felt unbelievably warm and hard in her hand, and she gently flexed her fingers around it, finding it difficult to believe that something so solid did not have a bone to support it. She loosened her grip slightly and began to move her hand up and down on its length slowly, and even if she didn't know what she was doing, whatever it was, Sheerness seemed to find it utterly enjoyable.

He started to quiver as she stroked him, and his concentration had become solely focused on what she was doing. Since he wasn't really intent on kissing her anymore, she let her lips trail across his jaw on her way to his ear. She could hear him breathing harshly and feel his hands clutching spasmodically where he held her. And then, when she gently grazed his earlobe with her teeth before sucking on it, something so remarkable happened, Psyche's eyes sprang open in surprise.

"Oh, Psyche, *mon dieu!*" gasped Sheerness in astonishment.

He tensed and inhaled deeply before he let out the breath again with a soft, shuddering groan. She felt him begin to spasm, and something warm dripped onto her hand as she stroked him. Psyche's cheeks colored as she slowly realized what had happened, and she stopped what she was doing and buried her face in the crook of his neck in embarrassment. She really didn't know what else she should have expected. Perhaps because she had never done it before, she had thought it would be more complicated. Sheerness lay beside her breathing raggedly, a film of perspiration on his skin. He eventually smoothed a hand across her shoulder and lifted her face to kiss her gently.

"I'm sorry," she said quietly. "I didn't mean to...to...."

"I know," said Sheerness softly and kissed her tenderly on the forehead. "You never do," he sighed. "Do you have a handkerchief?"

Psyche's forehead wrinkled confusedly as she tried to concentrate on the question, finding it almost too difficult to comprehend despite its simplicity. Regardless of what had happened, she was going to sleep. She had only minutes left before she was out completely. She couldn't fight it anymore.

"Top middle drawer," she said slowly.

Sheerness moved away from her momentarily and leaned over the side of the bunk to retrieve a handkerchief from the drawer. He took her hand in his and wiped it off, and then he cleaned himself. He dropped the handkerchief onto the floor for the time being, and he pulled Psyche close to his side.

"Are you angry?" she asked groggily.

She was very limp as he rested her head onto his chest and took her hand in his. He chuckled softly at her question and tightened his arm around her.

"Ah, no, *chere*," he said gently with a soft smile. "In case you didn't notice, I *did* enjoy that."

She was settled heavily against him, her breathing steady and slow, and he wasn't sure she had heard him. She was sound asleep. He smoothed a hand over her back and kissed the top of her head before closing his eyes tiredly.

He thought she was going leave him miserable again, but she had surprised him, much to his relief and delight. He should have warned her, but he was afraid she would stop. He knew how drowsy she was; there wouldn't have been time for anything else, and he had wanted her so bad…whatever way he could have her. She hadn't known what was going to happen, and it had startled her. Judging from her question, she had been more concerned about whether or not it was what he had wanted rather than by what she had done.

He thought about what she had said before she distracted him. Surely, she had to be mistaken. He didn't understand how she could know what would be required. He didn't want to go to Constantinople, and he didn't find sailing back around Peloponnesus and up the western side of the country just to get *close* to Ioannina very appealing either. He didn't want to chase across the countryside to get permission. It would be time better spent looking for things.

Sheerness sighed and smoothed his hand down her side to her hip. He felt more relaxed than he had in days, weeks even, and he was glad she was there. For the time being, he brushed aside the fact she had been the cause of most of the strain he had been under in the first instance. He could ponder that after he got some sleep, if he still wanted to.

Psyche's statement that he would need a firman proved to be correct. He spoke to several agents in Athens, both English and Greek, but they only confirmed what she said. Even Lord Elgin had needed to go all the way to Constantinople, personally, to get permission from Mahmud II. Sheerness didn't intend to do anything so grand as dismantle the Athenian Acropolis, and he was hopeful he would be able to find someone to go to Constantinople to pursue his approval for him.

It sounded simpler and less expensive than it was. A big problem was that Sheerness did not speak Greek…not modern Greek. It didn't take him long to realize the difference between modern and ancient Greek wasn't so much in how it was written but more in how it was spoken, which was why he had been able to understand Chrissoula's letter. He was slowly becoming accustomed to it, but he still didn't understand it well enough to speak it himself or understand someone else. He certainly didn't speak Turkish, so he had to have a translator and someone knowledgeable about the politics. It was like searching for a pebble at the bottom of the ocean. Everyone wanted to be compensated for their efforts, whether they proved to be helpful or not. After spending several days trying to make arrangements, he was no closer. It *was* beginning to look like he would have to go to Constantinople, and he wasn't looking forward to it.

He spent his days away from the ship, often not returning until very late at night. Always when he did return, Psyche was sleeping. He had not been able to talk to her since the night they docked in Piraeus. He was always relieved when he got back to the *Medea*, and he tiredly climbed into bed to hold her. She had not been taking her sleeping draught—he could tell by how she slept, but he always returned too late for her to be awake. He could see how she was occupying her time during the day; the walls of her cabin were covered with sketches and watercolors. They were very good, and he would look at them each morning before he left and choose his favorites.

Most of them were of buildings on the Acropolis, and he wondered how she had managed to gain access. It was a military fort, and it wasn't a place someone could just casually stroll. In the end, he decided he would rather not know. He would look at the pictures wistfully because they were of things he wanted to see himself but couldn't. Not all of the pictures were of buildings; some were of people: soldiers, local residents, Freddie, several members of the crew…including Stockbridge.

Sheerness knew the bosun was her escort when she left the ship from talking with Stockbridge himself. Just because he didn't get to talk to *her* did not mean he didn't talk to anyone else. But the bosun was reticent when it came to details of what she did during the day. It was difficult for Sheerness to fight the suspicion it was something he should be concerned about, and since he couldn't talk to Psyche to find out what she was doing, Sheerness was left with taking whatever information the bosun would provide to him.

Sheerness was frustrated after a week of no luck making arrangements. He was to the point that he was about ready to admit defeat. He was becoming resigned to sailing to Constantinople. It was an interesting city, he was sure, but it was not among the places he had wanted to go. The thing he found so discouraging was that he would have no guarantee of success even once he made the journey. The crew was enjoying their time without duties, but Sheerness had not traveled the distance he had to spend all his time talking to people from sunrise to sunset.

On Wednesday when Sheerness woke up, he was startled to find Psyche propped up on her elbow looking at him, wide awake and apparently that way for some time. Her face was tanned from the time she was spending in the sun, and it made the green of her eyes glow. She looked absolutely stunning, and Sheerness missed just looking at her. Her gaze was pensive as she looked at him, a slight frown furrowing the space between her brows. He lifted a hand to the side of her neck and brought her mouth to his for a soft kiss. When she raised her head, the frown was still there.

"Is there anything I can do to help?" she asked quietly.

Sheerness scoffed with a wry smile and shook his head. He traced his finger along her collarbone to the hollow at the base of her neck. The edge of one breast was exposed at the opening in the front of her shift, and he ran his finger down to skim along the softness of it. Psyche grabbed his hand. She gave him an assessing glance, and Sheerness could see she wasn't going to be distracted.

"Are you sure?" she asked solemnly.

"Unless you're friends with a Turkish pasha who can be easily bribed, then I don't see what you could possibly do," said Sheerness dryly.

He kissed her soundly and sat up on the edge of the bunk, rubbing a hand over his face. He looked at the new pictures she had hanging on the wall. Some of the older ones had been removed to make room. The new ones were not of the Acropolis. It appeared to be a cemetery of some type, and he wondered why she had painted it.

Psyche sat up on her knees behind him to knead his shoulders. It felt wonderful, and he tried not to lean back and impede her work. Psyche could feel the knots of tension in the muscle beneath her fingers, and she worked them until it was smooth and supple. When she was finished, she wrapped her arms around him and rested her chin on his shoulder, putting her cheek against his, looking at the pictures as well.

"Did you enjoy seeing the Acropolis?" he asked her mildly.

"It was nice," she said neutrally.

"Just nice?"

"I don't think it's the same as when Myron saw it. It was sad, actually."

"Sad?" quipped Sheerness, and he turned his head to look at her.

"Elgin took a lot. The frieze and the metopes from the Parthenon…much of what was left, I'm sure. One of the caryatids from the Erechtheion. He completely shattered another and just left it lying on the ground. What war hasn't obliterated, Elgin did a fine job of trying to finish off," she said disgustedly. Her expression turned gloomy. "I almost wish I hadn't seen it."

Sheerness kissed her on the cheek. "I'm sure you don't mean that."

Psyche sighed and shook her head. "No, I suppose not, but it just makes me so angry he's done that."

"You seem to forget that's why we're here, too," said Sheerness evenly.

"*I'm* not," said Psyche simply. "If I don't take one piece of rock home, I'm happy. Why do I *need* to take it home with me? Am I going to learn any more from having it in my back yard than I would looking at it where it belongs?"

"Perhaps Elgin took it to preserve it for future generations," said Sheerness stiffly. "You said yourself a lot of it has been destroyed by war."

Psyche snorted derisively. "I am *not* going to believe Elgin did what he did out of any altruistic ideals. He's taking it to his *home*. Who's going to see it there? Certainly not the people it belongs to."

"The people it *belonged* to are long dead and gone," said Sheerness tightly, and he stood up to begin getting dressed.

"No, they're not. Look out the window and you see Greece. They belong to *Greece*, not Britain. What if someone came to England and decided they wanted to take the sculpture and whatnot from the ruins at Bath back to their country? What about Stonehenge? Canterbury Cathedral?"

"No one would do that, and you're being silly," said Sheerness with an amused smirk.

"You don't know that," countered Psyche quietly. "Imagine the highly improbable for the sake of argument, and one day England was conquered by a foreign power. We have no dearth of old ruins, some of them damaged in wars. Along comes someone from this other country, who sees it and decides we don't need it…we won't miss it. It's old and broken, so who will care? But *you* would care, *wouldn't* you?"

Sheerness finished buttoning his waistcoat and turned to look at her with a troubled frown. Psyche reached into a drawer on the side of her bed and held out her brush. He reluctantly took it from her to brush his hair in the mirror.

"It's well and good if you're taking things to save them and actually preserve them. But just to take them as some mark of accomplishment or personal pride, to gain them just because you *want* to?" Psyche raised her hands from her sides and shook her head. "That's wrong."

Sheerness turned from the mirror to return her brush. Then he pulled her toward him where she still knelt on the bed, giving her a gentle, yet thorough, kiss. He lifted his head and swatted her on the bottom before he released her.

"I *still* need to have permission," he said with a slight smile, and Psyche watched as he left her cabin.

She folded her arms across her chest and sighed fitfully, a thoughtful frown on her face. She didn't know if what she said had made any impression or not. She had never used that particular argument before. Their relationship had changed so much since they had discussed the topic at all she couldn't tell if it had made a difference. She supposed he didn't *completely* disagree with her. She thought he would be willing to state his reasons if that were the case, but at least he wasn't arguing just for the sake of doing so anymore.

Psyche finally looked at her watch and shook her head. She needed to shower and get dressed. She had things to do. She had given Sheerness a week to get things sorted on his own, and she had seen everything she wanted to see in Athens in the meantime. She was ready to go to Thessaloniki. She had, at least, asked him if he needed her help, and he had told her what he needed. Now she was going to give it to him. She looked in her drawer and pulled out one of the outfits like Chrissoula's and laid it on the bed to air out the creases. It wouldn't do for her to go where she intended looking rumpled.

She had finished her shower and was almost dressed when Freddie brought breakfast. She would put on the rest after she ate. Freddie tilted his head and looked at her curiously, but he didn't say anything. He had learned she never wore normal women's clothes. He stayed to chat while he fed Waddlesworth as she ate breakfast, and he was able to take her tray when he left. Psyche had eaten quickly. She didn't know how long this would take. She wasn't going to see ruins; she was going to see a person…someone who was not easy to visit, and she didn't know what kind of reception she would have.

After Freddie left, she got a drawstring bag she had purchased in Valletta from one drawer, and then she went to the drawer with her kits and pulled out her box of allowance. She smoothed a hand over the lid contemplatively for a moment before she opened it and counted out coins to put in the bag. She wasn't using the money as a bribe in the literal sense, but it might be necessary.

Once she had the money in the bag, she put away the box and finished getting dressed. She put her hair into a knot at the back of her head after she'd braided it and tied on the silk scarf. She put in her earrings and the ornate necklace that matched them. After she put on her slippers, she put on the heavy velvet coat, and then she grabbed her spectacles, the bag with the money, and the drawstring bag that carried her own money. She looked at herself in the mirror, and she decided she looked as presentable as she ever would.

She left her cabin after putting Waddlesworth into the shrouds. She went to the deck to find Stockbridge and put on her spectacles to protect her eyes against the bright, late-morning sun. He wasn't difficult to locate. He was at the railing, still whittling his mermaid, but the carving was almost finished. He turned when he heard her approaching, and his eyebrows shot up in surprise.

"You're a little dressed up to go looking at dilapidated buildings," he said with a slight grin.

"Stockbridge, we're going to see a man about a firman," she said mildly.

"Indeed?" he quipped amusedly. "Does the captain know?"

"Not really, no," said Psyche calmly as she helped him untie the ropes from the cleats to lower a launch into the water. "But he said the only way I could help was if I knew a pasha who could be easily bribed." They lowered the small boat into the water, and then she turned to look at him with a grin and a wink as she began to climb down to it. "It just so happens I think I do."

Stockbridge looked down at her as she gracefully hopped into the boat and took a seat, carefully arranging the silk of her dress to avoid wrinkling it. He noticed she was carrying two bags, and one appeared to be very full and heavy. His forehead wrinkled when he thought about what she might be carrying in there, but she was nonchalant. That was for the best and would be sufficient to protect her. He didn't have time to see Blossom about a pistol, and then he would have to explain why he wanted it. Psyche wouldn't want him to. He climbed down the ladder to get in the launch and began to row them ashore.

"I've never asked you, Stockbridge, but I'm curious: are you married?"

Stockbridge threw his head back and laughed. "No," he drew out.

"Why is that funny?" asked Psyche curiously.

"What woman would have me?" he asked amusedly.

Psyche's eyes widened, and she shook her head. "I don't know. Unless you have problems I've failed to notice. Gambling? Drinking? Womanizing?"

"I *am* bossy," said Stockbridge evenly, as if it were something that should be completely obvious.

"Well, perhaps you just need to find a woman who can stand up to it…maybe one who will give it right back."

"I have yet to find one of those," said Stockbridge with a charming smile. "You would suit, but I think your interests lie elsewhere."

Psyche lifted an eyebrow. "Whatever do you mean?" she asked innocently.

Stockbridge chuckled. "Not one thing," he said pleasantly. "Now, let me ask *you* something."

"Yes?" she asked archly.

"How did you come to be on the *Medea*? The captain has never said."

Psyche waved a hand through the air dismissively. "My sister locked me in a trunk and stowed me away."

Stockbridge looked at her disbelievingly. "You're not serious."

"I am," she said with a nod. "Actually, she drugged me first."

"Now I know you're bamming me," scoffed Stockbridge. Psyche continued to look at him in perfect seriousness. "Does she not like you?"

It was Psyche's turn to laugh. "It does sound as if she doesn't on first telling, I have to admit, but she loves me very much. She didn't intend for things to go as horribly wrong as they did."

"When the crew first learned you were aboard, when they saw your condition, there was speculation the captain had kidnapped you." Psyche's eyes widened in alarm. Stockbridge shrugged and tilted his head sideways with a smile. "Now they know better."

"Do they?" she chortled.

"Well, it's obvious the man is nuts about you, but they're fairly sure you would have broken his arm if he'd tried to kidnap you even still."

"Aha," said Psyche noncommittally as they reached the dock.

Stockbridge climbed out and tied off the boat, and then he reached down to help Psyche climb out. They walked down the quay to the stairs and found a cart for hire.

"*Boreíte na mas párete sten katoikía tou pasá Duman, parakaló?*" she asked pleasantly.

The driver looked at her speculatively for a moment, but he nodded and started the cart being pulled by a single horse. The drive to Athens was slow, and Psyche and Stockbridge spent much of it talking about their families—her large one, his nonexistent one. She mentioned Chrissoula at one point, and an idea began to form in the back of her mind. They soon arrived at a large villa with lush, landscaped gardens full of palms, olives, and citrus. Psyche looked up at the daunting edifice. She paid the driver, and she and Stockbridge stepped down after she asked the man to wait.

"You *know* the person who lives here?" asked Stockbridge in amazement.

"Somewhat," hedged Psyche. "My father knows him very well, but it's been a few years since he's seen him. I've personally never met Duman Pasha, but I'm on excellent terms with several members of his family."

Stockbridge looked at her uncertainly as they walked up the low set of steps to the colonnaded front of the house. She pulled on a rope connected to a nearby bell and gave the bosun an encouraging look. Before long, a servant answered. She was a native Greek, but Psyche wasn't sure if she was from Attica or some other part of the country. Her clothes suggested she was from somewhere in the Aegean Islands, but Psyche wasn't sure which one.

"Can I help you, my lady?" asked the young maid.

"We would like to see Duman Pasha, please," replied Psyche pleasantly.

"Is he expecting you?" she asked suspiciously.

"No, but if you would please tell him that Lady Psyche Savage is here, I think he will want to see me."

The maid continued to look at her doubtfully, but she nodded and held open the door for the strangers to enter the house. They walked into the cool interior to a large foyer, a set of stairs leading up to the first floor at the back of it. To the left, there were columns that separated a large sitting area covered with cushions and rugs, a table in the center holding an ornate houka, a fireplace large enough to roast a boar on the back wall. The wall to the right was completely sealed except for a doorway, and another doorway went to rooms further beyond the stairs.

"Wait here," said the maid quietly.

Psyche nodded with a smile and watched as the maid left through the doorway to the right.

"Where did you learn to speak Greek?" asked Stockbridge curiously.

"My maid, Chrissoula, is from near Thessaloniki, and we have a few other servants from Corfu." Psyche turned to look at him seriously. "I don't know if Duman Pasha is going to let you come with me. My father has said he's very distrustful, with good reason."

"I don't like the sound of that," said Stockbridge flatly.

"I'll be fine. The man is at least as old as my father, and no match for me, I'm sure," said Psyche with a grin. She shrugged. "Besides, he may let you. I just thought I would warn you."

Psyche continued to look at the sitting area to the left. It was very comfortable and informal, and it would be fantastic for the type of entertainment the Turks and Greeks both enjoyed: dancing and good food. The maid returned with a bemused expression.

"Duman Pasha said he will see you right away," she said in amazement.

Psyche smiled happily. "Wonderful! Thank you," she said pleasantly.

Psyche and Stockbridge followed the maid down the hall to the right, and they came to a door to a room on the back of the house. The maid opened it and gestured for them to enter. The two of them walked into the brightly lit room, and Psyche was surprised to see Sheerness already there with another gentleman she didn't recognize. The pasha sat behind a large desk with the two visitors sitting in front of it, but when Duman saw Psyche, he grinned widely and stood up from his seat to come around the desk.

"Lady Psyche Savage!" he said happily. "I would know you anywhere. You have your mother's eyes and your father's hair...not to mention his chin," he said with a laugh. Psyche was startled when he pulled her toward him for a warm hug and to kiss her affectionately on both cheeks.

"Duman Pasha, I'm so glad you would see me," said Psyche quietly, a bit overwhelmed by his warm greeting.

"How could I refuse to see the daughter of one of my oldest and dearest friends?" he asked reprovingly. "Your father has done so much for me. Now, you must tell me: how are my children?"

"They are wonderful," said Psyche happily. "Sacit has gone to Bermuda with Gregory, of all places, but we hope they will be returning to England very soon. I've been there myself, and I imagine he is enjoying the weather after all the rain and cold," she said with a smile. Duman nodded agreeably. "Rajeesh, our butler, will soon be retiring, and his son Tannaz will be taking his place, and Basir will be taking Tannaz's position as the under-butler. And Cari has begun training a new girl to take her place in the kitchen because she is going to be taking an indefinite amount of time away from her duties."

"Whatever for?" asked Duman concernedly.

Psyche grinned. "You are going to be a grandfather…if not already."

"Allah Allah!" laughed Duman. "I am too young to be a grandfather."

"Yes, my father says the same thing," said Psyche with a wry grin.

"*You* have children?" he asked, looking her up and down disbelievingly.

"No, my twin, Pandora, had twins of her own in June, and my brother, Dorian, has a wife expecting one very soon as well."

"Oh, my! All of these babies!" He looked past her to Stockbridge curiously. "Is he your husband?"

"No, Duman Pasha, he is not. He is only a friend and protector."

"Ah. So, where are your parents?"

"They are still in England."

"You have come all this way alone?" asked Duman concernedly.

"Not really," said Psyche evasively. "Myron was supposed to come with me, but he died in June."

"What?" asked Duman in shock. "How terrible!"

"I have actually come all this way with Lord Sheerness," said Psyche, and she turned to look at him in his chair. He had an irritated expression, a muscle ticking in his jaw as he clenched it.

"You have come with *him*?" asked Duman disbelievingly. "*He* is your husband, then?"

"No, Duman Pasha, I'm not married," said Psyche patiently. "It's all a jumble how I came here with him. Let us suffice to say it was Myron's dying wish that I should see Greece, so here I am," she said with a half-smile.

"Ah," said Duman, smiling in understanding. "We will have some coffee, and you will tell me what I can do for you."

He went to ring a bell on his desk. The maid returned, and he told her to bring coffee. Psyche was astounded at the difference between his demeanor when he talked to her and when he talked to the maid. With her, he was jovial and warm; with the maid, he was stiff and arrogant.

"Do we need all these people here?" he asked her pleasantly.

Psyche looked at the other three men. Stockbridge, she was sure, wouldn't mind if he had to wait elsewhere. She didn't know the man with Sheerness. Sheerness, however, would have to stay, even if he had no inkling what the conversation was. So far, she had been chattering with Duman in Turkish, a language Sheerness didn't know how to speak, and no one else had said a word. She turned to look back at Duman.

"Stockbridge, the man I came in with, will not mind leaving, if you could arrange for him to have some dinner. Lord Sheerness should stay, since the matter I came to see you on also concerns him. I don't know the other gentleman, so I couldn't speak for him," said Psyche evenly.

"Fine. You and the English earl will stay; the other two will *go*," he said, making a brief shooing gesture with his hands.

The maid returned with a tray with coffee, and she set it on the edge of the desk. She turned to look at Duman, and he began to issue her directions in Greek. Psyche turned to look at Stockbridge.

"She's going to take you somewhere to feed you," said Psyche quietly as she leaned close to his ear. "The other gentleman will be going with you. Since he is with Sheerness, I *think* he speaks English. The captain and I will stay here. Enjoy your dinner, and hopefully this will not take long."

Stockbridge nodded agreeably. He would have been uncomfortable leaving Psyche alone with the pasha, even if he did seem friendly, but she would be safe with Sheerness there. The other man, who still had not been introduced, stood up to leave as well, apparently having understood the conversation either between Psyche and Duman, or Duman and the maid. Either way, he knew he was expected to leave. Sheerness started to rise with a put-out expression. Psyche's lips twitched amusedly as she looked at him.

"No, Sheerness, you get to stay," she said mildly. His face registered surprise, and he settled back into his chair.

After Stockbridge and the other man left with the maid, Duman actually served their coffee himself, and then he went to sit behind his desk.

"Now, *anything* you need, you just tell me what it is," said Duman with a smile, tapping the top of his desk soundly with his finger.

Psyche walked out into the late afternoon sun and immediately put on her spectacles. She wasn't surprised the man with the cart had left, probably long ago. She took off her coat and draped it over her arm with a sigh and calmly started walking down the drive to the gate and the road. She had paid attention on the ride up, and even though it was a long walk, they would find another ride before long. If not, there was still plenty of daylight.

Sheerness and Stockbridge looked after her with disbelief as she began to walk, but they both stepped off the porch to follow her, Sheerness taking off his own coat and unbuttoning his waistcoat. He came up beside her and grabbed her arm to stop her.

"What just happened?" he asked confusedly.

"What do you mean?" asked Psyche calmly as she started to walk again.

"All of that," said Sheerness, waving his arms perplexedly. "I've been trying to see that man all week, and it was just wasted on a *social call*?"

Psyche laughed and shook her head. "You said the only way I could help was if I knew a Turkish pasha who could be easily bribed." She lifted the heavy bag still on her wrist and shook it. "I would say *easily* and *cheaply.*"

"What?" said Sheerness in stunned disbelief.

"Duman is going to get your firman, and it will be good for anywhere in the Ottoman Empire...not just Greece...*anywhere*."

"Bloody hell!" hooted Stockbridge. Sheerness gave him a dark look. "Sorry."

"How do you know?" asked Sheerness suspiciously.

"Because I asked him to," said Psyche simply.

"Wait a tick," said Sheerness disbelievingly, coming to a dead stop in the middle of the road. "He's going to get a firman, issued by the sultan, granting me permission to remove antiquities from *anywhere* in the empire?"

"Me, too," said Psyche blithely over her shoulder as she continued to walk. "There will be, however, some limitations."

Sheerness started walking again and quickly came up beside her. "What kind of limitations?"

"Well, we can't have you carting off the rest of the Parthenon or the Great Sphinx and whatnot, now can we?" said Psyche amusedly. "He'll try to arrange it so you'll have permission to remove anything you find that is not of documented historical importance. Hence, nothing on the Acropolis or Giza. You'll have to find your own goodies."

"Bloody hell!" hooted Sheerness in astonishment. He looked at her suspiciously. "Why is he doing this? How do you—obviously—seem to know him? And *why* didn't you mention you did the minute we docked in Piraeus?"

"I didn't mention I knew him because you didn't ask for my help...not until today." Psyche shrugged. "Actually, you *still* didn't ask for my help, but close enough. I've never met Duman Pasha before today, but he is very good friends with my father, and three of his children work for my family. He also owes my father a debt of gratitude because of said children, so if one of *his* children needs a favor...," finished Psyche leadingly.

"Unbelievable," said Sheerness in quiet amazement. "And he's doing this because he owes your father?"

"It's a pretty big debt," said Psyche vaguely. "I offered to pay him, at least for his expenses, but he would have none of it."

"How much did you offer him?" asked Sheerness curiously.

"One hundred guineas," said Psyche calmly.

"What?" yelped Sheerness. "One hundred—" He lowered his voice. "Do you mean to tell me you're carrying one hundred guineas in that bag?"

"Yes. I have about thirty pounds in notes and coins in the other one."

"Are you crazy?" he asked her calmly. "Really? Are you? What can you be thinking carrying that much money?"

"Well, I didn't think I would be carrying it all back to the ship with me," defended Psyche. "And it's not like anyone *knows* I'm carrying it...except you and Stockbridge." She gave him a peeved glare. "And no, I am *not* crazy."

"Where did you get that kind of money anyhow?"

"It's part of my allowance," said Psyche neutrally.

"What allowance?"

"My allowance Pandora packed for me. She gave me what would be the equivalent of my allowance from August through December." She shrugged as she continued to walk. "I'd only just found it the morning we docked in Valletta. Frankly, I was hoping Duman Pasha would take the money, so I wouldn't have so much of it."

"I'm not even going to ask how much you have," said Sheerness dully with a shake of his head.

"Good...because I wouldn't tell you anyhow," said Psyche airily.

Stockbridge walked along beside them listening to their arguing with barely controlled amusement. It was better than watching a comedy at Drury.

"So, back to the matter at hand," said Sheerness calmly. "When will we receive our firman?"

"Oh, I couldn't say for sure. It will take until tomorrow at least for Duman to be ready to go to Constantinople, probably longer. You know better than I would how long it will take for a ship to sail from Piraeus to there. Then, there has to be an audience with the sultan through his advisors, and *he* might need to think about it. Then, however long it will take for a ship to sail from Constantinople to Thessaloniki."

"What about Thessaloniki? Why would it be going to Thessaloniki?" asked Sheerness suspiciously.

"Because that's where *we* will be," said Psyche calmly, and she stopped to pull a rock out of her slipper. She wished she'd worn her walking boots.

"Who says?" hooted Sheerness.

"I do," said Psyche flatly. "I've seen all I wanted in Athens, and there's not much more *you* can do until you get your hot little hands on your firman. If I'm going to be stuck somewhere until we get it, I would rather it be in Thessaloniki." Psyche put her hands on her hips and looked at him. "I bet you haven't even decided where you want to go yet, have you?" Sheerness's jaw tightened, and Psyche shook her head and started walking again. "Were you going to stay in Athens the whole time? Granted, there are a lot of things to see in Athens, but it only took me a *week* to see them all."

Sheerness stopped in the middle of the road again and watched as Psyche and Stockbridge walked on. She was right. Until he got the firman, there wasn't anything more he could do. She was content to look at things, but he wasn't. If things had not gone well with Duman Pasha, he would have been prepared to sail to Constantinople tomorrow. He was disappointed he wouldn't be able to look at the Acropolis. All he had been able to do was see it from a distance as he went about the city chasing after a simple piece of paper, a piece of paper it apparently would have been quite easy to obtain if he had asked for Psyche's help from the beginning.

And he did owe her. Before she had arrived at the pasha's, things had not been going well. The man had been intransigent and firm in his refusal to help Sheerness. When she walked in, Duman had become wreathed in smiles and had stayed that way until they walked out the door. She had saved him...again, and she made it look so uncomplicated and effortless...again.

"Sheerness! Come on! We found a cart!" yelled Psyche from over the hill.

Sheerness shook his head and began to jog toward the sound of her voice. He supposed they would set sail for Thessaloniki tomorrow.

Chapter Twenty Six

The *Medea* sailed with the tide the next morning. Sheerness didn't get to spend a lot of time at the Acropolis after their visit to Duman, but Psyche surprised him when she located the cart. Instead of going directly back to the ship, they went to the Acropolis. She bribed the commander of the fort, as she had been doing all along, to let them in, but the amount was a pittance. Psyche explained they were much more amenable to letting one in if all one intended to do was *look*.

Sheerness walked away from it feeling much the same way she did. What Elgin hadn't taken had been damaged in his quest for removing things. Rubble lay everywhere, not all of it caused by Elgin. When Sheerness imagined how it must have looked when it was new, when not a stone was out of place, compared to what he could actually see with his eyes, it *was* saddening.

By nightfall they were on their way to the northern Aegean. They had passed just around the northwestern edge of the Cyclades and the southern tip of Euboea. They were nearing the southernmost island of the Sporades, Skiros, when Psyche and Sheerness went below to have supper with the rest of the officers. Once they managed to navigate through the islands, there would be nothing between them and Thessaloniki except water. Sheerness expected they would be there by sometime the following afternoon.

Psyche was finally able to get him to sit down and discuss what he hoped to accomplish with his firman. He still wasn't sure where he wanted to look, but Psyche made him let her look at his maps and began to take notes. They were both familiar with the history of ancient Greece, but some things would need to be taken only as suggestions or wishful thinking rather than fact. She knew of a few places she wanted to visit, but as her purpose was more inclined to looking rather than taking, it was easier for her to make up her mind.

Sheerness let her use his maps but only if she put them away properly. If he found so much as a new wrinkle in one of them, she wouldn't be allowed to use them anymore. Psyche rolled her eyes and shook her head exasperatedly. One of these days, she would find out why he was always so fastidious. She didn't consider herself a slouch, but compared to him she was. Even Pandora, who was tidier than Psyche, would appear disorganized and slovenly next to him. It was a simple enough matter for him to keep *his* cabin spic-and-span— he was never in there. He was always on deck or in the officers' mess during daylight hours, and he slept in *her* cabin. When he said what he did about his maps, it seemed he thought she was incapable, and that annoyed her.

She lay down on her bunk to sleep after looking out the window for some time. Sheerness would be there eventually. He still didn't knock, and he was there every night. While they were in Piraeus, she had been asleep by the time he was back to the ship. Last night, he had returned to the ship when she did, just as the darkness became complete, but he still didn't come to her cabin until after she was asleep. She had no notion of what he did that kept him so occupied, but she wasn't going to stay awake worrying about it. She had enough other things on her mind to keep her awake without adding something to them that was none of her business.

She was mostly asleep by the time he came in. She vaguely heard when he opened the door, but she wasn't going to move and find out if he actually had. She could have just been dreaming it, and then she would be awake for no reason. She stirred somewhat when he climbed onto the bunk, and she was aware of when he took away the pillow she was holding to pull her close. He had his arms around her waist, and he had put one of his legs over hers. He nuzzled her neck and the side of her face, and then he put his mouth close to her ear.

"Psyche?" he whispered.

She frowned slightly in her sleep, but she didn't open her eyes. "Hmm?" she sighed.

"Are you asleep?" he asked, smoothing a hand down her side to her hip.

"Mm-hmm," confirmed Psyche groggily, and she snuggled closer to him to drift off again.

He started kissing the side of her neck, up to her jaw, and his hand at her hip moved up her side to cup her breast. Psyche's frown deepened. As tempting as it was, she wanted to sleep. If he had come to her cabin even thirty minutes earlier, she would have been easier to convince to stay awake. She waveringly lifted her free hand and blindly splayed it over his face.

"Shh. Sleeping," she mumbled, considering the matter settled.

Sheerness looked at her hand in astonishment. She apparently *was* sleeping. He had thought when she answered that she was awake. Perhaps there was a part of her that was conscious, but the rest of her was not. Sheerness took her hand away and kissed her palm before laying it onto her stomach and putting his arm back around her waist. He nestled his head closer to hers on the pillow and rested his nose against her cheek. He could never seem to get done with his work early enough to catch her awake, and she was always still sleeping when he got up in the morning. Perhaps once they reached

Thessaloniki, once they had to stay still and wait for the papers from Constantinople, he would be able to find the right time.

By the time Psyche went to the deck the following morning, they had navigated through the Sporades and were well into the Thermaikos Gulf. Psyche kept her eyes, for the most part, on the landscape passing them on the portside of the ship because it was closer, and she eventually recognized something that made her heart begin to beat excitedly. She closed her book and climbed out of the launch and went up to the poop deck.

"Do you know what that is?" she asked Sheerness, pointing at a tall peak in the distance.

He looked at it. "It's a mountain," he said dryly.

"Do you know *which* mountain?"

He looked at her suspiciously. "No," he drew out.

"That's Mount Olympus," said Psyche with a grin, bouncing on her feet.

"No, it isn't," said Sheerness calmly.

"Yes, it is," countered Psyche tartly, and she restrained herself from sticking out her tongue. "Chrissoula said she could see it from her home."

Sheerness took another look at the mountain. It wasn't quite what he expected. When he thought of Mount Olympus, he imagined snow-covered heights mystically shrouded with clouds. While he did see a few wispy clouds floating near the summit, it was certainly not *shrouded*, and it wasn't covered with the glacial hoariness he had envisioned. He looked at Psyche doubtfully.

"I don't think that's Mount Olympus," he said flatly.

"Suit yourself," said Psyche blithely, and she walked down the steps and climbed back into the launch.

Sheerness looked from her to the mountain again and tilted his head. It was supposed to be there somewhere, and he didn't see any higher peaks. It was close enough to the sea it would be visible from the water. He had to admit (reluctantly) that she was right. He tried to ease his disappointment by reasoning it was only the beginning of September. It wasn't the right time of year for snow to cover anything, not even mountaintops, in this kind of climate.

Not long after they began to edge past the mountain, their course changed to a more northeasterly direction. They would eventually turn even further east to enter the Gulf of Thessaloniki. If the mountain was indeed Mount Olympus, Thessaloniki couldn't be more than a few hours away. They would be there no later than two that afternoon, even if the wind were to slacken.

Psyche continued to watch the coast as they passed, looking at the occasional villages. The shore was, for the most part, fairly level below the mountains, but as they began to turn further east, the range dropped down to the shore, creating cliffs, some as high as thirty or forty feet. Not long after they passed one tiny village situated where the cliffs were further back from the sea to provide a wide strip of white, sandy beach, there was a house...at least, Psyche *thought* it was a house, built on the edge of the cliff as it rose almost forty feet above the sea and far higher than the land to either side of it.

It jutted onto an escarpment at one edge of a naturally-protected cove, the inlet about forty feet wide, before more jagged rock rose out of the water on the other side to join the cliffs as they began to subside. The house was built on many levels, some of them more than one story, and there was an unusual, octagonal tower that had three or four floors at the very tip of the promontory. It was made mostly of bare stone, but in some places the surface had been covered in white-washed stucco. There were balconies and protected verandas facing the water, and there were trees of different types everywhere to provide shade. Psyche was enchanted *and* impressed.

But the viewing was brief. About the time she saw it, the *Medea* turned due east, and it went behind the ship, out of her sight. She sighed wistfully. She imagined the house had incomparable views—of Olympus, the water…everything, especially from the top of the tower. And the cove was probably perfect for swimming. For a time she wondered who might live there, whether they were Turks or Greeks or perhaps neither, but she only thought about it briefly before she climbed down from the launch and went to the berth deck for dinner. Meals could have had Freddie bring food to her cabin, but it was rather silly to have Freddie do that when all she needed to do was walk down the stairs to the deck below and get it.

The crews' bedazzlement had lessened during the time that had passed since she had fixed the pump, much to Psyche's relief. They were all friendly and respectful, but they no longer bobbed and bowed as she went past, and they didn't speak as if she were the queen. She didn't often eat her dinner, or any other meal, on the berth deck, and the first time she had, it caused an uproar. She had done it frequently enough that now she had no trouble going to Meals for her food, finding a likely table, and taking a seat to enjoy her meal.

She usually selected a location midships because the light from the hatch let her continue to read her book. She had started on the third volume of Pliny the Younger, and it contained information on Pompeii and Herculaneum, enough that she thought she might like to see them. His uncle's notes on the eruption of Vesuvius would have been more insightful…if he hadn't died in it.

After she finished dinner, Psyche was undecided about what she wanted to do next. She wanted to look at Sheerness's maps, but she also wanted to work on piecing together the shards of vase. Then she wanted to be on the deck to see Thessaloniki as they docked. She wasn't sure how far away they were, so she didn't know how long she would have. She would ask Sheerness, and then she would decide what do next based on what he told her. She only knew she would be leaving the ship almost immediately once they moored.

She walked up the stairs to the deck and looked toward the bow once she reached it. She was so startled she jumped when she saw a harbor quickly approaching. She hadn't realized they were that close. It at least made her indecision unnecessary. She wasn't going to have time to do anything more than walk up to the poop deck for a better view and be out of the way of the crew as they drew in the sails and prepared to drop anchor. She put on her spectacles and tucked her book under her arm and went to stand beside

Sheerness as he watched the crew going about their work. She lifted her watch to look at the time. It was nearing 1:30.

After she had stood beside him for a few minutes, Sheerness turned his head to look at her with a neutral expression.

"That *was* Mount Olympus," he said dully.

Psyche kept her features calm and put a hand to her lips and coughed to hide an amused smirk. Then she scratched her forehead.

"Yes, I thought so," she said evenly. "We've reached Thessaloniki?"

"Indubitably," said Sheerness mildly. "You'll want to see Chrissoula's brother, Nikos, was it?"

"Oh, absolutely," said Psyche definitely.

"Do you know where he lives?"

"Not exactly. He doesn't actually live in Thessaloniki, but it's the closest, largest port."

"So where does he live?" asked Sheerness dryly.

"I'll have to ask."

"What do you mean: you'll have to *ask*?" quizzed Sheerness in a moderately annoyed tone.

"I'm sure he's well-known. Chrissoula never told me exactly where he lived…just near Thessaloniki. Duman Pasha knows where he lives."

"Then why didn't you ask *Duman Pasha?*" shot Sheerness mockingly.

"Because I didn't need to," said Psyche shortly, "and even if it does take a while to find him, it's not like we have anywhere we need to go, is there?"

Sheerness tightened his lips and clenched his jaw. "What makes you so sure he's going to let you stay with him…even if you do find him?"

"I don't know that he will let me stay with him, but he will know how to find us once I find *him*, and it will be easier for Duman Pasha to give the firman to Nikos than it will be for him to give it to us. Aside from that, Chrissoula has mentioned me to him, so I'm sure he will at least want to meet me."

"Hunh," said Sheerness darkly.

Thessaloniki was larger than Piraeus and Athens combined. It started at the water's edge and continued up the gradually rising hill in the valley where it was located. When she saw the size of it, Psyche realized she had set a harder task for herself than she had anticipated. She believed Nikos was well-known, but she wasn't sure he was known well enough to find him in a city that large.

The most practical way to start her search would be at the waterfront and steadily work her way inward. There were a few places she did *not* want to go, and one of them was easy enough to see over the walls around the city. The one thing that offered her consolation was that Sheerness didn't know how to speak the language…any of them. That would be safer for Nikos. Sheerness wasn't going to let her go without him, but there were things she hadn't had the chance to explain to him, things she hadn't realized she would *need* to explain until that moment.

They were able to moor the *Medea* at a dock, which would make it less time-consuming to get to and from the ship. One other thing that would make this a better port than Piraeus was the city's larger size. The crew still didn't know the language, but it would be easier to find things to occupy themselves without getting into mischief. If they spoke Spanish, they *might* be able to make themselves understood well enough by the local population, for the most part, but Psyche didn't think many of the crew spoke more than English.

Once they were tied off, Psyche went to her cabin to tidy her appearance and grab her drawstring bag from the top of her desk. She put Waddlesworth out the window after giving him the bread she had saved from dinner. She was wearing her gansey and split-skirt in shades of mauve. As an afterthought, she tied a silk scarf over her head and grabbed a coat. She heard Sheerness go to his cabin and leave again while she was in her own cabin, and she found him waiting on the deck when she reached it.

"So, do you have any idea where to begin looking for the man?" asked Sheerness neutrally.

"I think here, near the shore, would be the best place to start. A lot of his business is done on the water, and I'm sure he comes here frequently." The gangway had been lowered and put across to the dock. When they reached it, Psyche looked at Sheerness with a serious expression. "While we're here, until we find Nikos, do *not* mention Chrissoula. Not even to me," she said quietly.

"Why?" asked Sheerness perplexedly.

"Does that matter right now?" she asked evenly.

Sheerness narrowed his eyes suspiciously as he looked at her. He had the impression that even though Chrissoula and her brother no longer lived in the same country, they were still on the best of terms, so he couldn't understand why Psyche didn't want him to mention her—at all—until they found Nikos. Whatever the cause, he could see it troubled Psyche. Still, it would be an easy enough thing for him not to do. She would just have to explain later.

"No, I suppose not," he said dully.

"Thank you," said Psyche with relief. She linked her arm with his as they walked down the dock.

"I think, if you want to start here, the best place to begin would be the customs house. If most of his *business* is done on the water, as you say, it would have to go through there before going into the city."

"That sounds likely," said Psyche agreeably. For the most part, he was a fisherman, and that *would* go through customs, but there were other things he carried that would not.

They found an officer standing not far from the entrance to the building. He looked at them curiously when they approached him, but he was nice enough. He was even more surprised when Psyche did all the talking, but he wasn't familiar with Nikos Andreanopoulos. He had, in fact, only started working at the customs house that week. Psyche asked if he could offer any suggestions on who else they might ask, possibly someone who had been working there longer, but he did not. The other officer had just left to take his dinner. He might be back in two hours. Psyche thanked him for his time, and they continued down the pier.

There was a small fishing boat tied off near the customs house, and she decided to ask the owner if he knew Nikos. She didn't want to ask every person on the pier whether they knew him, but there had to be someone who did. It took her a few tries to find the right language, but it didn't help. He got ready to leave as she was talking to him, but he said he didn't know Nikos. Psyche sighed and scratched her forehead and turned to look at Sheerness.

"Your Spanish is atrocious. I thought you spoke it better than that," said Sheerness in puzzlement.

"That was Ladino, not Spanish," said Psyche evenly. "You did notice the man I was talking to didn't have a problem understanding me?"

"Hunh," said Sheerness noncommittally. "Do you intend to ask every person you meet whether they know Nikos? I was asking because if that's the case, we could be doing this until the sun goes down and most of tomorrow."

"No, not everyone. When the other officer returns from his dinner, we can ask him. In the meantime, it wouldn't hurt to ask a few other people, maybe see a few things."

Sheerness decided to indulge her. They had spent more than a week in Athens on his business, and it truly wasn't as if there were anywhere else they could go until Duman Pasha got the firman from Constantinople.

"So who taught you Ladino?" asked Sheerness as they walked along the quay in front of the city walls.

Psyche looked at him distractedly for a moment. "The same person who taught me Greek," she said finally.

"And what about Turkish?"

"Duman's children."

She looked at the people as they walked by, trying to find someone who seemed like they might know Chrissoula's brother. She wasn't confident there was a specific *type* of person he would associate with; she could only go by the things Chrissoula had told her about Nikos and their family. He did a lot of fishing, but that wasn't his only source of income. He, in fact, didn't need to work for his livelihood at all, but Chrissoula's family was no more prone to idleness than her own. The things he did that earned the most money were not common knowledge and not something Psyche could ask about of just anyone.

She would occasionally ask someone, but none of them admitted to knowing him, even if they did. Psyche sometimes got the impression the people *did* know him. She let them keep up their pretense, but she made no secret of who she was, where she was from, and that she would be staying aboard the *Medea* in the harbor. Her intention was that hopefully one of the people would let Nikos know she was there, even if they wouldn't tell her how to find him. Still, she was puzzled why no one wanted to admit they knew him or even knew *of* him. Despite some of his activities, he was, as far as she knew, considered to be a respectable, upstanding member of the community.

After they had asked several people and entered the city proper, Sheerness looked at her doubtfully. "This is not promising," he said dryly.

"It doesn't seem so," said Psyche neutrally.

"I thought you said he was well-known."

"He *should* be, and I'm sure he is." She gave him a long-suffering look. He was one of the wealthiest Greeks in the area, and that anomaly alone should have made him familiar. "He's not a pasha or a bey, but he's not obscure."

"Then why does no one seem to know him?" persisted Sheerness.

"I don't know," said Psyche testily. "Thessaloniki is a large city. We simply haven't asked the right person yet."

"Hmm," said Sheerness dully. "You could be right...I suppose."

"Really?" said Psyche tartly. "Are you actually conceding I might be right about something? That's utterly shocking!"

"Funny," said Sheerness with a scowl.

They began to near the tower, and Psyche would rather go in a different direction. She had never seen it personally (obviously), but she had been told enough about it that she recognized it. She didn't want to go near it. Just the thought of it set her teeth on edge, and there were things she was afraid she might hear if she got too close.

"Now, *that's* interesting," said Sheerness as it caught his attention.

"Mm-hmm, lovely," said Psyche dully. "Let's go this way," she said as she tried to steer them another way.

"I want to see that."

"No, you don't," said Psyche flatly.

"And why not?"

"It's a prison," said Psyche shortly. "You wouldn't want to take a tour of a bridewell, would you?"

"How would *you* know it's a prison?" argued Sheerness as he looked at it. He couldn't see anything to indicate that was its purpose.

She stopped and looked at him. "I *know*," she said firmly.

Sheerness raised an eyebrow. "The number of things you will owe me explanations for is quickly growing," he said stiffly.

"I will explain. I promise I will," she said earnestly, "but not right now. Especially not here," she said as she looked at the tower, one of the tallest buildings to be seen. She worked very hard to control a shudder.

The old Byzantine edifice disturbed her. Her secrecy and knowledge of things like the local prison disturbed *him*. He wondered if coming to Thessaloniki was such a good idea after all. Perhaps it might have been wise for him to have asked more questions, but until today, he hadn't realized he needed to. He might not be able to ask about Chrissoula or the tower, but he could ask about other things.

"So, how long has your father known Duman Pasha?" he asked mildly, finally letting her turn him in another direction.

Psyche looked at him in surprise at the question, but she was relieved he was going to let her lead them away. Her forehead wrinkled thoughtfully. "Twenty-five or thirty years, I think."

"Really? That long?" he asked in amazement.

"At least."

"If he's a pasha, why do three of his children work for your family?"

Psyche raised an eyebrow. She wasn't sure she wanted to tell him, but it was harmless enough. It was one thing she wouldn't need to explain in private.

"They're illegitimate," she said calmly.

It was Sheerness's turn to raise an eyebrow. "That still doesn't explain why he would let them go to England or let them work for your family."

"Duman married his first wife shortly before my father met him. Then he married two more. That's not unusual. He also had a mistress…again, not unusual. Her name was Samira, and he had six children with her. The unusual didn't happen until Duman decided to marry Samira and make *her* his chief wife. The current one, Meryem, of course, was having none of it. She poisoned Samira and killed three of the children before Duman could stop her." Sheerness's eyes widened in shock. "My father was here at the time, and Duman asked him to take the other three children where they would be safe because even though Samira was dead and the children were illegitimate, Meryem still saw them as a threat to her own position. So, my father took Sacit, Basir, and Cari to England."

"*Merde alors!*" said Sheerness breathlessly with a shake of his head. "What happened to Meryem?"

"She's still Duman's chief wife," said Psyche evenly.

"You mean *nothing* was done, even though she murdered four people?"

"Meryem is of noble blood. Samira was a commoner *and* an adulteress, and her children were—are—bastards. I would like to say Meryem was executed for her crimes, but she was avenging her honor."

"Oh, that's not right," said Sheerness slowly in disbelief.

"No, it isn't," agreed Psyche dully, "but that's the way it is." She gave him a solemn look. "You do understand things are different here? These people are *not* like us…not really."

"No, no, I know that," said Sheerness quietly with a troubled frown.

She squeezed his arm and gave him a wan smile. "It's not all bad, either."

Sheerness smiled wryly and tilted his head sideways. She was right, but even to him, someone to whom honor meant a great deal, Meryem's actions and that nothing was done to her were detestable.

Psyche would occasionally ask someone if they knew Nikos, but she suspected their best option would be waiting until the other officer returned from dinner. In the meantime, she saw no reason why they couldn't look at the city itself. There weren't as many old ruins in Thessaloniki as there were in Athens, but she was thrilled to know she was in Macedonia, the birthplace of Alexander the Great. They had not walked very far, however, before Psyche heard an odd rumbling noise and looked at Sheerness.

"You didn't have dinner, did you?" she asked knowingly.

"No," admitted Sheerness sheepishly.

"I'm sure we can find a taverna. You're lucky it's today instead of tomorrow."

"Why is that?" he asked curiously.

"Because almost everything here is closed on Saturdays." Sheerness raised an eyebrow. "Thessaloniki has a very high Jewish population, more than half, and Saturday is their Sabbath. But you knew that, right?"

"Yes, actually, I did know that about Saturday," said Sheerness with a slight smile.

"Aha! This place!" said Psyche, pointing to a building they were passing. Sheerness looked at it doubtfully. "Are you sure?"

"Oh, absolutely," said Psyche as she steered him through the doorway. "What are you hungry for? I had dinner on the ship, but I would love some *loukoumathes* and retsina."

"That sounds fine," said Sheerness agreeably.

Psyche tilted her head sideways with a frown. "Really? Are you sure you wouldn't like something more substantial?" Then she realized he had no idea what it was. "Did you not eat any of the food while we were in Athens?" He scowled at her. "I'm not trying to be obnoxious, but honestly, the food *is* one of the best things about this country."

The proprietor greeted them and asked them to find a table and said he would be with them in a moment. Psyche thanked him, and they selected a table near the large front window and sat down. There were several other occupied tables, and it took a while before he was able to get to them.

"*Kaló apógeuma. Autó pou boreí egó na párei gia sas?*"

Psyche ordered Sheerness a nice dinner and dessert for herself, as well as a bottle of retsina. He soon returned with the wine and the glasses. The food would take a little while. The owner, Mr. Theotokis, poured their wine and left them to it, promising he would return with their food. After he was gone, Sheerness looked at the wine, and then he gave Psyche a suspicious glance.

"Go on. Drink up," said Psyche with a grin. "Thousands of years of production cannot be wrong."

"What is it?" he asked, still eyeing the glass distrustfully.

Psyche took a sip from her own. "Retsina. It's wine, and if it was good enough for Plato and Archimedes, I don't think you'll have a problem with it."

Sheerness slowly picked up the glass and took a small sip. It didn't taste the way he expected. By appearance, it was white, so he was expecting it to be dry, possibly even sweet. He could say it definitely wasn't sweet. Even after another sip, he couldn't say for certain whether it was dry, either. There was a hint of some type of citrus, possibly lemon, but the most overwhelming note was something he couldn't place. He couldn't decide if it were a spice, the wood the barrel was made of, or even a bad batch of grapes. He also couldn't decide if he liked it, not even after he'd finished the glass and poured another.

"This has a peculiar flavor," he said as he took a sip from the new glass. "I can't put my finger on it. It leaves an almost resinous sensation in my mouth."

Psyche chuckled. "Aleppo pine resin is usually added to the must during fermentation and filtered out before it's bottled."

"Ah," said Sheerness with a nod. "That would explain it."

"Do you like it?"

"It's growing on me," he said with a grin. "What about the citrus?"

"That is something specific to this particular vintner, but I think it's citron." She took a sip from her own glass. "I think it will go well with your dinner."

"Which will be?" he asked leadingly.

"You're about to find out," said Psyche with a smile as Mr. Theotokis approached with a tray.

He placed several plates onto the table and left them to their meal after Psyche requested he bring another bottle of wine. She took the plate of *loukoumathes* for herself, but the rest was for Sheerness: *dolmades* with rice and ground pork, *spanakopita*, *horiatiki*, and a variety of *souvlakia* with *tzatziki* and fried potatoes. Psyche saw the uncertain expression on his face, and she helpfully informed him of what everything was. He still looked overwhelmed.

"It is all delicious, and most of it is edible with your fingers. No one will say a word," assured Psyche with a teasing grin. "Get to it, or Mr. Theotokis will be insulted."

Psyche picked up one of the *loukoumathes* and started to eat. Sheerness finally tried the *spanakopita*, and she almost laughed at the look of complete surprise that came over his face when he discovered it was delicious and unlike anything he had ever tried before. From that point on, he didn't require any further coaxing to eat his dinner, and Psyche watched with amusement as he tried to eat everything he had been brought. Mr. Theotokis brought the second bottle of wine while he was eating, and Sheerness looked at Psyche.

"Tell him this is by far the best meal I've ever had," said Sheerness enthusiastically.

"Really?" chortled Psyche. She looked at Mr. Theotokis. "He said this is the best food he has ever eaten."

Mr. Theotokis looked at her in surprise. "Is he serious?"

"He's English," explained Psyche.

"Ah," said Mr. Theotokis with a nod and a smile. "And what about you? I don't think you're from here either, even if you do speak as if you grew up in Sfendami."

"No, I'm from there as well, but I have friends from here who made sure I would not be quite so uncouth should I visit," she said with a grin.

Mr. Theotokis laughed. "If it weren't for your clothes, no one would ever suspect you're not a native."

"Thank you," said Psyche with a pleased smile. "Mr. Theotokis, you have obviously been here for a while, and in your business, I am sure you meet a lot of people. I was wondering if you might be able to help me find someone."

"I will try," said Mr. Theotokis agreeably.

"I am trying to find a man named Nikos Andreanopoulos. Have you ever heard of him?"

"Oh, sure, sure, I know him," said Mr. Theotokis with a grin.

"Marvelous," said Psyche with relief. "Can you tell me how to find him?"

"He does not live in Thessaloniki, but I get my fish from him."

"Do you know *where* he lives? It is really important I find him."

"He lives between Methoni and Makrigialos on the Gulf, but I could not say exactly where; I have never been."

"That is all right, Mr. Theotokis. You have been very helpful. Thank you," said Psyche with a grateful smile.

Sheerness looked at her enquiringly after the man left. "You told him more than I liked the food."

"You noticed that?" she asked with a grin. "We need to teach you Greek."

"Well?" he quipped, ignoring her comment.

"He knows Nikos, and he was somewhat able to tell me where he lives."

"Do you believe him?"

Psyche raised an eyebrow. "Of course. Why wouldn't I?"

Sheerness shrugged and continued to eat. "You've been trying to find someone who knows him for a couple hours now, and we just happen to stop somewhere to eat that the owner knows him?"

"There *is* such a thing as coincidence," said Psyche as she finished her wine. "When we return to the harbor, the other officer will be back, and I can ask him, too, if that will make you feel better." Psyche didn't like that he seemed to be implying she had been deceitful.

"Hmm," said Sheerness doubtfully. "Are you sure *you* don't know where he lives?"

"Of course I'm sure," said Psyche flatly. "What possible reason could I have to lie about knowing where he lives?"

"One wonders," said Sheerness dryly.

"Ooh!" groaned Psyche aggravatedly. "Are you done?"

"Yes," said Sheerness, patting his stomach with satisfaction. "If I eat one more thing, I will pop."

"*One* can hope," said Psyche tartly. She waved for Mr. Theotokis to come over and smiled pleasantly. "Thank you for the lovely meal. How much do we owe you?"

"Three piastres," said Mr. Theotokis.

Psyche was surprised it wasn't more and handed the coins to him. She and Sheerness left the taverna, but instead of going back to the harbor, Psyche wanted to see more of the city. She was confident Theotokis had given her good information, even if Sheerness wasn't. She would have to look at, or have Sheerness look at, his maps when they got back to the ship. She wasn't familiar with the two cities Theotokis had mentioned. Well, she had heard of Methoni, but she didn't know where it was, or even if it was the same one.

Once she got the information from Theotokis, Psyche didn't bother to ask anyone else if they knew Nikos. She might have been able to find someone else to tell her something more specific, but it wouldn't be necessary. Once they located the two cities on the map, if she could convince Sheerness to go there, it would be more likely they could find someone in one or the other who would know exactly where he lived.

Psyche enjoyed her walk through the city. There were lots of old churches and mosques, and they hadn't walked far before they found the Kamara.

Psyche was fascinated by the carving and the size, and she wished she had brought a sketchbook. She wouldn't have had time to do it justice though. She hoped she could come back at some point and make a drawing or painting. After they left the Kamara, they turned west, and they eventually turned back to the south, making their way to the harbor. She looked at her watch as they approached the customs house and saw with some surprise that it was almost five. The officer should have long since returned.

She was relieved to see he had. He was as friendly as the other officer, and he did know Nikos. Unfortunately, he couldn't give her much more information than Theotokis had. All he could add was that the house could not be missed, for whatever that was worth. She thanked him for his time, then she and Sheerness made their way to the dock. Psyche took the scarf off her head and draped it over her arm with the coat she hadn't needed and sighed tiredly. She had enjoyed her walk, but she was ready to sit down for a while.

There was a ketch moored across the dock from them as they neared the gangway, and it wouldn't have caught Psyche's attention if it weren't for the man standing near the bow, obviously looking at her with a wide grin.

He was very attractive. He was tall and muscular, dressed in loose-fitting white cotton trousers and shirt with a black vest. His shoulder-length hair and eyes were black, and he had a well-trimmed beard and mustache. He stood with his feet balanced apart, his hands clasped casually behind his back as he watched her approach, and Psyche couldn't determine if he was Greek or Turkish. She gave him a hesitant smile in return as she continued to walk toward the ship. He looked at her as if he knew her, and Psyche wasn't sure how she should respond to that.

What happened next took her completely by surprise. He leapt from the boat onto the dock, and before she had time to react, he grabbed her around the waist and lifted her in the air to spin her in a circle.

"Oi! Unhand her!" said Sheerness angrily as the attack surprised him, and his shout made the crew come to the rail and look at the commotion.

The strange man laughed happily as he continued to spin with her, and Psyche's eyes rounded in alarm as she wondered if he was unhinged.

"*Thea!*" he said jubilantly, and he finally put her back on her feet and kissed her soundly on both cheeks, keeping his arms around her waist.

"Nikos?" she said breathlessly.

"*Soztá,*" he said softly with a grin.

Psyche laughed delightedly and hugged him around the neck. "We have been looking for you all day!"

"What is this? Take your hands off her!" roared Sheerness, and he pried Psyche out of the man's arms. He found her hugging and kissing a strange, *handsome* man she was obviously happy to see a little disturbing.

"Oh, Sheerness, relax," chortled Psyche. "This is Nikos Andreanopoulos."

"Really?" said Sheerness with a scowl, folding his arms across his chest.

"Does he not speak Greek?" Nikos asked Psyche in surprise.

"Classical Greek," said Psyche, "and no Turkish or Ladino."

"I am," said Nikos in English to Sheerness.

"How did you know it was me?" asked Psyche.

"I would know Thea anywhere," chuckled Nikos. "You *are* a goddess!"

Psyche blushed. "Flatterer!" She looked at Sheerness's dark countenance, and her jubilance dampened somewhat. "Nikos Andreanopoulos, this is Sebastian Nichols, the Earl of Sheerness."

"Ah," said Nikos slowly with a smile, giving him an assessing glance. "I've heard of you." He held out his hand. "Good to meet you," he said definitely.

For a moment, Sheerness looked as if he weren't going to take the offered hand, and Psyche clenched her hands at her sides to refrain from smacking him on the back of his head. There was no need for him to be rude. He finally took Nikos's hand and shook it briefly with a nod.

"How long will you stay?" asked Nikos of Psyche.

"I don't know. At least three or four days, probably a lot longer. Duman has gone to Constantinople to get a firman for us, and he will be bringing it here—to you, actually—once it is arranged. I hope that is all right?"

"Most excellent," grinned Nikos. "You will be my guests until then, yes?"

Psyche's expression turned uncertain, and she looked at Sheerness. He did not seem to like Nikos, and he didn't appear pleased Psyche had been able to find him. She wanted to see Ioanna and the girls, but Sheerness looked most unhappy. She couldn't really go without him, but she would if she had to.

"Can we? Please?" she asked him earnestly.

Sheerness was jealous, and it was something that was becoming common with Psyche, even when she did nothing to provoke it. She desperately wanted to go, and she would go with or without him, but he was not going to allow that. Whether she wanted or liked it, she was under his protection. Regardless of what she knew of the man from Chrissoula, Nikos was a stranger, and even if she did seem to instantly trust him, Sheerness did not…not for a minute.

He didn't know how long it would take Duman to get the firman, but Higginbotham and the rest of the officers could keep things under control until they returned, and it wasn't as if he couldn't come back—daily, if necessary—to see to things himself. He would make sure of where they were going, just in case. He rubbed a hand over his chin and scratched the back of his head.

"All right," he said finally, and his expression softened somewhat when he saw how happy it made Psyche. "Where?"

Nikos pointed toward the setting sun. "Due west. We sail until we reach land again, and we should leave soon if we are to make it by nightfall. The *Athena* is fast but not that fast."

Psyche frowned, but she nodded. She was puzzled why Nikos had conveniently arrive exactly when and where he did. She didn't believe for a moment she looked unique enough that he would have known her from any other woman, regardless of how strangely she was dressed. She shrugged. She would ask him once they got under way.

She went aboard to her cabin and stood with her hands on her hips as she tried to decide what to take with her. She would need clothes, but she wasn't sure which ones. She pulled things out of the drawers and tossed them on the bed. Once she had everything in one place, she had to decide how she was going to take it. She didn't want to pack it into a trunk, but she wasn't sure how else it was going. She had purchased a smaller trunk while she was in Athens, which she had stored inside one of her larger ones, deciding she needed it for gifts and other things, including the cinerary urn. That trunk would be better, if she could get everything to fit, and she could carry it herself. She did manage to get everything in: clothes, art and writing supplies, the kits she thought she would need, and presents.

She closed the lid and looked out the window. Waddlesworth was sitting on the channel, waiting to be brought in, and she looked at him with some dismay. She didn't know what to do with him. She couldn't take him with her, and she also couldn't let him stay cooped in her cabin the whole time she was gone. She set him down on his cushion, and then she lifted her trunk and carried it from the cabin. She went topside and was only standing for only a minute when Stockbridge walked over to her and took the trunk.

"You didn't have to do that," said Psyche with a grateful smile.

"You looked like you needed help," he said with a grin.

"Actually, I'm looking for Freddie. Have you seen him?"

Stockbridge nodded with his head toward the stairs to the berth deck. "He's below helping Meals with supper."

"Thank you. I'll be right back."

Psyche walked down the stairs and found Freddie at a table near midships (the one Psyche herself usually preferred) peeling potatoes. She sat down across from him and asked if he would be willing to watch Waddlesworth for a little while. His face became concerned when he found out she was going away, but Psyche explained she would be coming back...soon. She thought about taking both Freddie and Waddlesworth with her, but Freddie was needed on the ship, and it would be best if the duck stayed, too. Freddie brightened somewhat when she told him there was no one else she trusted to take care of the duck, and she knew he would be in good hands. She tousled his hair affectionately as she stood up, and then she walked back to the deck.

Stockbridge wasn't where she had left him. She looked over the railing to the dock and saw he had already taken it to be put onto the *Athena*. Nikos was standing on the dock with what Psyche was beginning to see was a typical pose for him—his feet balanced apart, his hands clasped behind his back. Sheerness was there as well, but he wasn't speaking to Nikos and looked as if he were trying to ignore him. Psyche frowned and walked down the gangway. She didn't like to see Sheerness so mean, and she couldn't understand why he was. She put on a pleasant smile as she neared, and Nikos grinned when he saw her.

"You are ready to go, Thea?" he asked jovially, offering her his hand.

"I am," said Psyche blithely. She looked at Sheerness with a stiff glance. "Are you coming?"

He gave her a silent nod and stepped aboard the boat. He turned and held out his hand, and Psyche took it to leap aboard herself. Nikos got on after unfastening the ropes from the dock, and he shoved at the edge of it with his foot to get them started turning around before he raised the sails to catch the wind. Sheerness did at least help Nikos get the boat under way, but his apparent dislike and distrust were puzzling.

Psyche put on her spectacles to shade her eyes, and Nikos laughed when he saw them. She removed them and let him try them on, and he agreed they were helpful. Sheerness tightened his jaw as he watched them. She had never let *him* try her glasses. Psyche spent most of the trip sitting near the helm, talking to Nikos. She tried to include Sheerness, but since he did not understand Greek well, he spent most of the trip sitting on the front of the cabin midships with a morose expression.

Nikos had learned of her arrival from Stefano, the fisherman she had asked not long after she began her search. He had immediately sailed to Nikos's home to let him know a strange woman was asking after him, and because he had known from Chrissoula that she was coming, Nikos realized who it was and sailed for Thessaloniki. He would have been there sooner, but it took Stefano two hours to reach Nikos, and then it took him nearly that long to sail to Thessaloniki. He was no less puzzled than she over everyone's reluctance to admit they knew him, but it did depend on *how* they knew him.

The ketch was fast, at least as fast as the *Medea*, and as they sailed due west, they soon neared land. As the sun began to slip behind the mountains, Psyche removed her glasses and put them in her bag. The house she had seen on the cliff became clearer as they approached, and Psyche asked Nikos if he knew who lived there. He gave her a grin and chuckled.

"I do."

"Oh, goodness! Oh, wow! Really?" said Psyche excitedly, and she tried not to jump up and down like a child in a sweet shop. Nikos laughed at her enthusiasm. Psyche turned to look at Sheerness. "He lives there!" she gushed.

"Hunh," said Sheerness noncommittally.

Psyche clasped her hands to her chest as they approached, and Nikos and Sheerness reefed the sails as they neared the entrance to the cove. They were going just fast enough once they entered, Nikos guided the boat to a short stone pier that jutted into the cove and brought it to a gentle stop. He jumped out and tied off, and then he jumped back on to retrieve Psyche's trunk. Sheerness grabbed the sack he had with his own things and stepped onto the pier, and then he turned to give Psyche his hand and help her onto the pier as well.

They weren't standing there long when she heard a shriek from the top of the stairs that led up to the house, and she looked up to see a woman coming down with a baby propped on her hip and four girls trailing behind. Psyche grinned and bounced on her feet excitedly as they neared, and she hugged the woman with a laugh and kissed her cheeks.

Ioanna was exactly as Psyche had imagined she would be. She was slender but curvaceous and shorter than Psyche by almost six inches. She had dark brown hair she had braided and wound into a knot low at the back of her head, with an olive complexion that made her bright blue eyes almost seem to glow.

Chrissoula always said her sister-in-law was very beautiful, and she hadn't been exaggerating. Ioanna and Nikos were a very striking couple. Ioanna reached up to brush a hand over Psyche's cheek affectionately.

"Thea, it's so wonderful to have you here," said Ioanna with a smile.

"Thank you," said Psyche dipping her head. She looked at the baby Ioanna had at her hip. "Ah, look at you," sighed Psyche. "Little Yelena."

The baby girl was about seven months old. She had her thumb in her mouth, but she simply had it resting there as she looked up at Psyche with round, curious eyes the same color as her mother's. Then she smiled and giggled and reached out her arms. Psyche took her as Ioanna looked on in surprise. Then Psyche turned to look at the other four girls.

"Let me see if I can guess who you are," she said with a smile. Chrissoula had told her about all of them, the oldest being born not long after Chrissoula had left for England.

Psyche looked at the tallest girl, who was almost eight, and she giggled and hid her smile behind her hand. "You are Stefania, yes?" The girl giggled again and nodded her head. "Oh, my younger brothers would be enchanted."

Then Psyche moved to the next two…identical twins who had just turned five. "Now, this is going to be difficult, but I *do* have a little experience with this," said Psyche with a grin and a wink. "Hmm, I am going to guess you are Evangelina, and you are Euphamia." The girls giggled and shook their heads. "Oh! So *you* are Euphamia, and *you* are Evangelina?" They nodded. Psyche took note of the most obvious difference between them: Evangelina had a small mole just near her left ear.

And then she came to the next-to-youngest, who was almost three. She had her father's dark hair and eyes, and she was looking at Psyche with a shy smile, holding Evangelina's hand. Psyche knelt down, balancing Yelena on her knee, and looked at the girl with a friendly smile.

"That will make you Odette," said Psyche softly. The girl smiled and hid her face behind her sister's arm, and she nodded.

Psyche chuckled and stood up. She looked at Ioanna and Nikos. "You have beautiful girls." Then she looked at Sheerness, who was dumbfounded. "Sheerness, this is Nikos's wife, Ioanna. Ioanna, this is Sebastian Nichols, the Earl of Sheerness." Ioanna smiled and nodded. "And these are their lovely daughters." She tickled Yelena under the chin, and the baby smiled. "Yelena, Stefania, Euphamia, Evangelina, and Odette."

"Ti kávete?" said Sheerness, and Psyche looked at him in surprise.

"Come! You are just in time for supper," said Ioanna with a smile. "We will have a proper welcome for you tomorrow. Tonight, we will eat and get you settled in." She herded the girls with her hands, and they started up the stairs at a trot, laughing and giggling all the way.

Psyche had settled into her room and sighed with contentment as she looked around herself. Nikos and Ioanna had put her in a room near the top of the house with lots of windows and a door to a terrace facing the ocean. The bed was unbelievably huge, covered with pillows and blankets and edged in netting to draw against the mosquitos. She was full from the hearty supper Ioanna had provided, and she had taken a proper bath in by far the largest tub she had ever seen. She had unpacked and put away her things, and she almost felt as if she had come home.

She was tired but not sleepy, and she walked onto the terrace to listen to the water lapping against the shore far below. After she stood for a time, she walked back into her room and left the door open to still here the sound of the ocean. She was about to take off her dressing gown and attempt to go to sleep when a sound from the doorway onto the terrace made her turn to look.

It was Sheerness. He was in the room next to hers, and their rooms were in a wing separate from that where Nikos and Ioanna and their family had rooms. Although Psyche felt it was unintentional, it gave the two of them far more privacy than they should have. He was dressed for bed, which meant he wasn't wearing anything, and Psyche tilted her head sideways in thought.

"I have something for you," she said finally.

"Do you now?" said Sheerness suggestively.

Psyche rolled her eyes with a half-smile and went to her trunk. She pulled out two paper-wrapped packages and took them to him. He was surprised; he thought she had been teasing. He went to sit in a chair near the fireplace and untied the first one and unwrapped the paper.

"I think they will fit," said Psyche nervously.

Sheerness pulled out white cotton trousers. There were two pair, like the ones Nikos wore. He opened the other package, and there were two shirts and two embroidered vests, one black with silver thread, the other dark blue with lighter blue thread. She was right—they would fit, and they would be comfortable, too. He looked from the clothes to her and lifted an eyebrow.

"I got them in Athens. Do you like them? I don't know why I bought them," she said with a shrug as he continued to sit without saying anything. "I thought you might want a souvenir...I guess," she finished lamely and began to chew on the side of her thumb.

Sheerness set the things aside and stood up. He walked toward her and pulled her close, moving her thumb to give her an affectionate kiss.

"I *do* like them. Thank you," he said softly with a smile, kissing her forehead.

"You're welcome," said Psyche relievedly, and she raised a hand to her mouth to cover a yawn.

Sheerness took her by the hand and pulled her toward the bed. Psyche was nervous about him sleeping in her room, but they were secluded. It should be safe. She took off her dressing gown and crawled to the middle of the bed. It was unusual having that much mattress, and it would take a while to become accustomed to it. Sheerness snuggled up beside her, and she rested her head on his chest.

"Psyche?"

"Hmm?" she asked absently, her hand smoothing over his chest.

"Are you going to explain why I couldn't mention Chrissoula while we were in Thessaloniki and how you happened to know that tower was a prison?"

Psyche raised her head to look at him. She needed to tell him, but she wasn't prepared to at the moment. She looked at him thoughtfully, and then she leaned forward to kiss him softly, smoothing a hand down his cheek. She lifted her head and gently tapped her finger against his chin.

"Not right now," she said quietly.

"Then when?"

"I don't know. Just...not right now," she repeated, nestling her head beside his on the pillow, her chin resting against his shoulder.

Sheerness sighed and smoothed his hand over her hip. "Why didn't you tell me he was married?"

"Who?" asked Psyche perplexedly.

"Nikos. Why didn't you tell me Nikos had a wife and five children?"

"You didn't ask," said Psyche tiredly. "Was it important?"

"It was to me," he said dully.

"Why? What difference does it make?" asked Psyche, propping her head up on her hand to look at him in puzzlement. His jaw set firmly, and he wouldn't look at her. Then Psyche knew what it was. "You were *jealous*?" He added a frown. "Why? Why do you *always* seem to be?"

"I don't know," sighed Sheerness frustratedly. "You're always so *friendly* with people. Sometimes a little too friendly."

"I've never—" began Psyche vexedly, and she closed her eyes and shook her head. She turned over on her side with her back to him and curled up in a ball. "I can't change who I am," she finally said quietly.

She curled one of her arms beneath her head under the pillow and closed her eyes as silent tears slipped from the corners of them. She had ever done anything to give him cause to believe she was light, but that's what he seemed to think. She had never shown any more attention to other men than she would her own brothers...less even, because they *weren't* her brothers. *He* was the only man she had ever made love to, the only one she had ever wanted to. She couldn't even imagine anyone else, but apparently he thought it was all *she* thought about, and it hurt to know that's what he believed. That her talking to other men or being friendly to other men made him jealous did not make her feel warm and fuzzy inside; it made her feel as if he didn't trust her and didn't have a very high opinion of her morals.

She couldn't change the way she was. She could not live her life self-conscious about how she should act toward someone on the chance Sheerness might become jealous. It wasn't fair to the other person, and it wasn't fair to her. He would either have to come to terms with it, or he would go insane.

Sheerness eventually turned on his side behind her and pulled her close, twining their fingers together. She sighed tiredly as he nuzzled her neck as he usually did before placing a kiss just below her ear. She was tempted to push him away, but she needed to be held, even if he was the one who had caused the pain in the first place.

Chapter Twenty Seven

When Sheerness woke the next morning, he was startled to see that Psyche was no longer in bed. She wasn't even in the room, and when he smoothed a hand over the place where she had been beside him, it wasn't even warm to prove she had been there. The sun was up and had been for a while. He didn't have Psyche's watch, and there wasn't a clock in the room, so he wasn't sure of the time. He rubbed a hand over his face and stood up. Once he had dressed and shaved, he would go looking for her.

He started back to his room when he remembered the packages and went to get them. The paper was gone, and the clothes were neatly folded in the chair. He frowned and looked around. That didn't seem like something Psyche would do; she wasn't prone to tidiness. It often seemed the exact opposite.

He slipped on a pair of the pants and tied the string. The cloth was very finely woven, and so soft it could have been silk. They weren't cheap. And she had bought them for him as a gift. Just because.

He had upset her. It wasn't her fault he was always in a state of jealous suspicion. She was kind to everyone: men, women, young, old, rich, or poor. If he were honest, he would admit he wasn't only jealous when she was nice to other men. He begrudged even the attention she paid to children or animals, as if they were taking her affection and leaving none for him. It was wrong and crazy to feel like that, and he had to stop before he drove her away.

He looked down at the cove as he went across the terrace to his room; the *Athena* was not at the pier. He looked out into the gulf, and he could just see what he thought was the ketch near the horizon to the south. He frowned slightly in curiosity as it disappeared, and then he went to his room to get dressed. Psyche said Nikos fished; that was probably where he had gone.

Sheerness did find Psyche eventually, after losing his way a few times. She was in the garden at the front of the house where the ground was level, playing with the girls. She had Yelena on her hip as she pushed the twins in a swing, and Stefania and Odette were playing with two dogs, one black with tan and white patches, the other cream with white patches, and a litter of puppies that was a mixture of the two. They were singing a song in Greek, interrupted occasionally by giggles as someone made a mistake.

He stood at the top of the stairs that led to the garden watching them before he went down to take a seat on a wooden bench near the bottom, shaded by a tree. Psyche had her back turned to him as she pushed Evangelina and Euphamia, and he smiled and casually draped his arm across the back of the seat as he listened to her sing. He had only heard her once before, and he recalled it had been passable. This time was no exception.

He wasn't there long when Odette spied him sitting on the bench, and she got up to walk toward him, a string of puppies following behind her. She looked at him curiously as she drew near, and she carefully climbed onto the seat beside him, folding her hands primly in her lap. Her legs were still too short to bend at the knee on the seat, and the puppies that had followed her jumped up from the ground to try to catch her feet as they just barely stretched over the edge. She sat quietly for a minute before she looked up at him.

"*Poioi eínai eseís?*" she asked quietly.

Sheerness frowned as he looked at her. It was a sad state of affairs when a three-year-old could speak Greek better than he could. He wasn't sure what she was asking, and so he wasn't sure what to say.

"*Pōs legestai?*" she tried again.

"Ah, *mé léne* Sebastian," he said with a slight smile.

Odette frowned as she looked at him. "*Den miláte ta elleniká?*"

"*Ochi polú kalá,*" said Sheerness dryly.

Odette's face brightened, and she scooted closer to him on the bench, getting on her knees. She put a hand on his arm to draw his attention and pointed down at the puppies rolling around and playing on the ground.

"*Koutábia,*" she said helpfully. She touched the bench itself. "*Págkos.*"

Then she proceeded to name the different parts of his face, touching each one with her little hand, and the different parts of his body. Then she tugged on his hand and hopped down from the bench to lead him around the garden, pointing out different things and naming them for him. He was actually finding her Greek lesson helpful, but he wasn't sure how much he would retain.

At some point during Odette's lesson, Psyche became aware he had come to the garden, and she watched as the little girl, standing less than half his height, guided him around by the hand, pointing at things. What tickled her most was the intent expression on his face as he listened to everything the toddler was saying. He might have been receiving instruction from Socrates for all his attentiveness. Their tour eventually brought them to where Psyche pushed the girls on the swing.

"*Koúnia,*" said Odette as she pointed at it. "Euphamia *kai* Evangelina *eínai dídyma. Adelphés.*" Psyche's lips twitched. Then Odette pointed at her. "Thea. *Omorphos.*" Then she pointed at Sheerness. "Sebastian. *Omorphos.*"

Sheerness frowned. He didn't understand the meaning of the word. He looked at Psyche for translation, and she chuckled.

"She thinks you're pretty." Sheerness pursed his lips to hide a smile and rolled his eyes. "So, are you learning anything?"

"A bit," said Sheerness noncommittally. He lifted Odette in his arms. "*Eycharisto, mikrós.*"

"*Parakaló,*" replied Odette with a smile, and she gave him a kiss on the cheek. "*Philí,*" she giggled.

Sheerness looked at the dogs, which were all once again gathered together. "These are interesting dogs," he said mildly.

"They're honey dogs and have been around thousands of years. I've seen them on vases. They're adorable and very smart," said Psyche admiringly. "The puppies are old enough to leave their mother," she said thoughtfully.

Sheerness looked at her blankly, and then his eyes rounded in alarm. "No."

Psyche gave him an innocent look. "No what?"

"No, you cannot have one," said Sheerness firmly.

Psyche gave Yelena to Stefania, and she bent down to pick up one of the puppies, a black- and white-spotted male that had a fleabitten gray pattern where the colors overlapped. She put him up to her cheek.

"Look at this adorable little face," she said coaxingly. "Have you ever seen anything so cute?"

"Yes, I have. His name is Waddlesworth, and he nearly gnawed my finger off," said Sheerness flatly.

"Sheerness, ducks do not gnaw; the worst they can do is grind."

"Tell that to my finger," muttered Sheerness.

"Fine," said Psyche airily. "*You* tell him he can't come with me."

She held the puppy up to Sheerness's face. The dog began to lick him affectionately on the cheek, and Sheerness heaved a long-suffering sigh as he looked at her. He finally rolled his eyes and groaned in surrender.

"All right, enough," he sighed. "What about your duck?"

"What about him?"

"How is he going to react to a puppy running about?"

"I'm sure they'll get along fine," said Psyche dismissively.

"Hunh," said Sheerness doubtfully.

Psyche put the puppy back down to rejoin the rest of its litter, and she took Yelena back from Stefania. The baby laid her head on Psyche's shoulder and started to doze off, and Psyche smoothed a hand over her back. It was time for her nap, and Psyche was ready for breakfast, as were the girls.

"Ioanna should have breakfast ready by now," she said as she rounded up the girls. "She was busy this morning getting things ready for tonight, but she said to try back in a couple hours."

"What's tonight?" asked Sheerness confusedly as they went up the stairs.

"Nikos and Ioanna are holding a party in my honor," said Psyche with a grimace.

"Imagine that," said Sheerness dryly with a smirk.

"It wasn't my suggestion," defended Psyche.

"Mm-hmm," said Sheerness doubtfully.

"I've told you I do *not* like being the center of attention."

"And yet you always seem to be," said Sheerness mockingly.

"I'll trade you," said Psyche flatly.

"Nah, don't think so," drawled Sheerness with a grin. "I'll take obscurity any day."

"Humph," said Psyche unhappily.

Psyche and the children led him through the maze that was the house. He tried to remember his way, but it was impossible. They came to a large, open room, and it was the kitchen, rather than a dining room. Ioanna was there with three other women, and they were talking as they bustled around cooking. Ioanna looked up from kneading a large bowl of dough when they entered, and she smiled and wiped her hands on her apron.

"Someone was sleepy," said Psyche with a grin. "Have you managed to get things under control?"

"Oh, yes," said Ioanna. "Nikos has gone to invite people, and they will invite people...," she said with a smile as she took Yelena.

"It really isn't necessary for you to go to all this trouble."

"Ah," said Ioanna negligibly, waving a hand through the air. "We don't have gatherings often enough, so this was the perfect excuse." She grinned. She looked at Sheerness assessingly and then at Psyche. "How is his Greek?"

Psyche chuckled. "Odette was giving him lessons in the garden, but I'm not sure how much he understands. He doesn't know Ladino or Turkish."

"He knows not to...?" she asked concernedly.

"I've somewhat told him, but I'll try to explain it fully before tonight."

"Yes, do that," urged Ioanna. "Poor thing. He's looking a bit at ends," she chuckled, "but, my goodness! He's very tempting. If I weren't married...."

"Ioanna!" gasped Psyche in astonishment. She looked at Sheerness, but he seemed mostly unaware of what they were saying, and she sighed with relief. Ioanna chuckled at Psyche's panicked expression.

"Go sit at the table on the terrace. It's not fancy, but it will be fine until dinnertime. We should have enough things out of the way by then to give you a proper meal," assured Ioanna.

"Whatever you have made will be more than adequate," said Psyche with a smile. "I am ravenous."

The girls had already gone to the large, sturdy table on the covered veranda accessed through a set of doors leading off the kitchen and began to eat. The terrace overlooked the garden rather than the sea, but it was every bit as scenic. There was a large pool inlaid with an intricate mosaic fed by a hot spring, which also provided the water for bathing in the house. The flowers were in bloom, and the citrus-scented air was buzzing with the sound of honeybees as they went about their work. Psyche loved this house. The weather was wonderful, the scenery was fantastic, and she felt that if she could never go home again, this was exactly where she would want to be.

She took an available seat and a plate and put on omelette with artichoke and feta, *keftethes*, *kataifi*, and *stafithopitta*. She was very ready to eat. She had been up for hours, and her stomach was rumbling. Sheerness took the seat beside hers, close to the slightly taller seat for Odette near the end of the table. Stefania poured milk for herself and her sisters and was sitting across from Sheerness on the other side of Odette. He was only one who didn't have food. Ioanna came out with cups of coffee for Psyche and Sheerness.

"Thank you so much," sighed Psyche. Ioanna chuckled and shook her head as she looked at all the food Psyche had put on her plate and went back to the kitchen. Psyche looked at Sheerness. "It's not going to serve itself," she said with a grin.

"I don't know what everything is," he said dully.

"Why don't you ask Odette?" she teased with a chuckle. She leaned past him to look at Odette. *"Ti einai ekeino?"* she asked, pointing at the omelette.

"Avgha me feta kai agkinára," supplied Odette.

Psyche looked at Sheerness. "Omelette with feta and artichoke," interpreted Psyche. *"Ti einai ekeina?"* she asked, pointing to another dish.

"Keftethes," said Odette, Euphamia, and Evangelina with a giggle.

"They're somewhat like sausages and somewhat like meatballs."

"Ti einai ekeina?" asked Sheerness as he pointed to a dish.

"Kataifi," said the girls.

Psyche's forehead wrinkled. "There's not really an English translation. They're somewhat like buns or biscuits, made with almonds and lemon syrup."

"Loukoumathes?" he asked as he pointed to another dish.

"Exactly," said Psyche with a grin. "Honey puffs."

"Ti einai ekeina?" he asked as he pointed to the *stafithopitta* on Psyche's plate.

"Ti einai ekeino," corrected Psyche mildly. *"That,* as opposed to *those. Stafithopitta.* Raisin cake."

Once everything had been named for him, Sheerness made his choices and put the food on his plate. It was, as it had been the night before, delicious. He agreed with Psyche that the food was one of the best things about Greece. The flavor was different; the combinations and types of ingredients were different. He could only assume Psyche was so familiar with it because of Chrissoula. While they were in Athens, he hadn't eaten unless he was on the ship because he simply didn't know what things were. While he didn't consider himself to be finicky, there were certain things he absolutely was not going to eat.

Psyche talked with the girls while they ate, and he was able to somewhat participate. Because the girls were younger, their vocabulary was not as broad as an adult's might be, and it was easier for him to determine what was being said. He also was not completely ignorant of the language, and this sort of *immersion* in its use would be the best way for him to become familiar with the modern form. That was how Psyche had become so fluent in most of the languages she knew; there was something to be said for having a native speaker talking to one as opposed to learning from a book.

After their late breakfast—or early dinner—the girls went back to the garden. Psyche offered to show Sheerness the tower, and he wondered how long she had been awake. She had no trouble finding her way to the kitchen from the garden, so she had to have been to the room at least once already. He did want to see the tower. It was, by far, the most interesting part of the house to him, and he imagined the view from the top was spectacular.

As he followed Psyche through the house, taking the shortest route—which meant passing across a terrace occasionally—Sheerness was puzzled by Chrissoula's position as Psyche's maid. Nikos was wealthy, and it was unlikely he had been made that any other way than through inheritance...especially the house. If Chrissoula was not illegitimate, Sheerness could not understand how she became a servant, in England *or* Greece.

"This is where they'll have the party tonight," said Psyche as she led him into the bottom floor.

It was large—not as big as some of the ballrooms in London or the larger country homes (including his), but it would hold quite a few people. There were two doorways, the one they came in and another that led onto a large terrace on the opposite wall. There was a huge fireplace on another wall, a fire burning there with several spits holding different types of meat. There were finely carved granite columns at the corners of the octagon that supported a rib-vaulted ceiling unlike anything Sheerness had ever seen before. Because of the eight points, once they intersected in the center and because of the vaulting, it resembled a dome. It was stuccoed and frescoed like a cathedral, but the bacchanalian scene depicted was most definitely not religious.

There was a low, circular table that filled much of the room, smaller in circumference than the tower with plenty of space to walk around the outer edge, and empty in the center to create an inner circle about thirty feet in diameter. There were no chairs, only large cushions to sit around the outside. The ceiling was high, taking the distance of the ground floor and the first floor. There were four large chandeliers that hung down and several sconces around the walls to provide lighting, but for the moment, none were lit. On the wall opposite the fireplace began the stairs leading to the next level, and Sheerness followed Psyche around the edge of the table to take them.

"This tower was the original house, built well before the Turks took control of the country. It's been in Nikos and Chrissoula's family since that time, and each generation, until recently, has added a little bit more to create the labyrinth it now is," said Psyche with a grin.

"I have noticed it has a maze-like quality," said Sheerness dryly.

"The ceiling in here was bare stone like the walls until the seventeenth century, but then someone decided it needed a little...modification."

Sheerness chuckled. "Is *that* what it is?"

"Ioanna says the local priest refuses to come in here," chortled Psyche.

When they reached the landing for the next floor, they were standing in a space that followed the octagonal shape of the tower with several doors leading from it. Psyche took him to the next set of steps, which led them to the top of the tower, edged by a wall that came barely to his waist. On the side facing the sea, there was another set of steps that led up to the top of the wall with a small platform about four feet square. There was no railing, but it looked as if there might have been at one point.

"That's peculiar," said Sheerness, climbing to the top of it.

"Yes," agreed Psyche neutrally. "At one time, it was used as a sort of lookout for family returning from sea, enemies approaching from land or the water. It's not really necessary anymore."

Just as Sheerness expected, the view was spectacular. He could see everything for miles all around. He looked to the water below and marveled at the distance. It could be seventy feet, and the water was a crystalline blue-green. He could see all the way to the bottom and could distinguish between the sand, seaweed, and rocks, and he could see several fish. He was about to climb down the stairs when something on the bottom caught his attention.

"There's a statue down there...under the water!" he said in astonishment.

Psyche didn't go to the edge to look, and she wasn't surprised. She would look at it at some point, but not from the top of the tower and not that day. She looked at the cove. The tide was out, but even still, the water at the base of the cliff outside the cove was at least thirty feet deep, and it was a long way to fall.

"I know it's there," she said quietly.

Sheerness turned to look at her and hurriedly walked down the stairs. "Did you see it earlier? Why didn't you tell me?"

"No, I haven't seen it yet, but there's no reason to be so excited. Yes, it's as old as it looks, but it was purposely put there, and it's not going anywhere."

"Why?" he asked perplexedly.

"It's a grave marker," she said evenly, and she went to take a seat on the stairs leading to the edge.

Sheerness frowned. "All right, I'll bite. Whose?"

Psyche looked at him solemnly. "Chrissoula's."

"What?"

Psyche gave him a wan smile. "I have yet another Grecian tragedy for you, and once I tell you, that's it. It stays *here*," she finished firmly.

Sheerness gave her a troubled look. "If you insist," he said evenly.

"Oh, I do." Sheerness raised an enquiring eyebrow. "Chrissoula's family has lived here for hundreds of years, and they have held onto it by *any* means necessary. They are, and always have been, Christians, but if you were to ask anyone, they would swear her people are Muslim. That's one of the reasons they've retained possession of their land despite the unfairness of Ottoman rule of Greece. It's a secret that more than one person has died for over the years...and killed for." She gave him an assessing glance. "Do you understand why this needs to stay here?"

"Yes, I think I do," said Sheerness quietly.

"Nikos and Chrissoula's mother was a Smyrniote, and so is Ioanna. The people who are like the Andreanopouli, Crypto-Christians, have a very small and tightly knit set of others like them that they trust with their secret. While the Orthodox faith will welcome you back to the fold if you stray, if you are Muslim and found practicing another faith, at least in the Ottoman Empire, you're dead. For the men in the family, it is important for them to marry women of that ilk to make things easier when they're raising their children, which is one of the reasons both Nikos and his father went all the way to Smyrna to find a wife. Nikos might have found a woman closer to home, but since it worked out so well for his father…. For the women, it's not so very important. Property passes through the males, so if the females have to marry an outsider, it's not such a tragedy…except in this instance.

"When she was seventeen, Chrissoula's father tried to find a man for her to marry, but she fell in love with a Muslim. She thought he loved her, too, so against his better judgment, her father agreed to the marriage. Things went well for about a year, until Chrissoula told her husband the truth. Her husband killed her father, and then she killed him."

"Mon dieu!" blurted Sheerness in shock.

"She had no choice. In addition to killing her father, her husband was going to tell everyone her secret. More people would have died. Chrissoula had trusted him completely and told him *everything*, including the names of other families. One guilty life in exchange for a hundred or more innocent seemed a worthy sacrifice.

"Chrissoula and her husband lived in Thessaloniki with his family. She was charged with both murders and taken to the tower. It's called the Red Tower because of the blood spilled by victims of the torturers and executioners. She only spent two weeks there, but she has scars." Psyche shuddered, and Sheerness sat down on the step beside her and put his arm around her shoulders. "She was there that long rather than being executed immediately because of Duman Pasha and my father. Duman and my father were friends with Chrissoula's father, and both of them were visiting. They gave Nikos time to get permission, as her senior male relative, to execute her himself."

"Bloody hell," sighed Sheerness breathlessly.

"Once Nikos got it, he brought Chrissoula here, to their home. When it was high tide, he led her here, to the top of this tower, tied her in a sack, and threw her off the cliff," whispered Psyche brokenly.

"Jesus!" breathed Sheerness, his face stricken.

He moved to the step behind Psyche to put both his arms around her and cradled her against him, placing his cheek against the top of her head. Psyche inhaled sharply and cleared her throat. She was almost done. Just a little more to go, and then she could try to forget about it again.

"There were witnesses, the local officials, and I believe there was even someone from Constantinople. It had to look convincing, and it was a long way to fall. That alone could have killed her, but if it hadn't been done, Chrissoula would most definitely have died. Nikos had given her a knife, and under the water on the side of the cliff, even at low tide, is an entrance to a cave that has no other way in or out. Nikos and Chrissoula used to play there when they were children. Once she got free from the sack, she swam to the cave and waited for nightfall. When it came, she swam to my father's waiting ship, and he took her to England.

"To Greece, she is dead, and she can never come back. If it were ever discovered Nikos didn't kill her, the Ottomans would kill him. No one here, other than Ioanna and Duman Pasha, knows she's still alive. The girls know their parents get letters from someone in England, but they think she is only a distant relation. She is rarely, if ever, even mentioned by name."

She raised her head from where she had been resting it against his knee and looked up at him somberly.

"Do you understand now why I didn't want you to mention her while we were in Thessaloniki until we found Nikos? I had no way of knowing who knew him and who didn't, and if the wrong person found out...."

Sheerness nodded. "Why didn't you tell me this before?"

"It's not something I think about," said Psyche evenly, "and it didn't occur to me that I should until yesterday when we got here."

"Is Duman Pasha a—what did you call them—a Crypto-Christian?"

"No, he's Muslim, but he is inclined to tolerance instead of oppression for other religions. It's one of the reasons he's friends with my father."

"So, is that everything?" asked Sheerness with a slight smile.

"There are a few things about Nikos, but they can wait." Sheerness looked at her suspiciously. "They can wait," repeated Psyche.

Sheerness leaned forward and kissed her, and Psyche put a hand to the back of his head, twining her fingers in his hair. It was getting longer, the ends starting to curl. She couldn't decide if she wanted it long again. She was used to it being short. He had shaved that morning, and the scent of his shaving lotion was still intoxicating, almost like an aphrodisiac. She wanted him so much she could scarcely think of anything else, and she sighed at the back of her throat when his hand moved up her side to rest just below her breast. She turned and wrapped her arms around his neck, pressing close against him, and she almost purred as his hands moved down her back to grab her bottom.

She opened her eyes in surprise when he broke their kiss and turned his head, tilting it sideways as he listened to something. Then she heard it, too. Childish giggling and shouting coming from the cove below. Nikos had returned, and the girls had gone to meet him. Psyche rested her forehead against his jaw and closed her eyes. The moment was gone.

"We need to teach you to dance," she said finally.

"I *know* how to dance," said Sheerness flatly with a scowl.

"Not Greek dancing. They don't dance the minuet, waltz, or anything else we do in London. We need to at least teach you the *syrto* and the *karsilama*. After that, we'll see if we have time for the *kalamatianos*." Psyche looked at her watch. It was close to one in the afternoon. "I don't think we will."

"Humph. Do your worst," he said with a challenging grin.

Psyche spent the rest of the afternoon teaching him the steps to the traditional Greek dances. She also tried to explain the etiquette involved.

Despite her comments on the subject in the past, he was an excellent dancer and learned without much difficulty. They took a brief rest for dinner, but it was well after six when she was done with her lesson. He would be passable, at least good enough that he wouldn't feel uncomfortable dancing.

They had finished on the terrace off the kitchen, and when they went back in, Nikos was with Ioanna, teasing her by holding the bowl she had been working with over his head, well out of her reach. When they came in, Nikos grinned and handed the bowl back to his wife with a kiss, and she smacked him on his arm and pursed her lips to hide a smile before she went back to work.

"You have learned to dance?" he asked Sheerness.

"I think so," said Sheerness agreeably with a half-smile. Nikos was very likeable, jovial and humorous. He had been unfair to be so standoffish.

"Good!" said Nikos happily. "We will have *mezedes* and *kleftiko* and *ouzo* and retsina, and then we will have *syrto* and *karsilama*, and maybe a little *tsifteteli*, eh?" he said with a grin and a step, snapping his fingers.

Psyche's eyes rounded. "I'm not sure about that," she said quickly.

Ioanna chuckled and looked over her shoulder. "A certain someone mentioned something about that," she grinned. "Did you bring it?"

"I did, but—" began Psyche.

"Then we shall have it," boomed Nikos with a laugh. *"Opa!"*

"Yes, that sounds like fun," said Sheerness as he noted Psyche's panicked expression. There was apparently a Greek dance she didn't know either.

"A-all right," stuttered Psyche resignedly.

Psyche looked at herself in the mirror in her room one last time with a bit of indecision. She was tempted to put on something else. The only comfort she had was in knowing she would not be alone. Ioanna looked forward to dancing, too, and there would be others, but Psyche was sure she would be the only one wearing this. She could have saved herself the concern if she had left it on the ship, and she couldn't for the life of her understand why she had brought it. It *was* very beautiful, and she expressed a moment of admiration for Chrissoula's handiwork.

The outfit was composed of several pieces, more than what she would have for a gown at home. There were two skirts, one made of dark purple silk embroidered with gold foil at the bottom edge. Over that was another made of iridescent chiffon that changed color from burgundy, to amethyst, and then to gold as it moved under the light. It, too, was edged at the bottom in gold foil. Both were flowing and billowy, but not revealing, except that they both rested just at the top of her hips, barely covering her birthmark. Tied over that at her hips was an amethyst scarf encrusted with beads and covered in delicate embroidery in gold, trimmed with crocheted and tasseled fringe on the edge.

The shirt, which Psyche realized was what Chrissoula had been working on at Wilderland, was made of rich purplish-red velvet covered with intricate embroidery in gold foil at the neck and across the bodice. About halfway down the sleeve, just above the elbow, the velvet ended and was replaced by silk chiffon like that of the overskirt, edged in gold foil, and it flared out as it came down to her wrist and further beyond in a triangular fashion that reminded Psyche of a frilly lace cuff.

The thing about the shirt, however, that caused her distress was its length. It ended just at the bottom of her ribs, leaving a space of six to eight inches between the end of it and the top of the skirt. Part of that was disguised by the crocheted and tasseled fringe at the bottom of the shirt, which matched that on the scarf at her hips, but there was far more skin showing at her midriff than she was accustomed to seeing in an outfit that was otherwise very modest. The neckline was not even as low as that on most of the gowns she wore at home and the bodice no tighter. It was just the skin in the middle. Unfortunately, it was somewhat important to the dance to have that exposed.

But she wasn't going to share it all night. She had a matching scarf, for dancing, but she would use it to hide her stomach until it was time for it to come out. It was made of the same fabulous chiffon and once she tied it over her shoulder and draped it attractively, it served her purpose. The area at her midsection was lighter, but it wasn't apparent the cause was bare skin.

She put in a pair of earrings made of finely filigreed silver with three pendant pearls each. She didn't recall ever seeing them in her jewelry box at home, but they were beautiful and suited the outfit. Without Chrissoula there, she wasn't able to create a complicated hairstyle, but she came up with something suitable. She braided most of it and coiled it low at the back of her head. The hair around her face was left loose, and the natural ringlets curled softly to attractively frame her features.

"Wow, you're wearing a dress," said Sheerness in admiration as he came into her room from the terrace.

"I do occasionally," said Psyche dryly as she turned to look at him from the mirror. "Besides, I *had* to wear this one."

Sheerness was wearing one of the outfits she had given him, and he had selected the black and silver vest. He was wearing a pair of low-heeled slippers that suited the outfit, much better than his boots would have, and she hadn't thought he might have brought something like that with him. He had made an effort to tame his hair, but it was growing longer and more unruly. He was more than presentable, and Psyche felt her heart flutter as she looked at him.

"That's a very nice color for you," he said casually.

"Really? Thank you," said Psyche in surprise. She couldn't recall if he had ever paid her a compliment before.

"Do you know how to get to the tower from here?"

"Of course," said Psyche with a half-smile.

"Good, because I don't," said Sheerness with a chuckle. "Shall we go, then?" he asked as he held out his arm for her.

"Absolutely." They left to walk down the hall, and Psyche looked up at him. "I don't think there are going to be any Muslims here tonight."

"Why would you think that?" he asked with a thoughtful frown.

"Nikos said we will have ouzo and retsina. Muslims don't drink alcohol."

"Perhaps there will be other things without alcohol for them to drink," said Sheerness mildly.

"Maybe," said Psyche thoughtfully, "but I don't think so because I am sure Nikos intends to drink alcohol himself."

"We'll have to wait and see," said Sheerness with a grin.

"I guess so."

She led him down a short hall to a set of stairs. He recognized them and had a general idea of where they were going, but then they turned down a different hall and went down another set of stairs. By the time they reached the tower, he was lost. There were other people arriving as they did, most coming up the stairs that led from the cove to the tower terrace. There were several boats moored below and torches around the edge of the terrace and along the stairs. Sheerness could hear Greek and Ladino, but no Turkish.

Ioanna was standing not far from the doorway when they entered, and Psyche was relieved to see she was dressed much the same...except her shirt did not have a gap at the midriff. She smiled when she saw Psyche and kissed both her cheeks before taking her by the hands to examine her from head to toe.

"That scarf doesn't belong there!" said Ioanna with a chuckle.

"It does for now," said Psyche with a smile, her cheeks coloring a bright red. "I'll take it off later, but I feel *exposed* without it."

Ioanna laughed. "I'm very jealous. That is a beautiful costume, and that you have the body to wear it...."

"I would much rather it was made like yours," said Psyche with a smile.

"Ah, after five children, there are certain things that should *not* be seen in public," chuckled Ioanna. She looked at Sheerness. "*He* is very fine this evening," she said with an appreciative grin. "Where did he get those clothes?"

"I bought them," said Psyche hesitantly.

Ioanna raised an eyebrow and chuckled. "Come! You and Sebastian will sit by us," she said, linking her arms through theirs to guide them around the table to their seats.

It took Ioanna awhile to get them to their seats because she stopped to introduce them to people along the way. Psyche didn't think there was room for anyone else to sit down. Somewhere between thirty and forty people were there, and being of that number seated on cushions rather than chairs put them about as close together as they could be without being cramped. The table was divided into four segments to allow servants to move around, provide access to the doorways and fireplace, and places for people to get to the middle.

A group of musicians sat playing in a corner, and the room buzzed with laughter and conversation above the music. The atmosphere was unlike anything Psyche had ever experienced before, and she tingled with excitement. Everyone was friendly and happy, and the undercurrent of backbiting and intrigue that was rampant in London was nonexistent here.

Psyche sat down on a cushion beside Nikos, and he smiled and leaned toward her to kiss her cheeks. Sheerness sat on the other side of her, and he leaned past her to shake Nikos's hand.

"Thea, you are lovely," said Nikos affectionately.

"Thank you, Nikos," said Psyche with a blush.

"What would you like to drink?"

"Ouzo, please," said Psyche with a grin. She turned to look at Sheerness. "Would you like some?"

"Some what?" he asked blankly.

He was looking around himself with a befuddled expression. Psyche had been prepared by stories from her parents and Chrissoula. Sheerness wasn't sure what to make of it. He looked at the ceiling and what was going on around him, thinking the comparison was not far off the mark. He would enjoy himself if he didn't try to understand everything and compare it to what he was accustomed to in Britain. A little alcohol would help. Psyche looked at Nikos.

"He would like ouzo, too." She looked at Sheerness and smiled as she handed it to him. "Drink it slowly," she advised.

Sheerness looked at the glass suspiciously. Psyche took a sip of her own. When he saw her drink it without any ill effects, he tried his. It was different, but he liked it. The flavor reminded him of anise biscuits, and although he could tell it contained alcohol, it didn't seem like it had much more than wine. He drained the glass and held it out to be refilled. Psyche looked at him in surprise, a piece of flatbread dipped in hummus halfway to her mouth. She had Nikos refill the glass, and she gave it back to Sheerness hesitantly.

"You really want to slow down with this; eat some food," she said mildly. "It can sneak up on you."

"Hunh," said Sheerness doubtfully.

"Have it your way," said Psyche diffidently as she went back to her food.

She leaned behind Nikos to speak to Ioanna, and both of them laughed at whatever she said. She turned back to Sheerness to see he had emptied his glass again, and she moved the bottle of ouzo closer to him with a shake of her head so he could serve himself. She had tried to warn him, but he would find out soon enough. Ouzo contained no less alcohol than his brandy or whisky. Its smoothness and sweet flavor didn't make it any less intoxicating.

She explained what everything was, but he wasn't sure what to make of everyone reaching into the same dish. Some things were put on an individual plate in front of a person if they required a utensil to consume. For the most part, the dishes were shared, and people took from them as they liked. After Psyche raised an enquiring eyebrow, Sheerness shrugged and started to eat. She made sure to tell him that the baskets of flowers were *not* food.

Psyche tried to keep him involved in the conversation as she talked with Nikos and Ioanna, and the ouzo was having an effect on him. What kind, she wasn't sure, but it seemed to be for the better. An older woman was seated on the other side of him, and Psyche watched with amusement as she flirted with Sheerness. He couldn't understand half of what Mrs. Pappas said, so Psyche tried to make sure he didn't inadvertently agree to something he shouldn't.

As people got up to dance in the open center of the table, Sheerness got to see what the flowers were for. When the dancers did something particularly entertaining, the onlookers threw the flowers as a sign of appreciation. He was overwhelmed by the joy and passion for living that filled the room, and it was almost as intoxicating as the ouzo. Even as lax as the mood was, there were certain points of etiquette to follow, but nothing nearly as involved as what was expected in London. He again looked at the ceiling, and this was as close to the kind of revelry portrayed there as he would ever likely get. He loved it.

Psyche sat beside him talking and laughing, and she would clap her hands and snap her fingers as the music played. If there was singing, she would hum along. He had never seen her so happy and relaxed, and if he had never met her before that night, he would have believed she was among her own people. For her, seeing the people, being here in this moment, was the most exciting part of going to Greece. Seeing ruins, finding new ones, would be a pleasure, but coming here to Chrissoula's family would be her greatest memory.

The two of them were eventually coaxed into getting up to dance the *syrto*. Despite his mild state of inebriation, Sheerness was able to remember the steps, and it was much more fun to dance with a group as he was doing than he had thought it would be while Psyche was teaching him. The music made the difference. There was something about it that stirred him, a timeless, ancient quality that made him feel as if the Greeks of antiquity were there with them.

The musicians played traditional instruments like the tambouras, sandouri, gaida, and zurna, but there were also a lute, mandolin, and violin…and three drummers. Psyche had explained what the instruments were called, but some of them looked like what he had seen on vases and mosaics. The progressions and patterns were different from what existed in Western music, and it evoked something primal in him as he listened that caused a disorienting sensation and made the whole evening seem almost dreamlike.

The party lasted for hours, and Sheerness couldn't recall ever having so much fun. Nikos convinced him to get up and dance the *tsamikos* with just the men. Psyche hadn't taught him that one. It involved kicking and leaping, and Psyche laughed amusedly as Sheerness tried his best to do it justice. She threw flowers and shouted *"opa!"* appreciatively, and she chatted enthusiastically with Ioanna and Mrs. Pappas as the men danced. Psyche was glad Sheerness was enjoying himself. She would have felt disappointed if he didn't.

Then it came time for *tsifteteli*. Psyche was unsure of how Sheerness was going to react. Ioanna tried to coax her out, but Psyche was reluctant. She had worn her costume, but that didn't mean she *had* to let everyone see her dancing in it. Then Sheerness joined Ioanna in trying to get her to dance, and Psyche sighed resignedly. She did *like* the dance, but Sheerness was in for a shock. She began to remove her scarf and leaned toward him speak in his ear.

"Just remember you told me to do this," she said quietly. She smiled nervously at Ioanna and left her scarf behind as she stood up.

Psyche was relieved she and Ioanna weren't the only ones getting up to dance. Psyche felt the more other women there were, the less conspicuous she would be. They also weren't the only ones wearing a suitable costume, and that put Psyche even more at ease. That she drank a few glasses of ouzo didn't hurt, either. It was one thing to dance with Chrissoula and her sisters and quite another to dance in front of other people.

Psyche did her best to ignore the astonished look on Sheerness's face when he saw parts of her clothes were missing. She tried to forget everyone else except the other dancers and concentrate on the music; otherwise, she wouldn't get through it without hives. The musicians were good, and she gave herself over to the rhythm they played. One of the things she enjoyed about *tsifteteli* was that there were no set patterns. There were specific movements, but it was all improvised, determined only by where the music guided each dancer.

Sheerness felt his mouth go dry as he watched Psyche. *Danse du ventre.* He'd read about it and knew that's what it was. There was something hypnotic about the way she moved, the sinewy—almost snakelike—grace as she danced, and she was oblivious to everything but the music, as if she were in a trance. It was sensual and earthy, elemental and arcane in a way that shocked him and yet irresistibly excited him, too. Her hesitation had nothing to do with inability. She had no difficulty with the dance and even had a costume for it. He now understood why she said she *had* to wear that dress.

When he managed to tear his eyes away, he could see he wasn't the only one enthralled. There were other women dancing, receiving attention as well, but everyone's eyes always returned to Psyche. Unwillingly or not, she was the center of attention, something she claimed to dislike immensely. She was a wonderful dancer, and it was a thing of beauty to behold.

He remembered what she said before she got up. *Jealousy.* She knew he would be jealous. She had given him the opportunity to let her bow out of it, even if she hadn't explained why, but he had insisted. When she told him what she did, it had been her way of telling him that she wouldn't tolerate anger from him. If he felt any, and he did, she didn't want to hear about it. *He* had made the decision; she was only complying with his wishes, much to his chagrin.

While her dancing attracted everyone's eye, he was the only one who watched her with such an utterly carnal interest. He saw admiration and joy, and there was desire as well, but he didn't think there was anyone there who wanted her more than he did. And there was envy. It was obvious they were together, and the men were envious. It didn't make Sheerness feel better.

The song ended, and when it did, the musicians immediately began another. To his surprise, the men got up and also started to dance. They didn't dance like the women, but in an accompaniment that was flirty and no less suggestive. Nikos clapped him on the shoulder to let Sheerness know he was expected to dance. Psyche looked at him with an amused grin when she saw his uncomfortable expression, and she shimmied her shoulders and crooked her finger teasingly, making him shake his head and roll his eyes as he walked around the edge of the table to go to the center.

Psyche spent the next half hour teaching him *tsifteteli.* He was a more apt pupil than he pretended. It was simply that he enjoyed putting his hands on her hips and feeling them gyrate. It felt no less provocative than it looked, but he could only feign ignorance for so long before she became suspicious. Once he quit behaving as if he didn't know what he was doing, Ioanna took him away to see how well he'd learned. As Psyche danced with Nikos, she wondered if he had faked his lack of skill. He seemed to be doing very well with Ioanna.

They eventually went back to their seats for more ouzo and more food. Psyche would give Sheerness an assessing glance occasionally, trying to gauge just how well he had been able to cope with seeing her dance. He seemed very relaxed, much more than she had ever seen before, which made her wonder if it wasn't an act. If it was, she would soon find out. People soon began to bid their farewells. Psyche didn't have a watch to know the time (the watch on a chain would have been out of place with the costume), but it had to be late by how tired she was. She hadn't stayed up past midnight since leaving London, and she was sure it was well beyond that. After she yawned two or three times, Ioanna laughed and leaned behind Nikos to speak to her.

"Stop that! You know those are contagious."

"I'm sorry. It has just been awhile since I've been up this late."

"Then you should go to bed."

"Are you sure?"

"You don't need to be the last one standing," chortled Ioanna.

"All right," said Psyche with a grin. "You notice you did not have to argue too strenuously to get me to agree?"

"I did notice that," laughed Ioanna. "Go to bed, and take him with you," she said, nodding to Sheerness over Psyche's shoulder with her chin. "I don't imagine he would stay too long without you anyhow."

"No, I suppose he wouldn't."

"Do not expect breakfast to be any earlier tomorrow," said Ioanna with a smile. "Would you like it brought to your room?"

"No, I'll come looking for it…same as today; I may not be in my room anyhow because I thought I might go for a swim tomorrow morning."

"Mm-hmm," said Ioanna agreeably. She kissed Psyche's cheeks, and then she tugged the back of Nikos's vest, and he turned to look. "Thea is leaving."

"Good night, Thea," said Nikos, kissing her cheeks. "You had fun, yes?"

"The best time of my life!" said Psyche enthusiastically.

Nikos laughed amusedly. "There's still time," he said humorously. "I will see you tomorrow. Maybe we will go see a few things on Monday."

"Absolutely," she said agreeably. She turned to look at Sheerness and leaned toward him. "Are you ready to leave?"

He nodded silently and stood up. Ioanna and Nikos stood up as well, and she kissed him fondly on both cheeks. Nikos grinned hugely and shook his hand before giving him a bear hug. Sheerness was startled by the display of affection, but he smiled and clapped Nikos on the shoulder. When Mrs. Pappas saw him leaving, she got up to kiss his cheeks as well, which made him blush, and Psyche rubbed a hand over her mouth to hide her amusement. The woman was sad to see him go, and when she kissed Psyche's cheeks, Mrs. Pappas made sure to tell her she was very lucky. Psyche didn't want to contradict her.

Chapter Twenty Eight

Sheerness kept his arm linked through Psyche's as they walked to their rooms. Considering how much ouzo he had drank, while he couldn't say he was drunk, he wasn't sober enough to find the way back on his own. Psyche had drank almost as much, so he couldn't understand why she was not fazed. She seemed tired but not drunk. Her tolerance for alcohol astounded him.

"Did you enjoy yourself?" she asked as they walked down the hall.

"Yes, I did," said Sheerness definitely. "It was…different but a lot of fun."

"Good. I'm glad you had fun. You don't seem like you do very often," said Psyche without thinking, and then she skipped a step and looked up at him. "I'm sorry. I suppose I shouldn't have said that," she said quietly.

Sheerness tilted his head sideways as he looked at her with a thoughtful frown. "I suppose you're right," he said dully.

Psyche wasn't sure which item she was right about: his not having fun or her not mentioning it…or both. They came to the door to her room, and he opened it for her to go in before following her and closing it behind him.

He stood not far from it as he watched her get ready for bed. She folded the scarf and put it in a drawer, which she left open as she removed the beaded scarf at her hips and the overskirt and folded them in as well. She took off her earrings and removed the gold combs holding up her hair and put them into a wooden box sitting on top of the dresser. He was astonished to see her putting things away. It was so unlike her, as it had been with the clothes folded neatly in the chair. She took off her sandals and saw him still standing by the door, watching her with a bemused expression.

"What?" she asked slowly, giving him a slight smile and raising an eyebrow as she walked closer to him to put the shoes in her trunk near the door.

"You're putting things away," he said curiously.

Psyche quirked her lips and moved closer. "I do that," she said matter-of-factly.

"No, you don't," said Sheerness decidedly, shaking his head. "Your cabin is constantly cluttered. It drives me insane sometimes the way you leave things lying about."

Psyche moved even closer and stood on her tiptoes to kiss him softly. She looked up at him with a teasing smile. "So quit coming into my cabin," she whispered, "or quit being so fussy."

She wrapped her arms around his neck and kissed him, nipping at his bottom lip before she ran her tongue across it. She then darted her tongue into his mouth to tease it against his, and his arms went around her waist. She moved her lips from his to glide them across his chin to his jaw and down to his neck, and he sighed longingly.

"I am not *fussy,*" he said softly. "It is simply much easier to find things if you put them away where they belong."

Psyche undid the strings that held on his vest, and she slid it down his shoulders as she continued to kiss his neck and the part of his chest exposed by the collar of his shirt, but the garment wouldn't go past his elbows as he kept his arms around her waist. She removed one of her arms from around his neck to slide her hand up the front of his shirt to smooth it over the muscle underneath, and she moved her lips back to his to kiss him hungrily.

She pressed herself even closer and soon had him pinned against the door. She got him to let go of her long enough to completely remove his vest, and she tossed it over her shoulder onto the floor unconcernedly. She lifted the front of his shirt to begin kissing his chest, and she heard him gasp as she licked one of his nipples before grazing it with her teeth.

"Now, see here," he sighed. "That's why you lose things."

Psyche lifted her head with a seductive smile, and she wrapped her arms around his neck and lifted her feet to twine her legs around his waist. She curled her fingers in his hair and moved against him achingly as she kissed him soundly. She lifted her head and clung to him with her legs as she used her hands to begin pulling his shirt over his head.

"Shag now. Talk later," she whispered desperately, and she only had his shirt halfway over his head, still covering his eyes as it too stuck at his elbows, before she started kissing him again with a sigh of longing.

Psyche continued to tug at his shirt and finally got it off to join the vest on the floor. This time, Sheerness didn't say a word. She kept one arm around his neck while she used her other hand to unfasten the buttons on the front of her shirt, and she shimmied her shoulders to slide it off and let it drop to the floor.

Sheerness put his hands under her bottom and walked toward the bed as she moved to one of his ears to tease the lobe. He was astounded by her unrestraint, but he was willing to accommodate her. When he reached the edge of the bed, he laid her onto it and undid the fastening on her skirt to pull it off. He looked for somewhere to lay it when she wrapped her legs around his thighs just above his knees, and she took it out of his hands to toss it aside.

She reached out for the strings on his trousers and gave them a tug to untie them, and then she moved her legs higher and used the heels of her feet and her toes to loosen the pants and make them fall to the floor. Sheerness looked at her in surprise, and Psyche gave him a leer as she used her hands to undo her braid. Sheerness leaned forward to smooth a hand down the front of her body, and she arched her back toward his touch with a sigh. She moved one of her legs higher up his back and pushed at it with the heel of her foot, and he almost lost his balance and fell on top of her.

"Just how flexible are you?" he asked wonderingly.

Psyche laughed softly and sat up, her legs still wrapped around him. She grabbed his arms and pulled on them, and she finally got him to climb onto the bed. He put his hands under her shoulders to move her further onto the mattress, and then he raised her back off the bed as he leaned forward to take the tip of one breast into his mouth. Psyche almost purred. She twined her fingers in his hair and smoothed one of her legs along his side as he stayed bent over her on his knees. She felt quivery and breathless as he continued to tease her breast, and when he ran his lips up her neck to her mouth to kiss her ravenously, she clung to him weakly with longing.

He began to kiss his way down her body, and his hands smoothed over her thighs and underneath her to cup her bottom. As he worked his way lower to her stomach, she felt him move first one of her legs to drape it over his shoulder and then the other, smoothing his hands up her legs to her breasts to knead their fullness and toy with the nipples with his fingertips. Then Psyche felt him raise her hips from the bed until only her head and shoulders rested against the mattress, and he began to tease her with his mouth. Psyche moaned and arched her back as exquisite sensations began to move through her body.

"Oh, wow!" she gasped in surprise, and Sheerness almost chuckled and lost his concentration when she made a gurgling sound of pleasure low in her throat unlike anything he had ever heard before.

She writhed helplessly as he continued to tease her, clutching at the blankets with her fingers, and Sheerness could feel the heels of her feet pressing into his back and imagined her toes were curling. When she climaxed, her back arched even further off the bed, and he thought she was going to levitate completely off it. He was gratified by the expression of utter delight on her face as she quivered, and her body glowed with a soft sheen of perspiration, a few tendrils of hair clinging to her forehead. He slowly eased her back onto the bed and moved his lips to her breasts before nuzzling her neck.

Psyche lifted her hands to smooth them across his shoulders and down his back to run her fingernails lightly across his buttocks. She heard him inhale sharply, and it created an erotic sensation of its own when he lifted his head slightly to blow with a cooling exhale across the dampness on her chest and stomach. She brought her hands back to his shoulders and then up to his hair, and she caressed his cheek rubbing her nose against his and giving him a tender kiss. She moved her hand down his chest, tweaking one of his nipples softly between her fingers before she went lower to take his erection in her hand. Psyche heard the breath catch in his throat as she touched him, and she looked at his face above hers to see his jaw tighten as his eyes closed in pleasure.

She surprised him when she let go of him and deftly rolled them over on the bed, and Sheerness found their positions reversed. He groaned excitedly at the back of his throat as she kissed him heatedly, and he felt her settle herself onto him with a teasing nip to his lower lip. She continued to kiss him as she started to raise and lower herself, and then she lifted herself up and balanced her hands against his chest as she moved, her head thrown back pleasurably. While he enjoyed the sight, she was moving far too slow.

It was his turn to surprise her when he first brought them both up to a sitting position, and then as he wrapped her legs around his waist and braced his hands against her bottom, he moved on his knees across the bed and laid her back against the pillows. The sensations she felt as he moved across the bed still inside her were exquisite, and she clung to him weakly as he knelt above her. He bent his head to one of her breasts and sucked the tip into his mouth, grazing the areola with his teeth as he teased the nipple with his tongue. Psyche cried out and arched her back as her hands clenched at his shoulders. He moved one of her legs at his waist up to his shoulder and thrust into her solidly as he continued to tease her breast.

"Oh, God, Sebastian!" she choked out on a whimper, and he lifted his head to look at her concernedly. She moved her hands to his hair to pull his mouth to hers for a desperate kiss. "Oh, no, don't stop!" she pleaded as she moved her hips against him.

Sheerness grinned rakishly as he began to move again, and he watched with pleasure as her expression changed to one of wanton abandon. She bit her lower lip, and her hands clutched at his arms spasmodically as she felt herself building toward another orgasm. Her breath came out in short, panting gasps as he continued to thrust in and out of her with sure, solid strokes, and she looked up at Sheerness with a marveling expression, gently running her fingertips over his features just as the first waves of ecstasy began to wash over her.

"Sebastian," she sighed softly. Psyche felt dizzy and breathless as she continued to orgasm with an intensity that left her quivering and weak, her entire body throbbing and covered in sweat, her heart racing and feeling as if it were going to beat out of her chest.

As Sheerness watched the astonishment on her face and felt her spasm and shake beneath him, he began to come as well, and his features were no less wondering and euphoric. He groaned low in his throat and shuddered as the pleasure rolled over him, and Psyche lifted her head to kiss him tenderly at the corner of his mouth. He weakly rested his head against her breasts, gasping for breath, wrapping his arms around her waist, and Psyche eased her leg from over his shoulder and cradled him gently with her arms around his shoulders. She kissed the top of his head and sighed tiredly with a satiated smile.

Once his breathing returned to a somewhat normal tempo, he raised himself up and moved off of her, propping himself up on one elbow to look down at her and trace her features with a fingertip. He bent down to give her a soft kiss and smiled boyishly.

"Now, *that* was fun," he said softly as he tweaked the end of her nose.

Psyche popped one eye open in surprise, and then she began to laugh slowly and reached for a pillow to lob at his head playfully.

"You're impossible," she chortled.

"I do believe you've mentioned that before," he said quietly, tracing his finger down her neck to her chest, running it down her breastbone to her navel. Psyche quivered slightly, and he could feel chill bumps on her skin. "Cold?"

"A little," she said softly as she looked at him.

He adjusted the blankets over them and pulled her close to his side. Psyche began to feel warmer immediately, but she also began to feel sleepier. She snuggled closer against him and lifted her head to place a kiss against his jaw and smoothed a hand over his chest.

"Psyche?"

"Hmm?" she replied drowsily.

"Why didn't you tell me what *tsifteteli* was?" he asked quietly.

Psyche raised her head to look at him and saw his troubled frown. She smoothed a soothing hand over his cheek and gave him a gentle kiss. She knew he wasn't as unbothered as he had seemed; she would have been surprised if he truly wasn't upset. Her expression grew thoughtful as she chose her words.

"I didn't tell you because it's just a dance," she said evenly.

"It is *not* just a dance," he said flatly.

"But it is," insisted Psyche. "Would knowing what it was beforehand have made you any less jealous?"

"I wouldn't have been so determined to have you dance it," he said dully.

Psyche shrugged. "But I still would have," she said gently.

"To see you dressed like that...all those men looking at you," said Sheerness with a distressed frown.

Psyche put a finger to his lips and climbed on top of him, giving him a sound kiss. Sheerness looked at her in surprise.

"Who am I with right now?" she asked him earnestly, smoothing a hand over his cheek. "Who was I with all night?" She began to place kisses down his neck to his chest. "Who am I with every night?"

She moved to one of his nipples and worried it with her teeth, and Sheerness sighed and lifted his back from the bed, becoming aroused again. She moved her lips back up his body and nuzzled his chin before kissing him hotly, and then she moved to one of his ears to nibble at the lobe. He weakly raised his hands to her hips and sighed her name as she placed kisses down his neck to his shoulder and down his chest again. And then she settled herself onto him and began to move.

"Who is inside me?" she whispered seductively in his ear before she nipped at the lobe with her teeth.

"I am," gasped Sheerness breathlessly as she rode him, her pace steadily quickening, and his hands clutched at her hips spasmodically as she continued to kiss his neck and tease his earlobes.

"No one else, Sebastian," she sighed, and she kissed him fiercely as she twined her fingers in his hair.

Psyche cried out his name as she began to climax, its arrival taking her by surprise, and as he felt her begin to spasm, Sheerness joined her, the pleasure so intense it was almost painful. Psyche had her face buried in the crook of his neck, one of her hands resting tenderly against his cheek. She was gasping for air, limp and sweat-soaked as she lay curled against him, and Sheerness felt his chest tighten emotionally as he smoothed a gentle hand down her back. That was, he realized, the closest she had ever come to admitting she had any kind of feelings for him. He lifted her palm from his cheek to place a kiss in the center of it, and Psyche lifted her head to look at him, blinking sleepily. He brushed the hair away from her face to kiss her softly on the lips before rubbing his nose against hers affectionately.

He carefully lifted her off him onto her side, and then he settled in behind her after he adjusted the blankets over them, one arm beneath her head under the pillow, the other wrapped around her waist. He nuzzled her neck before placing a kiss below her ear, and he twined his fingers with hers as he pulled her tightly against him, closing his eyes. She was already asleep, and he smiled softly in amusement.

"I love you," he whispered, resting his nose against the back of her neck.

Psyche's forehead wrinkled as she was almost asleep, just at that point between a dream and consciousness when she could easily go either way. She was exhausted, but his words almost brought her back to being fully awake. He had said it so quietly, she couldn't be certain he had meant her to hear it or not, but she was fairly sure she hadn't imagined it. If he hadn't wanted her to hear it, then why would he have said it? Unless he meant it.

Psyche woke, as usual, just as the sun was rising. Sheerness slept on, pressed closely against her, his breathing warm and steady against the back of her neck. Ordinarily, it was a pleasant, comforting sensation, but after what he said as they were going to sleep, it troubled her. After the day of Myron's funeral, in the solarium, he had never said it again…until last night. He hadn't mentioned marriage again, either. In the meantime, her feelings for him had changed…or at least had become more solidified.

She tried to hold still until she was ready to get out of bed because she didn't want to wake him. She wasn't ready to talk to him yet. She had to decide how she was going to react. If he had said it without intending her to know, she supposed she should act as if she didn't. But it would mean he *did* love her, and she had been wrong…so very wrong. If he had said it meaning for her to hear it, would that mean he planned to renew his attempt to get her to marry him? Or had he said it for her to hear it but still *meant* it? The simplest way to settle the matter would be to come right out and ask him, but that would be too easy, and as the whole matter hinged on her doubt of his sincerity, she wasn't sure he would give her an honest answer.

And she loved him. The feeling she had on the swing that seemed to have happened a lifetime ago had come to pass. She tried not to think about what would happen once they returned to England because she didn't believe it could end well. She couldn't live without him, but she couldn't marry him if all he wanted was someone to provide an heir, no matter how much she loved him. She still had her pride…for the moment.

The sun started to rise higher as she lay thinking, and she soon felt it had been up long enough to warm the water in the cove. She could go swimming in the pool in the garden, which would be hot regardless of the time of day, but she had things to see in the cove and just outside it. The pool could wait for another day. The swim would also help clear her head, and she would have plenty of time for a long swim before breakfast.

She carefully eased her way out of bed, and she didn't breathe again until she was out without waking Sheerness. She bustled around the room picking up discarded clothes, folding hers and putting them away, folding his and setting them at the foot of the bed. She didn't know why he thought she didn't put things away. She put things away, when she had places to put them…when she wasn't using them…when she didn't have other things on her mind. She pulled out the sari she had brought with her, made of beautiful amethyst-colored silk with a *choli* of an eggplant color. It would be perfect for going to swim because it would be easy to take off and put back on, even if she was wet, and it just lent itself to the weather.

She moved back to the side of the bed and looked at Sheerness sleeping there as she coiled her hair up out of the way. He had shifted in his sleep after she got out of bed and turned more onto his back. As she gazed at his relaxed features, his hair hanging down on his forehead, Psyche thought he looked as innocent and boyish as Philip…and just as vulnerable. She had discovered he was that, in so many ways.

She went to the door to the terrace and carefully closed it behind her. She went down the stairs that led to the terrace below and steadily made her way down the outside of the house to the cove. The temperature was warming, and she looked forward to a good swim. The tide was in, and the cove deepened quickly. There was a shelf around the edge where the water didn't get beyond five feet deep, but closer to the center, and at the inlet, it was just as deep as the water outside the cove along the cliff.

The *Athena* was moored at the pier, but the other boats were gone. She didn't know if Nikos intended to take the boat out that morning, but she expected not. It was Sunday, and even if he let everyone think he was Muslim, as an actual Greek Orthodox, doing anything close to work on Sunday would be avoided. Considering how late he had been up the previous night, Psyche doubted he would be up early, even if he weren't going anywhere.

Psyche walked onto the pier and looked down. It was long enough that the water was deep at the end and along much of the side to keep the boat from running aground when it was moored during low tide. Psyche stuck her toe in and decided it was warm enough, at least near the surface. There was a ladder nearby that she could use to climb out. No one was around that she would be nervous about seeing her naked, except for Nikos, and she was sure he would be gentlemanly. She took off her clothes, uncoiled her hair, and dove in.

Her belief that the water was warm near the surface proved right. It was comfortably warm to about five feet then gradually became colder but not unbearably so. She paddled around for a few minutes to stretch her muscles, and then she went for a small opening in the wall of the cove near the tower, too small for a boat but easily navigable for a swimmer. The current was strong outside the cove, but not too difficult to manage close to the cliff.

She floated on her back toward the tower, occasionally looking below her in the water. She could see schools of fish darting about beneath her, occasionally squid or cuttlefish or shrimp, but she was looking for the statue. When she found it, she dove for the bottom. Chrissoula had never seen it, and Psyche wanted to tell her exactly how it looked.

When Psyche reached the bottom, she held onto the statue to keep herself anchored. It was a nymph of some type, clad in a chiton. She sat on a pedestal, her legs folded beneath her, one hand balanced on the ground at her side, the other resting on her hip. She looked downward, her features thoughtful with a slight smile. It was a very beautiful work, made in marble. Nikos had found the perfect monument, and it did look like his sister. Psyche had no notion of where he got it, but the British Museum would be envious.

Psyche thought she saw something move from the corner of her eye and turned her head to look, but it had been only a blur. It was probably a fish, or a school of fish, surprised to have their world invaded by a human. She looked at the statue again one last time and made her way back to the surface. She took note of the entrance to the cave as she passed, and she would go back to it after she went to the top for some air. She didn't have enough to make it this trip. It was her understanding the tunnel was a fair length. She felt a current move past her back and heard the sound of bubbles behind her, and Psyche frowned and turned to look. Again, there was nothing there.

When she reached the surface, she looked around herself, but she didn't see anything. She didn't see any boats nearby, which definitely might have caused concern, considering she was swimming naked outside the cove. When she looked below herself in the water, she didn't see anything. She had seen crabs scuttling around on the seabed, and she could still see them, as well as urchins and other small creatures, but whatever had swam behind her was nowhere to be seen. It had either been a school of fish or something much larger, and she had not imagined it. The motion she had felt was too strong to have been caused by a single, small mullet. Fish didn't bother her, but being outside the cove did make her nervous about sharks.

She'd never actually seen a shark before, not a live one, but she had heard about them. Gregory had brought back a dead one after a sea adventure. It was enormous, with rows and rows of sharp teeth, and it wasn't something Psyche wanted to meet in the water. Chrissoula said there were sharks in the Aegean, but she hadn't mentioned how big they were or what kind. She hadn't seemed concerned about them, but after seeing the one Gregory had caught, Psyche had her qualms. Chrissoula had mentioned other animals—rays and moray eels, but even after saying what they were capable of doing, she didn't seem concerned about them, either. Now that Psyche was here and thought about what her maid told her, she was having second thoughts.

After she swam around on the surface a little longer, contemplating whether or not she should swim back to the cove and come back to look at the cave later, when she had someone nearby, she decided to take her chances. She had been floating for several minutes and had not seen anything. She dove back under the water and went to the entrance of the cave. It was a dark, gaping hole, about five feet in diameter, positioned about a third of the way up the side of the cliff from the bottom. Psyche got the oddest sensation she was being watched, but when she looked around, there was nothing. She shook her head and swam into the cave.

Chrissoula had described the way. It was a long tunnel that gradually widened and curved upward to the left. There were no off-shooting branches, so there was no way to get lost. Psyche swam through, keeping her distance from the walls, just in case there were small places for animals to hide that liked to live in dark caves and eat unsuspecting passersby. The light from the entrance eventually began to diminish, especially once she started upward, and Psyche could tell she was doing so as the pressure in her ears began to change. But as she swam up, she could see light again, and her eyes filled with amazement as she breached the surface and had reached the cave proper.

Chrissoula said she and Nikos called it the Cave of Wonders. As Psyche looked around herself, she could see why. It was true the only entrance was through the tunnel, but it wasn't dark. It was apparently very close to the side of the cliff, and over time there had been holes broken by one means or another. None were large enough for a person to fit through, but they allowed light to enter, and it looked like a night sky lit by a constellation of stars. The walls of the cave were a glaring white limestone, and when the light shone through the holes, it reflected off to make the inside of the cave very bright.

There was a small beach at the back, and Psyche swam to it and climbed out to rest. The water inside the cave was colder than outside. She could hear birds chirping and singing, what seemed to be dozens of them, which used the holes to enter and build nests in its sheltered environs. There were stalactites and stalagmites, some joining one another to form columns, and they sparkled like diamonds from the light reflecting off the water dripping on them.

It *was* wonderful. She could only imagine how much fun it must have been to have this secret place to play as children. Psyche was sure Nikos and Chrissoula weren't the first children (or people of any age, for that matter) to have found it, considering how long their family had lived here, but to have a place to go for solitude must have been marvelous. Like the solarium she and Pandora shared. In the end, it had been Chrissoula's sanctuary. Psyche lay back on the sand and looked around herself for a moment before she closed her eyes and listened to the birds. It was loud, but also—bizarrely—very peaceful.

≪ ≫

Sheerness slowly woke with a slight frown as the light from the windows shined against his face to warm it uncomfortably. He rolled over to reach for Psyche, only to find she wasn't there…again. He opened his eyes and raised himself on his elbows to look around, but she wasn't in the room. His clothes sat in a neat pile at the end of the bed.

He was finding these changes in her behavior disconcerting. First, there was the neatness. Now there was the rising early and not being there when he woke. She had been at the park to ride well before anyone else, the same as he did, and he got the impression she was there for some time before he arrived. Until they got to Thessaloniki, she hadn't been waking up until after he did. He missed that. And he was troubled she wasn't telling him where she was going, almost as if she didn't want him to go with her.

He had expected her to still be there, and that had disappointed him. Last night had been remarkable and worth every second he had waited. Now he wanted more. He was convinced Psyche had feelings for him. He wasn't sure what kind. Last night, lust was a strong possibility. He was willing to take that for now. She had tried to assure him that whatever was between them was exclusive; that gave him hope there was something more than physical attraction. But he couldn't find out if she was never there.

He sighed and pulled on his clothes. He would go to his room to change, brush his teeth, *try* to brush his hair, and make his bed look as if it had been slept in…just in case anyone was looking into that. Then he would go looking for Psyche. Hopefully it wouldn't take him as long as it had yesterday.

Psyche eventually decided to leave the cave. She wasn't sure how long she had been there, and she wasn't sure what time it was at all. If she was at least in the cove and it was time for breakfast, Ioanna would be able to find her and let her know. No one would find her in the cave. Her stomach was starting to rumble, so breakfast could not be so very far away.

The water was a bit of a shock as she slipped back into it. She hadn't noticed how cold it was when she had come out because it had been a gradual change, but she could certainly tell now. She swam down the tunnel, and it was easier to see her way out. The water temperature began to change for the better, and she was grateful. She would go back to the cove for a bit. Then she would go in search of breakfast, if Ioanna didn't call her first.

When she came back to the side of the cliff, she almost inhaled water in surprise and paused just inside the cave. Waiting outside the entrance was a small pod of dolphins. They had to be what she had felt before, and they *were* waiting. She wasn't imagining it. There were four of them: three adults and one tiny (in comparison) baby. They were looking at her curiously but no less so than she at them, and it didn't seem they intended to harm her.

After watching them for a few seconds, she couldn't wait any longer and had to go for air. She was surprised when they followed her. When she reached the top, she took a deep breath and floated on her back to rest. She was curious why she had been unable to see them. The adults were longer than she was tall, and although dolphins were fast swimmers, the water was clear enough she should have been able to see them. She suspected they had swam into the cove through the same opening she had used, as if playing hide-and-seek. Until she went into the cave, they could have hidden in there as well.

As she floated on the surface, they swam around her in a circle. Psyche smiled in wonder at her newfound swimming companions. One would occasionally spray a fine mist through its blowhole before taking a breath, and Psyche grinned. She wondered if they would follow her to the cove. She was sure they had already been there because there was no other way they could have hidden from her so quickly otherwise. After she rested a few minutes more, she went back under the water and began to swim for the opening. She smiled to herself when she saw they were indeed going to follow. This would be something interesting to tell her family. They had all *seen* dolphins before, but none of them could brag they had gotten to *swim* with them...except her.

Psyche still had some air left after they made it to the cove, and she went to the middle and floated under the water as the dolphins continued to swim around her. One swam very close, and she reached out to smooth her hand along the animal's back near its dorsal fin, finding the texture of its skin fascinating. It was slick without being slimy and felt almost like her own skin under the water. Psyche went to the surface to take a breath, but she went under again, staying on top only a minute or two. The dolphins were extraordinary, and that they were there with her was surreal.

Sheerness was crossing the terrace to his room when he casually glanced down to the cove to see if the *Athena* was still there. Seeing that it was, he started to continue on his way when he spotted the bright purple on the pier. When he looked beyond it, he saw Psyche in the middle of the cove, and *fins* were circling her.

He felt a surge of panic, and he began to make his way as quickly as he could down to the cove, his eyes never leaving her. His heart went into his throat as he watched her go beneath the surface, and one of the fins dipped below to follow her and moved very close. She was being pulled along beneath the surface. He was about halfway there and could see no quicker way to get to her. When he reached the next terrace, he was startled to find Nikos standing there, watching, his hands clasped behind his back.

"Bloody hell!" gasped Sheerness in surprise.

Nikos looked at him with a grin. "Thea has made new friends."

"What?" said Sheerness in consternation.

"Dolphins are very lucky, you know," said Nikos casually. "To have one breach the wave at the bow of your vessel is a sign your voyage will be successful and safe."

Sheerness watched in astonishment when, at that moment, Psyche and the animal burst to the surface and rose high into the air. He heard her laugh joyously as she released the dolphin's fin and did a somersault in the air before diving back below.

"To have them befriend you like this," continued Nikos as he waved his hand toward the cove, "means you are *very* special."

"Dolphins?" asked Sheerness dully. Nikos nodded. "They'll drown her," said Sheerness worriedly.

"If my sister taught her to swim, she can hold her breath almost as long as they can. We sponge dive and spear fish in my family…a long tradition, and if you can't hold your breath at least four minutes, you're useless. I think they see a kindred spirit in Thea: an animal that can swim like a fish but still has to surface to breathe air." Nikos chuckled.

Sheerness looked at her with the dolphins. She was enjoying herself and not in any danger. It was fascinating to watch as she held onto a fin, sometimes being pulled along the surface, sometimes dipping under it, but clearly having the time of her life. He was familiar with dolphins; he saw them all the time at home, but he couldn't recall anyone saying they had been *swimming* with them.

"Is there anyone or anything that dislikes her?" he asked in bewilderment.

Nikos looked at him and roared with laughter. "I don't know! You know her better. All I have is what I am told in letters, but it is my understanding she is generous and humble…and honest to the point of it being ridiculous. I've also been told she is very empathetic and judges herself more harshly than she judges anyone else. I don't know what the dolphins see in her," he said with a grin, "but I find qualities such as those very difficult to dislike."

Sheerness continued to watch her. Even from this distance, he could see she was naked. It seemed absolutely right she should be that way swimming with the dolphins, but he wasn't sure he liked Nikos seeing her that way. For his part, Nikos didn't even seem to notice. She could have been dressed in black wool from head to toe for all the concern he showed. Actually, that might have attracted more of his attention. Sheerness did notice, however, that the jealousy he would have wallowed in yesterday didn't seem to be there, and he was amazed…and relieved. He didn't like feeling that way, and Psyche found it unwarranted. Nikos turned to look at him.

"You should go for a swim, too. It will be at least an hour or two before Ioanna has breakfast ready." He grinned. "She's still sleeping. I was going to do a little fishing, but I can wait," he said with an amused smile.

Sheerness tilted his head sideways and nodded. It was a good idea, and he could be with Psyche. Nikos clapped him on the shoulder and left. Sheerness continued on his way to the cove, and he discovered that finding his way on the outside of the house was easier than inside. Psyche didn't see him; she was engrossed in the dolphins. He pulled off his clothes next to hers and dove in.

If Psyche didn't know he was there, the dolphins did. One swam over to investigate while the others stayed with Psyche. It swam around him in a few small circles, and then it dipped under the water and swam beneath him before coming up behind him to nose him in the backside, almost as if hurrying him along. Sheerness looked at it nervously as it swam away to rejoin the others.

Psyche was treading water, and the dolphins weren't far away, their heads above water as well. They were making high-pitched squeaks and clicks, almost as if they were talking. Psyche was talking back in Greek. He smiled amusedly as he neared her. Of course, being in Greece, the dolphins would *have* to speak Greek.

"Are you sure they don't speak Italian…or Arabic?" he called humorously when he was about ten feet away from her.

Psyche turned to look at him in surprise before she gave him a slow smile. "Being the refined, intelligent creatures they are, I would say it *has* to be Greek." One of the dolphins squirted water at her face and squeaked and shook its head, almost as if it were laughing. "But given their quirky sense of humor, it could just as easily be French."

He laughed. "*Maman* would have something to say about that."

"She would probably agree with me," chortled Psyche.

The dolphin that had nudged him slapped its tail on the surface of the water to splash Sheerness in the face, and he looked at it in surprise as it swam away.

"I don't think he likes me," said Sheerness as he eyed it warily.

"*She*, actually, seems to like you…*a lot*," said Psyche mildly. "I think they're all female." She nodded her head at one swimming toward the inlet to the cove in a wide circle. "I know she is because she has a baby."

"How do you know she has a baby?" asked Sheerness doubtfully.

"Because it's with her. Go under and look."

Sheerness eyed her curiously, as if he thought she might be teasing, before he went under the surface. It was almost too far away to see, even in the clear water, but he could just make out a smaller form swimming beside the adult, and it was obviously nursing. He came back above the water to look at Psyche.

"So why do you think they're *all* female?" he asked dryly.

Psyche shrugged. "I don't know. It's not as if I've any knowledge of telling one sex from another, but it just seems likely. They get along well together, and they don't seem to be aggressive enough to be male."

Sheerness raised an eyebrow and quirked his lips. "Really?"

One swam between them on its side, and Psyche reached out a hand to rub along its belly as it went past. The one with the baby continued to swim in a wide circle, and Psyche suspected they were going to be leaving. She didn't think Sheerness's arrival was the cause; they were ready to find food. She was ready to find food herself. She had been playing in the cove with the dolphins for a while, and now she was ravenous. She watched with a sigh as they left the cove and swam away.

"Was it something I said?" asked Sheerness wryly.

Psyche grinned. "Hungry, I imagine, and they certainly wouldn't eat *you*. It would give them indigestion."

Sheerness slapped water at her with his hand and grinned. Psyche splashed him back with a giggle and swam away on her back, kicking more water at him with her feet. He looked at her in surprise and swam after her. Even with her early start, he was easily able to catch up because she was swimming on her back and he was not. When he caught her, he grabbed her around the waist and dunked her head under the water. She came up sputtering, a shocked look on her face, and she grinned wickedly as she returned the favor.

She used his thigh to push off and spun around to swim away underwater. She looked behind herself to see him coming after her and smiled as she continued to swim. When she heard splashing over her head, she looked up to see he had surfaced and swam past her. She frowned and went to the top as well. They were in a small grotto near the base of the tower where the top of the cliff overhung the bottom slightly, almost creating a cave, but only in that it made the small nook very private. It couldn't be seen from anywhere except the water. The sun reached it to warm the water to a nice temperature, and the shelf around the edge of the cove provided a comfortable place to sit.

"That's cheating," she huffed.

Sheerness laughed to see her so nettled. "I wasn't aware we were racing."

Psyche paddled over to the shelf and sat. The tide was going out, and she was able to sit with the water just coming to her collarbone. It was nice to sit for a while. She had been swimming for a couple hours, and she was tiring. Added to that was hunger pangs. Her fingers had long since become pruny. She was ready to get out and would do that after she rested a few minutes.

Sheerness swam over to her and put his hands on the shelf to either side of her hips, theoretically trapping her. He smiled at her and wiggled his eyebrows mischievously. Psyche smiled with a silent laugh and shook her head. He leaned toward her to kiss her, and Psyche sighed softly at the back of her throat, one of her hands moving to curl in the hair at the back of his head while the other moved to his shoulder. Without her hands to hold her still against the rock, her body floated up to brush against his, and the combination of sensations she felt was indescribably pleasurable.

He moved them a little higher on the shelf using his hands, and he trailed his lips down her neck to her chest to lave his tongue against a nipple, and Psyche arched toward him ecstatically. She should be worried about someone seeing them, but at the moment, she could care less. All she could think about was him and the exquisite feeling of him next to her, touching her. The weightlessness of the water, the feel of it lapping against her as it gently moved her body against his, made her forget anything else.

Sheerness kissed her hungrily as he slowly glided into her, and Psyche moaned as this new source of pleasure made it all almost too intense. She anchored herself against him by loosely hooking one of her legs over his, and she grew dizzy as he slowly moved in and out of her. She was literally floating in a sea of ecstasy, and she thought she was going to faint.

She released a strangled cry as she began to orgasm, and Sheerness covered her mouth with his to muffle it as he continued to thrust into her. She clung to him weakly as wave after wave sent shocks through her body until she felt him tense and groan against her lips as he reached his own end, his movements slowly stopping. Both of them were panting as he ran his lips down her neck before resting his forehead tiredly against her shoulder.

Every time they made love, it was like a sensory whirlwind for Psyche. She felt disoriented and satiated, and she could think of nothing else except him and the *next* time. He was like an addiction, and that couldn't be good. She couldn't sleep without him in some fashion, be it imaginary or actually having him with her. She could deny him nothing when he was with her like this, and that worried her.

"I'm hungry," she said dully.

"You'll have to wait another hour or so. Ioanna's still sleeping."

"Must be nice," said Psyche enviously.

"Aren't you sleeping well these days?" asked Sheerness with a frown.

"As well as I ever have," said Psyche calmly. "Why?"

"You were up before me yesterday and today. I just thought something might be bothering you."

Psyche shrugged dismissively. "I'm always awake before you. It's just here I have things to do."

"You are not always awake before me."

"Yes, I am," said Psyche slowly. "I may not be up and moving around before you, but I am awake."

"Do you mean to say all this time you've just been *pretending* to be asleep when I've left your cabin in the morning?" he asked shortly. Psyche blushed uncomfortably and nodded. "All this time, I could have been…we could have been…?" he trailed off disbelievingly.

"What?" asked Psyche curiously, lifting an eyebrow.

"Nothing," said Sheerness flatly, clenching his jaw. "Why? Why have you been acting like you're asleep when you're not?"

Psyche felt her heart starting to thump against her ribs in panic. She could tell him the truth and have him angry, or she could tell him she didn't want to give him the reason with the same result. The question she had to ask herself was: which would be worse for her? As a general rule, the truth was always best, but in this instance, she wasn't so sure. Unfortunately, those were her choices; he hadn't really left an option for a half-truth or an *alternate* truth. The part she could get by without telling him to preserve her self-respect wasn't going to make the other part any better.

"Well? Are you going to tell me, or are you trying to come up with a story?" he asked stiffly.

"I don't tell *stories*, if you are using it to imply that I lie. I'm debating whether I should tell you anything at all," said Psyche angrily, "and it would serve you right if I didn't."

"Don't do me any favors, then," said Sheerness coldly.

"Believe me, not telling you *is* the favor," shot Psyche exasperatedly. Sheerness rolled his eyes and shook his head disbelievingly. "Don't you think that if I don't want to tell you, I might have a good reason? And why is it such a catastrophic thing that I did pretend to be asleep?"

"Because it's dishonest."

Psyche's face blanched. He couldn't leave it alone. Perhaps it had been dishonest, but it wasn't lying...not really. There was one reason she had done it, and then it had become a habit she had started to enjoy. She should never have told him because now she couldn't anymore. It would be one less way to defend herself, one less place of sanctuary. She looked away from him and sighed tiredly.

"I did it because I didn't want to have sex with you," she said woodenly.

Sheerness felt as if she had just slapped him. Of all the things he thought she would say, that was not among them. She was right: it would have been a favor not to have told him. And he had no doubt...no doubt, she was being purposely *brutally* honest. Yet it was obvious she had wanted to last night. She had seduced him. Just now, she had wanted him. There had never been a time when he felt he had forced himself on her...not once.

"I'm sorry you find it so repugnant," he said brusquely.

Psyche turned to look at him in dismay. "It isn't that. It's never been that," she assured.

"Then don't you think a simple *no* would have sufficed? Was it necessary to resort to dishonesty?" he bit out through stiff lips.

"It wasn't dishonest, and yes, it was necessary," said Psyche firmly.

"Why?" Psyche looked away from him, her cheeks coloring brightly, and she drew her knees to her chest and wrapped her arms around them protectively. "Why couldn't you just say no?"

"Because I can't say no to that...not from you," she choked out, and she put a hand over her mouth and shook her head, not quite believing she had just told him. Her cheeks were tingling...they were so red, and she wished the rock she sat on would open up and swallow her.

Sheerness's eyebrows rose in astonishment, and he tried not to laugh. She was disturbed by the entire conversation, particularly that bit of information. It put the whole thing into an entirely different light for him, though.

"You didn't mean to tell me that, did you?" he asked in measured tones, trying to contain his mirth.

Psyche couldn't look at him or speak, and she shook her head. If her emotions weren't so completely involved in what they were discussing, she might have been able to find some other—honest—excuse to provide to him, but she was finding it difficult to think straight at the moment. She didn't like that. There were reasons she needed to be able to say no, and since she couldn't seem to bring herself to do it, pretending to be asleep had been her way to avoid it altogether. Now there was one more thing she couldn't use to defend herself.

Sheerness's amusement waned as he looked at her. She was embarrassed to have blurted that out. And ashamed. She had a trapped look as she sat there curled up as she was. He didn't know why she had told him. He was sure she hadn't meant to, and someone else would not have. It was almost as if she had been incapable of *not* telling him, as if it had been involuntary. He had been told it was physically impossible for her to lie. He was beginning to wonder if that might be true after all.

It was obvious it distressed her that he knew. Just because she couldn't say no didn't mean she *wanted* to say yes. He did understand that...truly. Now she was afraid he would take advantage of it. To know she couldn't refuse him was tempting, but he couldn't bring himself to use it. There were any number of reasons why not, and he wasn't going to try believing she couldn't refuse because she loved him. That, too, was tempting, but finding something irresistible didn't mean one had affection for it. He understood that as well.

He reached out a hand to brush it across her cheek, and he wasn't surprised when she flinched away from him.

"I'll forget you said it," he said quietly.

Psyche looked at him, her expression serious. "No, you won't," she said solemnly.

"Then I'll at least try not to let it go to my head," he said dryly. That coaxed a wan smile from her, and he gave her a gentle half-smile of his own. He carefully reached up to run a finger along her jaw to her chin and looked into her eyes. "Whatever *you* want," he said softly.

Psyche looked at him reflectively, and she leaned forward to kiss him tentatively on the lips, brushing her fingers down his cheek. She didn't really believe him, but he seemed sincere. She could hope. He said he would forget, but that was a lie, even if unintentional. Whether he would use the knowledge was something she would have to wait and see. For now, she couldn't resist, but if he started to use it, he would find out just how *pig-headed* she could be.

Chapter Twenty Nine

By the time Psyche and Sheerness left the cove and dressed, she was almost weak with hunger. She was willing to eat just about anything, and she hoped Ioanna had breakfast ready. She would even settle for a piece of bread, anything to make the sensation that her insides were gnawing themselves stop. Sheerness looked at what she was wearing in surprise.

"A sari?" he asked her doubtfully.

"Why not?" asked Psyche evenly with a shrug.

"Where did you learn to wear a sari?"

"From Shailesh. She's the daughter of our butler, Rajeesh, and also one of our maids. Where did you learn what one was?"

"I've actually been to India."

"Really?" she said in surprise. "Tannaz and Shailesh say it's always very hot and humid there, and the mosquitoes fly around like flocks of birds."

"That about sums it up," said Sheerness with a grin. "I like the food better here, though."

"I hope Lilly is doing well there," said Psyche absently, her face forming into a frown as they walked up the stairs from the cove.

"Who's Lilly?"

"Well, she used to be Manson, but now she's married a soldier named MacNeil stationed in India. Her sister, Victoria, married Lord Drake, who Lilly was once engaged to herself."

"Oh, yes," said Sheerness slowly in recollection. "That is all rather odd. I don't know Drake very well, but his wife…," he trailed off and shook his head.

"What?" asked Psyche with a frown.

"She's not all there, I think," said Sheerness thoughtfully.

Psyche's eyes rounded in amazement. "That's what Pandora and I think, too. Well, all of my sisters think that, actually. Arachne doesn't even believe Lilly married Sean, but there was a letter, so it *must* be true. I don't imagine

Lilly likes India much," said Psyche with a shrug. "It must be hard for her to live there, not knowing the language or having any family, and she's not capable of fending for herself."

"Yes, but she's married."

"To a *soldier*. The man can't stay home and see to his wife, and in a place like that—"she shook her head—"it's like putting a lamb in a den of wolves."

"That's a bit melodramatic, don't you think?"

"You've been there," said Psyche matter-of-factly. "You tell me."

Sheerness frowned consideringly. She was right...up to a point. Actually, she was closer to the mark than he would care to admit. Most of the natives were friendly, but there were others who loathed the English. If you weren't strong enough, India could swallow you whole.

"Nikos said he would take us to see a few things tomorrow. I don't know what he has in mind, but as he lives here, he's bound to know of some interesting places. Climbing Mount Olympus would be fun."

"Climbing Mount Olympus?" hooted Sheerness amusedly.

"Why not?"

"I don't think that would be as easy as it sounds. I can't recall hearing of anyone ever climbing it before."

"Well, maybe no one was along who could write," said Psyche practically. Sheerness looked at her and started to laugh. "Well, just because no one's ever written they've done it doesn't mean they haven't. How many things do you think there are in history that have happened that no one knows happened?"

"Too many to count, I'm sure."

"All right, then," said Psyche simply.

She was leading them through the house to the kitchen, and as they approached it, she was thankful to smell food. Her stomach rumbled noisily, and Sheerness looked at her and laughed amusedly. Psyche's cheeks pinkened, and she pretended she hadn't heard a thing. Ioanna and another woman were in the kitchen, and she looked up and smiled when she saw them come in.

"Good morning, Thea," said Ioanna cheerfully. "I was just about to send Stefania for you. Food is on the table, and I'll have coffee for you soon."

"Thank you," said Psyche gratefully.

Ioanna looked at what Psyche was wearing. "I think you've missed the current fashion by more than a thousand years," she teased.

Psyche giggled. "It's still all the rage in India." She tugged on Sheerness's arm to go to the terrace.

Nikos was there with the girls, and he had Yelena sitting in his lap while she gummed a piece of *loukomathes*. Her face was sticky, as were her hands, and she had drool down her chin that dripped onto her father's sleeve. She looked up at Psyche and grinned with her one tooth and held out her treat in offering. Psyche chortled as she sat down beside them and tweaked the end of Yelena's nose affectionately.

"You eat it, little one," said Psyche amusedly. "I'll get my own. Thank you."

Ioanna came out with two cups of coffee, and Psyche smiled appreciatively as she put food on her plate. She was starving, and she wondered if she needed to start secreting things in her room to snack on to tide her over between when she woke and when everyone else did. Chrissoula would usually bring her a cup of tea and some biscuits at home when she came in to help Psyche dress after her ride, just something to keep her from becoming too hungry before the family had breakfast. At Pandora's, it was coffee with toast and strawberry preserves, Psyche's favorite. On the *Medea*, she couldn't wander on the berth deck in search of food, and she didn't feel comfortable nosing about in Ioanna's kitchen. Maybe breakfast would be earlier tomorrow. That would help. Freddie had started bringing her breakfast a little earlier while she was aboard ship, but nine was still too long to wait. Here, the last two mornings, breakfast hadn't been ready until almost eleven. That was far too long.

Psyche devoured her food as slowly as she could, but she was so hungry, it was difficult. She ate until she almost didn't want to move. *Full as a tick* was an expression that came to mind. Luckily, there was plenty to eat, but no one else ate nearly as much. That made her feel gluttonous. She would have to find a way to eat before breakfast, or this was going to become common. It wasn't very ladylike, but when one was starving, manners weren't something that ranked very high on the list of concerns.

Everyone was done eating, and the girls had already left the table to play in the garden when Ioanna came out carrying handfuls of letters.

"I'm sorry I forgot about this, but these came before you arrived," she said with a grin. "It was one of the ways we knew you would be here eventually," she chortled.

Psyche's eyes rounded in surprise as Ioanna handed her a pile of what seemed to be dozens of letters. "Oh my goodness!" she gasped. "I never thought anyone would write me. I hope this didn't put you to too much trouble. You must let me know how much it cost."

Ioanna chuckled and shook her head. "It's been interesting and worth the expense, wondering who we would get a letter from next. For a while, almost every day, someone was sending you a letter." She reached into a pocket on her apron and held out five or six to Sheerness. "These came for you, too."

He was startled. Like Psyche, he hadn't expected anyone to write, and he certainly hadn't expected they would be sent to Nikos and Ioanna.

"Thank you," he said quietly as he took them.

Psyche started to tear them open and begin reading them at the table, but she decided to take them to her room. She had brought her things with her to write, just in case, and she could answer them once she finished. She looked at Sheerness curiously. He wasn't impatient to read his own. He looked at the letters in his hands with a bemused frown then glanced at Nikos.

"I was wondering if you could take me to Thessaloniki today. I need to see how my crew is doing."

"Of course," said Nikos and stood up from the table. "Let me tend to a few things, and we'll go. Thirty minutes?" Sheerness nodded, and Nikos left.

Psyche frowned. He was leaving now? "Aren't you going to read your letters?" she asked confusedly.

"They will still be letters when I get to them," he said evenly.

Psyche looked at him in puzzlement, but she was impatient to read her own. The crew was fine without him, but she could understand his concern. She stood up, holding her letters. Sheerness stood as well to go with her. He still didn't know how to find his own way, and he needed to change.

"Do you want to come with?" he asked as they walked to their rooms.

"No, thank you. I have these to occupy me," said Psyche, hefting the letters in her hands.

Sheerness grinned. "Yes, those will take care of your time for the rest of the day, I'm sure."

"Tell everyone I said hallo," she said calmly, "and can you see how Freddie is doing with Waddlesworth?"

"That could be arranged," said Sheerness mildly.

Sheerness opened the door to Psyche's room once they reached it, since her hands were full, and he followed her in. She saw the bed was made and turned to look at him.

"You didn't do that, did you?" she asked him suspiciously.

"No, actually, I didn't," he said dryly with a slight smile.

He hadn't made his own bed look slept in. He wouldn't have completely mussed the covers, but he would have at least wrinkled them...flipped a corner on the counterpane, just something to make it look as if it had been used. It was obvious it hadn't been, and he hoped it would not cause gossip.

"Good, the maids would be upset if you did their work," said Psyche with a grin as she went to put the letters on the writing table near the fireplace.

Sheerness came up behind her and put his arms around her waist, kissing her neck before he rested his chin on her shoulder, looking at the unbelievable amount of correspondence she had received. She put her arms over his and relaxed against him, leaning her head against his. This was nice, just being together. There was no arguing, no sexual tension, just *intimacy*.

"I'll see you when I get back," he said quietly, turning her in his arms to kiss her softly. "I have to go change."

Psyche ran her fingers down his cheek to his chin then tweaked his nose. "Have fun," she said with a grin.

Sheerness looked at her in surprise, and then he chuckled and shook his head as he released her, going to the door to the terrace to go to his own room.

Psyche looked after him for a few minutes, and then she sat at the desk to look at her letters. She flipped through them, trying to decide how to organize them. Ioanna had stacked them as they had been received, which might or might not be the chronological order for them. Psyche decided to sort them by who sent them. Once she had them opened, before she read them, they would have a date, and she could sort them by when they were written.

The thickest pile was, by far, the letters she had received from her twin. The next was that from Chrissoula, and then her parents. She had received at least one letter from every member of her family, including—much to her delight—Gregory. There were letters from Amalie, the Yeardley children, Sheerness's mother, Georgiana, Sir James, Lord Georgie, and a few others from people she hadn't even written, people she hadn't been aware even knew where she was going. She was overwhelmed by the number of letters. There were almost four dozen.

Once she had them sorted by sender, she had to decide which ones to open first. Although the ones she wanted to read most were those from Pandora and Chrissoula, Psyche felt the best thing would be to read them from least to most important. It took her some time to determine what that was. It obviously meant that those from her twin and her maid would be last. The ones from her parents, her family, Sheerness's family. The ones sent from people she hadn't written were least important. She would start with those.

She was preparing to open the first one when there was a knock on the door. She looked at it thoughtfully for a moment from her seat before she got up to answer it. Stefania was there with Evangelina.

"Mamma said it's time for dinner," said Stefania with a giggle.

"Goodness! Is it really?" said Psyche in surprise.

She went to the dresser for her watch. It was after two. She couldn't believe it had taken so long just to organize the letters, but now it was done. After dinner, she would come back to start reading and write answers. She put her watch around her neck and left with Stefania and Evangelina.

When Psyche came back from dinner, she had a basket with a variety of baked goods. She had explained her dilemma to Ioanna, and she had laughed amusedly. She provided Psyche with things she could eat before breakfast because, Ioanna explained, even when she wasn't running behind, it still wasn't served until ten. Psyche was grateful for the food, and it would be more than enough for several days. It would also be nice to have on hand should she get hungry between dinner and supper, which was usually served around eight or nine. With one problem solved, Psyche started reading.

The first few were easily dealt with. They were mostly wishes for a safe and pleasant trip and belated sympathy for Myron's death. They didn't warrant a reply. Lord Georgie's was much the same, but she composed a quick answer back and let him know she thought Lucy would much prefer somewhere like France or Italy for a honeymoon, since he had asked. Lucy didn't strike her as someone who would appreciate ancient Greek ruins, but the shopping of either of those countries would be to her liking.

The letter from Sir James was very nice and full of wishes for success in her endeavors. He still hadn't found any useful information on where the map on her necklace might lead, but he could tell her where it would *not*. That was actually helpful. It told her where she needn't bother looking. She sent a letter back, and although she did ask a few questions, she didn't expect she would receive an answer in time for anything he might reply with to help her. She didn't know how long Sheerness intended to stay in Greece, but she didn't expect it would be for the length of time it would take her letter to go all the way to England and for Sir James to send an answer back.

She then read the one from Georgiana. It was brief and not very cheerful. She thanked Psyche for her touching letter and gave her sympathy regarding Myron. From the tone of it, Psyche never would have guessed there was a relationship between Myron and Georgiana. She told Psyche how Lorelei was doing, and that she was glad to be back in the country. Then toward the end of it, to Psyche's shock, Georgiana said she was expecting a child in March. The poor woman would now be truly bound to her husband. While he was currently in prison, he wouldn't be there forever. Before, when it was just her and Lorelei, she might have stood a chance of escaping him one day. Not with a child. Psyche replied, offering congratulations, but the words seemed hollow.

She moved on to the letters from Sheerness's family. She had only one from the countess, but it was nice, and it was also one she had not solicited. The main thing his mother told Psyche was that his birthday was the eleventh of October and that she would appreciate it if Psyche would wish him many happy returns. Psyche chuckled and shook her head. She didn't know how his family celebrated birthdays, but it always involved more than just wishing many happy returns for her own. She would surreptitiously investigate what they did do for birthdays, and then she would plan something of her own. She wrote a reply and added it to the ones for Sir James, Lord Georgie, and Georgiana, and she tried to keep in mind that she should write another letter to Josephine after his birthday to let her know how it went.

There were two from the Yeardleys, all of them writing their own bits in the same letter. Philip wasn't able to do much more than sign his name and say hallo, but he included pictures. Josie and Jerome had taken turns on who was the major and minor composer for each missive, and Psyche chuckled at the differences in the two. Jerome's was more formal and polite. Josie's was airy and full of details about things they had been doing. Psyche missed them, almost as much as she missed her own family. She wrote back and included a picture of her own, one of her sketches of the Erechtheion, for Philip.

There were three from Amalie, mostly filled with news about her family and her impending marriage to Westerkirk. She, too, made sure to let Psyche know her brother's birthday and that he was very fond of chocolate. Psyche took that to mean she should look into having a cake made for him involving that as a major component. She wasn't sure where they would be on his birthday, so she would have to ask Meals as soon as possible if he had any on board. If not, she would have to find some. She didn't expect they would still be with Nikos and Ioanna. It was unlikely it would take Duman that long to get their firman. At least, Psyche hoped not. She wrote a response to Amalie and moved on to the next letters, those from her siblings.

While she was reading the letters from Sheerness's family, she noticed they thanked her for letting them know how he was. She hadn't gone out of her way to mention him; usually it was just something in passing. She had to wonder if he hadn't been writing them himself. She couldn't imagine going so far away from home without letting her family know how she was and what she was doing; it wouldn't even enter her mind. She made a mental note that she would make sure in her future letters to his family to tell them specifically news about him, if he wasn't going to do so himself.

She started with the youngest to oldest on the letters from her siblings, even though she could see from the dates it wasn't the order they had been written. It just seemed fair. Each of her younger brothers had written one apiece, and all were enthusiastic about hearing of her "adventures." Psyche chuckled. One would think she was a swashbuckler from their excitement. She told them about finding the treasure on Pantelleria and getting to swim with the dolphins, but that, unfortunately, was the extent of her adventures. She didn't mention rescuing Freddie from drowning or breaking a man's arm in Valletta. Those were things she didn't want to mention because her brothers would tell her parents, and it would only worry them to know things like that.

Persephone had written her two letters, which surprised Psyche. She might have expected *one*, but *two* was remarkable. They were brief, but full of suggestions on things to do—or not do—while wearing britches and evading bandits. Psyche chuckled. Trust Persy to be practical and not at all girlish. Psyche responded with appreciation for the suggestions on britches and bandits, and she *did* let Persephone know about Freddie and Valletta with the strict warning she couldn't breathe a word to their parents. Persephone would comply and infinitely appreciate the adventures.

Psyche received one from Eurydice, dated from before she would have received Psyche's letter wishing her a happy birthday. She let Psyche know their parents had firmly agreed to let her go to Vienna…after the close of the following Season. She would have to wait that long for Myron's mourning to be over, and Leilah Mahone, their mother's friend whom Eurydice would be staying with, wouldn't be ready for her to arrive until then. Psyche was thrilled to learn the news. Dicy had wanted to go to Vienna almost as long as Psyche had wanted to go to Greece and Egypt. She wondered if finally getting to make *her* journey was what had made their parents relent about Eurydice's. Psyche penned her response excitedly, wishing her sister loads of congratulations. She asked for details on what Eurydice intended to do once she got to Vienna, but Psyche had no doubt she would learn that once she returned home.

There were two letters from Arachne, and Psyche found them to be the most informative regarding what her family was really doing. Hers was the first to mention Gregory had returned from America for a short time not long after Psyche left. He had brought Annabelle with him, and Arachne assured Psyche that she would like her instantly. Being the writer that she was, Arachne was able to provide a good description of her new sister-in-law in temperament, and as a treat, also being a very accomplished artist, there was a drawing for Psyche to know how she looked. Psyche shook her head as she examined the picture.

Annabelle looked exactly like someone Psyche imagined Gregory would marry. She was pretty without being saccharine, having light auburn hair and beautiful brown eyes. It was funny, but Psyche thought in appearance that she was a combination of her sisters Persephone and Eurydice. She was very much like Psyche and her sisters, according to Arachne, capable of doing feminine duties but not limited to them. Psyche couldn't wait to meet her. She wrote a response to Arachne, thanking her for the picture and letting her know about the dolphins.

She next read the letter from Gregory. He was sorry he wasn't able to see her and hoped he would soon be home for good. Annabelle was looking forward to moving to Wales from Bermuda (Psyche couldn't imagine why, considering the weather), but they couldn't finalize their plans until the end of the war. He had made arrangements to be home for Christmas, and he hoped Psyche would meet his wife then. Psyche would have loved to write a letter back to her brother, but it was difficult enough to get letters sent home to Britain. Finding a way to get one to Bermuda wasn't likely.

There were two from Dorian and one from Selena next. Both were happy at the impending arrival of their baby, and Psyche was sad she would not be home when he (or she, as Selena thought it would be) was born, at the end of October or early November. Work had been completed on the lodge near the middle of August, and they had settled in. Psyche looked forward to seeing it. The lodge had not been much used before their father gave it to Dorian and Selena, and Psyche hadn't seen it since work had started on it. She wrote responses to both of them and added them to the growing stack.

With her siblings out of the way, Psyche could move on to the ones from her parents. There were several from both of them. She looked at her watch and was startled to see it was after seven. She had been so intent on what she was doing that she hadn't noticed it was becoming too dark to see properly. She was also a little cool. She built a small fire on the hearth first, and then she lit the lamp on the desk.

It was actually nice to get up and move around. She had become stiff from sitting so long. She opened the doors to the terrace and went out, rubbing at her arms in the slight breeze. She looked at the cove, but the *Athena* hadn't returned. It wouldn't be long, though. How much could have possibly gone wrong on the *Medea* in the short amount of time Sheerness had been gone? Someone had lit the torches lining the cove to provide Nikos a beacon to find his way, and Psyche wondered if Ioanna did it herself. After she stood a few more minutes, enjoying the sound of the water, she went back to her room and closed the doors. The sound was peaceful, but the breeze was chilly.

Psyche tried to decide whose letters to read first: those from her mother or her father. There were three from both. She opened all six and sorted them by date. She thought to start with whoever had written first, and that was her father. He had written his first letter on the thirteenth...the day she left. In that one, he expressed concern but wished her a safe and pleasant journey. He expected to hear of wonderful things when she got home and hoped to see some as well. He said Pandora had explained what happened and that he held Psyche blameless. He also said he thought it would be, in the end, the best thing all around. He would explain everything to her mother, not to worry.

His next letter, however, took Psyche by surprise and caused her a great deal of confusion. It was filled with frantic concern for her safety and demands she write immediately to let him know she was all right. There was no explanation for the worry, other than that he would take Pandora to task. Psyche looked at the date. The twenty-third. It had been written well after the first one. Considering the date, he would have received her own first letter to him and her mother.

She read the last one, dated the twenty-fifth. It *was* a response to her first letter…somewhat. The tone had mellowed slightly, but he still seemed angry with Pandora for what she had done. He also still seemed convinced Psyche was unwell. Her frown continued to furrow her brow as she looked at the letters. She had mailed one from Melilla, but it hadn't been long enough to receive an answer for that one, let alone the ones from Valletta or Athens.

Psyche quickly read through the three from her mother. They followed much the same pattern as her father's. The first one, dated the seventeenth, expressed parental concern but also well wishes and no worry. The next two, bearing the same dates as those sent by her father, were almost hysterical with fear for her safety. Neither parent mentioned news regarding her family, not even that Gregory had been to England, something that should have been high in their thoughts. It was all concern for *her* well-being.

In her father's first letter, there was no anger for Pandora, not even irritation. In the next two, he was furious. Her mother didn't seem furious, but she was terrified for Psyche. Psyche couldn't understand it. If Pandora had explained what had happened, and he wasn't angry *the* day he discovered it, what had happened in the intervening time to change his mind?

Psyche stood up and began to pace, chewing on her thumb thoughtfully. She was disturbed her parents were so worried. It also concerned her that they were both very upset with her twin. Psyche herself had tried to explain things in her first letter home to them tactfully, just in case Pandora had *not* told them everything. From her father's first letter, it sounded like she had. She had also told them both *not* to be angry with Pandora and that she was fine.

She hadn't mentioned what happened as a result of her sister drugging her and stowing her in a trunk. Psyche hadn't felt it was something she should mention because it had been a misunderstanding on her part and nothing to do with her twin, and she was fine now. She wasn't even worried about the dark anymore, and her fingernails had grown back. It was completely survivable. Even if it were something she should mention, it would not be something she would write about in a letter. There were some things people should not find out that way. Psyche considered what had happened to her one of them.

She stopped pacing long enough to reread the last two letters from her parents. The ones from the twenty-third were *very* emotional. The two from the twenty-fifth were emotional, but they seemed to be somewhat mollified. What had happened? She wanted to read the letters from Islington, Chrissoula, and Pandora, but how she should respond to the letters from her parents was going to take more thought. She flipped back through the ones from her siblings and Sheerness's family. The most recent ones were from Damon and Selena. None of the letters from the rest of her family or friends had gone through the same change of tone as those of her parents.

She started to pace again, her thumb at her mouth, the other arm wrapped around her waist. Had she not written them soon enough? She had sent a letter home at the first available opportunity. Considering the date of her father's and mother's second letters, the post was traveling uncommonly good, but she was fairly certain their third letters were written in response to her first. What had happened between the twelfth—or to narrow it down even further, the seventeenth, when her mother wrote *her* first, completely normal letter—and the twenty-third?

Sheerness came in from the terrace and surprised her mid-pace. He saw her frown and looked at her concernedly.

"What's wrong?"

"Ah," said Psyche, waving a hand. "Correspondence issues."

Sheerness looked from her to the letters on the desk. There were still several unopened, but it she had made significant progress.

"Anything I can do to help?" he asked mildly.

"Are you aware of anything that might have happened between the seventeenth and twenty-third of last month?"

"No," said Sheerness with a frown. "Nothing comes to mind. Why?"

"Ooh, parental concerns," said Psyche aggravatedly, scratching her forehead.

She looked at her watch. It was time for supper, and she could tell because she was very hungry. Psyche kept her frown. It didn't make any sense. She would have been able to understand if the first letters were the third letters, but to have them going from calm to panicked instead of the opposite left her bumfuzzled. She had written a letter every time she mailed letters home, and it would be soon that she would receive another letter from one or the other of her parents. She would make sure to write them a letter specifically reassuring them of her well-being, and then she would decide how to proceed after she received their next letter. There was no way for her to soothe them quicker. She wished there were.

"Shouldn't your parents be concerned about you? I mean, isn't that what parents do?"

Psyche raised an eyebrow. "Yes, I suppose, but I'm finding theirs a bit odd." It was Sheerness's turn to raise an eyebrow. "Well, they started with what I would consider a *normal* level of concern and moved to outright frantic. It's just odd." Psyche shrugged. "How is everyone?"

"Waddlesworth is fine," said Sheerness with a grin. "Freddie puts him out twice a day, and none of the crew has reported losing a single digit."

"I didn't expect they would," said Psyche simply. "And what about the rest of the crew otherwise? I'm assuming no one has fallen ill or been taken to jail?" She was distracted about her parents, but there was little she could do.

"No, everyone is fine," said Sheerness mildly.

Psyche looked at the letters on her desk she had yet to open from Pandora, Chrissoula, and Islington. Now she had seen the ones from her parents, she wondered if theirs would follow the same pattern. She didn't know why they would. Sheerness could see the letters from her parents bothered her and was curious what they might have said. She didn't seem willing to tell him, but he did suppose it wasn't any of his business. Psyche looked at her watch at almost the same time someone knocked on her door. She looked from it to Sheerness.

"I don't think you should be in here," she whispered.

He smiled and shook his head as he went to the door to the terrace. He thought about simply ducking down on the other side of her bed, but he did have things to do in his own room.

Psyche waited until he had silently closed the door behind him, and then she went to the hall door. This time it was the twins together, and Psyche felt a pang as she looked at them. Both girls giggled as they looked at her with an expression of mischief.

"Mamma said it's time to eat," they said in unison with a smile.

"Lovely. Thank you," grinned Psyche. She watched as they skipped holding hands down the hall to Sheerness's door before closing her own.

She could hear them telling him the same thing, and then very soon after, she heard them skipping down the hall, chattering and laughing as they went. Her room was still chilly, and she went to the fireplace to add more wood. She never would have thought Greece would be cold enough for a fire, but the chill bumps that made the hair stand up on her arms proved otherwise.

She thought about changing into one of her ganseys and a split skirt, but supper was ready, and she was hungry. Being tired did not help. She was glad the meal would be served on time, and she looked forward to going to bed. Perhaps if she got to bed early enough it would make up the difference for not falling asleep quickly and rising at dawn. She stood in front of the fire for a moment to warm herself and chewed on the side of her thumb thoughtfully as she looked at the letters on the desk. She had just about decided she would take a quick peek at the ones from her sister when Sheerness came back.

"Mamma said it's time to eat," he said with a chuckle in Greek.

Psyche grinned. "Your pronunciation could use a little work, but what can you expect when you learn from five-year-olds?"

"Very funny," said Sheerness dryly with a grin.

Psyche took his arm as they left the room to walk down the hall. "So did you and Nikos get on well?"

"We did, actually. He said we could go to Mount Olympus tomorrow, if you truly are interested. He can't recall anyone successfully climbing all the way to the top either, though not through lack of trying. His grandfather claimed he had, but no one believed him. Nikos said *he* tried to climb it and almost made it, but there was a snowstorm, and he had to turn back."

"That could be fun. I can think of a few people who would be envious."

"Me, too," said Sheerness with a grin, "but he said it will take at least two days, and he also said it gets very cold."

Psyche grew thoughtful. "Myron would have done it," she said determinedly after a moment.

Sheerness looked at her and raised an eyebrow. "If you're sure you really want to do it. Nikos and I could go by ourselves."

Psyche grinned at him. "Do you not think I can do it?"

"Just the cold and the camping."

"I can tolerate it for a night or two."

Sheerness was doubtful. She had a fire burning in her room, and while it was cool outside, the weather wasn't near what he would consider cold.

"You should let him know you intend to come with us, then."

Psyche looked at him in surprise. "You two are getting on well enough you planned to go *without* me?"

Sheerness chuckled. "Don't look so insulted. I'm not as insufferable as you think I am."

Psyche snapped her teeth together. She couldn't say she had never said he was because she had…repeatedly. She hadn't said so recently, for quite some time actually, but a lot had changed. She couldn't say she'd changed her mind now; it was too soon for her to say it without making it seem it was because he was having sex with her.

"I believe I told you other people like you," she finally said evenly.

"Hunh," he said dully. "And what about you? Do you like me yet?"

"You have your moments," said Psyche seriously, and then she winked at him and smiled as they walked into the dining room.

Nikos and Ioanna's dining room was different from the ones in England. It was far more informal. It was like the family sitting room without the sitting furniture. If they needed to dine formally, they used the tower. Psyche liked their attitude toward eating; it was very similar to that of her own family.

Supper was very good. They had *dolmathes; saganaki;* the ever present salad, *horiatiki;* a soup called *fakes,* made with lentils; rabbit *stifado; spetsofai;* and fried potatoes. Psyche ate a little bit of everything, but there were some things, particularly the *dolmathes, saganaki,* and *spetsofai,* that required seconds. It was all delicious. Then Ioanna served *galaktoboureko,* a custard dessert with layers of phyllo, and Psyche thought she was going to burst. She could eat Greek food for the rest of her life, but if she continued to eat it in such great quantities, she would be quite rotund. She would die happy, though.

Psyche told Nikos she planned to go with him and Sheerness the next day to Mount Olympus. He agreed it would be great fun, but he mentioned, just as Sheerness did, that it could be very cold. Snow was not impossible at the higher elevations, even this early. Psyche understood, but she still wanted to go. She had brought clothes with her that would be warm enough.

After supper, Psyche wanted to take a bath. She had been in the water quite a bit, but a bath in the hot spring water would warm her and make it easier to sleep. Sheerness would help, but she was still disturbed by the letters from her parents. She could do with all the relaxing she could find; she hadn't brought her sleeping draught.

When they got back to their rooms, Sheerness offered to help wash her back or anything else, but Psyche said no, thank you. It might have been nice, but Psyche didn't believe she would get much washed. She put on her dressing gown before she went, and Sheerness had a hard time not delaying her. He was amazed by her nonchalance at being naked. She showed no hesitation in taking off her clothes while he was there, but then she hadn't been nervous about it when they were swimming that morning, either. He watched her leave with a thoughtful expression and scratched his forehead.

He started to leave her room and go to his own, but then he saw the letters on her desk. He shouldn't, he knew, but they were right there. He flipped through the ones she had folded and sealed. Not any surprises there, except for the one to his mother. He looked at the pile she had opened. There were two, actually: one for those from her parents and another for the rest.

The pictures were in another pile, and he picked those up to look at them. The artists had signed their names, and he ran his fingers over the ones from Philip. They were very sweet. Sheerness had received a letter from his niece and nephews, but Philip hadn't sent him a picture. He wondered who the girl was in the picture Arachne had sent. She almost looked like one of Psyche's sisters, but he knew it wasn't. He had met all of them, even the youngest, Persephone, and this was not the same girl.

He looked at the open letters. He shouldn't. He *really* shouldn't, but he couldn't stop himself. She would be awhile in the bath. He clenched his hands at his sides for a few minutes in an effort to restrain himself. He groaned softly and shook his head before he picked them up and began to read.

Sheerness was amazed by the people who had sent her letters: Countess de Lieven, Thomas Young, the Duke of Sussex, and, to his astonishment, the comte d'Artois. He wondered why replies to these people weren't among the ones she had written. Two princes, a princess, and one of the greatest minds of their time, and she didn't seem to think their heartfelt words warranted an answer. Yet she did Sir James and Lord Georgie. He found their letters interesting, but he didn't know why Psyche thought theirs were more important. He hoped she told Georgie that Lucy would loathe Greece.

He read through the ones from his family and her family. That took some time, even as quickly as he read, because there were so many. He was surprised both his mother and his sister had told her about his birthday, and he wondered what she intended to do with that information. Myron had told him when hers was…a long time ago. His sister still seemed very intent on marrying Westerkirk. His mother and Amalie both thanked her for letting them know how he was, so she must have at least mentioned him. The letters from Josie, Jerome, and Philip were amusing, and while the one they had sent to him was affectionate, their letters to her were less formal. He was amazed by the things people told her, that everyone, including his mother, valued her opinion highly enough to ask her questions about things he never would have suspected.

The letters from her own family were no less interesting and informative, at least about her family. He discovered who the girl was in the picture and could only assume it was a good likeness. Arachne's work was too precise to think it wasn't. Sheerness came away from reading the letters feeling warm from all the love and affection shown by her siblings and just a little envious. His family was close; they cared for each other a great deal, but it was never expressed so freely as it was in Psyche's family. It hadn't been since the death of Monique and his father; even before then it had not been this unfettered. There was no judgment, no expectations, just love and encouragement.

He looked at the door again cautiously. It had taken him quite a bit of time to read through all the letters in that pile, and he had still not read the ones from her parents, the ones that had bothered her and made him most curious. She had been barefooted, and the floors were made of stone. If she came while he was reading them, she might catch him. She would be upset to find he had invaded her privacy so thoroughly, as she would have if she had discovered he'd read the letters from Pandora and the maids, but he had to know.

He picked up the pages and read them quickly, but when he was done, Sheerness wasn't puzzled. He knew exactly what had happened, especially when he saw the dates on the letters. Just because it didn't puzzle him did not mean it didn't worry him, and he could see why it disturbed Psyche. He could only hope she wouldn't figure it out too quickly, if at all, because she would be furious when she did.

Sheerness put the letters exactly as he'd found them and added wood to the fire before Psyche was through with her bath, but only just. He had become chilled himself, and he was watching the flames with a troubled frown when she returned. The only letters that remained would have to be from her twin, her maid, and probably Bardsey as well. When she read them, if they were anything like the letters *he* had received, she would know. Her parents hadn't mentioned what had caused their frantic concern, but he doubted that would be the case for Pandora. He had still been stinging from the letter he received from Bardsey when he returned from Thessaloniki. The ones from her parents and her twin had not been quite so bad, but Sheerness had reason to worry.

He composed his features into something less pensive when he heard her open the door. He couldn't let her find out he had read her mail. It was easier for him to let it slip to the back of his mind as she moved closer. Her hair was still slightly damp from being washed, and the scent of her perfume tendriled toward him to make his heart skip a beat and move to a quicker pace.

"Have you been waiting for me this whole time?" she asked in surprise as she put away the things she had taken with her.

"Not really, no," said Sheerness quietly with a slight smile.

"That's good," said Psyche with a chuckle. "I couldn't imagine it would have been much fun."

The frown she had worn throughout most of dinner was gone until she glanced to the letters on the desk as she walked past it toward him in front of the fireplace. It wasn't as deep as it had been, but it returned. She was thinking, reasoning, and she was much too smart not to realize what the answer had to be. He needed to distract her and give himself more time.

He pulled Psyche close to nuzzle her neck. She had a beautiful neck, and it always smelled so good. He couldn't believe no one else was unable to resist doing the same thing. He placed kisses along her jaw to her lips, and Psyche sighed as she slowly wrapped her arms around his neck, leaning closer to him. He reached down to untie her dressing gown before smoothing his hands up her waist, over her breasts to her shoulders to slip it off and let it fall to the floor.

Sheerness picked her up and carried her to the bed. Psyche pulled back the covers, but she didn't get under them as she lay on her side, propping herself up on her elbow to watch him undress. She groaned disbelievingly and shook her head as he draped each piece of clothing he removed over the chair by the desk, placing his boots beside it, and Sheerness chuckled at her obvious impatience. He climbed onto the bed toward her, and Psyche smiled as he moved slowly.

"I can just go to sleep," teased Psyche, starting to get under the covers.

"No, you won't," said Sheerness softly with a wolfish grin as he reached her and pulled her against him. "I can keep you awake."

"You do that," agreed Psyche wholeheartedly.

She arched toward him and put her leg over his thigh as he dipped his head to her breasts. She smoothed a hand over his shoulder to his back, lightly playing her nails over the muscle. It raised chill bumps on his skin, and she moved her hand lower, raking her nails across one buttock to the back of his thigh, and Psyche was startled when he began to laugh.

"Are you ticklish there?" she asked in astonishment.

"No," denied Sheerness as he moved his lips up to her neck.

"Really? Are you sure?" asked Psyche impishly. "I could swear that when I did this—" She raked her nails across the back of his thigh again, and she was rewarded by another laugh. Psyche giggled. "*You* are a terrible liar."

Sheerness grabbed her hand and gently pinned it near her head on the pillow as he rolled her over on her back and settled between her thighs. Psyche chortled again and moved her other hand to his other thigh and tickled it. Sheerness laughed and tried to move out of her reach before he began to tickle her ribs. Psyche laughed and began to squirm. She surprised him when she managed to bring up her leg and pin his arm to his side.

"Truce!" she chortled, panting for breath.

"No quarter," growled Sheerness and bent his head to kiss her hungrily.

Psyche moaned softly and moved her free hand to curl it in his hair. Her leg that pinned his arm loosened, and he rested it at the knee in the crook of his elbow, smoothing his hand down her calf in a caress. Sheerness lifted his head to look at her.

"Where did the hair on your legs go?"

Psyche blinked in surprise. "Do you *really* have to know that right now?" she asked exasperatedly.

"Not really," said Sheerness with a grin, "but I'm *very* curious."

Psyche tried to bring his mouth back to hers, but he moved it instead to her neck and on to the shoulder where he had her hand pinned. He lifted his head and looked.

"You've no hair under your arms either!" he said in astonishment as he lifted her other arm to look under it as well.

Psyche groaned frustratedly and shook her head, nudging him several times in the backside with the heel of her foot.

"Not now," she moaned. Sheerness chuckled. "You're a tease," she pouted.

Sheerness began to play with one of her nipples with his fingers and took the other into his mouth. Psyche gasped and arched toward him, tightening her fingers in his hair. When he suddenly stopped, Psyche thought she was going to start crying. Sheerness grinned wickedly.

"So, where did it go?"

"I use a depilatory Pandora made," she said flatly.

She astonished him when she brought her knees up to her chest, put her feet onto his shoulders, and easily flipped him off of her onto the mattress with a thud. Before he had time to react, she leapt on top of him and pinned his arms to his sides using her knees and hands. After a few more adjustments, she had them effectively held with just her knees.

"Do you know what will happen to a man who teases a lion?" she asked softly, giving him an evil smile.

"N-no," he said nervously.

"He'll get his hand bit off," she purred.

She leaned toward him as if she were going to kiss him but stopped just short of doing so. When he lifted his head to close the distance, she moved hers back just out of reach. She moved toward his ear along his jaw, almost but not quite touching him, and she lightly grazed her teeth against the lobe. She heard him gasp, and she grinned wantonly as she continued to keep her distance, sometimes touching him briefly but not giving him what he wanted.

She smoothed her hands across his chest, lightly raking her nails across it. She tweaked his nipples playfully, and he involuntarily arched his back and sighed. She tilted her head back to let her hair feather across his erection, and he groaned as he tried to get his arms free. That wasn't going to happen until *she* was ready to let him. She had put her knees on a spot on his arms that placed pressure at just the right point, effectively paralyzing the lower half and preventing him from moving the upper. She was waiting for a certain expression to come onto his face. It wasn't there yet.

She leaned forward and finally kissed him lightly, brushing her lips against his before running them down his chin to his throat. She moved her bottom back until it rested against his erection, and she felt him jump at the contact. She wiggled slightly to rub herself against him, and she heard him release a strangled groan. She grinned as she lowered her head to his chest to nip at one of his nipples as she continued to rub herself against him. He was writhing under her as he tried to get free. She looked up at his face through her lashes as she laved her tongue against his nipple. Almost, but not quite there.

She reached behind her with one of her hands and barely ran her fingers over his erection. He was gasping for air as she lightly stroked him. Psyche balanced her hands on his thighs and poised herself above him. She just barely brushed herself against him, settling just onto the tip and not letting him go any further. She glanced at his face and saw the expression she had waited for. He wanted her desperately, so desperately he might begin sobbing at any minute.

"Psyche, *mon dieu!*" he groaned in a strangled voice. "Please!" he gasped.

Psyche smiled tenderly as she settled onto him completely. She lifted her knees from his arms and braced herself as he flew up from the bed to kiss her ravenously. She slowly wrapped her arms around his neck and responded in kind. Her breath caught in her throat as he turned with her and tossed her back against the pillows, rising up on his knees. He firmly grabbed her hips to raise them from the bed and plunged into her deeply.

She smiled and sighed blissfully as his expression became one of pleasure mingled with what might be relief. He was almost frantic as he thrust into her, and Psyche braced her hands against the wall above her head to hold herself steady. She released her breath with a quiet sigh of happiness as she began to climax. She quivered and closed her eyes with a soft smile as it vibrated through her, and she opened them again when Sheerness tensed, tightening his hold on her hips as he began to shudder from the intensity of his own release.

He slowly lowered her back to the bed, and he smoothed his hands over her thighs before he leaned forward to kiss her softly. She lightly played her fingers over his shoulders up to his hair before she rested her palms against his cheeks. He was covered in sweat and exhausted, and it would be a while, if ever, before he tried to tease her like that again. He lay down beside her and pulled her close against him, and then he adjusted the blankets over them with a tired sigh. Psyche laid her head on his chest, giving it a soft kiss and wrapping her arm around his waist, resting her hand at his hip. Within minutes they were both sound asleep.

Psyche awoke with a start. For a moment she was disoriented as she tried to remember why she had awoke so suddenly from a sound sleep, but then it came back to her. She felt a surge of panic go through her as she sat up in bed to look at Sheerness with an incredulous expression.

"Oh, my God!" she gasped. She pounded on his chest with her fist, and Sheerness awoke with a startled glance.

"What? Psyche, what are you doing?" he asked in bemused astonishment.

"What did you do?" she asked breathlessly. "What have you *done?*" She pounded on his chest again angrily, and he grabbed her hands to hold her still. "You *bastard!* It was none of your affair! You should have let them be!"

"They were sitting right there! I was curious!" he said defensively.

Psyche went still, her breath catching in her throat. "What?"

"You shouldn't have left them lying around if you didn't want them read," he said slowly, still disoriented by his rude awakening.

Her eyes flew to the desk. "You read my letters?" she asked tonelessly.

"Isn't that what this is about?" asked Sheerness darkly.

"No, this is about whatever it is you wrote to my parents, or it was," said Psyche coldly. "*What* did you tell them, and who *else* did you tell?"

"I told them the truth. I told them you were trapped in a trunk for three days without food or water, and then when you woke up in the middle of a storm, you went so out of your mind you attacked me and Dr. Felton and that you had mangled your hands and your knee trying to get out. I also told them you were unable to sleep and were afraid of the dark now…or you were."

"Bloody hell!" gasped Psyche, and she felt queasy. "What else?"

"That's all."

"Who else? Who else did you tell?" she asked breathlessly.

"Your sister. I told her what happened, and I also gave her a piece of my mind about her scruples."

"Oh, my God!" she sighed. "It was none of your business! You shouldn't have told anyone anything!"

"Well, it didn't seem like you were going to, and someone needed to!"

"It wasn't Pandora's fault, and my parents didn't need to find out about something like that *in a letter from three thousand miles away!*" she roared. "What the hell were you thinking? My brother has only been dead three months! And you *write them a letter* telling them something like that? No wonder they're going out of their minds. You *idiot!*" Psyche got one of her hands loose and smacked him on the side of his head.

Sheerness grabbed her hand again. "It seemed like a good idea at the time!" he yelled back. "You could have died! They needed to know that."

"But I didn't die, did I? It was *none* of your affair! They're *my* family! Now my parents are worried sick and furious with Pandora because *you* thought it was a good idea at the time…after I told you it wasn't Pandora's fault and that *you* had no right to be angry with her!"

"Well, we can't all be *perfect* like you!" he spat.

"I never said I was perfect," said Psyche flatly.

"No, but you think you are, don't you?"

"No, I don't. I would be the last person to think I was, and my opinion of myself is irrelevant at the moment," said Psyche tiredly. "I will have to write to them and explain what happened and reassure them I am well and hope that will be enough. It's not as if I can go home tomorrow and let them see for themselves." She rubbed her cheek against her shoulder to wipe away her tears since he still held both her hands to keep her from hitting him again. "And what about my letters? Were they entertaining enough for you? Did you learn what you wanted to know?" she asked sarcastically.

"You shouldn't have left them sitting out," he said flatly.

"If I had known I would have to worry about you prying into my things, I wouldn't have," she said quietly. "I have never once gone through your things…ever, not here, not on the *Medea*, not even when you were sick at your home. I have never even asked you a question about your personal affairs. I thought if there was something you felt I should know, you would tell me; if not, it wasn't any of my concern. The least you could have done was extend me the same courtesy."

"I thought it would help me to understand you better," he said stiffly.

"You should have *asked* me if there was something you wanted to know. I would have told you. It wasn't necessary to read my mail."

"How do I know you wouldn't have lied to me?"

Psyche looked away from him and closed her eyes painfully. She took a deep breath and shook her head before she looked back at him resolutely, trying her best to maintain her composure. She pulled her hands out of his and crossed her arms in front her chest.

"Please, go," she said quietly. "Go mess up your own bed for a change."

"We need to talk about this more," argued Sheerness.

"I'm done. You betrayed me. That's all I need to know. You appear to have nothing else to say for yourself that would make me change my opinion, so I'm done."

"That's not fair," he said softly.

"Don't—" began Psyche loudly, and she took a deep breath to calm herself. "Don't tell *me* what's fair!" she said, poking him in the chest. "*You* are trying to blame *me* for *your* faults, so *don't* try to tell me I'm not being fair!"

"What about Mount Olympus?"

"Go with Nikos tomorrow. Stay gone forever for all the difference it will make to me. At the moment, I'm hoping you fall off a cliff, but I want you to leave my room now, please."

"Psyche—"

"Go away!" she bit out. "I will forgive you eventually…probably, but you can expect me to be mad for quite a while."

Sheerness clenched his jaw on a retort. She was right. She really was. There was nothing he could say to excuse what he'd done. Not even that he loved her was an excuse. She was angry, but he had also hurt her, and he had known all along she would be when she found out.

Maybe it was for the best he would be gone for a few days. He would be less likely to get into any more trouble that way. He finally nodded his head briefly and sat up. Psyche had her face turned away from him, and he quickly leaned toward her and kissed her cheek before she had the chance to move. He stood up and went to get his clothes and boots. He started to say something as he reached the door to the terrace, but he simply sighed instead and left.

Psyche curled up in a ball in the middle of the big bed and cried quietly, pulling the blankets up to her chin. There had been something he could have said that would have made her forgive him right then, but it apparently hadn't even occurred to him. Instead he had been intent on blaming her. If he had admitted what he had done was wrong, if he had apologized, she would have still been worried about how she was going to calm her parents, and Pandora as well, Psyche was sure, but she would have felt far less wounded by what he had done. He had never apologized for anything he had ever done to her that was wrong. Not once. And she wasn't going to ask him to. If he was incapable of realizing on his own that he owed her an apology, it would be pointless to ask him for it. He wouldn't mean it.

She had never thought he would read her mail. It had been one thing to flip through her letters to see who she had written, but for him to actually *read* things other people had written to her, things that were meant to be private, left her feeling violated. Every time she had gone to his cabin, she had been so careful not to look at anything that might be personal because she didn't want to feel as if she were invading his privacy. She had trusted him enough to think he would do the same. It hurt her to know he apparently had no trust in her. He was jealous and suspicious, and he seemed to have no respect for her at all. She didn't know how she could have possibly begun to believe he might have meant it when he said he loved her.

And he still thought she was a liar. She actually wished she were capable of lying without consequence; it would make her life so much simpler. Yet no matter how often she told him she didn't lie, he wouldn't believe it, not even after that morning. He couldn't possibly believe she would have admitted what she did if she could have lied instead. Still, after what he had gotten her to say even without believing her, perhaps it was just as well he didn't. Her admission had cost her an amount of her self-respect. Many more questions like that, and she would lose it all. She could see him testing it if he knew, just to see what would happen, like a boy pulling the wings off a butterfly.

Chapter Thirty

Psyche eventually cried herself to exhaustion. The sun was up for an hour or two when she woke, but considering how little sleep she had gotten, that extra bit of time made no difference. She wished she had brought her sleeping draught. She would have taken some and gone back to sleep. At the moment, she was craving oblivion. If she was asleep, she wouldn't have to think, or if she did think, she wouldn't care.

She could only assume Sheerness and Nikos were gone to Mount Olympus. Considering how far they had to go and how long it would take, at least Nikos would have wanted an early start. The quickest way to get there was sailing down the coast and making their way inland. Psyche was going to regret she didn't go, but wouldn't have been able to enjoy it...not now. She wouldn't enjoy much of anything until she got a letter from her family that wasn't full of hysteria. With Sheerness there, it would have made it even more difficult. In the daylight, she was still hurt and angry. She hoped by the time he returned, she would at least be able to speak to him civilly.

She rolled over to look out the windows and doors at the terrace. The sun came in to warm her room comfortably, and the fire had burned out at some point without any concern from her. She sighed and got up from the bed. She went to get her dressing gown from the floor near the fireplace. It was funny how he had to have all of *his* things picked up and put away, but he showed no concern for leaving hers lying about. She put it on and went to the terrace. She looked down at the cove, and as expected, the *Athena* was gone. She could see the dolphins playing below, but she didn't feel like joining them. She just couldn't bring herself to laugh at the moment.

After a few minutes of watching them swim, she went back inside and closed the doors. She put on her lavender and mauve gansey and the matching split skirt, and then she braided her hair after she brushed her teeth. She put on her watch and looked at it once she had it in place. Breakfast would be ready in about an hour, and she wasn't hungry. The thought of eating anything didn't appeal to her at all. She wasn't even tempted to eat something from the basket Ioanna had given her the day before. That was quite a change from the way she had been feeling for weeks.

Psyche went to the desk and looked at the unopened letters. There were six from Pandora, three from Chrissoula, and two from Islington. She needed to open them, but she was almost afraid of what she might find. She could only imagine Pandora saying she would be there as quickly as she could. Although Psyche missed her and would love to see her, to have her worried enough to set sail immediately left Psyche feeling guilty.

She penned a reply to her parents first, assuring them that Sheerness's report of things was much exaggerated…more than likely. She specifically told them she was in the best of health and perfectly happy, and she hoped that would finally allay their fears. They knew she wouldn't lie, not even in a letter. Psyche then opened all the letters from her sister, maid and brother-in-law and arranged them by date. She started with the ones from Chrissoula.

Two of them had been sent before she even received Psyche's first letter. They were full of suggestions for things to do while staying with Nikos, places to see, things she would like Psyche to check at the house to find out if they had changed. There was also a reminder to keep track of her courses. Psyche shook her head with a slight smile. She had been minding them, meticulously, and there was no reason for Chrissoula to tell her why; although, Psyche had to wonder why her maid had never mentioned that she suspected something might be going on between her and Sheerness. Psyche had no concern Chrissoula would tell her parents, but Psyche had to wonder exactly how long she had known. The third letter was written in response to Psyche's own, but she made mention of the problems that had resulted from Sheerness's letters to Pandora and her parents. Chrissoula said she was concerned to hear things the way Sheerness described them but felt confident Psyche would have told her if she had been in as much danger as he made it seem.

She was right…up to a point. Psyche hadn't mentioned it because it was no one's fault but her own. While it could have been catastrophic, it wasn't, and while it had been traumatic, she was fully recovered. Psyche replied, assuring Chrissoula she was well and much enjoying her stay with Nikos and Ioanna. She also let Chrissoula know she would make paintings of all her nieces. Her skill was not as good as Arachne's, but it wasn't terrible. She was simply better at portraying inanimate objects…like ruins.

Psyche picked up the letters from her twin with a deep indrawn breath. Four were written before Pandora would have received Psyche's first one and two after. The first four were in Pandora's typical meandering fashion, and Psyche enjoyed reading them. They contained news about her nephews and Jezebel's new foal and reassurances their parents weren't angry or worried about Psyche's abrupt, unplanned departure.

The second two, written after Sheerness caused havoc, were not so calm. Pandora didn't seem as panicked as their parents, at least not in tone, but she wanted Psyche to write her immediately and let her know how she was and what really happened. She was also profusively apologetic, which meant Pandora was more upset than her words would lead someone else to believe. Pandora rarely apologized, which was why when she did offer regrets, the recipient could be sure they were given with the most heartfelt sincerity. To have her apologizing the way she was, pleading for forgiveness, confirmed for Psyche that her twin was just as (if not more) upset.

Psyche replied with a bit of hesitation. She didn't want to tell Pandora everything, but she would tell her as much as she could. Before she did, she assured her sister she was not at fault and that it wasn't something she would have ever mentioned in a letter had Sheerness's actions not made it necessary...if at all. Psyche wasn't even sure what Sheerness had told her. He told Psyche what he had written, but she couldn't be sure without having seen it. She told Pandora that his writing the letters had definitely been unsolicited and that she was furious with him for having done so. Psyche offered an apology of her own for him causing Pandora and their parents so much anguish.

With that out of the way, she moved on to the two from Islington. Both of them had been written after Sheerness's and hers. He thanked her for her birthday wishes, but that was the extent of what would be considered polite conversation in the letters. He was furious with Sheerness. He did not hold Psyche at fault, but he recommended boxing Sheerness's ears or any other suitable, physical form of punishment she felt worthy for the things the man had said about Pandora. He asked her to inform Sheerness that she was accident prone. The two letters were only written a day apart, and his anger had not lessened any after a night's sleep. His letters actually did the most for brightening her outlook. He did ask her to let him know how she was, but he didn't seem overly concerned the way everyone else Sheerness had notified seemed to be. Psyche replied with a fond smile and assured him she would do her best to comply with his wishes.

After she was done tending to her mail, she decided to go eat breakfast. It was time for it, and while she still didn't an appetite, she had to eat something. There was no more she could do to repair the damage Sheerness had caused, and it would be pointless to make herself sick. Ioanna had a cup of coffee waiting for her when she reached the kitchen, and Psyche took it gratefully. Ioanna frowned when she saw the dark circles under Psyche's eyes.

"Are you not feeling well?" asked Ioanna concernedly. "I was wondering why you didn't go with Nikos and Sebastian. You were so looking forward to it last night."

"I'm fine. Just tired," said Psyche evenly.

"Perhaps some food would make you feel better," soothed Ioanna.

"It might," said Psyche doubtfully.

"Are you missing Sebastian already?" teased Ioanna.

"I thought I could do with some time away from *Sebastian*," said Psyche dryly. "He's caused no end of worry to my family, and I can't make them feel better because I'm here."

"Well, if there is nothing you can do about it, why worry? Eat. Drink your coffee," said Ioanna cheerfully. "When we're done, we will go for a swim in the pool. Yelena is not quite big enough to swim in the cove yet." She pinched Psyche's cheek affectionately and grinned. "We will have a wonderful time by ourselves without *men.*"

Psyche chuckled and went to the terrace. Ioanna was right. If there was nothing she could do to change it, it was pointless to worry. She could still be angry with Sheerness, but she wasn't going to spend her time dwelling on it. She would eat breakfast, and then she would go for a swim. Then she would start the paintings for Chrissoula. Maybe if Sheerness was gone long enough, he would realize what he needed to do to make things right. If not, she would simply follow Islington's recommendation and box his ears.

≪ ≫

Nikos moored the *Athena* at Plaka. From there, the bottom of Olympus was only about a five mile hike. Ioanna had sent them with plenty of food and water, even more than what they would need. After the two of them divided things between two packs, Nikos secured his boat, and they started out.

The view of Olympus was impressive as their path led them steadily uphill from the shore. The climb would gradually become steeper, but at the moment, it was gentle, relatively speaking. After about an hour-and-a-half of walking, they made it to Litochoro, a small village nestled at the base of the mountain. From that point on, the climb would only become steeper and slower.

As Sheerness looked at it, he could see the mountain had several peaks, not just one, which meant it would more appropriately be called a massif, and he had no notion of which one Nikos intended to attempt. Sheerness would be satisfied with any of them, and it didn't even have to be the tallest one. He had almost changed his mind about going after the argument with Psyche, but he had reasons of his own making the climb, and time away from her would be good for both of them. He wanted her to forgive him, and he didn't know what he could do to make her do that other than doing what she asked.

As they walked, Nikos pointed things out he thought that Sheerness might find interesting, regaling him with stories heard from family and friends. Sheerness thought Litochoro was an interesting town with spectacular views. Nikos amusedly told him he needed to wait until they started to climb the mountain before he made a firm decision.

They made their way up the mountain following a river valley that seemed the most natural course to take. Nikos explained it was the Enippeas River, which eventually reached the gulf near a place called Gritsa. It was the only river originating on the mountain that contained running water year-round. There were others that had flow during the late winter and spring from snow melt and rains, but not this time of year. There were a few foot bridges that crossed back and forth over the river along the gorge occasionally, but after they reached a certain point, those would disappear.

The path they were taking was the same one Nikos had used before, when he tried to make the climb alone. It was the same path his grandfather had taken for the climb which he had claimed his entire life he had successfully made as a young man. Nikos wanted to get as far as they could, but he didn't want to camp above the treeline. That would require carrying wood from lower down the mountain to build a fire, and they would *need* a fire. Even at a lower elevation they would need one; it was easier to build one if they didn't have to go far for fuel. Nikos thought they would at least make it halfway up before they had to stop; then they would try to finish the next day. His main concern was that the higher they went, the more unpredictable the weather would become.

They stopped to eat and take a rest not long after they left Litochoro. It was ten in the morning, and neither of them had eaten since leaving the house. Nikos said there was a monastery further up the gorge where they would stop for dinner, but they wouldn't stop again until it was time to make camp for the night. Ioanna had provided them with bread and cheese, fruit, raisins, nuts, and *souvlakia.* They also had *loukomathes* and *baklava,* which they both enjoyed for breakfast. They carried plenty of water, and until they left the Enippeas Gorge, they could replenish their supply as necessary. Nikos had brought some *tsipouro,* but they would wait until they stopped for the night before having that with their supper. It wouldn't do to try climbing while intoxicated a mountain no one had supposedly ever successfully climbed before.

As they started out again after their stop for food, Sheerness idly wondered what Psyche was doing. He imagined she was still busily composing letters to her family in an attempt to repair the damage he had caused. He had never thought when he wrote the letters that it would create such turmoil. She was right. He shouldn't have done it. He should have minded his own business. But he had been so worried after what happened to her; he obviously had not been thinking rationally. He could not now understand why he would have possibly thought her parents would want to find out something like that in a letter. She was right: he was an idiot.

Against his better judgment, he had looked in on her before he left. She had looked so small and fragile curled up in the middle of that impossibly big bed. It was obvious the silent tears she had been crying when he left had continued for quite some time. He had carefully climbed onto the bed to give her a soft kiss on the lips, and he had thought he was found out when she shifted in her sleep. She was too exhausted to wake up that easily, but he had left before he tempted fate further. He was sure she was still furious, and if she had found him there, pounding on his chest or smacking him on the side of his head would have been the least she would have done.

She said he betrayed her. He could only assume she had trusted him...at least in some fashion. Now he had ruined it. He didn't know how he was going to fix it. She had told him if he wanted to know something, all he had to do was ask, but there were some things he didn't want to know. If he didn't ask, then he wouldn't have to give up. He could keep believing what he wanted. She said she didn't think she was perfect, but he didn't know how that could be true. He thought she was, and trying to live up to her expectations was exhausting. No matter what he did, it either made things worse or made her unhappy. Now he wasn't sure any of it had made a difference.

"So Thea decided she didn't want to go?" asked Nikos after a time when it seemed his traveling companion was losing interest in what he was saying.

Sheerness blinked at the question. "What?"

"Thea? She changed her mind about coming?" asked Nikos slowly.

"Yes," said Sheerness dully. "I managed to change it for her."

Nikos raised an eyebrow. "You didn't want her to come?"

"No, I wanted her to, and she wanted to, and she's not happy she didn't."

"Was she not feeling well, then?" asked Nikos in confusion.

Sheerness took a deep breath and shook his head. "No, I did something that made her angry, and she told me she had hopes for me falling off a cliff."

Nikos roared with laughter. "Did you deserve it?"

Sheerness smiled self-deprecatingly. "Most definitely."

Nikos laughed even harder. "Did you apologize?"

"What?"

"Did you tell her you were sorry, or did you make her angry on purpose?"

"I don't think she wants to hear it," said Sheerness dully.

Nikos chuckled and clapped him on the shoulder. "My friend, one thing I have learned from being married: saying you're sorry is always appreciated, especially when you mean it." Nikos gave him an amazed glance. "Don't tell me you never have; I'm sure you've upset her at least *once* before now."

Nikos actually knew Sheerness had upset her more than that. His sister's world revolved around Psyche and her family, and he had heard of the goings-on in London over the past two years between the two of them. It gave him and Ioanna no end of amusement. It was like getting a new installment of a dramatic serial every time they got a letter from Chrissoula. It was one of the reasons they had been looking forward to finally meeting them.

Sheerness stopped mid-stride and looked at Nikos in stunned consternation. "I did apologize...once, but it wasn't because of anything I'd done that had upset her...not really."

"She still talks to you?" asked Nikos in disbelief. "Maybe Englishwomen are different, or maybe Thea is different, but if I never apologized to Ioanna, she would serve me tripe for dinner every night, never sleep with me again, and probably cut off my thumbs."

Nikos started walking again, whistling a cheerful tune, and Sheerness followed after him with a thoughtful frown after adjusting his pack on his shoulders. Sheerness had always considered himself to be intelligent, but after what Nikos said, he was left feeling thick. He had never apologized to her for anything, and there were so many things he had done to hurt her that he regretted. While she was always saying she was sorry, sometimes for things that hadn't bothered him at all, and she always sincerely mean it, not once had he ever admitted he was wrong.

Why *was* she still talking to him? He always did things that were mean or hurtful or disappointing, and she just accepted it. She forgave him, even without his saying he was at fault. He had come to take it for granted. Somewhere in the back of his mind, he had come to expect it and perhaps even take advantage of it. She was always there. Sometimes she would be angry, but she always forgave him, and she sometimes accepted responsibility for things that were his fault.

As he and Nikos continued their climb up the gorge, Sheerness felt so utterly guilty. He was tempted to call the entire excursion to a halt and go back to the house. He didn't because he had a reason for going, aside from Psyche not wanting him near her for the time being. And he didn't really know what good it would do at that point. She had said there was nothing further he could say and that she would eventually forgive him. She always had in the past, but what if this time was it? What if this time he had finally pushed her too far, taken advantage of her one too many times?

It was shortly after two when they reached the monastery, Aghios Dhionisios. The monks who lived there were nice and happily welcomed them to have a meal. It was simple fare, but as Sheerness had noticed with all food in the country, it was hearty and delicious. After they rested for a short time and ate their meal, they started on their way again, steadily climbing up the gorge. The monks wished them luck and success for their adventure, but Sheerness could see they didn't think the two of them would do it.

When they left the monastery, a fine mist had settled while they were inside. It wasn't impossible to see, but it would make the climb more difficult. The weather was still, for the most part, comfortable, but it was possible they would encounter some type of precipitation, either rain or snow, or possibly even sleet. Up until then, they had been taking their time, walking and talking, stopping for an occasional drink of water. Once the mist settled, Nikos decided they needed to move quicker. He had a place in mind for them to stop for the night, but it was after three when they left Dhionisios, and they were only halfway there. The peaks weren't visible through the clouds, and the weather looked similar to the last time Nikos had tried, when there was a snowstorm.

Nikos thought they could make it to where he wanted to stop, at the head of the gorge on the side of the mountain, before nightfall, but only if the weather held. The mist would complicate matters, but mist was a tolerable problem provided it didn't rain or snow. They were following a footpath that led from the monastery to their intended destination, but it was not very well kept. Occasional rockslides had covered it in some places, and in others it was overgrown with saplings. Still, it was better than having no trail at all, and there were still bridges to cross over the river when necessary.

"Have you ever climbed a mountain before?" Nikos asked mildly.

"Once, in Switzerland," said Sheerness calmly. It had been much taller than Olympus, and there had been a guide.

"Switzerland. They have tall mountains," said Nikos with a grin.

"A few," agreed Sheerness with a grin of his own.

"Maybe *you* should be leading the way."

"No, no," chuckled Sheerness. "You've climbed this one before, so I will gladly let you lead."

"You do realize no one is ever going to believe us if we make it," said Nikos amusedly. "My grandfather claimed to his dying day that he had made it, all the way to the top of Mytikas, and no one ever believed him."

"That's fine with me," said Sheerness. "We will know we did."

"He said he left something behind up there, which was one of the reasons I had wanted to climb before."

"Oh? What did he leave?"

"His crucifix…sitting on the Throne of Zeus."

"Hopefully the weather will hold, and you will be able to retrieve it," said Sheerness with a grin.

"Maybe," said Nikos as he glanced around them at the mist and up at the sky. "Things are not looking so good. I think Zeus and the other gods are trying to make up their minds whether they will let us."

Psyche had fun playing in the pool with Ioanna and the children. She was amazed by how accomplished even Odette was at swimming. Psyche had learned to swim when she was quite young herself, but she hadn't become nearly so capable until after Chrissoula came when she was ten. Even Yelena, tiny, seven-month-old Yelena, already knew how to hold her breath and swim under water. Part of it was reflexive, certainly, but it wouldn't be long before the baby was swimming better than some adults. She already did, actually.

After the swim in the pool, Psyche worked on her paintings of the girls. She completed one of Stefania and began one of Euphamia and Evangelina. She had thought to do individual portraits, but they were as inseparable as she and Pandora had been. Having them pose together kept them from fidgeting nearly so much as they did when they were apart. She was painting the pictures in the garden, and the puppies and dogs featured in her work. Ioanna thought she had done a wonderful job on the one of Stefania. If she had time, Psyche would do more as a gift for Ioanna and Nikos. It was difficult to get the girls to sit still long enough for one picture, let alone for another.

Once the sun started to set, Psyche took her things back to her room and would start again the next day. She went to the terrace to look toward Olympus, and her brow furrowed worriedly. The top was shrouded in clouds, and she could see an occasional flicker of lightning. The sky over her own head was clear and had been all day. She hoped the weather on the mountain wasn't as bad as it appeared, at least for Nikos and Sheerness's sake.

She truly didn't want Sheerness to fall off a cliff. She might have felt so when she said it last night, but that had disappeared about five minutes after he left her room. He might have hurt her and made her angry, but she didn't want him to come to any harm. Even the anger had begun to lessen over the course of the day. The hurt hadn't yet, but there was no point in staying angry. It wouldn't change what he had done. Her parents would still be worried, and she would still be unable to do anything. She would be devastated if something happened to him, even now.

Supper was delicious, as usual. They had *piroski,* boiled crabs and shrimp, grilled pork chops, cabbage rolls, okra with tomatoes, and fried zucchini. They also had an interesting dish called *soupa soupion*, a soup made from cuttlefish and wine. It was an interesting color, almost black, from the ink in the fish, but the color was no less interesting than the dish itself. Psyche wasn't sure she would like it, but she was surprised. It was very rich and spicy. Psyche wouldn't want to eat it every day, but it was tasty.

After supper, she stayed with Ioanna to help her clean up. Ioanna said it wasn't necessary, but Psyche felt like she should, and it would delay her on going to sleep. She didn't know how well that would work, since she didn't have her sleeping draught...or Sheerness. Even if he had been there, she couldn't say he would be sleeping with her. Since he wasn't, wondering was irrelevant.

The time soon came when Psyche had to go to bed. She went to her room, but she wasn't tired. She should have been. She hadn't slept much last night, and she had swam in the pool for a few hours. She was wide awake. She climbed onto the bed and lay on top of the blankets, hugging a pillow. It wasn't helping. Thinking of Sheerness didn't help because he was the reason she couldn't sleep. She got under the blankets, still holding her pillow against her, but she resigned herself to not going to sleep any time soon...if at all.

Sheerness and Nikos crawled out of the tent to find the ground covered with a light powdering of snow hiding a thin layer of ice. They had reached the point where Nikos wanted to camp, built their fire, and eaten supper before the weather turned nasty. The wind had howled all night, and even in the dawn it was still blowing briskly. The sky was clear and cloudless, and while the air was very cool, it looked as if the day was going to be perfect for climbing top. The freezing rain that had turned to snow at some point during the night was gone. Both men felt once the sun was up a little while, the ground would thaw.

The place where they camped was a small shelf protected by trees. There was a beautiful waterfall nearby where a spring emerged from the mountain. When Sheerness knelt beside it to wash his face, he had never tasted water so pure or felt any quite nearly as cold. It was an excellent location for them to camp, and the trees had protected them from the brunt of the winds and the rain. One of the other things about the camp was that it would be easy to find, something that would be important on their return trip.

They ate their breakfast quickly, leaving the tent in place and most of their belongings behind. Nikos carried a coil of rope, provided Sheerness with a small pick that matched his own, and a small sack carrying the food they would eat for dinner. Each of them carried a full canteen of water, and they had put on the warmest clothes they had brought with them. Regardless of whether or not they actually scaled the summit, they would have to be back to the camp by nightfall. One consolation was that it would (or should) take far less time to go back down than it would to go up.

It was almost 7:30 when they left the camp, starting up the mountain in a northeasterly direction. They were somewhat following a ridge, making their way through a forest thick with pine and oak. The air was cool beneath the trees, but the physical exertion kept the two of them warm, and the trees had protected the ground from becoming covered with snow and ice.

The trek up the ridge was slow but not hazardous, and Sheerness enjoyed the walk. There were several flowers unlike any he had ever seen before blooming near the bases of the trees and in the occasional glades. At one point, a shadow moved across his face, and he lifted his head to see a large eagle soar overhead, coasting on the winds that seemed to be constantly blowing. The trees blocked much of the view, but what could be seen was stunning.

They had been climbing almost three hours when they stopped for rest. There was a small, flat plateau they selected to take their ease. It provided the perfect location to look across the countryside above the treetops, giving them a good view of what would be ahead of them. The ridge continued up the side of the mountain to a point between two peaks where it looked as if there was another plateau. The peaks to the left of it were the ones Nikos intended to climb, the tallest ones, and to Sheerness, it seemed the most difficult.

After they rested about thirty minutes, they started again. They would have dinner once they reached the plateau. The weather continued to hold, still windy and cool but sunny, and Nikos and Sheerness both began to grow excited that they might reach the top. Sheerness didn't care if anyone ever believed he had done it; he wasn't doing it for notoriety.

He wished Psyche was with them. She wouldn't have had a problem with the climb. She was in better physical condition than he was. He knew, though, that having her there would have been problematic. It would have required two tents, more food, and she would hate the weather. He would take something back for her, maybe a rock from the very top. It was something she would like.

Psyche woke at sunrise, as usual. It was unfortunate because that meant she had only slept two or three hours. She had tossed and turned most of the night, and then when she would just start to doze off, she would jolt awake again. She had not had nearly enough sleep, and it made her cranky. She didn't like feeling that way. She ate some *baklava* from her basket, brushed her teeth, and got dressed. She would swim in the cove and hoped that would lighten her mood. It was doubtful, but she could try.

The water in the cove was colder than two days ago. Not unbearably so, but Psyche considered going to the pool. It wouldn't be cold, but it was much smaller and shallower. She would swim in the cove for a while; if it still seemed too cold, then she would go to the pool.

She thought about swimming out to see the statue, but there would be time to do that again before she left. She didn't know how long it would take Duman to get the firman, but it had been less than a week. It might be another week at least before he was able to come to Makrigialos to deliver it. She had great confidence in his abilities, but she didn't expect miracles.

She hoped the dolphins would come play, but they didn't. It was unusual when they had played with her the first time, and she wouldn't be surprised if they were never there again. There were lots of small fish in the cove, and Psyche couldn't stay still long. When she did, they would nibble at her. As the only time she was usually holding still was when she was floating on her back, the location they usually went for was her bottom, and it was disconcerting to have them nipping at her there. They would tug at her hair as it floated around, almost like a fishing line, and after one of the larger ones pulled at it quite vigorously, she decided it was time to get out. It would be good for the dolphins to come, if only to clear out the fish that wanted to eat *her*.

The swim did much to improve her attitude. She felt refreshed from the coolness of the water, and the exercise was good for her. She still considered going to the pool, but she had spent a couple hours in the cove. That was long enough. After she put on her clothes again, she looked at her watch. It was time for breakfast. She was looking forward to it that morning, even after the *baklava* before her swim. The exercise had helped.

As she walked to the kitchen, she idly wondered how Nikos and Sheerness were faring with their climb. When she had gone onto the terrace to go to the cove, she had noticed a light covering of snow at the top of the mountain, but the sky was cloudless. If they did make it to the top, she wondered if she would be able to see them. She wouldn't with her naked eye, but if she had a spyglass or something similar, she wondered if it would be possible. It wouldn't be the same as being there, but it would be exciting to see. It would also give Ioanna some comfort to know her husband was, at least until then, safe.

Ioanna had coffee waiting for her, and she chuckled when she saw the younger girl's dripping hair and damp clothes.

"You're not human," she chortled, "you're a mermaid…or a siren…or a sea nymph."

"I'm not a siren," giggled Psyche. "You *don't* want to hear me sing."

"Then you're a mermaid or a sea nymph, perhaps a nereid."

"I suppose," said Psyche with a grin. "My whole family is that way, though. We love the water—sailing, swimming, fishing. And it doesn't even have to be a body of water. We like rain, snow, any of it. It's as if we *thrive* on it. My sister, Arachne, loves to swim more than I do, and she doesn't care if it's freezing cold."

"Yes, I'm married to someone like that," grinned Ioanna. "Let's go eat."

"Yes, please," agreed Psyche wholeheartedly.

"Do you have anything you want to do today?"

"I thought I would finish the painting of Euphamia and Evangelina and do one of Odette. I'll do one of you and Yelena together, if that's all right?"

"Of course," said Ioanna with a nod. She took Yelena from Stefania so the older girl could eat and gave Yelena a piece of *stafithopitta*. "Anything else?"

"Well, I was wondering, would you happen to have a spyglass or something like that?"

"We have several, actually," chuckled Ioanna with a raised eyebrow, taking a sip from her own coffee. "Why?"

"I thought I would go to the top of the tower and look at the mountain. They should reach the top today, if they make it, and I wanted to look at it, just to see if I can see them when they do."

"Oh, that could be fun," said Ioanna with a grin. "I have an idea or two for other things we can do if they make it; they might even be able to see."

"Really?" asked Psyche curiously.

"We can try flashing a mirror, and if that doesn't work, I have fireworks."

Psyche giggled. "Yes, they might see the fireworks, but let's hope it doesn't scare them so much they fall off the mountain."

"That *would* be awful," said Ioanna, chuckling herself.

"Do you have a spyglass that powerful?" asked Psyche in surprise.

"We have a telescope your father gave to Nikos's father as a gift. I believe he gave it to Stavros for him to look at the stars and such, but I imagine it would work for this. It's stored in one of the rooms on the floor before the top of the tower. We've never used it ourselves, so it's just been collecting dust for the past ten years or so."

"Oh, wow, an actual telescope! That will work wonderfully."

"Then after we eat, we will go to the tower and set up the telescope for our first inspection of the day before you get to your painting. If they make it, I'm sure Nikos will stay on the top as long as possible, so if one or the other of us goes to check every thirty minutes or so, we're bound to see them."

"That sounds like an excellent plan," agreed Psyche, taking a bite of her omelette with ham, peppers, and zucchini.

≪ ≫

"We've made it to the Plateau of the Muses!" said Nikos excitedly. "I did not make it this far the last time I tried!"

"The Plateau of the Muses?"

"This was where the nine Muses were said to live, looking down on us mortals to shower us with inspiration or punish us by taking it away," said Nikos with a grin. "Calliope, Clio, Erato, Terpsichore, Urania, Euterpe, Thalia, Polyhymnia, and Melpomene. This is where they lived."

Sheerness looked around himself. The plateau was shaped like a shallow bowl, and at the moment it was covered with one or two inches of snow, the dried, golden grass peeking through. At its lowest point, it contained water at some time during the year, probably only in the spring. He found it hard to believe there was such a large expanse of relatively flat area so close to the top of the mountain. As he looked at one of the peaks to the right, he squinted for a better inspection and realized there was some type of small building, barely discernible, at its peak.

"What is that?" he asked in astonishment.

"The peak itself is called Profitis Ilias. It was named after the Prophet Elias, who is said to have built a small chapel at the very top almost a thousand years ago. The one that is there now was built in the sixteenth century. That used to be the mountain the ancient Greeks went to to make sacrifices to the gods, who lived up there," he said as he pointed to the higher peaks to the left, the ones he intended to climb.

Sheerness was awestruck to be standing where he was. This place, revered by the ancient Greeks as the home of the gods, and he was standing there, looking at it. He could put his hand to the ground, and he could *touch* it. It was overwhelming. Psyche would have loved to be there; she *should* be there.

"Come, we'll eat dinner just there, I think," said Nikos as he pointed to an outcropping of rock near the edge of the plateau where the snow had melted and dried. "We will rest, and then we will climb the Throne of Zeus!"

Nikos was cheerful. He always seemed jovial, but having made it this close to the highest point of the mountain made him very merry. An occasional cloud swirled around the summit, but they didn't last long. It did look as if there was nothing to stop them from reaching the top. Even the snow that covered the plateau was almost nonexistent on the bare rock of the peaks. His enthusiasm was contagious, and even though Sheerness was disappointed Psyche wasn't there, he couldn't help but feel excited.

The two men talked about the best way to reach the top as they ate. The eastern face sloped gently for a distance, but then it turned into an almost sheer cliff. Nikos had brought rope, but not enough, and neither wanted to try going that way. They decided the easiest way would be a steep ridge that jutted out close to where they were sitting. It would still not be easy, but it would be easier than scaling the front. Once they finished their dinner and gave it a chance to digest, they started for the throne.

As they neared it, it was daunting. The jagged edges that appeared to be easy hand and footholds didn't look so very on closer inspection. They began their ascent, and they would be able to traverse from one peak to the next once they got to the top, but they had to get there first.

At one point, Sheerness almost removed his boots. They protected his feet from the sharp rock, but they were slippery and offered little traction. After one slip almost made him go over the face, he stopped and was in the process of pulling them off when he realized he would have no way to carry them if he did. They didn't have laces to carry them over his shoulder, and he needed his hands. He would have to keep them on, unfortunately. It was like climbing up a knife edge with butter slathered on his feet.

Even with shoes that were unsuited, they made it very near the top in what Sheerness considered a respectable amount of time. The most difficult part didn't come until they were almost there, a fissure between where they were and the summit. There was snow inside the crevice, but neither thought it was packed enough to try climbing over it. That was when Sheerness did take off his boots. He held them in his hands and leapt to the other side. It was a move that proved far less hazardous without the boots. When Nikos saw Sheerness make it, he did the same.

"We made it," said Nikos breathlessly with a dumbstruck expression. He was almost too excited to speak.

"Bloody hell," gasped Sheerness. "We're at the top of Mount Olympus."

Nikos roared with laughter, and both men were giddy. Except for a point a few yards higher, they were standing at the highest place in the country, somewhere no one else had supposedly ever been before. Sheerness looked around at the surrounding countryside. The air was clear, and he could see for miles. He could see Litochoro far below at the head of the gorge. When he looked north, he could see another city and small villages along the coast.

"Look, there's Katerini," said Nikos, pointing to the city. "You can't see it from here, but the house is not far beyond that."

He began to look around at the rock beneath their feet. He was looking for the crucifix. His grandfather had sworn he left it right in the middle. There was no snow along the ridge, and not far from where they stood, he saw the sunlight glint on something metallic so dimly he almost missed it. Had it been cloudy, he would have. He made his way over to it and knelt to pick it up after moving a rock that had been put on top of its chain to hold it in place. The silver was tarnished from exposure to the elements for almost seventy years, but it was definitely a crucifix, attached to a chain of rosary beads made of amber. He gently ran the beads through his fingers with a wondering smile, too emotional to speak. He crossed himself and kissed the crucifix before he stood and turned to look at Sheerness.

"Old Damiano wasn't lying after all," said Nikos quietly.

"And you shall know the truth, and the truth shall make you free," said Sheerness with an amused smile.

"No one's ever going to believe this," said Nikos, shaking his head.

"You do; I do; your family will. The rest doesn't matter."

Nikos laughed jubilantly. "You're right."

From the corner of his eye, Nikos saw a bright flash to the north, and he turned to look in that direction. Whatever it was disappeared before he turned his head. As he watched, beyond Katerini, it flashed again. He started to chuckle amusedly and raised his hands to begin waving hugely. Sheerness looked back up from the valley below to see Nikos's wild gesticulating.

"What are you doing?"

"Waving to the audience," said Nikos, pointing to the flashing light.

"What is that?" asked Sheerness, almost to himself.

Sheerness could see the flashing light, bright but far away on the edge of the sea. He couldn't tell what it was, but it seemed to be some sort of signal. It would flash two or three times, stop, and then flash the same number again.

"I think Ioanna and Thea are saying hallo," said Nikos, continuing to wave.

Sheerness looked at it uncertainly. How would they even know he and Nikos had made it to the top? His next question was: what were they using? It wasn't a lamp. There wasn't a light invented that was bright enough to be seen from that far away. Then he realized what it was: a mirror. It would have to be a very large mirror. He couldn't think of any other reason anyone would be flashing a mirror in their direction unless they were indeed trying to signal someone on top of a mountain…like him and Nikos. He lifted a hand from his side and waved hesitantly.

"They're never going to see that," chuckled Nikos amusedly. "Wave *big!*"

Sheerness waved his arms. He still doubted the motions would be seen from that far away, but it was possible, if the men could be seen from that distance in the first place. The two of them waved until their arms grew tired, and the flashing light finally stopped. Sheerness went to a nearby rock and sat down to rest. The thin air and activity left him feeling out of breath.

"I'm going to scout along the ridge that way," said Nikos, pointing toward the rest of the mountain, "and make sure it is passable. I think it is the only way we will easily get down from here."

"I'm going to sit here for a little while, I think," said Sheerness, putting a hand to his side where a stitch had developed.

Nikos chuckled and shook his head. He was panting slightly as well, but he wasn't nearly as tired as Sheerness. Nikos began to carefully pick his way along, whistling a happy tune, and Sheerness grinned in amusement. He didn't think he had ever met anyone who was always so *happy.* Nothing seemed to disappoint the man. Sheerness wished whatever it was that always made Nikos so cheerful could be bottled and doled out to those in need…like himself.

After he got his breathing to a more even tempo, he reached into the pocket on his coat and pulled out the letter. It had become worn on the outside edges from the number of times he had picked it up and fingered it contemplatively over the past few months. This was the reason he had made the climb even after Psyche wasn't going. There was a no more perfect place to finally read it than here, on the Throne of Zeus. He had brought it with him, determined to read it *somewhere* on the mountain. He took it as a sign it was meant to be when they reached the top. It was Neath's letter, the one he had not been able to bring himself to read.

Sheerness took a deep preparatory breath and carefully broke the seal. He took his time unfolding it, and he didn't immediately begin to read once he had. He scratched at his forehead uncertainly for a few seconds, and then he looked down at the pages in his hands.

"*Barneville, I am sure if you are reading this, I am gone. I realize my abrupt departure will be one more shock for you to muddle through, and— believe me—no one more than I wishes that were not so. Obviously, things did not go the way I intended, and it was no fault of yours. You* did *try to talk me out of it. The one time I let honor take precedence over anything else, and it did not end well. Damn.*

"As this is the last you will ever hear from me, I suppose I should make it profound without being preachy, sincere without being sappy, and—above all—useful. You will have to forgive me if I do not achieve my objectives. I never thought I would have to write something like this, least of all to you, and the amount of paper it took to write it is definitely not equivalent to the number of pages you will read.

"Old men do not have to write letters like this; they die peacefully in their beds, surrounded by loved ones. I wish that for you. I hope you live to accomplish everything you ever wanted and even longer to do the things you had only imagined. That is about as sappy as I will get…I hope.

"You are often too stodgy for your age, and it's your own blame fault. Just because you have a responsibility to duty and honor does not mean they are the only things you have. They never were for me. They did not even rate on the list of things I felt were most important in my life, but I think you know that. There really are things more important, and the rest will follow…trust me. So, every once in a while, for me, do something just because. It can be quite a lot of fun, and you don't have nearly enough of that. Whoever told you it was not allowed was so very full of it. Just because it is fun does not mean it is wrong.

"And do not be afraid to admit when you are wrong. Actually, just quit being afraid…all the time. You are always worrying about things you cannot change, and you will work yourself into an early grave if you don't stop. I don't want to see you again for a very long time, so end all of that now, before it's too late. Everyone makes mistakes. Things happen whether we want them to or not. No one has the right to expect they can control everything. Sometimes a catastrophe can be a blessing in disguise. You do see where I am heading with this, right?

"Not everything has to be perfect, and not everything that seems to be is. Perfection is relative in any case. Sometimes things just are the way they are, and without the flaws, they cease to be. That includes you. You were my best mate, and I loved you, faults and all. I don't think I would have nearly so much if you were perfect. Perfect is boring.

"Tread carefully with Psyche. She is as close to perfection as you will find on Earth, but she does have her limits. She is loving, generous, forgiving and humble, and she will bear things with grace that would make a grown man cry, but do not ever take it for granted. Like any goddess, her wrath can be terrible. You have been consistently hateful to her in your quest to find her flaws, and it has been the only bone of contention I have ever had with you in our many years of friendship. She is not going to break if you push her too far; she will retaliate. My advice to you is to simply accept her as she is. I've heard being struck by lightning can be painful.

"I can tell you this now without fear of reprisal, but use this knowledge with great care. If she ever breaks out in hives, she's lying. Be careful what you ask her because she will almost always choose the truth over hives, but too much honesty can come with a very high price. If you are going to force the truth from her, the least you better do is repay it. I will refer you to the *previous paragraph for what will happen if you do not. All you have to do is believe in her.*

"On that note, I believe it is time for me to bring this to a close. I have no final requests from you other than that you should have fun, be happy, and quit being mean to my sister. I thought I would reiterate just in case it wasn't clear. I am sorry we will not be going to Greece and Egypt together. That would have been a grand adventure, I am sure, but you should definitely go without me. Good luck with the war and all that. Your friend, Neath."

Sheerness wiped his eyes on his sleeve and smiled as he folded the letter back and put it in his pocket. In his head, he could hear his friend, and it was like Neath was there with him. He should have read it a long time ago, but he was glad he had waited. Neath would have appreciated the venue. He sat looking around himself feeling more at peace than he had for a long time.

Nikos soon returned, hopping across the rocks like a mountain goat, a grin on his face. Sheerness grinned back.

"We should get going," said Nikos. "We shouldn't have any problem getting down."

Sheerness stood up and took one last look around. There was a cloud bank gathering around the top of the mountain, and while it didn't look as if it intended to stay, much less bring rain or snow, it was getting late into the afternoon. They would make it back to their camp just before nightfall.

"We will have some *tsipouro* to celebrate," said Nikos as they started along the mountaintop. They hadn't had any the night before, and now there was a wonderful reason to open it.

"What is *tsipouro*?" asked Sheerness curiously.

Nikos laughed humorously. "Only the best stuff in the world."

Chapter Thirty One

The weather that night was better than the night before, but the following day was not. A rainstorm began soon after they packed their things and started down the gorge. They made it as far as Aghios Dhionisios before they had to stop. The rain made the way down the mountain very slick, and both of them agreed it would be better to lose a few hours' travel waiting for it to stop than to risk losing even more by one of them being injured.

The monks were, as they had been on Monday, hospitable. They provided the men with something to eat and a fire to warm themselves and dry out. The monks were curious when they discovered Sheerness was English, and they wanted to hear about his country. Nikos had to translate. Sheerness's knowledge of Greek, while improved, was still not up to snuff for discussing things like geography, politics, or religion. As they were friendly, Sheerness didn't want to say the wrong thing and offend them, and he was glad they didn't ask any questions he was unable to answer through Nikos.

They were also surprised, and pleased, to learn the men had successfully made it to the top. Nikos had his grandfather's crucifix, which Father Ioannis, the head of the monastery, blessed for him after giving it a good cleaning. Sheerness carried in his pocket two shards of rock he had picked off from the top of Mytikas...not from the *very* top; he didn't want to make the mountain shorter. One was for Psyche, and the other was for him. Father Ioannis offered to bless them as well, and Sheerness let him. It could only help.

Sheerness also had, in a sack that used to contain food, a few things he discovered in a cave on the way back down. They were not items left by anchorites. He would have left them if they were. They weren't as spectacular as the items Psyche had found off Pantelleria, but they were interesting. There were several coins of various denominations, some tablets covered in ancient Greek, and a few small pieces of jewelry, including a cuff bracelet and a ring. He also found several pieces of broken pottery, and he had carefully collected all he could find and put it into the bag. He wasn't sure what could be done with them, but he thought he might as well take everything that was there.

Sheerness did take the time to examine the cave. It appeared to be natural, and it didn't seem to have been modified—no carving, no painting, just the artifacts he found at the back of it. He wouldn't have looked for any manmade decoration if Nikos hadn't made him. Nikos didn't disagree with removing the objects, but he did have Sheerness try to remember where everything had been, even the pottery sherds. He said it might be important. Sheerness didn't see how, but he did what Nikos suggested.

Sheerness realized what he was doing was theoretically illegal. He had yet to receive his firman; if he were caught removing the items from the country without it, they would be confiscated. He had no notion of what would happen to him. He'd rather not find out. Duman was getting the firman, so it was only a matter of time. Sheerness wouldn't be coming back to Olympus. If he didn't take them now, someone else would find them and remove them.

The afternoon wore on as they waited at the monastery. The rain showed no signs of stopping. Considering the elevation, it was probably raining at the house, too. Sheerness wondered what Psyche was doing. She liked spending much of her time outdoors, even if all she did was read. He had been away from her for three days, and he missed her. Even if she was still angry when he got back, he was looking forward to seeing her.

The weather did not want to cooperate. It was late afternoon when the rain finally stopped, and while it had stopped early enough to make it to Litochoro, it would be too dark by the time they reached the town to make it to the *Athena* at the coast. Reluctantly, they would have to stay the night at the monastery. It would be comfortable, at least better than sleeping on the ground. They were welcome, but it was one more night away from home. They thought about trying to make it, but both realized their chances were unlikely.

After supper, they were shown to two small rooms beside each other in the wing where the novices were housed. The mattresses were stuffed with straw, on frames with ropes, and the blankets were made of simply spun wool, but two nights sleeping on the ground made both men appreciate anything that kept them off of it. They said good night and agreed whoever woke first would wake the other for them to get an early start. If they left early enough, they could be back to the house by noon.

Psyche had a quiet day. She again did not sleep well, and she couldn't swim because of the rain. She finished her painting of Ioanna and Yelena and started on the second set she intended to leave for Nikos and Ioanna. She completed the picture of Stefania and had started another of Euphamia and Evangelina. The second round of portrait painting was going much better, perhaps because the rain made it impossible for the girls to do anything but sit still in the house.

The previous afternoon was fun, watching the summit of Mount Olympus. They had set up the telescope on top of the tower, and it proved to be just as powerful as Psyche had hoped it would. It wasn't strong enough to see every detail, but fine for distinguishing between chamois and other wildlife on the mountain and a person. They hauled up a large cheval glass stored in the room with the telescope to use as a signal. Both women were excited when they saw the men reach the top. The telescope showed them enough to see the men, but if it hadn't been for the differences between them, Psyche and Ioanna wouldn't have been able to tell which was which. Psyche operated the mirror while Ioanna watched the telescope, and both laughed triumphantly when the men waved back. It had been a good way to pass the time.

The women had expected Nikos and Sheerness to return on Wednesday, but when the rain continued to fall in heavy sheets all day, they realized it would be unlikely. They hoped the men had at least found a cave or an overhang to shelter under. Ioanna was confident she had sent them with plenty of food, so they would at least not go hungry. She knew of the monastery, but she didn't expect they would get there in the rain. Of course, she didn't know where on the mountain they had started from that morning.

Psyche was growing attached to her new puppy, and it made her happy when Ioanna said she was welcome to take him to her room, which she did after supper. Psyche took him with her when she went to have her bath, and he spent his time rolling around and playing with a piece of rawhide Euphamia had given to him.

Psyche was still undecided what to name him, but something would come to her. As with Achilles and Waddlesworth, there would be some characteristic of the dog that would tell her what his name should be. He was very cute, lovable, and playful. He was also very smart, and Psyche looked forward to introducing him to Bo, another smart dog. Naming him Spot would not do him justice. He would let her know what it should be.

After her bath, she carried him to her room, and he ran from one side of it to the other, still playing with the rawhide. Once she was dressed for bed and brushed her teeth, Psyche took him to the terrace. As small as he was, he was already housebroken. She would need a plan for what to do on the ship. She brought him in after he was done and took him to the bed. He walked around on the soft surface for a few minutes after Psyche had lain down, but he finally settled himself near her feet and closed his eyes with a huge sigh.

Psyche wasn't so lucky. Even having the puppy didn't help. She tried not to toss and turn so as not to wake him, but it wasn't easy. She really wished she had brought her sleeping draught, but she had never thought she might need it. She hadn't since Sheerness had started sleeping with her…not usually. Since Sunday, she didn't know if she would sleep with him again any time soon. She should have brought it, but she had become complacent about her relationship with him. That was a mistake.

After tending to her mail, she had packed it into her trunk. She wasn't going to let him use the excuse she had left it out again. It had been a poor reason the first time, but if he read her correspondence again, it would be due to outright snooping rather than any kind of temptation she might provide. And, as much as she was able, she would mail her own letters to prevent him from looking through them. It wasn't as if she *wanted* to be secretive, but if he didn't trust her, she wasn't going to promote or reward it.

She did miss him, even as upset as he had made her, and she was impatient for him to come back. Psyche couldn't believe she felt that way. She wasn't angry anymore, and the hurt had settled into something she would have to tolerate. She had known it would happen eventually from the minute she had accepted her feelings for him. It was something she had taken as part of the bargain, but she was *not* going to let it become a regular occurrence, at least not by her own actions. As she thought about it she realized if this was the worst he would do to her, she should consider herself lucky.

She could only hope he would stop being so afraid. She was beginning to believe that's what it was. He was afraid she would do something she shouldn't. What, exactly, she didn't know. She loved him and would never do anything to intentionally hurt him, but it seemed that was what he was expecting. She could only wonder what someone had done to make him so distrustful, to make him think she was going to do the same. She didn't know what else she could do to convince him it wasn't going to happen. He would have to sort out on his own, though, because there was nothing she could do.

The puppy finally woke up after an hour or two of her trying to go to sleep. He walked up to her face and licked her nose a few times before he settled onto the pillow she was holding and curled up close to her stomach. Psyche smiled and gently petted him. Having his warm, little body snuggled up to her seemed to help somewhat, and she was eventually able to fall asleep.

Psyche woke up to something cold and wet rubbing her face. The puppy licked her face and rub his nose against hers, and she scrunched her eyes closed in a feeble attempt to ignore it. She finally squinted one eye open and ruffled his fur to let him know he had accomplished his goal. He barked at her once before bounding away over the bed, and Psyche sat up, rubbing a hand over her face. It was sticky from dog slobber, and she would need to wash it after she let him onto the terrace. She was glad the sun was up before he woke her, which meant she did manage to get a decent night's sleep…at least, for her.

She washed her face and brushed her teeth before she got dressed, and then she took the puppy to be with the other dogs. She walked down to the cove for a swim, but when she dipped her toe in the water, it was too cold. She went to the garden to swim in the pool. Its temperature was much more to her liking. She could see Ioanna getting things ready for breakfast, and Psyche waved at her as she swam. By the time she got out, she was starving.

She walked through the house to the kitchen, and as usual, Ioanna had a cup of coffee waiting for her.

"No swim in the cove?" asked Ioanna with an amused grin.

"Too cold," said Psyche with a chuckle.

"Where is your puppy?" asked Ioanna, looking around her feet.

"I thought he could use some time with the other dogs."

"Have you named him yet?"

"I do have something in mind, but I haven't decided."

"I suppose you could keep calling him *koutabi*," said Ioanna as she grabbed a plate of *keftethes* to take to the table, "but he won't be that forever." She took Yelena from Stefania after getting her own plate and gave the baby some *halva*.

Psyche spooned some eggs with cheese and peppers and some *keftethes* onto her plate and shook her head.

"I think he wants to be called Cupid."

Ioanna looked at her in surprise and started to giggle. "Really? *Cupid?*" she chortled.

"Yes," said Psyche with a resigned sigh. "I tried to find something else, but that's what he wants to be called."

"Well, if that's what he *wants* to be called," said Ioanna, her lips twitching.

≪ ≫

Nikos and Sheerness left around eight after being fed a simple breakfast of porridge with honey and goat's milk. They were to Litochoro by ten and had the *Athena* under way before noon. It wasn't as early as they had hoped. They thought they would be to the house by then, but it would be early enough.

Nikos didn't want to go anywhere once he got home, but he told Sheerness if the weather was good the following day, he knew of a few places that might be interesting. He pointed out their general locations as they sailed past. There wasn't a lot to see, but there were a few things. Most were easily reachable and several could be visited in a day, but Nikos thought they should wait until they got back to the house to discuss it with Psyche.

It was then that they got on the subject of the statue at the bottom of the cliff. Sheerness was quite interested in it. He had yet to examine it, but it appeared to be an excellent work. When Nikos explained where it came from, Sheerness was excited to discover it had not been the only one, and they weren't the only things where Nikos had found it. But Nikos wouldn't give him the exact location, telling him only that it was quite a distance away, at least two days sail. Nikos would *think* about whether or not he wanted to tell Sheerness where it was, but it wasn't something Sheerness needed to be overly concerned about until he received his firman. That was something that should wait until they returned to the house to discuss with Psyche.

When the tower came into view, Sheerness was almost as excited to see it as he would be had it been his own home. It wasn't the place, really; it was who was there. The wind couldn't fill the sails fast enough to suit him, and it seemed to take hours before they lowered them to guide the boat into the cove. No one was about as they reached the pier and tied off.

"Ah, so good to be home," sighed Nikos as he leapt onto the pier.

"Too right," agreed Sheerness with a grin.

They climbed the stairs to the house, and as they went in, they could hear the muffled sounds of children laughing. It was obvious from the distant sound that they weren't inside but in the garden, a fact that was confirmed as the men went to the front of the house and opened the door to go down the stairs to the garden. Stefania was pushing Odette in the swing as the twins played with the dogs nearby. Ioanna sat holding a sleeping Yelena on a nearby bench as Psyche painted their picture, which appeared almost finished. The black and white spotted puppy was playing with a piece of rawhide at her feet. Sheerness was struck by how domestic and peaceful it seemed and how much he enjoyed it.

"I am gone for more than three days, and no one is there to meet me when I return?" boomed Nikos in pretended ire.

"*Pappa!*" squealed the girls happily, immediately stopping what they were doing to race toward him, laughing and giggling.

"That's better!" chuckled Nikos, going down the stairs the rest of the way and setting down his things to kneel and receive their hugs and kisses.

Ioanna got up from her seat and sedately walked toward him, patiently waiting her turn. Nikos stood up from hugging the girls, still holding Odette, and Ioanna leaned toward him to give him a quick kiss.

"*Geiásou, e agápe mou,*" she said quietly. "Are you hungry? We were just about to have dinner."

"I want to wash first, but I am starving," said Nikos with a grin.

"What about you, Sebastian? Are you hungry?" asked Ioanna with a fond smile, looking over her husband's shoulder to where Sheerness still stood several steps from bottom.

"Yes, I am, thank you," he said quietly.

Psyche put away her painting supplies and stood up to look at him with a wary expression. She at least did not seem angry anymore. She walked toward Nikos and smiled, giving him kisses on both cheeks.

"*Phew!* You smell like a wet goat!" she chortled, jerking her head back.

"Isn't that attractive?" asked Nikos with a chuckle. Psyche scrunched up her face distastefully and shook her head. "Then I will go wash right away."

Ioanna linked one of her arms through her husband's with a chuckle. She turned to look back at Psyche as they started up the stairs. "Dinner will be in about an hour, then," she said with a smile, but then she caught a whiff of the odor Psyche had noticed and grimaced. "Maybe."

Psyche laughed as she watched them leave. Sheerness moved down the rest of the stairs to the garden to make room for the family to pass, and he stood a few feet away from her. He looked frowzy. If Nikos didn't shave for a few days, it wasn't noticeable because of his beard. On Sheerness, however, it was entirely obvious. His hair was a tangled mess, and when the wind blew from his direction to hers, she noticed he, too, was in serious need of a wash. She was sure he had absolutely no idea. She rubbed the side of her finger on the end of her nose and bent her head slightly to hide the amused twitching of her lips before calmly clasping her hands behind her back.

"So, the mountain troll returns," she said evenly.

"I missed you, too," said Sheerness sarcastically with a scowl. He didn't know if she had missed him, but he had honestly missed her.

"Humph," said Psyche airily. "Did you have fun?"

"Yes, I did," he said calmly, his expression thoughtful. "I brought this back for you," he said as he reached into the pocket on his coat to hold out the shard of stone.

Psyche looked at it with an arched eyebrow and moved closer to take it from him. "It's a rock," she said blankly.

"From the top of Mytikas, the tallest peak on Mount Olympus. Well, not from *the* top. I didn't want to make it shorter…a few inches from the top, then," he finished lamely. Sheerness shrugged as she looked from the stone to his face in surprise. "I thought you might like it," he said quietly.

Psyche stood on tiptoe to give him a brief, soft kiss on the lips, brushing a hand down his cheek. "Thank you," she said softly.

She went to collect her painting things and put the box under her arm. She looked around for her puppy and saw him playing with the others. That was good. She would take him to her room after supper, like she did the night before. She had a few more touches to add to the painting of Ioanna and Yelena, but she didn't need them to sit any longer for her to do it. She would take care of it once she reached her room, and then she would give the paintings to Nikos and Ioanna at dinner.

Once she came back to Sheerness, she put a finger into her mouth to wet it and held it up in the air, looking around herself with a nod.

"What are you doing?" asked Sheerness confusedly.

"I'm checking for wind direction. I want to stay upwind of you," she said with a grin.

"Why?"

"Nikos isn't the only one who smells like a wet goat. Where have you two been sleeping?"

"On the cold, hard ground, mostly," said Sheerness dryly as he adjusted the sack on his shoulder as they started to walk up the stairs. "Last night, we slept in a monastery."

Psyche heard the pieces of pottery bumping together in the sack, and she looked at him curiously. "Did you bring back a whole sack full of rocks?"

"No, just one for you and one for me," said Sheerness mildly. "I found a treasure in a cave."

"A treasure? On Olympus? That doesn't make sense," said Psyche confusedly with a shake of her head.

"And why can't I have found a treasure?" argued Sheerness.

"Because Olympus is a holy place—or it was—to the Greeks. They wouldn't take a treasure there. You might have found a horde of some type, but I doubt it was all put there at once." She saw his petulant expression, and she sighed patiently. "I am not trying to demean whatever it is you found, and I hope you will let me see it, but I think it will require a little closer examination before you can say for certain it's a *treasure.*"

"Why wouldn't I let you see it?" he asked with a frown.

"Because it's yours," said Psyche simply.

"Now, *that* doesn't make sense," said Sheerness flatly.

"Why doesn't it?" asked Psyche with a raised eyebrow. "You don't think I'm capable of offering a worthy opinion on anything related to antiquities, so if I've nothing to contribute, why would you let me see it? It's not as if I would look at it when your back was turned."

Sheerness colored in discomfiture as she inserted the verbal knife and twisted it. He had repeatedly belittled her abilities, not quite going so far as to outright call her stupid, but he had often questioned her intelligence. He had known at the time he was doing it that she *wasn't* stupid or incapable, and the reasons that had motivated him were pitiful at best. It was too late to say he hadn't meant it because then he would have to explain why he *had* done it. He wasn't ready to do that yet. As for her saying she wouldn't look at his things while his back was turned, he didn't know if she had intended it as a jibe for his doing that very thing to her, but it certainly felt that way. And while she was no longer angry, while she may have even forgiven him, she had not forgotten yet.

"I'd love for you to look at my horde," he said with a charming smile.

Psyche gave him a scrutinizing glance. He was being entirely too nice. "If you're sure," she said doubtfully.

"Absolutely," said Sheerness firmly with a grin as he opened the door to her room and followed her in. He carried the sack to her bed and set it down. "I'll leave it here while I take a bath, and you may look to your heart's content."

"All right," said Psyche, still eyeing him suspiciously.

She set down her painting things on her desk, and then she jumped in surprise when she turned to find him standing just inches away. He pulled her close and bent his head to kiss her before she had time to think. She raised her hands to push him away, but as she put them onto his shoulders, her arms instead went around his neck. Her legs went to jelly as he explored her mouth with his tongue, and she suddenly didn't care what he looked or smelled like. He finally ended the kiss with a nibble to her lower lip and rubbed his nose against hers affectionately.

"Hallo," he said with a slow smile.

"Hi," replied Psyche breathlessly, feeling slightly flustered. "Oh, God, you *really* need a bath," she said quietly, her nose wrinkling.

Sheerness laughed and let her go. "Where is it?"

"Go down the first set of stairs you come to, and go left. Then, go up the next set of stairs you come to, and go right. It's the first door on the left." Sheerness gave her a lost look, and Psyche shook her head with a sigh. "Go get what you'll need from your room, and I'll show you."

Sheerness smiled with relief. "Thank you."

"You'll have to find your own way back," called Psyche after him as he left through the door to the terrace.

Psyche shook her head as she turned back to her desk. The house was large and had lots of stairs and hallways, but it was simple to figure out once one knew which parts were built when and what the underlying geography was. If that failed, it helped if one could remember one's way. Apparently, Sheerness had difficulty with that, and Psyche couldn't understand how he managed to keep the *Medea* on course.

She quickly added the final touches to the painting of Ioanna and Yelena while she waited for Sheerness and added it to the other three paintings. She cleaned her brush in the wash basin and packed it back into her paintbox, and then she put that away in her trunk. She started to put the paintings in, too, but she was afraid she might forget them if she did. She left them on her desk and looked at her watch. He was taking a long time just to grab a change of clothes. She was going to see what was taking him so long when he came back.

"And I thought *I* was slow," said Psyche tartly, but she grinned to soften her words.

"I had to put away my things," defended Sheerness, "and I did it as quickly as I could."

"Hmm," said Psyche skeptically. "Your things would still be there after you came back, you do realize?"

"Now I don't have to worry about it," said Sheerness patiently.

"Fussy, fussy, *fussy,*" teased Psyche with a grin, shaking her head slowly.

Sheerness clenched his jaw and scowled at her. "I am not," he said testily.

"Are, too," chortled Psyche, and he tightened his lips into a firm line to hold back further retort, as if he realized that was exactly what she wanted him to do. "Come on, then; let me show you where the bath is," she soothed.

He was too easy to tease for her to resist, especially about his insistence on putting everything in its place. Pandora liked to have everything put away and organized, too, but she was not nearly so fastidious as Sheerness. Psyche had a higher tolerance for clutter than her twin, but she liked things put away where they could be found. With Sheerness, it seemed he felt compelled to do it...right then. Psyche took enjoyment in teasing him about it, finding it occasionally bothersome but endearing all the same.

Sheerness walked past her desk and saw the paintings. He almost picked one up when he stopped himself and looked at her. "May I?"

"You can look at them after you wash," said Psyche, crossing her arms over her chest calmly. "Thank you for asking, but you are a stinky troll. My eyes are starting to tear up, and I don't think I can bear it much longer."

"Is it really that bad?" asked Sheerness as they left the room.

"You can't smell it?" she asked as she led him down the hall, taking the first set of steps down and turning to the left when they reached the bottom.

"No, I can't," said Sheerness dully.

"I don't know what it is. I'm sure it's from much more than not washing for three or four days. Did you sleep in stinkweed?"

"No," said Sheerness flatly.

"I'm sorry. It does seem I am harping, but my goodness!"

She led him up a set of stairs and went right when they reached the top, leading them into an older wing of the house with views onto the garden. She opened the first door on the left and held out her arm toward the room in invitation for him. Sheerness was surprised to feel steam. The walls and floor were covered with polished, warm pinkish-orange granite. There was a small vestibule at the front with low benches made of the same stone, followed by a short, narrow hall with a lower ceiling than that in the vestibule and the rest of the room beyond. In four niches, two to each side of the hall, were scantily clad female statues in various poses, scaled to life-size.

Psyche smoothed her hand down the raised arm of the first one on the left, made of a soft white marble that was almost creamy yellow. Her back was turned to the viewer, the back of her gown raised to expose her buttocks and thighs. She was looking backward over her shoulder and downward as if she were admiring the view herself. One arm gracefully held up her robe, while the other rested in front of her out of sight from behind.

"Aphrodite Kallipygos."

She touched the one to the left, made of unusual black marble, dressed in a remarkably detailed robe. It looked as if it were being blown by an imaginary wind, hugging against the front of the figure's legs and slightly billowing behind. The figure had a sheer veil covering her face that seemed so real Sheerness thought he could touch it and feel the gossamer.

"Nyx," said Psyche admirably. "Extremely rare."

She moved to the next one on the right, made of a white marble so bright it was almost painful. The figure was bare from the waist up, except for the himation draped loosely over her shoulders. She wore a crown from which nets hung to veil her hair, and she bore a trident with her left arm.

"Amphitrite," said Psyche with a chuckle. "Had I lived in ancient Greece, I think I would have worshipped her."

In the last niche on the right stood a figure composed of a granite that almost matched that of the surrounding stone, only more flesh-colored. The robe was as finely sculpted as that on the statue of Nyx, and Sheerness thought they might have been done by the same sculptor. She stood with one foot slightly in front of the other, the leg bent at the knee, giving the figure a sinewy shape. One hand was raised to her neck, the other stretched forward as if she were going to touch something. The features on the face were finely sculpted, and she was looking toward her extended arm with a pensive expression. Sheerness thought of the four, this was the most beautiful.

"I had to ask Ioanna who this one was," said Psyche, running her fingers over the figure's outstretched hand. "I thought she might be another Aphrodite or possibly Hera, although this is not a typical pose for either of them that I'm aware of. I knew it wasn't Athena or Demeter."

"So, who is it?"

She turned to him with a grin. "Psyche." She cleared her throat. "The bath is through here," she said over her shoulder, leading him into the room.

Sheerness saw the tub. "That's not a tub; it's a pool," he said in disbelief.

The top of it was only slightly raised above the floor, a rectangle about six feet by twelve feet, faced in the same stone as the rest of the room. There was a set of steps leading into it, and around the edge beneath the water's surface was a shelf where a bather (or bathers) could sit. There were tendrils of steam curling up from the water, and a slight current flowed across from one short end to the other. The room itself was lit by a large skylight in the ceiling and a bay of windows on the back wall, providing a view of the garden beyond.

"I don't think you intend to add oils and such to your bath, but if you do, there are sluice plates at the supply and drain ends to keep the water from changing. You can also use them to allow the water to cool by either waiting or adding cold water from the pump over there supplied from the cistern." She pointed to a pump in a niche in the corner.

"This is extraordinary," said Sheerness in fascination. "Where does the hot water come from?"

"There is a hot spring on the property. Nikos's ancestors harnessed it a long time ago. It supplies the water for the pool in the garden, the baths—of which there are four, I think, and hot water for use in the kitchen. The spring originally drained into the gulf, and it still does after taking all these indirect routes through the house."

"Wow," said Sheerness softly in awe.

"I know," said Psyche with a grin. "I want one at home." She walked over to a wardrobe made of cypress wood on the wall to the left and opened the doors. "Towels and flannels are in here. You can put them in the hamper in the bottom after you're done. There are also sponges if you'd prefer." She thoughtfully tugged at her bottom lip. "I don't think there's anything else I need to tell you. Can you find your way back to your room?"

Sheerness gave her a blank look. "Uh, maybe."

"Seriously?" gasped Psyche with some exasperation. "Love a duck!" she chortled. "How long will you need?"

"Thirty minutes?"

Psyche looked at her watch. "I'll come back to get you in thirty minutes."

"Thank you," said Sheerness with a grin.

"Humph," said Psyche noncommittally as she turned to leave.

Psyche hurried back to her room and the sack on her bed. She moved it to the floor and sat down beside it, loosening the drawstring at the top. The contents were a jumbled mess, and she couldn't tell what she was looking at. From someone who liked to have everything in its place, this was decidedly disorganized. She groaned frustratedly and began to separate items into piles: sherds in one, tablets in another, jewelry in another, and then coins. Once she had everything separated, then she began to examine the items in detail.

There were several pieces of jewelry, the smallest being a gold ring with a ruby. The rest were heavier: a wide, gold cuff bracelet, etched with a scrolled pattern; an armband, also of gold, fashioned like a dolphin with amber eyes; a necklace made of electrum and lapis lazuli; and two necklaces made of gold and stone beads. They were all pretty pieces, but told Psyche nothing about Sheerness's horde. The only thing she could see was that they were all pieces of jewelry worn by women.

She began to sort through the coins, but looking at her watch showed she wouldn't have time. She had to get Sheerness. She put everything back in the bag, but she hoped to come back to it after dinner. She didn't want to go through the effort of sorting everything again. The only things she did pick up were the pieces of jewelry and coins. Those would be easy enough to re-sort, and while she wouldn't need to worry about Nikos and Ioanna's servants stealing them, they were things that might be too tempting to resist. She put them in the sack, and then she put the sack in her trunk out of sight.

Psyche made her way to the bath quickly. She was a few minutes late but not enough to make a difference. She started to knock but changed her mind and simply walked in. Sheerness never knocked on her door—not on the ship, and not here, either. It was rude to barge in without permission, but as he seemed to take for granted she didn't mind him coming into her room whenever he liked, among other liberties he had taken with her privacy, she felt she owed him a small dose.

Her determination only carried her so far, however. After she closed the door behind her, Psyche hesitantly walked further into the room. She went past the statues in the short hall and gingerly poked her head around the corner. When she saw him, her eyebrows rose in disbelief, and she walked over to the edge of the bath and sat down, her lips twitching amusedly.

He was reclined on one of the benches, one arm propped onto the edge, and he was sound asleep. He had at least washed first, but he hadn't shaved. Psyche let her eyes travel from one end of him to the other appreciatively, particularly below his waist where she hadn't been able to examine things under good lighting. That was educational and intriguing. Looking at statues and other art or seeing her brothers had prepared her, but it was different looking at the man she had sex with, the man she loved. She agreed with Odette: he was pretty, even with four days' growth of beard.

Psyche dipped her fingers into the water and flicked the moisture at his face. He didn't move. She tried again with a little more water to the same effect. She finally cupped her hands and splashed water onto his face, but it didn't work out as she anticipated. He woke with a start and flailed around. When he did, his hand flew up, and his knuckles made solid contact with Psyche's chin. It wasn't as forceful as it could have been or intentional, but it knocked her off balance, making her fall onto his lap with a splash and a startled squeak. Sheerness was no less surprised to find her sprawled there, her legs still hanging over the edge of the tub.

"That was interesting," said Psyche, her features stunned, and she gingerly reached up to rub her fingers over her chin. "I bet I'll not do *that* again."

"*Merde alors*," gasped Sheerness in alarm. He looked down at her concernedly. "Are you all right?"

"Yes," said Psyche calmly.

Sheerness grabbed her chin to look at it. "Are you sure?"

"Ow," said Psyche slowly and succinctly, and she glared at him. "Not when you do things like that."

She grabbed the edge of the tub and eased herself off his lap and stood. Her sari was dripping wet, and she slipped off her sandals and moved them to the side before the water drained to the bottom edge and got them wet. She began to unwind the material as she went over to the wardrobe to retrieve a towel. She dropped the sodden silk into a pile on the floor and added the *choli* before wrapping the towel around herself. She picked up the silk and undershirt and carried them over to the tub, where she wrung the water she could out of her garments on top of Sheerness's head.

"Your thirty minutes are up," she said flatly. "I have four words for you: left, down, right, up."

With that, Psyche grabbed her sandals and left the room, her back straight. As she walked down the hall to her room, she made a mental note to never try waking him again unless she had to. It was only what she deserved. She shouldn't have barged in; she should have knocked. She shouldn't have been looking at him, either. He hadn't meant to hit her, but perhaps it was Fate's way of telling her she had been naughty. She didn't need to be told twice.

When she got back to her room, she put on her pink mohair gansey and the burgundy split skirt. Then she took her sari and undershirt to the terrace and draped them over the edge of the railing and secured them with rocks to dry. They would be wrinkled, but she could borrow an iron, she was sure. She looked at her watch and was relieved to see it was still working. They were going to be late for dinner.

Psyche sighed frustratedly and went back to the piles of pottery and tablets sitting on her floor. The sherds would take some work to sort out. She didn't know how many pieces there would be were the pottery all put back together. The tablets would be easier. They were all about the same size, about four inches across and seven inches long. All of them were still in one piece, except for a few with chips missing along the edges. Some were misshapen, though, bent or skewed. Their texture was unusual as well. They were mostly smooth, but they also had a grainy texture that was in no way uniform. Some were grainy on the front, some on the back, and some along the edges. They appeared to have been damaged before the clay dried—obviously, for the ones that were deformed. It was curious they would be in a cave on Olympus. It was unlikely a potter would have set up shop there and left a midden pile.

She picked up one of the tablets that was in fairly perfect condition and looked at the writing. The message was brief and to the point, and Psyche had no trouble translating it. It was a request to Aphrodite to grant the composer, Iphigenia, success in winning the love of a man, Praxiteles. Psyche rolled her eyes and shook her head. She put it aside and picked up another, written by a woman named Delphina, also to Aphrodite, asking that the beauty of her youth be restored. Psyche raised an eyebrow, and after she read two or three more, she grew excited. They all appeared to be prayers to the goddess, requesting her assistance in one fashion or another for things that fell under her sphere of influence. Psyche was beginning to believe Sheerness *had* found a treasure but not of the type he thought.

She jumped when there was a knock on her door, and she answered it. Stefania was there, and she looked at Psyche in puzzlement.

"What happened to your purple dress?"

"I got it wet," said Psyche simply. She didn't need to provide the full details to the eight-year-old.

Stefania shrugged, knowing how often she managed to mess up her own clothes. "Mamma said it's time for dinner."

"All right. I'll be there as soon as Sheerness is done with his bath."

"Who?"

"Sebastian."

"Oh," said Stefania. "I'll tell Mamma," she called over her shoulder as she began to skip down the hall.

"Thank you," called Psyche before she closed the door.

She went back to the piles on the floor. The rest of the tablets would take some work to decipher because of their condition, but she didn't doubt they would be along the same lines as those she had already read. She started sorting through the pottery, turning all the pieces over to see the outside. She was able to sort out at least three different containers when Sheerness came through the door to the terrace. She was bent over the pieces of pottery on her hands and knees, and she looked up at him in surprise.

Sheerness looked at the clutter on her floor and shook his head. He didn't see the jewelry or coins, and he looked for the sack everything had been in and didn't see it either. He was now shaved and smelled much, much better.

"Where's the rest of it?"

"In my trunk for safekeeping," said Psyche as she got up from the floor. "We're late for dinner."

Sheerness carefully stepped over the things and looked down at the piles. "Aren't you going to pick that up?"

"Not right now. I want to look at it some more, if you don't mind."

"No, I don't mind. I thought you'd be more interested in the coins and the jewelry though," he said curiously as they walked down the hall.

"I did look at it, but the pottery and the tablets are more interesting." Sheerness raised an eyebrow. "I think I figured out what you found…maybe."

"Really?" he said in surprise.

"Possibly," said Psyche tentatively. "How big was the cave, and where were the things you found? Were they scattered everywhere or in one location? Was there any kind of painting or carving inside or outside the cave?"

"It wasn't very big. The entrance itself was fairly large—I had no trouble walking in standing upright, but the cave was only about twenty feet deep. Everything I found was at the very back of the cave, fairly well in a pile, except for a few pieces. There wasn't anything inside the cave or outside the cave as far as painting or carving, although it did seem to have a grown up path that led to it, and there were three very large boulders around the mouth of it, like a lintel, that made it look as if the entrance had been marked." Psyche had started to grin as he spoke. "What?"

"I think you found Aphrodite's wishing well."

"Come again?" he asked blankly.

"I think you found the ancient Greek equivalent of a wishing well, specifically for wishes people wanted granted by Aphrodite." Sheerness raised a skeptical eyebrow. "Well, I noticed all of the jewelry was *women's* jewelry, which by itself is not unusual since men have never really been prone to as much adornment as women. I haven't had a chance to look at the coins, which would be useful for providing the range of time it was used. The clay tablets, though, are fantastic. I translated several already, and the ones I looked at are all prayers to Aphrodite: make this man or woman fall in love with me; let me have my beauty back or take someone else's away; make me irresistible to men or women. I'm curious about the pottery, but it will take some time to piece together. I think it was only used as containers for the jewelry and coins. Twenty feet is a long way to throw something that light, especially if you're tossing it backwards over your shoulder."

"Why would you think that's what it is?"

"The condition of the tablets and where everything was found in the cave; what is written on them; and the condition of the pottery. The tablets are all marred in some fashion from damage caused before they hardened. The objective, I am assuming, would have been to throw the tablet or offering into the cave from the mouth of it, since it would be considered a sacred place, off limits to mere mortals. If what you threw hit the back of the cave, your wish would be granted, but if it didn't, better luck next time."

"Do you really think it could be that simple?" he asked doubtfully.

"Does it have to be something complicated?" asked Psyche evenly. "There are examples of prayer tablets found other places, and it doesn't take a genius to determine that's what the ones are that you found. The pottery wouldn't be in the condition it is had it been gently laid inside the cave, and the tablets wouldn't be either." Psyche shrugged and grinned. "In any case, I think you can resume calling it a treasure again."

"Oh," said Sheerness dully.

Psyche looked at him in surprise. "You seem disappointed."

"I am, actually," said Sheerness. "You're sure they're all prayer tablets?"

"Well, there are still several I haven't translated, but I don't doubt they'll be along the same lines as the others I read." She looked at him with a frown. "You did find some lovely pieces of jewelry, too, although there's no knowing what the supplicants were asking for when they tossed it in…unless we can prove which piece of pottery they were in and the pottery has an inscription." Psyche raised an eyebrow. "What were you hoping they would be?"

"I don't know. Lost plays, a treatise from a scientist of some type."

"Sheerness, it would be unlikely for you to find something like that in a cave on the side of Mount Olympus. It would be interesting, but improbable. I like what you really found much better than some boring treatise from a scientist, and most Greek plays are overrated. If it will make you feel any better, I did find one with a short, erotic poem."

"What?"

"*I* was certainly intrigued and entertained. The tablet was warped, so I hope the man got his wish. If I were Aphrodite, I would have given it to him just based on his creativity. Considering what it was he wanted, it *would* have taken a miracle for him to get it. Coincidence and nature would not have cooperated."

"*What?*" said Sheerness confusedly.

They were nearing the entrance to the kitchen, and Psyche pulled him to a stop to whisper in his ear, just in case the girls (or even Nikos and Ioanna) were nearby. As she recited the poem to him, his eyes began to grow rounder, and his face began to color a flaming shade of red. He was excited by the closeness of her mouth to his ear, but when it was combined with the words she spoke, to hear something like that coming out of her mouth, as if she were reciting something as mundane as Anne Bradstreet, made it difficult for him to breathe. She finished the poem and looked at him plainly.

"Do you understand what I meant now?" she asked calmly. Then she looked at his face, and her cheeks began to turn a shade of pink as well. "Oh," she said softly. "I'm sorry."

Psyche thought he was going to turn blue. He seemed to have completely stopped breathing, and she wasn't sure if it was from shock, anger, or possibly something else. In any case, if he didn't start breathing again, he was going to faint. She had one hand on his chest, the other on his shoulder, and she moved the one she had there to his back and whacked him soundly between the shoulderblades once.

"Breathe, Sheerness," she said quietly.

He did as she asked, and she watched with concern as he moved away from her and went to lean his forehead against the cool stone of the nearby wall with his eyes closed and his jaw clenched, his palms raised and balanced against it as well. He hadn't said a word, and Psyche was worried. She went to put a concerned hand on his shoulder, and she was surprised when he flinched away from her.

"Don't touch me," he said softly.

Psyche's eyes widened in dismay, and she could feel her eyes starting to sting from tears. She bit her bottom lip to keep it from trembling and nodded at his turned back.

"I'm sorry. I didn't mean to offend you," she said quietly. "I'll…I'll just go into dinner, then. I'm sorry," she whispered again, and she clenched her hands at her sides as she went through the doorway into the kitchen. Luckily, there was no one there, and she did her best to regain her composure and form her features into something less mortified as she walked across the room to go to the terrace.

Chapter Thirty Two

Nikos and Ioanna were fascinated to learn about Sheerness's find. Psyche was able to conduct a semi-normal conversation, even after Sheerness came to the table some minutes later. Both of them were somewhat subdued; Sheerness participated in monosyllables. She hadn't thought he would find the poem so unseemly. But then it wasn't the poem that had disturbed him but her recitation of it. It wasn't the sort of thing a *lady* would be likely to say, but she hadn't been thinking about that. Her sisters would have found it entertaining. She had thought it to be rather innocuous. Apparently, she was wrong.

While they were eating dinner, she discovered her chin was developing a bruise. Actually, she didn't discover it; Ioanna did.

"What happened to your chin?"

Ioanna had thought the slight smudge had been just a shadow, but when it didn't change as Psyche moved her head, she realized it was a bruise. She had also noticed Psyche and Sheerness were being rather quiet. She knew the two of them had argued before he went to Mount Olympus and that Psyche had been upset by whatever had caused it. She didn't want to believe Sheerness might have struck Psyche; she found him to be very careful with her, if a bit possessive. Ioanna noted the way Psyche's eyes rounded at the mention of it, the way her hand flew to her chin. She also saw Sheerness's reaction, the way his head jerked as he turned to look at her, the color draining from his face. Ioanna knew that whatever Psyche might say to the contrary, he had done it.

"I have a bruise?" asked Psyche blankly. She was truly surprised it was there, but it did feel tender. "I guess I got it bumped harder than I thought. As my brother-in-law often says, and I will readily admit, I am accident prone. Activities that seem perfectly harmless can be dangerous for me. It's rather embarrassing, actually. As for how it happened, let's just say it involved a lot of water."

"Really?" said Ioanna doubtfully.

"Absolutely. It's not as bad as it looks." Psyche gave her a reassuring smile. "I wouldn't have even noticed if you hadn't mentioned it." Then her eyes rounded as a thought occurred to her. "Oh, darn! I've forgotten something for you in my room. I'll be right back."

Psyche rose from her seat and hurried to her room to get the paintings from her desk. She had left them there so she wouldn't forget them, but she had anyhow. Sheerness had managed to distract her again. She had noticed that; he was detrimental to her concentration. When he was near, it difficult to think about anything else. She doubted he was affected the same way by her. It wasn't fair. She should be mad at him, for countless reasons, but instead she was unhappy because *he* was angry with *her.*

When she got back with the paintings, Ioanna wasn't surprised by them, but Nikos was. They were both pleased, but they didn't know where they would hang them. Sheerness finally got to see them. He didn't think her work was as detailed as Arachne's, but they were good likenesses.

After dinner, Psyche offered to help Ioanna clean, but she had one of the maids to help her. Psyche decided to go back to her room to look at the tablets and sherds. She would not tell Sheerness if she found any more poems. She was about to stand up when Nikos broached the idea of going to see some nearby ruins starting tomorrow. Chrissoula had mentioned a few to Psyche, and Psyche was aware of a few of her own. Some of them were too far away to visit on a day trip, and while he seemed agreeable, Psyche didn't want to take Nikos away from his family overnight again so soon.

Their discussion became fairly involved and lasted longer than Psyche had anticipated, but they had their itinerary planned for the next several days. Even if Duman didn't arrive at some point while they were looking, they would still have plenty to do. Psyche was very much looking forward to it. By the time she was able to leave, the sun was well on its way to setting. When she looked at her watch, she saw with some surprise it was after seven. Sheerness had again not said much, although this time, it was because of the language.

He silently walked with her back to their rooms, and while Psyche was still unhappy, she was content to let him remain that way. At least he wasn't yelling at her. She was hoping he would go to his own room. He didn't seem angry, but he hadn't taken her arm to escort her to dinner or back to their rooms. He walked instead with his hands clasped behind his back, a slight frown on his otherwise impassive face. She tried not to let it concern her. She had already apologized, and there was nothing else she could do.

She wasn't surprised when he opened the door and followed her into her room, and she still couldn't understand why he took for granted she wouldn't mind. She didn't mind…not really, but it irked her somewhat that he took it for granted. The air had become cooler with the setting sun, and the first thing she did was carefully pick her way over the tablets and pottery to build a fire. Once she had that done, she lit the lamp on her desk and turned to survey the things on the floor. While she could see them lying there, she wouldn't be able to do much without natural light. There wasn't enough of that.

Then she looked out the door to the terrace and saw the purple on the railing and remembered her sari. She went to the terrace and folded it up. Surprisingly, it was fairly free of wrinkles, and she thought she could get by without ironing it after all. She brought it and the *choli* back into her room to put away. Sheerness had taken a seat in the chair by the fireplace. He had unbuttoned his waistcoat and sat with his chin propped on his hand, his legs stretched out in front of him, watching the fire intently. She still had nothing to say—not any more than he did—as she stepped over the items on the floor to put the sari in the dresser.

She turned her attention back to the things. She didn't want to leave them lying there until tomorrow or whenever she could look at them again. She suspected it would be several days, and they looked like just the sort of thing Cupid would love to scatter everywhere if given the chance. But she didn't want to put it all back in the bag with the jewelry and coins. She also didn't want to combine the tablets she had read with the ones she had not or the pieces of pottery she had already sorted.

She stood looking down at everything, thoughtfully chewing on the side of her thumb as she tried to determine what she could use to keep them separated. When she decided what would suit, she happened to glance at Sheerness and saw to her astonishment that he was sleeping. She groaned silently and shook her head. He could stay that way. *She* wasn't going to wake him.

She went to her dresser for two pairs of stockings in different colors, but as she looked from them back to the piles, she realized they wouldn't be big enough. She put them back in the dresser, and then another idea came to her. She left her room and went to the kitchen. Ioanna had several small, woven baskets used to collect fruit and nuts from the orchard. After Psyche explained why she needed them, Ioanna parted with four of them and told Psyche supper would be ready at 9:30. Psyche took the baskets to her room and put all the items on her floor into the baskets. Then she put the baskets on top of each other near her trunk by the door, out of the way.

She hadn't been quiet as she worked, and she thought the noise would wake Sheerness, but he slept on. She still didn't want to wake him, not after what had happened last time. She looked at her watch. She still had another hour-and-a-half before supper. If he wasn't awake by then, she would try to come up with a way to wake him. In the meantime, she would find something to keep herself occupied.

She went to look at her desk, but there was nothing there. She had put it all away to reduce temptation for Sheerness. Even her letters to be mailed back home were gone, hopefully on their way to their intended destinations. Stefano, the fisherman she had met her first day in Thessaloniki, had stopped by on Tuesday, and Ioanna had arranged for him to see to their being mailed. Psyche had at first been reluctant to entrust him with it, but she had relented after Ioanna assured her that he was completely reliable. Psyche had wanted to get them mailed as quickly as possible. She was still waiting for new letters to arrive from her family, and she didn't have a book. She hadn't thought she would need her work on the necklace, so it remained in the cabin on the ship. Other than painting or drawing, she had nothing to do.

She sighed and retrieved her sketchbook and pencils from her trunk. She turned the chair at her desk so the lamplight reflected onto it over her shoulder as she faced Sheerness sleeping in the chair by the fire. She began to draw him, adding only a few suggestive lines at first, then gradually beginning to add more detail. She had never drawn his picture before. She had pictures of several members of the crew, some of complete strangers, but none of Sheerness. The reason behind it was that she hadn't had him sitting still for a long enough period of time, and probably that he wouldn't like her doing it. But he was asleep now, and as long as she kept her sketches out of sight, he wouldn't find out she had done it. She didn't really know if he would mind, but it would be best not to find out.

Drawing kept her occupied quite well for the remainder of the time before supper, and she just managed to get done as it was time to go eat. She looked from the drawing to Sheerness a few times after she was finished and decided it wasn't a bad likeness. She took her things to her trunk, and then she put the desk chair away. She looked at Sheerness thoughtfully. She didn't know how she was going to wake him, but she would have to think of something.

She tried calling his name a few times, standing a safe distance away, but it didn't work. She moved a little closer and nudged his boot with her foot. Other than shifting slightly, he showed no sign of noticing. She nudged his foot and called his name at the same time, and he continued to snooze. Psyche was growing irritated, partially from jealousy over his ability to sleep so soundly. She was tempted to just let him sleep and go to supper without him, but she couldn't. How could he sleep like that?

She warily edged a little closer to the chair. She wanted to stay out of arm's reach, just in case he started flailing. She *was* accident prone. She might have been able to excuse away the bruise on her chin, but *two* marks would be difficult to dismiss to clumsiness, even if they were caused by it. He wasn't doing it intentionally, but she didn't want Nikos and Ioanna to think he was beating her. She moved behind the chair and leaned around the side where his head was propped up. She knocked his hand from beneath his chin and quickly straightened up behind the chair. That finally worked.

"What?" he said with a start, looking around himself.

After he was done flailing, she came around. "It's time for supper."

Sheerness looked at her confusedly. "Why were you behind the chair?"

"I thought I could do with a shield," said Psyche tartly. "Let's go before we're late again."

Sheerness nodded dazedly, still half asleep, and stood up. He did take her arm as they went down the hall, but he was not completely awake. Psyche glanced up at him.

"Are you unwell?" she finally asked.

"I don't *feel* unwell," said Sheerness evenly. "I'm just tired."

"Hunh," said Psyche noncommittally.

Supper was the usual informal affair with good food and conversation. Sheerness did try to participate more than he had at dinner and while they talked about the ruins, but he still seemed withdrawn. She eventually shrugged and took him at his word that he was tired. Perhaps he was. He *had* climbed a mountain. Although, Nikos didn't seem to be so affected. By the time Psyche finished dessert, she was tired herself.

Sheerness looked at her curiously when they went toward the front of the house rather than their rooms after everyone had said goodnight.

"Where are we going?"

"I'm going to get my puppy," said Psyche as she opened the door.

The door led onto a covered terrace where the dogs slept at night. They all stirred and started to yap when they saw her, but Cupid was the one she wanted. She picked him up and ruffled his fur affectionately as he squirmed excitedly in her arms, trying to lick her face.

"Hallo, puppy!" she crooned. "How's my good boy? How's my Cupid, hmm?" She closed the door and started to their rooms.

"Cupid?" said Sheerness dully.

"Yes," said Psyche in between pets and cuddles with the puppy.

"You named your dog *Cupid*?" quipped Sheerness incredulously.

"Yes," said Psyche calmly, trying to get the puppy to settle down.

"Psyche and Cupid," stated Sheerness flatly.

Psyche stopped and turned to look at him, her eyes widening in realization. "Oh, no," she said breathlessly.

"Oh, yes," drawled Sheerness. He laughed at her expression of dismay as they resumed walking. "Don't tell me that wasn't your intention," he chortled.

"It wasn't," said Psyche with a frown. "Everyone here calls me Thea, and it was what he wanted to be called."

"He's a dog. He can't talk. It wasn't as if he *told* you to call him that."

"The name suited him, just like with Achilles and Waddlesworth."

"Hunh," said Sheerness doubtfully. "You can change it to something else."

"No, I can't. That's his *name,*" said Psyche patiently. "It would be like me telling you that your name is *George* now. Do you feel like a George?"

"Not especially," said Sheerness with an amused smile, "but I didn't choose my name."

"Oh, I bet if you were to ask your mother why she named you Sebastian, she would tell you it was the name that suited you."

"Actually, it was her father's name," said Sheerness flatly.

"Well, it still suits you," said Psyche airily. "You *look* like a Sebastian. You *act* like a Sebastian."

Sheerness laughed heartily. "How is that, exactly?"

"I don't know. Like you."

Psyche put the puppy down after they went into her room, and he happily began to run from one side of it to the other as he had done the night before. Psyche went to her dresser and retrieved a shift, the burgundy one, and then she leaned over to remove her sandals and took them to her trunk.

"And what about you? Do you feel like a Psyche?" asked Sheerness as he watched her remove her sweater and put it away.

"I suppose," said Psyche with a shrug as she looked at him over her shoulder. "I feel like me, and I've never met anyone else with my name...."

"What about the mythological one?"

Psyche paused in removing her split-skirt for a moment to look at him and blinked before she giggled and removed her pants with a shake of her head.

"My sisters are nicer than hers, and I don't have the patience to sort a room full of grain. I also don't sleep well," she grinned as she put her clothes away.

"And what about being too perfect for mortal man?"

Psyche giggled again. "That's funny. What other kind is there?"

"No, no," said Sheerness impatiently. "Being too perfect?"

"I already told you that I'm *not* perfect. No one is," said Psyche simply. "If we were, we wouldn't be here."

"You don't really believe that," said Sheerness doubtfully.

"Absolutely, I do," said Psyche firmly. "Anyone who thinks he or she is perfect is a fool." Psyche started to take off her chemise but paused to look at him. "Besides, perfect is boring."

She pulled off her chemise and grabbed her shift from the top of the dresser. She had it over her head and was about to pull it down the rest of the way when Sheerness stopped her.

"Wait. You've done something to your back."

Psyche had stopped with her arms raised, and she turned her head to look at her back over her shoulder. Sheerness blinked and swallowed when it brought the statue of Aphrodite in the bathroom to his mind. *Aphrodite of the Beautiful Buttocks.* She was that, and he couldn't believe he had never admired them before. She had a slight frown as she looked, trying to see what he saw. She looked over the other shoulder. It was apparently in a location that would require her to be an owl in order to see it because she couldn't. It didn't *feel* like she had done anything. She looked at him with a puzzled frown.

"Where?"

"Right there. On your hip. Don't tell me you can't see that."

When she realized what it was, she shook her head and dropped her shift into place. She turned around to look at him with a slight smile.

"You mean my birthmark?" she asked as she started to take down her hair.

"You have a birthmark?"

"All my life...well, except for the first three or four days."

"Why haven't I noticed it before?"

"You tell me," said Psyche with a grin as she put down her brush. She quickly washed her face and brushed her teeth, and then she went to the door to the terrace to let Cupid out for a few minutes. "Go make wibble."

She left the door open and went to add more wood to the fire. It had burned low while they were at supper, and opening the door let in a cool draft that raised the hair on Psyche's arms. She turned to see Sheerness looking at her with a bemused expression. Psyche raised an eyebrow.

"What?"

"Does your twin have one?"

"One what?" asked Psyche confusedly.

"A birthmark."

"No, and she wouldn't let you see it even if she did," chortled Psyche. "Why do you ask?"

"Is there any other way to tell the two of you apart?"

"I should hope so. We're completely different people." Sheerness raised an eyebrow. "You mean physically, just by looking?"

"If you were standing beside each other wearing the exact same dress, would you look any different from each other?"

"Since we've never done that before, I couldn't say. My family would know the difference. If you look long enough, we have different mannerisms that are obvious, and she is left-handed, while I'm right-handed. We've never fooled Islington."

"You *have* worn the same dress before," said Sheerness flatly.

"No, we *haven't*," sighed Psyche patiently as she let Cupid back in and closed the door.

"You did so. Last year," said Sheerness irritatedly.

"No, we *didn't*," said Psyche exasperatedly. "They were both white dresses cut the same, but the embroidery was different, our jewelry was different, and our hair was different. Your family had no trouble telling us apart, but there were people who did. Some people have trouble telling us apart even when our clothes are completely different, but that's because they don't know us." She shrugged. "Or they don't care."

"I want you to tell me, once and for all, yes or no: was that your sister on the terrace last year?" asked Sheerness in measured tones.

"Yes."

"And my cravat? Who did I give that to?"

"Me."

Sheerness balled his hands at his sides with a slight disbelieving shake of his head as he clenched his jaw.

"So you've been lying to me all this time," he stated quietly.

"No, I *haven't!*" spat Psyche, deciding enough was enough. "You just didn't ask the right question! You asked me if I told her what happened on the terrace, and I told you no. I didn't have to tell her because she was there...not me! I've told you before that you need to learn how to ask a question, and for the thousandth time, I *don't* lie!" Psyche scratched her forehead and sighed wearily. "I am very tired of constantly defending myself to you, which I've also told you, so could you just stop...please?"

She turned off the lamp on her desk with the intention of going to bed. She was through arguing with him. He could leave or he could stay. She didn't care. At least now she wouldn't (or shouldn't) have to be concerned about him mentioning that blasted terrace ever again. It was his own fault for not being able to tell the difference between them. She picked up Cupid and put him on the bed, and then she climbed onto it as well. She didn't look at Sheerness, but she was again beginning to hope he would leave.

She fluffed her pillows and crawled under the covers. Cupid played near the foot of the bed, but he would settle down, just as he had the night before. She turned on her side in the direction opposite from Sheerness. She closed her eyes and angrily wiped the tears off her cheeks, and she realized things never really changed...*he* never changed.

Cupid finally settled at the foot of the bed, his snout hanging off the edge of it. Other than the crackling of the fire, there were no other sounds, but she knew Sheerness was still in the room.

She kept her eyes closed and tried to go to sleep, but she knew she wasn't. She wasn't surprised when she felt him climb onto the bed. What did surprise her was when he climbed onto it on the side she was facing and lay down facing her on his side under the blankets. She tried to turn over and ignore him, but he put a hand on her shoulder to stop her.

"Just go away," she whispered tiredly.

"I've upset you," he stated quietly.

Psyche looked at him angrily. "Shouldn't I be?"

"I was the one deceived," he said evenly.

"Only because you let yourself be," she said bitterly. "You had no trouble telling us apart when you wanted to be *mean*." Psyche tried to turn over again, but he still held onto her shoulder. "Let me be."

"I'd like an apology."

Psyche's eyes widened in shocked incredulity, and she felt as if someone had knocked the wind out of her. She didn't want to believe she had heard it. He had to be making a poor attempt at a joke because he couldn't be serious. As he continued to look at her, she realized rather sickeningly that he was.

"How dare you?" she said breathlessly. "Oh, you are a mean, self-centered, hypocritical *prick*, aren't you?" She gave him a self-deprecating smile, her eyes glittering, and she sat up to look down at him. "All this time, I was beginning to think I might be mistaken about that."

"That's harsh, don't you think?" he asked tightly, sitting up as well.

"Not yet," said Psyche evenly. "You treat me as if I'm stupid, as if nothing I say or do matters, as if you are *amazed* I can even put a logical sentence together. You go out of your way to demean and belittle me, to do whatever you can to make me unhappy and force me to tears. You invade my privacy and take for granted that everything—and I mean everything—I have is yours without any concern for whether I mind. You have absolutely no respect for me. You're jealous and possessive, and you think I intend to fuck every man I see. And yet you...and yet *you* want *me* to apologize because my sister knocked the wind out of you when you tried to kiss her, and you are so damn full of yourself you couldn't tell it wasn't me!"

Psyche was so enraged she backhanded him without thinking about it. She watched with *satisfaction* as a trickle of blood appeared at the corner of his mouth. Her face was streaked with tears, her chest heaving emotionally, and she began to push him off the bed using her hands and feet whatever way she could. He didn't try to stop her or defend himself as she pummeled him. He let her beat on him, moving him toward the edge of the bed, his features ashen.

"Get out! Get out! *Get out!*" she sobbed, and she finally got him to topple onto the floor over the side.

Cupid woke up while she was pushing Sheerness, and the puppy ran back and forth at the end of the bed, barking excitedly. Sheerness didn't move from the floor where she had landed him, his back against the side of the bed, his legs stretched out in front of him. Psyche collapsed on the bed, her body quivering emotionally and racked with sobs. Her distress was made even more acute because she regretted what she had done, now that it was over. She felt guilty, and it wasn't fair.

"I shouldn't have done that. I'm sorry," she choked out.

That finally provoked a reaction from Sheerness. He flinched as if she had struck him again and groaned. His face throbbed from her first blow, and she had bruised a few of his ribs, but none of that injured him as badly as hearing her apologize in that miserable, dispirited whisper. She could have done worse, and he would still feel like he deserved it. Contrition only described a fraction of what he was feeling.

He slowly eased himself off the floor after a few minutes, grimacing at the pain it caused in his ribs, and climbed onto the bed. Psyche was curled up in the middle of it, her face buried in the mattress, her arms folded under her head, and Sheerness watched as she continued to weep, her shoulders shaking. Cupid had settled into her side and had what could only be called a mournful expression, his head resting on his front paws. He lifted his head slightly when he saw Sheerness and made a slight noise that was a cross between a growl and a whine before he got up and moved back to the foot of the bed.

Sheerness carefully moved closer to Psyche and curled up behind her to gently put an arm around her waist and pull her close. He was propped up on his elbow so he could lean over to whisper in her ear. She struggled to move away from him, but all the fight had left her.

"Shh," he soothed. "I'm sorry," he whispered softly. "I am so sorry for everything I've ever done to cause you pain, and I know I have caused you so much. I have no worthy excuse for any of it. You are kind and gentle and giving, and I am sorry I took advantage of it...so sorry that I didn't even think of what it cost you all the times you have forgiven me. You *always* have," he said emotionally, "and I feel so fortunate...and so unworthy."

Psyche turned over to stare at him with a solemn gaze. He looked so forlorn and remorseful, and she believed him. It was more apology than she had expected, and it had been worth the wait. The right side of his face was starting to swell, and there would be a bruise on his cheek. She hesitantly reached up to carefully wipe the blood off his chin that had trickled down from his lip, and then she lifted her head to place a soft kiss at the corner of his mouth where she had busted it and along his cheekbone. She saw him wince as he shifted his weight on his elbow, and she looked at him concernedly.

"Bruised ribs, I think," he said quietly.

Psyche's expression changed to one of dismay, her lower lip trembling. "Oh, my God! Why didn't you stop me?" she gasped.

She sat up and helped him lie back against the pillows, and she gingerly ran her fingers over his ribs. It was easy for her to tell which ones hurt from the way he flinched when she touched them. She crawled off the bed and went to the wash stand to retrieve a wet flannel and brought it back to gently press it against the right side of his face.

"Why didn't you stop me?" she repeated softly.

"I asked for it," he said evenly.

"No, no, you didn't," said Psyche sadly with a shake of her head.

Sheerness put a finger to the side of her chin to make her look at him. "I did ask for it, and I deserved even worse."

"I'm sor—" began Psyche, but Sheerness put his hand over her mouth.

"Stop saying that!" he said exasperatedly. "Please!"

Psyche blinked in surprise and nodded her head. "You're going to look terrible tomorrow," she said quietly.

"I'll live," said Sheerness dryly, giving her the ghost of a smile.

Psyche ran her fingers across his cheek to his chin and leaned forward to kiss him softly, smoothing her fingers down his throat to rest over his heart. She trailed her lips across his jaw to his ear and heard him inhale sharply and release it slowly. The hand he had resting at her left hip tightened on her shift.

"Psyche, I don't think I'm up for that," he sighed.

She placed kisses down his neck to his chest, where she grazed one of his nipples with her teeth, and her fingers traveled lower to skim across his semi-erect member before she took it gently into her hand. She felt him quiver, and he hardened even more. She moved her lips back to his, and he kissed her longingly. She grinned wantonly as she untied the strings on her shift and pulled it off.

"Oh, I think you are," she purred.

"Psyche," whispered Sheerness, his tone disbelieving.

He reached up to smooth his hands across her breasts and down to her hips to pull her on top of him, and Psyche leaned forward to kiss him passionately. He cupped and squeezed her breasts before teasing the nipples with his thumb and forefinger. Psyche moaned low in her throat and curled her fingers in his hair. He slowly sat up with her still across his lap and ran his lips down her neck to take a breast into his mouth, nipping and sucking at it hungrily. Psyche's head tilted back in pleasure with a sigh, and she rubbed herself against him achingly, her fingers tightening even further in his hair. She bent her head forward to run her lips down his neck to his shoulder, and she bit and sucked on it in imitation of his actions with her breast.

Sheerness twined his fingers in her hair and pulled her mouth back to his before raising both of them to their knees. He moved his hands down her hips to cup her bottom and pull her against him, and Psyche could feel his erection pressed against her stomach. He moved behind her, and she leaned her head back against his shoulder as he nuzzled her neck, his hands going to her breasts. He spread her thighs wider using his knees, and Psyche sighed low in her throat when he moved his hands to her hips and guided her backwards to settle her onto him.

Psyche reached back over her shoulder with one arm to curl her fingers in his hair and tilted her head to kiss him desperately as she gyrated against him. Sheerness groaned softly, and he moved his hand up her side to skim his fingers along the edge of her breast and up her arm to gently disentangle her fingers. He took her other hand, and then he bent her forward onto her hands and knees. He placed kisses along her jaw to her neck as his hands massaged her breasts, and then he kissed her shoulder before he straightened up and smoothed his hands along her back to grab her hips and thrust into her.

Psyche moaned pleasurably as her fingers tightened into the blankets. She had been unsure about letting him take her this way, and she could tell from the care he had taken in leading her into the position that Sheerness knew. But now, as she felt him move in and out of her, his thrusts steady and deep, she decided if it wasn't *the* one she liked best, it was a very close second. When he moved one of his hands to begin teasing her button, she quickly decided it was her favorite…so far. Sheerness moved his other hand from her hip to her shoulder as his pace began to quicken, and Psyche could tell from his occasional moans of pleasure that this was a particular favorite of his as well.

When she began to orgasm, she cried out his name, and for God, and she thought she was going to faint as the rapture coursed through her veins. She smiled happily when she felt Sheerness tense and issue utterances much the same as hers when he began to orgasm just as the last tingling shocks of her own began to ebb.

He bent forward slowly and placed kisses along her spine to her shoulder. His breathing was ragged, much the same as Psyche's, but there was a slight hitch at the end of each inhale as the bruising on his ribs made it painful for him to take too deep a breath. She didn't take it personally when he collapsed onto his back on the bed. She leaned forward to kiss him softly before rubbing her nose against his, and then she straightened to pull the blanket up to his waist.

Psyche was actually not cold. Between the fire and recent activities, she was covered with a film of perspiration, and the thought of covering up with a blanket was unappealing. She pulled it up to her waist and lay on her stomach, resting her head on her arm for a few minutes before she rose up on her elbow and propped her chin on her hand to look at Sheerness.

He lay with his eyes closed, a slight frown between his eyebrows, a nerve ticking in his jaw. He was going to have a bruise, but it wasn't his face that was bothering him. Sheerness slit one eye open to look down at her when he felt her placing gentle kisses along his side.

"I can't do that again right now," he said tiredly.

Psyche looked up at him and giggled. She softly ran her fingers over his ribs and bent forward to kiss him on the lips, and then she reached up to comb her fingers through his hair.

"You thought you couldn't the first time, either," she teased.

"Aha, I thought I couldn't before. I'm sure I can't right now."

"If you say so," said Psyche airily. "I wasn't expecting you to. I was only trying to kiss it and make it better."

Sheerness chuckled silently and grimaced. "Ow. This isn't a skinned knee, and I'm not five."

"Oh, I know," said Psyche practically. "A skinned knee hurts much worse, and I couldn't do this if you were five."

She leaned forward to kiss his navel, wrapping her lips around it and massaging the indentation with her tongue while adding a moderate amount of suction. Sheerness stopped breathing, and his hands balled into fists as he felt a jolt of indescribable pleasure. Psyche let go and straightened back up, walking her fingers up his chest playfully.

"Where did you learn to do that?" he asked breathlessly.

"I just thought it would be fun," she said casually with a shrug, but she did make a mental note that he obviously liked it. "Of course, if you *were* five, this could be fun." She leaned forward and blew a raspberry on his stomach. "Actually, this is quite fun." She did it again. She looked up at him with a raised eyebrow. "How old are you anyhow?"

"One and thirty," said Sheerness, trying not to laugh again.

"Really?" said Psyche in surprise.

"The last time I checked," said Sheerness dryly.

Psyche fought a yawn, covering it with the back of her hand. She lay back down on her stomach, resting her head on her arm. She blinked sleepily as Sheerness turned his head to look at her. She lifted her hand to trace her fingers over his lips to his chin before resting it on his chest with a gentle pat.

"Good night, Sebastian," she said drowsily.

"Good night, Psyche," he said softly. "Are you going to be here when I wake up in the morning?"

"Mm-hmm. Sleep sweet, Sebastian."

Sheerness covered her hand on his chest with his own and closed his eyes, but he wasn't sleepy. He wasn't sure if that was what Myron meant by being struck by lightning, but it had certainly been painful. He didn't know how he had avoided it until now. He remembered the conversation between the sisters at Almack's and realized he had pushed her beyond the point she could tolerate things. He felt guilty she had to *beat* an apology out of him, but she still hadn't asked for one; she had only put clearly to him why he didn't deserve one. If he hadn't finally made her lose her temper, if he hadn't apologized, would she have still forgiven him?

He ran his fingers up and down her arm where it rested on his chest and looked at her sleeping face. Her lips were curved into a slight smile, and she seemed completely at peace. He didn't know how she managed it. She was so beautiful, it sometimes hurt his heart to look at her, and at that moment, with her hair spiraling out around her, the graceful curve of her back exposed, he felt his chest tighten. She made him so happy it was frightening, frightening because he didn't know how he would live without her. Having her there had made him realize he couldn't.

Sheerness finally started to drift off, but as he did, his forehead wrinkled. How would *she* know a skinned knee hurt worse than bruised ribs?

Cupid woke Sheerness in the morning. The puppy was sitting by his head, licking at his chin incessantly. Sheerness squinted one eye open to look at the puppy, and then he turned his head to look at Psyche. Just as she had said, she was still there, and it didn't look as if she had moved all night. He turned his head to look out the windows and door to the terrace. The sun was up…barely, which meant it was far earlier in the morning than he would like to be awake.

Cupid still sat looking at him, his head tilted sideways, his tongue lolling out. Sheerness sighed tiredly and grabbed the puppy and carefully eased himself off the bed to take him to the door and let him onto the terrace. He felt stiff, his ribs hurt, and when he ran his fingers over his right cheek, it felt tender. He went to the mirror on the dressing table to look. It was covered by an impressive bruise, but it wasn't swollen. He went back to the door and let the puppy in, and Cupid began to run from one end of the room to the other.

Sheerness climbed back onto the bed beside Psyche and stretched out on his side and propped himself up on his elbow. She really hadn't moved. Her cheek still rested on the back of her hand, and the hand she had placed onto his chest had still been there before he had moved. The only thing different was that she was no longer smiling. The blankets had shifted when he got up, and they just barely came up to cover her bottom. The red of her birthmark just above the edge of the white sheet caught his attention.

He moved his head closer to examine it. He couldn't believe he'd never noticed it before last night. Granted, when she was naked, her back was not what attracted his attention. But he hadn't noticed it the night she danced either, and her hips had been mesmerizing. It apparently had been covered…somehow. It was very low on her right hip, just above the beginning swell of her bottom. It wasn't very large, barely more than an inch in length and less than that in height. It was dark pink in color, just like a strawberry, with uneven margins and smooth on the surface of her skin. As he looked at it, turning his head this way and that, his eyebrows shot up in disbelief. It was undeniably, unmistakably shaped like a reclining sphinx. Even with his terrible close vision, he had no trouble seeing it.

Sheerness smoothed his fingers over it, and then he bent his head to kiss it. Then he began to place kisses along the skin exposed by the edge of the blankets before starting up her spine. The back of her really was as beautiful as the front, and the birthmark didn't detract from it in the slightest. He found it very erotic. Actually, there was nothing about her that he didn't. Psyche woke up at some point while he was kissing her back, and by the time he reached her shoulder, her smile had returned. She turned over onto her back and put a hand to the side of his head to pull his mouth to hers for a kiss.

"*Kaleméra, o erastós mou,*" she said softly.

"I like that," said Sheerness with a grin as he nuzzled her neck.

He brought his lips back to hers, and Psyche lifted his face away to look at his cheek. He looked like he had been beaten (which he had been). She gently ran her fingers over it before giving it a soft kiss, and then she trailed her lips over to his ear to nibble at the lobe. He brought his hand up her hip to one of her breasts and teased the nipple with his fingers until it hardened, and then he took it into his mouth to worry it further until Psyche arched her back toward him and sighed his name, wrapping her arms around his head weakly. He moved to nuzzle the valley between her breasts before teasing the other with his teeth, lapping at it with his tongue.

Psyche moved one of her hands down his side to his hip before letting it slide down to skim across his arousal, and his hips thrust toward her touch spontaneously. She was going to move her hand back up to his chest, but she closed her fingers around his erection instead, moving her hand up and down slowly before circling the tip with her thumb. He groaned low in his throat and thrust his hips excitedly as she continued to touch him, but he soon moved her hand away and pulled her toward him.

He put her leg over his waist and slowly glided into her with a soft sigh of pleasure. Psyche worked her other leg beneath him to wrap around his waist as well, and she smoothed her fingers over his cheeks before tangling them in his hair and kissing him hotly. She watched his face as he began to drive into her, the way his jaw tightened with intense concentration, his expression one of pleasure mingled with lust and something much more gentle. Her breath came out in disjointed gasps and sighs, one arm around his neck and clinging to him weakly as he moved in and out of her with long, deep strokes. The palm of her other hand rested against his cheek, and she moved her fingers feverishly along his jaw in a caress before moving her lips to his for a kiss.

Her body tensed and began to quiver as she climaxed, and it became all the more exquisite when she looked at Sheerness's face as he released a moan and came with her. She ran her fingers through his hair as they shook together, and he rested his forehead against her chin. Their mating was always so intense and passionate, and it didn't seem to be showing any signs of lessening. In some ways that gave Psyche great joy; in others, it frightened her.

They lay twined together as they attempted to regain their breath. They were sweat-soaked and pleasantly exhausted, and Psyche was waiting for the beat of her heart to settle back to a normal rhythm. She ran her fingers down one of his arms where it curved around her waist and gave him a soft kiss. Sheerness wrapped his arms around her tightly and nuzzled her neck.

Psyche could hear Cupid running around, playing with his piece of rawhide. She turned her head to look for him and thought she should let him outside. She started to move away from Sheerness, but he held onto her firmly.

"Where do you think you're going?" he asked with a wicked smile, running a hand over her shoulderblade.

"I need to let Cupid out before he messes on the floor," she said with a half-smile, smoothing her fingers down his cheek.

"No, you don't. He woke me up before I woke you up, and he has already *made wibble*, as you called it." Sheerness grinned. "I guess it would be unpleasant to drink."

"No doubt," chortled Psyche. "How are your ribs? I am assuming they are feeling better."

Sheerness shrugged and moved a hand over her hip. "Not especially, but I've had worse." Psyche raised an eyebrow enquiringly. "I've had a few broken before…once…a long time ago...in India."

His expression grew distracted as he smoothed his hand over her thigh where it still rested at his waist. Psyche looked at him curiously, but he didn't elaborate. She wanted to ask what had happened, but it didn't seem to be something he wanted to talk about. She didn't want to pry. He looked up at her with a thoughtful half-smile and ran his finger over her chin, where there was a smudge of light purple from him hitting her in the bath.

"I have a question for you," he said mildly. Psyche arched an eyebrow with a somewhat wary expression. "How do you know a skinned knee hurts worse than bruised ribs?"

Psyche blinked in surprise and giggled, finding the question unexpected and amusing. "Because I've had both." It was Sheerness's turn to raise an eyebrow. "I *am* accident prone, and I've fallen out of trees, off horses, off ladders, a bit of over-enthusiasm sparring."

"Sparring? As in *fighting*?"

"Well, not fighting, really. Not like boxing. *Wǔshù.*" Sheerness looked at her blankly. "It's a Chinese martial art; that's what *wǔshù* means, and there are different forms. It depends on who is your *dà shī* and what form he learned." Sheerness looked lost again. "Your master or teacher."

"And who was yours?"

"Keung. He taught everyone in my family…is still teaching."

"Hunh."

"I haven't practiced since I left London," she said with a frown, and then she clicked her teeth and shrugged. "Of course, there's not anywhere big enough on the ship. Still, I suppose I could do my stretches and such."

"Is that why you're so flexible?" Psyche nodded. "And the flips and somersaults?" She nodded again. "And this is a *martial* art?"

"Well, there are some weapons, too: swords, staffs, bows, blowguns."

"*Blowguns?*" blurted Sheerness in disbelief.

Psyche nodded enthusiastically. "Myron is really good with a blowgun." Her expression clouded. "Or he was," she said quietly.

"And where did Keung learn?"

"You ask a lot of questions," said Psyche archly.

"I'm just curious," said Sheerness evenly. "I assume you'd tell me to mind my own business if it bothered you."

Psyche sighed and smoothed her hand down his shoulder with a thoughtful expression. "Keung was an apothecary in China before he came to work for my family, and before that he was a monk."

"But not in the military?"

"You must know Buddhism isn't the same as Western religions."

"Of course."

"Well, there you go," said Psyche with a teasing grin.

"I don't see how learning to do acrobatics and bend every which way could possibly help you defend yourself."

"Aha, but I also learned other things, like how to do this—" She put her fingers at a spot on his wrist and applied a slight amount of pressure. It didn't take much effort, and she wasn't pressing hard, but he willingly let her move his arm wherever she wanted because the pain was almost unbearable. She let it go and placed a kiss where her fingers had been.

"That's what you did to Myron, isn't it? That night?"

Psyche nodded. "That's fairly innocuous, but helpful. I could show you others, but they would hurt really bad."

"No, thank you," said Sheerness with a grin. "So you learned *wǔshù* from Keung. Chrissoula taught you *tsifteteli* and how to swim?"

"Yes."

"What other interesting skills did someone teach you?"

"I think that's all that might be considered out of the ordinary."

"Hunh," said Sheerness doubtfully.

"What?" asked Psyche with a half-smile. "I'm good with languages, antiquities, and animals, but I wouldn't consider those unique. I'm passable at art. I have no musical skill. Just ask Eurydice. I can't cook. I can barely sew. I can load and shoot any gun you give me, but don't expect me to hit anything." She shrugged. "What else is there? You obviously have something in mind that hasn't occurred to me but seems out of the ordinary to you."

Sheerness smoothed his hand over her hip and leaned forward to nuzzle her neck, and then he looked at her pensively. He really was curious, too curious for his own good, but he had to know, since she seemed willing to talk.

"Sometimes…when we're together…you do things, and I just…wondered if someone might have…taught you."

Psyche looked at him in disbelief and tried to push away from him, her lips tightening angrily, but he held onto her firmly. He moved his mouth close to her ear and smoothed a hand down her back soothingly.

"Shh. I know I was your first," he whispered gently, and he placed a kiss at her temple. "I know." She finally quit struggling, and she leaned back to look at him confusedly. Sheerness kissed her warmly and ran his fingers over her bottom. When he lifted his head, he gave her an appreciative smile. "It is just that I am very…*impressed* with some of the things you do, and I know there are women who earn their livelihood with far less talent."

Psyche blinked in surprise, her cheeks turning pink. "Thank you, but it's mostly due to plain old enthusiasm," she said quietly.

"*Mostly?*"

"Well, I've read books, and I've talked to Chrissoula. Then I've talked to Maiyin and Lucia when I had questions as well, but I haven't had anyone actually show me how things are done. My parents are open-minded, but not *that* open-minded."

"Who is Lucia?"

"My mother's maid."

"Why her and Maiyin out of all the maids who work for your family?"

"I don't think I should tell you that," said Psyche hesitantly, her cheeks coloring even further.

"What books?"

"I don't think I should tell you that either," said Psyche quietly, and her cheeks were almost red as she blushed to the roots of her hair.

"Don't you trust me?" he asked teasingly with a grin.

Psyche looked at him soberly and lightly smoothed her fingers down his cheek. "I do."

"Then why don't you think you should tell me?"

"It's not something you need to know right now...maybe...eventually."

"All right," said Sheerness with a frown. "What kind—"

Psyche put her hand over his mouth. "No more questions. You're nosy." She grinned at him saucily. "Just enjoy it."

"I can do that," said Sheerness wholeheartedly after she removed her hand. He smoothed his hand down her neck to her chest, settling his hand between her breasts. His face grew pensive. "Why don't you ask *me* any questions?"

"I ask you questions," said Psyche calmly, running her fingers through his hair. He really needed a haircut.

"You didn't even ask how old I was until last night."

Psyche smiled as she began to run a hand over his chest. "Oh, you mean that kind of question."

"Aren't you curious?"

Psyche gave him a half-smile. "I can be *very* curious," she said softly, trailing her fingers over his shoulder, "but I also don't believe in prying."

Sheerness pulled her close and began to nuzzle the valley between her breasts. She could feel his smile as he nipped at the side of one of them before licking it with his tongue. "You have my permission to ask me whatever you'd like, but I reserve the right not to answer."

Psyche sighed and closed her eyes, her head tilting back as he played with her breasts. She did have questions to ask him, but none were coming to mind at the moment.

"What is your favorite color?" she sighed.

"Anything blue." He moved his lips up her chest to her neck and began to tease her ear.

"Favorite flower?" she gasped.

"Roses." He trailed his lips along her jaw to nip gently at her chin, and Psyche clung to him weakly as he went back to her breasts.

"Favorite food?"

"Anything *cow.*"

"Greek or Roman?"

"Hmm. Greek," murmured Sheerness definitely as he weighed her breasts in his palms.

"Marble, granite, or limestone?"

"Marble." He ran his hands along her hips and shifted them against his. "You need to come up with something complicated," he drawled with a leer.

"I can't concentrate," she sighed. Sheerness chuckled and rolled over to place her beneath him. "What's your middle name?"

"Philippe. Still not hard enough."

Psyche ran her hand down between them and wrapped her fingers around his erection.

"Oh, yes, you are," she purred. Sheerness groaned with pleasure and amused disbelief, and he nipped at her neck in retaliation. "Very well," she sighed. She was becoming dizzy and quivery as he teased her, and she wasn't able to think of much except her need for him. She tried to think of a question to shock him. "How old were you the first time you were with a woman?"

"Aha," he said with a grin, "that's more like it. Fifteen."

"Fifteen?" exclaimed Psyche in surprise. "Who was she?"

"A bawd in Canterbury."

"Do you remember her name?"

"Sally Wiggins."

"How many women have you been with?"

Sheerness sat up on his knees and moved one of her legs to his shoulder and began to kiss his way from her ankle to her knee along the inside of her calf. He was about halfway there when she asked the question, and he stopped to look at her, running his fingers along the other side of her calf to her thigh and along her bottom. Psyche squirmed. He seemed to be calculating the answer, his face thoughtful as he continued to lightly run his fingers up and down her leg.

"A score or so," he answered before turning back to kissing her leg.

Psyche lifted her other leg from around his thigh and nudged her foot at his other shoulder to get his attention.

"That many?" she blurted incredulously.

She supposed it really wasn't a terribly large number, but it sounded enormous to her, considering she had only ever been with one man and had no intention of being with another. She had never, and would never have, thought to ask her brothers how many women they had been with for comparison. Sheerness looked at her astonished expression with a lazy smile.

"Were they *all* bawds?"

"No." He ran his hand up her thigh and across her stomach to one of her breasts.

Psyche had a thoughtful frown, and while she was still wanting him, her mind was spinning.

"When was the last time you were with a woman before me?"

"Years," said Sheerness dismissively with a grin.

"Really?" Sheerness nodded with an amused smile. "How many?"

"I don't know. Three or four, maybe five."

"That long?" He nodded again, still amused by her amazement. "Why?"

Sheerness kept the leg he had been kissing over his shoulder and moved the other back around his waist and thrust into her. He leaned forward to kiss her lustily before raising his head with a teasing grin.

"I was waiting for you."

Psyche rolled her eyes and smiled affectionately. "You are such a *terrible* liar," she chortled. She smoothed her hands over his cheeks before running her tongue up the indentation in his chin to his lips and covering them with her own. "You are so going to hell," she whispered.

He began to move in and out of her with a wicked smile. "More than likely," he sighed, "but I will die *very* happy."

Psyche forgot about everything else as he plunged into her, and she moaned as her hands fluttered over him frantically. She ran one of her hands along his side to his hip and trailed her nails across his buttock before splaying her fingers there. She found it indescribably erotic as she felt the muscle tighten and relax as he drove into her, his pace becoming steadily faster. She loved the sound of the sighs and moans he made as he drew steadily nearer to his climax, and she choked out his name breathlessly as she reached her own, her back arching off the bed in a spasm of delight, her hands gripping him tightly when she felt as if she were going to fall off. She felt him tense and begin to quiver as he released a long, shuddering moan, and he let his head come to rest weakly against her shoulder, his forehead nestled into her neck.

"Oh, you sweet, sweet woman," he sighed, breathing tiredly as he placed a kiss on her neck just below her ear.

Psyche smoothed her hands over his shoulders, her eyes closed sleepily. "Sure, you say that now I've thrashed you," she teased with an affectionate smile.

Sheerness chuckled and lifted his head to give her a tender kiss on the lips. "Absolutely," he whispered.

Psyche opened her eyes and looked up at his face. He was gazing at her with a gentle expression, and she moved her fingers up his neck to run them softly over his face. He was sweat-soaked, and his hair was a wavy, unruly mess, but he had never looked more precious to her. She tweaked the end of his nose gently.

"We need a bath," she said with a smile.

"Together?" he asked in surprise.

"It could happen," Psyche answered agreeably, giving him a wink.

Chapter Thirty Three

Luckily, they had woke early. Bathtime proved to be a drawn-out activity that didn't involve a lot of washing. They went to the bath room after Psyche put Cupid onto the porch with the rest of the dogs. By the time they were done, they were ready to go to bed…to sleep. Unfortunately, they couldn't because they were late for breakfast. They couldn't have a nap after because they were going to look at ruins with Nikos. It was something they wanted to do, but if they hadn't planned it the day before, they would have stayed at the house in bed as much as possible.

At breakfast, both Nikos and Ioanna (and the girls) had no trouble seeing the bruise on Sheerness's cheek. Ioanna also saw the way the two of them would look at each other with a slight, affectionate smile when they made eye contact. She had no doubt they had made peace—whatever their disagreement, and the bruise was part of the reconciliation. She thought amusedly that they were very Greek for people from England. If he had given Psyche the bruise on her chin, it was unlikely to happen again. But she had to hear what explanation they would have for the mark.

"Now what have *you* done to get a bruise?" she asked curiously.

Sheerness looked at her uncertainly, his cheeks coloring brightly. Psyche's lips twitched as she took a sip of her coffee. She watched as he sat tongue-tied while trying to decide how to explain what happened. After a minute of his silence, Psyche decided to intervene.

"He fell out of bed," she said amusedly.

She looked at him with a raised eyebrow and a half-smile. It was the truth without being the whole truth. It was plausible, and it was just embarrassing enough to explain his hesitancy in answering. Nikos and Ioanna both laughed, and Sheerness grinned sheepishly, looking appropriately chagrinned.

As with her story for what had happened to her chin, Sheerness had it demonstrated what Bardsey had meant about her not lying. She was capable of giving an *honest* lie…if there were such a thing. Her explanations were *truthful* but not the complete *truth*. It was an impressive talent, but he had to wonder how many times she had used it with him. Had she done it every time he thought she was lying? Or was it more or less often than that? Discovering she didn't lie by simply not telling the whole truth made him even more suspicious about the things she said than had she been telling outright lies.

After breakfast, Psyche and Sheerness went back to their rooms to get the things to take with them on their trip. Sheerness didn't have anything he needed, but Psyche wanted to take her sketchbook and pencils, and she also wanted to take her spectacles. Sheerness followed her to her room and watched her collect her things. He had only been up a few hours, but he was already tired. Added to that was his deliberation about Psyche's ability to tell the truth and still lie, so he was rather silent. Psyche noticed and looked at him. She thought he might be upset about the excuse she gave Nikos and Ioanna.

"Should I have not told them you fell out of bed?" she asked, giving him a pensive look.

"No, that was fine," he said mildly. "All things considered, that was better than what I would have told them."

"Glad I could help," said Psyche with a grin.

She turned back to the box on her dressing table, trying to decide which pair of spectacles she wanted to wear. She wanted some that actually corrected her vision, but she didn't want to use her clear ones because the sun would be bright for most of the day. She had on her mauve and lavender gansey with the matching split-skirt. She decided on the ones made of a dark purple amethyst.

"Can I try those on?" asked Sheerness curiously. Psyche looked at him in surprise but smiled and held them out. He tried them on and immediately felt more blind than usual. "How can you see in these?" he chortled as he moved his head around before taking them off to give them back to her.

"It's easier outside, and it's also helpful if you're nearsighted like I am."

"You're nearsighted?" he blurted in surprise.

"We can't all have perfect vision like you," said Psyche tartly. She reached into the box and pulled out a pair with smoky quartz lenses that were almost black. "Try these. They don't have any correction."

Sheerness took them from her and put them on. They made the room much darker, but they at least did not make it harder for him to see. Actually, to his surprise, they helped…a lot. He found that hard to believe if they weren't made to correct anything because he did *not* have perfect vision.

"That's better," he said with a grin. "Who made these for you?"

"Pandora makes all my spectacles. You're welcome to wear those. I only use those to keep the sun from making me squint, not if I actually need to *see* something."

"Thank you." The two of them left through the door to the terrace. "Your *sister* makes your spectacles?"

"Other than my first pair, she always has. She makes mine, Arachne's, and my father's."

"Are they nearsighted, too?"

"Arachne and my father are farsighted. Damon seems like he will be also, but we're not sure correcting it would do more harm than good right now. Myron was nearsighted like me, but he would never wear his glasses." She smiled fondly. "He would always borrow mine. He was such a dandy."

Nikos was waiting on the pier, and he laughed when he saw them wearing the spectacles. He wouldn't have minded a pair himself, but he couldn't see through them when he had tried them before.

Ioanna sent a basket with dinner, and the day was perfect. The weather was warm, a pleasant surprise after the coolness of the night before. Psyche was sweating in her gansey, and as they sailed down the coast, she wished she had worn something cooler. Sheerness wore his usual outfit of breeches, shirt and waistcoat, but he soon removed the waistcoat and pulled his shirt out of his waistband. Nikos had on a white cotton shirt and trousers with a black waistcoat and thick-soled sandals. As the two men continued to work the sails, Psyche watched enviously as they both removed their shirts. She didn't like to be cold, but she also didn't like to be too hot, and she was stifling.

She could have gone into the cabin, where she would have some shade, but then she wouldn't be able to talk to Sheerness and Nikos. Besides, she was enjoying the scenery, and it wasn't just the landscape floating by on the right, either. She sat on a bench at the stern, out of the way while they worked and still able to watch and talk. Sheerness's right side and back were covered with bruises, but Nikos pretended not to notice. She was sure Nikos didn't believe Sheerness had fallen out of bed, but with it said, everyone had a respectable way of denying it had happened any other way.

She was fairly certain Nikos and Ioanna knew Sheerness was sleeping in her bed. It was patently obvious to the maids that his bedroom was always straight as a pin, particularly his bed, while hers was not, especially her bed. Changing the sheets on it was surely no easy task. They would have to change them even if she were sleeping alone, but not as often as now. Psyche tried to console herself about the extra work by reasoning that since they never had to make his bed it evened out. She didn't doubt it had been mentioned to Ioanna, and Psyche was relieved Ioanna (and by extension, Nikos) was not bothered.

She did have to wonder *why* they weren't. The Greek view of a man and woman sleeping together if they weren't married was no less dim than it was in Britain. If anything, it was even more scandalous. But Psyche didn't want to ask. As with the bruise, it gave everyone the option of respectable deniability, and Psyche appreciated that. She was sure her family would, too.

Nikos guided the boat to shore and tied off at a small quay. The first place they were going was Dion. It was supposedly an impressive site in antiquity, and Psyche had heard of it, but there wasn't a lot to see these days. After hiking the three or so miles from where they had tied the boat to the ruins, Sheerness was disappointed to see that most of it was submerged in a marsh swarming with mosquitoes. Psyche thought it was wonderful. She could see the tops of columns and pillars rising above the reeds and grasses, portions of broken walls and other architecture. While Sheerness and Nikos walked around, Psyche found a comfortable place to sit and sketched. She first did one of what the site currently looked like and another of what she envisioned it might have looked like in its glory. They stayed a couple hours before going back to the boat.

Psyche thought the site showed great promise for excavation, and she sighed wistfully because she wouldn't be there to see the result and how closely her sketch compared. Doing justice to the job would require more resources than she had on hand and Sheerness was willing to expend. The water would have to be drained and kept from inundating it again, and that would take lots of workers. Sheerness had the crew of his ship, but he wouldn't press them into excavation, not that they would do so willingly. Dion was of documented historical importance, so Sheerness wouldn't be able to remove anything, and she couldn't convince him to go to the expense and effort of uncovering it just to see what it looked like. She would, but that wasn't why he had come.

By the time they got back to the *Athena,* it was time for dinner. Ioanna had sent *souvlakia, tzatziki* and pita to make *gyros,* pickled okra, different types of olives, *boureki,* and tiny *kreatopita.* With that were a couple bottles of red wine produced from their own vineyard. It was a wonderful meal, and Psyche and Sheerness both thought the wine was excellent. Once they had eaten all they wanted, they untied the boat and started back north.

The next place they went was Pydna. There was even less to see than there had been at Dion, but both Psyche and Sheerness were aware it had been the site of a few important historic battles, including one involving Olympias, the mother of Alexander the Great. Even with nothing to see, both of them were thrilled by their surroundings, to know they were standing in a place of such epic importance. Psyche found it slightly disorienting to have something she had read about converge with what she was seeing. It almost made her dizzy, and she hoped it wouldn't happen every time they went somewhere.

The sun was starting to set by the time they set sail again, and that was when Psyche was glad she had worn her sweater. It started to become cool again. The sky was almost completely dark just as the *Athena* was guided into the cove to be tied off at the pier. It had been a satisfying day's activities, even though they had not had time to see Methoni, a little further north of the house. They could always see it tomorrow…or the next day.

She got the impression Sheerness had liked seeing Dion and Pydna, but it had frustrated him that he had been unable to *take* anything. Apparently, their discussion about being able to go home with *souvenirs* had not left a lasting impression. That disappointed her. It was too much to have hoped for, and it was something he would have to come to understand on his own.

It was late enough that Ioanna was almost done preparing supper when they got back. Psyche and Sheerness had just enough time to freshen up before it would be time to eat. He started to return the spectacles he had borrowed, but Psyche said he could hold on to them. She had no doubt he wouldn't lose them, and it wasn't as if she didn't have more even if he did.

Supper was wonderful, as usual, and Sheerness got to try *soupa soupion.* He was hesitant, but Psyche convinced him to try a bite. He was surprised that it tasted wonderful but agreed it was too rich and spicy to eat all the time. They also had roast lamb, *spanakopita,* and stuffed zucchini flowers.

Psyche started to nod off at the table, she was that full and tired. She collected Cupid from the porch, and he was so happy to see her that she was barely able to hold on to him because he squirmed so much. Psyche shushed him, and he sneezed at her as a sign of protest, but he did finally settle down enough to allow her to carry him. As soon as she put him down, he went in search of his rawhide, which he found hiding under the bed where he had left it that morning.

Psyche began to undress and managed to remove all of it but her chemise before Sheerness grabbed her around the waist and started to pull her toward the bed. Psyche giggled and tried to drag her feet, but his legs were longer, and he was stronger, so it wasn't difficult for him to lift her and carry her.

"Wait. I have to let Cupid out…unless *you* want to clean up the mess he'll make," she chortled.

Sheerness let her go with a smile, and she retrieved Cupid to let him onto the terrace with a slow laugh. She was cold running around in her chemise, and she didn't leave the door open after she let the puppy out. She had built a fire, and she went to stand in front of it while she waited. Sheerness came behind her to put his arms around her waist and began to nuzzle her neck.

"Aren't you tired at all?" she sighed.

"Not *that* tired," he drawled as he moved his hands up her ribs to cup her breasts. He moved his mouth to her ear. "Are you?"

"I might be able to stay awake long enough for that," she teased. When he asked in that velvety baritone, she couldn't possibly refuse.

"I won't be offended if you say no," said Sheerness softly.

Psyche turned in his arms and put hers around his neck, giving him a seductive smile before running her tongue up his neck to his chin and giving him a sound kiss.

"Why would I want to do a thing like that?"

"Huzzah," growled Sheerness lowly, grabbing her bottom and pulling her close for a lusty kiss.

"Hold that thought over there," chuckled Psyche, stepping out of his arms and pointing him in the direction of the bed.

Once Psyche let Cupid back in, she turned to find Sheerness already undressed and on the bed waiting for her with a grin. That might have been the quickest she had ever seen him get undressed except when she had undressed him herself. Psyche giggled as she slowly sauntered toward the bed.

"You want me bad," she purred with a lecherous grin.

"Oh, yes," affirmed Sheerness with a nod as he watched her remove her chemise and toss it onto the floor with a flourish. "I intend to shag you rotten."

"Huzzah," sighed Psyche as she crawled across the bed toward him.

Psyche woke up the next morning when the sky was still gloomy. She could hear the distant rumble of thunder and was disappointed they wouldn't be able to see any ruins. Cupid hadn't awakened her, so she couldn't understand why she was awake. She should be exhausted. Sheerness had kept his word, and they had made love until they were just too tired to do it again. Because of the impending storm, Psyche couldn't be sure what time it was, but she suspected she had only managed to get three or four hours sleep. Sheerness slept on, curled behind her, his arm draped over her waist.

Then as Psyche was awake for a few minutes more, she realized what had disturbed her. She should be relieved, and she was most assuredly that, but disappointment competed with it and almost won. She consoled herself by accepting it would only be a few days. Chrissoula would applaud her for keeping track of it so well. She had even thought to bring her supplies, even when she hadn't considered she might have needed her medicine kit. Her courses had come right on schedule.

She carefully eased her way out of bed, but she didn't think she would wake Sheerness. He slept like a hibernating bear even when he wasn't exhausted, and he was definitely that. Cupid woke up when he heard Psyche stirring, and to avoid the risk of the puppy waking Sheerness, she let him onto the terrace. She also added more wood to the fire. Then she tended to what she needed to, trying to be as quiet as she could. By the time she was done, the sky had brightened a little, but it was obviously going to rain…a lot.

She let Cupid back in after she put on a dressing gown, and he promptly started to play with his piece of rawhide that was looking quite gnawed on. Psyche was wide awake, and it was pointless to try going back to sleep. Sheerness had shifted after she got up, and she couldn't resist making another drawing to pass the time. She went to her desk where she had unintentionally left it the previous evening and retrieved her sketchbook. She carefully eased the desk chair closer to the bed and sat, propping her feet on the edge of the mattress to use her thighs as an easel and began to sketch.

He had rolled onto his back, one arm flung above his head, the other stretched out on the mattress where she had been. The blankets barely came up to his waist, and one of his legs was bent at the knee beneath them. His head was nestled into the pillows, his face turned slightly toward her, his expression entirely peaceful and innocent, and his hair tousled from sleep (among other things). She couldn't have placed him into a more perfect pose had she tried.

Psyche drew methodically, listening to the thunder. She would look up occasionally when there was a bright flash of lightning, but the storm didn't bother her. She enjoyed a good thunderstorm…on dry land anyhow. She felt peaceful while she worked, enjoying the quiet, the only sounds being those of the storm, the fire crackling, and Cupid playing with his rawhide. Then the rain finally came, accompanied by a strong wind, to soothe her even more. After working on the sketch for an hour or so, she was finished. Sheerness slept on, and he hadn't moved. She put her sketchbook and pencils away, and then she took Cupid to be with the rest of the dogs.

When she returned to the room, Sheerness had finally changed position again. The arm that had been flung over his head was now across his chest. They still had a few hours before it would be time for breakfast, so Psyche was in no hurry to have him awake, but she was envious he was able to sleep so well. She didn't know why she should be—*everyone* slept better than she did. She crawled onto the bed and lay on her side, propping herself up on her elbow as she watched him sleep. She had done it before, and she never grew tired of it. She could watch him sleep for hours—had watched him sleep for hours.

But he wasn't a late sleeper either, and she watched as he slowly began to wake. His eyelashes fluttered on his cheeks as he took a deep breath, and then his eyes were open. He looked at her and smiled sleepily, and then he pulled her toward him to kiss her tenderly. He smoothed his hand over the silk of her dressing gown covering her hip and leaned his forehead against hers.

"How long have you been awake?"

"Hours," she said negligibly.

He leaned back to look at her with a slight frown. "Did you not sleep?"

"I did until I woke up," she smiled, smoothing a hand over his frown.

Cupid wasn't on the bed, and it didn't sound like he was in the room.

"Did the puppy wake you?"

"No, actually, I woke him."

A loud clap of thunder made him turn his head to look over his shoulder. "Was it the storm, then?"

"No, this is perfect weather for sleeping, and I was awake before it even started." She ran her fingers through his hair. "You need a haircut," she said absently. "I can do that for you today if you'd like."

"Sleeping isn't all this weather is good for," said Sheerness coyly, wrapping his arms around her and draping one of his legs over hers.

Psyche giggled and tweaked the end of his nose before giving it a kiss. "I have to agree with you, but I don't think we can or we should."

Sheerness untied her dressing gown and flipped it out of his way behind her back, exposing her for his appreciative viewing. "I know we *can,* and I definitely think we *should.* " He kissed her hungrily and ran his hand down her back to cup her bottom.

Psyche moaned low in her throat, and she moved her hands to his shoulders. She almost forgot why it was that they couldn't, but it did finally come back to her. It took a lot of effort to break the kiss and look at him.

"Any other time, I would say yes, please, but not right now," said Psyche mildly.

"Why not?" asked Sheerness confusedly. "Are you ill?"

"No, I'm not ill. It's just I've—what was that euphemism you used? Oh, now I remember. I've *gotten my flowers.*"

Sheerness moved away, his cheeks turning red, and he couldn't look at her. Psyche didn't know why it made him so uncomfortable. She took in his reaction with a raised eyebrow. It was somewhat humorous, but it also hurt her feelings a little when he withdrew from her, as if she had some sort of disease.

She tried not to take it personally, but it wasn't easy. Sheerness did finally look at her, and he frowned.

"Are you sure?" he asked doubtfully. "You don't *act* like you are." He looked her up and down. "You don't *look* like you are."

Psyche laughed. "I am having my courses, and is there a particular way I'm supposed to act or look when I am? It's a perfectly natural, biological process, not an infection." Sheerness pursed his lips. "Should I be hiding myself away in a dark room or a cave until it's done?"

"No, but you don't *look* like you are."

"And I'll ask again: how am I supposed to look?"

"Shouldn't you have on something to…I mean…isn't it…?"

Psyche made a moue of distaste. "You mean the belt and whatnot?" Sheerness nodded. He didn't like this conversation at all, but he would have to adjust to it if they were going to spend any length of time together. There was only one way to avoid it, and she wasn't going to let that happen. "Eww. I use something much better…at least to me it is, but you're turning green, so I won't say another word unless you insist."

"No, I'll take your word for it," he said weakly.

Psyche brushed a hand down his cheek and leaned forward to give him a brief kiss. He didn't try to move away. The first time, she might excuse it to surprise and forgive him. The second time, he would sleep in his own room.

"Will you tell me why you're so squeamish?" she asked impishly.

"Shouldn't I be?" he asked incredulously.

"Oh, you mean because you're a *man*, and it's a *woman's* bodily function, one of those secret things that go into sex and making babies and all that?"

"You make me sound like a prude," he huffed.

Psyche giggled. "You're no prude, just a man."

"You make that sound even worse," he said with a frown.

Psyche kissed him soundly, and he finally responded back. "Oh, believe me, I very much appreciate that you are a man."

He pulled her close and ran his hands over her bottom. "So there'll be no swiving today?"

"I'm afraid not," confirmed Psyche sadly, "nor tomorrow, or the day after that, or the day after that, and probably not the one after that either."

"Five days? How can I possibly not touch you for *five* days?"

"You will survive," assured Psyche with a chuckle. "It's not as if you'll have withdrawals."

Sheerness nuzzled her neck. "Yes, I will," he groaned. "I already am."

"You're not making this any easier for me," she sighed with long-suffering.

Sheerness looked at her in surprise. "You still want to?"

"I would ask why you think I wouldn't, but I won't. I'm surprised you're not more familiar with things like this, given the fact you had two sisters—"she smiled impishly—"and your…*experience* with women."

"Yes, well, Monique and Amalie are—or were—not like you." He smoothed a hand down her back and looked at her reflectively. "For someone so well-bred and innocent, you're very worldly…far more than I would have suspected." Psyche frowned. "I don't mean that as an insult…truly. As for my *experience* with women, I wasn't around them long enough to worry about things like this, and I didn't care to be."

Psyche shrugged. "I forget the males in my family are exceptional." Sheerness frowned. "Oh, don't look at me like that. You're exceptional, too, just in a completely different way." He grinned boyishly.

"So, what are we going to do instead?"

"Do you mean now, the rest of the day, tonight, or the next five days?"

"All of them."

"I'm going to have a bath, and you're welcome to join me." She ruffled his hair. "Actually, I think you *should.* Then, it will be time for breakfast. You need a haircut, unless you're intentionally letting it grow long again. Since we aren't going anywhere, I thought I would look at your horde some more, take a few notes on the translations and whatnot. As for tonight, this sex all the time is a recent development, and I seem to recall just snuggling is quite fun.

"For tomorrow, depending on the weather, Nikos wants to take us to Pella, and then to some place to the west of here after that. You'll need to check on your crew, and I thought I'd go, too, because I haven't seen everyone in ages, and I miss Waddlesworth and Freddie. I have some shopping I'd like to do in Thessaloniki. Beyond that, I couldn't say." She grinned at him. "See, we can keep ourselves occupied without being *occupied.*"

"Yes, but this is much more entertaining," said Sheerness with a leer before taking one of her breasts into his mouth.

"Focus, Sebastian," sighed Psyche, tangling her fingers in his hair and pulling his head away. "Perhaps you should stand in the cold and rain for a few minutes," she teased. "Maybe we shouldn't bathe together."

"No, no, I can do this," said Sheerness determinedly, taking a deep breath. Psyche gave him a teasing, doubtful smile. "I can."

Over the following days, Psyche was proud of his fortitude. He was hankering, she could tell, but not any less than she. She had previously thought it was over quickly enough, but time seemed to drag. Every morning and night, Sheerness would look at her hopefully, and Psyche would shake her head. The wait was interminable. They did enjoy just holding each other, but Psyche had to agree sex was more entertaining. There were ways she could have helped him bide his time, but it wouldn't have been fair.

Sheerness let her cut his hair, despite his misgiving. It was only hair, and it would grow back. He had grown accustomed to it short, and anything would be better than what it was. He normally entrusted the task to Clements, but his valet was in England, having a much-needed holiday. He was amazed when she set to the task with several pairs of scissors *and* a razor. He expected her to leave him bald (which, after some consideration, he felt wouldn't be a *bad* thing), so he was surprised by the end result: a professional cut and the best shave he'd ever had. He wouldn't tell Clements and hurt the man's feelings.

Sheerness did ask her, finding she had yet another hidden talent. She explained she treated it like trimming topiary…somewhat. His hair was wavy, like hers, but it was a soft wave, and once it was cut shorter than a certain length, it was easier to manage. As for the shaving, until Pandora created her depilatory cream, that was how all the girls removed the hair from their legs, except for Arachne, who had always preferred sugaring like their mother. When Psyche explained what that was, Sheerness winced, just the thought of it sounding painful. Needless to say, all the girls were quite skilled with a razor except Arachne.

It rained again on Sunday, and they had to remain at the house, but it was a gentle rain for most of the time, unlike Saturday—too wet and dreary to go walking in or sailing, but Psyche convinced Sheerness to go for a swim to see the cave. It was quite a distance for him, and he was amazed as he remembered the story Psyche had told him about Chrissoula. Swimming to the cave almost took the maximum length of time he could hold his breath, and Psyche's ability to hold hers for far longer was impressive. The cacophony of the birds was louder than it had been the last time Psyche was there, and she suspected more of them were taking refuge from the rain. Before the noise had been soothing, but it soon began to give them a headache. They didn't stay long. Sheerness found the cave beautiful, though, and fascinating.

On Monday, the sun was out again, and Nikos took them to Thessaloniki for Sheerness to see to his crew and for Psyche to shop. As much as he was able to demonstrate it, Waddlesworth was happy to see her, and Freddie absolutely was. He looked forward to meeting Cupid when Psyche told the boy about the puppy, and he readily offered to help take care of him as well. After her absence of more than a week, the rest of the crew was happy to see her, too, and everyone greeted her cheerfully. It took a while to reach her cabin because she had to stop and talk with nearly everyone on her way there. She retrieved her medicine kit to take with her. She didn't know how much longer they would be there, but having it might be helpful.

While Sheerness was busy talking with Bothi, Broughton, and Stockbridge, Psyche went to the berth deck to have a quick, secretive conversation with Meals regarding things he had on hand in the stores. She was disappointed (but not surprised) to find he didn't have any chocolate. She asked if he knew of somewhere in Thessaloniki to buy some, and she was happy that he did. She gave him money to buy it and a few other things, and Psyche's plans for Sheerness's birthday surprise began. She had a little over three weeks—plenty of time, but there were some things that would have to be arranged as soon as possible because she had no notion of where they would be when it was his actual birthday. None of it would work if they weren't on the ship at all.

After tending to things on the ship, Sheerness and Psyche went shopping. Acutally, Psyche went shopping; Sheerness only watched in open-mouthed astonishment. She bought more art and writing supplies, some glue, towels and flannels, several bolts of fabric, various items of clothing, house goods, a goodly amount of ouzo, and a multitude of other things he soon lost track of.

For every purchase, she haggled with the seller, even when Sheerness thought the price they were asking was a fair one. It reminded him of a fishwife on market day, and he couldn't believe she was doing it. She had to explain it was expected; the people would be offended if she didn't make an effort. Most of the things she arranged to have delivered to the ship, but some would be going with them to the house.

Nikos took care of his own errands while they were in Thessaloniki, and one of them was checking at the customs house for mail. Psyche also gave him a few to be mailed. Sheerness was slightly bothered she didn't asked him to do it. When they met back at the dock, Psyche was excited to find she had letters from home. Not as many as before, but a very nice handful nonetheless. There were two each from her mother and father, three from Pandora, and one each from Chrissoula, Arachne, Eurydice, and her younger brothers. There were also letters from Amalie, the Yeardley children, Josephine, and Sir James. Sheerness had only two, which he put in his pocket unconcernedly.

After Psyche and Sheerness left instructions with people on the ship, they boarded the *Athena*. The crew happy and healthy, but they had to be growing bored sitting in the port day after day. Psyche hoped it wouldn't be long before they had work to do. She was content to stay with Nikos and Ioanna, but Sheerness and his crew wouldn't like to stay in Thessaloniki forever. Perhaps soon Duman would return from Constantinople with the firman.

Under ordinary circumstances, Psyche would have waited until she was back to the house to read her letters, but she didn't feel she could. She sorted them, placing the ones from her parents, then Pandora, on top and began to read. She opened the ones from her father first, arranging them by date.

She began to feel better as she read. The first was written between the time he had received her first letter from Vigo and the second from Melilla, and the second was written in response to it. He was still concerned, but his tone had turned to a tentative relief. As she had mentioned no difficulties, and her second letter had been full of excitement about her trip, he had to believe she was well, and she was. She hoped her first letter from Thessaloniki, the one in which she specifically assured him of her health and happiness, wouldn't take long to reach him. The two from her mother were along the same vein.

The first two from Pandora were still very concerned; although, the third one, written after she had time to receive Psyche's letter from Melilla, had a less anxious tone and was almost written in her twin's typical meandering style. She was overjoyed to hear news of Freddie and apologized for not providing handkerchiefs. She found the news that Waddlesworth had also been stowed away amusing. After Psyche read it, she felt almost giddy with relief. The excited and happy tone of her own letters had allayed her family's worries, even if they had yet to receive her letters specifically addressing them.

Chrissoula's letter, written in response to Psyche's from Melilla, was even less concerned, but her maid hadn't been overly worried even after learning of what had happened. She was glad Psyche was enjoying her journey and expected to hear more in further letters and in person once she returned home.

She asked Psyche to give everyone a hug and a kiss for her. As for Sheerness, Chrissoula suggested Psyche charm the crew into mutiny and have him thrown overboard. Luckily, it hadn't come to that.

Psyche waited until she was back to the house to read the rest from her siblings, Sheerness's family, and Sir James. The ones from her parents, Pandora, and Chrissoula were the ones she felt could not wait. Sheerness gave her some time alone to tend to her correspondence and blessedly did not ask what the letters contained. He got the impression from her cheerful mood the news had been favorable, and he was relieved. He really was regretful about causing her and her family so much worry. He had only letters from his mother and Alex, but he didn't want to read them in front of Psyche.

The letters from her siblings were cheerful and unconcerned, as her parents hadn't mentioned what happened to her to them. Damon thanked her for her birthday wishes, and he was sad she had missed the wonderful party. Eurydice also thanked Psyche for wishing her many happy returns. At the time she wrote the letter, she didn't know what her parents intended to do for her birthday, but she thought it unnecessary for them to go to a lot of effort. She always did think so, and every year she had at least a cake and was happy. Arachne mentioned Psyche had a pair of her spectacles by mistake, which she was sure Psyche would notice as soon as she put them on. They were the smoky quartz ones that were almost black, and while Arachne didn't expect her sister to send them back—as she had others, she thought she should mention it.

Psyche frowned after she read that, knowing they were the ones she had loaned to Sheerness, and yet he hadn't seemed bothered by the corrective lenses. Psyche wondered how he could have seen through them at all. Arachne had very poor near vision...probably from all the reading and writing she did. The men of society thought she had a dreamy expression, one of the things they found charming about her. The truth was: Arachne was almost blind as a bat when looking at things that were near without her glasses, and the *dreamy* expression was caused by her inability to focus her eyes properly. How *had* Sheerness managed to see with them?

Psyche pondered the question for a while, but she finally shrugged and moved on. She would ask for the spectacles and offer a different pair. While she had no doubt he could keep track of them, she didn't want to take the risk with glasses that weren't hers. If he couldn't see through them, it was pointless for him to have them anyhow.

The letters from Sheerness's family were cheerful and unconcerned, and Philip included another picture. Psyche chuckled as she read the letter. Jerome was upset his uncles had decided he should be sent to Eton when the time came. Psyche agreed with him. All the boys in her family went to Harrow. Jerome wanted to go to Harrow because his father had gone there. Psyche assumed Sheerness and Alex wanted him to go to Eton because they had. She only knew that Sheerness had gone to Oxford, like Myron. Come to think of it, she didn't even know what he had studied. She could only believe it involved antiquities or languages, but she could be wrong.

Josie thought her brother was being whiny and that he should be grateful he got to go to school at all. Philip didn't want to go to school. When he grew up, he wanted to be a tree, and that didn't require an ability to read *or* write. Psyche laughed until tears streamed from her eyes when she read that. Still, she thought she might ask Sheerness about Eton, perhaps intervene on Jerome's behalf. She wasn't sure what good it would do.

Once she responded to the letters and answered them, she put them in her trunk. Sheerness hadn't shown any interest in her mail, but he hadn't when he'd read it before, either. The only thing she left out was the picture from Philip. Sheerness might enjoy seeing where his nephew's aspirations were going to take him. It was a large, old, leafy oak. He was anticipating a long and happy life, which was all anyone could hope for.

When she showed Sheerness the picture, he shook his head and laughed. His nephew's decision on his future career would change by the time he wrote his next letter and several times more beyond that before it was something that actually became important. It was one of the freedoms of being five *and* being a younger son. It was one of the things Sheerness envied about Alex. He had no expectations placed upon him as far as responsibility. Sheerness had never had that luxury.

Psyche mentioned Jerome's unhappiness with going to Eton. She was right that it was the school Sheerness and Alex had attended—and their father, but his mind wasn't set on it. She mentioned that Cosmo and Christopher would be going to Harrow soon and that Jerome might appreciate going to a school where he would already have friends. Sheerness said he would think about it, but Psyche was fairly certain he would change his mind.

For the third night, they had to be satisfied with just holding each other. It was frustrating in some respects, more so to Sheerness than Psyche. She enjoyed sex, but she also liked the intimacy of just being close to him. For Sheerness, it had become similar to the apple tied to the string in front of the horse or the beggar looking in the window of the bakery. At least they were both getting sleep, which Psyche had to admit neither of them had been. What was she going to do in a fortnight when she had to tell him no for other reasons? He was already growing impatient, and she could no longer pretend to be asleep. She would have to think of something.

On Tuesday, Nikos took them north to Agii Apostoli, what once was ancient Pella. There was more to see than there had been at Dion, even though part of it was covered by a modern city. Psyche had to wonder how much of the ancient one had been destroyed to create it. She understood the living had to take precedence over the dead, but preserving history was important. One couldn't know where one was going if one didn't know where one had been. She wondered if in the future (not in her lifetime) someone would move things to find out what was beneath it all. There were beautiful mosaics and columns, and Psyche made several drawings of what was there and what she imagined it must have been like long ago. All in all, it had been a worthwhile trip. Sheerness had enjoyed seeing it, but he was growing impatient.

Psyche had noticed he was steadily becoming impatient about everything, even though he kept it hidden well. He wanted to have sex, and he couldn't. He wanted to take things from the places they visited, and he couldn't. He wanted to know everything there was to know about her, and he couldn't. Most of it would be resolved in due time. They would be able to make love again in a matter of days, one or two at the most. Their firman would give them permission to take things, within reason, and it wouldn't be long before Duman arrived with it. He had the sultan's ear, but it took time. It had been almost two weeks since he left. It would be beyond the end of the month before he accomplished it, and that was an estimate based on things going wrong. Still, even without the firman, she had her find from Pantelleria, and he had the one from Olympus. Both were respectable discoveries. She supposed they weren't *big* enough for him. Eventually, they would go to Egypt and find what was on her map. She was very close to finding the location with Sir James's help.

As for knowing everything about her, that was impossible. Yet it seemed that's what he wanted. He was constantly asking questions about everything, and while she didn't mind giving him the answers, sometimes she just wanted to tell him hush. She didn't understand why he had to know. He reminded her of a little boy with the incessant questions. She was curious about him, too, but it wasn't important, not important enough to pry. She didn't think he was asking to be invasive, and she didn't think he even realized how bothersome it was. By Tuesday night, Psyche had had enough. They were walking back to their rooms after supper, and after she had collected Cupid from the porch, he begin asking her questions about things that, while totally innocuous, were unimportant for him to know. At least, she thought so.

"Sheerness, can you, please, quit asking so many questions?" she sighed tiredly.

"Why? Does it bother you?" he asked with a frown.

"It's beginning to," she said quietly. "I appreciate that you're curious, but there's a fine line between curiosity and intrusion. You're starting to cross it. Actually, if I were anyone else, you would have crossed it about five dozen questions ago."

"Why don't you want to tell me? Are you hiding something?"

Psyche clenched her jaw and shook her head. "As many questions as you've asked, I can flatly tell you no and quit being silly. You don't need to know everything about me, not any more than I need to know everything about you. Sometimes you need to just accept things the way they are. It's not important to always know why...especially not with people."

"Am I being unfair? Do you want to ask me anything?"

"No," said Psyche as he opened the door. "Nothing is coming to mind."

"Are you sure? Why don't you want to?"

"Sheerness, enough!" groaned Psyche. "You're making me tired. If you persist in asking me all these questions now, what will there be to talk about later? And since you ask *me* so many questions, by the time you're through, even if I had any, I'm just longing for *silence.*"

"I didn't realize it was so offensive," he said stiffly. "I'm only curious."

Psyche sighed exasperatedly and smoothed a hand over her forehead. "Why are you? Why do you want to know everything about me?"

Sheerness looked away from her, his jaw clenching. Psyche threw her hands up in aggravation and got ready for bed. At least he wasn't asking questions. She didn't understand why he persisted in asking and expecting her to answer when he didn't want to answer any she might ask him. Other than the ones she had put to him on Friday morning, he had been resistant to telling her anything the few times she had. That *was* unfair. She unbraided and brushed her hair after she put on her shift and brushed her teeth. Sheerness was standing in front of the fireplace, leaning a hand against the mantle, looking at the flames of the dying fire. Psyche walked behind him and put her arms around his waist, resting her cheek against his back.

"You can't have all of me, but I'll give you as much as I can."

Sheerness turned to look at her. She had a pensive expression, and he softly smoothed his fingers down her cheek before pulling her close to hold her tenderly. As he thought over the past few days, he realized he had been harrying her. He just wanted to know everything about her to make it easier to live up to her expectations. He wanted to know what she liked, what she didn't, and what she thought because he didn't want to disappoint her. His constant prodding must have felt smothering and unnerving.

"I'm sorry I've been so nosy. From now on, just tell me to shut up," he said softly, resting his cheek on top of her head.

Psyche smiled and tightened her arms around his waist. "I will take that under advisement." She could hear Cupid playing with his piece of rawhide. "I need to let the puppy out before bed," she said as she looked up at him, placing a kiss on his chin, "and you aren't even undressed yet."

"What's the point these days?" he asked on a sigh.

Psyche tweaked the end of his nose as she stepped away from him with a teasing smile. "I like seeing you in the buff," she said practically.

"Mm-hmm," said Sheerness with a slow grin as he unfastened the buttons on his waistcoat. "Do I make you hot? Oh, wait—that was a question."

Psyche turned back from letting Cupid out and walked toward him, smiling wantonly as he pulled off his shirt. "Boiling," she drawled.

"Is it time yet?" he asked hopefully.

"No," she sighed as she added more wood to the fire. "Maybe tomorrow night." She turned to watch as he took off his pants. "And you know what they say," she said with a grin.

"What's that?" asked Sheerness with a slight frown as he folded his pants to place them onto the chair with the rest of his clothes.

"A watched pot never boils," chortled Psyche.

"Oh, you are just positively evil," chuckled Sheerness.

Psyche giggled. "I think that would be the *kettle* calling the *pot* black."

"Boo," said Sheerness slowly with a wry grin. "No more." He grabbed Psyche by the arm and pulled her toward him just as she was going to let Cupid back in and gave her a lusty kiss, his hands resting on her bottom. "You are *so* going to be sorry tomorrow night."

"Maybe," said Psyche with a soft smile as she ran a finger over his chin. "I hope so."

She let Cupid in and put him on the bed, and he did his usual running around before settling down with his nose hanging over the end. Sheerness smoothed a hand over his fur a few times and climbed onto the bed to join Psyche. He snuggled close behind her and wrapped his arms around her waist, giving her a squeeze before placing a kiss on her neck just below her ear.

"Where is Nikos taking us tomorrow?" he asked quietly.

"I'm not sure," said Psyche with a yawn. "He just said it's a place he knows of not far from here, a little north and to the west."

"How does he know about all these places?"

"Ask me again tomorrow," said Psyche tiredly, snuggling against him.

"Could you not wiggle against me like that?"

"Could you not play my diddey like that?" chuckled Psyche drowsily.

"I am astonished by your knowledge of slang, Lady Psyche Savage," said Sheerness archly, but he moved his hand back down to her ribs.

"Brothers," mumbled Psyche, almost asleep. "Good night, Sebastian."

He kissed her neck again. "Good night, Psyche."

The next morning, Nikos had them meet him at the front of the house, earlier than time for breakfast, once they had collected their things. They walked through the garden, and Psyche was surprised when he took them to a stable where there was a carriage pulled by two horses waiting.

"I didn't know you had horses!" she exclaimed.

Nikos chuckled. "Just these two, and they do everything."

The carriage wasn't fancy and was more like a wagon. There was no front seat but rather two, lightly padded benches facing inward with an awning-type roof to shield the occupants from the sun or rain. There was a basket with things for their dinner and breakfast under one bench and a box containing lanterns and other things beneath the other. Psyche didn't know if that box was there all the time for use with the cart or if Nikos had put the things there for their outing.

The ride was scenic as they traveled inland, and Psyche enjoyed seeing more of the interior of the country. There were groves of olives and nuts, particularly pistachios and almonds, and citrus, and they also passed several vineyards. There weren't many estates, and most of the villages were sparsely populated. They passed through Makrigialos to Sfendami and then a small village called Piakia before fording a river. Psyche loved the smell of the air. It was spicy and exotic and clean, and completely different from the air at home.

Nikos explained as they traveled further west that most of the land they saw belonged to the bey of Palatitsia, and the place where he was taking them was near two villages, Koutles and Barbes, which the bey "owned." Psyche found it odd to think someone could actually *own* a village, but then she reasoned that even in Britain, the nobility—while not having a deed or patent—often had villages near their country estates that somewhat—for lack of a better term—fell under their *patronage.* The inhabitants typically worked for them, and the land the village was built on had originally been part of the noble's demesne. But they weren't *owned*, and the villagers weren't serfs.

The ride took a little over three hours, and when they arrived, Psyche wasn't sure what she was looking at. There were a few ruins, tumbled columns and decayed stone walls, but there were several small hills, almost as if monstrous colonies of ants had built mounds a long time ago. As she looked at the mounds, her head tilted sideways thoughtfully. They reminded her of the tumuli in Britain. Some of them, on closer inspection, had a lumpiness that made it possible to distinguish there was something more than dirt there. She turned to look at Sheerness, but he obviously didn't see what she did. He had a disappointed expression, and he thought this, next to Pydna, was the most disappointing excursion they had made yet. She looked at Nikos after they stepped down from the carriage with a curious frown.

"Where are we?" she asked wonderingly.

"You see them, don't you?" said Nikos with barely contained excitement.

"I do," said Psyche with a nod, "but I'm still not sure where we are."

"My sister said you're very familiar with Greek history. You've studied maps and read about the ancient cities?"

"Ye-es," said Psyche slowly with a frown. "We've seen Dion, Pydna, Methoni, Pella, and now we're looking at what?" she asked rhetorically.

She put her hands on her hips and turned in a circle, looking around herself. The back side of Olympus sloped toward them. They were at the end of a wide ravine, standing on a relatively flat plateau dotted with the barrows, including one she had first mistaken for a small hill but realized was the largest tumulus she had ever seen, covered with elms and shrubbery. Some of the mounds had been disturbed, but it hadn't happened recently. She didn't see anything to determine where they were. She was sure there was more beneath the soil, but at the moment she was looking at a giant cemetery.

Macedonia was an area that had been of particular interest to Psyche because of Alexander the Great. Actually, she was more interested in the *women* in his life, like his mother, sisters, and wives, and the part he had played in the creation of the Ptolemaic dynasty in Egypt. She went through the things she knew about ancient Macedonia, particularly its geography, and she began to chew on the side of her thumb and pace.

Sheerness stood with his head tilted sideways, watching her, wondering what it was about this place that had Nikos so excited and Psyche so bothered. He was not impressed. It would have been a further journey, but they would have been better served by going to Edessa or even back to Thessaloniki. There were fewer ruins here than there had been any place else they had gone. Psyche continued to pace with a thoughtful frown, and then she stopped mid-stride and turned to look at Nikos.

"You cannot mean it?" she said breathlessly.

"I think it is," said Nikos with a grin.

"Ohmygosh, ohmygosh!" squealed Psyche, jumping up and down.

"Will someone, please, enlighten me?" asked Sheerness flatly.

"You mean you don't know?" asked Psyche disbelievingly.

"I wouldn't be asking if I did," said Sheerness dryly with a slight smile.

"This is Aigai," said Psyche, so excited she seemed to vibrate in place.

Sheerness looked at her doubtfully. "Why would you think that?"

"Sheerness, it's so obvious," said Psyche with amused exasperation, grinning. "Think about where we are." She waved her hand in the direction of the mounds. "Look at the tumuli…everywhere. And the ruins. Even without seeing everything, and I can tell there is more buried here than is visible, it's obvious this was a major center of habitation or worship. Aigai was both, and it was supposed to be located somewhere hereabouts." She turned to look at Nikos. "How did you find it?"

"Chrissoula and I did, a few years before…," he trailed off. "We thought the little mounds were curious, so once when we came, we dug into one. There wasn't much in it because it had been plundered long before we got here, but it piqued my interest. I began to read and look at maps, and then I knew. I've never told anyone. I didn't find out until after Chrissoula…." He shrugged. "By then, it didn't seem important anymore."

"Oh, this is fantastic," sighed Psyche, putting a hand to her heart.

"We should have some dinner, then we can explore, yes?" said Nikos.

"Oh, I don't know if I can wait," said Psyche slowly.

Nikos chuckled. "It has been here for more than two thousand years; another hour is not going to make a difference."

Sheerness's stomach rumbled, and he rubbed a hand over it. "I agree."

He had a slight frown as he looked around himself while Nikos retrieved the basket from the carriage. If they were right, if this was Aigai, it would be one of the most spectacular discoveries ever made. It had been the capital of the region for a long time and was the burial place of the Macedonian royal family belonging to the Argead dynasty. Not Alexander the Great, but several members of his family and his ancestors and others who came after him.

As Psyche and Nikos chose a spot to have their meal, Sheerness looked at the small mounds. Most of them had been disturbed. He could see that from the way they were misshapen. Nikos admitted he and his sister had plundered at least one. Some could have collapsed upon themselves over the centuries, and at least part of the site had been destroyed by the Romans. Still, it could be one of the richest finds made, and the city might be known from history, but the site itself—*this* site—was not of documented historical importance. This could be *the* place for both he and Psyche to find something they felt was useful.

They ate their dinner quickly, impatient to look around. Psyche wanted to look at the large tumulus. Sheerness wanted to look at the small ones. Nikos wanted to find the one he and Chrissoula had dug into to find out what kind of changes the past twelve years had made. Psyche could barely sit still to eat, and she looked at the hill nearby with longing and speculation, tilting her head this way and that as she gazed. If her hands weren't occupied with her food, she would be chewing her thumb.

Psyche didn't wait for her food to digest before she got up to walk toward the large mound. She walked along the edge of it, looking it up and down. Then she walked up the side of it. She would occasionally bounce with her feet and examine the roots of the trees. She went about halfway up and paced out an area, and then she began to pull at the bushes and grass beneath the trees in a location that was remarkably bare of roots on the surface. Sheerness and Nikos looked at her curiously from where they were at the small mounds.

"What is she doing?" asked Sheerness slowly.

"Hmm," said Nikos thoughtfully. He walked to the carriage to pull out some shovels and a pick. "I *thought* we might need these," he said with a grin as Sheerness looked at him questioningly, and he went to join Psyche on the tumulus.

"Why are you pulling up the undergrowth on this hill?" asked Sheerness as he reached them. "I don't think they're antiques."

Psyche giggled. "This isn't a hill. It's a mound, and I think I've found a place beneath it that's hollow."

"What?" blurted Sheerness in surprise.

"This is a tumulus, just like the others, only much bigger, and I just have to wonder: what's buried under it?" grinned Psyche as she used one of the shovels to dig up the roots to a particularly stubborn laurel.

"Are you sure?" asked Sheerness doubtfully.

Psyche sighed and shook her head and pulled him by the hand a little further away. "Stomp your foot right here." Sheerness raised an eyebrow but did as he was told. It sounded like a hill to him. She then took him back to where Nikos was steadily digging with the other shovel. "Now stomp your foot here." He did, and he could hear a faint echo.

"*Merde alors,*" he said in astonishment.

"Absolutely," said Psyche with a grin.

Sheerness took the shovel from her and began to dig with Nikos, both of them soon removing their shirts as they toiled. While they were digging, Psyche tried to sift through the dirt they removed on the chance there might be items hidden in it. It proved a wise decision, as she found several circular, dirt-encrusted pieces of metal she suspected were coins, among other things. They would occasionally hit something made of stone, and in the process of digging the hole, they managed to discover three stelae, one of them painted, the other two with raised carving. Psyche carefully moved everything they uncovered to the side to keep it from being reburied under the dirt they removed.

Eventually, they hit a piece of stone far larger than the stelae, and judging by the smoothness of the piece of limestone, it had not occurred naturally. Sheerness and Nikos removed the dirt around the sides of the hole they had dug and searched for the edges of the stone they had found. It was marginally smaller than the hole, which was big enough for the two men to stand in and shovel without hitting each other and a little over three feet deep. It had taken them a while to dig, but it was just nearing one. Once they had the edges cleared, the two men jumped out and looked down at the stone with Psyche.

"That's going to weigh a lot," said Psyche thoughtfully.

It was a piece of limestone, about three feet on each side, and it abutted the edges of others that were probably of the same size. It was part of a roof, but Psyche could only speculate about its thickness. If it *was* part of the roof, it couldn't be more than four inches thick simply because of the architectural soundness involved, but that would still put it at possibly weighing as much as four hundred fifty pounds at its worst. If they were lucky, it would be only about two inches thick, which would still make it weigh close to two hundred. How were they going to lift it?

Nikos walked back to the cart and returned carrying some rope, wedges, and a long, iron pry bar. Psyche grinned when she saw him.

"You were ready for anything," she chortled.

"Actually, I keep most of this stuff on the carriage all the time, simply because the roads in Greece are atrocious."

Once they cleared away enough dirt to stand on the abutting stone and have leverage, Nikos and Sheerness worked the pry bar between the stones and lifted. The stone was—while not two inches thick—not four, and it was one of the less dense types of limestone. Nikos and Sheerness worked their way around the edges of it, lifting and inserting wedges, and once they had it raised high enough to work their hands under the edges, the two men were able to lift it without the rope and put it out of the way on the edge of the hole.

Psyche stood on the edge of the excavation, looking down at the black, gaping square with excitement, but also with misgiving. How deep was it, and what was in it? She wanted to know, but then she *didn't* want to know. Nikos went to the cart and brought back two lanterns. He soon had one lit, and then he looked up at Psyche.

"You want to do the honors? You did find it, after all," he said with a grin.

Psyche looked at the opening uncertainly. She did want to see what was inside. After some hesitation, she stepped into the hole and took the lantern from Nikos. She knelt down, bracing one of her hands on the edge and hung the lamp into it. She then bent over at the waist and looked in. She tried to ignore the distance to the floor below, but she couldn't quite bring herself to do it. Even as she looked at the wondrous things dazzling her in the light of the lantern, she felt herself going dizzy with vertigo. Sheerness had to grab her by the shoulder and pull her back before she toppled in.

Chapter Thirty Four

"Are you all right?" asked Sheerness worriedly, noticing the way her features turned pale and her out of focus expression.

"Just over-excited maybe," she said with a sheepish smile.

He grinned slowly, still unsure. "That good?" he asked hopefully.

She handed him the lamp. "Look for yourself," she chortled.

Sheerness bent down through the hole and looked around, having none of the fear of heights that plagued her. He looked for several minutes, and when he straightened, he wore an astounded look.

"That's…that's fantastic," he said slowly.

He handed the lantern to Nikos. As Nikos looked around, he slowly began to chuckle, and by the time he was upright again, it had turned into a full, belly-splitting laugh.

"Oh, Thea, your feet have divined something *divine*!" he chortled. "Tykhe has smiled on you!"

Nikos tied the rope around a nearby tree. He pulled on it several times to make sure it was secure, and then he tossed the end into the hole. Psyche just had to go in, but she wasn't sure she could. The distance to the floor wasn't far—less than ten feet. It was just a question of whether or not she could make herself forget the ten feet and go in. She stood up and climbed out of the hole.

"I want to look around first, and I want to make drawings before we move anything. Let me go get my things from the carriage."

Nikos and Sheerness looked at each other. She was behaving strangely, but perhaps she *was* simply over-excited. They would be able to see better once both lanterns were lit and they were actually in the tomb, but just looking around through the opening had left both of them awed.

As Psyche walked down the hill to the carriage, she was quickly trying to decide what she could do to get herself in the hole and to the floor without fainting. It wasn't so much the height that concerned her; it was the fear of falling. That was always the case, which was why heights above water didn't bother her. By the time she made it back with her art supplies, she had decided she would keep her eyes closed and keep in mind that the quicker she got down the rope, the closer the floor would be. She set her things on the slab they had removed and looked at the hole nervously. She had climbed into the bilge on the ship without any problem, but then again, it was barely six feet deep at the keel, and most of that had been disguised under the surface of two feet of water. She looked at Sheerness.

"You can go first," she said quietly.

He frowned dubiously. "Are you sure?"

"Absolutely," said Psyche, nodding her head quickly. "You go first."

Sheerness looked at her assessingly for a minute, but he finally shrugged his shoulders and took the rope in his hands. Once he was standing inside the tomb, Nikos lay on his stomach and leaned into the hole to hand down the lanterns. Psyche was still unsure, but she took the rope in her hands. She sat on the edge of the opening and hung her feet over the side, and then with a deep breath she closed her eyes and slipped over the edge. She didn't look down as she eased herself down the rope, and she sighed with relief when she felt Sheerness put his hands on her waist and helped her down the rest of the way.

"Thank you," she said with a brief smile.

"Is that why you wanted me to go first? To help you down?" he asked with a grin.

"Of course," said Psyche with a wink. "I wanted something soft to land on if I fell." It was not a lie.

Nikos leaned in again for Sheerness to take her art supplies. Psyche picked up one of the lanterns and looked around as Nikos made his way down the rope. The room was packed with treasures, and Psyche was amazed by what she saw. There was no door, so the only way in was the way they had come. The tomb was small, a rectangle that looked to be a little more than six feet wide and ten feet long, which was one of the reasons it was so full.

They couldn't leave behind the things they had found. Psyche hoped they would come back and dig even more, but now that the tomb was exposed, it made it vulnerable to robbery. Even if they put the slab back and refilled the hole, it would be obvious the ground had been disturbed. The site didn't appear to be known, but someone traveling through might notice and decide to find out what it was. If they left the things behind, they might never see them again. That would be a shame.

She looked at the walls and sighed. The upper halves of three were covered with frescoes in excellent condition. The colors had faded a bit, but the detail was clear. Psyche would do her best to make her copies accurate. The bottoms of the walls were painted dark red, divided from the upper parts by a blue-green border painted with griffins and flowers. Even without all the grave goods, Psyche had no difficulty telling this was a royal tomb, and she was fairly sure the occupant was a woman. The frescoes weren't what she would expect for a man. She could be wrong. Just glancing around, she could see belongings that weren't likely for a woman, but not necessarily. It all depended on the woman.

"Fabulous," said Sheerness as he looked around. "Absolutely fabulous."

"This is like Ali Baba's Cave of the Forty Thieves," grinned Nikos.

Psyche took her art supplies from Sheerness and set them on the floor near her feet. She took a pencil and her sketchbook and quickly began to make a drawing showing where things were located. She didn't add a lot of detail because things in the far corners, even with two lamps, weren't very clear. She had a general idea of what she was looking at, and as they began to remove things, she would take notes on where they were located in the room. Once she had the layout sketch completed, she would wait until they had everything out before she worked on her paintings of the frescoes. It would be easier then because she would have to sit down to paint; she didn't have room right now.

"Do we have room for all this on your carriage?" she asked Nikos.

"We will make it fit," he said with a grin.

"How are we going to get it out?" asked Sheerness.

"The picnic basket will do for something to place the smaller items into, but we will have to figure out how to carry them home. There is more than a basketful of items," said Psyche, looking around with her hands on her hips.

"Obviously," said Sheerness with a grin.

"Considering their age, we can't have them rattling around loose."

Nikos went to the rope. "I'll arrange something. You wait here, and I'll be right back." Psyche and Sheerness watched as he climbed the rope and disappeared into the daylight. He looked into the hole at them. "Don't go anywhere," he chortled. A few minutes later, they heard the carriage departing.

Sheerness turned to look at Psyche. "Where do you think he's gone?"

"Don't know," said Psyche dully. "My guess is he's gone to find something for us to carry this back to the house. Palatitsia, Barbes and Koutles are nearby. Maybe he's going to one of them." She turned to look at Sheerness with a grin. "In any event, he'll be back, and he'll have exactly what we need."

"Hunh," said Sheerness noncommittally. He looked at the fresco. "The abduction of Persephone, you think?"

"Without doubt. So, do you think this is a woman's tomb, or a man's?"

There were several objects he recognized immediately as being weapons or related to arms. "I don't know. I'm thinking it was a man's, but the painting is all wrong for that."

"That's what I thought," said Psyche in amazement, her eyes widening.

Sheerness grinned. "Don't look so surprised."

She looked into the corner behind her. "This throne is absolutely gorgeous, and I can't believe it's still in one piece. We'll have to be careful removing it."

Sheerness pulled her close and rubbed his nose against hers. He was without his shirt, and his skin was sticky and cool from the sweat that had dried there from the shoveling he and Nikos had done. Psyche put a hand to his cheek and brushed her lips against his softly with a slight smile.

"You're going to need a bath when we get back home," she said quietly.

Sheerness removed her hand from his cheek and flopped it in front of her eyes. "You're one to talk," he chuckled. Her fingers were filthy, dirt caked under the nails from her sifting through it.

Psyche cleared her throat with a wry grin and stepped away from him. "So, let's see what we have here," she said brightly.

There was a large marble sarcophagus near the back wall. The sides were sculpted with a ring of nymphs, and Psyche couldn't tell if it portrayed a particular scene from mythology or if it was just decorative. Each figure was carved differently, so they were specific characters, but determining who they were would take more time than they would have in the tomb. When she first saw the sarcophagus, had it been smaller, she might have thought it was a cinerary urn, but this was not the right region for those. It had three sections to the lid, and each one had been carved with a different scene, like panels.

Psyche started to chew on her thumb thoughtfully as she walked toward it but quickly took her hand away when she tasted dirt. She picked up one of the lanterns and set it down nearby to give herself more light. She ran her fingers over the top of the lid on the left. She smiled slightly when she realized it was Tykhe and Nemesis along with a few other characters, including Aphrodite. It was probably the seduction of Helene, and Psyche thought it was odd someone would choose that as a decoration for a tomb. The middle panel was easy enough to figure; it was Hekate with Cerberus. The one on the right was a depiction of Demeter with Pan. Psyche looked at the figures of the nymphs around the edge. She began to suspect they were Lampades, nymphs of the underworld. It would make sense.

She put her hands on the lid with Tykhe and carefully lifted it off. She blinked her eyes in surprise.

"Oh," she said softly.

Sheerness came behind her and looked in as well. "*Mon dieu,*" he gasped.

It was a small box made of what appeared to be solid gold. The top was embossed with a twelve-pointed star. The lid was hinged, and there were shallow indentations on the sides where the hands could be placed to lift it. Psyche didn't do that, but she did carefully open the lid. It barely made a noise, and she lifted it until the top rested against the back of the sarcophagus. The contents were covered by a blue and gold cloth, and after a brief hesitation, she slowly shifted it to reveal cremated remains. She tilted her head sideways with a slight frown as she looked at what was there.

"So little," she whispered, looking at the fragments.

"Yes, well, cremation tends to do that," said Sheerness dryly.

She looked up at him where he was standing over her and shook her head. "No, that's not what I meant." She looked into the box and carefully removed one of the larger fragments of bone. "This is a femur...almost complete. Can you tell me what's wrong with it?"

"What's a femur?" asked Sheerness blankly.

"It's the thigh bone, the longest bone in the human body, and you can't mistake it for any other, not when it's nearly whole like this one."

Sheerness looked at the bone she held in her hand. It was less than a foot long. He looked down at his own thigh and back to the bone thoughtfully, and it was then that he realized what she meant.

"A child?"

"A baby," she said quietly as she put the bone back in the box, recovering it with the cloth and closing the lid.

She removed the lid to the second compartment and found another gold box carved with the same star. She opened the lid and found the remains covered with a purple and gold cloth. When she pulled it back, she found a gold diadem carved with myrtle flowers so detailed she might have thought it was the real thing dipped in gold sitting on top of the bones and ashes.

"Ah, the woman," said Sheerness wryly.

Psyche closed the coffer and moved to the remaining compartment. When she removed the panel, she wasn't surprised to find yet another gold box. When she opened the lid, the remains were covered with another blue and gold cloth. When she pulled it back, there was a silver circlet plated in gold. She picked her way through the fragments, looking for something that might tell her a little about whose remains they were. She found a piece of the jawbone, but not enough to tell her if it was a man or a woman. She found a piece of the front part of the skull, part of the brow and a portion of the eyesocket.

"I think this is a man, but there's not anything big enough for me to be sure at such a cursory glance," she said distractedly, still picking through the bones.

When she didn't find anything after a few more minutes of searching, she put the cloth back, closed the lid, and stood up to look at Sheerness.

"So, do you want my initial assessment?" she asked evenly.

"I await it with baited breath," said Sheerness with a teasing grin.

"This is a family—a man, a woman, and their baby. The only one that was fully of royal blood was the woman, but she wasn't a queen."

"What makes you think that?"

"She was the only one with her remains covered by a purple and gold cloth. Purple is, and always has been, thought of as the color of royalty because the dye for a true purple is so difficult to make, which makes it incredibly expensive. Had the husband been a king, or a prince of royal blood for that matter, he would have had his remains covered by purple as well, and so would the baby. Also, her remains are in the center compartment, which makes me think she took precedence over her husband. If he were the royal one, she would have been in one of the end compartments like their child. She wasn't a queen because there weren't any...at least not any that ruled in their own right; perhaps as a regent, but not as the actual *annointed* queen."

"So who are they?" asked Sheerness with a grin. He silently admitted he couldn't find any fault with her reasoning.

"That will take far more time than I've just spent to determine, and it's not important right now," she answered back with a grin of her own. "Maybe after we've uncovered a few more tombs, hopefully as intact as this one, we'll be able to create some sort of identification for these individuals."

"*More* tombs," said Sheerness happily. "I like the sound of that."

"Yes," said Psyche dryly, tweaking his nose, "I thought you might."

Psyche and Sheerness spent their time cataloging the items in the tomb. Sheerness didn't think they needed to, but Psyche felt it was necessary to list everything they found, where it was located, and a brief description. She didn't make a sketch of an item unless it was fragile and might be easily damaged while being moved. There weren't many things like that, as most were made of silver or gold. As Psyche looked at the items in the tomb, she began to get a sense of who the people were that were buried there, even if she as yet didn't know their names. They had just finished when Nikos returned.

"Look out below," he called.

Psyche and Sheerness looked up as Nikos dropped down several bundles of straw. They moved them to the side for Nikos to come down, but he remained where he was. He held a crate over the opening, and Psyche caught it with a grin and moved it to the side. They soon had several sitting in a stack. After Nikos dropped down a pile of cloths, he climbed down to join them.

"Nikos, if there's ever a crisis, I am with you," chortled Psyche, and Nikos laughed. Sheerness clenched his jaw, feeling an unexpected stab of jealousy.

They steadily packed everything into the crates after lining them with the straw. They wrapped the items in the cloth and put them into the boxes, covering them and filling in the spaces around them with even more straw. Psyche tried to pack things in an orderly fashion, putting things grouped together in the tomb in the same crate as much as possible. They soon had everything packed except the throne, sarcophagus, and the coffers inside.

Nikos and Sheerness climbed the rope out of the tomb, and then Psyche tied the rope to the boxes for them to lift out and take to the wagon. It took a while, but they soon had all of them out, leaving behind only the things that were too large to fit into a crate.

Sheerness came down to help with the throne. It wasn't easy to tie securely. Of all the things found, because it was made of wood, it was one of the most fragile. The matching footrest was small enough to put in a crate, but the throne was barely going to fit through the opening in the roof. They did cover it with one of the cotton cloths before they began to tie it. Hopefully, it would survive being removed and carried to the wagon. After Sheerness climbed out to help Nikos lift it, Psyche watched anxiously as it disappeared through the hole, and she didn't start breathing again until it was safely out.

Psyche took the remaining crate and cloths to pack the coffers. As for the sarcophagus itself, she didn't know how they were going to get it out. It was too long to fit through the hole lengthwise…unless they removed another slab. Not only that, while Nikos and Sheerness were strong, they weren't strong enough to lift it out, not even if Psyche helped…which wouldn't be much help at all. It was made of marble, and even though mostly hollow, there was no mistake it would be heavy. The lids easily weighed fifty pounds apiece. Assuming the marble for the lids and sarcophagus had come from the same quarry—and Psyche had no reason to think they hadn't—that was going to put the sarcophagus weighing six hundred fifty pounds or so. If they couldn't figure out a way to remove it today, they could always come back tomorrow after they'd had a while to think about it.

Sheerness came back down, and they first sent up the crate with the coffers, then each of the lids. Nikos came back down then to look at the sarcophagus with them. They all stood looking at it silently, wondering what they were going to do with it.

"So, how much do you think it weighs?" asked Sheerness, looking sidelong at Nikos.

"More than *we* can lift," said Nikos with a grin. He looked past Sheerness to Psyche. "How much do you think it weighs, Thea?"

"Seven hundred pounds…maybe," she sighed tiredly.

Sheerness looked at her in surprise. "That much? Really?"

"You don't think it will?" she asked dryly.

"It doesn't seem that big," said Sheerness doubtfully.

"It's marble," said Psyche drolly. "You felt how much the lids weighed. Think about it."

Sheerness did. "Oh."

"I think this is something we should let Autos and Aute take care of for us," said Nikos after a moment of thought.

"Him and her?" asked Sheerness blankly.

"The horses," said Nikos with a grin.

"How are we going to get it to the carriage once we get it out of here?" asked Psyche, the thought just occurring to her.

"We can use a sledge to at least get it to the carriage, but we'll have to think of something else to lift it on," said Nikos.

"Will we have time?" asked Psyche concernedly. "We could just come back for it tomorrow."

"Sure, we have time for it," said Nikos with an assuring grin. "The sledge won't take long."

He went up the rope to get started, and Psyche decided to start on her drawings and paintings of the frescoes on the walls. She didn't know how long it would take for the sledge, but once he was done and they started lifting the sarcophagus and moving it to the carriage, she wouldn't have time. She needed something to do, and this seemed likely. She first did quick overall pictures of each one, and then she began details of the individual elements: Hermes running before the chariot holding Hades and Persephone; the female on her knees behind it, watching with dismay at the abduction; the despair of Persephone's mother, Demeter; and Fate.

She had never seen examples of Greek frescoes of this age. There were plenty of mosaics, and no dearth of Roman works, but she didn't think she'd ever seen Greek. She did her best to paint what she saw, and duplicating things like this, making architectural renderings and replicas, was where she excelled in her art. As Sheerness watched, he was impressed, not only with her speed but also her accuracy. It explained how she had managed to make so many while they were in Athens, and her work in this area was far better than her portraits. By the time Nikos had made the sledge, she was done with her work and had packed away her things.

Her clothes were filthy and she had a large streak of dirt across her cheek, not to mention the dirt under her fingernails. She also looked tired. She hadn't stopped to rest since she had entered the tomb, and she had been there for hours. It was going to be well after dark before they made it home. Yet she was perfectly content. It wasn't even the riches they had found that caused it, either. Had they found nothing but shards of broken pottery and disintegrated wood, she would have still been just as happy. As she had told him, that wasn't what interested her. The thing about this tomb that excited her most would be discovering the story behind it. The *why*. Sheerness had to admit the stories behind the things they had found so far made them all the more exciting to him as well. She was right about one more thing, but this time, it was something he was glad she was.

Removing the sarcophagus proved to be no easy feat. Lifting it out and getting it safely onto the carriage took almost as long as it had taken to remove all the other objects combined. The hardest part wasn't even lifting it out of the tomb but lifting it onto the cart. Nikos had moved the cart beneath a nearby tree with a strong overhanging limb before unhitching the horses. Once it was lifted out and placed onto the sledge, he had the horses pull it over to the tree, where he rehung the rope over the branch to lift it to the necessary height, and then he and Sheerness guided it into the space Nikos had left for it. It was hard to believe, but everything in the tomb fit. However, there wasn't much room left for people. Psyche would have to sit on Sheerness's lap unless Nikos rode on one of the horses.

Sheerness went back into the tomb to hand the lamps up to Nikos because his reach was longer, and after she took one last look around the now-empty chamber, he helped Psyche climb the rope, and Nikos helped her out. She did not look down. There was not much adjustment for her eyes to make because the sun was setting. Sheerness climbed out shortly after her, and then he and Nikos placed the limestone slab back into place. They debated whether to replace the dirt, and Psyche won with the argument they needed to put at least some of it back because if it rained the roof could leak and ruin the frescoes. Nikos and Sheerness found digging again unappealing, but they conceded she had a point. They replaced half of it. Nikos then used the rope to lash down the things on the carriage, and Psyche got her first look at it.

"Oh, my giddy aunt," she said in surprise, at first not seeing anywhere to sit, as the back was almost full with orchard crates and furnishings to the awning. It was going to be a slow ride back to the house.

They had to climb into the carriage from the front, and Psyche did have to sit on Sheerness's lap. They weren't even to Piakia when Psyche fell asleep, her head drooping onto Sheerness's shoulder. She had been on her feet working in the tomb for several hours, but he and Nikos were the ones who did all the manual labor, so Sheerness found it amusing she was the one who fell asleep. He kept his arms around her waist to keep her from slipping off as he talked with Nikos.

Nikos tried to move along as quickly as he could and delayed lighting the lanterns for as long as possible. There wasn't a lot of fuel left after having them in the tomb for so long. Eventually, they had to be lit. The moon was only in its first half, and while its light illuminated the road, it wasn't enough. By eight, the lanterns *had* to be lit. Fortunately, they were already to Sfendami. When they got to the house, Nikos pulled the carriage into the barn. After the horses were unhitched, he closed the doors.

When Sheerness woke Psyche, the first thing she noticed was the crick in her neck. The second was how grimy she felt. She hadn't realized how dirty she was before her nap took her away from it. She was hungry, but what she really wanted was a bath. Luckily, by the time they were home, Ioanna was still thirty minutes away from having supper ready.

Psyche and Sheerness hurriedly went to their rooms for their things then went to have a bath. Sheerness would have liked to do more than wash, but Psyche made him stay on task. She wanted to oblige him...desperately, but they didn't have time. As much as she disliked having to tell him, she wasn't sure it was time. His expression reminded her of the disappointment a small boy might show on discovering someone else had taken the last piece of cake. She sympathized, but it was also amusing.

At dinner they told Ioanna of the wonderful things they had found. Then they talked about how they were going to get the things to the hold of the *Medea*. Most of it could be loaded onto the *Athena* easily enough, but the sarcophagus would take some effort. They also had to decide whether they wanted to go back tomorrow or wait until they had the firman. As much as Psyche wanted to go back, it would be best to wait. She wanted to look at what they already had. Sheerness, of course, thought they should go back. Having the firman was only a formality. Psyche didn't want to tell him that while she had every confidence in Duman's abilities, he was not the sultan, and the final decision would rest with him. He could just as easily say no as yes. They would know soon enough.

Psyche and Sheerness walked back to her room after supper, and he was tired. He wouldn't be too tired for sex, but he didn't think it was going to happen whether he had the strength or not. Psyche seemed calm, and he didn't know how she could wait so patiently. He didn't know how much longer he could bear it, and today was supposed to have been the last.

He tried not to watch as she got ready for bed because seeing her naked was difficult. Bath time had been almost unbearable. She, on the other hand, watched appreciatively as he got undressed, and he couldn't understand why she couldn't be overwhelmed by the same kind of longing he felt for her, at least just a little. She obviously enjoyed seeing him naked, but she didn't look like she wanted anything more. If she did, she was good at hiding it.

They got into bed after Psyche let Cupid in from the terrace. Psyche snuggled into his side, laying her head on his chest, and put one of her legs over his. Sheerness closed his eyes and clenched his jaw, and he began to breathe in and out slowly through his nose. Certain parts of him weren't tired at all, and having her pressed close to him was making them very hard to control. Psyche noticed his stiffness as she lay there, and she lifted her head to look at him, noting that he was concentrating very seriously on something.

"Are you all right?" she asked concernedly.

"I'm fine," he answered quietly, keeping his eyes closed.

Psyche frowned. "Are you sure?" she asked worriedly, smoothing a hand down his cheek to his chest.

"Just go to sleep," he said stilly.

"But—" she began hesitantly.

"Psyche, please, hush," he cut in patiently.

"Fine," she said after a moment through stiff lips. She flopped over with her back to him and punched her pillow angrily before nestling her head into it.

Sheerness looked at her turned back and rubbed a hand over his face. He hadn't wanted to make her angry. All he wanted was to sleep so he could forget about her lying beside him. He started to apologize, but if he did, she would turn over and touch him again. Having her angry was going to be the least painful way for him to get through the night.

Psyche, meanwhile, had a deep frown etched between her eyebrows as she tried to go to sleep. She didn't know what was bothering him (actually, she had a suspicion), but he didn't have to be mean. She had thought about giving him some relief, but now he could wait. At this rate, he would be lucky if she let him make love to her in a week, much less tomorrow. They could have that night, but now he could suffer. The only thing she was going to miss was cuddling. It made it much easier to go to sleep. It was going to be a long night.

Psyche woke up feeling very snug. At some point during the night, Sheerness had curled up behind her and put his arm around her waist. Cupid was sleeping curled up in a ball against her chest. She was hot from the two bodies pressed against hers. The sun was barely up, and she didn't know when they had moved. It had taken her a couple hours to fall asleep, and Sheerness was asleep long before her. He hadn't been touching her, let alone holding her.

Cupid woke when he felt her stirring, and after he licked her nose once, he stood up and stretched then trotted to the edge of the bed and leapt to the floor. He wanted to go outside, but Psyche didn't want to move yet. After a minute or two, though, she needed to let the dog out. She eased off the bed and went to open the door, where Cupid was waiting with his tail wagging excitedly. She went to the fireplace and added a few pieces of wood, and then she used the pot and washed her face. She let Cupid back in, and then she went back to the bed and climbed on, sitting cross-legged as she watched Sheerness sleep, her chin propped on the palm of her hand as her elbow rested on her knee.

Sheerness shifted in his sleep, reaching for her, but of course she wasn't lying there anymore. He frowned slightly, and then he opened his eyes and looked around, only to see her looking back at him with a raised eyebrow.

"Do you never sleep?" he asked her quietly.

"Sometimes," she said mildly, reaching down to trace a finger over the veins in the back of his hand where it rested near her knee.

Sheerness turned his hand and gently grabbed her by the wrist to pull her toward him. She didn't seem tired, but he didn't know how she managed on the little sleep she got. He brushed the hair back from her face and kissed her softly. Psyche shifted and lay down, pressing against him, putting one of her legs over his thigh. She could feel his erection through the blankets and sighed longingly as she ran her hand down his side to his back. Sheerness tore his lips away from hers and rested his forehead against her chin, his breathing uneven.

"You're killing me," he groaned, rolling onto his back and moving away from her, putting a hand over his eyes.

Psyche's lips twitched amusedly, and she unfastened her shift and pulled it off. She climbed on top of him and started to place kisses down his neck to his chest, and she felt him jump when he realized she was naked. His hands flew to her waist to push her off, but Psyche put her hands to his arms and wrapped them around her as she teased one of his nipples with her teeth.

"Oh, God, *please*, tell me it's time," he whispered breathlessly.

"Oh, yes," drawled Psyche with an impish grin, looking up at him through her lashes and pulling the blankets away. She kissed her way back up his chest to his neck and chin. "It was time last night," she said as she placed teasing kisses against his lips. "I was trying to tell you, but you told me to *hush*."

"And am I ever sorry about that," sighed Sheerness feelingly, claiming her lips hungrily as he rolled over to place her beneath him.

He took the tip of one breast into his mouth, and Psyche sighed with satisfaction as she curled her fingers in his hair and arched toward him. He was frenzied as he explored her body with his hands and mouth, and Psyche had a soft smile of affection and pleasure as he touched her. He was like a child in a sweet shop, as if he couldn't decide what he wanted first because it all looked and tasted so good. Psyche had one of her feet hooked around the back of his thigh, and she rubbed against him longingly with a soft moan, running her nails across his back and down to his buttocks. He had just plunged into her with a sigh of relief and gratification when there was a knock on the door. Both of them jerked their heads to look at it in surprise, and Sheerness dropped his forehead to her shoulder, giving it a shake of disbelief and frustration.

"Oh, no, no, no," he moaned softly.

Psyche shushed him and ran a soothing hand through the back of his hair and across his back, giving him a gentle kiss to his temple. She sympathized.

"Just a minute," she called.

Sheerness rolled off of her with an irritated sigh, draping his forearm across his eyes. Psyche quickly covered at least the lower part of him with the blankets before she grabbed her dressing gown from the foot of the bed and put it on as she headed for the door. Her heart was racing as much from what was interrupted as anxiety at someone discovering Sheerness in her room. Her cheeks were flushed and her eyes were bright, and she probably had a guilty expression. She looked back at the bed briefly to see Sheerness hadn't moved, and she carefully opened the door, trying to keep whoever was standing there from seeing into the room. She looked down at Stefania, her features excited.

"What is it, Stefania?" asked Psyche pleasantly.

"Pappa wanted me to tell you Duman Pasha has arrived," said Stefania hesitantly.

"Wonderful!" said Psyche excitedly. "I'll tell Sheerness. Thank you!"

"No problem," said Stefania, and she turned to trot down the hall.

Psyche closed the door and ran toward the bed, doing a flip onto it before crawling across it to climb on top of Sheerness, quickly removing her dressing gown and pulling away the blankets. Sheerness lifted his arm to look at her, noting her excitement.

"What?" he asked breathlessly as she settled herself onto him.

"Duman Pasha is here," she said distractedly as she began to raise and lower herself onto him.

Sheerness grabbed her hips to still her with some effort. Psyche looked down at him frustratedly and bit her nails into his chest.

"Ow!" he hissed. "He's back from Constantinople?"

"Yes," groaned Psyche as she gyrated against him. "Must move…now," she sighed desperately as she leaned forward to kiss him.

Sheerness smoothed his hands down her thighs in a caress with a self-satisfied smile as she started to move again. "Absolutely."

Psyche and Sheerness sat looking at Duman with astonishment. They had read the firman, Psyche reading the copy in Turkish, Sheerness the one in Italian. It didn't say what they expected. While it did give them permission to remove antiquities from the Ottoman Empire, there were severe limitations on where they could originate. They couldn't come from a place of documented historical importance, and, if interpreted correctly, they couldn't come from the land. The phrasing was obscure, but that was the impression they had from both versions of the document, and also what Duman thought. That meant the things Sheerness had found on Mount Olympus and the things from the tomb at Aigai could not rightfully be theirs. As for Egypt, the sultan had no issue with them removing antiquities from there in any fashion, but he would leave the decision for that resting solely with Muhammad Ali, the wali ruling the country.

"Maybe he just means *above* ground," said Sheerness hopefully.

Psyche looked at him. "Well, we could use that as our interpretation should we get caught being naughty, but I don't think that *is* what he meant." She chewed the side of her thumb thoughtfully. "I don't think we should take back the things we've already found," she said with a resigned sigh, "but I don't think we should try to find any more."

"Lady Psyche, I'm very sorry to have failed you in this," said Duman sadly. "I should have tried to convince him more strenuously."

"Duman Pasha, I'm sure you did everything you could, and you *did* get the firman for us. Having even this one is better than none at all," said Psyche with a soothing smile. "We shall have to just be more creative about where we look in Greece and hope Muhammad Ali Pasha is a generous soul."

"I could go back to Constantinople and try to reason with Mahmud, perhaps get him to change his mind," offered Duman determinedly.

"No, no," said Psyche quickly, giving him a smile and scratching her forehead. "I think we should take what we have and be grateful we got it at all." She gave him a wry grin. "It would be our luck you would go back to make him change his mind, and he would change it for the worse. Best to leave well-enough alone."

"You're sure?" he asked, giving her an assessing glance.

"Absolutely, Duman Pasha. Thank you for all you've done."

He smiled warmly. "You are quite welcome." He glanced at Sheerness, who was sitting with an unhappy frown, rereading the firman. "And what of him? Has he become any less supercilious since I saw him last?"

Psyche grinned. "He has his moments." She shrugged. "I think we've made progress."

Duman chuckled. "Good, good. A man with that much hubris is simply asking for someone to smack him down from his pedestal."

"I'm working on it," said Psyche softly.

Duman stood up, and so did Psyche and Sheerness. He kissed both her cheeks and gave her an affectionate hug. He started to just shake Sheerness's hand, but he kissed both his cheeks as well with an amused chuckle.

"You must stop by to see me in Athens before you go home," said Duman with a smile. "We did not get to spend nearly enough time together."

"I'll try my best," assured Psyche.

"Then *I* am sure I will see you," called Duman over his shoulder as he left.

Sheerness looked at Psyche after he was gone. "What was that about?"

"What?"

"What were you two talking about?"

"Oh," said Psyche, waving a hand through the air dismissively. "He offered to go back to Constantinople and try again, but I told him he might make it worse. He also invited us to stay with him for a few days in Athens on our way home. I'm sorry it didn't go as expected."

"I suppose we should make plans to return home," said Sheerness evenly.

Psyche looked at him in surprise. "Why? We haven't gone to Egypt yet. Even if we can't take anything else back with us, there are still plenty of things to see." She tweaked the end of his nose with a grin. "You give up too easily."

"No, I don't," said Sheerness tightly, scowling at her.

"Such a face," teased Psyche with a grin.

Psyche decided what he needed to take his mind off things was a swim. The water in the cove was a bit too cold for Psyche, so they went to the pool in the garden. They had already eaten breakfast with Duman before getting the firman. After Duman left, they talked with Nikos, and Psyche briefly explained what had happened. He agreed they should keep the things they had found, and he watched them scamper off to the pool with a thoughtful expression.

Psyche thought something else to do that would make Sheerness feel better was have more sex. Once they were done with their swim and went back to her room, it wasn't difficult to convince him. It was fortuitous they were able to have sex again just as Duman arrived to deliver his disappointing news. Had he arrived a day or two earlier, Sheerness would have been in a very foul mood. At least now he was consolable.

After the swim and more sex, Sheerness was, if silent, at least not bad-tempered. He thought the turn of events was unfair, but he didn't feel as if he were denied something to which he was entitled. They were almost through with dinner when Nikos mentioned something.

"So, what are your plans now?" he asked them.

"I still have places I would like to see in Greece," said Psyche evenly. "I've never felt it was necessary to take things. I'd like to see Delphi, Thebes, and Delos before going to Egypt, but other than that I haven't any ideas." She smiled. "The best part of my trip was seeing you and Ioanna, so I'm happy."

"And what about you, Sebastian?"

Sheerness looked up from his plate. "We have found some wonderful things, and although I would like to find more, I can be satisfied with what we have."

Nikos looked at Ioanna, and she gave him a slight, secretive smile and a brief nod of her head. Nikos cleared his throat, his lips twitching.

"You asked where I acquired the statue at the bottom of the cliff. I told you it was several days sail and we would wait and discuss it with Thea. Now we'll discuss it," grinned Nikos. Psyche tilted her head sideways thoughtfully as she looked at him. Sheerness hadn't mentioned he had talked to Nikos about Chrissoula's marker. "Where it came from is a place that falls within the restrictions of your firman, even if you take it in its literal interpretation."

"What?" asked Psyche in surprise.

"The place where it came from is *under water*," grinned Nikos.

"Definitely *not* land," Psyche chortled.

"There is no gold or silver. At least, I don't think there is, but you will find it every bit as rich." He looked at Sheerness. "I can't tell you how to find it, exactly, other than that it is near Delos. I'll have to show you."

Psyche looked at him in dismay. "But we could be gone for days! Weeks even! We couldn't take you away from your family for that long."

Ioanna smiled. "Take my husband, *please*," she chortled. "He has been pining to get away for an adventure, and the girls and I will be just fine."

Psyche bit her lower lip uncertainly. "Are you sure?"

"Of course," grinned Ioanna.

Psyche turned to look at Nikos. "Do you really want to do this?"

Nikos shrugged. "Sooner or later, the ruins will be found. I would rather you find them than someone else."

Chapter Thirty Five

The *Medea* sailed from Thessaloniki on Saturday. After Nikos told them of the site, he and Sheerness sailed to the port and let the crew know to begin making ready for sail. Sheerness had Meals resupply the food stores and had Broughton oversee all other necessary stores. He talked to Laing about putting the door back on his cabin. With Nikos occupying the cabin that would have been Myron's, it seemed like the sensible thing to do…especially if Psyche was going to sleep in Sheerness's cabin. He hoped she would.

On Saturday morning, Higginbotham brought the ship from port and sailed it into the tiny cove. Psyche watched from the top of the tower as the ship arrived, and she admired his ability as the ship glided into the enclosure and came to a stop not far from the pier. Psyche wondered if they would have enough room to fit it back out again. *That* would really take skill.

With the crew there, loading the things from Aigai wasn't a problem. Nikos led them up the path from the cove to a covered walkway that went to the front of the house. Although the sarcophagus was too heavy for two men, a crew of six sailors had no trouble. Psyche went to the hold with Higginbotham to oversee storing everything. She didn't want it too close to the animals because of the waste, but she also didn't want it too near the heat of the boiler. They would need room for the things at the site Nikos was taking them to. Something told her it was going to be *large*. By the time everything was situated to her satisfaction, her nerves were frazzled.

Before the crew left, Ioanna insisted on having them come up to the tower for dinner. It wasn't as fancy as what she had served for the party she gave for Psyche and Sheerness, but it was out of the ordinary for the sailors. Meals didn't serve Greek dishes, and Psyche didn't think many of them had frequented the tavernas in Thessaloniki because of the language. They enjoyed the food, but being waited on made them uncomfortable…and so did the ceiling.

After the crew was fed and back to the ship, Psyche, Sheerness, and Nikos said their goodbyes to the Andreanopoulos women. Yelena didn't want to let go of Psyche's neck, but she convinced the baby she would be much happier staying with her mamma. Psyche also had Cupid tucked under one arm. They would be coming back to bring Nikos home, but the sooner she got the puppy used to being aboard ship, the better. It would give her a chance to make sure having him there would work. Some dogs were suited to sailing and some weren't. As her family had never had pet dogs, she didn't know which were which, and they didn't have dogs like Cupid in Britain in any event.

It was shortly before two when they sailed out of the cove and back into the gulf. Psyche was surprised that Sheerness let Higginbotham direct getting the ship under way. She thought he would have missed ordering people about. She still had a firm hold on Cupid, who was wiggling in her arms, but she didn't want to let him loose and getting under the feet of the crew. Until he learned to mind his manners, she would have to find something to use as a leash. She stood on the deck waving to Ioanna and the girls on the pier until they were out of sight behind the rock walls of the cove, and then Psyche went to the after cabins to introduce Cupid and Waddlesworth.

The meeting went well, but they would have to make some adjustments to each other. It was a good sign when Waddlesworth didn't hiss at Cupid, but he quacked loudly when he first saw the puppy. For his part, Cupid didn't try to chase Waddlesworth. He did give him a friendly lick on the side of his head. A few days in each other's company would be all that was needed for them to become friends.

Psyche had missed her cabin. She didn't realize until she was in it for a few minutes. The room at Nikos and Ioanna's had been lovely, and that, too, had felt like home, but after spending nearly a month in the cabin, it had become familiar and comforting. There were all her things she hadn't taken with her, and for a time she simply sat on her bunk and enjoyed being in her own domain again. She was going to miss the big bed, though.

She desperately needed to do laundry, and after a quick glance at her watch, she thought she might have time. She went onto the deck and looked around before going to the berth deck to get her things. She had a brief chat with Meals about plans for Sheerness's party while she was there and was happy to learn it was going nicely. He had gotten the things they needed in Thessaloniki, and everything was going according to plan. Meals would have some sailors bring her the things she needed to her cabin in a trice.

Psyche spent the rest of the afternoon washing and doing a bit of sewing while she waited for them to dry. Sewing was not among the pastimes she normally indulged, but this was *necessary* sewing rather than recreational. She was nearly out of the small muslin bags she used when she had her courses. There was no one else to make them for her, and they could not be purchased.

She had to take Cupid out a few times onto the deck, and she realized something would have to be done after the first trip. The second time, she took him to the bow of the ship where there were places of ease to either side. The hole was small, but the seat itself was large, and Psyche put him on top of one. He stood looking at her with his head tilted sideways in puzzlement, and then he looked down through the hole to the sea passing beneath it. Several of the nearby sailors nudged each other to direct their attention to what Psyche was doing, most of them shaking their heads with amused smirks. Sheerness and Nikos stood watching with the other officers on the poop deck, and Sheerness looked at her with only slight disbelief. He was starting to learn better. Several of the sailors quickly exchanged small wagers on whether or not she would get the puppy to do what she wanted.

She was partially successful. He raised his leg to urinate, but it didn't go in the hole. It did, however, go over the side of the ship, which still accomplished Psyche's objective. He then carefully squatted over the hole to do the rest of his business, and Psyche giggled and offered him lots of praise and petting. She turned to carry him back across the deck and saw the varying expressions of amazement and hilarity. Her cheeks turned pink, and she smiled weakly as she went back to her cabin. When he needed to go again shortly before dark, Psyche took him directly to the bow, and Cupid repeated the procedure and received praise from Psyche yet again. She had only marginally thought it would work, and she was extremely happy it did. Cupid was a very smart dog.

After their supper of lamb stew, Psyche took Cupid on deck one more time before going to her room. With Nikos there, she didn't know how the sleeping arrangement she shared with Sheerness was going to continue. He had the door installed on his cabin again. She was making no assumptions about why he had done so, and she was not going to simply invite herself into his bed. She didn't think he would mind, but having Nikos in the room across the alcove caused her some anxiety. At his house, she and Sheerness had been able to share her bed without making it blatantly obvious. On the ship, Nikos would have to be a fool not to realize the two of them were sleeping together. Nikos was no fool.

After she got ready for bed and brushed her teeth, she climbed into her bunk and put Cupid onto it. It took him some adjustment, but he soon got comfortable in the far corner at the foot. She heard Nikos and Sheerness come down from taking a walk around the deck and go to their respective cabins. She cuddled her pillow and closed her eyes, but she wasn't trying to go to sleep. Not yet. She would wait a while for Sheerness to come in. He had to update the log and give Nikos time to go to sleep. At least, Psyche hoped he would give Nikos time to go to sleep.

The wait went on and on. After what seemed like more than an hour, she started to doze off. She was almost asleep when she vaguely heard her door opening. She turned over when Sheerness finally climbed onto the bunk. She yawned hugely as she ran her hand down his cheek to his chest and pressed herself against him.

"I was almost asleep," she said groggily, giving him a soft kiss.

Sheerness untied the strings on her shift and pulled it over her head then grabbed her by the hips to press her close against him. He nuzzled her neck before moving his lips to hers.

"You should have gone to my bed," he said distractedly as he took the tip of her breast into his mouth.

Psyche buried her fingers in his hair and draped her leg over his hip with a soft sigh. She was still half asleep, and she felt almost dizzy between trying to wake up and the sensations she felt as he touched her.

"I didn't realize I was invited," she sighed, her breath catching as he turned them over to place her beneath him.

He raised himself up on his elbow and smoothed a hand down her cheek to one of her breasts before moving it to her thigh to put her leg around his waist.

"I will *always* want you in my bed," he said silkily, dipping his head to kiss her thoroughly. "And while your bunk is good for cuddling and sleeping, it is too small to suit me for other things."

He slowly started to kiss his way down her body, and after he had worked his way back up from her knee along the inside of her thigh, he put her leg over his shoulder as he began to tease her with his mouth. Psyche moaned in pleasure and arched her hips toward him, one hand going to his head while the other clutched spasmodically at the blankets.

"I love it when you do that," she sighed breathlessly before she lost the ability to say much more that was intelligible.

When she began to orgasm, Psyche bit the inside of her lip to keep herself from crying out. She wasn't sure how thick or well-insulated the walls were. She didn't want Bothi or Nikos to hear. She quivered uncontrollably as it worked its way through her body, and she felt weak and satisfied as he worked his way back up to her lips. She moved the hand she had in his hair to the side of his face, her palm resting against his cheek tenderly as she kissed him appreciatively, running her foot along the back of his thigh. She felt him start to laugh, and she smiled against his lips and moved her foot away.

"Sorry," she whispered. "I forgot about that."

Sheerness gave her a few nibbling kisses as he settled himself more solidly between her thighs.

"If you were already in my cabin before Nikos and I came below, no one would know you're in there," he said as he continued to kiss her face and neck.

"That is true," sighed Psyche absently. She could feel his erection pressed against her, and conversation was not high on her list of priorities. She reached down between them to take him in her hand, and she heard his sharp intake of breath as she slowly started to guide him into her. "We'll have to see if that will work when we come back."

"Back?" said Sheerness blankly, lifting his mouth from her neck to look at her with a frown.

"We leave to go to Delphi and Thebes in the morning, and then we'll meet the ship again at Chalcis after we travel over land," said Psyche evenly, reaching up a hand to smooth it over his frown and gyrating her hips against him with a wanton smile. "You do remember that conversation, don't you?"

"Yes, but—" Sheerness's frown deepened with displeasure as realization struck. "Oh, bloody hell," he groaned.

"Yes," drawled Psyche as she wrapped her legs around his waist and gyrated against him again. "You had better get it out of your system because it's going to be a while. I would rather have you greedy tonight than grumpy for however long we'll be gone." She pulled his mouth to hers and kissed him. "So, shag me rotten…please…now," she sighed with a hint of frustration.

Sheerness smiled rakishly and began to move. "Yes, ma'am."

The three of them left the ship the next morning carrying blankets rolled up and slung over their shoulders, just in case they were unable to find an inn to stay at for the night while they were gone. The weather was warm, so sleeping outside wouldn't be too uncomfortable…unless it rained. Psyche carried her medicine kit, the box containing her art supplies, and a change of clothes. She also had a knife in its sheath stuck into the top of one of her boots, hidden beneath the length and folds of her olive-colored split-skirt. Nikos carried a rifle in an elaborate fringed and beaded holster slung over one shoulder as well as a bag with a shoulder strap containing his own clothes and ammunition. Sheerness carried a sack containing food and another with his clothes. He also carried a pistol in a holster strapped at his waist, hidden beneath his coat, and the ammunition in the bag with his clothes. Nikos thought it would be best if they were armed because they might encounter bandits. Sheerness had almost made Psyche stay on the ship, but it was an argument he would lose. He hadn't even tried to convince her.

Higginbotham would sail the *Medea* down the Evoikos Gulf to dock at Chalcis, where he would await their arrival. The three of them weren't sure how long the journey would take. Sheerness told his first mate not to become concerned unless a week passed and they had not arrived. Sheerness didn't anticipate it would take that long, which was why he had told Higginbotham not to become worried until then. It was their intention to secure transportation. None of them wanted to actually *walk* the entire way.

They went south once they were on land, and Nikos led the way with a carefree spring in his step. They could see mountains rising on the far side of the plain they crossed. Psyche had a general idea of where they were, as did Sheerness, but Nikos knew exactly where they were going. Sheerness was curious how Nikos knew his way around the country so well, how he knew where all of these ancient ruins were located. England was dotted with ancient ruins, and Sheerness doubted there was anyone in the country who knew where they *all* were. Nikos could just be knowledgeable about the ones on the eastern side of the country, close to the Aegean, but it puzzled him.

The plain they crossed was almost barren. The soil was sandy, and there weren't many plants. It was covered with a tough grass for the most part, dotted here and there by small bushes. Trees grew at the base and up the sides of the mountains, but not where they were walking. Sheep grazed, being tended by their owners, but none paid any mind as the three walked.

"We're not climbing *over* the mountains, are we?" asked Psyche charily as they walked along.

"No," said Nikos with a grin. "There's something I want to show you, and then we will go along the edge of the mountains to a village and find a cart or something. It's somewhat on our way, so I thought you might like to see it. I'm surprised you haven't figured out where we are yet."

"Another guessing game?" said Psyche with a grin.

"This place where we are walking used to be under water. That's why it's so barren. All of the salt left behind makes it difficult for anything to grow." He picked up a stick and swung it at the grass as they passed. "There aren't any ruins, but there *is* something else."

Sheerness frowned as he looked around. He could see a pass through the mountains, and it appeared to be the only way to get past if that was what one wanted to do. He scratched his forehead thoughtfully. He knew where they had departed the ship and what was supposed to be in the area. As the base of the mountains loomed closer, when Nikos brought them to a stop beside some hot springs, he knew where they were.

"Thermopylae," he said quietly.

"*Soztá,*" said Nikos with a chuckle.

Nikos was right. Other than the springs, there was nothing to prove this was the place where so many ancient, historically important battles took place, the most well-known and legendary being that between the Spartans and the Persians. Psyche knelt down and put her hand in the water. It was very hot, much hotter than the spring at Kastro Andreanopouli. It was also very clear, and Psyche could see the rocks at the bottom, their surfaces bleached white from the heat and minerals. The surface rippled with eddies created by the heat and force of the spring. Steam curled several feet above it before dissipating into the air.

They didn't stay long before Nikos moved them on. There was a small village less than a mile away, and it took them about an hour once they reached it to find someone willing to provide a horse and cart. It didn't come cheaply, and what they got for their money wasn't impressive. The horse was old and stubborn but of a suitable size and good conformation. The owner assured them the animal would serve them well. The cart was very small and barely big enough to carry the three of them and their meager belongings. It had two wheels and sat fairly low. There was no awning or roof to shield them from the elements, but there was room behind the seat to put their things rather than having to carry them on their laps. The three of them on the bench seat at the front was crowded. As barely adequate as the cart and horse would be, it had been difficult for the owner to part with. Hopefully, the money they (actually, *she*) had paid would allow the man to buy or build something better.

The journey to Delphi was quicker than it would be had they walked, but it wasn't as fast as they would have liked it to be. Had they been in England riding their horses, the trip would not have taken more than three hours. With the horse and cart, it was going to take twice that. There was no other way to reach it, though, and the path they were taking was the shortest route. The countryside was peaceful, and they were yet to encounter any of the bandits

Nikos had mentioned, much to everyone's relief. They stopped around two for dinner and to give the horse a chance to rest not far from a town called Amfiklia. They weren't even halfway to Delphi yet.

Psyche gave the light chestnut horse half the pear she had, and he became her new best friend. She wasn't sure how old he was…at least fifteen. His owner had been vague on that point. His owner hadn't been able to provide a name, either, which she didn't think was unusual, but Psyche named him Sunny, shortened from *suntrophos*. Neither Nikos nor Sheerness thought the name would have come from his disposition.

Sheerness shook his head when he found out. He couldn't believe she had acquired yet another animal. She was going to expect to take the horse onto the ship, and he wouldn't be able to tell her no. For someone who had come on this journey without the expectation of taking anything home, she was gathering quite a collection of things: antiquities, all manner of items from her shopping excursions, and animals. She was running out of room in the trunks in her cabin and would have to buy more. It baffled him.

It was close to six in the evening when they reached the village that was partially built on the ruins of ancient Delphi. As they rode through, Psyche could see bits and pieces from the site that had been used to construct some of the buildings. She might have been a little more understanding had one of those buildings happened to be an inn, but none were. The further they traveled through the town, the more disappointed Psyche was when she realized she was unable to see anything of the ancient site…except for the pieces of it the people of the village had used.

"That's disappointing," she muttered.

Nikos looked at her where she sat between him and Sheerness on the seat with a slight laugh. "Not quite what you were expecting is it?"

"No," sighed Psyche sadly. "One would think you would be able to see *something*, that someone would have tried to preserve *some* of it." She raised her hands from her lap. "It's all gone—buried…or reused. Nothing survives but the name." She blinked her eyes to clear away the tears. "I understand people need to survive, but have they no pride in where they come from?"

"Centuries of servitude to an uncaring master will do that to a people," said Nikos quietly.

Psyche put her hand on his forearm and gave it a brief squeeze. "One day it will all be back," she said with a slight smile.

"Soon, I hope," said Nikos with a chuckle. "Let it be soon." He urged Sunny to a faster pace, guiding them toward a ravine between the two sheer cliffs facing them. "Those are the Phaedriades, something that *cannot* be reused," said Nikos with a grin. "We'll camp near the only other thing that has survived, the Castalian spring."

"It's still here?" asked Sheerness in surprise.

"Oh, yes," said Nikos jovially. "I'll get us as close as I can, but we won't be right beside it. We should have time before dark to snare a rabbit or two for supper and make a temporary shelter."

"With what?" asked Sheerness in puzzlement.

"There are lots of trees," said Psyche practically.

Sheerness raised an eyebrow. "Yes, but we have no rope, no canvas, and no axe."

"We'll have to see then, won't we?" said Psyche with a grin.

Nikos pulled the cart to a stop at the face of the cliffs. After Sheerness helped her down, Psyche unharnessed Sunny and found a likely place for him to graze. Nikos left to make snares. For a moment, Sheerness stood beside the cart, looking back and forth between the two of them uncertainly. Once Psyche had the horse situated, she turned to look at Sheerness.

"Do you want to help?" she asked with a grin.

"With what?"

"Building the shelter, of course," said Psyche simply.

"Shouldn't Nikos do that?"

"I can do that," said Psyche dismissively. "Didn't you ever build pretend forts when you were a boy?"

"No," said Sheerness flatly.

"What did you do for fun, then?" asked Psyche perplexedly. Sheerness scowled at her. "Did you not have fun then, either?" The scowl deepened even further. "Never mind," sighed Psyche.

She looked at the nearby trees and found three that looked likely, saplings growing a decent distance apart. There was some vine growing around another not far away, and she retrieved a decent length of it and draped it over her shoulder to have at the ready.

"You grab that tree—" she instructed him as she pointed to one of the saplings—"and bend it toward this one—" she jiggled the one closest to her— "while I grab this and bend it toward yours."

Sheerness raised an eyebrow but did as instructed. Once the tops of the trees overlapped each other, Psyche had him hold them while she bound them together with the vine. Once they were fastened, she had him let go, and the two saplings formed an arc. Psyche retrieved more vine, and then she grabbed the third sapling and bent it toward the arc of the first two and had Sheerness hold it down while she fastened it.

"That is not a shelter," said Sheerness flatly.

Psyche sighed and shook her head. "I'm not done yet."

She looked around and for fallen branches of the right length and dragged them over to put in the open spaces between the saplings, forming a frame. Once she had enough, she broke off leafy limbs from other trees and draped them across the frame until it was fairly solid.

"It's not very waterproof, but it should work for blocking the wind and giving us some protection from wild creatures," said Psyche as she gave it an assessing glance, resting her hands on her hips.

"What wild creatures?"

"Do you mean the ones that might try to eat us or all of them?" asked Psyche with a grin. Sheerness folded his arms across his chest. "Bears, boars, wolves, foxes, lynxes, and jackals. It's starting to get a bit late in the year for them, but there are snakes, too."

"You're not serious."

"I am perfectly serious. Oh, and let's not forget about men."

"Aren't you worried?"

"No," she chortled. "Most wild animals are more afraid of you than you are of them, and just having a fire will keep most of them away. Having the shelter will reduce the number of directions they might come from, just in case." She looked at him disbelievingly. "Have you never camped before?"

"Not before I came here," said Sheerness flatly.

Psyche walked toward him and put her hand to his cheek before giving him a soft kiss on the lips. She didn't say anything as she looked at him, but her expression was almost pitying.

"Now we'll build a fire," she said evenly.

She started to turn away when Sheerness grabbed her by the hand and pulled her close to kiss her. When he finally ended it, Psyche looked up at him with a somewhat dazed expression before tweaking the end of his nose and giving him an impish smile.

"That wasn't the kind of fire I meant," she teased.

Sheerness rolled his eyes and shook his head with a wry smile as she went to gather wood. She collected some of the nearby rocks to make a ring, and once it was together, her eyes rounded with dismay. She looked at Sheerness.

"Did you bring a flint?"

"No," said Sheerness with a shake of his head.

"Nikos probably has one, but I wanted to get the fire built now."

She tugged at her bottom lip before she shrugged. She took a piece of wood and scraped the bark off of it in a place with her knife. Then she took another piece of wood and used the knife to slightly sharpen the end of it. She put the piece missing bark near the bottom of the things she had gathered for the fire, and then she took the sharpened one and poked it down through the center to make contact with the other piece. She removed the lace from one of her boots and found a flexible piece of branch to tie the string to, making something that looked very like a bow. She looped the lace around the end of the wood she had pointed upright through the pile and began to spin the tip against the other piece quickly. Sheerness watched in puzzlement.

"What are you doing?"

"I'm lighting the fire," puffed Psyche as she spun the piece of wood.

She slowly started to smile as a small curl of smoke began to rise up, and then it turned into a grin as the leaves and lichen on the bottom ignited. She looked up to see Sheerness's amazed expression.

"Don't tell me you've never seen that before," she said incredulously as she began to re-lace her boot. "I thought everyone knew how to do that." Sheerness scowled again. "Very well, apparently not," she said dryly.

By the time Nikos returned carrying two rabbits skinned and prepared for cooking on a stick, he was pleased to see they already had a good fire and an excellent shelter. He had two other sticks in his hand to use for setting the spit on. He put them in the ground on either side of the fire and put the rabbits over it to begin cooking. He turned to look at Sheerness.

"This is a fabulous shelter," said Nikos jovially. "Very roomy."

Sheerness looked from him to Psyche where she sat on a nearby rock by the fire. "Actually, you've Psyche to thank for that...and the fire. The closest I've come to camping is going to school at Oxford."

Nikos looked from one to the other then laughed with hilarity. Sheerness admitted it was funny a *woman* was more capable at preparing a camp than he was. They sat talking around the fire while they waited for the rabbits to cook, discussing what they would do tomorrow. Other than looking at the spring, there would not be anything to see in Delphi. Nikos told them there wouldn't be much more to see at any of the other places they wanted to visit either. Psyche tried to contain her disappointment. At least she would be able to say she had been there. Nikos didn't think they would make it to Thebes (or Thivai, as it was now called) tomorrow, but they would at least be able to find an inn...maybe. Psyche didn't care, as long as it wasn't raining...or too cold, which it wouldn't be provided there was a fire.

When it was time to go to sleep, Psyche put a rock near the fire to warm before arranging her blankets with her feet facing it. She moved the rock to the bottom end to keep her toes warm. Sheerness arranged his blankets so that he was sleeping at the back of the shelter just in case an animal approached, with the top end close to Psyche's. Nikos arranged his with his head toward the front and his feet near Sheerness's.

After Psyche took off her boots, she climbed under her blankets and put her feet near the rock. Nikos had turned on his side facing the wall of the shelter, either because the light from the fire bothered him or to give her and Sheerness privacy. When she tilted her head back slightly, Sheerness was looking back at her with a half-smile. After he spared a brief glance to Nikos, he lifted himself up to give her a quick kiss. Psyche thought that was rather bold. She laid her head onto her arm with a slight smile and yawned as he continued to watch her, his eyes blinking sleepily. Her own eyelids began to droop, and every time they closed, she would blink them open until she couldn't open them anymore. Once she went to sleep, Sheerness let himself do the same.

Psyche woke up feeling cold and stiff. She had a crick in her neck, and all she could tell about her right arm was that it had gone to sleep. There was a weight sitting on it. She opened her eyes with a frown and saw that at some point during the night, Sheerness had decided to use her arm as a pillow. She tried to wiggle her fingers, but they wouldn't move. She raised her left hand to her neck to massage the stiffness out of it. Then she sat up slightly and carefully eased her arm from under his head, trying not to wake him.

Once Psyche had her arm back, she had a proper stretch, and she bit her lower lip as the tingling began in her arm. She hadn't slept well, but she didn't think it was all due to the hardness of her "bed." She could recall bits and pieces of the disturbing dreams she'd had, but not enough to remember what they had been about. Even awake, they left her feeling anxious. It had been a long time since she'd dreamt like that, and she didn't like it at all.

The sun was barely up. Nikos and Sheerness still slept. Psyche didn't see any reason to wake them. She put on her boots and tucked her knife into one of them. She crawled out of the shelter and put more wood on the embers of their fire. She sighed with relief and held her hands out toward it to begin warming her fingers once it caught and began to do more than smoke. She grabbed one of the canteens to take a sip of water, noticing it was nearly empty. She didn't know if the water at the spring was potable. It used to be.

Thinking about water and having a drink made Psyche realize she needed to relieve herself. She stood up from her seat on a rock near the fire and went to find a private spot to take care of it. She checked on Sunny as she walked past him, going toward the ravine and the spring. He seemed well-rested, if not spry, and he would appreciate some water. She would take him to the spring, but she would wait for the men to wake up first. If they weren't awake by the time she got back to camp, she would *make* them wake up.

She had finished taking care of things and had just put her clothes back into place when she heard the snap of a twig breaking under something heavy behind her. It might have been an animal, but there was a difference between the noises created by wild creatures and people. The noise had sounded like it came from a human animal. She was concerned but not frightened, thinking it could be Nikos or Sheerness, but she was only marginally surprised when three men she didn't know came into the open.

One of them carried a rifle much like the one Nikos had. The other two carried long knives. They weren't swords because the blades weren't long enough and too wide, but they were not daggers. These had to be some of the bandits Nikos had warned about. From the looks on their faces, she had no doubt what they wanted. It was probably the smoke from the fire she had rekindled that had drawn the bandits' attention to their presence. The camp was too far away to make a run for it, but she could see the smoke from the fire; it was easily within shouting distance. She didn't know if Sheerness would hear her, but Nikos might. Her mind began to whir as she analyzed the situation. She still wasn't ready to panic. She had an advantage.

"Good morning, gentlemen," she said calmly and loudly, giving the men a pleasant smile.

The man with the rifle leered as he pointed it at her. The other two men moved to positions to either side behind her.

"If you scream, we'll kill you," said the man with the rifle.

Psyche smiled coyly. "Why would I scream?" Then her eyes widened as if a thought occurred to her suddenly, but of course it hadn't. She was trying to buy herself time, to give Nikos and Sheerness a chance to get there just in case she *couldn't* defend herself. "You *cannot* mean you are bandits?"

The men all laughed evilly. "If you let us take what we want, we might let you live," said the bandit with the gun.

Psyche remained pleasant. "If you're going to kill me whether I give you what you want or not, why would I want to be dishonored before I die? You really don't want to do this," she said evenly.

The bandit with the gun, the leader, looked her up and down, wiping at the side of his mouth with a finger as if he were drooling. He tucked the butt of the rifle beneath his arm, no longer aiming it at her, nodding his head slowly as he started to approach her.

"Oh, yes, we do," he leered.

The other two men each took one of her arms. Psyche waited until the leader was close enough before she used their hold on her for leverage to lift her feet from the ground, using one of them to have the toe of her boot connect soundly with the man's chin in the soft tissue behind the bone, compressing his windpipe. He collapsed to the ground, gasping for air he couldn't have, his rifle firing as he dropped it. The move startled the other two men enough that Psyche was able to work her way out of their grasp. She took the arm of one holding his knife and applied a pressure grip, forcing him to drop it as she used her other hand to land first a blow to the windpipe of the other bandit and then another to his solar plexus. He, too, collapsed to the ground. She then changed her grip on the arm of the one she held and twisted it out and behind him before she casually leaned on it with her elbow and broke it. He dropped to his knees, screaming from the pain, and Psyche gave him a blow to the back of his head, rendering him unconscious like the other two.

"I told you that you didn't want to do that," she said mildly.

Nikos and Sheerness both woke up at the sound of her first greeting to the men. They started walking toward the sound of conversation, but at the gunshot, they started running, arriving just as Psyche dispatched the second two bandits. It was over so quickly, they were unable to do more than watch. Psyche turned to look at them when she realized they were there, her hands at the ready, but she relaxed when she saw it was them.

"Marauding bandits," she said brightly with a slight pant.

Nikos went to collect their weapons and to make sure they were still alive. He stood up from the last one and turned to look at her in amazement.

"Remind me never to make you angry," he said with a grin.

"Oh, I wasn't angry," denied Psyche, her eyes rounding in surprise when Sheerness pulled her to him in a tight, relieved embrace. "I can't think straight enough to do things like that when I'm angry." She looked up at Sheerness with a slight frown as he continued to squeeze her tightly. "Can we go look at the spring since we're this close?"

Sheerness let her go and turned Psyche to look at him, his face incredulous. "You mean right now?"

"Of course," said Psyche practically. "We should bring Sunny with us so he can have some water, and the canteens need to be refilled. These men won't stay unconscious forever, so I thought we should go look while we can."

"She has a point," grinned Nikos. "I'll put these in the cart—" he shook the weapons in his hands—"and get the canteens and the horse."

Sheerness looked from Psyche to Nikos's departing back, his expression still disbelieving. "Am I the only one here who understands you could have been killed?" His eyebrows shot up even further as he watched Psyche approach one of the bandits to take the canteen he carried and pour its contents onto the ground. "Now what are you doing?"

"We need the water in the canteens to drink. I want to keep some as a souvenir," she said distractedly as she shook the canteen to drain out the last of what was in it. She would rinse it as well before putting in the spring water. She looked up at Sheerness with a gentle smile. "They couldn't have killed me; they were too preoccupied by what they wanted. If I were someone else, then, yes, I could have been." She ran a soothing hand down his cheek and gave him a quick kiss on the lips.

"What were you doing away from the camp on your own?" Psyche raised an eyebrow and tilted her head sideways with a slight smile. "Never mind."

Nikos returned with Sunny, and they went to the spring. It wasn't easy to get the horse to the water, but they managed it. It was some of the best water Psyche had ever tasted, and she put as much into the canteens as she could. The ruins were pretty, especially with the oleander and laurel, but Psyche would have loved to see the ruins of the actual sanctuary, the temple of Apollo or the sanctuary of Athena Pronaia and other things…*anything.*

They stayed long enough to resupply their canteens and water the horse, and then they walked back to camp. The three men were still unconscious. For a time, they contemplated tying them up and notifying the authorities in the village, but the only thing they had was vine. Psyche didn't think it would hold them, not if they *wanted* to get away. They would pack up their things, and then they would mention the men to the people in the village, should anyone there be interested in going to investigate.

They put their things on the cart, and then Psyche used her knife to cut the vines holding the saplings together to make the shelter. The three small cypress trees sprang back to their original positions, none the worse for wear, other than the brush left on the ground. They made sure their fire was out, and they ate some of the bread and cheese Sheerness had brought in the sack for breakfast.

The villagers of Kastri, as the town was known, were appreciative to learn the bandits had been laid low. The local leader quickly sent some men to get them before they escaped. These three had been worrying them for some time, waylaying not just Turks and Muslims, but the natives as well. Nikos didn't tell the villagers that Psyche was responsible for bringing the bandits down. It would be embarrassing for all parties involved.

They left Kastri shortly after eight. Much of the way was slow because of the mountains and valleys. There were several villages they passed through, and they found a taverna in one to stop at for dinner. As they approached Livadia, the land became more level, but the sun was setting by the time they could see the city. It was almost dark by the time they reached it.

They were able to find an inn, a small one. Much to Sheerness's consternation, when Nikos arranged for their room—and it was for only one—

he put forth the story that Nikos and Sheerness were brothers and Psyche was married to Sheerness. Psyche's eyes rounded as Nikos conversed with the innkeeper, but she understood why. Psyche traveling unmarried and alone with two men, neither of whom she was related to, would have resulted in them being unable to get any room at all. Considering how small the inn was, since they were family, it simply made more sense for them to be in the same room. All three sharing a room in an inn wouldn't be any different than sharing the shelter the previous night.

They were shown to a room near the top of the stairs on the first floor. It wasn't large, but it was big enough to contain a full-sized bed and a small cot. Psyche took her things without a word after the innkeeper left and placed them beside the cot. It didn't look very comfortable, but it would be better than the ground, and she could use her blankets to make it softer.

"You should have the bed," said Nikos as he watched her.

"I agree," said Sheerness.

Psyche giggled. "And that will either leave both of you sleeping on this very small cot, or one in the cot and one on the floor." She shook her head. "*I* will sleep on the cot, and you two will have the bed."

"But you should have the most comfortable place to sleep," argued Sheerness. "It's ungentlemanly for it to be any other way."

Psyche raised an eyebrow. "Quit being silly. I'm sleeping on the cot." Nikos and Sheerness started to argue, and Psyche held up her hand. "It would be impractical for me to sleep in that bed by myself when it's big enough for two people, so quit arguing. For the last time, I am sleeping on the cot."

Sheerness would have argued further, but the stubborn way she looked at him said Psyche wasn't going to change her mind. It was only that he knew she had a hard time going to sleep; that uncomfortable cot wasn't going to make it easier. He and Nikos looked at each other and shrugged resignedly. If she was satisfied with the arrangement, there wasn't much they could do about it.

After they settled into their room, they went in search of a place to eat. There was a taverna not far from the inn, directly beside it actually, and they enjoyed a simple meal of *fakes*, baked lamb with potatoes, and cabbage rolls with two bottles of retsina. The rabbit and a few things from the sack of food Sheerness had brought from the ship had been fine for supper the night before, but their meal at the taverna was much more satisfying.

When they got back to their room, Psyche took off her boots and climbed under the blankets on her cot. After sleeping on the ground the night before, she felt like she was lying on feathers, and she had a pillow. To make it easier, she took some of her sleeping draught. After going weeks without using it, its effect was almost immediate. She was asleep within minutes.

They left from Livadia the next morning when the taverna wasn't open, so they had more cheese and bread from the sack. They hoped they would find a taverna at some point along the way for dinner. Once they made it to Thebes, and they would reach it before sunset, Chalcis wouldn't be far. They would spend the rest of the day and the night in Thebes, and then they would go to Chalcis and meet the ship tomorrow by early afternoon.

Psyche hated to think it, but she was finding the trip a waste of time and energy. All they had seen were springs. Her sketchbook remained empty. She had liked seeing Thermopylae; there wouldn't have been more than the springs there anyhow. It would have been unlikely for them to find anything else. She had her canteen full of water from the Castalian Spring at Delphi, but she had hoped to see more. It had saddened her to see it the way it was, both because there had been nothing *to see* and because the people of Greece had been reduced to using their heritage—something that should be preserved—for building materials. They took something of a detour and passed through Chaeronea on their way to Livadia, another battlefield with nothing to see. The lion that had been erected as a memorial for the Sacred Band of Thebes was toppled and in pieces. Psyche was left feeling as if she had arrived too late or too soon, and because of the firman, there was nothing she could do about it.

The journey from Livadia to Thebes was a level and easy road...except for the massive potholes they would encounter occasionally...and the herds of sheep and goats...and camels. Psyche had never seen camels before, other than in pictures, and they were the oddest-looking creatures she had ever seen. After they encountered a trader pulling a string of them along on his way to Athens, Sheerness and Nikos were beginning to believe Sunny was the most gentle-natured animal on four legs. Even Psyche, who had a soft spot in her heart for any animal, thought they were the most foul-tempered and nasty-smelling brutes ever. Perhaps their unpleasant disposition was caused by their chore, but somehow Psyche didn't think so. She wasn't even the least bit tempted to take one home.

They went through some cities on their way to Thebes that in ancient times had been thriving metropolises: Haliartus, Thespia, Leuctra. There was nothing there. Nearly four hundred years of Turkish control of the country had reduced them to little more than villages. She could see from his expression that Nikos was also saddened. Everyone knew Greece was the cradle of civilization, but one couldn't tell to look at it today.

The city of Thebes itself, however, was the greatest disappointment of all. It was tiny. There was a taverna, but there was no inn, and any ruins that might exist were buried. The best arrangement they could make for sleeping was in the barn of the taverna owner. He had at least taken pity on them and wasn't going to charge them for it, only for stabling Sunny, and Psyche thought he was being generous. She didn't mind sleeping in a barn. It wouldn't be as comfortable as the inn, but it would be better than the ground. If it were to rain, they would at least (theoretically) be somewhere dry.

She could see that Sheerness was glad this was their last night. He had admitted he had never slept outside, but he obviously hadn't slept in a nice, comfortable bed his entire life; he had to learn to sail somehow, and that didn't happen in a drawing room...or at Oxford. He didn't complain, and he wasn't in a bad temper, but he was missing his bed. Actually, she was, too.

After their simple but satisfying meal at the taverna, the three of them went to the barn not far away and climbed into the loft. There was plenty of straw, and between their blankets and keeping on their clothes, it wasn't too scratchy. Actually, Psyche thought it was even more comfortable than the cot. She arranged some of the straw into a nice pillow and nestled into it on her side.

The three of them were sleeping in a row with a foot or two between them, Sheerness in the middle. Psyche thought it was odd how there seemed to be some unspoken understanding that he should be the one sleeping closest to her. It seemed Nikos did know there was something between the two of them, and Sheerness was asserting his possession, almost as if he were still jealous. Psyche didn't like the thought of that, and she tried to put it out of her head. He didn't act as if he were jealous, at least not overtly, but there were sometimes things he did or said that made her wonder.

He was lying on his left side, watching her, and Psyche smiled at him sleepily, trying to put her troubled thoughts to the back of her mind. It wouldn't help her go to sleep. Sheerness reached out his hand to trace his finger down her cheek to her chin, and Psyche grabbed his hand to place a kiss on the palm before letting it go. He grinned and mouthed the words *tomorrow night*. Psyche rolled her eyes with an amused smile before she closed them and tried to sleep. She could only imagine how he was going to react when he found out he would *only* have tomorrow night before he would have to wait yet again.

Chapter Thirty Six

They were later reaching Chalcis than they thought they would be, but it was still only mid-afternoon. They took a ferry across the strait to the harbor, and the ship was easy enough to locate. Even after several months, it was still bright and shiny, and Sheerness was like a mother hen with her chicks; he *knew* his ship. Loading Sunny into the hold was uneventful, and both Higginbotham and Stockbridge scratched their foreheads when they learned he was to be part of the cargo returning to Britain. There was room for him, and the other animals would provide him with plenty of company.

Once he was lowered in, Psyche went down to make sure he was settling in; he had already made friends with the milk cow and her calf. Psyche was sure he would get on with the rest of the horses her family owned. They had one pony in particular that was older and far more crotchety, which Psyche thought at the age of thirty he had every right to be. Perhaps between the two older animals, they might even teach Achilles some manners. It was unlikely but possible. And it wasn't really that her horse was ill-mannered; he just liked to eat and had the skill to untie himself to search for food when the situation warranted. Maybe what he needed to learn was some patience.

Rather than abandoning the cart on the quay, they found someone who looked like he could use it and gave it to him. It was hard to believe someone could actually *need* a cart such as theirs, that it could be an improvement over something else, but they did find someone. The man would not simply take it from them, so Psyche accepted one of his finely woven wool blankets in exchange. She thought she was getting the better end of the deal, while he felt the same. He had been carrying his wares on the back of a mule. Now he had harness for the mule and a cart to carry himself and his things. Psyche wasn't too sure the mule was going to feel relieved, though.

Once they had everything squared away, the *Medea* set sail, heading south through the strait to the other end of the Evoikos Gulf. For a time, they considered sailing slightly to the east around the edge of Euboea to Eretria, but after Nikos said there was nothing to see, not even a village, Psyche and Sheerness decided to forego it, thinking they'd had enough disappointment for one week. Instead, they would sail on and stop at Marathon, yet another battlefield. It would be dark by the time they made it, so they would set anchor once they reached it and go look at the site in the morning.

Waddlesworth and Cupid were happy to see Psyche. They were getting on well. Freddie had done an excellent job looking after them, but Psyche hoped it would be a while before she had to leave them again. Perhaps it was all the time she had spent at Kastro Andreanopouli, but she missed staying in one place. She looked forward to sleeping in the same place for a while.

Psyche was sitting on the coffer by the window, holding her necklace up to the dying sunlight, a slight frown between her eyebrows as she looked at the map on the back of the amber, her chin resting in her palm. Now that she was in one place again, maybe she could back to work determining where it led. She had the information from Sir James and Sheerness's maps, but she was beginning to wonder if she would ever figure it out. She turned her head to look at the door when there was a knock, and she hopped down from the coffer to open it, finding Nikos there. He looked at the necklace in her hand.

"Not Greek," he said with a grin.

"No," she agreed with a grin of her own. "It's a map to a place in Egypt…I think, but I can't figure out where it is." She took him by the hand and led him over to the window. "Come take a look." She held it up to the light for him to look at the amber, and she watched the surprise flicker in his expression.

"That's amazing," said Nikos. He turned the amber the other way with the triangular pendant at the top and the beaded chain at the bottom.

"Why are you looking at it upside down?"

"No, Thea, why are *you* looking at it upside down?" chortled Nikos as he continued to gaze at it.

"What do you mean?" asked Psyche confusedly.

"It's a necklace, yes?" Psyche nodded. "If you were wearing it on your neck and held it up to the light, which way would you have it? The chain is too short to hold it this way," he said, turning it with the chain at the top again.

The color drained from Psyche's face, and she felt as if her heart had stopped beating. "Oh, my giddy aunt," she said breathlessly. "I am *such* an idiot." She went to her desk for the enlarged drawing, turning it upside down. "Oh, God, that makes so much more sense now."

Nikos grinned and held out the necklace. Psyche took it and impulsively gave him a hug around the neck and a peck on the cheek. Sheerness walked through the open door just as she released Nikos to put the necklace and map on her desk. To Sheerness, it disturbingly looked as if she were intentionally putting distance between them…like he was catching them doing something they shouldn't have been. Neither appeared to be showing any guilt or concern for his having walked in, but he knew how deceptive that could be. A nerve began to tick in his jaw as he clamped his teeth together.

"Nikos just made me feel absolutely silly," said Psyche with a grin.

"Did he now?" said Sheerness stiffly.

"I'm rather embarrassed to admit it, but all this time I've been looking at my map upside down," she said, her cheeks coloring.

"Which map?" asked Sheerness blankly.

"The one on my necklace, of course."

"Oh?"

"I was looking at it and showed it to Nikos when he came in, and he turned it the other way...the *right* way. I can't believe I've been looking at it wrong all this time." She glanced at Nikos. "What did you come in for again?"

"It's not important. I can ask you later," said Nikos mildly. It had to do with the party, and now Sheerness was there, he would have to wait.

Sheerness looked at them suspiciously. Psyche still acted completely innocent, but Nikos's statement seemed a bit secretive. Nikos excused himself to wash up for supper, closing the door behind him. After he was gone, Psyche walked toward Sheerness and put her arms around his neck, giving him a sound kiss before nipping at his bottom lip with her teeth playfully. She tilted her head back to look at him, taking note of his guarded expression.

"Is something the matter?" she asked with a hesitant smile. "You're looking awfully dour."

"Am I?" he asked softly, resting his hands at her hips.

Psyche smoothed a hand down his cheek. "I know you're not happy going all these places and not being able to *take* things, but we'll be somewhere you can soon. Now I'm looking at the map in the right direction, that will give us another place...possibly...if someone else hasn't already found where it leads and removed everything...and if Muhammad Ali Pasha will let us."

Sheerness continued to look at her pensively. She still acted as if nothing were amiss. Perhaps he was just being jealous and suspicious for no reason. She thought his distance was caused by disappointment over their useless, three-day trip, or so it seemed. Nikos *was* old enough to be her father. If Sheerness looked at it objectively, she had never shown interest in anyone but him. He didn't know how she felt about him; the uncertainty made it difficult for him to believe she wouldn't place her affections elsewhere. He moved his hands down to cup her bottom and pulled her against him.

"Are you coming to my room?" he asked, giving her an assessing glance.

A slight frown formed between her eyebrows. "Do you not want me to?"

He bent his head to nuzzle her neck. "We've had this discussion," he said silkily before kissing her thoroughly. "Need me to refresh your memory?"

"We'll be late for supper," she sighed. The next four days were going to be difficult. "You can remind me later."

He gave her a wolfish grin before tweaking the end of her nose. "Oh, you can count on it."

Psyche went to take a shower after bringing in Waddlesworth and taking Cupid to the deck one last time. She thought about leaving the puppy in her cabin, but he wouldn't stay in there alone. Freddie had told her the puppy had slept with him while she was gone because he whined when he was shut up in her cabin; it made it hard for Bothi to get any sleep. She made sure her cabin door was latched so it wouldn't come open at some point during the night while she was gone. She didn't ordinarily go through such preparations before taking a shower, but she wasn't leaving Sheerness's room once she was done…not until morning.

It was nice to have a shower, and she could hear Cupid running back and forth across the floor, playing with the rubber ball she had bought for him. Actually, it wasn't obvious he was running around unless he slipped and skidded into the side of the shower with a thud or rolled the ball into it. The piece of rawhide from Nikos and Ioanna's had become too shredded, and Psyche thought the ball might last longer. He seemed to like it.

After her shower, she sat in the chair by the fire to dry her hair and brush the snarls out of it. She dried out her towel and folded it, and then she looked at the bed. She couldn't decide which end was which. She put Cupid onto it; he walked back and forth for a few minutes before settling onto the left side in one corner. That was good enough for Psyche. She pulled back the blankets from the other end, added a few pillows, and climbed on.

"Outstanding," she sighed as she settled into it with a smile.

The mattress for her bunk was soft, but this one was softer, and all the pillows and blankets were snuggly, made of silk and cashmere. Those fabrics were highly impractical on a ship, but Psyche loved it anyhow. Added to all of that was that it smelled like Sheerness. It was heavenly. After thinking about it for only a second, she pulled off her shift and settled back into it completely naked. It was every bit as luxurious as she had imagined. She buried her face in the pillow and inhaled. Before she even realized she was tired, Psyche was sound asleep.

Sheerness walked into his cabin and could tell immediately that Psyche had showered. He looked at his bed and saw her in it, her shift draped over one of the side panels. She didn't stir when he came in, and he walked to the bed to look down at her. Sleeping. He shook his head disbelievingly. He would wake her eventually, but he would do his paperwork and shower first, since there wasn't anything (or anyone) requiring his immediate attention. He couldn't wait until morning, but he could wait an hour…probably.

He poured himself a brandy and took off his waistcoat before going to his desk to light the lamp and open the top. He spared a brief glance over his shoulder to the bed before he retrieved his spectacles from their case and put them on. He made his entries in the log and wrote a few letters. He didn't know when he would have another chance to write them or when he would be able to mail them, so he might as well get them out of the way. The amount of correspondence Psyche maintained had made him realize his own was lacking.

Once he was done, he put away his spectacles and straightened the things on his desk before closing the lid. He quickly took a shower, noting that he needed a shave. He thought about taking care of it before bed but decided he would ask Psyche to do it tomorrow; she gave an excellent shave. The first time, he had been nervous, but by the end of it he had been very relaxed and found the whole experience very sensual. He stepped out of the shower and dried off, draping his towel over the door to dry.

He didn't notice until he got into the bed that Cupid was there, curled up in a ball near the front panel. It surprised him, but he didn't mind. It was a big bed, and the dog was small and good at keeping himself out of the way. He gave a startled jump when he realized Psyche was awake—somewhat.

"Did I wake you?" he asked quietly as he adjusted the blankets and propped himself up on his elbow to look down at her.

Psyche smiled sleepily and put her hand to the side of his neck with a slight shake of her head. "Not really…the steam did. I would have gotten woke up at some point anyhow." She smoothed her hand from his neck to his cheek and yawned as she tried to become more alert. "You need a shave. I'll do that for you tomorrow, if you'd like." She smiled seductively. "I love your bed."

Sheerness grinned and bent his head to nuzzle her throat. "Do you now?" he asked amusedly. "What have you been missing all this time?"

He ran his hand up her hip to her side before palming one of her breasts. Psyche leaned into his touch and pulled his mouth to hers to kiss him enthusiastically. She gave a gentle push to his shoulder and rolled over on top of him, trailing her lips across his jaw to begin nibbling at his earlobe. Sheerness sighed happily and smoothed his hands up her hips and along her sides to her back. She began to make her way down his neck to his chest, and he shuddered as she began to tease one of his nipples and lightly trailed her nails down the center of his stomach before wrapping her fingers around his erection.

"Oh, what have *I* been missing all this time," he sighed.

He put a hand to the back of her head and guided her mouth back to his to kiss her hungrily. Psyche moaned low in her throat and rubbed herself against him longingly. Sheerness shifted lower on the bed and took one of her breasts into his mouth, laving the nipple with his tongue until Psyche whimpered and weakly clutched the fingers of one hand in his hair, the other grasping the edge of the end panel. He smoothed his hands down her sides to her hips and slowly began to raise her onto her knees as he kissed his way down her stomach. He soon had her positioned with her knees on the pillows to either side of his head, and Psyche quivered pleasurably as he began to tease her with his mouth.

"Oh," she sighed, her tone one of surprise and bliss as her grip tightened on the end of the bed.

He had one hand balanced on her bottom to hold her still as he played her, gently gliding two fingers from the other hand inside her. She was hot and wet, and he moaned softly at the back of his throat as he felt her thighs tremble excitedly. Psyche bent her head to look at him, feverishly running her fingers through his hair. The shutters were still open on the stern, and she could see his face in the light of the nearly full moon. Watching him, seeing the expression of enjoyment on *his* face as he teased her caused an erotic pleasure of its own. When he opened his eyes to look at her, Psyche began to shudder uncontrollably and cried out his name with a strangled whimper as she began to orgasm. Sheerness could feel her spasm around his fingers, and he gently smoothed his hand from her bottom across one of her thighs.

Psyche eventually lifted herself off of him and leaned down to give him an adoring kiss, smoothing her fingers down his cheek. She lifted her head to give him an impish grin.

"I have absolutely no basis for comparison, but you are *very* good at that," she said amusedly.

Sheerness chuckled with a slow smile. "Every man needs a talent."

Psyche giggled and began to place kisses down his neck to his chest, teasing his nipples. "*Any* time you want to practice," she said between nibbles, "I'm your girl."

She ran her tongue down the ridge of muscle at the center of his stomach and wrapped her lips around his navel, massaging it with her tongue. Sheerness groaned pleasurably, loving the feel of her mouth and the teasing sensation as her hair feathered over his skin. He sucked in air through his teeth and tensed as she softly played her fingers across his hip to take his erection in her hand, slowly smoothing her thumb around the tip before wrapping her fingers around the shaft and beginning to move her hand up and down as she continued to kiss his navel.

Psyche looked up at him in surprise when he put his hand over hers to stop her. He rose up on his knees and pulled her toward him to kiss her hungrily before lowering his head to nip at her breasts. He moved behind her, and Psyche smiled silkily as he bent her forward onto her hands and knees and plunged into her with a blissful moan. He gripped one hand at her hip and the other at her shoulder as he thrust into her, and Psyche buried her fingers into the covers spasmodically, her breath coming out in short panting gasps of pleasure. A shiver worked its way up her spine, and she bit her lip to keep herself from crying out too loudly as she orgasmed, and she thought her arms were going to collapse beneath her. Sheerness tensed momentarily as he began to come, and Psyche smiled satisfactorily as she heard him release a soft, shuddering groan. She adored the sounds he made.

Sheerness smoothed the hand at her shoulder down her back before he bent his head to place a kiss on her birthmark. He collapsed onto the bed with a tired sigh and pulled her mouth toward his for a kiss. Psyche snuggled into his side and draped one of her legs over his, propping her cheek onto the back of her hand on his chest. He reached up to brush the hair out of her face and saw her satisfied smile as she looked at him.

"Lord Sheerness, I think you're a *very* talented man," she purred, her eyes blinking sleepily.

Sheerness actually blushed and gave her a slight smile. "Perhaps we should go three days without more often."

Psyche's eyes widened. "Do you really think so?"

Sheerness grinned wickedly and shook his head, smoothing his hand down her back to cup her bottom. "Absolutely not," he said softly. Psyche's face grew pensive. "What?"

"Four days without, then…maybe?" she asked hopefully.

Sheerness frowned. "No. Why?"

"Because after tonight that's how long you'll have to wait," said Psyche quietly, watching her finger as she traced it distractedly across his chest.

"What? Why?" His eyebrows shot up. "It can't be that time again already. It's only been a week."

"No, it's not time for my courses, but it is somewhat related," she said evasively, still watching her finger.

"In what way?" he asked confusedly, grabbing her hand to stop her.

She looked at him directly then. "Have you any illegitimate children running around?"

Sheerness looked at her in surprise, finding the question unexpected and far more personal than she was prone to asking. "None that I'm aware of, thank God," he answered slowly after a time.

"Then I don't think now would be a good time to start, do you?"

His face paled. "You mean…?" he trailed off.

"I'm thinking Friday would be the worst possible time, but it's better to be safe than sorry." She looked at him. "Even tonight is chancy."

"How can you be so sure?" he asked suspiciously.

"This is one of those secret things that goes into making babies and all that it's helpful for a woman—any woman—to know. I'm sure."

"You could just marry me," said Sheerness softly.

Psyche sat up and looked away from him, wrapping her arms around her knees as she pulled them up to her chest. "No, I can't," she said quickly. She looked back at him over her shoulder. "And I'm not discussing it right now, so do not ask," she said flatly.

Sheerness clenched his teeth together as a nerve began to tick in his jaw. He closed his eyes and took a deep breath in and out through his nose to regain control of his temper. It seemed she still had no intention of marrying him, even after all this time, and from that, he could only infer she still didn't love him. *What* did she *want* from him? Still, if this was the only way he could have her, then he would have to be satisfied with it for now.

Psyche, meanwhile, was trying to control her own temper. She shouldn't have told him the real reason, but she couldn't lie. She had hoped he would be supportive rather than thinking it would be an excellent way to convince her to marry him. Now her concern was that he knew she could become pregnant within the next four days. With her difficulty telling him no, and no real physical reason to do so, it would give him the perfect opportunity to make it impossible for her to refuse to marry him, killing two birds with one stone by gaining a wife and an heir in one go. She was already taking a serious risk, but any time in those four days would just be asking for it.

"Four days?" he asked quietly after a time. "Can't we just miss Friday?"

Psyche turned to look at him, giving him a slight smile. "No. I'm sorry. *Truly* I am." She lay back down on top of him and smoothed a hand down his cheek before giving him a gentle kiss. "And tonight is chancy."

"How chancy?" asked Sheerness casually, smoothing his hands across her back. He was thinking less than four-to-one.

"You want odds?" asked Psyche dryly, raising an eyebrow. Sheerness nodded. "About even, I think."

Sheerness brushed her hair out of her face to look at her concernedly. "But we…. You…."

Psyche kissed him soundly. "Too late to worry now," she said quietly, running her finger along his jaw to his chin. "Considering you've already gone three days and will have to go four more, I don't think you want to look a gift horse in the mouth." She kissed him again and grinned. "*I* like the odds."

Sheerness looked at the top of her head as she placed tiny kisses on his chest, a slight frown between his brows. "I know you don't want to talk about it, but if you were to…become pregnant, would you…marry me?"

Psyche lifted her head to look at him, her expression grave. She started to say something before looking away and grabbing her bottom lip with her teeth as she thought some more, and Sheerness began to wonder if she was going to answer at all. She finally looked back at him.

"Yes," she answered quietly.

It surprised him to hear her say that. He had expected her to say not just no but never. To know she had made love to him even though she stood a good chance of becoming pregnant, just so he wouldn't have to wait, made him realize his belief she was indifferent had to be wrong. His heart was pounding in his chest as she continued to look at him with that solemn gaze. He was hopeful, which was more than he had been before. He could see from her expression, though, that she was waiting for him to use it. While there was a part of him that wanted to, he couldn't. For now, it was enough to know. He ran his fingers over her cheek to the side of her head and pulled her mouth to his to kiss her tenderly before rubbing his nose against hers.

Sheerness startled Psyche when he rolled onto his side and placed her onto the mattress. He reached down to pull the blankets over them and nestled close behind her, putting his arm beneath her head under the pillow and wrapping the other tightly around her waist. He nuzzled her neck before placing a kiss on it, and then he whispered in her ear.

"I still want you in my bed."

Psyche's eyes widened, and for a moment she couldn't breathe. She had to blink several times as she felt the sting of tears, and she bit the inside of her lip as a drop escaped from the corner of her eye onto the pillow. All this time, she had thought he was lying when he said he loved her, and now she wasn't so sure. Psyche was beginning to believe she had made a horrible mistake.

After breakfast, Psyche and Sheerness set out with Nikos for Marathon. They saw the burial mound, and then they walked a little further inland toward the mountains, where Nikos took them to see a cave. Psyche found the cave more interesting than the battlefield. It was a sanctuary of some type, and after looking for a little while, she realized it was dedicated to Pan. That had prompted a chuckle from her. Pandora would also find it amusing, and Psyche would have to make sure she told her twin about it in her next letter.

When they returned to the ship around mid-afternoon, the three of them had dinner as the *Medea* sailed south along the Attican peninsula, heading for Cape Sounion. The weather was pleasant, but even for the Aegean, fall had arrived. She was growing concerned the water wouldn't be warm enough to look at ruins…at least, not for her. By the time they reached Cape Sounion, the sun was setting, but there was only one thing to see, up the hill from where they stopped the ship and plainly visible on the promontory.

The *Medea* dropped anchor in the small bay, and they went ashore in one of the launches. They walked up the hill to look at the Temple of Poseidon. It was large and impressive, even though it was missing most of its architecture and had nothing left above the Doric columns except for the architrave. Psyche made a few quick sketches and a watercolor with the sun setting behind it before going for a closer look. At the base of one column, Psyche saw something that made her eyes narrow angrily.

"Ooh, the nerve of that man!" she hissed.

"What?" asked Sheerness.

"I did not travel three thousand miles to find *his* name carved on a two-thousand-year-old temple!"

"Who?" asked Sheerness blankly.

"Byron," said Psyche exasperatedly. She looked at Sheerness. "Don't tell me you can't see that." She pointed at the name plainly carved on the base.

"Oh," said Sheerness as he looked at it. He turned to look at her with a grin. "Do you want to carve yours?"

"No, I don't," she said flatly. "For a man who claims to adore the Greeks so much, he certainly doesn't seem to have any respect." She turned to look at Nikos. "What do you think?"

Nikos grinned. "I think in two hundred years, people will travel from all over the world to see it." Sheerness laughed silently at the consternated look on Psyche's face at the thought of it. "Come. I think we should be getting back to the ship. It will be dark soon."

They left for the ship and made it back just as full dark arrived. Sheerness had intended to sail for Delos once they had visited the temple, but on seeing it had already become dark, he decided they would stay where they were and sail in the morning. They would be there by early afternoon, and that would be soon enough. There were a lot of ruins on the island, but if they couldn't see them all tomorrow, they could simply look at more the next day. The ruins Nikos was taking them to were near Delos, so there was no need to hurry.

When they got back to the ship, Psyche went to her cabin to write. Her stack of correspondence was growing again, and she would have to mail the letters soon. The one she wanted to make sure she wrote was to Sir James, informing him that she had discovered what her mistake had been with the map, thanks to Nikos. He hadn't mentioned whether or not he had realized the error as well, but she suspected not. She was curious to see how closely the locations he had ruled out would align with the actual site.

They would be at Delos tomorrow, and then afterward they would go to the underwater ruins. Psyche didn't know how long that would take, and it would occupy much of her time once they located them. She would have to look at the maps of Egypt and find her site before they got to the country so she would know whether it would be worth the effort to ask for permission to remove things. There would be no point if it was somewhere long since discovered.

After supper Psyche took Cupid on deck, got ready for bed, and went to Sheerness's cabin. Psyche had woke feeling awkward that morning, and she hadn't been able to pretend she was asleep to avoid it. Sheerness hadn't seemed any different, and Psyche hadn't wanted to point out that something *had* changed…at least for her. She still wasn't sure, so she wasn't ready to talk about it yet, to offer her humblest apology.

Psyche stood in the middle of the cabin, scratching her forehead for a minute after she put Cupid onto the bed. The room was still spic-and-span, and she still didn't know how. She had given Sheerness the shave he needed as they traveled between Marathon and Cape Sounion, and she had found out he kept the things for that in the top drawer of the chest with the mirror. Other than the decanters on the commode on the starboard side, there was nothing out. She was yet to ask him why everything was so neat…why it seemed he *needed* it that way.

She finally shrugged and climbed onto the bed after removing her dressing gown. She yawned and stretched and snuggled under the blankets. It was like sleeping in a nest, the mattress was so comfortable and cozy, and the best part was the smell. She had slept well past sunrise; Sheerness had to wake her. It was extraordinary. Granted, it had taken her a while to fall asleep, but even under usual circumstances, she was still awake as the sun came up. Sleeping beyond that was something she could easily become accustomed to.

She was just on the point of dozing off when the door opened. She thought about moving, but she didn't want to. Sheerness would be in the bed soon enough. She felt him approach before walking away and heard him moving around the room. The clink of glass as he poured himself a drink. The sound of his desk opening. The sound of the chair being pulled back as he sat down. Psyche frowned with her eyes closed. He thought she was asleep. It was true she didn't immediately need him in bed, but she did want him there. She had been doing well going to sleep even without him. Then she heard a sound that was familiar but not expected, and her eyes opened.

Psyche lay for a moment thinking. She could have been mistaken, but it would explain a lot. After some hesitation, she cautiously raised herself up to look over the panel. He sat with his back turned as he wrote in the log. She could see letters and papers folded neatly and tucked into pigeonholes at the back of the desk with a space in the center where the log would go and a few other notebooks were located. In one corner on the desktop was a small wooden box, standing about five inches tall, eight inches wide, and a foot long. It didn't have a hasp or a lock, but it had a keyhole on the front. There was a key on a ribbon hanging from the knob of a drawer, and she wondered if it was for the lock. She was curious about that box, but it hadn't caused the noise.

Psyche looked at Sheerness as he continued to write. He paused for a moment, as if in thought, and turned his head slightly. The light from the lamp glinted off something. Spectacles. She thought she had heard the spring on a case being opened, a sound she heard quite often from her father and Arachne. He had to be farsighted, since she'd never noticed problems seeing things in the distance…unlike her, which would explain why he had no trouble seeing with Arachne's set that Psyche had taken by mistake. It also explained a great deal more. After watching a few minutes longer, Psyche lay back down and began to chew on the side of her thumb thoughtfully.

She didn't know for certain how bad his vision was, but if Arachne's spectacles worked, she had to believe it was pretty awful. That would account for the problems he'd had finding his way around Nikos and Ioanna's house. Why he couldn't see the map on the back of the necklace. Why he liked to have everything put in its place, so he'd know where to find it even if he couldn't see it. Why she'd never once seen him read anything, because he couldn't without his glasses. And it would explain why he had been unable to tell the difference between her and Pandora at the ball. Anyone able to see would have noticed the differences, but he couldn't because they hadn't been blatant enough. It all made so much sense now, and Psyche felt worse because she had blamed a lot of it on faults that didn't exist.

What puzzled her was why he wouldn't wear his glasses. She could understand (somewhat) why he wouldn't wear them at social functions, but there was no reason for him not to wear them *now*. His crew and officers wouldn't think anything of it. Neither would Nikos. She certainly didn't because she wore them herself, and she would choose being able to see over what people might think any day. He had never struck her as being vain. She had accused him of having perfect vision, and he hadn't corrected her. From that, she could only assume he didn't want *her* to know. It was perplexing.

Psyche was so lost in thought, she didn't hear he'd finished his work and gotten ready for bed until he climbed onto the bunk. She jumped in surprise when she felt it shift, and she turned over to look at him.

"I thought you were asleep," said Sheerness in an accusatory tone.

"I was…almost," said Psyche quietly. She gave him a slight smile. "I was just too comfortable to move."

"Hunh," said Sheerness doubtfully as he got under the covers.

He nestled Psyche into his side, and she laid her cheek on the back of her hand on his chest to look up at him. He ran his fingers through her hair and brushed it out of her face before running his finger along her cheek. She didn't seem like she had been almost asleep, and he had to wonder if she had seen his glasses. She raised her head from where it was resting to give him a lingering kiss before nuzzling his chin lovingly. Sheerness looked at her through narrowed eyes. The way she continued to look at him with that thoughtful expression was making him terribly suspicious, but she had behaved oddly all day, from the minute he had to wake her up.

"It's difficult to sleep with your eyes open," he finally said dryly.

"I know," she answered practically. She moved her other hand to start tracing a finger through the hair on his chest.

"I thought you were almost asleep."

"I'm not sleepy now," said Psyche distractedly as she continued to watch her finger. She stopped to look up at him. "Are you?"

"Psyche, is there something bothering you?"

"Well, I'm in a bit of a personal quandary, but I wouldn't say it's *bothering* me. Why?"

"Absolutely no reason," sighed Sheerness, raising a hand to rub his eyes tiredly. He opened them to see her still watching him. "Since you're not sleepy, perhaps you can tell me how Nikos knows about all these places he's taken us to see."

"You could ask Nikos," said Psyche with a wry grin as she resumed running her fingers over his chest. "You are friends, aren't you?"

"Ye-es, but I'm asking you, and please, stop that," said Sheerness quietly.

Psyche looked up at him through her lashes, and she curled her hand into a ball and tapped her knuckles against his chest lightly before letting it drop.

"It's something of a pastime. He got a classical degree at university in Bologna, so he decided to use it for something. He's been trying to locate all the ancient sites in Greece and document them, their condition, possibility for excavation or preservation. There's not much that can be done under the Ottomans, but he wants to have the information anyhow."

"He went to university?"

"You seem surprised."

"I suppose that would explain why he's so knowledgeable," said Sheerness softly, almost to himself.

"You make it sound like you think of him as some rustic," said Psyche tartly as she adjusted herself into a more comfortable position, lying more solidly on top of him.

"No, I don't. He doesn't *act* like he went to university." Psyche raised an eyebrow. "He's very unassuming."

"Oh, you mean he's not *pedantic* enough to have gone to university." She bit her tongue to refrain from asking him if that was why he sometimes behaved the way he did. "Knowledge is good enough for its own sake. It's not necessary to flaunt it. If all you do is learn something to let everyone else know you have, it's almost as useless as not learning anything at all."

"Then why do you act like you know everything?"

"I don't act like that," said Psyche evenly. "I don't know everything. It's not necessary, and I haven't the time or the energy. I know languages; I know antiquities. I know just enough about a few other things from the interests of my family to occasionally be helpful, but I'll never pretend to know something I don't, and I will readily admit when I don't know the answer."

Sheerness looked at her thoughtfully. She really was modest about her accomplishments. There was so much she knew, far more than he did, but she never treated him like she did. It was all due to his feelings of ineptitude. It was all so effortless to her, and that was why he always felt like such a dunce. She didn't have to struggle to find an answer, so she didn't feel it was necessary to prove she had it. She didn't seem to realize not everyone was like that.

"You said Nikos was a smuggler. Why would he go to university just to be a smuggler?" he finally asked.

Psyche ran her finger across the dimple in his chin. "I said he was *somewhat* like a smuggler," she said absently as she moved up to trace his lips. "He doesn't trade in ill-gotten goods."

"Then what does he smuggle?" asked Sheerness, his question somewhat muffled beneath her fingers.

She kept her fingers in place over his mouth as she looked up at him from what she was doing. "People."

"What?" blurted Sheerness in a shocked tone, and luckily her fingers were over his mouth to soften the loudness of it.

"Shh!" hissed Psyche exasperatedly. Sheerness scowled, thinking slave trading was far worse than smuggling. She tapped her fingers against his lips before she removed them.

"Explain," said Sheerness flatly.

"The Ottomans have to get their soldiers from somewhere. An empire as vast as theirs, they've got to have a large army to defend it. Some volunteer, but not enough to meet the need, so they have something like impressment. The Greeks call it *paidomazoma*…child gathering."

Sheerness started to say something, and Psyche put her fingers back onto his lips. "If you're a Christian in the Ottoman empire, you pay taxes on your land, taxes on trade, and taxes to worship. You're good enough for the empire to want your money, but they would never have you in their army. Still, the soldiers have to come from somewhere. Christians have to give a tribute of children. Every Christian community has to give one son in five to be raised Muslim and enlisted into the Janissary corps." Psyche shrugged. "Some don't mind because it gives their sons the opportunity to advance far beyond what they would as Christians, but it's not as if they're really given a choice.

"Chrissoula told me stories of families who crippled their sons to keep them from being taken away. It's one of the reasons Nikos and Ioanna are happy they have nothing but girls. They don't worry about the conscription because they're supposedly Muslim, but they *are* Christian. If they had sons, they would feel obligated to surrender one because it would be cowardly and hypocritical to do otherwise. Nikos helps families get their sons somewhere safe, taking them to relatives outside the empire or to relatives who have no sons. It's one more thing the Ottomans would kill him for." She smiled wryly. "He thought he may as well hang for a sheep as hang for a lamb."

"That's how he travels around the country to find all these ruins, isn't it? Traipsing from one end of it to the other smuggling children?"

"By land or by sea," said Psyche absently as she laid her cheek back onto her hand and suppressed a yawn. "Hopefully he won't have to much longer."

"Why?"

"There's a resistance growing. The Ottoman empire's grown bloated and inefficient. Nikos knows people…people like him, smart and full up. They need help, though, from people like us…from Britain. It's just not right these people have to live the way they do. It's enslavement." She yawned hugely then, unable to control it any longer. "I may talk to my father when we get home." She blinked sleepily. "*He's* the one who knows everything."

Sheerness smoothed his hand over her back with a slight smile before he moved it to the back of her head to guide her mouth to his and kiss her. Whatever her personal quandary might have been, she had managed to move beyond it, or at least put it from her mind for the time being. She kissed him back languidly, and Sheerness moved his hands to cup her bottom and shift her completely on top of him. She sighed at the back of her throat as he pressed her against him, and she moved her hands to either side of his face and lifted her head to look at him.

"We can't do this," she whispered.

"I'm only kissing you good night," said Sheerness softly.

Psyche lowered her head to give him a tender kiss before easing off of him. She turned onto her side and grabbed his arm to put it around her waist and have him snuggle behind her.

"Good night, Sebastian," she sighed.

He kissed her neck and squeezed her gently. "Good night, Psyche."

Psyche didn't want to get up…again. Sheerness wondered if she was unwell. When he had to wake her yesterday, he at first thought she was pretending because she was always (usually) awake before him. It wasn't easy to wake her, which was why he knew she really was asleep. This morning took several attempts, and the one thing that worked was the one thing they couldn't do. It took all of Psyche's effort to stop, and she was awake by then.

"I may have to sleep in my own cabin until Monday," she sighed.

Sheerness grinned boyishly and lay on top of her, squishing her into the mattress. Psyche giggled and started to squirm, and he rolled off of her onto the bed before they got into trouble again. He got up and started to dress.

"Well, if all we're going to do is sleep," said Sheerness as he tucked his shirt into his trousers.

Psyche raised herself up on her elbows. "I meant by myself."

"No," drew out Sheerness slowly as he pulled on his waistcoat. "Just quit making me have to be inventive to wake you up."

Psyche climbed off the bed and walked toward him to help with his collar. Once she had it adjusted to her satisfaction, she ran her fingers through his hair to straighten it before tweaking the end of his nose.

"Do you have something in your mattress or pillows, like hops?"

Sheerness chuckled and shook his head. "No. Why?"

"There's just something about your bed that makes me want to sleep. It's extraordinary, really. I've even had dreams."

His eyebrow shot up in surprise. "You don't usually?"

"I used to have nightmares when I was small, but then I quit sleeping so much, and they went away." She scratched her forehead. "I had one for the first time in ages the night we stayed at Delphi, but I don't remember much of it. Probably something silly, I'm sure. Then, last night and the night before, I had dreams. Not nightmares…just dreams. I can't recall that ever happening before, so that was why I wondered if your pillows had…." She trailed off and tilted her head sideways when she saw his expression. "What?"

Sheerness pulled her close and smoothed his hand down her cheek. "Everyone needs to dream, *chere*. If my bed makes you sleep well enough to do that, then that's where you need to be. You don't get enough sleep, and I don't know how you manage." He gazed at her solemnly. "I worry about you."

Psyche blinked. "Oh," she said softly. She covered his hand on her cheek with her own and stood on her tiptoes to kiss him gently. "Thank you," she said uncertainly. Telling him she was fine wouldn't make him worry any less, and nothing else came to mind.

Sheerness sat in the wing chair to pull on his boots, and Psyche went to use the water closet. By the time she came out, he had on his boots and had started to make the bed.

"I can do that." Sheerness glanced at her with a doubtfully raised eyebrow. "It won't be *flawless,* but since it will just get messed up again tonight…."

Sheerness turned back to making the bed, and Psyche walked behind him to goose the back of his thigh. He chuckled and sidestepped out of her reach, turning to face her.

"If you're really not fussy, as you continually protest you aren't, then you will leave this instant and let me make the bed," said Psyche with a teasing grin. "Otherwise, I'm going to start calling you Sheerness the Stodgy."

He chuckled again. "That's better than Barneville the Bastard." Her cheeks colored, and Sheerness grinned. "You thought I forgot, didn't you?"

"It used to be very appropriate," said Psyche flatly.

"So does that mean you like me now?"

"You're trying to distract me while you make the bed so I won't be able to," pouted Psyche.

"Possibly, but that still doesn't answer my question," said Sheerness mildly as he put Cupid onto the floor to continue making the bed.

"Yes, I like you, even when you're impossible…like right now."

Sheerness stopped then and grabbed her by the arm to pull her close for a warm kiss. Psyche looked up at him wonderingly when he lifted his head to gaze at her searchingly.

"Do you mean that?"

"Yes, you're being quite impossible right now," said Psyche breathlessly.

"No, no, that you like me."

Psyche frowned slightly. "Of course I meant it. How can you still not believe I have never lied to you?" she asked chidingly.

To her surprise, his jaw tightened angrily, and he let her go to walk to the door. He paused with his hand on the knob and turned to look at her.

"I could ask the same of you," he said quietly before he opened the door and was gone.

Psyche stood looking after him for several minutes with a stunned expression, trying to recall every conversation they'd ever had. She numbly sat on the edge of the bunk when she began to realize he never had…at least, not that she could tell, not to a serious question. Other than her not believing he loved her or that he wanted to marry her because of it, there was nothing else. He had been mean. He had been hypocritical. He had taken liberties with her privacy. He had simply not replied if she asked a question he didn't want to answer. She couldn't truly say she had ever caught him in a lie. That she didn't believe him on that one thing was what bothered him.

Psyche eventually stood up to finish making the bed. She started to leave the room when her eyes settled on his desk. She looked from the desk to the door uncertainly, and then she went to the desk. She opened the lid and looked for the spectacles case. She opened it and pulled out the glasses and lifted them to look through. She was astonished. Psyche thought his vision might be *worse* than Arachne's. No wonder he couldn't see where he was going without them. No wonder he hadn't been able to tell the difference between her and Pandora. Now that Psyche knew he couldn't see, her sister's trick had been most unfair. Pandora would agree and would never have done it had she known. Psyche put the glasses back in their case and put it back exactly where she had found it.

She looked at the box and tilted her head sideways. She put her hand on the lid then pulled it back. She already felt guilty about invading his privacy by looking at his spectacles, knowing Sheerness didn't want her to know he wore them. She started to lift the lid on the box; it was unlocked, but she only opened it a fraction before she closed it without looking at what was inside and closed the top of the desk. She didn't need to know. She might *want* to know, but she didn't *need* to.

Psyche spent most of the morning after breakfast looking at maps of Egypt. She was determined to find the place on her map. Once she started looking at it in the right direction, she was quickly able to rule out several locations, most of them places that had already been found. She grew excited that it might be a place that was undiscovered…and undisturbed. By the time Freddie brought her dinner, she had ruled out most of the Nile north of Giza.

She could hear Sheerness and Nikos having dinner in the officers' mess. She thought about joining them but decided against it. She hadn't talked to Sheerness since he had left that morning. She wasn't intentionally avoiding him…not really. At least, that's what she tried to tell herself. In actuality, she *was* avoiding him because she felt guilty. She hadn't believed him, and she had looked through his things without his permission. She wasn't sure she could look him in the eye yet...not without coming down with hives.

They reached Delos well into the afternoon. They would have a few hours to explore before sunset, but just by looking at the island from the deck, Psyche didn't think that would be long enough. There were ruins everywhere, and there was far more beneath the sand. She looked forward to exploring, and she didn't care if she got to take any of it with her or not.

On the side they approached, the western side, there were two small islands and two spits of land jutting out toward them that seemed to be harbors. They glided into the larger of the two and set anchor. It was deep enough they were able to put down the gangway onto the land and walk off the ship. Psyche had her art supplies and looked around herself as she adjusted her spectacles, wondering where they should begin. Sheerness (wearing Arachne's glasses that Psyche decided he should be allowed to keep) and Nikos stood beside her.

"This is incredible," said Psyche softly. "Who knows what is buried under the sand. No wonder Myron wanted me to see it."

The three of them walked further inland, stopping occasionally to look at things. They found evidence of dozens of buildings, temples, squares, and cisterns. Psyche was constantly making sketches, occasionally making notes on the page for things she found particularly fascinating. They found parts of columns exquisitely carved with bulls and garlands of flowers in one area, and Psyche couldn't recall ever seeing anything quite like it. To her, they seemed almost Egyptian. Not far beyond it, they came to a trail that led them to yet another sanctuary. All three stopped and looked in astonishment.

"Oh, my," gasped Psyche amazedly, her eyes rounding.

"Suddenly, I'm feeling very inadequate," said Sheerness softly after he cleared his throat uncertainly, and he reached over almost instinctively to put his hand over Psyche's eyes.

Psyche pushed his hand away and glared at him. Nikos looked from one to the other and roared with laughter. They were looking at a sanctuary for Dionysos. There were two square stone pillars with carvings around the sides. On the front of each was what might be a bird...only it was topped by a phallus instead of a head. The pillars were meant to be topped by identical statues. One had been knocked to the ground and lay broken and mostly covered by sand. The other, however, remained in place, and it was—by far—one of the most bizarre things Psyche had ever seen. It was a huge, erect, phallus, with testicles and what might be stylized pubic hair forming the base to keep it balanced on top of the pillar as it jutted into the air at an angle. Psyche flipped to a page in her book and began to sketch. Sheerness looked at her in disbelief.

"You're not making a drawing of it!" he said in astonishment.

"Why not? I think it's fascinating. I've never seen anything like it. It's enormous!" Psyche blinked when Sheerness blushed. "Well, I've seen several examples of the small winged phalluses used as votives. I even have one at home in the solarium, but this...this is extraordinary!"

"Psyche!" groaned Sheerness, closing his eyes and shaking his head.

"It is!" she persisted as she made her sketch. She turned to look at Nikos on the other side of her. The whole time the two of them had been *discussing* the statue, he had been shaking with silent laughter. "What do you think?"

"I think in two hundred years, people will come from all over the world to see it."

Psyche's lips twitched at the shocked look on Sheerness's face. She made her sketch, and they continued on. They found an agora not far beyond the sanctuary, which they cut across at a diagonal, and not far beyond that, they found what might have been a lake. It was surrounded by a stone wall, but it was dry. Adjacent to that to the west was a row of lion statues. Psyche made another sketch. The wind and elements had eroded them, and yet they were still beautiful and majestic. Some were missing limbs, and the faces were almost completely gone from others, but Psyche thought they were spectacular, still standing watch after thousands of years. They reminded her of sphinxes, and she pondered again the almost Egyptian element to the island.

They circled around the northern edge of the dry lake and spotted a cave on the hill not far beyond the complex to the south. The sun was setting, but the large hole in the side of the mountain wasn't far away, and they went to look before going back to the ship. When they reached it, they turned to look at the ruins below them, and the view quite took Psyche's breath away. There was so much there. She could see from the ripples across the landscape that there was so much more still buried. She would be happy to just dig and explore, to find out what was there, to expose all of that history.

The cave was in the side of the hill. After looking at it, seeing the way it was built up, Psyche knew it was a sacred cave, like the one Sheerness had found at Olympus. Inside was dark, but there was enough light to see it was carved and decorated. Any offerings that might have been left had long since vanished; the cave was too easy to access for anything valuable to have remained once the people who thought of it as a sacred place had gone.

A long time ago, Delos had been thought of as the birthplace of Apollo and Athena, one of the most holy places for ancient Greeks, with an oracle considered secondary only to Pythia at Delphi. Then the Romans came, and then the Christians, and then the Turks, and anything that remained of the country's history was left to be buried beneath the sand and forgotten, either because of its pagan idolatry or because remembering it would instill pride and resistance to domination.

Psyche was saddened as she looked down the hill. It was so unfair, and she could see from Nikos's face that she was not alone. Psyche reached over to take one of his hands to give it a gentle squeeze and smiled sympathetically. His expression lightened when he realized she had seen how morose he had become, and he squeezed her hand back before giving her a grin.

Sheerness hadn't missed the silent communication between Psyche and Nikos as they stood there, and he felt a gnawing in the pit of his stomach as they began to make their way back down the hill through the ruins to the ship, even though Psyche took his arm and smiled at him affectionately as they walked. There was an intimacy between Psyche and Nikos that Sheerness wasn't sure he liked. She had great respect for Nikos and felt a certain bond with him because of Chrissoula, and they shared the same views about antiquities and how they should be treated. It left Sheerness feeling shunted to the side in her attention once again.

When they were to the ship, Sheerness looked at Psyche enquiringly.

"So, do you want to look at Delos more, or would you like to go on?"

Psyche looked from him to the island. There was so much to see, so much to be found, but it would all be for naught. She knew he was impatient to see Nikos's ruins, the ones Sheerness could take things home from that he found *useful.* He had been generous in letting her see all of the ruins they had visited, even though he had found them disappointing, especially since he hadn't been able to keep anything. She sighed wistfully as she looked. Maybe one day she would be able to come back and look again, perhaps after some other explorers had uncovered even more of what was there. She looked at Sheerness.

"We can continue on," she said finally.

"Are you sure? It wouldn't hurt for us to stay another day or two if you'd like to look more."

"No, it's your turn now," said Psyche with a smile. She turned to look at Nikos. "We do need directions, though."

Nikos grinned. "You can see where we're going from here." He pointed to the small island slightly past the second spit of land that jutted out to form another harbor. "There's a small cove there. That is where we need to go. We can wait until morning or go now, but since it isn't that far…," he trailed off.

"It doesn't seem necessary to go now," said Sheerness, "not to raise the anchor and drop the sails to go that far when supper is almost ready. First thing in the morning."

"Absolutely," said Psyche with a grin.

Chapter Thirty Seven

Psyche woke to bright light shining through the windows. She felt hot as the sun poured in. She squinted her eyes open slowly to let them adjust to the light, and she looked around herself in surprise. Sheerness wasn't there, and it was late. If he had tried to wake her, she couldn't remember, and she felt groggy from the amount of sleep she had gotten. She never slept that long unless she was ill, and it was disorienting for everything to be so bright when she first woke up.

She climbed off the bed and went to the water closet, and then she made the bed as neatly as she could before taking Cupid to her room. When she picked up her watch to put it on after she dressed, she was startled to see it was after nine. She never slept that long. She had just finished braiding her hair and brushing her teeth when Freddie came in with her breakfast. He happily took Cupid to the deck while she ate, and Psyche opened the window to let out Waddlesworth, noting they had moved to the island. She could no longer see Delos, looking at the steep cliffs lining the cove. Well, she assumed it was the cove, and they weren't moving.

Psyche started to turn back from the window, a piece of bacon in her mouth, when she looked down at the water. It wasn't very deep where they were, and like most places in the Aegean, it was a clear, crystalline blue. She could easily see the bottom, and what she saw made her choke on her food.

"Oh, my giddy aunt," she wheezed.

She didn't know if it was high tide or low, but twenty feet beneath the surface was a temple, remarkably intact. There were toppled columns and the roof had collapsed, but it was a tholos surrounded by a garden of nymphs. Even though parts were tipped over and some of the statues were broken, it was all there. Psyche hurriedly finished eating and raced from her room.

When she reached the deck, she squeaked in surprise and immediately turned to go back to her cabin, her cheeks turning pink in mortification. There were naked men everywhere. She didn't think any of them had seen her, but she had certainly gotten an eyeful. The only one, thankfully (or not), who stood out in her mind was Stockbridge. Good looking *and* that? He was going to make some woman a very happy wife, whether he was bossy or not. Psyche could only assume Sheerness had told the men they could go for a swim while the ship was stopped.

Psyche went back to her cabin and looked out the window. She gazed at the ruins below wistfully. She watched two men swim around the ruins, and she could see it was Sheerness and Nikos. She was envious. *She* wanted to be down there, and she hoped they didn't move anything before she had the chance to make drawings. Thinking of that, she grabbed her sketchbook and climbed onto the channel.

She sketched quickly, drawing as much detail as she could. After a moment, she groaned and went back into her cabin to retrieve her spectacles and came back out just as Sheerness had surfaced for air and gone back down. The green tint shaded her eyes, and the corrective lenses helped. There was more than what she was seeing from above, particularly beneath the tumbled roof, but until someone rigged her ladder, she would have to stay where she was. Once she had an overall drawing completed, she started to make sketches of individual details that stood out on the metopes, then on to the statues that lay or stood around it.

She had just finished one drawing and was starting another when Sheerness came to the surface below her. He had been going to the stern or around to the starboard side of the ship the last few times he came up. Psyche thought his limit seemed to be about three minutes. That wasn't very long. He looked up at her and grinned, treading water.

"You're awake," he said mildly.

"Yes, for some time," said Psyche testily, putting her pencil behind her ear.

"Can you see it?"

"Of course I can," she said flatly. "I'm certainly not making sketches of the cliffs. Could you get someone to hang my ladder?"

"Is something bothering you?"

"I slept late, and there are naked men running around on the deck. What could possibly be bothering me?"

"How do you know there are naked men on the deck?"

Psyche's cheeks turned pink. "I saw them," she mumbled. "There are some people you just should *not* see in the altogether. A warning would have been helpful."

"I tried to wake you, but after the third time, I decided it would require far more drastic measures than you would have liked." He grinned. "Does the crew know you saw them?"

"I don't think so, but can you get someone to get my ladder, please? I don't want you moving one stone until I've taken a look."

"Yes, ma'am," chuckled Sheerness. "I shouldn't let you sleep so long anymore. You become awfully grumpy when you get enough rest."

"It's just I'm up *here* when I want to be down *there*," said Psyche, pointing at the ruins.

"The water's cold," warned Sheerness amusedly.

"I don't care."

Sheerness chuckled. "All right. I'll get someone to hang your ladder."

"Thank you," said Psyche with a slight smile as she watched him swim under the ship to go to the other side.

She climbed back into her cabin, bringing her sketchbook. She looked through her drawers for the chemise she had sewn into a swimming costume. It was unfair the men were allowed to swim naked but she wasn't. Sheerness and Nikos had on trews, so he realized she would wake up eventually.

Psyche waited until the sailors attached her ladder and climbed up the shrouds before she put on her chemise. It was harder to put on than she remembered. Either it shrank or she had eaten too much baklava at Nikos and Ioanna's. She did get it on, and she retrieved one of her towels from the coffer and climbed back out her window.

She looked at the water hesitantly for a moment. Sheerness had said it was cold, and she wasn't sure he had been teasing. It *was* the first of October, but they were in the Aegean. The water in the cove at Nikos and Ioanna's had become too cold before they left, but that was several hundred miles further north. She finally shrugged because she couldn't spend all day pondering whether to jump or not. She took a preparatory breath and dove in.

The water was so cold it shocked her. She had tried to prepare herself, but not well enough. It was colder than the water in the cove, and that had been too cold for her. But she wasn't going to let it stop her from taking at least *one* look at the ruins. She went to the surface to adjust herself to the cold, making sure her fingers and toes weren't going numb, and then she took a breath and headed for the bottom.

As she neared the ruins, they were even more spectacular than they had been from the surface, and they were unlike anything she had seen before. All of the stone was marble, but it wasn't all white. There were shades of green, pink, and black. Some of the metopes and triglyphs still had faint traces of paint, but they were, for the most part, bare white marble. She examined some of the statues, and then she looked beneath the pieces of the roof into the cella, which was still mostly upright, protecting what was inside. The grillwork and doors were still there, if a bit bent out of shape, and those definitely required closer examination.

She saw a large mosaic, in excellent condition with only a few tesserae missing, nearly eight feet in diameter. The part that amazed her was that it seemed to be on a solid piece of stone rather than several, which explained why it had remained intact through whatever calamity had caused the tholos to sink into the sea. Beyond the mosaic was the cult statue, and Psyche's eyes widened. When she saw it, she knew it was a temple of Poseidon. In one hand of the statue, gripped in front of him as he sat on a rock looking regal and dour, was a gold trident.

Psyche felt a movement behind her and turned to see Sheerness. She pointed toward the surface, and he nodded as they rose to the top.

"Ohmygosh! That's incredible!" was the first thing out of Psyche's mouth as soon as her head was above the water.

"It certainly is," agreed Sheerness with a grin.

"I've never seen anything like it. That marble is just…it's just…well, it's just gorgeous." She gasped in astonishment. "And those statues! The mosaic!"

Sheerness chuckled at her enthusiasm. "I couldn't agree more."

Nikos surfaced not far away and swam toward them. He could see from Psyche's awed expression that she had been down to look inside the temple.

"You like it?" he asked with a grin.

"Oh, Nikos, it's wonderful!" sighed Psyche. "Do you think it was part of Delos?"

"Possibly…more than likely, considering the proximity. To have a temple for Poseidon all to itself would make sense—in a way—considering Delos was dedicated, for the most part, to Apollo, and everyone knows the two did not like each other…mythologically speaking." He grinned. "I suppose it's appropriate it sank into the sea."

Psyche looked at Sheerness. "So, which parts do you think will be *useful?*" she asked with a half-smile.

Sheerness exchanged a glance with Nikos. "All of it."

Psyche's eyes widened in surprise. "What?" she asked in disbelief, looking from one to the other of them. "You want to raise the entire thing? Why?"

"Because I want to take the mosaic, but to get that, I'll have to move nearly everything else, so I thought, why not take it with and reconstruct it?"

Psyche looked at Nikos. He seemed to be in agreement. She had become fairly good at assessing what he was thinking even if he outwardly appeared to be his typical easygoing self. She was not detecting any tension. She was unsurprised Sheerness wanted to take the mosaic, and she was sure he would take all the statues, including the one of Poseidon. It would be an interesting project to rebuild the tholos, but it was *a lot* of marble.

"I don't think the *Medea* can carry it all," she said hesitantly.

"Nonsense, there's plenty of room," said Sheerness dismissively.

"Just because there's *room* for it doesn't mean the ship can carry it. You know that," said Psyche calmly. "It's marble…all of it. Do you have any idea how much it's going to weigh?"

"No, but I don't think it will be a problem," said Sheerness stiffly.

"If you take it all apart, how are you going put it back together? Have you devised some plan for numbering the stones, diagramming the pieces so you at least have how they look *now* to start from?"

"No." Psyche watched as a nerve began to tick in his jaw in irritation.

"If you have to take the entire thing, then let me do some surveying first for us to determine how much this is going to weigh and the best way to get it on the ship so it can be put back together. I know the *Medea* can carry a lot, but those statues are going to weigh at least eight hundred pounds apiece. And that mosaic you're so determined to take with you is going to be at least two tons." Sheerness looked at her disbelievingly.

"I don't want to be a killjoy, I really don't, but marble lasts as long as it does because it's *dense*, and that means *heavy*. The temple will stay on the bottom of the sea if you overload your ship and sink it." She tweaked the end of his nose and gave him a cajoling smile. "Let me look at things…at least for the morning," she pleaded.

His expression softened when he saw that she really was only trying to be helpful. "All right," he finally agreed. "You are better at that sort of thing."

Psyche blinked in surprise. She might have to mark down this precise date and time somewhere. He had just admitted she could *do* something…*better* than him. That made her feel warm and fuzzy inside, and her cheeks turned pink. For a moment or two, she didn't even notice the water was cold, and she smiled happily.

"I'll be as quick as I can, I promise," she said determinedly. She started to swim toward her ladder. "The nice thing is that I'll be able to do most of it out of the water."

"I told you it was cold," chuckled Sheerness.

Psyche spent the rest of the morning with her notebook and sketchbook on the channel outside her window. She had Sheerness and Nikos swim down to take measurements when she needed them. The water was too cold to suit her, and the thought of getting back in didn't appeal to her in the slightest.

She didn't want to count each individual piece of stone, so she estimated. The numbers weren't promising. Fitting the tholos into the hold wouldn't be the problem. She was afraid it was simply going to be too heavy. Once she had the estimates of weight, she made a list of the items in order of importance, so if it *was* going to be too heavy, the pieces of lesser importance, like the roof tiles and supports, the ashlar stones comprising the walls of the cella, and even the stone of the stylobate, could be left behind if necessary.

As it neared dinnertime, Sheerness climbed the ladder to sit beside her on the platform. Psyche had changed into her green sari after her brief swim, and she felt comfortable in the slight breeze that blew occasionally. She looked up at him from jotting down notes with an affectionate smile. She could see chill bumps beginning to rise on the skin of his arms, and she reached over to grab her towel she had hung in the shrouds to dry and handed it to him.

"Oh, this is nice," said Sheerness appreciatively as he wrapped it around himself and rubbed it with his hands, enjoying the softness and the warmth of it from the sun.

"Egyptian cotton. It has a nice long fiber," said Psyche mildly

"So, how goes it?" he asked curiously, leaning over slightly to look at what she had written. Psyche seriously doubted he could see it.

She looked at him levelly. "I don't think you're going to like it."

Sheerness frowned. "That bad?"

"You know better how much the *Medea* can carry, but the calculations are very high." She looked at her watch. "It's time for dinner, so why don't we go in, and I can tell you what I've found." Nikos came to the surface just then, and Psyche looked down at him with a grin. "It's time for dinner, *adelphos*."

"Good. I'm starving," he said happily, and he went back under the water to swim beneath the ship to the other side.

She put her pencil behind her ear and stood up after closing her notebook. They went through the window to her cabin, and Sheerness pulled her close to kiss her warmly once they both stood on the floor and she had put her books on her desk. Psyche wrapped one of her arms around his neck, and she could feel the cold water dripping down from his hair onto it. He ended the kiss and rubbed his nose against hers affectionately, and Psyche giggled. He lifted his head to look at her.

"What?"

"Your nose is cold and wet like a puppy dog," she chortled. He grinned and bent his head to nuzzle her neck, and Psyche cringed and laughed, trying to push him away. "That's cold!"

"Are you going to need me to go back in the water again?"

"That depends," said Psyche as she ran her fingers down his cheek.

"On what?"

"On what happens after you hear what I have to say," she said mildly as she ran her fingers down his neck to his chest. "You might want to have Bothi and Stockbridge join us, since they'll be doing some of the work."

"Mm-hmm," said Sheerness in distracted agreement. Her hand had moved beneath the towel to his side, and he was only marginally paying attention to what she was saying. "How much longer do we have to wait?" he sighed.

Psyche looked up at him. "Tomorrow night, I think," she said quietly.

"Is that four days?" he asked with a slight frown as he tried to remember. He couldn't think straight when she was touching him.

"Not technically," said Psyche, "but yesterday around eleven in the morning was *the* time, so tomorrow night should be long enough."

Sheerness raised an eyebrow. "What do you mean *the* time?"

"Well, I get a cramp in my side just before I…*hatch* an egg, one might say, and then it goes away as soon as I do. That happened around eleven or so yesterday morning."

Sheerness's eyes widened in disbelief. "Do you mean to say you can tell the exact *moment*?"

"Provided I'm awake," said Psyche with a slight nod. Her face grew thoughtful. "Actually, tomorrow *morning* might be long enough," she said almost to herself.

Sheerness looked at her in amazement. He didn't think all women kept track of their cycle as closely as that, and he didn't think they could. He ran a hand down her cheek before giving her a soft kiss on her forehead.

"Let's go eat," he said quietly.

"That can't be right," said Sheerness, shaking his head.

"That's my conservative estimate," said Psyche evenly. "I honestly think it may weigh more."

"But it's not that big," said Sheerness disbelievingly.

"But it's all stone, and it's an entire building. You should be surprised it doesn't weigh more than five hundred fifty tons."

Psyche, Sheerness, Bothi, Stockbridge, and Nikos sat at the table in the officer's mess after dinner, discussing what Psyche had determined. She had checked her figures several times, and Pandora was much better at math than she was, but Psyche didn't think she was wrong. This wasn't a complicated calculus equation, just simple multiplication and division. She could give him a more exact figure if he insisted, but that would involve counting and weighing everything, and she felt fairly confident it wouldn't be off by much.

"Can the *Medea* carry it?" she finally asked.

Sheerness sighed gustily and scratched his forehead thoughtfully. "She can, but we'll want to offload all the ballast. With a load like that, provided your calculations are accurate, we won't need it." He continued to frown as he thought about it.

"My second question is: can your windlass or capstan and whatnot lift it? The mosaic, as I said, is going to weigh at least two tons by itself. It is, by far, the heaviest thing down there, but some of the other stones will weigh a ton apiece, and there are *a lot*. Are you sure you don't want to leave some of it?"

"No, no, we may as well take it all. The ship can carry it," said Sheerness distractedly. He looked at Bothi and Stockbridge. "Can we lift two tons?"

Higginbotham ran a hand across his chin. "It'll be tricky." Stockbridge nodded in agreement. Higginbotham looked at Psyche. "How big is this mosaic?"

"It has an eight foot diameter, and it's six inches thick, I think,"

"Oh, that is going to be tricky," said Higginbotham gravely. "Blocks of stone are simple enough. Hoisting something that big around on its narrow edge...." He sucked in air through his teeth and shook his head. "It's not impossible...just devilishly difficult."

"We should onload as much of the rest as we can before the mosaic," suggested Stockbridge. "The weight of the rest will add counterbalance. If we try to lift something that heavy without enough weight to balance it, it's liable to tip the ship over."

Everyone nodded agreement, and Psyche sighed resignedly. She thought the entire venture was going to be a mistake. She felt something was going to go horribly wrong...somehow. She stood up from the table, and all the men rose when she did. Sheerness raised an enquiring eyebrow as he looked at her.

"I need to find Laing and borrow a grease pencil. I've got some numbering to do," she responded to his unspoken question.

Psyche climbed onto the bunk and settled under the covers tiredly. She had spent the rest of the afternoon, for the most part, underwater. She had a numbering system for the stones, grouping them by the architectural structure they made, which corresponded to a plan in her notebook. Once they were back to England and it came time to reconstruct the tholos, it would be like putting together the pieces of a three-dimensional puzzle, with the numbers directing how they should go. As much as she loved swimming, Psyche was done. She had taken a shower to thaw out, and she felt waterlogged. The rest of the work raising the temple could be done by Sheerness, Nikos, and the crew. She shouldn't have to go back in…she hoped. She intended to stay on the ship where it was dry and help Bothi and Stockbridge in the hold.

All afternoon as she worked, she had been unable to escape the gnawing sensation something was going to go wrong. She couldn't place her finger on what it was that bothered her, whether it was the concern they were going to overload the ship or something else. She just *knew* raising the temple was a bad idea. She didn't know why she knew, but there it was. The feeling she had was almost disorienting because she felt like what was happening had *already* happened. She didn't like that feeling. It happened to Arachne and Eurydice all the time, but Psyche had managed to muffle it…except this time.

She was almost asleep when Sheerness came in. She groggily turned onto her back and lifted herself up to look over the panel at him. He came to the bunk and sat on the edge of it, running a finger down her cheek to her neck.

"You look exhausted," he said quietly.

"I am," agreed Psyche with a yawn.

"I could have helped this afternoon."

"I know, but it was easier for me to do it myself rather than try to explain it." Sheerness tightened his jaw. "That didn't sound right. I just meant I already knew how I wanted them numbered. It might have gotten out of order with two of us, even if it might have gone faster." She grinned. "You can put it back together." She tugged at the front of his waistcoat to pull him toward her for a kiss. "Besides, you'll be in the water plenty soon enough."

"I can't wait," said Sheerness dryly. He stood after giving her another kiss.

"Are you coming to bed?" she asked casually.

"Eventually," sighed Sheerness. "I've got paperwork, and I want a shower. You should go to sleep."

Psyche settled back onto the mattress beneath the covers and smiled sleepily. "I can do that. Wake me in the morning," she mumbled after a jaw-cracking yawn.

Psyche woke up to the pleasant sensation of Sheerness placing kisses down her neck as one of his hands slowly moved up her thigh and the other massaged one of her breasts through the opening in her shift. She smiled softly with her eyes still closed and wiggled her bottom against his arousal. He moved his lips up her neck to tease the lobe of her ear before whispering in it.

"Good morning, sleepyhead."

Psyche turned onto her back to look up at him. She was sound asleep when he came to bed, not even remembering what time it was when he did.

She smoothed her hand along his chin to his jaw before moving it to the side of his neck to pull his mouth toward hers for a kiss. She sighed at the back of her throat as he untied the strings to her shift and moved his hand to cup her breast before teasing the nipple with his thumb. He lifted his head to look at her.

"Can we?" he asked hopefully.

"Oh, yes, we can," purred Psyche with a grin. "For the next two weeks, you may shag me to your heart's content."

Sheerness bent his head to nuzzle the valley between her breasts, and Psyche could feel his smile. "If I did, I would never get anything else done."

"Oh, really?" chortled Psyche. "You'd grow tired of it."

Sheerness pulled off her shift and laid it over the panel on the side of the bed. He settled on top of her between her thighs and kissed her thoroughly. He lifted his head to look at her with a boyish grin.

"You're very *fun* to shag. I couldn't imagine ever growing tired of it."

Psyche smiled and smoothed her hand down his cheek. "You're impossible."

"But I think you like it," drawled Sheerness as he lowered his head to begin kissing down her neck toward her breasts.

"Absolutely," she sighed.

Over the next few days, they worked on bringing the more uniform pieces of stone to the surface. The tiles of the roof were set aside to be placed on top because of their fragility, but the ashlar for the walls of the cella, followed by the stones of the stylobate, were steadily hauled over the side and lowered into the hold. The entire process reminded Psyche of a game of jackstraws. The columns and capitals were moved to the side, and work steadily progressed. By Tuesday, the mosaic could be easily seen, and she made a sketch as soon as it was. She was concerned a piece of stone might fall and shatter it.

Everything was going remarkably well. The unease Psyche had felt at the beginning of the project lessened as the days wore on without incident. The ship was becoming weighted down, but Higginbotham knew his job well, as did Stockbridge, and her worries they would overload the ship waned. She spent the majority of her time sitting on the stairs into the hold, watching as the stones were lowered in. If she wasn't there, she was on the deck looking over the side, making sure that Nikos and Sheerness were all right.

On Sunday before Sheerness and Nikos started to work, Psyche made Nikos promise he would look after Sheerness. Sheerness was capable and sensible, but he just wasn't able to hold his breath long enough to suit Psyche. He had to come to the surface for air twice for each time Nikos did. With practice he would get better, but certainly not in a day or two. It had taken her years to be able to hold her breath as long as she did. She would have felt better if they had a diving bell, but retrieving antiquities from the bottom of the sea had not been something Sheerness had anticipated.

Psyche did go down at least once a day for a brief visit, usually in the afternoon when they were almost through for the day and giving the water the maximum amount of sunlight exposure to warm up to a tolerable level. She would look for any small items that might have been uncovered. So far, she hadn't found anything.

By the end of work on Friday, Sheerness thought they might have removed enough to raise the mosaic, if not first thing on Saturday, then by the end of the day. The columns, their capitals and bases, the decorative stonework of the metopes and guttering, and the roof tiles and supports had all been moved to the side. There were still several stones left of the stylobate, some of which were under the edge of the mosaic and couldn't be moved until it was, but Psyche agreed the mosaic could be raised now without unbalancing the ship.

Sheerness was always exhausted by the end of the day, but he found the energy to make love before falling asleep and usually in the morning as well. While Psyche enjoyed it, she thought it might be better for him to conserve his energy. They had lowered one of the launches for Sheerness and Nikos to rest rather than going to the deck or treading water. Several of the crew also took turns going below to help move the stone and load it. The only time Sheerness was aboard during the day was when he and Nikos came up for dinner. He seemed driven to load the temple as quickly as possible. The weather was becoming cooler—the water certainly was, but Psyche thought they had time. She didn't understand the need to rush.

So far, the weather had been pleasant and sunny. That was unusual, but Psyche was glad it was cooperating, since Sheerness seemed to be in such a hurry. It wouldn't stay that way for long. They were in the rainy season, and while the temperature might not become frigid, it was soon going to become cool enough that getting into the water wouldn't be wise. It had already become too cold for her, and while the weather was pleasant, she was glad to have her ganseys.

Work continued on Saturday the same as it had all week. They would remove a few more of the other pieces of stone before lifting the mosaic, simply because they weren't able to get the rope around it to lift it without doing so. The sun was shining particularly bright, and Psyche thought she might have been more comfortable wearing a sari or an abaya rather than the breeches, shirt, and waistcoat she had on as she stood on the deck watching. She wasn't sweating, but the sun was beating down on her head.

Sheerness and Nikos had come up for dinner and gone back down again. Sheerness decided the mosaic would be the last thing they would raise for the day. Psyche was looking forward to having it in a dry spot to examine it. The tesserae still seemed to be well-attached, and she hoped that having it out of the water wouldn't cause damage to the mortar holding them on. She had her sketches, and all the pieces were there, so if they were to come loose, she should be able to reattach them if necessary. It was a beautiful picture with keys and swirls resembling waves around the edges in an alternating pattern toward the center, where dolphins and hippocamps frolicked. The workmanship was exquisite, and Psyche had no problem understanding why Sheerness wanted to take it. *She* wanted to take it.

The statue of Poseidon had been moved to the side and placed with the statues of the nereids, and his trident had been pried from his hand and stored in Sheerness's cabin. It was beautiful metalwork, with delicate filigreed scrollwork all over the surface. The tines had removable sheaths that revealed sharpened points beneath. It was an actual, usable trident and something Psyche thought was unique. She was surprised it hadn't disappeared long ago. The temple was hard to miss beneath the surface, and the gold would have made it worth the danger involved to remove it.

Psyche went to the hold as they prepared to lift the mosaic. She had already discovered from Higginbotham that he intended to put it directly midships, but she wanted to be there when it arrived. Higginbotham had directed the crew to place the stone in even layers, starting in the middle and working toward the edges, almost like a pyramid. As the layers had built up, he had the stone move inward from the bow and stern, almost like stairs, so a person could walk over them from one end of the hold to the other.

Psyche heard creaking, and the ship pitch slightly to portside as they started to lift the mosaic. Her heart pounded excitedly in anticipation as she waited. The noise and tilting had made her nervous the first few times it happened while they were lifting the stone, but the *Medea* always righted herself. Psyche was accustomed to it, and now she barely noticed. The pitching had lessened as the ship became heavier to counteract it, but this time it was tilting almost as far as it had the first day.

She was standing beside Higginbotham, and as the ship began to lean, she looked at him and grinned happily.

"You've been waiting for this, haven't you?" he asked with mild amusement.

"Oh, yes," drawled Psyche. "Not as much as the captain, but I am—"

There was a loud boom above their heads. The ship shuddered and yawed, throwing Psyche into Higginbotham and both of them to the sleepers on the deck of the hold. After a moment of confusion, they looked at each other in alarm and quickly stood to run to the stairs toward the main deck. Psyche tried to fight the panic she felt, but she knew something had gone horribly wrong.

There was a lot of confusion when they reached the deck, but it wasn't chaos. The crew was working feverishly to gather the lines they had been using to raise the mosaic. The boom for putting cargo into the hold was a splintered mess. Felton was tending to one of the sailors, Bolen, whose upper arm was bleeding badly from the broken end of the boom putting a gash into it. Psyche ran to the side of the ship where Bandy and Watkins were climbing up. Nikos surfaced shortly after, gasping for air, and she watched as he swam toward the ladder using only one arm, the other cradled against his chest.

"Where's Sheerness?" she called anxiously.

"He's caught beneath the mosaic," he gasped as he reached the ladder, and nearby crewmen began to help him up. As he neared her, Psyche could see that the arm he held close was bent at an odd angle. "His foot. I couldn't...I couldn't get him loose," he panted.

"Bloody hell!" gasped Psyche, and the skin on her face began to tingle as the blood drained out of it. "Felton! Help Nikos!" she yelled as she started to remove her shoes and clothes. "Get that damn thing lifted!" she shouted as she was down to her chemise and dove over the side into the water.

Psyche swam to the bottom as quickly as she could. Sheerness was struggling desperately to get his foot free. When the boom broke, the mosaic had plummeted back to the bottom and settled almost into the same position it had been in originally, but it had pinned Sheerness's foot beneath it. The stone of the stylobate had the mosaic lifted from the seabed. His foot was stuck in a space between the larger and smaller stones, not crushing it, but there was no way to get his foot through the crevice. The mosaic or the stone had to move.

Psyche's heart pounded anxiously when she saw his terrified expression. He was running out of air, a process happening all the more quickly because of his continued efforts to get loose. As soon as she was near, she grabbed him by the shoulder and pointed at her face. Her cheeks were puffed out with as much air as she could fill them with, and she hoped it might buy him some time to let the crew raise the mosaic. They wouldn't have to lift it far, only two or three inches would be enough. She put her mouth to his, and she felt him take the air. It wasn't going to be enough, not if the crew didn't hurry.

She put a soothing hand to his cheek, and then she spied a metal prybar lying nearby. She swam to it and picked it up, carrying it back to where his foot was pinned. She put the pointed tip between the two lower pieces to move them apart, but she wasn't strong enough. If she could break the stone, she could work the pieces loose. She began to pound it against one of the stones. Small chips were coming loose, but not big enough or fast enough.

Sheerness made a noise, and Psyche turned her head to watch in helpless horror as he started to drown. She felt as if her heart were going to explode as she felt a surge of panic, and she desperately renewed her efforts to break the stone. Sheerness began to struggle less and less until he went completely limp in the water, his eyes half-closed, one small bubble of air escaping from his mouth. Psyche fought the urge to scream as she continued to pound on the stone. She could feel her own supply of air running out, but she couldn't leave him, not now.

Just as she managed to fracture off a larger piece of the stone, the crew started to lift the mosaic, and Sheerness floated loose. She dropped the prybar to grab him by the arm and swim toward the top as quickly as she could. As she came nearer, trying to surface close to the ship, she adjusted her grip on him, slipping her arm beneath one of his to turn his back toward her and for his head to lean onto her shoulder while she tilted his chin to raise his face above the water when they surfaced.

"*Help me!*" she screamed as soon as she filled her lungs with air, towing Sheerness toward the ladder. His head lolled lifelessly against hers, and she could feel the hot saltwater of her tears mingling with the coldness of the sea.

Several pairs of hands reach down to lift them out of the water, and it felt like an eternity before they were on the ship. Psyche looked around desperately as they laid Sheerness on the deck on his back. She needed a sack of grain, a log…something…a person.

"Stockbridge, lie down!" she ordered quickly. "Crosswise, there!" she said as she pointed toward Sheerness's head. Stockbridge looked at her in surprise, but he did as he was told. "You two, help me get him turned over on his stomach across the bosun. Quickly now!"

Two sailors standing nearby did as they were told, laying Sheerness across Stockbridge's chest while Psyche raised one of his arms to rest it beneath his forehead. Once he was in place, Psyche moved to his back and pressed at his ribs with all her weight, pushing the water out of his lungs and stomach. It seeped out of his mouth onto the deck in a steady stream that slackened as she raised up, only to increase again as she repeated the action. Felton knelt beside him to take the wrist of his other arm and check for a pulse. There wasn't one, and he looked up at Psyche with a grave expression. The captain was dead.

Psyche repeated the squeezing action three or four times until she didn't see any more water coming out of his mouth, and then she grabbed Sheerness by the arm to flip him over onto his back and raised his arms above his head. After she made sure his tongue was out of the way, she straddled him at the hips on her knees and put her hands to either side of his chest, pressing upward and inward on his ribcage in an effort to get air into his lungs.

She fought very hard to control her urge to sob as she worked, but her face was streaked with tears, her expression one of desperate determination. There was an ominous silence as she worked, other than the occasional faint whisper as someone prayed. She couldn't understand why he wouldn't breathe. It seemed to have been forever, but it hadn't been that long.

"Come on, Sebastian, breathe for me, sweetie," she whispered as she continued to press on his ribs.

Felton felt his wrist again. There was still no pulse. He wasn't going to breathe without a heartbeat. "Lady Psyche," he said quietly, "his heart's not beating." He started to reach out a hand to her soothingly. "Perhaps you should—"

"No!" said Psyche fiercely. "He's not going to give up on me this easily. I'm not going to let him." She looked at Stockbridge. "I need to lay him flat."

Stockbridge quickly slid out from under Sheerness, and Psyche pulled his arms back down to his sides out of the way. She tilted his head back and opened his mouth, and then she pinched his nostrils closed and covered his mouth with hers to blow into it, watching his chest as the air filled his lungs. If he wasn't going to breathe, then she would do it for him. And if his heart wasn't going to beat, she would *make* it. After she breathed into him a third time, she moved her hands to his chest. She felt along the bottom edge of his ribcage until she found his sternum, and then she placed the heel of one hand just above it and clenched her other hand over it to press down with both of them on his breastbone as hard as she could in several heartbeat-like pushes.

Felton started to move toward her to pull her away, but Stockbridge put out his arm to stop him. If the captain was already dead, then what she was doing wasn't going to hurt him, and it was something she felt she needed to do. He had seen the pressing she had started with before, but this was something new. He had not missed the way Sheerness's chest had rose and fell as she breathed into him, but Stockbridge wasn't sure if trying to make his heart beat by pushing on his chest was going to accomplish anything. Instead of trying to move Psyche away, Felton went to Sheerness's other side and put his fingers to the captain's neck to check for a pulse. There was still nothing.

Psyche breathed into him again twice before moving back to his chest to compress it again. The sailors standing nearby, as well as Stockbridge and Felton, heard the faint cracking sound from his ribs as she pushed. To the doctor's amazement, he could feel a faint beat begin beneath his fingers as she did it. After she moved back to breathe into his mouth again, it didn't stop. When she started to move back to his chest, Felton held up his hand to stop her.

"Breathe again. I have a pulse; he needs air."

Psyche's expression began to grow hopeful, and she breathed into him again. Felton could still feel the faint, fluttery beat beneath his fingertips, and as she continued to steadily blow air into his lungs, it began to grow marginally stronger. After several breaths, she put her ear to his mouth to listen for any sign that he might be breathing on his own. There was still nothing. She bent her head to breathe again, and she began to cry with relief when she felt him begin to cough, and he took a rattling breath into his lungs on his own. He continued to cough, and Psyche rolled him onto his side as he vomited the air and remaining contents from his stomach.

"Let's get him below," said Felton, looking at Psyche in amazement.

Stockbridge and Watkins quickly helped the doctor lift Sheerness from the deck. Psyche stood up to follow them, and Nikos moved in front of her. He held her clothes and shoes in one hand. The other arm was bound with a splint in a sling around his neck. Psyche took her clothes from him.

"I'm sorry," he said quietly.

She brushed her hand down his cheek before squeezing his shoulder. "It wasn't your fault," she said soothingly with a slight smile before she walked past him to go below.

Chapter Thirty Eight

Psyche took her clothes to her cabin and grabbed a dressing gown. She arrived in Sheerness's cabin just as the doctor was preparing to bleed him. She shuddered as thoughts of the last time a doctor performed the procedure on him came to her mind. She moved to the side of the bed and put her hand over Sheerness's arm.

"No bloodletting," she said flatly.

"But—" began Felton.

"*No* bloodletting," she repeated firmly. "You'll have to go through me. Do you really want to?" she asked evenly. Felton looked askance at her. "His left ankle was pinned beneath the mosaic, and I'm sure I cracked a few of his ribs. But, there will be no bloodletting...*or* laudanum." She put her hands on her hips. "Anything else, I'm willing to listen."

"He needs laudanum for his lungs. All that water, the coughing, the risk of pneumonia." He lifted the blanket to look at Sheerness's ankle. It was starting to swell. While it wasn't broken, it was badly lacerated and at least sprained. "His ankle is bad, and I *know* you cracked a few of his ribs. Think of the pain."

"Have you nothing besides laudanum?" asked Psyche exasperatedly.

"What else is there?" asked Felton dryly. "It's the best thing for both."

"No, it isn't," said Psyche flatly. "I'll be right back."

She muttered under her breath as she went to her cabin to get her medicine kit. It was sad that she knew better than a practicing physician. Granted, some of the things she had were not items a typical British doctor had, but still, laudanum wasn't the panacea they persisted in believing it was. The relief it brought came at the risk of a very high price, and she knew people who had paid it. She took it to the great cabin and opened the desk to set it down.

"What is that?" asked Felton.

"*My* medicine kit," she said quietly as she turned to look at him. "I don't want to insult you, Dr. Felton. My brother had the highest regard for you, so you obviously know what you're doing, but I cannot let you give the captain opium or bleed him." Stockbridge was standing nearby, and she looked at him. "Can you get the fire lit...and the lamps, please?"

The bosun nodded and set to work. Felton looked at her doubtfully. She had saved the captain's life; she had brought him *back* to life. Not once had she ever come to him with a complaint of any kind, something completely atypical. He could only assume it was due to her little wooden box.

"Now, what does he need, and I'll see if I have something that will suit," she said tiredly.

Psyche put her ointment on his ankle and bound it tightly. As for the pain (and Psyche wasn't so sure he was feeling much of anything at the moment) and the need to dry his lungs, she got a glass of water and mixed in some drops of her pain medicine and the one Keung had made for influenza. He was reluctant to drink it once she roused him to semi-consciousness, but he finally did, grimacing before drifting off again. She took it as a sign of how far gone he was when his waking was not accompanied by the usual startled flailing.

Once he was medicated and his ankle tended, Felton said the only thing they could do was wait. He told Psyche she could re-dose Sheerness with the medicine as needed, but there was nothing to be done for his ribs except give them time to heal. The next seventy-two hours would tell the tale. If the captain continued to breathe well, and hopefully improved, he would probably be fine. As for when he would regain full consciousness, Felton couldn't say; he had never treated someone who had been brought back from the dead.

By the time they had finished tending to Sheerness, it was completely dark. He was breathing well and sleeping peacefully. Felton stayed with Sheerness while Psyche went to her cabin to change clothes. Once she returned, he left to inform Higginbotham and the other officers about the captain's condition. He told her to get him if Sheerness showed any signs of getting worse. Stockbridge would tell the crew, and Psyche asked him to have Freddie keep an eye on Waddlesworth and Cupid. She would be staying with Sheerness.

Psyche pulled the chair from his desk beside the bed. After she adjusted the blankets and added a few pillows to lift him slightly higher, she sat on the chair and took his hand in both of hers. She smoothed it down her cheek before placing a kiss on the palm and holding onto it tightly. She listened to the slow, steady sound of his breathing...no rattle, no trouble, just the sound of him sleeping, a sound that was familiar and comforting to her. His face was tranquil, and he showed no signs of being in pain or distress. His dear, sweet face that had grown so precious to her.

Her features slowly crumpled and her shoulders began to shake as she started to cry. She had almost lost him. For a moment, she had experienced what her life would be like without him, and it had been more unbearable than she could have imagined. He would have died never knowing how much she loved him. He still could. She stood up and leaned over to place a kiss on his forehead, and then she moved her lips to his ear.

"I love you," she whispered as she brushed a hand down his cheek.

She lifted her head to look for any sign he might have heard her, but there was nothing. She retook her seat and covered his hand with hers, watching him, willing him to get well.

She was still watching when Freddie came in carrying a tray with food and a pot of tea. She wasn't sure she could eat. There was a bowl of broth for Sheerness, but Psyche wasn't sure she would be able to wake him. She would try, though, because he needed to eat. After Freddie placed the tray on the open desk, he hesitantly walked toward her where she sat by the bed.

"Is he going to be all right, ma'am?" he asked quietly.

Psyche eased Sheerness's arm back under the blankets as she stood up to go pour herself a cup of tea. She gave Freddie a soothing smile and brushed the hair out of his eyes.

"I don't know," she said softly. "Ask me again tomorrow. Thank you for looking after the animals for me."

"Oh, any time, ma'am," said Freddie with a slight smile. "See you."

"Goodbye," replied Psyche to his departing back.

She brushed a hand down Sheerness's cheek before going to the water closet. When she came out, she went by the bunk before going to the desk. Meals had provided lamb stew, bread, and cheese. She broke off a piece of bread and dipped it in the stew. She ate mechanically; only knowing that she *needed* to eat made her willing to go through the effort. Even at that, she was only able to manage half of it before she couldn't eat anymore. She would try to finish later. Freddie wouldn't be coming back for the tray.

After she finished her tea and poured herself more, she lifted the bowl of broth and the cloth covering the tray and took it to the bed. She carefully sat on the edge to avoid spilling the broth and set the bowl onto the nearby chair until she saw whether or not she would be able to wake Sheerness to eat it. She put a hand to his cheek and leaned toward him.

"Sebastian," she called softly.

He didn't stir, and she tried again a little louder. His head moved slightly on the pillow. She called his name one more time and watched his eyelashes flutter on his cheeks as he tried to get them open. She grabbed another pillow to raise him to an almost sitting position to make it easier for him to eat, and then she grabbed the bowl of broth from the chair. When she turned back to face him, he was still more asleep than awake, but he was alert enough to eat. His eyes were glassy, his features confused, as she lifted the bowl to his lips.

"Drink up," urged Psyche. He did as he was told, even if he didn't know what he was doing.

When he was finished, Psyche set the bowl aside and removed the extra pillow after she used the cloth to wipe up the little bit that had dripped from the corner of his mouth. He blinked sleepily, and she brushed a hand down his cheek soothingly. He didn't have a fever, but he was still confused. Given the circumstances it was understandable, but he hadn't said a word the entire time she fed him. She leaned forward to give him a soft kiss.

"I love you," she whispered.

When she lifted her head, she saw that he had fallen back to sleep. Psyche sighed tiredly and adjusted the blankets over him. She took the empty bowl to the tray and got her cup of tea. She took her seat by the bed and resumed her watch. She wanted to be by his side in case he needed anything.

Psyche woke with a start. She had eventually put the desk chair back and moved the wingchair closer to have something more comfortable to sit on. She had finished her dinner and taken the tray to the dumbwaiter in the officers' mess, retrieving a blanket from her room on the way back. She had managed to stay awake most of the night, but she had dozed off at some point during the wee hours. She hadn't intended to go to sleep at all.

Sheerness hadn't moved. She had checked that he wasn't running a fever, and she had roused him long enough for more medicine, but he still lay under the blankets...sleeping. She stood up and leaned over to brush the hair off his forehead. The sleep was good for him, but it made her anxious that he didn't stir at all. When he was awake the night before while she fed him, he had looked at her as if he didn't recognize her. She hoped it was temporary because she couldn't imagine what she would do if it wasn't.

She added more wood to the fire then went to the water closet. She came back out and massaged a kink out of her neck as she looked at her watch. It was barely five. She heard the rumble of thunder and suspected that was what woke her. It wasn't because Sheerness had said something. She looked at him on the bed and adjusted the blankets. It was time for more medicine. She wasn't sure it was necessary, but it wouldn't hurt, and it was so much the better if it helped. The pain medicine tasted horrid, but it was better than laudanum and worked just as well for pain.

She opened the lid on her kit on the desk. She set out the two bottles and poured a glass of water from the pitcher on the commode. It was almost empty, and she put it on the desk to remind herself to refill it after she gave Sheerness the medicine. She put the drops in the glass and sat on the edge of the bed. She put a hand to his cheek and leaned close to his ear.

"Sebastian," she said softly, nuzzling his temple.

He started slightly with a deep breath and grimaced from the pain in his ribs. She watched as his ridiculously long lashes fluttered against his cheeks before his eyes opened, and he turned to gaze at her sleepily. She moved her hand from his cheek to run it through his hair.

"It's time for more medicine," she said quietly, giving him a soothing smile as she lifted his head from the pillows to put the glass to his lips. He started to turn his head away distastefully after only a few swallows, and Psyche took that as an encouraging sign. "Drink it all, Sebastian," said Psyche as she continued to hold the glass, giving him an assuring look. He did so reluctantly, and he made a moue of disgust and shuddered when he was finished.

She continued to sit beside him, running her hand through his hair after she had lowered his head back to the pillows. He had a confused frown between his brows as he looked at her, and he was still very sleepy...and weak.

"What happened?" he whispered.

Psyche looked away from his gaze as she adjusted the blankets. There was nothing wrong with the way they were already arranged; she simply couldn't look at him for the moment.

"You had an accident, but you're going to be fine," she replied quietly. He apparently didn't remember, but Psyche thought that was for the best. It would be so much the better if he never did.

"Was anyone else hurt?"

"Nikos broke his arm and Bolen got a nasty cut, but everyone's going to be fine," assured Psyche.

"I feel so weak," said Sheerness, and he winced as he tried to move his legs and the weight of the blankets put pressure on his ankle.

Psyche put a gentle hand to his chest. "You need to lie still," she said quickly. She leaned forward to give him a soft kiss. "Sleep now," she whispered. She began to lightly run her fingers across his forehead, soothing away the frown. "You're fine now. Just go to sleep," she said slowly.

He didn't want to, but he wasn't able to fight it. She smiled as she continued to smooth his brow, and his eyes eventually drifted closed again. Now that he had talked to her intelligibly, she thought he should sleep. If he were awake, he might try to move, get off the bed even, and he needed to wait awhile longer because of the sprained ankle and cracked ribs.

Once she was sure he had gone back to sleep, Psyche took the pitcher to the officers' mess and refilled it. On her way back to his cabin, she went to her own room to retrieve her crutches. She didn't think he would need them, but she might as well bring them for when he was ready. She could be wrong about him needing them; he would eventually need to use the water closet.

The sky had lightened somewhat since she woke, but it had started to rain, and the thunder and lightning continued. The ship rocked slightly at anchor, but they were sheltered in the cove. It didn't seem the storm was going to be severe. She took her seat again and wrapped the blanket around herself as she watched him sleep. She curled her feet beneath her and rested her chin on her hand while she rested her elbow on the arm of the chair. She should have been bored just watching him sleep, but she wasn't. She couldn't think of doing anything else.

She jumped when there was a soft knock at the door. She looked at her watch as she went to answer it and was startled to see it was already nine. She opened the door to Freddie standing there with a breakfast tray. She smiled and moved out of the way, going to open the desk to let him set down the tray.

"Is he going to be all right?" asked Freddie as he looked at Sheerness.

"Yes," said Psyche with a smile, "I think he will be." Freddie's face brightened remarkably. "Is your uncle up and about?"

"Oh, yes, ma'am."

"What about Dr. Felton?"

"He's up, too. He's having breakfast."

"Can you tell him I'd like to see him when he's finished, please?"

"Of course, ma'am," grinned Freddie, and he skipped from the room and closed the door.

Psyche looked at the tray. There were pancakes and bacon, a pot of tea, and a bowl of oatmeal with honey. Under normal circumstances, she was sure he wouldn't find oatmeal appetizing, but it was probably what Felton had told Meals to prepare for him. She would eat after she fed him. She poured herself a cup of tea and took the bowl to the bed. She placed it on the chair for the time being and sat on the edge of the bed. She put a gentle hand on his chest and called his name. He was easier to wake, and he started in surprise...not with the usual flailing, but she was encouraged to see him behaving more like himself. She smiled affectionately when he looked at her confusedly.

"Time for breakfast," she said quietly, smoothing a hand down his cheek.

He nodded, and Psyche leaned forward to carefully adjust the pillows and help him sit up. She heard him gasp as she moved him, and when she looked at his face, he had a slight grimace of pain. She would give him more medicine after he ate. She picked up the bowl and saw his displeased expression. She dipped the spoon into the bowl and raised it to his mouth, which he stubbornly clamped shut.

"Doctor's orders," she cajoled, waving the spoon. He wasn't moved. "Come on. You *need* to eat. Please?" He finally relented at her worried expression and opened his mouth. Psyche smiled with relief. "Thank you."

He gave her a sullen look as she made him eat the entire bowlful, and Psyche's lips twitch amusedly from time to time because he reminded her of a little boy. When he was finished, she dropped the spoon into the empty bowl with a pleased smile and leaned forward to give him a kiss. She straightened up and tweaked the end of his nose before hopping off the bed to take the bowl to the tray. After she set it down, she took a sip from her tea, and Sheerness was upset when he saw her pick up a piece of bacon to nibble on as she went to pour a glass of water from the pitcher. She ate a second piece as she retrieved two bottles from her medicine kit. Then she added some drops to the glass and brought it to him on the bed.

"Why can't I have bacon?" he asked petulantly.

Psyche held the glass to his lips. "Because the doctor said so," she said with a slight smile. "Drink up." He pouted, and Psyche giggled, finding his display of rebellion so relieving she was giddy. "I *can* make you," she warned amusedly. "It will help you feel better," she said softly. "If you drink this and quit behaving like a little boy, I will give you a piece of bacon."

Sheerness drained the glass, and Psyche smiled wryly as she got up to put the glass back and bring him a piece of bacon. She held it out to him, and he took it with a smile. He was still weak, and though he was awake, he was becoming tired. Still, she didn't think he was in danger of getting pneumonia, even though Felton had said seventy-two hours. She lifted the blanket to look at his ankle. The binding minimized the swelling, and she had put a pillow beneath his foot to elevate it. There was no discoloration in his toes, and they didn't feel too cold or hot, so it seemed it would heal without complications.

She replaced the blanket and put her head to his chest to listen. His heartbeat sounded the same as ever, and his lungs were clear as he breathed. He would mend, and she was so grateful. He was showing great improvement already.

"I need to…," he began when she looked up at him, and she watched his cheeks color with embarrassment.

"Yes, I was afraid of that," said Psyche dryly. "I brought my crutches, but I don't think you're strong enough yet."

"Yes, I am," said Sheerness determinedly. "Bring them to me."

Psyche gave him an assessing glance. He wasn't strong enough, but he could be just as stubborn as she was. He would *have* to make an attempt. She got up to get the crutches. By the time she came back, he was trying to sit up and put his legs over the side. It was painful, and it was making him dizzy. Psyche sighed and leaned the crutches against the side of the bed. She put herself under his left arm and carefully braced a hand against his side to help him stand. He began to weave, and Psyche almost fell as she supported him.

"I don't want to hear another word about how pigheaded *I* am," she grunted as she helped him to the water closet.

He didn't have the energy to reply because it took all he had not to fall over. She got the door open and helped him in, and then she closed it. She went back to the desk to eat more. She would give him a few minutes to tend to things. She was starving. She ate her last piece of bacon and started on her pancakes, sighing blissfully. She was almost finished when Sheerness opened the door. She helped him to the bed and under the blankets. She fluffed his pillows before settling him back. He would never admit it, but it had exhausted him. He blinked sleepily as she sat on the edge of the bed beside him.

"How long was I asleep?"

"Since I woke you this morning or altogether?" asked Psyche as she began to smooth a hand across his forehead.

"Altogether," he sighed. He was going back to sleep, despite his wishes to the contrary.

Psyche shrugged negligibly. "Not long. Twelve hours, fifteen at the most." She gave him a gentle kiss. "You should sleep more."

"I want to…," he trailed off as he fell back to sleep, the thought forgotten.

Psyche gave him another kiss and a slight smile. "Not today, sweetie."

She looked up when there was a knock on the door. Felton was there when she opened it. She stood out of the way to let him come in.

"Freddie said you wanted to see me?" He gave Sheerness a critical look on the bed. "Has he been awake at all?"

"Yes, he's been awake, and he ate his oatmeal…whether he wanted to or not. He's just tired from a trip to the water closet. I have a few things I need to do, and I didn't want to leave him unattended. Would mind watching him for me? I won't be long."

"Of course. Take all the time you need." He gave Psyche an assessing once-over. She had dark circles under her eyes, and there was a slight strain to her features. "Have you had any sleep?"

"Some," said Psyche vaguely with a slight nod.

"You need more," said Felton sternly. "Might I suggest that one of the things you tend to be a nap?"

"You might," said Psyche with a cheeky grin as she retrieved the tray to take to the dumbwaiter. She went to the door and looked back at him. "No bleeding or laudanum while I'm gone, either, hmm?"

The rain had stopped for the time being, and Psyche went to the main deck to speak with Higginbotham. Laing was overseeing the rebuilding of the boom, and they were making significant progress. She wasn't sure they would be done that day, but it would be very close, if the weather would cooperate. She let the first mate know Sheerness was recovering. Then she asked if they were going to start bringing up the rest of the temple once the boom was repaired. Higginbotham told her that would wait until either Sheerness or Nikos was well enough. Psyche believed that would be longer than they could afford to wait; it would be weeks. Psyche told him to let her know when it was repaired, and she would go down to oversee things. She wasn't looking forward to it, but it had to be done.

After she spoke with Higginbotham, she went to see Meals. There was a hush when she came down the stairs to the berth deck. It only lasted for a moment before the men resumed their conversations, but they all watched as she went to the other end of the deck where Meals was preparing dinner. She wasn't sure what about her recent actions had caused the hush. That she had saved Sheerness was the most notable thing. That she had stripped down to her chemise in front of them and cursed, and it was obvious she was involved with the captain. Psyche tilted her chin a little higher and calmly walked across the deck. She didn't think there was a man among them who thought less of her.

She only wanted to let the cook know the captain's birthday party would go ahead as planned on the appointed day. He was recuperating, and while he might not be back to normal, he would be well enough for cake and presents. Meals grinned and promised he would make sure everything was ready.

Psyche went to her cabin for a book and started to go back to the great cabin. After she closed the door to her own, she stopped in the alcove. She hadn't seen Nikos since yesterday. She went his door and knocked. There was no response. She tried again, and there was still no answer. She frowned. She supposed he could have been on deck. He felt responsible for what had happened to Sheerness, and he did have a broken arm. She went into Sheerness's cabin, and Felton stood up from the wingchair when she entered.

"You didn't take a nap, did you?" stated Felton reprovingly.

"No, I'm not sleepy," said Psyche evenly.

"Just because you're not sleepy doesn't mean you don't *need* sleep," said Felton testily, his lips tightening into a firm line. "I *am* a doctor. You would do well to listen to me."

"I promise I will sleep at some point today," said Psyche calmly. "Doctor, have you seen Nikos?"

"Yes, I have. He had breakfast and went to his cabin."

"Oh," said Psyche in surprise, her frown returning. He could be sleeping, but she had knocked. "How is he?"

"That was a nasty fracture to his forearm, but it will heal, provided he doesn't try to use it too soon."

"Good," said Psyche distractedly. It almost seemed Nikos was avoiding her, and that concerned Psyche. She smiled automatically. "Well, I'm sure he's just resting, then."

"You should do the same," said Felton firmly as he went to the door.

"I will," swore Psyche. Felton looked at her doubtfully before he opened the door and left.

Psyche went to the bed to adjust the blankets and smooth a hand down Sheerness's cheek. She could tell Felton had examined him. It didn't bother her, and it reassured her that Sheerness was going to be fine when the doctor didn't mention any concerns. She curled up in the chair with her book and flipped to the page she had marked. She could have been looking at maps or artifacts, but reading didn't require as much of her attention, and she wanted to be there for Sheerness. She would give him an hour or two before she woke him for medicine, provided he didn't wake by himself before then. It would be about time for dinner as well.

She read her book, occasionally glancing up from the words to Sheerness as he slept. He would shift at times, moving a hand or one of his feet, but he didn't wake. She went to the water closet at one point, but for the most part, she sat reading and watching him sleep. She was on the verge of dozing off when there was a knock on the door. She inhaled with a start and looked at her watch. It was dinnertime.

Freddie grinned when she opened the door and carried the tray to the desk.

"I taught Cupid a trick," he said happily.

"What did you teach him?" asked Psyche as she lifted the cloth on the tray. Broiled grouper, potato cakes, and garden peas…for both of them. And beer.

"I taught him to sit up on his hind legs and wait until I give him a treat."

"That's very good," said Psyche with a grin. "You taught him that just since yesterday?"

"Oh, no, ma'am. I started working on it while you were gone to Delphi. Now he does it perfectly."

"I'll have to see later," chortled Psyche. "Have you seen Nikos today?"

"Not since breakfast this morning. I don't think he's feeling very well with his arm and all."

"If you see him, will you tell him I'd like to see him, please?" asked Psyche earnestly.

"Yes, ma'am," said Freddie, and he left the room.

Psyche chewed on the side of her thumb thoughtfully for a minute after he had gone. She was worried about Nikos. She thought he would have come at least once already to see how Sheerness was doing. He could speak to Felton or Higginbotham, but Psyche thought he and Sheerness were friends. It was very unlike him.

She finally walked over to the bed and sat on the edge of it. She bent forward to call Sheerness's name, and she had to jerk back quickly as he flailed about before releasing a groan and grimacing. He looked at Psyche confusedly, and she gave him an apologetic smile.

"It's time for dinner," she said quietly.

"I'm not eating more oatmeal," he said darkly.

"Not right now, no," grinned Psyche. "For dinner, you're having fish and beer, but if you throw a tantrum, you'll have oatmeal for supper."

She bent forward to help him sit up and placed more pillows behind him. She started to move away, and Sheerness used one of his hands to keep her arm around his neck and moved the other to the back of her head to kiss her ardently. Psyche nuzzled his face affectionately when he ended the kiss and leaned her head back to look at him with a warm smile.

"You *are* getting better," she drawled.

She got the tray with their food. She balanced it onto the top of his thigh and hers to use as a table, and they ate their dinner. She was overwhelmingly happy to see him able to feed himself. She surreptitiously kept an eye on him to make sure he ate every morsel. He didn't eat quickly, but he did clean the plate and drained his tankard. Psyche took the tray back to the desk when he was finished. She got a glass of water and put some medicine into it, taking it back to the bed. He eyed the glass petulantly.

"Do you want honey or syrup with your oatmeal?" threatened Psyche airily. He took the glass and drained it.

"Pah! That is rank!" he said disgustedly when he was done and gave the glass back to her.

Psyche smiled and took it back to the cabinet and refilled it with plain water for him to clean out his mouth.

"It's the valerian," she said mildly, "but it's not addictive like laudanum, and it's strong enough for cracked ribs *and* dislocated shoulders." Sheerness raised an enquiring eyebrow as he drained the glass. "Not me…Islington." She took the glass back to the cabinet, and then she came back to the bed. "Do you need to use the water closet?"

"Yes, please," he responded meekly.

Psyche helped him in. While he was there, she took the tray to the dumbwaiter. He was able to manage much better this time, and she thought he might be able to try using the crutches next time. She went to the desk to close the lid and smoothed her hands over the top of the box sitting there. She had looked at it curiously for the past day, but she had still not opened it. She closed the desk and turned to look expectantly when Sheerness opened the door. She helped him to the bed and settled him under the covers. The trip had tired him again, but not as badly as that morning. He gave her a studious glance once he was comfortable.

"You didn't sleep well last night, did you?" he asked mildly.

"No, I suppose not," said Psyche evenly. She wasn't going to tell him she had only slept for an hour, and even that had been unintentional.

He patted the bed beside him. "Come have a snooze."

"Oh, but—" she began.

"I am going back to sleep whether I want to or not, so I won't need anything. Don't make yourself ill," he reasoned quietly.

Psyche looked at him contemplatively for a moment, and then she carefully climbed onto the bed. She curled up beside him, and he smoothed his hand down her thigh and draped it over his, leaving his hand in place. She wrapped one of her arms around his and looked up at him as he closed his eyes. Her own began to droop closed, the whatever-it-was of his bed quickly working its magic. Within seconds, they were both sound asleep.

Psyche jerked awake groggily. She put a hand to her forehead confusedly and looked around herself. It was dark; the lamps hadn't been lit, and the fire was almost out. She looked at Sheerness to see that he was still sleeping. There was a knock at the door to the cabin, and she realized a previous one must have been what woke her. She carefully eased off the bunk and went to answer the door. Freddie was there with the dinner tray.

"Did I wake you, ma'am?" he asked uncertainly.

"Yes, Freddie, but don't worry. I shouldn't have gone to sleep in the first place. Come in," she said quietly, moving for him to carry in the tray.

She opened the desk for him to set it on, and then she added wood to the fire. She grabbed a rush and lit a few lamps then turned to look at Freddie.

"I'm sorry I didn't come see the trick you taught Cupid," she said softly.

"Oh, that's all right," said Freddie with a smile. "I don't think he's liable to forget." He clasped his hands behind his back and rocked slightly on his heels. "I have some messages for you."

"Yes?"

"Uncle Bothi wanted me to tell you the boom has been repaired, and I told Nikos you wanted to see him."

"What did he say?"

"He said he would come see you." He saw Psyche's troubled expression. "Didn't he?"

"I don't know. I fell asleep shortly after dinner, and you just now woke me up. He might have come while I was sleeping." She shrugged dismissively. "I suppose we'll eventually get our ducks in a row."

"Oh!" said Freddie, his eyes rounding, "speaking of ducks. Waddlesworth has come by an odd habit."

"What's that?"

"He's taken to riding around on Cupid's back."

"What?" said Psyche, her expression one of disbelief and amusement.

"Well, the dog doesn't mind, but Waddlesworth will get on his back, and Cupid will run up and down the berth deck with the duck riding along."

Psyche's shoulders shook with silent laughter. "Well, I suppose it does make for a quicker journey than waddling along by himself."

"Yes, ma'am," chortled Freddie.

"Run along now. I'll take the tray to the dumbwaiter when we're through. If you see Nikos, can you let him know I'd still like to see him, please?"

"Of course," said Freddie agreeably as he closed the door.

Psyche looked at the tray. It was roast chicken, potatoes, and carrots, with a basket of rolls and apple pie for dessert. There was also a bottle of wine. She stretched and looked at her watch. It was 9:30. She moved the wingchair back by the fire, leaving her book on the cushion. After her nap, Psyche felt confident she could sleep on the bed. It wouldn't be necessary to stay up. She sat on the edge of the bed, but rather than calling his name or shaking his shoulder, Psyche leaned forward to give Sheerness a soft kiss, slowly working her way down his neck. She felt him stir, and one of his hands moved to her waist. She lifted her head to look at him and giggled.

"So *that's* the secret! You're not a fish out of water at all! You're Sleeping Beauty!" she chortled, tweaking the end of his nose.

Sheerness rolled his eyes and shook his head. "Very funny."

"It's time for supper. Are you hungry?"

"Yes...provided it's not oatmeal."

"No, it's chicken and apple pie," said Psyche with a grin.

"Then I'm starving," said Sheerness, trying to sit up in the bed.

He wasn't able to adjust the pillows because it required him to twist his torso, an action that was unpleasant, and Psyche helped him sit up before she went to get the tray.

"Wine, too?" said Sheerness happily when he saw the bottle.

"Well, you do have just a few cracked ribs and a sprained ankle. It's not as if you're at death's door," grinned Psyche.

"Hunh," said Sheerness noncommittally as he began to eat.

Psyche poured them both a glass of wine, and they ate their supper. His appetite remained good, and she watched with satisfaction as he ate everything on his plate and drank most of the bottle of wine.

After her comment about the extent of his injuries, it was obvious he still didn't remember what had happened. Psyche wasn't going to mention it unless he asked. So far, he had shown no interest in finding out. Once he was feeling better, which would probably be very soon, he was going to ask. Maybe he would ask Felton. Psyche didn't think she would be able to tell him.

When they were finished, Psyche took the tray to the desk. She would take it to the dumbwaiter eventually, but it could wait. She mixed up more medicine for him and carried it to the bed.

"I don't think you're well enough for a shower, but I could arrange something if you need a wash," said Psyche as she sat on the bed and handed him the glass. Sheerness thought about it and shook his head, eyeing the glass with dislike. He finally took a breath and downed it without stopping. "Water closet?" she asked as she took the glass and went to refill it with plain water.

"Yes, please," croaked Sheerness, and he shuddered. "It does help...a lot," he said with a grimace as he took the glass of water and drank it, "but I don't know if I can stand it anymore."

"The only alternative is laudanum. Would you rather have that?"

"No," said Sheerness flatly. "I sleep enough as it is." He sat up and moved to the edge of the bed and put his feet on the floor.

"Do you want to try the crutches?"

He was doing better. Sheerness nodded, and Psyche gave them to him. He placed them under his arms and stood, but when he tried to swing his legs, supporting his weight with his arms, he groaned and nearly fell. He would have fallen if Psyche hadn't been there. She took the crutches and put them away, and then she put herself under his arm. His dizziness may have gone. He was stronger. But, cracked ribs wouldn't heal overnight. If his ankle weren't sprained, he would be able to get around well.

"I think you're no longer going to need the crutches by the time your ribs are well enough for you to use them," said Psyche gently.

"You might be right," grunted Sheerness as they reached the water closet.

Once Psyche saw him safely inside, she picked up the tray and took it to the dumbwaiter. Everyone else had finished eating, and the table had been cleared. The lanterns were off, and the room was dark. As she went through the alcove, she paused outside Nikos's door. She almost knocked, but she needed to get back to Sheerness to help him to the bed. Maybe she could talk to Nikos tomorrow. She was concerned about him. She got back to the cabin just as Sheerness opened the door to the water closet.

"Where did you go?" he asked in a tone that suggested she had abandoned him.

"I just took the tray to the dumbwaiter," she answered mildly. "There's no sense in it sitting there all night."

She helped him onto the bed and settled him in after fluffing the pillows, and then she closed the top of the desk and added more wood to the fire. She came back to sit by him and brushed the hair off his forehead before running a hand down his cheek and bending forward to give him a kiss.

"Are you coming to bed?" he asked sleepily as he ran a finger along her jaw to her chin and up to her lips.

"I'm not sleepy right now," she said softly, "not after that nap."

"I wasn't planning on letting you sleep…at least, not right away."

Psyche sucked in air through her teeth and gave him a teasing smile with a shake of her head. "I don't think you're well enough for that."

Sheerness gently grabbed her by the wrist and pulled her toward him to kiss her hungrily. "Why don't you come to bed and find out?"

"You're impossible," said Psyche with a grin. "You can't even walk."

Sheerness gave her a wicked grin and moved a hand to one of her breasts. "I don't need to walk."

Psyche dipped her head to kiss him before she looked at him tenderly. "It's a tempting offer, Sebastian, but I think you should sleep."

"I've been sleeping all day," he pouted, and then he yawned hugely.

Psyche began to place tiny kisses all over his face. "Because you need it," she whispered gently. "I will stay right here until you go to sleep, and then I'll come to bed when I'm tired." She smoothed a hand across his forehead. "I won't be long, and I promise we can try in the morning."

Sheerness still frowned, but he was slowly falling asleep. There was something about the way she brushed her hand across his forehead that was almost hypnotic. He was sleepy, but he could have stayed awake if she had given him a reason.

"But—" he mumbled.

"Shh. Sleep now," she crooned. "In the morning, Sleeping Beauty," she teased.

Sheerness smiled as he drifted off. Psyche pursed her lips amusedly as she looked at him. She couldn't believe she had never tried to wake him that way before. He had awakened her that way, but even if he hadn't, she had never been prone to the flailing he did. She still didn't understand why it worked, but it was a way to wake him that was not only safe but she enjoyed it, too.

After she was sure he was asleep, she went to sit in the chair by the fire. She curled her feet under her and put the blanket over her lap and started to read. She wasn't long for going to bed, but if she tried now, even with the ease she had of sleeping in his bed, she would toss and turn at least a few times. She didn't want to disturb him. Perhaps in thirty minutes, particularly with the boring portion she was wading through in her book, she would be ready. She *was* looking forward to snuggling.

It didn't even take thirty minutes. After about twenty she dozed off and was awakened by the sound of her book making a thud as it dropped from her hand to the floor. She rubbed a hand over her eyes and retrieved the book. She stood up and stretched her arms high over her head. She folded the blanket, and then she went to her cabin to get dressed for bed, leaving the door open. She didn't leave the door to her own cabin open, just in case Nikos or someone else happened by, but she did have it cracked so she would be able to hear Sheerness call for her should he wake while she was gone. Once she was dressed and had brushed her teeth, she opened her door at the same moment Nikos came into the alcove from the officers' mess.

"Oh!" gasped Psyche in surprise. "I thought you were in your cabin."

"I couldn't sleep, so I went on deck for a while," said Nikos quietly.

"I'm so glad I saw you," she said with relief. "I've been so worried. Are you all right?"

He touched his forearm in the sling lightly and gave her a slight smile. "This is a new one for me. I've never broken this one before."

"Does it hurt? Do you need something for pain?"

Nikos smiled. "No. I have a bottle of ouzo."

Psyche smiled, but she was still concerned. He did not seem to be himself. "Are you sure you're all right?"

"I'm fine," assured Nikos. He looked to the open door of Sheerness's cabin. "Felton said he is going to be fine, too?"

"Yes, he's almost back to his old self again, except with cracked ribs and a sprained ankle," said Psyche with a grin.

Psyche watched in dismay as his face crumpled and his shoulders began to shake. She wrapped her arms around him and rubbed his back soothingly. Nikos buried his face in her shoulder and tightly put his arm around her waist as he cried, and Psyche frowned worriedly as she tried to calm him.

"Shh, *adelphos*, what is this about?" she crooned.

"I'm so sorry," he choked. "I broke my promise."

"Oh, no," she soothed. "I'm sure you tried. I'm sure you did everything you could. I should never have asked it of you. It was too much to ask." She kissed his cheek comfortingly and continued to rub his back. "It wasn't your fault. I've never thought it was your fault." She got him to calm down enough to lift his head and look at her. She gave him an assuring smile and put a hand to his cheek. "I told you that."

"You forgive me?"

"Nikos, there is nothing to forgive, but if you need to hear me say it: I forgive you, yes."

"Thank you," he said, smiling with relief.

Psyche thought she heard a noise behind her from Sheerness's cabin, and she turned to look. She didn't see anything, and from what she could tell, Sheerness hadn't moved. She looked back at Nikos and smoothed a hand over his cheeks to wipe away the moisture.

"He's really going to get well?"

"Absolutely," said Psyche with a nod.

"Are we still going to have—?"

"Yes, we are," she cut in. She hadn't seen Sheerness moving, but he could be awake and listening. She didn't want to spoil the surprise.

"Don't you think we should tell him?"

"No. Why do it now? We've been at this for weeks, and it will only be a few more days. Let's not ruin it."

"No," agreed Nikos with a grin, and Psyche was finally relieved to see he was back to himself.

"I'll see you tomorrow. They've gotten the boom repaired, and now that Sheerness is on the mend, I'll have to go in the water." She gave him a teasing grin. "It is a shame when it takes only *one* woman to do the job of *two* men."

Nikos chuckled amusedly and kissed both her cheeks. "Good night, Thea."

"Good night, Nikos."

≪ ≫

Sheerness lay on the bed listening, his hands clenched, a nerve ticking in his jaw. He had never felt so betrayed. He was so angry he couldn't think and so heartbroken he couldn't breathe. He really hadn't thought she would do something like that...not really. She had managed to lull him into believing she was his alone, and he had been gullible enough to trust her.

He was awakened by Psyche's book thumping to the floor. He had watched her leave, never imagining she had gone for a tryst. He thought she had only gone to dress for bed, but then he heard voices in the alcove. He had raised himself above the side panel to see her embracing Nikos passionately. It had stunned him so much he had dropped back to the pillows, his vision blurring for a moment. He hadn't been able to hear everything they were saying but enough to know they had been carrying on for some time…weeks. He had to wonder how long. Did they start the day they met in Thessaloniki? Or was it after the two men returned from Olympus?

He was so lost in thought, he missed the sound of Psyche coming back to the cabin and closing the door. He didn't realize she was back in the room until she had turned off the lamps and carefully climbed over him onto the bed. The blood was rushing in his ears, and he almost flinched when Psyche curled up beside him beneath the blankets, snuggling into his side before brushing a gentle hand down his cheek and giving him a soft kiss.

She was so calm and unconcerned, it galled him. He didn't know how she could so blithely go from being in the arms of one lover to another without a twinge of conscience. When she ran a hand down his arm to twine their fingers together before resting her cheek against his shoulder, Sheerness couldn't bear it another minute. If she were a man, he would beat her. He would display his anger in such a way that it would be impossible for her not to realize he knew.

He turned over on his side and pulled her tight against him. She was almost asleep, and her eyes flew open in surprise. She smiled slowly and put a hand to his cheek.

"I thought you were asleep," she said softly.

Her expression was guiltless, relaxed. If he didn't know better, he never would have suspected. She could have continued to string him along, play him for a fool, and he would have believed…because he wanted to. Not anymore.

He put a hand to the back of her head and pulled her mouth to his to kiss her roughly. She tensed in surprise at the hardness of it, but she didn't stop him and did her best to respond. He nipped at her lower lip viciously and felt her wince. He moved his lips down her neck to where it joined her shoulder, and he bit and sucked at the tender skin there, leaving behind a lovebite.

"I thought we were going to wait until morning," she said hesitantly as she trailed a hand up his shoulder to the back of his head.

She was overwhelmed by the intensity of his embrace, and she was trying to relax and follow where he led her. He had wanted to make love when she made him go to sleep, and she wanted him, too, as always. It would be better if he waited. She hadn't expected he would need her so desperately. Her concern was that if he didn't slow down, he might hurt himself.

He tugged at the strings of her shift, and his hand groped beneath the silk to harshly clamp onto her breast before he painfully pinched the nipple.

"Ow!" she gasped, a frown forming. "You're being too rough."

He ignored her and moved his lips down her chest to take her breast into his mouth, biting and sucking on it in a way Psyche did not find pleasurable. He moved his hand down her thigh to grab her bottom, pressing her close to grind his pelvis against hers. She tensed and flinched, and the frown she wore began to deepen. She was beginning to believe he didn't *want* her to enjoy it, and she couldn't understand why.

"Ow, Sebastian, you're hurting," she whispered, and a knot of panic began to form in the pit of her stomach.

She tightened her fingers in his hair to pull his mouth away from her breast, and he moved his lips back to hers to kiss her violently, plundering her mouth with his tongue before grinding his lips against hers to cut the tender skin on the inside against her teeth. She put her hands to his shoulders to push him away, but he held onto her tightly.

The thing she began to suspect loomed larger, and the sting of anxious tears started in her eyes. She didn't want to believe what she thought was true. He had never been like this before. There had been times when their lovemaking had been intense, almost rough, but it had always been mutual. The wildness had been caused by passion and need. This was different. He seemed angry, as if he were intentionally trying to hurt her.

She gasped in surprise when he roughly turned her onto her stomach and pinned her arms above her head. He placed a pillow beneath her hips and forced her thighs apart with his knees. She struggled to turn over and move away from him, but he settled onto her with most of his weight, trapping her against the mattress. The position was uncomfortable, and her face was buried against the pillows, making it difficult to breathe. She fought to turn her head and gasped for air, a frightened whimper escaping from her when she did.

"No, please, Sebastian! I'm not ready," she cried quietly, but he paid her no attention.

As she craned her neck to look at him over her shoulder, she could see the cold, cruel expression on his face, and she knew then without question that he had no intention of her enjoying this. She winced and bit her lip as she felt him thrust two of his fingers inside her, and she tried to get away from him. He had her effectively pinioned. He kept her arms raised above her head, and he had settled his knees onto the backs of her thighs, keeping her legs spread apart. He removed his fingers and lifted his hand to his mouth to spit on it. He rubbed it onto his erection and positioned himself and thrust into her.

"Oh, God, no," she whimpered.

Psyche buried her face in the pillows and screamed before she started to sob uncontrollably. The pain was exquisite as he drove into her, and she cringed away from the sound and feel of his harsh breathing close to her ear. It was purely animal, and Psyche felt sick with shock and horror. She tried to pretend it wasn't her, that it wasn't Sheerness. She didn't want to believe he would do this. She felt him tense and release a shuddering moan, and he dropped his head to bite and suck at her neck, leaving another mark. He then moved his lips to her ear and savagely wrapped his fingers in her hair to keep her from moving away.

"You're *mine*!" he whispered viciously. "No other man can do that!"

Psyche flinched, and he rolled off of her onto the mattress. She lay still for several minutes, her face still buried in the pillows, numb with shock and anguish, her body aching. She slowly moved her arms to raise herself, and she blindly crawled off the bunk, weaving slightly on her feet with dizziness and the threat of her legs collapsing beneath her. She grabbed her dressing gown from where she had draped it over the side panel and instinctively put it on, wrapping her arms around her waist protectively when she was finished. She looked at him lying on the bed. His eyes were closed, but she could tell from the nerve ticking in his jaw that he wasn't asleep.

"I am *not yours*," she said quietly. "I am *no* man's possession. And you are right: no other man could have done that. Only you could make it hurt quite so much." She rubbed a shaking hand over her forehead. "I don't owe you anything anymore, and if you try to lay a finger on me again, I'll kill you." She turned and walked toward the door. "I want to go home now," she said tonelessly as she opened it and then closed it behind her.

Chapter Thirty Nine

Psyche walked into her cabin and locked the door. She went to the washstand to pour some water into the basin, and then she took off her clothes and washed herself. She winced and sucked in air through her teeth as she cleaned between her thighs, but she spent extra effort wiping the area anyhow. Once she had washed, she got another shift and dressing gown from the drawer, putting those she had been wearing in the pile of dirty clothes.

She crawled onto the bunk and curled into a ball in the corner, wrapping a blanket around herself and pulling her knees up to her chest. She began to chew on the side of her thumb, staring blankly at the wall across the cabin. She felt numb. She couldn't even bring herself to cry.

He had raped her. It couldn't compare to what Hendon had done to Georgiana, but that's what Sheerness had done...taken her by force against her will. He had done it to debase her, to make her feel used. He had done it to punish her...as revenge. For what? Judging by his words, it seemed he thought she had been unfaithful. She wasn't surprised he thought that. He had never trusted her. He had always—even when he hadn't overtly shown it—been suspicious of her fidelity. With Sir James. With Stockbridge. With Nikos. With any man. He was always jealous and possessive...and untrusting, It stemmed from some insecurity that was beyond her to mend, despite everything she had tried. But Psyche never thought he would be capable of raping her.

There had been times when she had made him angry...furious, but he had always restrained himself from causing her physical harm. Even this time, he hadn't struck her; the physical pain was relatively inconsequential, but the anguish she felt was a much greater wound than he could have caused had he used a knife. She had truly come to believe he loved her. She had trusted him. She had thought his reading her mail and upsetting her family would be the worst he would ever do to hurt her. She was left feeling desolate because she loved him, and she couldn't make it *stop*. It wouldn't go away, and she desperately needed it to. She couldn't still love him after what he had done; it wasn't fair.

Now she was left in a quandary. She couldn't stay, and yet there was no way for her to go, not if he didn't want to let her. Eventually, he would take Nikos home, and when he did, she would stay there. Nikos and Ioanna would see to getting her home safely; she knew that. Thessaloniki was a big port; other ships from Britain were frequently there. It was only finding the right one to get her back to England. Once she let her family know she and Sheerness had parted ways, if she hadn't managed to find a way home on her own, they would come for her.

She couldn't understand what she had done to make him do what he did. She went over and over in her mind every little thing she had done or said, and she was unable to determine *what* she had done. In the end, she began to realize it was something she would never figure. She wasn't going to ask him to explain. She didn't want to talk to him or see him again. She couldn't possibly bear it.

Psyche jerked awake at the sound of someone knocking on her door. She had drifted off sometime after dawn. She still sat curled up in the corner of her bed, and when she moved, her body ached all over. She gingerly crawled off the bunk and went to the door, putting her hand on the knob.

"Who is it?" she asked quietly.

"It's Freddie, ma'am."

Psyche opened the door and poked her head out to see the boy standing there alone with a tray of food.

"Oh, Freddie, I'm so sorry you brought that for me. I'm not feeling well right now, and I couldn't possibly eat it."

Freddie's face grew concerned. "What's wrong?"

"I'm just feeling a bit under the weather. That's all."

"Do you want me to fetch Dr. Felton?"

"No, no, that's not necessary. I'm just going to stay in my cabin. I'll be feeling better tomorrow."

"Are you sure?"

"Yes, Freddie." Psyche gave him an apologetic look. "Can you let your uncle know I'll not be going in the water today?"

"Of course, ma'am."

"Thank you. I won't be hungry today, so don't worry about bringing me trays at dinnertime or supper either. If I change my mind, I can go to the berth deck and get something. All right?"

"Yes, ma'am."

He was worried, and Psyche tried to give him her best reassuring smile. "I'll be better tomorrow. I promise."

"What about the captain?"

"He can take care of himself," said Psyche flatly.

"A-all right."

She gave him an apologetic smile. "Goodbye, Freddie."

"Goodbye."

Psyche closed the door and locked it. She went back to her bunk and lay down, hugging one of her pillows. The nausea she had felt was mostly gone, but the thought of eating made her stomach churn. She would eventually have to eat, but at this point she wouldn't be able to keep it down. The thought of doing anything—eating, talking, moving—did not appeal to her at all.

Psyche was staring blankly at the wall across from her when there was another knock on her door. She didn't know how long she had been lying there. The sun was still shining, but she didn't know if it was morning or afternoon. She didn't care. She lifted her head to look at the door. She didn't want to answer it. She didn't think it was Freddie. She slowly climbed off the bunk and went to the door.

"Who is it?"

"It's Dr. Felton."

Psyche frowned. She had told Freddie she didn't need the doctor. There was nothing wrong with her that he could fix. She cracked the door open to look at him.

"Yes?"

"Forgive me for intruding, Lady Psyche, but Freddie said you were feeling unwell. I know you told him you didn't need to see me, but I thought I should look in on you."

Felton looked at her concernedly. She had looked tired the day before. She was now worse. Her features were pale and drawn, dark circles under her eyes that were dull and listless. She was still in her dressing gown, despite it being afternoon, and she had not brushed her hair. She appeared to be on the verge of collapse, troubled by something more than just lack of sleep.

"I'm fine," she said flatly.

"I'm sorry, but you don't look fine," returned Felton in the same tone.

"Well, I *will* be fine," she said quietly. "I just need to be left alone."

After Freddie told him Psyche was feeling unwell, he went to check on the captain. Sheerness was out of bed and dressed, hobbling about with the use of a crutch. He was busy all morning overseeing raising the ruins, directing members of the crew who had volunteered. The first thing raised was the mosaic that had nearly killed him. He was in a terse mood, but he seemed to be healing well. Felton suspected it was pain that affected his temperament. Now it appeared Psyche had made herself ill tending to him. Felton sighed. He couldn't make her let him examine her.

"Very well," he said finally, giving her a compassionate smile. "If you decide you need my help, you know where I am."

"Thank you, doctor," said Psyche softly. She closed the door and locked it.

She rested her back against the door and closed her eyes tiredly. She missed the solarium. It was at the top of enough stairs that most people found it not worth the effort to make the climb to disturb her. If they did, she could sit the helm outside the door, and they would know she wanted to be left alone and would let her.

She walked back to the bunk and climbed onto it again listlessly, curling into a ball. She had felt the ship rock periodically throughout the day and knew they had resumed lifting the ruins. Neither Nikos nor Sheerness was capable of going into the water, so she could only assume the crew was doing it. Sheerness was up there. She had heard him leave his cabin, the sound of the crutch thumping against the floor unmistakable. She idly wondered what kind of progress they had made, but she didn't really care. Not now. She just wanted to lie there and forget everything…just forget it all.

She lifted her head to look at the door, and then she looked at the ceiling. Her medicine kit was still in Sheerness's cabin. She got up from the bed and put her ear to the door. There were no sounds, and she quickly unlocked it and opened it. The door to Sheerness's cabin was open, and she hurried in, first going to the water closet and then to retrieve her kit, keeping her eyes averted from the bed. She went back to her cabin and closed and locked the door.

She took the kit to the table and opened the lid. She brushed her fingers over the bottles before lifting out the largest one from the bottom. She poured a glass of water, and then she looked at the bottle in her hand contemplatively. She had never thought she would do this. She *knew* the risks, but as the day had progressed, she had begun to understand the appeal. Just once. Just for a little while. She *needed* to forget. She removed the stopper and added several drops, ignoring the instructions. She swirled the glass to mix it, and then after a brief hesitation, she lifted it to her mouth and drained it, grimacing at the bitter flavor when she was done. She set down the glass and slowly made her way across the room to her bunk. By the time she lay down, it had already started to take effect, and she sighed with relief as her thoughts began to unravel and float away on a fluffy white cloud of oblivion.

Nikos went to the door of Psyche's cabin and knocked softly. He knew she was in there, but he didn't hear any sound. Both Freddie and Dr. Felton had said she was feeling unwell. No one had seen her out of her room, and Freddie said she hadn't eaten breakfast or dinner. Now she hadn't eaten supper. He didn't want to intrude, but he was concerned. She was fine the night before.

He frowned and knocked again. Both Freddie and Felton said she had answered when they knocked. He waited a few minutes and tried again, softly calling her name. There was still no answer. He tried the knob, and his frown deepened when he found it was locked. Sheerness had not been below since he went to the main deck after breakfast. He'd taken dinner on the berth deck, and after supper, he had gone back up for his nightly stroll despite his ankle.

Sheerness had been in a foul mood all day. He had, for the most part, completely ignored Nikos. When Sheerness had talked to him, his words had been clipped and his expression disdainful. Nikos had been puzzled by his behavior, but he supposed it could be due to pain. When someone mentioned Psyche was unwell, Sheerness hadn't shown any concern. The captain had not been to see how she was, and that perplexed Nikos more than anything. Something was not right.

Nikos tried the knob again, jiggling it in the hopes that the catch of the lock would unfasten, but it stayed firm. He examined the door on its frame, noting the way it was slightly off-square. He put his hand on the knob and leaned his shoulder against the door, and with a shove at the right point, he was able to get the door to open. The room was dark, and when he looked around the corner to the bunk, he saw Psyche curled up in a ball on her side, her eyes closed.

"Thea?" he called softly. She didn't respond, and he walked closer to the bed. "Thea?"

Nikos hurried back to his cabin to light a rush and brought it back to light the lamp on the wall over her bunk. Once he had it lit, he was able to see that she was breathing, slowly but shallowly. Her face was pale, and even beneath the sootiness of her lashes, he could see the dark circles under her eyes. He gently shook her shoulder and called her name. She stirred slightly but didn't wake. He left her cabin and went to the officers' mess to knock on Felton's door. The doctor was still awake reading, and he opened it shortly after Nikos's summons.

"I'm sorry to bother you, doctor, but you need to see Thea."

Felton nodded and followed him to the cabin. He, too, tried to wake her by shaking her shoulder, getting the same response. He felt her forehead and found no fever. He put his fingers to the side of her neck to check her pulse and found it to be rapid and thready. He lifted each of her eyelids one at a time to look at her pupils, and he frowned when he saw the almost pinpoint dilation of them. He looked around himself and saw the open medicine kit on the table, one bottle sitting out beside it. He went to look at the bottle. The label was in Chinese, which, of course, was useless to him. He removed the stopper and smelled the contents, and then he looked back at Psyche on the bed.

"She's taken laudanum. Too much, I think," said Felton, rubbing a hand across his chin as he put the bottle down and went to sit beside her on the bunk and check a few more things.

"She wouldn't take laudanum," said Nikos firmly.

"One wouldn't think so, but that's what is sitting on the table," said Felton distractedly as he continued his examination. He shook her by the shoulder firmly. "Psyche!" he called sharply. Her head lolled, and she tried to force her eyes open. "I don't think she's taken a fatal amount, but more than someone who's not an addict should take in one dose." He turned to look at Nikos. "She isn't, is she?"

"Absolutely not," said Nikos darkly.

"She obviously didn't follow the recommended dosage, so I don't think she took it for pain. She hasn't eaten all day, so she might have had some type of stomach complaint as a reason for taking it. I think she intentionally took more than the recommended amount, but I'm not sure she intended to have quite this kind of effect. At least, I don't believe she did. Why do you think she would have taken it?"

"I don't know," said Nikos quietly, but he was beginning to have his suspicions. "Will she be all right?"

Felton rubbed his hands on his thighs and stood up. "She will be. As I said, she took more than she should but not a toxic amount. All we can do is wait for it to wear off." He pulled out his pocket watch and looked at it. "We don't know when she took it other than sometime between when I checked on her and now. She should be fine by morning."

"You're sure?"

"Of course," said Felton with a slight smile. He straightened her out on the bunk and covered her with the blankets. "You or the captain can keep an eye on her, but I don't think it's necessary." He started to leave the cabin.

"Thank you, Dr. Felton," called Nikos softly as he looked at Psyche sleeping on the bunk.

"Not a problem," replied Felton, waving over his shoulder as he left for his cabin.

Nikos's lips tightened into a grim line as he watched her sleep. She had been fine last night. She hadn't seemed ill or upset. She was happy Sheerness was getting well, and she had been her usual caring, sympathetic, gentle soul. The only thing Nikos was able to reason was that whatever had happened to cause this had occurred *after* he had seen her. As far as he knew, the only person she had been with beyond that point was Sheerness. Given his taciturn mood of the day and her seclusion, Nikos knew the man had caused it, and he didn't appear sorry for it.

Nikos's head jerked to the doorway when he heard Sheerness enter from the mess. He stalked to the alcove and grabbed the younger man by the shirt and slammed him against the wall, pinning him there with his broken forearm in its splint against his neck, the hand of his good arm pressing against Sheerness's chest.

"What did you do to her?" Nikos growled.

At first Sheerness was astonished by the attack. He could see the anger in Nikos's face. He had never imagined the Greek would be capable of it, but as bright as his happiness was, his fury was no less dark. Sheerness grimaced in pain at the pressure on his chest, but he gave Nikos a mocking grin.

"What's the matter? Are the goods too damaged for you now?"

Nikos put more pressure on Sheerness's neck, shifting his forearm closer to his elbow above the break rather than below it.

"What are you talking about?"

"The two of you are carrying on together."

Nikos gave him a disdainful sneer. "When would we have been able to? You follow her around like a dog on a leash! She can't go anywhere without you!"

Sheerness glowered at him. "I saw the two of you last night, so don't try to pretend you're so innocent and noble," he said coldly.

"Oh, what have you done?" gasped Nikos.

"I saw you," bit out Sheerness. "She said you had been at it for weeks."

"She was forgiving me…because I felt guilty for breaking my promise to look after your worthless hide!" growled Nikos. "And what she has *been at for weeks* was planning a surprise birthday party…for you!"

Sheerness looked at him doubtfully. His mother and sister had both told Psyche about his birthday. He had caught her in hushed conversations with members of the crew—particularly Meals—since they had returned to the ship, conversations that would immediately end when he came near. Every time, she would try to act as if nothing were amiss, but she would turn slightly pink and have a guilty expression…as if she were trying to keep a secret, something too close to lying for her conscience to bear. But he wasn't ready to believe Nikos had been distraught last night.

"I would hardly say a few cracked ribs and a sprained ankle are something to become overwrought about," spat Sheerness.

Nikos looked stunned. "Jesus! You don't remember, do you?"

"Remember what?"

"You honestly don't know what happened," said Nikos, looking at him in disgust.

"There was an accident. I can only assume I was hit by the boom."

"What's the last thing you *do* remember?"

"Tying off the mosaic to lift it."

Nikos shook his head. "You fool. You stupid, pathetic fool," he said with a mocking grin, and he stepped back from Sheerness and let him go, as if he found the thought of touching him repulsive. "When the boom broke, my arm got tangled in the rope and was fractured. Your foot got pinned beneath the mosaic, and you sprained it unsuccessfully trying to get it loose."

Nikos scratched his forehead thoughtfully. "When Thea found out you were trapped, she dove into the water to save you, giving you the very air from her lungs. She tried to break the rocks around your foot to get it loose while the crew tried to lift the mosaic off you, and she was there alone with you when she *watched you die*." Sheerness looked at him in stunned disbelief, and the color began to drain from his face.

"You were dead when she brought you to the surface. She got the water out of your lungs, but you had no heartbeat. The doctor wanted her to leave you, but she wouldn't give up. Your ribs are cracked because she *made* your heart beat again. She watched you lose your life, and then she gave it back to you!" Nikos shook his head and swallowed emotionally. "She stayed up watching over you, wearing herself thin until you were safe, and this—" he hissed angrily as he grabbed Sheerness by the front of his shirt and pulled him into Psyche's cabin—"this is how you repay her…by trying to destroy her!"

Sheerness looked at her lying on the bed. He felt nauseous, and the blood was rushing in his ears as he began to grow dizzy. She was sleeping in a position she never used, her complexion waxy and pale. The two men had been arguing loudly, and she hadn't stirred.

"What's wrong with her?" he asked breathlessly.

"She hasn't slept, she hasn't eaten all day, and then she took an overdose of laudanum…all because of *you!*"

Sheerness's chest began to heave, and his vision blurred. He swayed on his feet and staggered to the window to open it and vomit. He wretched until nothing more would come up, and then he dry-heaved for several minutes. He was horrified and disgusted with himself, and he felt helpless because he didn't know how he could possibly atone for it. He finally closed the window and turned to look at Nikos, his face ashen.

"I didn't…I didn't know," he said brokenly.

"Should it have mattered?" spat Nikos. "Whatever you did to her, she's never done anything to deserve it."

"No," choked Sheerness with a slight shake of his head. "I'm sorry I thought that you and she were…that the two of you were…." He swallowed to fight back another wave of nausea. "I shouldn't have."

Nikos waved his hand through the air impatiently and glared at Sheerness. "I'm not the one you hurt. I'm not the one you betrayed."

"She's never going to forgive me."

"Do you think she should?" asked Nikos coldly. "How many times have you done things to hurt her, hmm?"

"Too many," whispered Sheerness.

"If she does forgive you, it would be more than you deserve. You don't deserve her!"

Sheerness closed his eyes and dropped his head, and a nerve began to tick in his jaw. "I know that," he said quietly.

Nikos narrowed his eyes critically as he looked at Sheerness. He was still young; he could still learn. His sister called her *thea* because of her boundless capacity to love and forgive. Sheerness did truly seem regretful about what he had done, but the decision would be solely hers.

"If she does take you back, I had better not ever find out you have hurt her again. She is far more forgiving than I am." Nikos turned on his heel and left the room, closing the door behind him.

After he'd gone, Sheerness looked from the door to Psyche on the bed with a lost expression. He finally hobbled over to the bunk and sat on the edge of it. He lifted a trembling hand to smooth it down her cheek and brush the hair away from her face, and then he began to shake all over before releasing a gasping sob. He took one of her hands in both of his as he started to cry. He had done this, and he couldn't escape the feeling that this time, she wasn't going to forgive him. She shouldn't.

Nikos telling him still didn't make him remember what had happened, but he knew it was true. There was only one thing he did remember, and he had thought it was a metaphor, as most dreams were. He had been terrified he was drowning, and then Psyche was there, gentle and caring, and he knew she would save him. He hadn't been afraid anymore. Now he knew it wasn't a dream. Anything beyond that was lost to him.

She had only said he'd had an accident. It had been so much more, and she hadn't told him. She had a knack for understatement that dovetailed well with her gift for telling honest lies. She had saved him…again…like always. And he had hurt her…again…like always. He wasn't listening to a thing Myron had told him. *Believe in her.* He didn't, and he should. *Accept her as she is.* He was always looking for the things she kept hidden, convinced there had to be something wrong with her, and he had always been so ready to believe the worst of her when there wasn't a worst. Spite and deceit were not in her. *Quit being mean.* Obviously, it had been his most blatant oversight.

Now he was going to lose her. What he had done was unpardonable, and he had no excuse. She had been terrified; it had been obvious. There had been no anger in her at what he had done. The sound in her voice had been wounded and bewildered…bereft, and now he knew why. He had punished her for something she hadn't done, and he hadn't even bothered to tell her what her imaginary crime had been. She hadn't deserved it; even if she *had* been guilty of what he'd thought, she hadn't deserved it. That she was innocent had made what he did all the more heinous.

Sheerness stood and rubbed a shaking hand over his forehead. He started to hobble toward the table with the intention of pouring what remained of the laudanum out the window, and his hip bumped against her sketchbook where it stuck out over the edge of her desk. It fell to the floor with a thud, the pages fluttering open. He did as he intended, removing the stopper and pouring out the contents before tossing out bottle and all, and closed the window.

He turned and bent down to retrieve the sketchbook, intending to put it back on the desk. He started to close it when he noticed the page it had opened to was a picture of him, asleep in the chair in front of the fire at Nikos and Ioanna's. He flipped through the pages and found another of him, sleeping in her bed. He found two more between the sketches of Sounion and Delos. Always sleeping. He had not thought she made drawings of him. He closed the book and put it on her desk, and then he took his seat beside her again.

He sat on the edge of the bunk holding her hand, watching her sleep for hours. Her breathing gradually changed, becoming deeper and more even, as the drug began to wear off. Her forehead creased with a frown that would come and go, and her eyelids moved as she dreamed. Whatever it was she dreamt, it was not pleasant, judging by her expression. He would reach over occasionally to smooth a hand over her brow, and it would lighten her sleep enough the dream would change or go away. The lamp over her bed eventually ran out of fuel, and the room began to lighten with the rising of the sun.

Shortly after dawn, her eyelids began to flutter, and she grimaced as she opened her eyes, putting a hand to her forehead at the pain she felt from the after-effects of the laudanum. Her mouth felt dry, and her stomach churned with a nausea completely different from that she had suffered before taking the drug. Then she realized someone was there holding her hand, and she started with surprise and panic when she realized it was Sheerness. She tugged her hand out of his and edged away from him.

"Get out of my cabin," she said flatly, looking at him with an emotion that bordered on revulsion.

Sheerness rubbed a tired hand over his face to combat the stinging he felt in his eyes. It was no less than he should have expected, and yet it pained him to have her look at him that way. She had looked at him in anger and indifference, but he had never known what it would be like for her to look at him with *hate*. He could never have imagined how hard it would be.

"You took too much laudanum. I just wanted to make sure you were safe," he said quietly.

Psyche's eyes widened slightly at his words, but she tilted her chin up and glared at him. "I'm fine. Get out."

A nerve ticked in his jaw, and he closed his eyes and swallowed a lump in his throat. He took a deep breath and looked at her pleadingly.

"I'm also here to beg you to forgive me," he said huskily. "What I did was more than just wrong; it was despicable. I have no excuse that would justify it," he said brokenly. "You always save me, and you always forgive me, and I know...I *know* this time I don't deserve it, but I don't know what I'll do if I lose you. So I am begging you to, please, give me one more chance."

Psyche sat with her back in the corner, and she closed her eyes and looked away from him as tears escaped from them to run down her cheeks. Her lower lip trembled, and she gripped it with her teeth to stop it. She shook her head slightly and took a deep breath before she opened her eyes and looked back at him accusingly.

"You hurt me," she whispered.

"I'm sorry."

"I trusted you," she choked out, "and you've never trusted me."

"I'm sorry," he repeated.

"How can I believe you won't do it again?" she sobbed.

"Because I swear, on my honor, that I never will," he said softly. "Please, forgive me," he whispered earnestly.

Psyche was torn. She desperately wanted to believe him. He seemed to be sincerely remorseful about what he had done. Yet she was afraid it would only last until the next time he became jealous. He was always jealous. She couldn't bear to have it happen again.

"I'm not yours," she said quietly. "You don't own me. I am with you because I choose to be."

"I know."

Psyche still wasn't sure she could do it again, but she loved him so much. She looked at him pensively. He had that lost and confused expression on his face, and Psyche knew there was another piece of him that had broken. There was so much in him that was good and gentle, and she wanted to believe he loved her. Until what had happened, she had come to believe it, but she didn't know how he possibly could if he didn't trust her. Still, the last few days had made her realize she couldn't live without him.

"I forgive you," she whispered.

Sheerness closed his eyes, and he looked as if a heavy burden had been lifted off him. He looked at her gratefully.

"Thank you. I will spend the rest of my life trying not to make you regret it. I only want to make you happy."

He had to understand he couldn't treat her like property and because she was with him by choice there was no need for him to ever doubt her fidelity. The jealousy and possessiveness had to end.

"I won't marry you," she said softly. "You'll have to marry someone else for an heir."

He looked at her in confusion and surprise at the statement, but he nodded acceptingly. "I don't care about an heir," he replied honestly. "I want you whatever way you'll have me. If you don't want to marry me, so be it." He gave her a solemn look. "Whatever you want."

Psyche narrowed her eyes as she looked at him. "What about your title? What about your father?"

Sheerness blinked and frowned confusedly. "What about him?"

"His dying request was that you marry and produce an heir."

"Who told you that?" he asked in surprise.

"Amalie."

"Am doesn't know what she's talking about," he said dismissively. Psyche raised an eyebrow. "She wasn't there." Psyche wasn't convinced. "She must have eavesdropped on one of the conversations I had with my mother, who wasn't there either, but even she knew that wasn't what my father wanted." Psyche folded her arms across her chest. Sheerness tightened his jaw and sighed patiently. "Yes, he did want me to marry, but it wasn't to produce an heir. He loved *Maman* and was very happy until the day he died." Sheerness looked away from her. "He thought if I found someone to marry, I would finally be happy, too."

"Aren't you?" asked Psyche softly.

"I wasn't," he said distractedly. He scratched his forehead. "I was sickly and bookish when I was a child, but I was happy. My father loved me, but he thought what was needed to properly groom me as his heir was to send me to India for a while…to harden me. It was hell on Earth, and I hated it. It accomplished what my father wanted, though, and I was never quite happy, or willing to admit it even if I were, once I came home. I was never the same, and my father knew he'd made a mistake sending me there.

"I met a girl while I was in India. Shobhita. She led me into a trap when I trusted her, and I nearly lost my life when I was attacked by Thuggee." He gave a self-deprecating smile and shook his head slightly. "She seemed so honest. She could lie so well, I believed everything she told me…right up until they put the scarf around my neck." He cleared his throat and shrugged. "My optimism and faith in the world dimmed somewhat after that. I've never told anyone what happened there…not my family…not Myron. Everyone just noticed I had changed. They didn't know why."

"You loved her, didn't you?" asked Psyche quietly.

Sheerness looked at her, his expression dispassionate and telling at the same time. "I thought so. I was young and naive. She was beautiful and deceptive." He picked at the blanket by his thigh distractedly. "Anyhow, my father thought if I got married it would repair that."

Psyche slowly crawled across the bunk toward him and moved onto his lap, straddling him on her knees. She brushed a hand down his cheek before lowering her head to kiss him softly. Sheerness was stunned to inaction. He quivered nervously as she continued to kiss him, nuzzling his nose and chin lovingly before lightly moving her lips back to his. She moved the hand she had resting at the back of his neck down his arm to put it around her waist, and he released a soft moan that was a cross between anguish and desire.

He felt her move her hands to remove his waistcoat and pull his shirt loose from his pants as she continued to kiss him, and he was still too uncertain to move. He knew what he wanted to do, but he was afraid, and his hands balled into fists at his sides. She pulled his shirt over his head to drop it on the floor and ran her hand down his chest as she started to place kisses up his shoulder to his neck.

"I don't want to hurt you," he sighed longingly.

Psyche lifted her head to look at him with a soothing smile, lightly running her fingers down his face before giving him a gentle kiss. She climbed off his lap to remove the boot from his uninjured foot and then the sock. She straddled his legs again as she stood on the floor, softly running her fingers through his hair as she began to kiss him again. He felt her hand unfastening the buttons on his pants, and he groaned when she lightly ran her fingers across his erection.

"Psyche," he whispered huskily.

She helped him to lie back against the pillows and removed his pants, carefully pulling them over his left foot, and then she unfastened her dressing gown to remove it and her shift. The breath caught in Sheerness's throat as he looked at her, and his chest tightened as she stood looking at him for a moment with a winsome smile.

"Oh, you *are* a goddess," he sighed.

Psyche climbed onto the bunk and bent down to kiss him, resting on her knees to either side of his waist. She lightly ran her fingers over his chest, teasing his nipples as she trailed her lips along his jaw to his ear before running them down his neck. She slowly made her way along his collarbone to the indentation at the base of his throat, and then she began to lingeringly kiss her way down his chest to one of his nipples. Sheerness sucked in air through his teeth and finally, weakly, moved his hands to clutch at her hips.

But then she began to move away as she continued down his stomach after teasing the other nipple, one of her hands sensuously moving up and down his side from his ribs along the front of his thigh to his knee. Sheerness shuddered pleasurably and moaned softly in his throat as she kissed his navel, and his hands clutched helplessly into the mattress. His hips rose excitedly when she took his erection into her hand, and when he opened his eyes to look at her, he gasped as she gazed back at him with a wanton expression, her lips slowly starting to trail away from his navel and move lower. He swallowed convulsively and clenched his jaw, and the smile on her face became all the more lecherous when she saw the effect it was having on him.

She took a slight detour to nibble at his hip before she made her way back across his pelvis, and Sheerness tensed and closed his eyes in anticipation as he felt the first warm, wet touch of her mouth on his erection.

"Ah, my God!" he groaned, and his hips bucked involuntarily as she began to play him.

Psyche almost giggled gleefully. She watched his face as she teased him with her mouth and hands, reveling in the expression of utter bliss he wore and the moans and sighs he breathed as she touched him. He reached for her as he neared his orgasm, attempting to pull her away, but she wouldn't let him. She took him deep into her mouth as he began to come, and his features were a combination of astonishment and rapture as he shuddered uncontrollably.

"Oh, Psyche, you—!" he gasped, and his words were cut off as he groaned pleasurably.

Psyche eventually kissed her way back up his body, wearing a self-satisfied smile as he would occasionally twitch as an after-effect from the intensity of his release. His breathing was ragged as he lay with his eyes closed, a nerve ticking in his jaw. She placed a kiss on it and moved her mouth to his, and he kissed her weakly in appreciation. She rubbed her nose against his affectionately and grinned.

"Happy birthday," she said huskily.

His eyes flew open in surprise. "Why did you do that?" he asked quietly. "You didn't have to do that."

"Because I wanted to make *you* happy," she said softly, smoothing a gentle hand over the frown that had appeared on his face.

The frown only deepened further. "But why do you…? How can you…?" He swallowed emotionally and took a deep breath. "I can't be perfect," he finally said defeatedly. "I tried, and I *want* to be, but I'm not, and I never will be. You're perfect, and you shouldn't have anything less. You deserve that."

"Sebastian, for the thousandth time, I am *not* perfect!" said Psyche exasperatedly. "I don't know what I can do to convince you. I can't sleep. I'm nearsighted. I can't tell a lie to save my life—well, I could, but I'd suffer for it. I'm afraid of heights. Actually, it would be the thump of my body on the cold, hard ground after the fall that terrifies me. Plato bores me to tears, and don't mention Plautus. I don't like being cold, and never try to make me sleep on a hard mattress. I loathe parsnips, and I think cravats are the most useless invention ever." She gave him a cajoling smile. "Does that sound perfect?"

"Yes," said Sheerness softly.

Psyche groaned. "Perfection is relative, which is why no one can be perfect. To truly be perfect, you would have to be seen that way by everyone, and if you were perfect, there'd be no reason for you to be here. *You* might think I'm perfect, but I'm not."

"But—" began Sheerness, and Psyche put her fingers over his lips.

"Sebastian, I swear if you say I am perfect one more time, I will slap you silly…birthday or not," she fumed.

Sheerness nodded, and Psyche removed her hand.

"I don't want you perfect, either. I want you just the way you are. I don't think I'd like you nearly quite so much if you were perfect," said Psyche softly, running her fingers through his hair before tweaking the end of his nose. "Perfect is boring."

"Myron told me that," said Sheerness quietly.

"He was right. He was my brother, after all," said Psyche with a wry smile.

Psyche was laying on top of him, resting on her elbows to either side of his head, her hair falling in a curtain around them. It was then he realized that even though she had never said she loved him, she had shown him repeatedly that she did. It didn't matter anymore. He didn't need to hear the words. She made him so happy. He didn't know what he possibly could have been thinking to ever want to hurt her.

"Why do you keep saving me?" he asked softly.

"Because I couldn't do anything else," said Psyche, gently running her fingers down his cheek.

She looked at him contemplatively for a minute, and then she got up from the bunk and went to her desk. She flipped through her notebook and pulled something out she had stuck between the pages and crawled back onto the mattress to hold it out to Sheerness. He looked from it to Psyche with a frown.

"What is that?"

"It's my letter from Myron," she said quietly.

"I can't read that," he said flatly, shaking his head.

Psyche got off the bunk again and grabbed her dressing gown from the floor. She left the cabin and soon returned. She held out something else to Sheerness, and he looked at her in surprise.

"Try it with these," she said softly, holding the case with his spectacles.

"That wasn't what I meant," he said uncomfortably. "I meant that it is your letter."

"I don't mind you reading it."

"No," said Sheerness flatly. "Why would you want me to?"

"Because he told me to look after you." She started to say something and hesitated, but then she went ahead. "He told me not to let you drown."

"What?" said Sheerness dully. He took the letter and the case from Psyche. He put on his glasses self-consciously and began to read.

"I didn't think he'd meant it literally at the time," said Psyche quietly, "but I guess he knew."

"How could he possibly know?" asked Sheerness distractedly as he scanned through the letter, getting almost to the very end before coming to the part about himself.

"We have dreams sometimes. It's a trait we inherited from *Babushka* Alexa, my father's mother. Arachne and Eurydice have them all the time, much to their and everyone else's annoyance. I used to, but not anymore. Most of the time, we just ignore them because it's no fun if you already know what's going to happen. Sometimes we dream and don't remember until what it is happens. It's not a very pleasant."

"And you think Myron knew?"

Psyche shrugged and chewed on the side of her thumb. "He might have, but there's no way we'll ever know."

"Is that how you knew Pandora was having twins? How you pick the winner of the Derby?"

"No," said Psyche slowly, and then she frowned thoughtfully. "At least I don't think so. Pan's stomach did this *thing*, and to me, it was so obvious there was more than one baby. As for the Derby winner, I narrow down my choices through statistics, but if I'm left with more than one, I always take the one my instinct tells me is going to win." She looked at him levelly. "I don't cheat."

"I never thought so," said Sheerness with an amused grin.

Psyche leaned forward to nibble on his ear, and then she nuzzled his cheek. "I like you in your spectacles," she purred.

"Do you?" blurted Sheerness.

"Oh, yes," she drawled seductively. "You wearing nothing but your spectacles and a smile makes me want to do all sorts of indecent things."

Sheerness might have thought she was teasing him if it weren't for the way she trailed her fingers across his chest and kissed and nuzzled his neck. He didn't know why he had been so worried about her seeing them. If he had known how much she liked them, he would have let her see them sooner.

"I'm sorry about the ball last year," she said as she continued to kiss his neck. "That wasn't very fair."

"It was my own fault. You didn't know. Your sister didn't know. I just wanted to kiss you so much."

Psyche gave him a teasing smile and did just that. "Why were you so mean to me?"

Sheerness sighed. "Because you seemed so perfect, I just knew there had to be something wrong with you, and it irritated me so much when I couldn't find anything. Everything seems so easy for you when it never has been for me, and I was jealous. Then, despite all that, I had feelings for you, and I didn't want to. Knowing you didn't care for me at all just made it even worse." He ran a finger along her jaw to her chin. "By the time I realized you were the one thing that could make me completely happy, I didn't know how to undo the damage. Myron was of absolutely no help; he said it served me right."

Psyche rubbed her nose against his affectionately. "Tell me you love me," she whispered.

"I love you," he whispered earnestly. "I fell in love with who I thought you were, and then I fell in love with who you really are so much more." He put a hand to the side of her face to make her look at him. "Do you believe me?" Psyche nodded with a teary smile. "Do you...do you love me?" He hesitated in asking the question because he wasn't sure what he would do if she said no. He thought she might, but at least for now he could pretend, even if she didn't.

"Yes…I do," she answered quietly, and her expression was somewhat troubled as she said it. "I love you, but I can't be with you if you're going to be jealous and possessive all the time. I just *can't.*"

"You won't have to worry about that anymore. I swear," he said with a silly grin.

"Won't I?" she asked with a puzzled frown.

"I didn't know how you felt about me. I was afraid you might find somebody else you *did* care for. I thought if I could keep you away from other men, that wouldn't happen. If I didn't share you with anyone else, then you would have to give all your love to me. Now I know, and I don't have to worry anymore."

Psyche looked at him chidingly. "How could you ever think I would want someone else?"

"I don't want to get slapped," said Sheerness, giving her a teasing smile. He smoothed his hands across her hips and cupped her bottom. "I'm perfectly happy with you not, but why don't you want to marry me?"

"Oh, we can…if you still want to."

"What?" blurted Sheerness. "But you said—" he began.

"That was when I thought you only wanted me for my ovaries."

"Your what?" he said blankly.

"My baby-making abilities," said Psyche with a grin, and she watched amusedly as his cheeks colored.

"So you will marry me now?" he asked hopefully.

"Yes, I will marry you now," said Psyche with a chuckle, giving him a happy kiss.

"Oh, thank God," sighed Sheerness with relief.

"What?" said Psyche, trailing her fingers through his hair.

"I wanted to marry you anyhow, but Bardsey threatened me with a gun."

Psyche blinked in surprise. "Why would he do that?" she asked in puzzlement. It was an activity she thought very unusual for her easygoing brother-in-law.

Sheerness's cheeks colored. "Because he saw us…in the garden."

Psyche sat up and put her hands to her cheeks in alarm. "Oh, my giddy aunt!" Her eyes widened even further, and she gasped when a realization struck her. "Pandora! She *knew!* She planned this whole thing!"

Sheerness smiled lazily and ran his hands up her sides to her breasts. "I don't think she planned all of it, *chere.*"

She put her hands over his and wiggled against him, giving him a teasing grin as he inhaled sharply. "How do you know? She thought you loved me, even before then. That's why she played that trick on you last year…to find out if you were good enough for me…and to make you give me your cravat."

"And why would she want to do that?" he asked, only partially interested in the answer. She had started to move her body on top of him, writhing sinuously, using movements he recognized from *tsifteteli*. It was very erotic, and he was becoming less and less interested in talking.

"Because we had a wager on who could get the most of them by the end of the season. She already had one or two, and I had none. She felt sorry for me."

"Lucky me," he drawled. He pulled up on her hips and slowly eased her down onto him. She started to writhe again, giving him a wanton smile. "Oh, that feels good."

"Can we go home now?"

Sheerness's eyes opened in surprise. "Right now?"

"Well, not right this instant. After we've raised the temple."

"Don't you want to see Egypt? What about your necklace?"

"Egypt will always be there. We still have the firman from Mahmud, and we'd have to talk to Mohammed Ali Pasha anyhow. I want to be home for Christmas."

"But—" started Sheerness with a slight frown.

"We can always go for our honeymoon," she reasoned softly as she began to move against him again.

"Mm," he smiled. "I like the thought of that."

"Besides, you are far more accident prone than I am. I don't think we could survive another country."

Sheerness tried to pretend he was surprised by his party. There was a large chocolate cake with brandy cream between the layers and chocolate frosting. His supper included roast beef, scalloped potatoes and Brussels sprouts, and Sheerness was astounded Meals had managed to pull together a meal so English. Psyche gave him a framed watercolor she had made of the temple of Hepahestus in Athens. He received a multitude of gifts from his officers and crew, a sign of their respect for him as their captain.

None of them were surprised when they discovered Psyche and Sheerness were betrothed, although they did their best to act as if they were. Nikos's mood brightened considerably earlier in the day when he noticed how happy the two of them were. As traumatic as the events of the past few days had been, their joy more than equaled it. Nikos, like his wife, thought the two of them were very Greek for people from England. He would have to write a letter to Chrissoula to let her know her wishes had been fulfilled.

Psyche had even more presents for Sheerness, which could only be given in private. She finally explained that she spoke to Maiyin and Lucia about sex because one had been a concubine and the other a courtesan. Needless to say, Sheerness was amazed and amused. She still wouldn't tell him what books she had been reading. He asked her if there was anyone in the employ of her family who didn't have some sort of nefarious or criminal past. After some thought, Psyche had to reply with not really, no.

They remained at Delos for another two weeks lifting the remains of the temple. Psyche didn't enjoy spending that much time in the water, but she didn't want to miss anything. When they were finished, the *Medea* sat much lower in the water and also went much slower. It was just as well they were leaving for home already; the return trip was going to take much longer.

Psyche finally got to see what was in the box on Sheerness's desk after he gave her a birthday party of her own almost a week after his. Much to her surprise, she found it contained things that belonged to her, including the necklace she had given him for mailing her letters. She found the stocking she had used for their race, multiple gloves, a fan, handkerchiefs, a few dance cards, and one or two other pieces of jewelry. There was a miniature she had given to Myron in the box, too.

Her brother had told Sheerness a lot of things about her, she discovered, including her birthday, her favorite color…and her middle names. Sheerness decided not to mention Myron had told him what happened when she lied. He wanted to find out if it would actually happen first. Psyche learned to her amusement that Myron had been blackmailing Sheerness to keep his silence about all the questions he had been asking. Psyche told him it would have been easier to believe him the first time he said he loved her if she had known.

They stayed another week with Nikos and Ioanna when they returned him home, but there was no more swimming in the cove for Psyche. It was fall, and regardless of whether or not it was the Aegean, it was too cold, especially after the two weeks she had spent for the most part submerged in it. She made several sketches of the bath room because she intended to recreate something similar once she and Sheerness were married. He thought it was an excellent idea. They both loved that bath room. When Psyche and Sheerness finally left for home, they promised they would write often.

They arrived in England shortly after the beginning of December. There had been letters waiting for Psyche at Kastro Andreanopouli, and she was able to answer back, letting everyone know they shouldn't write anymore because she was on her way home. The letters reached home before her, but she found out there were a few that had been mailed to her in Greece that she would have to retrieve when they went through the following year.

When they reached London, both her family and Sheerness's were there waiting. It wasn't difficult to know when the ship would arrive because Psyche and Sheerness had stopped at his home on Sheppey before continuing up the Thames. Psyche had thought for a time about simply surprising her family, but she wanted to see them as soon as possible. She had missed them so much, she couldn't wait to go all the way to Wilderland before seeing them.

The countess was happy to see them, as were Amalie and the children. Psyche was overwhelmed by the children's response when they learned she was to wed their uncle. When it was time for Psyche and Sheerness to continue on with the ship to London, the children hadn't wanted to let them go until Psyche explained they would travel by coach with their grandmother and aunt and Uncle Alex to meet them at the dock with the Aberdares. Amalie made it known that Psyche had been the one they wanted Sebastian to marry all along. She was very happy for them to be back because it meant she could proceed with making plans for wedding Westerkirk, which would happen on May Day.

Everyone was happy (and no more surprised than the crew) when Psyche and Sheerness announced they were betrothed. Both were dumbfounded that no one thought it sudden and unexpected. They themselves were amazed. Islington congratulated Sheerness on a job well done and had to mention he had doubts for a while. Then he let Sheerness know with an amused grin that the gun had never been loaded. Psyche made sure to scold both her twin and her maid for having a hand in engineering it, but she also had to give them a cheeky grin and her cheeriest thanks. The duke and duchess were pleased to welcome Sheerness into the family. They couldn't think of anything more fitting.

Psyche performed a bit of engineering of her own when she introduced Chrissoula to Stockbridge. She tried to hide her mischievous and victorious grin when the two of them were instantly taken with one another. She wasn't sure what gave it away, though, whether it was Chrissoula's tongue-tied silence or Stockbridge's bashful politeness. Psyche was satisfied they had both finally met their match.

She was overjoyed Gregory had returned from America. He would not, unfortunately, be able to stay until Christmas. He was due to set sail only days after Psyche arrived. She was sad to hear that but infinitely happy he was there when she returned. He had brought Annabelle to stay in Wales. She was expecting their first child in May, and he wanted her to be with his family. Once the conflict in America was settled, Gregory would be returning home to stay as well. He had had enough of war. Psyche was happy to meet her sister-in-law. She liked her instantly, and Arachne's painting had been an excellent likeness. Psyche looked forward to getting to know her better, and it seemed Persephone had found a much-needed female cohort.

Eurydice was full of talk about her plans for going to Vienna at the end of the following Season. The only thing she did not look forward to was the long journey by coach across the continent to get there. Psyche suggested Sheerness could take her by ship as far as Venice. It wouldn't be any longer than traveling over land all the way and much more comfortable. The only problem would be finding someone to chaperone her from Venice to Vienna. When Psyche mentioned it to her parents, they were confident something could be arranged. Eurydice was ecstatic.

Psyche told Sheerness they could spend a week or two at her family's palazzo in Venice, which did not see nearly enough use. He thought that was an excellent idea. They could stay there for a little while, then go stay with Nikos and Ioanna at Kastro Andreanopouli for a week or two, and then they could go to Egypt. It would be the perfect honeymoon.

Dorian was there without his wife, looking very proud. Selena had delivered Thomas Franklin Savage the previous week, and Dorian was pleased as punch. Psyche couldn't recall ever seeing her brother look so happy, except on his wedding day. Pandora had Myron and Alex with her, and they had grown so big, Psyche barely recognized them. She didn't have any trouble recognizing who was who; Myron was still the calmer of the two.

Sheerness was impatient to start making babies himself, and Psyche repeatedly had to explain they weren't married yet. As both of them were still in mourning, according to etiquette, they wouldn't be able to marry until nearly the end of the following season…a season which Psyche would, thankfully, not have to endure. If they were to start this early, it would be obvious what had happened, and while she didn't care about the scandal, it could make things difficult. She didn't think that was necessary. There would be plenty of time for that later, but it was going to be a long wait.

Author's Afterword

Oh, where to begin? Since I have already made this book so unbelievably long, I almost didn't want to add an afterword, but there are a few points I wanted to make…just in case you were wondering. I guess the main things I want to talk about are the condition of things in Greece during this time period—Aigai in particular—and one or two other things.

Archaeological exploration of Greece did not become a "thing" until after the Greek War for Independence, which began in 1821. All of the magnificent ruins tourists flock to see in modern times were barely visible until about the middle of the nineteenth century. Delphi was, for the most part, buried beneath the village of Kastri, pieces of the ancient site used to construct it. After an earthquake caused substantial damage to the town, authorities relocated the residents to a completely new site, and excavation of Delphi began in earnest in 1893. It was pretty much that way all over the entire country. Any ruins that were visible at the time this story takes place in 1814 was only due to nature and time not having completely covered them yet…except for the Acropolis in Athens. It was a military compound and had been for several centuries. Oh, the ignominy. I originally thought of how much fun it was going to be to have them visiting all of these sites, not realizing until I did the research that they didn't, theoretically, exist at the time. I think the way they really were actually presented more opportunity for me as a writer.

As for Aigai, located at modern day Vergina, its site was not determined until the 1850s, and excavation did not begin until 1861. It is believed that the tomb of Philip II of Macedon, father of Alexander the Great, was found at Vergina. Since the Argeads cremated their dead and we have no DNA samples, the only thing to go on is what the archaeological record indicates. It's not as if they left a plaque that said: "Philip is buried here." It would be nice, but that doesn't happen very often. I'm siding with the folks who think they found his tomb. You know the theory—if it walks like a duck and talks like a duck….

The tomb "discovered" by Psyche and Sheerness is the one called the Tomb of Persephone. When it was excavated by modern archaeologists, it was empty except for the frescoes and a few bone fragments. It is fairly certain that the tomb was plundered long before 1814, probably closer to the beginning of the first millennium. I didn't want these folks to walk away empty-handed, so I decided to have some fun making things up. I hope people who actually know the truth aren't too offended. As for the things they found when they opened it,

I went by the things that had really been found in some of the other burials at the site for a basis.

When I decided to have them find and raise an entire temple at Delos, that took a lot more work than I had ever anticipated. First, I had to decide what it was going to look like and how big it was going to be. Then, I had to decide how much it would *weigh.* That was the really fun part. No, actually, the really fun part was trying to figure out whether or not the *Medea* would have been able to carry it. Ack. I hope people who actually know something about the cargo capacities of ships are not saying: "You are *so* full of it." I tried my best, I really did. I know the *Medea* is not as big as a super tanker.

To touch on Psyche's ability to hold her breath for a very long time, it was possible. Just the other day, there was a segment on NPR about free diving. I don't want to misquote people, and I was in the middle of doing something else while I was listening to it, but I could swear I heard seven minutes mentioned. Actually, I thought I heard *seventeen*, but I know *that* can't be right. Psyche can hold her breath in the five to six minute range. Free divers and spear fishermen, based on the research I did on the subject, can hold theirs for longer. Dolphins can hold theirs in the five to eight minute range.

When it came to Nikos and Sheerness climbing Mount Olympus, I couldn't *not* have them successfully climb it, even if the first recorded successful scaling didn't happen until 1913, nearly one hundred years later. As Psyche said, just because it isn't recorded somewhere doesn't mean it didn't happen.

I think the last thing I want to mention is Psyche's use of what might be recognizable as something very similar to modern-day CPR to revive Sheerness. The movements she started out with that caused a bellows action were a method I found in a nineteenth century mariners' manual. What she did afterward is not modern CPR...similar, but not quite. It was something I felt someone with a moderate understanding of human anatomy might try, regardless of when usage of CPR became "standard." She had to have her happy ending, so I couldn't have the love of her life die from drowning.

There you have it. I'm sure there are probably other things people are wondering about, but as in the afterword for *Edinburgh*, I recommend you do the research yourself (like I did) if you have questions. I hope, again, that you had as much fun reading it as I did writing it. Until next time.

Emyll O'Bryan
May 5, 2008

About the Author

Emyll O'Bryan lives in a small, gray box on the edge of nowhere with an onion and two cats. She would say the middle of nowhere, but she knows someone who lives there. It's close but not quite within rock-throwing distance. She had dreams of becoming a member of a big-hair 80s band in her teens; started on an anthropology degree with ambitions of becoming an archeologist in her twenties; and decided in her thirties that she should just stick with what she knew: telling stories. She enjoys history (although anything after 1865 is current events to her), languages (both real and imaginary), cooking (mostly Italian and Greek), watching movies (a *good* sci-fi horror adventure), singing in the shower (it provides its own special auto-tune), and sleeping (*lots* of sleeping). Not necessarily in that order. She also finds it very peculiar to be referring to herself in the third person as she writes this but feels it would be bucking the system and just the least bit vain to do otherwise.

≪ ≫

Other Books by Emyll O'Bryan

Edinburgh – The Savage Brood: Book One (2015)